John Birmingham is the author of the cult classic *He Died With a Felafel in His Hand*, the award-winning history *Leviathan*, and the trilogy comprising *Weapons of Choice: World War 2.1*, *Designated Targets: World War 2.2* and *Final Impact: World War 2.3*. Between writing books he contributes to a wide range of newspapers and magazines on topics as diverse as biotechnology and national security. Before becoming a writer he began his working life as research officer with the Defence Department's Office of Special Clearance and Records.

John Birmingham refuses to build a website, but he has three blogs, CHEESEBURGER GOTHIC at http://cheeseburgergothic.com, THE GEEK at http://blogs.brisbanetimes.com.au/thegeek/ and BLUNT INSTRUMENT at http://blogs.brisbanetimes.com.au/bluntinstrument. If you ask him nicely, he might even answer your questions, but he will probably not read your manuscript. He's very lazy.

Also by John Birmingham

WITHOUT WARNING

JOHN BIRMINGHAM

PAN
Pan Macmillan Australia

First published 2008 in Macmillan by Pan Macmillan Australia Pty Limited
This Pan edition published in 2009 by Pan Macmillan Australia Pty Limited
1 Market Street, Sydney

National Library of Australia
Cataloguing-in-Publication data:

Birmingham, John, 1964–
Without warning / John Birmingham.

978 0 330 42498 1 (pbk.)

A823.3

Typeset by Post Pre-press Group, Brisbane, Queensland
Cartographic art by Laurie Whiddon, Map Illustrations
Printed in Australia by McPherson's Printing Group

Papers used by Pan Macmillan Australia Pty Ltd are natural, recyclable
products made from wood grown in sustainable forests. The manufacturing
processes conform to the environmental regulations of the country of origin.

This one's for the Burgers.

ACKNOWLEDGEMENTS

You know who you are. All the unusual suspects. My editors and publishers who put up with so much. Cate. Bri. Jono. Betsy. And all of the serried ranks behind them too. Marketing mavens, publicists (Hi Annie!), cover designers. I loves y'all. A big tip o' the propeller beanie to Russ Galen too, for making me think this idea through properly before he went and sold it.

Then there's my family, who put up with so much. Jane, Anna and Thomas. Every book I promise to be a bit less monstrous come deadline. Every book I lie. And there's all those friends and neighbours who stepped in at crucial moments to help get me off Planet Parenthood long enough to get a few more pages written. My parents, Jane's mum Pat, and a swag of uncles and aunts helped out there too. They all put up with so much.

For this book, there was also the hard chargin' crew at Clayton Utz, the rockingest little great big law firm anywhere, anytime, who put up with so much from me as their writer-in-residence. I'm still not sure why. I guess they're just cool. While on that topic, the happy funsters at *Avid Reader* in West End also, possibly unwisely, gave me some valuable writing space while I was itinerant by virtue of renovations. My thanks. I was pretty well behaved there though, so I guess, for once, they really didn't have to put up with too much.

There's Murph – or Mr Murphy to you. Mr S.F. Murphy of the great state of Missouri – who put up with so much as my principal researcher and at one point even graduated to co-author for a couple of pages in one particular battle. I owe him for pulling my fat out of the fire so many times it just ain't funny. Which reminds me to thank my good friend Mr Andrew McKinney of the Texas bar, who provided Lord knows how many thousands of dollars' worth of free legal advice re the line of succession, amongst other things.

And finally there's my blog buddies. The Burgers. Too numerous to name the guilty parties. And man, do they put up with too much, especially as deadline closes in and all they get, day after day, is entry after entry bitchin' about how tough I got it. Luckily, they're a ferociously disrespectful bunch of scurvy dogs and they don't let me get away with much. I bounce a lot of ideas off them. Get them to do a lot of unpaid research. And generally take them way too much for granted. But I'd be lost without them.

As always when I write my acknowledgements, I can't help but feel that I've left someone out. I really shouldn't do these late at night with a drink in hand. Whoever it is that I've forgotten this time, my apologies. Drop into the blog and tear me a new one. I'll give you a cameo in the next book.

CHARACTER LIST

PARIS

Caitlin Monroe (aka Cathy Mercure): Echelon senior field agent posing as international eco warrior and London-based political activist

'Aunty' Celia Wickstead: English member of The Sorry Committee

Maggie Leigh: American member of The Sorry Committee

Monique Duroc: French political activist, member of The Sorry Committee

Dr Stéphane Colbert: Groupe Hospitalier de la Pitié-Salpêtrière

Bilal Baumer (aka al Banna): Cell Master, al-Qaeda in Europe

Nicolas Sarkozy: French Minister of the Interior

Captain Marcel Rolland: 1er Régiment d'Infanterie

Bernard Lacan: Director, Action Division, DGSE

Wales Larrison: Echelon's Paris controller

Monty Pearson: chief of staff, BBC Paris bureau

Noordim ul Haq: Indonesian-born Jemaah Islamiyah commander

SEATTLE, WASHINGTON

James Kipper: chief engineer with Seattle City Council

Barney Tench: deputy chief engineer with Seattle City Council

Barbara Kipper: James's wife, and mother of six-year-old Suzie

Heather Cosgrove: engineering intern at Seattle City Council

Marv Basco: sanitation engineer at Seattle City Council

Dave Chugg: water engineer at Seattle City Council
Rhonda Thiess: secretary to the chief engineer, Seattle City Council
Aaron Metz: Microsoft executive
Malcolm Vusevic: Constitutional Convention delegate from Spokane, WA

NORTHCOM, GUANTANAMO BAY

Brigadier General Tusk Musso: US Marine Corps lawyer, acting commander of Guantanamo Bay Naval Base
Lieutenant Colonel George Stavros: aide to Musso, acting 2IC of Guantanamo Bay Naval Base
Ensign April Oschin: USN sysop, Guantanamo Bay Naval Base
Major Eladio Nuñez: Cuban Army officer
Lieutenant Jenny Kwan: US Marine Corps, Incident Response Unit
Sergeant Guilio Gutteres: US Marine Corps, Incident Response Unit
Captain Vincente Álvarez: Cuban Army officer
Professor Norman Griffiths: US National Laboratory
Lieutenant Dan McCurry: US Navy
Chief Petty Officer Strom Lundquist: US Coast Guard
Sergeant Les Carlyon: US Marine Corps
General Alano Salas: Venezuelan Marine Infantry commander

PACIFIC OCEAN/ACAPULCO

Pete Holder: Australian-born skipper of the *Diamantina*
Mr Lee: first mate on the *Diamantina*
Julianne Balwyn: daughter of English nobility, *Diamantina* crew member
Fifi Lamont: ship's cook on the *Diamantina*
Sergeant Narayan Shah: formerly of Her Majesty's Royal Gurkha Regiment

Corporal Birendra: formerly of Her Majesty's Royal Gurkha
    Regiment
Private Thapa: formerly of Her Majesty's Royal Gurkha
    Regiment
Private Subba: formerly of Her Majesty's Royal Gurkha
    Regiment
Private Sharma: formerly of Her Majesty's Royal Gurkha
    Regiment
Miguel Pieraro: contracted beef hauler for McDonald's
Rhino Ross: former CPO, United States Coast Guard
Dietmar Dietz: navigator
Henry Cesky: Brooklyn-based construction magnate
Larry Zood: internet pornographer
Phoebe St John: survivor, heiress, from Boston
Jason St John: survivor, heir, from Boston
Denby Moorhouse: Basel-based merchant banker
Marc Unwin: oil broker
Lars Havel: Norwegian ship's mate
Mariela Pieraro: Miguel's wife
Pankesh Daxa: Sri Lankan chief engineer, *Aussie Rules*
Rohan van der Meuwe: Dutch ship's engineer, *Aussie Rules*
Urvan Plost: Dutch ship's engineer, *Aussie Rules*

QATAR/KUWAIT

Bret Melton: former US Ranger, veteran *Army Times* foreign
    correspondent
Sayad al Mirsaad: Jordanian journalist with Al Jazeera news
    agency
Captain Christian Lohberger: US 7th Cavalry
Lieutenant Leo Euler: US 7th Cavalry
Sergeant-Major Bo Jaanson: US 7th Cavalry
Specialist Vincent Alcibiades: US 7th Cavalry
Corporal Tucson Shetty: US 7th Cavalry
Sergeant Fryderyk Milosz: Polish GROM squad leader
Colonel Rudi Molenz: Israeli Air Force pilot

PACOM, PEARL HARBOR, HAWAII

Admiral James Ritchie: US Navy
Captain Andrew McKinney: PA to Admiral Ritchie
Colonel Brian Maccomb: US Army's 500th Military Intelligence
    Brigade
Jed Culver: Louisianan attorney
Commander Damon Oakshott: US Navy, aide to Admiral Ritchie
Asher Warat: Israel's envoy to the United States
Governor Linda Lingle: Republican senator, Governor of Hawaii
Lieutenant General Stephen Francis Murphy: Commander, US
    Army, 25th Infantry Division

CENTCOM, DOHA

General Tommy Franks: Commander of the United States Central
    Command

BRUSSELS

General JL Jones: Commander of the United States European
    Command

SOUTHCOM, COMAYAGUA, HONDURAS

Lieutenant Colonel Susan Pileggi: Acting Commander,
    SOUTHCOM

FORT LEWIS, WASHINGTON

General Jackson Blackstone: US Army, Commander, Fort Lewis
Major Ty McCutcheon: US Air Force, aide to General Blackstone

Area affected by the Wave

SCALE

0 Kilometres 1500

ONE DAY

14 MARCH, 2003

1

PITIÉ-SALPÊTRIÈRE HOSPITAL, PARIS

The killer awoke, surrounded by strangers. An IV line dripped clear fluid through a long, thick needle punched into the back of her right hand. Surgical tape held the silver spike in place and tugged at the fine blonde hairs growing there. The strangers – all women, she thought dully – leaned in, their faces knotted with anxiety, apparently for her. But she stared instead at her hands as they lay in her lap on a thin brown blanket. They looked strong, even masculine. She turned them over, examining them. The nails were cut short. Calluses disfigured her knuckles, the heels of both palms, and the sides of her hands, from the base of both little fingers down to her wrists. The more she stared, the more unsettled she became. Like the women gathered around her bed, those hands were completely alien to her. She had no idea who she was.

'Cathy? Are you all right?'

'Nurse!' somebody called out.

The strangers, three of them, seemed to launch themselves at her bed. She felt herself tense up, but they simply wanted to comfort her.

'*Docteur! Elle s'est réveillée . . .*'

She felt soft hands patting her down, stroking her like one might comfort a child who's suffered a bad fright. *Cathy* – that wasn't her name, was it? – Cathy tried not to panic or to show how much she didn't want any of these women touching her. They looked weird, not the sort of people she'd want as friends.

And then, she remembered. They weren't her friends. They were her mission. And her name wasn't Cathy. It was Caitlin.

The women were dressed in cheap clothing, layered for warmth. Falling back into the pillows, recovering from an uncontrolled moment of vertigo into which she had fallen, Caitlin Monroe composed herself. She was in a hospital bed, in a private room, and in spite of the apparent poverty of her 'friends', the room was expensively fitted out. The youngest of the women wore a brown suede jacket, frayed at the cuffs and elbows and festooned with colourful protest buttons. A stylised white bird. A rainbow. A collection of slogans: *Halliburton Watch*, *Who would Jesus bomb?* and *Resistance is fertile*.

Caitlin took a sip of water from a squeeze bottle by the bed.

'I'm sorry,' she croaked. 'What happened to me?'

She received a pat on the leg from an older, red-haired woman wearing a white tee-shirt over some sort of lumpy handmade jumper. *Celia*. 'Aunty' Celia, although she wasn't related to anyone in the room. Aunty Celia had very obviously chosen this strange ensemble to show off the writing on her shirt, which read: *If you are not outraged you are not paying attention.*

'Doctor!' cried the woman in the doorway.

Maggie. An American, like Caitlin. And there the similarity ended. Maggie the American was short and barrel-chested and pushing fifty, where Caitlin was tall, athletic and young.

She felt around under her blanket and came up with a plastic control stick for the bed. 'Try this,' she offered, passing the control to the young girl she knew as Monique. A pretty, raven-haired Frenchwoman. 'See, the red call button. That'll bring 'em.' Then, gently touching the bandages that swaddled her head, she asked, 'Where am I?'

'You're in a private room, at the Pitié-Salpêtrière Hospital in Paris,' explained Monique. 'Paris, France,' she added self-consciously.

Caitlin smiled weakly. 'S'okay. I remember Paris is in France.' She paused. 'And now I am too, I guess. How did I get here? I don't remember much after coming out of the Chunnel on the bus.'

The large American woman standing over by the door to her room (*Maggie – try to remember her fucking name!*) turned away from her post. 'Fascist asswipes, that's how. Attacked us outside of Calais.'

'Skinheads,' explained Monique. 'And you were *magnifique*!'

'I was?'

'Oh yes,' the French girl enthused, as the others chorused their agreement. Monique looked no more than seventeen years old, but Caitlin knew her to be twenty-two. She knew a lot about Monique Duroc. 'These National Front fascists, Le Pen's bully boys, they stopped the bus and began pulling us out, hitting and kicking us. You stood up to them, Cathy. You fought with them. Slowed them down long enough for the union men to reach us and drive them away.'

'Union men?'

'Workers,' Maggie informed her. 'Comrades from the docks at Calais. We'll meet up with them and the others in Berlin, for the next rally, if you're up for it. We really gotta keep Bush on the back foot. Mobilise the fucking streets against him.'

Caitlin tried to reach for any memories of the incident but it was like grabbing at blocks of smoke. She must have taken a real pounding in the fight.

'I see,' she said, but really she didn't. 'So I beat on these losers?'

Monique smiled brightly for the first time. 'You are one of our tough guys, no? It was your surfing. You told us you always had to fight for your place on the waves. *Really* fight. You once punched a man off his board for . . . what was it . . . dropping in?'

Caitlin felt as though a great iron flywheel in her mind had suddenly clunked into place. Her cover story. To these women she was Cathy Mercure. Semi-pro wave rider. Ranked forty-sixth in the world. Part-time organiser for the Sea Shepherd Conservation Society, a deep green militant environmental group famous for direct and occasionally violent confrontation with any number of easily demonised eco-villains. Ocean dumpers, long-line tuna boats, Japanese whale killers – they were all good for a TV-friendly touch-up by the Sea Shepherds. But that was her cover. Her jacket.

She took another sip of cool water and closed her eyes for a moment.

Her real name was Caitlin Monroe. She was a senior field agent with Echelon, a magic box hidden within the budgets of a dozen or more intelligence agencies, only half of them American. She was a killer, and these women were . . . for a half second, she had no idea. And then the memory came back, clear and hard: these women were not her targets, but they would lead her to the target.

Al Banna.

Caitlin cursed softly under her breath. She had no idea what day it was. No idea how long she'd been out, or what had transpired in that time.

'Are you all right?' It was the French girl, Monique. The reason she was here, with these flakes.

'I'm cool,' said Caitlin. 'Do you mind?' she asked, pointing at the television that hung from the ceiling. 'I feel like I'm lost or something. How'd the peace march go?'

'Brilliant!' said the red-headed woman. Aunty Celia. She was a Liverpudlian with a whining accent like an ice pick in the eardrums. 'There was 'undreds of thousands of people. Chirac sent a message and all. Berlin's gonna be huge.'

'Really?' said Caitlin, feigning enthusiasm. 'That's great. Was there anything on the news about it? Or about the war?' she continued, pointedly looking at the television.

'Oh sorry,' muttered Monique as she dug another remote control out of the blankets on Caitlin's bed. Or Cathy's bed, as she would have thought of it.

A flick of the remote and the screen lit up.

'CNN?' asked Caitlin.

Monique flicked through the channels, but couldn't find the news network. White noise and static hissed out of the television from channel 13, where it should have been. She shrugged. There was nothing on MSNBC either, just an empty studio, but all of the French-language channels were available, as was BBC World.

'Can we watch the Beeb then?' asked Celia. 'Me French, you know, it's not the best.'

Caitlin really just wanted to carve out a couple of minutes to herself, so she could get her head back in the game. Her injuries must be serious, having put her under for three days, and although her cover was still intact, she didn't want to take any chances. She needed to re-establish contact with Echelon. They'd have maintained overwatch while she was out. They could bring her back up to –

'Eh up? What's this then?' blurted Celia.

Everyone's eyes fixed on the screen, where an impeccably groomed Eurasian woman with a perfectly modulated BBC voice was struggling to maintain her composure. '. . . *vanished. Communications links are apparently intact and fully functional, but remain unresponsive. Inbound commercial flights are either returning to their points of origin or being diverted to Halifax and Edmonton in Canada, or to airports throughout the West Indies, all of which remain unaffected so far.'*

The women all began to chatter at once, much to Caitlin's annoyance. On screen the BBC's flustered anchorwoman explained that the 'event horizon' seemed to extend down past Mexico City, out into the Gulf, swallowing most of Cuba, encompassing all of the continental US and a big chunk of south-eastern Canada, including Montreal. Caitlin had no idea yet what she meant by the term 'event horizon', but it didn't sound friendly. A hammer started pounding on the inside of her head as she watched the reporter stumble through the rest of her read.

'. . . *from a Canadian air base have not returned. US Naval flights out of Guantanamo Bay, at the southern tip of Cuba, have likewise dropped out of contact at the same point, seventy kilometres north of the base. Reuters is reporting that attempts by US military commanders at Guantanamo to contact the Castro government in Havana have also failed.'*

Caitlin realised that the background buzz of the hospital had died away in the last few minutes. She heard a metallic clatter as a tray fell to the floor somewhere nearby. Caitlin had a passing acquaintance with the Pitié-Salpêtrière. There had to be nearly three thousand people in this hospital and at that moment they were all silent, the only human sounds coming from the television sets that hung in every room and ward, a discordant clashing of French and English voices, all of them speaking in the same clipped, urgent tone.

'*The Prime Minister, Mr Blair, has released a statement calling for calm and promising to devote the full resources of the British Government to resolving the crisis. A Ministry of Defence spokesman confirmed that British forces have gone onto full alert, but that NATO headquarters in Brussels has not yet issued any such orders. The Prime Minister rejected calls by the Liberal Democrats to immediately recall British forces deployed in the Middle East for expected operations against the regime of Saddam Hussein.'*

'That'd be fookin' right,' Aunty Celia muttered to herself.

The reporter was about to speak again when she stopped, placing a hand to one ear, obviously taking instructions from her producer.

'Right, thank you,' she said before continuing. *'We have just received these pictures from a low-orbit commercial satellite that passed over the eastern seaboard of America a short time ago.'*

The screen filled up with black-and-white still shots of New York. The imagery was not as sharp as some of the mil-grade stuff Caitlin had seen over the years, but it was good enough to easily pick out individual vehicles and quite small buildings.

'This picture shows the centre of New York, as of twenty-three minutes ago,' said the reporter. *'Our technical department has cleaned up the image, allowing us to pull into a much tighter focus.'*

Caitlin recognised Times Square from above. She quickly estimated the virtual height as being about two thousand metres, before the view reformatted down to something much closer, probably about five or six hundred feet. The Beeb's IT guys were good. It was a remarkably clear image, but profoundly disturbing. Her brief curse was lost in the gasps and swearing of the other women. Fires, frozen in one frame of satellite imagery, burned throughout the square where hundreds of cars had smashed into each other. Smoke and flames also poured out from a few buildings. Buses and yellow cabs had run up onto the footpath and in some cases right into shopfronts and building facades. But nothing else moved. The photograph seemed to have captured an unnatural, ghostly moment. Not because they were looking at a still shot of a great metropolis in the grip of some weird, inexplicable disaster. But because nowhere in that eerie black-and-white image of one of the busiest cities in the world was there a single human being to be seen.

2

The lower reaches of the Cascades never failed to impress James Kipper. Dropping his backpack for a five-minute rest and a drink of water, he rewarded himself for the morning's trek with a moment staring down the long, deeply wooded valley up which he had climbed. Snow lay in patches along the well-beaten trail and dropped in wet clumps from the sagging branches of fir and pine which covered the gentle slopes below him in a dense green carpet. He loved it out here. Nature was so powerful, the hand of man so light, you could have been hundreds of years removed from the twenty-first century. The brisk but unseasonably sunny morning had made hiking up the remote valley a rare pleasure for the senses. The air was fragrant with sap and the rich, brown mulch of earth warmed by the sun for the first time in months. A breeze, just strong enough to set the treetops swaying, carried the natural white noise of a nearby stream, running heavy with an early melt. As he stood at the edge of a small plateau he could imagine the landscape below dotted with castles and mounted knights. As the father of a little girl just lately in school, knights and castles and fairytales were seldom far from his mind these days.

Kipper sucked in a draught of air so clean and cold it hurt all the way down into his chest. But it hurt *good*. The temperature hadn't snuck much past the mid fifties but he was well dressed for the hike, and could even feel sweat trickling down the inside of his arms. Another mouthful of icy spring water added pleasantly to the discordant sensations of being both hot and cold in parts. His breath plumed out in front of him and his stomach rumbled, reminding the engineer that it had been four hours since his last substantial meal, a bowl of pork sausages and beans cooked over the coals at his camp site a few miles down-range. Kipper unzipped his Gore-Tex jacket and fished around inside for the protein bar he'd stored in one of the many pockets before setting out that morning. It would be satisfyingly warm and chewy by now.

He frowned at the buzzing in one of the pockets. A second later the trilling of his satellite phone punched him back into the real world. The phone was a concession to his wife, Barb. Three days a year he was allowed to run around the woods by himself, but as a former New Yorker, Barb had 'issues' with his 'nature-boy shtick', and insisted that if he was going to go commune with the elves he should at least take a sat phone and GPS locator with him. 'So we can find your body, before the coyotes and buzzards are finished with it,' she'd said.

He took out the heavy lump of hated technology, scowling at the small screen as he realised it wasn't even her on the line. Judging by the number, the connection ran all the way back to City Hall.

Well, now I'm really pissed, he thought. Only his wife and the park rangers were supposed to have this number, and, true to her promise, Barb had never actually used it. But apparently she'd gone and given it to some pinhead at work. Unless of course it was telemarketers. *Please God, don't let it be telemarketers.*

He was simultaneously dreading and relishing the prospect as he answered. If this was some asshole in New Delhi trying to sell him a time-share apartment . . .

'Kipper, are you there?'

The chief engineer of Seattle City Council closed his eyes and exhaled. 'Hey Barney. This better be good, man.'

Whoever had decided there was something worth interrupting his precious hiking holiday tor had chosen the messenger well. Barney Tench was his closest friend and probably the only person who could call him right now, safe in the knowledge that he would survive the encounter.

'It ain't good, Kip,' said Tench, and now Kipper noticed the tremor in his friend's voice. Was he scared?

When Barney spoke again he sounded like he'd just survived a train wreck. Like he was terrified. 'It's fucked, man. Totally fucked. You gotta get back here right now. I know it's your break and all, but we need you – right now.'

Kipper shivered as a single bead of sweat trickled down his spine before hitting a patch of thermal underwear and being absorbed. 'What's up, Barn?' he asked. 'Just tell me what's going on.'

Tench groaned. 'That's it, Kip – nobody knows. Could be a war. Could be a fucking comet strike. We don't know.'

'A what?'

His surroundings were completely forgotten now. All of James Kipper's attention was focused down the invisible connection to his friend and colleague back in the city. A friend who seemed to have lost his marbles.

'What d'you mean "a comet or a war", Barney? What's going on?'

'The whole country is *gone*, Kip. All of it, 'cept us. And Alaska, I guess. Even Canada's gone – most of it, anyway, in the east.'

The ice water he'd just swallowed was sitting very heavily in his stomach, as though he'd gulped down a gallon of the stuff instead of just a mouthful. That might have been anger – he was beginning to suspect this was some sort of prank. Tench was famous for them. When they were rooming together in college, he'd fabricated an entire gala ball at the Grand Hyatt, convincing a couple of college babes to hand out 'free', 'strictly limited' tickets on campuses all over town. They'd got as drunk as lords sitting in the foyer, dressed in rented tuxedos, watching hundreds of students waving their bogus ball tickets in the face of a bewildered hotel manager. Barney Tench was more than capable of fucking with someone's head for a laugh. Especially Kipper's.

'Gone where, Barn?' he growled. 'You're not making any sense.'

'Just gone, Jimmy. Just fucking *gone*.' His voice was scaling higher with every word he said. 'Turn on your locator beacon. There's a National Guard chopper headed your way soon. They're gonna pick you up and transfer you to a plane somewhere. It'll get you straight in here. Council's called an emergency meeting.

All heads of departments. Governor's office is sending a team, although nobody can find Gary Locke. His schedule had him in transit today. In the air,' he added, as though that explained everything.

'Barney, is my family safe?' asked Kipper.

'They're fine, buddy, they're fine. Barb gave me your number. Look, I gotta go. The Guard can fill you in. I got a thousand calls to make now I found you. Just fire up that beacon, sit your ass down and wait.'

'Bar–'

But the line cut out.

'What the fuck was that about?' he muttered. Shaking his head, Kipper knelt in front of his pack and popped the snap lock on the pocket containing his personal locator beacon, a small lightweight ACR Terrafix unit. He powered up the little yellow device and couldn't help searching the skies, even though he knew his ride was probably still an hour away. Assuming it came at all, and Barney wasn't now roaring with laughter, about to fall backwards off his chair. Who knew?

Sub-zero air torrents high above him stretched a few scraps of cloud into long white ribbons, streaming away towards the coast. He caught sight of a giant hawk as it dived into the valley, wings folded back.

'Someone's about to get eaten,' he thought aloud.

Then he noticed the contrail, maybe twenty miles further north. The sky was crisscrossed with them during the colder months – great white arcs of vapour trailing the jet liners as they headed for Seattle, or the Pacific and the long haul to Japan or down to Honolulu. There seemed to be fewer than usual, just this one actually, and he had never seen a plane tracking so low over the Cascades before. His unease at the surprise call from Barney tightened into alarm as he watched the slow arc of the aircraft and realised it wasn't going to clear the mountains towards which it was headed.

'No,' he whispered, aware that he almost never spoke aloud on his hiking trips, and that he was positively yapping his head off today. 'No, don't.'

His mouth was dry, and he drank from his canteen without

thinking. The cold water hit his clenched stomach like acid, and for a second he thought he might vomit. That faraway plane, a thin tube of metal enfolding – what, a hundred, two hundred souls? – slowly, gracefully, inexorably speared itself into the side of a mountain, impacting just over the snow line, freeing great blossoming petals of dirty yellow flame to roll away into the morning air.

'Ah shit . . .'

Kipper shook his head and took a few steps towards the small, roiling ball of fire, before he stopped himself. He would never make it, and anyway he had to stay here and wait for the chopper. He apparently had his own disaster to deal with.

Still, he had to do something. He keyed 911 into his sat phone, glancing down momentarily to check he'd got the numbers right. He could at least call this in. Maybe someone had survived – a ridiculous thought, which he recognised as such as soon as he'd had it. But he couldn't just stand by with his thumb in his ass, taking in the view, could he?

'Nine-One-One, which service do you require?' The dispatcher sounded harried, and just as freaked out as Barney had been. But then, Kipper thought, that was probably her normal state of being.

'This is James Kipper, chief engineer, Seattle City Council. I've just seen a passenger plane crash. A big jet.'

The dispatcher's voice seemed almost mechanical, washed free of human affect by the multiple layers of impossibly complicated technology required to allow Kipper to speak to her from the side of this mountain in the middle of nowhere. 'Sir, what is your location and the location of the incident?'

As Kipper told her that he was in central Washington state, in the lower reaches of the Cascades, and read his location off the GPS beacon, the soft rumble of the titanic explosion finally reached him.

'Sir, please repeat. Are you outside the metro area?'

'Yes, damn it. I just watched this plane go down in the mountains. It was flying out of the east and it got too low, and – '

'Are you outside the Seattle metro area, sir?'

'Yes, I – '

'Your call has been logged, sir, but we cannot dispatch anyone right now. Please hang up and leave the line free for genuine emergency calls.'

And with that he was cut off.

'What the fuck!' he said, loud enough to startle a flight of birds from a nearby tree. A mass of snow, disturbed by their take-off, fell to the ground with a soft, wet crunch.

Twenty miles to the north, a pillar of dark smoke climbed away into the hard blue sky. A secondary explosion bloomed silently in the heart of the maelstrom on the face of the granite peak. Kipper was still staring at the phone in disbelief when the sound reached him.

SEATTLE, WASHINGTON

The car park of the Safeway on Broadway East could be a challenge at the best of times. Barbara's little Honda had picked up three mystery scratches or dents in there over the past six months. But today it felt like genuine hell. With one hand she was trying to control a heavily laden trolley sporting at least two malfunctioning wheels, while carrying a sobbing child on her other arm and attempting to redial Kipper's number on her cell phone. The parking lot was full of hysterics and loons, some of them normal people who'd gone over the edge, others professional nutbars who'd turned up with sandwich boards urging everyone to *REPENT* as the *HOUR OF DOOM* was *AT HAND!!!!* The signs looked quite professional, as though they'd been prepared much earlier for just this occasion. Barb had taken a small measure of childish joy from clipping one of the God botherers with the corner of her fast-moving, barely controlled metal shopping cart.

She was less pleased with the long scrape she gouged out of the paintwork as she stumbled and lost her grip on the cart just as they made it back to the car. 'Shit!'

Suzie, who at six years old was way too big to be carried, one-armed or otherwise, for more than a few steps, struggled to clamber deeper into Barbara Kipper's embrace. 'I'm scared, Mommy,' she cried.

Struggling with her daughter, Barbara lost her grip on the cell phone – a cheap clamshell model – which fell to the bitumen and broke in two. 'Oh shit! Oh . . . I'm sorry, sweetheart. Mommy's sorry. Just hop down, would you, and . . .'

Suzie, her head buried in Barbara's neck, shook her head and wailed, '*Noooo*.'

'Suffer the little children unto Him, good lady . . .'

Barb spun around to find that one of the religious nuts had followed her through the heaving crush of the car park and was holding aloft a small branch of some sort, waving it as if to bless her.

'Suffer the little – '

'I'll fucking suffer you to get the hell away from me, you goddamn freak! You're scaring the bejesus out of my daughter.'

She fixed him with such a baleful stare that he actually seemed to recoil as if struck, but Barbara, who was normally so conscious of others' feelings, felt not the least bit contrite. This place was a madhouse. It was like people had gone nuts or something when the news first came through, and these holy fucking lunatics were only making it worse.

Barb managed somehow to lower a clinging Suzie down to the ground while digging her keys out and thumbing the car's electronic lock. It opened with a reassuring *bleep-bloop*, lessening her fears that whatever had happened might have put the zap on all the electrics. Back in the store, some bearded panic merchant had jumped up onto a checkout to announce that an 'electromagnetic event' had taken out all the circuits, everywhere. Unfortunately for him, the automatic conveyer belt on which he was standing was entirely functional and it jerked forward, pulling his feet out from under him. The last Barb had seen of the man, he was lying on the floor of Safeway with a badly broken ankle.

His theatrics, combined with the almost instant viral panic that seemed to run through everyone, a couple of fender benders in the parking lot, followed by the inevitable blaring of horns, the trilling of alarms and increasingly ugly screams of abuse – it had all been enough to upset Suzie so badly she was shivering, begging to know where Daddy was, and whether it was 'Mine Eleven' happening again. Barbara Kipper soothed her as best she could while pushing the child into the back seat, where her stuffed panda, Poofy Bear, might at least provide some comfort.

She popped the hatch and transferred the shopping bags as quickly as possible, with no idea of how she was going to get away from here. The lot was a gridlocked nightmare, with people increasingly desperate to leave, backing and crunching into each other, while more turned up every minute, presumably to panic-buy a year's worth of discount Pop-Tarts and Cheeseburgers In A Can – the specials of the day.

A short distance away, two men were squaring up for a fight. An actual fight. One was huge, enormously obese, while the other looked tall and fit. God only knew what they were pissed at each other about. Perhaps the big guy got the last of the cheeseburgers. They circled each other, feinting and throwing out air punches, and then, much to Barb's surprise, the thinner of the two bent over and charged the other guy like a rhino, head-butting him in the gut. They went down in a tangle as police or maybe ambulance sirens seemed to be closing in from somewhere nearby. Barbara shook her head in disgust and threw the last of her groceries into the hatch.

Having unloaded the cart, she didn't dare push it back to the collection bay, for fear of leaving Suzie alone for even a moment. She could have killed Kipper at this point. He would choose this of all weeks to disappear into the mountains.

As soon as she voiced the thought in her mind, her heart lurched forward. *Disappeared*.

No, he wasn't gone too. He was fine. He'd left a hiking plan with her and the park rangers, and as soon as she'd called them they said there was no way he would have been anywhere near the edge of this . . . effect . . . event . . . whatever it was. It was on the far side of the mountains.

She began shaking anyway, an uncontrolled shudder that seized her whole body as dizziness threatened to steal her legs from under her. Biting down on a knuckle until she drew blood helped to focus her mind away from the terror that wanted to swamp her. The pain was something sharp and real, something on which to focus. And as soon as she did, Barb was embarrassed that she'd let herself get so frantic. She gathered up the broken pieces of her cell phone and tossed them into the front passenger seat before moving around to the driver's door. She was going to hit the shopping trolley if she backed out, but really didn't care. Getting Suzie away from here was more important.

'Is Daddy all right, Mommy? Is he okay?' she asked as soon as Barb had the door closed. It shut out some of the chaos and madness but meant that Suzie could see without any distractions just how disturbed her mother was.

'He's fine, sweetheart,' she said, as calmly as she could manage. 'His friends from work are phoning him and sending a helicopter just for him. To bring him home. He'll be back later, don't worry.'

'But what if he got *eaten*, Mommy. I heard a man in the store say everyone was *eaten*. Everyone.'

'Daddy is fine,' she repeated calmly, even as her head reeled with the insanity of it all. 'And nobody was eaten, Suzie. I don't know what's happened, but nobody was eaten. That's just silly talk. Now strap yourself in, sweetie. This is going to be very dangerous.'

The young girl snapped her seatbelt to show that she'd already done so, and Barb apologised for not noticing. She keyed the ignition (which worked perfectly, like those of all the other cars in the parking lot) and slowly but resolutely backed out of her parking space, pushing the trolley aside with the rear bumper. A few more scrapes and scratches, then.

The view out of the back window was bedlam, with people swarming and vehicles everywhere. Barb gritted her teeth and kept moving, even as she butted up against shoppers who didn't move out of her way. Some hammered on the window – one guy punching it so hard it cracked, causing Suzie to squeal in fear. But Barbara Kipper refused to stop, believing that to do so would see them trapped. She was only making a walking pace, but kept going. Not for the first time was she grateful to be driving a small car in this parking lot. Whereas SUVs and sedans soon got themselves jammed together, almost like broken teeth on a zipper, she was able to thread, very slowly and determinedly, through the crowd, until she made it to a small hedge line at the edge of the lot and gunned the little Honda right on through it. The car didn't like it much, and the scratching of branches on the paintwork was hideous. She almost certainly knocked the wheels out of alignment while mounting the kerb, but she was suddenly able to press the accelerator and break free onto Harvard Avenue. They bounced and hit the road with a terrible, metallic crunch. But at least they were out.

As they drove away in the heavy traffic, Barb was certain she heard the pop of gunfire. She couldn't help but keep looking at the phone, wondering if Barney had got through to Kip.

3

Somebody must have tipped off the ragheads, because they were wailing up a storm. Long ululating cries of '*Allahu Akbar*' rolled around the dusty confines of Camp Delta, drifting over the razor wire. General Musso heard them as tinny voices emanating from the speakers of a nearby computer in the situation room of the Naval Op Centre, at the southern end of the base. 'Operation centre' was a grand title for such a modest facility, a demountable hut with heavy grey air-con units rumbling away at the windows. It was a relatively mild Caribbean day outside. Late winter in Cuba was almost but not quite balmy. The brigadier general knew he could probably run up and down the nearest of the scrubby, low-rise hills that surrounded this part of the base without raising much of a sweat. But the room was stuffy. Dozens of laptops had been plugged into the existing cluster of workstations and they were all running hard, dumping waste heat into a space that was already overcrowded, with at least three times as many occupants as normal.

Having given up on the computers in frustration, Tusk Musso leaned over the old map table, gripping the back of a swivel chair, biting down hard on the urge to pick it up and throw it through the window. He was so angry – and, just quietly, so weirded out – that there was a fair chance he could have heaved that sucker all the way down to the water's edge. The bay was deep cerulean blue, almost perfectly still, and the chair would have made a satisfying splash. Unfortunately, Musso was the ranking officer on the base today and everybody was looking to him for answers. Guantanamo's naval commandant, Captain Cimines, was missing, apparently along with about three hundred million of his countrymen, and a whole heap of Mexicans and Canucks into the bargain. And Cubans too, Musso reminded himself. *Let's not forget our old buds just over the wire.*

'What are the locals up to, Georgie?' he rumbled.

His aide, Lieutenant Colonel George Stavros, delivered one brief shake of the head. 'Still hopping around, sir. Looks like someone really kicked over their anthill. Our guys have counted at least two hundred of them bugging out.'

'But nothing coming our way yet?'

'No sir. Santiago and Baracoa are still quiet. A few crowds building, but nothing too big.'

Musso nodded slowly. He was a huge man, with what looked like a solid block of white granite for a head, resting atop a tree trunk of a neck. Even that one simple gesture spoke of enormous reserves of power. He shifted his gaze from the antique, analogue reality of the map table with its little wooden and plastic markers, across to the banks of flat screens, which even now were refusing to tell him anything about what was going on a short distance to the north. The faces of the men and women around him were a study in barely constrained anxiety. They were a mixed service group about two dozen strong, representing all the arms of the US military that had a stake in Guantanamo, mostly Navy and Marines, but with a few Army and Air Force types thrown in. There was even one lone Coast Guard rep, mournfully staring at the map table, wondering where his little boat could possibly have gone. The cutter had dropped out of contact. It was easily found on radar, but would not respond to hail.

Musso had no permanent connection to Guantanamo. He'd been sent down to review operations at Delta, the first task of a new job, a *desk* job back in DC he really hadn't wanted. A genuine shooting war was about to begin, and here he was, on a fucking day trip to Gitmo, making sure a bunch of jihadi whackjobs were getting their asses wiped for them with silken handkerchiefs, not copies of the Koran. It was almost enough to test a man's faith, and more than enough to make this one regret the international law degree he'd taken as a younger marine. It had seemed like a good idea at the time. A fall back, his old man had called it, in case he didn't take to the Corps with any enthusiasm. Musso stood erect, folded his arms as though examining a really shitty used-car deal, and grunted.

'Okay. Let's take an inventory. What do we know for certain?' he asked, and began ticking the answers off on his fingers. 'Thirty-three minutes ago, we lost contact with CONUS for two minutes. We had nothing but static on the phones, sat links, the net, broadcast TV, radio – everything. Then, all of our comm links started functioning again, but we get no response to anything we send home. All our other links are fine – Pearl, NATO, ANZUS, CENT-COM in Qatar – but *not* Tampa. All responding and wanting to know what the hell is going on. But we have no fucking idea. I mean, look at that . . . What the hell is that about?'

The Marine Corps lawyer was waving his hand at a bank of TV monitors. They were all tuned in to US news networks, which should have been pumping out their inane babble twenty-four / seven. With the war in Iraq only days away, the global audience for reports out of America and the Middle East was huge and nigh on insatiable. But there was the Atlanta studio of CNN, back after a few minutes of static, devoid of life. The anchor desk sat in centre frame, and dozens of TV and computer screens flickered away in the background, but nobody from CNN was anywhere to be seen. The same over at Fox. Bill O'Reilly's chair was empty. Bloomberg still filled most of one monitor with garishly bright cascades of financial data, but the little picture window in one corner where you'd normally find a couple of dark-suited bizoids droning on about acquisitions and mergers was occupied by two chairs, what looked like some smouldering rags, and nothing else. Meanwhile another bank of screens, running satellite feeds from Europe and Asia, showed the studios there to be fully operational, and peopled by increasingly worried talking heads, none of whom could explain what was happening in North America.

'Anybody?' asked Musso, not really expecting an answer.

The silence might have become unbearable had it not been broken by a young ensign, who coughed nervously at the edge of the huddle. 'Excuse me, General,' she said.

Musso bit down on an irrational urge to snap at her, instead keeping his voice as level and non-threatening as he could. 'Yes, Ms . . . ?'

'Oschin, sir. I thought you might need to look at these. I've streamed vision from eighteen webcams onto a couple of monitors at my workstation. These cams are all in high-volume public areas, General. Grand Central in New York, Daley Plaza in Chicago, that sort of thing . . .'

Ensign Oschin, who was obviously uncomfortable addressing such a high-powered group, seemed to run down like a wind-up toy at that point. Musso noticed a couple of army officers glaring at her for having interrupted the big kids at play.

'Go on, Ensign,' he reassured her, giving the army jerk-offs a cold, hard glare. 'What's your point?'

Oschin stood a full inch taller. 'They're live feeds, sir, from all over the country. And there's nobody in them. Anywhere.'

That information fell like a lead weight into a dark, bottomless well, tumbling down out of sight. No one spoke as Musso held Oschin's gaze, seeing the fear gnawing away at her carefully arranged professional mask. He could taste a trace of bile at the back of his throat and he was unable to stop his thoughts straying to his family back home in Galveston. The boys would both be in school, and Marlene would be up to her elbows in blue rinse at the salon. He allowed himself the indulgence of a quick, wordless prayer on their behalf.

'Can you patch it through onto the main displays?' he asked.

'Aye sir.'

'Then do so, please, as quickly as you can.'

Oschin, a small nervy woman, spun around and retreated to the safety of her workstation, whipping her fingers across the keyboard in a blur. Other sysops, who'd been less successful in their own endeavours to raise anyone Stateside, snuck peeks over their shoulders at the results of her work as two large Sony flat panels hanging from the ceiling suddenly filled with multiple windows displaying scenes from across the US. Oschin appeared at the map table again with a laser pointer. She laid the red dot on the first window in the upper left-hand quadrant of the nearest screen.

'With your permission, General?'

'Of course.'

'That's the Mall of America, in Bloomington, Minnesota. Local time 1320 hours. You're looking at the main food court.'

It was empty. A small fire burned in one concession stand and it looked as though sprinklers may have tripped, but the image quality wasn't clear enough to be certain. It reminded Musso of an old zombie flick he'd watched as a kid. *Dawn of the Dead* or something. For some reason, his flesh crawled at the memory, even though he'd thought the movie was a dumbass piece of crap the first time he'd seen it. Oschin flicked the laser pointer over the next three windows as a group.

'Disneyland, California. Local time 1120 hours. You're looking at the concourse just inside the main entrance. Then you have Space Mountain in Tomorrowland. And finally Mickey's Toontown.'

Again, the pictures were poor in quality, but no less disturbing because of it. Not a soul moved anywhere in them. A breeze pushed litter around the main concourse, where some sort of golf buggy had run up on a gutter and tipped over. The young officer, her voice wavering, laid the red dot on a couple of piles of smoking rags. 'I think they may have been clothes, sir.'

Nobody replied, possibly because they all felt as sick in the gut as Musso. Oschin waited a second, then made her way through the rest of the image windows. Crown Center in Kansas City. Half-a-dozen cams from UCLA's Berkeley campus. A mortgage brokers' convention in Toledo. The main strip in Vegas – which looked like Satan's wrecker's yard, with cars all piled into each other and burning fiercely. Venice Beach. JFK Airport. The Strand in Galveston . . .

Musso arranged his features into a blank façade for that one. He'd already recognised the scene before Oschin had explained what they were looking at. Down in his meat, right down in the oldest animal parts of his being, he knew his family were gone.

Oblivious to the personal import of what she'd just shown them, Ensign Oschin carried on, cycling through a list of public gathering places that should have been teeming with people. All of them abandoned or empty, or . . . what?

'It's the Rapture,' whispered an army major standing directly across the table from Musso. He was one of the two who'd unsettled Oschin a few minutes ago. 'The end of days.'

Musso spoke up loudly and aggressively, smacking down on the first sign of anyone in this command unravelling. 'Major, if it was the Rapture, don't you think *you'd* be gone by now? And where are the sinners? Don't they get to stay and party? And last time I heard, this thing has a defined horizon, not too far north of here.'

Chastened and not a little put out, the major, whose name-tag read *Clarence*, clamped his mouth shut again.

Musso wished, for once in his life, that someone was giving him orders as opposed to the other way around. This was one football he didn't want to run with. He didn't know what to make of the video streaming out of his homeland. After 9/11 he didn't think anything could surprise him again. He'd been ready for the day he flicked on the television and saw mushroom clouds blooming over an American city. But this . . . this was bullshit.

'*Allahu Akbar. Allahu Akbar . . .*'

The distinct popping sound of gunfire in the middle distance crackled out of a set of speakers. Then came the screams.

'George,' growled Musso.

'I'm on it, sir.'

His second-in-command hurried out of the room to track down the source of this new disturbance. Musso waited for more shots, but none came.

'Okay,' he said. 'I'm not sending any more assets into this thing, whatever it is. I think we've established that it's a no-go zone.'

Both of the helicopters he'd ordered to fly north over international waters had apparently crashed soon after crossing the line that now defined the edge of the phenomenon.

'Okay. Let's call up Pacom . . .' he started to say.

'General, pardon me, sir. Permission to report?'

A fresh-faced Marine butterbar in full battle rattle appeared in the doorway, his dark features unaffected by the recent turn of events.

'Go ahead,' said Musso.

'It's the Cubans, sir. They've sent a delegation in through the minefield. They want to talk. Matter of fact, they're dying to. One of their vehicles hit a mine coming in and the others just kept on rolling.'

Musso stretched and rolled his neck, which had begun to ache with a deep muscle cramp. He was probably hunching his shoulders again. Marlene said she could tell a mile off when he was really pissed, because he seized up like the Hunchback of Notre Dame. *Marlene . . . Oh my god . . .*

'Okay,' he said quickly. 'Disarm them and bring them in. They're a few miles closer to it, whatever it is. They might have seen something we haven't.'

The lieutenant acknowledged the order and hurried away, weaving around Stavros, who returned at the same moment.

'I'm afraid a bunch of our guests decided to charge a guard detail,' he said, explaining the gunshots of just a few minutes ago. Things were moving so quickly that Musso had stopped caring about the incident as soon as it had failed to escalate. 'Two dead, five wounded. They've heard something is up. They think Osama's let off a nuke or something. The camps are locked down now.'

Musso took in the report and decided it didn't need any more of his attention. 'Folks, right now, I gotta say this. I don't think bin Laden or any of those raghead motherfuckers had anything to do with this. I think it's much bigger. But what the hell it is, I have no idea.'

The live feed from Oschin's webcam trawl stuttered along above his head. Mocking them all.

I wish it was just a nuke, thought Musso, but he kept it to himself.

4

The old sailboat was a twin-masted forty-footer carved out of thousand-year-old Huon pine from the Tasmanian highlands, a beautifully preserved museum piece. She'd placed third on corrected time in a Sydney–Hobart race way back in 1953, and in the decades since had logged enough miles to make it to the moon and back. In that time she'd been the plaything of a builder, a manufacturing tycoon, two dot-com millionaires, and Pete Holder.

Pete knew he was never going to be anywhere near as wealthy as any of the *Diamantina*'s former skippers – although the dot-com guys had tanked badly a couple of years ago and were probably down to their last two or three million now, hence the bargain basement price he'd paid for the old girl. Not that he could give a shit. The Australian Government issued his passports, but he considered himself a citizen of the waves, and for the past eight years, after taking a redundancy payment from his old job as a rig boss for Shell, he'd been devoted entirely to the pursuit of the world's most fantastic lifestyle. Mostly that involved meandering from one secret surf break to the next, putting in a few weeks at the Maldives, cutting down the Indonesian archipelago to Nias, or booming across the Pacific to chase triple overhead sets off northern California. And sometimes, of course, to pay for this life of pure indulgence, it meant loading the boat up with half a ton of compressed ganja and running the gauntlet of international supernarcs like the DEA and the AFP.

Even worse than them were the state-sponsored but highly autonomous shakedown artists like the crooked Indonesian Navy commodore he'd tangled with in Bali last year. Or the Peruvian *federales* he thought he'd paid off in Callao only to have them come back a day later saying they'd 'lost' his very generous bribe and would be in need of another to the same value within twenty-four hours – unless Señor Pedro felt like seeing out his days as a slave in a manganese mine deep in the jungles of la Montaña. Pete had transferred the money within two hours and never sailed into the territorial waters of Peru again.

As he watched Fifi and Jules moving around to clear away the remains of lunch, the veteran smuggler catalogued all of the near misses he'd survived over the years. It was a sobering exercise, one he forced himself to endure before every new payday, as a caution against hubris and stupidity. Bad luck he couldn't control, but with good planning and preparation he could at least minimise any opportunities for the ever fickle finger of fate to insert itself firmly into his anus. Hubris and stupidity, on the other hand, were completely avoidable. They were the principle mechanism by which natural selection thinned out his competitors, and he'd be damned if he were going to fall victim to them. Pete Holder was a survivor.

'Mr Peter, sir?'

Lee had snuck up on him again. A Malaccan-Chinese from a 300-year-long line of pirates, Mr Lee was always doing that. Pete tried to rearrange his features into a sunny smile, but Lee knew him too well and responded with a pitying shake of the head. Pete was notorious for his ill temper in the hours leading up to a job, and try as he might to control it, his face was always clouded over and dark until they were safely away. Frankly, he resented the necessity for the whole smuggling business and would have done almost anything other than getting a normal job to avoid it. But he couldn't, so here they were.

'Hey, Lee. What's up, mate?' Pete tried for a light tone, the sort of thing his fellow Tasmanian Errol Flynn might have pulled off if he'd gone into smuggling and full-time surf bummery. Instead he just came off as clipped and nervous. He noticed Fifi and Jules throw a curious glance back his way. They'd only been with him eighteen months, but like Mr Lee they'd learned to read his moods with an almost preternatural accuracy. It was the legacy of living so close together and taking things right up to the edge.

'Something is up, Mr Peter.'

'Okay. I'm waiting.' Jeez, he wished he could *loosen up*.

'The *Pong Su*, she is changing course, sir. She will not meet up with us if she continues on her new heading.'

Pete was dressed in ripped board shorts and a sun-faded sky-blue cotton shirt. The Tropic of Cancer was well north of them and the day would have been uncomfortably warm were it not for a gentle sou'-wester, which only just bellied out the sails but did little to dry the sweat pooling between the breasts of his female crew.

'Come see. I show,' said Lee.

Jules finished scraping a plate of grilled fish scraps over the side and used the dish to shade her eyes as she straightened up. 'Is there something the matter, Pete?' she called out in her rather posh English accent, the sort of accent his mother would have called 'all peaches and cream'.

'Dunno yet,' he answered. 'Could be. Let's be ready to split just in case. You and Fifi better kit up too, soon as you're ready.'

'Righty-o,' she said. The two girls set about their cleaning chores with added vigour. Both were athletic blondes in their early twenties and resembled each other closely enough that Pete had long ago taken to calling them 'the Twins', even though Jules was a Brit, a trust-fund exile from Surrey, while Fifi had run away from a trailer park in Oregon at the age of fifteen. They brought a rare and valuable mix of skills to the *Diamantina*. Jules had a masters in accounting from the London School of Economics, and her father, the late Lord Balwyn, was a two-time winner of the Fastnet race and a board member of the Royal Thames Cruising Yacht Squadron. Or he had been on the RTCYS board, until Scotland Yard had come calling at the Manor one day with a warrant for his arrest on a hundred and twenty-nine charges of fraud and tax evasion.

Fifi, the ship's cook, on the other hand, had not even finished high school and her only inheritance was genetic. Her mom, one of Larry Flynt's very first *Hustler* models, had bequeathed her some good looks and a mighty fine arse, but apart from an explosive temper and a morally flexible attitude to life's manifold challenges, that was about it. And compared to her mom, Fifi was still kind of uptight. She'd left home after her fourth 'stepdad', the aptly named Randy, a shiftless, unemployed crab-pot repairman, had suggested they have a threesome and go on *Springer* to tell their story. He'd heard they could score a trip to Chicago, a free stay in a motel, and two hundred dollars' cash for expenses. Fifi was on the road, with her thumb in the air, about half an hour later.

She was a great cook, however, and hell on mag wheels with a loaded weapon.

Pete could hear the Twins rummaging through the gun locker just beyond the forward bulkhead as he sat at the nav station and tried to make sense of the screens in front of him. Even with the air-con running, it was hot below decks, and the prospect of a transfer going bad gave the confines of the boat a claustrophobic feeling. The *Diamantina* was fitted out for high luxury, thanks to her former owners, the dot-com greedheads, and Pete was able to sink into a soft leather swivel chair adapted for maritime use from a Herman Miller original, but nothing about sitting in front of the flat panel displays in the small nook outside his personal cabin made him happy. He could see immediately what Lee was talking about as he watched a computer-generated track of the *Pong Su*, the North Korean freighter scheduled to swap four million dollars' worth of perfectly counterfeited US currency for a 'full stick' – one million dollars of the real deal bundled away in the *Diamantina*'s stronghold. That money represented the profits of three high-risk dope runs from Mexico up to California. It wasn't the sort of business they'd normally choose to get into, but the blow-out in Bali had left him few options.

Now it seemed he had fewer still. Forty minutes ago the *Pong Su* had deviated sharply off course, and was apparently running rudderless. It looked for all the world as though she'd lost steering.

'No good, Mr Peter,' avowed Lee. 'Look here, and here too.'

It was only then that Pete realised that the *Pong Su* wasn't the only ship in trouble. Five other vessels within the *Diamantina*'s radar bubble had all likewise veered off course and appeared to be heading out of the designated shipping lanes.

'Pete, you'd better come up on deck. There's something very strange happening off to the north.' It was Jules, with Fifi at her elbow. After cleaning up they had changed into their rig for the handover. Both were now dressed in ballistic vests and wearing combat harnesses weighed down with reloads for the Vietnam-era M16s and grenade launchers they would take from the armoury fifteen minutes before the rendezvous. But Pete Holder was beginning to doubt there'd be any rendezvous today, or ever.

'What do you mean "strange"?' he asked.

'I mean odd, weird, right out of the bloody ordinary, Pete. It looks like a storm front came out of that heat haze to the north, but . . . well . . . you'll need to see for yourself.'

Grunting in frustration, he pushed himself up out of the chair and hurried up on deck. Moving forward to the bow, shielding his eyes, he saw immediately what she meant. Far to the north of them, half the sky seemed to be taken up with the queerest, most exotic-looking storm front he'd ever seen. It appeared to sparkle and hang still in the air. It must have been a long way distant, because it appeared from beneath the horizon and climbed away into the stratosphere. Just standing, watching it, he felt insignificant and deeply vulnerable.

'Radio's not working!' Fifi called out from below.

'Radio's fine . . .' he started to say, then stopped. They'd been monitoring the airwaves for any US or Mexican government traffic, using the yacht's high-gain antennae to eavesdrop on Coast Guard and Navy signals – a constant background chatter. It was only when Fifi pointed out the silence from the radio that he realised he'd heard nothing in over half an hour. Frowning at the bizarre weather up ahead, he hastened back below decks.

Mr Lee was flicking switches and twirling dials on the M802 marine radio. It was only then that they picked up the babble of some commercial station down in Acapulco, where a DJ was reading in heavily accented English a local police order imposing an immediate curfew that would remain in effect until contact with the central government was 're-established'.

'Oh, bugger this . . .' muttered Pete at the unpleasant feeling of déjà vu. It transported him back to when he'd woken up late one morning, dockside in Santa Monica, after a hard night's partying with his then relatively new crew-mates. He'd spent nearly the entire day mooching around, drinking Irish coffee and napping off his hangover. It was 11 September, 2001 and he'd missed almost all of the day that had changed the world. Only Lee's return from the city in the afternoon had alerted him to the news from the East Coast. As he sat below decks now, sweat leaking out of his armpits and trickling down his sides, listening to an increasingly hysterical radio jock talking about '*la catástrofe*', and watching the strange, ghostly track of those five ships to the north, Pete Holder felt as though time had folded back in on itself.

'I dunno what's happened,' he said, 'but I've got a sick feeling about this. And about that weird fucking storm front. I'm gonna go with my gut. Mr Lee, let's make ready for a fast run, sou'-sou'-west. Keep a watch on the *Pong Su*. If nothing changes, we're gonna blow this off in fifteen minutes. I want to put some serious miles between us and . . . whatever.'

The *Diamantina* slipped through a light swell, pushed south-south-west by a freshening breeze. Mr Lee had the wheel, as phlegmatic in the face of world's end as he had been staring down the barrel of an M16 in Bali. Pete wondered what, if anything, would upset him. Not that it mattered, because between himself and the Twins there was plenty of freaking out to go around.

'Zombie Jew on a fucking Zimmer frame,' cursed Fifi.

'What?'

'It's redneck for "Christ on a crutch", Pete. Let's stay on the ball, shall we?' said Jules.

The three smugglers were crouched in front of the Samsung monitor, a brand new 23-inch flat screen Pete had picked up back in La Paz during a night of tequila shots and hard bar-tering with an Italian yachtsman of long acquaintance. CNN's Asian bureau, reporting out of the network's regional HQ in Hong Kong, was running in a small window that took up about a quarter of the screen. Jules had plugged into the live web feed via an iridium phone, and if they watched it much longer they'd need all the money in the hold to pay this month's bill. If it ever arrived.

Pete's eyes flicked over to the GPS window, which showed them retreating from the abandoned rendezvous with the *Pong Su* at eleven knots. The North Korean ship was still describing a long, lazy arc that would eventually see it run aground somewhere near Mazatlán, in the next day or so. Pete, the only one of them to have a seat in front of the display, had to rub his eyes. Like an addicted gamer, he'd been staring so hard at the screen he hadn't blinked in a long while. He shook his head as he rubbed the irritation away, his vision blurring slightly when he refocused on the window in which footage of a major highway crash was now being shown.

He couldn't get his head around these pictures, which had come in from a small Canadian news team – some guys out of Quebec, according to the dateline. The image seemed to be out of focus or something. He could tell they were looking at a big pile-up on a six-lane highway, but everything was indistinct, as though viewed through poorly blown glass.

'*The effect is stationary,*' the heavily accented Québécois voice-over assured everyone. '*Mounted Police at the scene are not allowing anyone to approach the phenomenon after the loss of the two fire engines.*'

Blurred, wavering vision of two fire tenders came up, both of them overturned in a deep ditch by the side of the road. A few hundred metres beyond them, a large pile-up of vehicles burned freely.

'Oh man, this is really putting the zap on my head,' Fifi muttered.

'We need to think this through,' said Jules, in her oddly cool, high-tone manner. 'This could be quite awful.'

Pete rubbed at his three-day beard, completely lost for an answer. For a few minutes, a little earlier, he'd actually thought of heading north to raid an empty city. He could have sailed into Santa Monica and picked up a super-yacht, provisioned her for a year, filled the leftover space with jewels and ammo. But CNN had convinced him otherwise. It was abundantly clear that you could go into the 'storm front' that had appeared to their north, but you'd never come back. What was the old Argentinian phrase? It 'disappeared' people.

'I think we might shoot through to my old stomping ground,' he said. 'Hobart looks far enough away to me. And I know people there. We can move this money in a flash.'

'But what if it starts growing?' asked Fifi, with a sharp edge to her voice. 'What if it just eats up the whole world, like the Blob or something?'

Pete gave her his most open, honest face. 'Then we're fucked, darlin'. Aren't we?'

'Pete . . .' It was Jules, if anything looking even more concerned than before. The worry lines between her eyes were virtual canyons now. 'How fast can we get to Hobart?'

'Why?' he asked. Jules had a post-graduate degree in keeping a stiff upper lip, probably thanks to her old man. If she thought something even worse was coming their way, it really didn't bear thinking about.

'Because nobody will want greenbacks if Uncle Sam's beamed up to the *Enterprise* and flown away for good.'

The bow of the yacht sliced into the face of a larger than normal wave, throwing them all slightly off balance. The *Diamantina* climbed up and over the crest, slamming down hard on the far side with a great, hollow boom. Fifi and Jules braced themselves against the nearest bulkhead. Pete hung on to the arms of his chair. On the computer screen, Stan Grant interviewed a physicist from the Hong Kong University of Science and Technology, but Pete Holder had already tuned out. Jules had a point: if this was a permanent deal, they had very little time before their hard-earned stick was worth less than a handful of Polish zlotys.

'You're right,' he said tonelessly. 'We have to get back onshore and change our money over. Do we know if the Caymans are affected? Or the Canal?'

'We can find out,' Jules replied, nodding at the screen. 'But Pete, I don't think we can get there in time. We have to get onshore as soon as we can. Somewhere big enough to convert the money, but far enough removed from whatever it is, that blind panic hasn't taken over yet.'

'Acapulco's still there,' said Fifi. 'But they're locked down, accordin' to the radio.'

'That might be a good thing,' shrugged Jules. 'If they keep a lid on things long enough, we might just get in and out. Otherwise we'll have to run down to Guatemala or El Salvador.'

Pete chewed his lower lip, sucking the salt from it as he pondered the unfolding disaster. A window displaying the Google news page refreshed, informing him that nearly three thousand stories had already been filed on the phenomenon – none of them from North America. The bright blue hyperlinks all led to European and Asian sites. One, from Agence France-Presse, reported that trading had been suspended on the London, Tokyo and Sydney stock exchanges. Just beneath it, a Novosti report from Moscow claimed that the Russian armed forces had all been called into barracks and placed on high alert. Pete adjusted his balance as the *Diamantina* slipped sideways down the face of another large wave. 'You're right,' he concluded. 'We've got to get in somewhere, fast. This feels like a big bucket of shit's about to tip over and bury the whole world. Let's head for Acapulco.'

'You sure?' asked Fifi, her usually sunny features darkened by real fear. 'That's close to the . . . thing.'

'I know,' said Pete. 'But I got friends there – well, contacts, anyway. And the effect's not moving.'

For now, he thought to himself.

5

The shock and awe was not long in coming. Coalition headquarters in Qatar was a focal point of communication links, neutron-star-dense, not all of them controlled by the military. Hundreds of journalists had gathered there to report on the upcoming invasion of Iraq, and many if not all of them enjoyed direct voice and data access to their own headquarters and, of course, to the wider global media. 'The incident', as it was now being referred to, had occurred shortly before a scheduled press briefing in the main media room, giving the assembled journalists just long enough to work up a fine head of craziness, and to warn their colleagues who might have been disinclined to attend the tightly scripted and mostly useless briefing that for once 'the follies' might be worth a look. Bret Melton couldn't believe the turnout. Normally this room was only half full, but today every seat was taken, and in the back half even the central aisles were packed. He doubted it had anything to do with the scheduled appearance of the British and Australian task force commanders, who were due to give their first joint conference with General Franks.

Indeed, neither Franks nor the junior Coalition partners were anywhere to be seen as a USAF colonel took the podium. Melton, a former Ranger, was a nine-year veteran of the *Army Times* foreign desk and knew most of the US military's Qatar-based flak handlers by their first names. He had never seen this air force bird before. He keyed on his dictaphone as soon as the officer appeared, ensuring that the first twenty seconds of his recording were taken up with the jabbering crescendo of 200-plus colleagues all shouting individual questions at the front of the room. He had no trouble resisting the urge to join in the raucous assault on the dignity of the briefer – what would be the point? Melton waited for the chaos to die down.

The colonel did nothing to calm the room. He merely placed a sheaf of papers on the podium and stood at ease, examining the unruly mob with cool detachment. Nearly a minute and a half after he had first entered the room, the reporters slowly, gradually, quietened down and resumed their seats like shamefaced school children. As if to make the point about who precisely was in charge, the colonel's eyes traversed his audience with a cold, mechanical detachment.

Melton readied his pen to take notes. His Sony recorder was working perfectly but that was exactly when you couldn't trust the damn things.

'Ladies and gentlemen, my name is Colonel Yost, and I will be taking your briefing tonight in place of generals Franks and Wall and Brigadier McNairn. They have been indisposed by developments but will make themselves available for questioning as soon as possible.'

An Italian TV producer sitting directly in front of Melton leapt to his feet and called out, 'When?'

Yost fixed him with a killing stare and waited a full three seconds before answering. 'As. Soon. As. Possible.'

A further glare delivered as a broadside to most of the room cut off any more interruptions.

'As you know, communications links to North America have been severed – not just from CENTCOM, but more generally, across both the civilian and military spectrum,' said Yost. 'Answering speculation as to why, how and by whom is not my responsibility today. It may be yours, but you won't get your answers here. CENTCOM is endeavouring to re-establish contact as quickly as possible. We have already confirmed links with the Pacific, European and – I emphasise – with *some* elements of the Northern Command. For those of you who do not know, NORTHCOM is the unified military command responsible for operations in the US, Mexico, Canada and the northern Caribbean.'

Melton didn't bother to jot down the explanation. He was familiar with all the US commands, having worked in each of them at some time, but he did note that Yost didn't claim to be in contact with NORTHCOM proper, just 'elements' of it. That could mean a big ass-kicking set-up like Fort Lewis, outside of Seattle, or it might mean he'd phoned a guard post somewhere on the outskirts of Anchorage or Guantanamo.

'Have you seen the photos, Colonel? The French satellite photos of your cities? Can you tell us what has happened to them?'

Melton recognised the voice of Sayad al Mirsaad, the Al Jazeera correspondent who was forever in danger of being thrown off the base. Yost levelled the same robotic stare at him as he'd used to silence the Italian provocateur, but Melton knew his Jordanian colleague wouldn't be so easily cowed. Mirsaad remained on his feet, hands on hips, almost inviting him to reach over and take a swing.

'They are gone, Colonel. It is all gone. An act of God, no less. How could it be otherwise?'

Yost jumped in before a flood tide of voices could drown him out. 'It could very easily be anything but, *Mr* Mirsaad. You are not there. You haven't seen anything for yourself. All you know is that you can't get a phone call through, and somebody is selling very expensive pictures of what looks to me like computer-generated video-game imagery. If I were you I'd go read your H.G. Wells before I pushed the panic button, sir.'

Melton smirked quietly as he filled his notepad with shorthand. He had to score that one to Yost, although the classical sci-fi reference seemed lost on the Jordanian as it was on most of the other foreign journalists in the room. Or at least those from non-English-speaking countries. For himself, he didn't mind a bit of trashy reading when he was stretched out in business class, thirty thousand feet up. He even admired Iain M. Banks's high-tone Culture novels as an unlikely blend of literature and SF. But he lived and worked in the real world, just like the men and women he wrote about, and while the *Army Times* correspondent couldn't possibly imagine what sort of technical clusterfuck or psy-war

hoax they were dealing with, he had no doubt that the explanation was more prosaic than alien space bats or the hand of God.

He hadn't had time to view the still shots on BBC World.
He'd been too busy trying (and failing) to get through to head
office back in Virginia. If he had to make a bet, however, he'd lay
his money on some kind of killer virus, probably written up by
guerrilla hackers in Russia or Malaysia as a protest against the
imminent war, not to mention as a personal shot at glory in the
bizarro underground. A hit like this, just days before the start of
the war, would instantly transform some spotty college drop-out
into a hyper-celebrity super-hacker. A pity for them they'd never
be able to cash in with Nike endorsements or a Coke ad. Best they
could hope for was a virtual hand job on some mal-ware chat site.
Fuckwits. Just a few months ago he'd freelanced a 3000-word fea-
ture on digital security for Stratfor.com that the *Times* didn't want.
He'd come away with mixed feelings; utter contempt for the social
misfits and losers who were the creators of so many of the most
destructive programs, and an unshakable certainty that some day
one of them was going to pull a stunt that did real-world damage
to real-world lives. Perhaps this was it.

Somebody from Agence France-Presse jumped to his feet
demanding to know – all the French reporters sounded like they
were always *demanding* this or that – how the Coalition expected
to maintain the integrity of their communications in any conflict
with Iraq, given the 'total collapse' of their network this morning.
It was a good question, one Melton had wondered about, and he
was surprised to see that Colonel Yost looked almost relieved to
get it.

'Our theatre-level networks remain fully functional, intact
and secure,' he said. 'General Franks is in complete control of all
Coalition forces in situ. That is simply not an issue. The US and
her allies are ready and willing to carry out any order from their
national command authorities. Whatever the mission, we will
accomplish it . . . Thank you. This briefing is at an end. You will
be kept informed of any developments via the media centre.'

Yost nodded curtly, gathered up his papers and walked away
from the rostrum as hundreds of seated reporters suddenly leapt
to their feet to hurl questions at him. Melton stood with them. In

the sudden outburst, all he'd heard was a single question shouted by Sayad al Mirsaad before anyone else.

'What national command authority? They're gone . . .'

It's an intensely frustrating experience for a newsman to find himself cut off from the biggest story of the day, and Bret Melton soon felt as though he was cut off from the biggest story of all time. That's not to say there was nothing to report from Qatar. The presser had broken up in chaos and the headquarters of the Coalition forces was seething with all the mad energy of a giant ants' nest that had been rudely kicked open. But in spite of all the activity as the military spooled up their response to whatever had happened on the other side of the globe, Melton knew that a more immediate story was available a short plane ride away: the inevitable eruption of the Arab world when it realised that America was gone.

It was unbelievable, insane, and completely fucking outrageous. It was *gone*.

He had eaten almost half a roll of antacid pills in the last hour as he'd tried to accept the situation. Sitting by himself in a crowded canteen roaring with the voices of dozens of reporters who'd crowded in for the free Wi-Fi and chilled air, Melton had surfed the web frantically looking for something – anything – that might expose this morning's news as a gigantic fraud. All he'd managed to do was convince himself that nobody, no state or group, and certainly no individual, could pull off such an enormous scam. The disappearance was real.

He thumbed another couple of Rolaids into his mouth, sucking at them despondently as he clicked through a series of windows. News reports. Canadian TV shots. Webcam feeds. He'd searched dozens of chat sites, which had 'lost' most of their participants hours ago, their last messages often ending mid-sentence. It was a visit to an online gaming site that convinced him, however. He had a little-used subscription to Blizzard.net that he'd set up when researching a piece about the possibility of using multi-player combat sims as a recruiting tool. Everywhere he went in the virtual world he found CGI avatars standing mutely, awaiting instructions from their creators. Beneath them, in the small windows given over to character dialogue, there were reams of increasingly bemused, uneasy, and then fearful comments from players who'd logged in from areas outside North America. Most tellingly, almost nobody was now online, the survivors having abandoned the game servers for news sites or perhaps even the real world.

'A dark day, my friend. A very dark day.'

Melton looked up from the eerie stillness of a window running a multiplayer version of Diablo. Sayad al Mirsaad, the Al Jazeera correspondent, stood over him.

'Do you mind?' he asked, indicating the seat in front of Melton.

'Of course not,' Bret said distractedly. 'Sit down, Sadie.'

His Jordanian colleague had given up protesting the American's use of the slightly offensive nickname, finally accepting some time ago that it was meant affectionately. He was regularly called much worse by some of Melton's countrymen.

'I can see from your face, you are a believer now, yes?' said Mirsaad, without a hint of irony. He and Melton were both educated men, both men of strong faith, and they had passed many late hours in Qatar discussing theology and politics.

The former Ranger shrugged and let his hand fly up in a gesture that was part resignation, part expression of utter futility. He didn't reply. Around him, the reporters all roared on, each holding forth on their own ideas and bullshit conspiracy theories. An unpleasant energy pervaded the room, setting Melton's teeth on edge. In contrast with the others, Mirsaad appeared to be as depressed as he was.

'Not everyone will think it's a bad day, Sadie,' Melton said at last. 'Some assholes are gonna be sending a lot of extra prayers upstairs tonight, thanking their God for getting rid of the great Satan.' He watched Mirsaad closely, but he seemed almost as upset as any American was.

'Then they would be fools,' replied the Jordanian. 'Ultimately everything is God's will, but this is not His work. In the affairs of men, the will of Allah is known through the actions of men. This . . . this is something else.'

Melton nodded. 'I think so too. But it doesn't mean – '

'Hey, shut the fuck up!' somebody yelled from across the room. 'It's Saddam.'

The name acted like a spell, laying a hush over the room as Melton twisted around in his plastic chair to get a view of a television screen high on the wall behind him. The Iraqi leader appeared there, beaming like a pirate king who'd fallen ass-backwards into a huge pile of both kinds of booty. The electronic watermark in the top right-hand corner of the screen belonged to the Al Jazeera network and the report was in Arabic.

'What's it saying?' somebody asked.

Melton glanced back at Mirsaad for a translation, but before he could answer, an educated English voice rang out over the heads of the crowd. A handsome, well-groomed young man with South Asian features and an impeccable Etonian accent stood on a chair to get a clear view of the TV. Melton thought he recognised him. A BBC producer.

'It's saying that Saddam appeared briefly before a crowd at one of his palaces about forty minutes ago,' the man called out.

The footage showed a beaming dictator. Melton thought he was smiling so much that if he'd been a cartoon character, the top of his head might well have fallen off. Dressed in army greens and sporting a black beret, he fired six rounds from a pistol into the air as a small coterie of unctuously smiling generals watched on and the hand-picked crowd exploded into spasms of joy and tyrannophilia. Saddam began talking and an Arab voice-over cut in, after a few seconds, paraphrasing him. The English producer translated as the roomful of journalists remained unnaturally still and quiet.

'He's saying that Allah the merciful, the Almighty, has swept the crusaders from the very heart of their castle . . . from the very face of the earth, which they defiled with their presence. He's calling on General Franks to come out of his spider hole, to fight right now. He's demanding that all of the Arab world rise up and throw out the invaders . . . and their dogs and puppets in Riyadh and Kuwait and Qatar . . . And he's promising to lead a coalition of the Fedayeen, the honourable, to drive the infidel and the apostate out of the holy lands.'

The Iraqi leader punched out a few more gunshots before

spreading his arms wide and retreating inside the palace. Probably to haul ass to an underground bunker before a Tomahawk caught him out in the open, thought Melton. He raised an eyebrow at Mirsaad, and the Jordanian nodded, confirming the accuracy of the BBC man's translation. Within a second, the room was in uproar again, even louder and somehow denser this time. Melton shifted in his seat and rolled his shoulders in a vain attempt to shrug off a growing sense of frustration.

He had no family back in the States. He was an only child and his parents, who'd had him late in life, were both dead. For the first time in what felt like a long and lonesome existence, he was glad to be on his own in the world. His work didn't lend itself to stable relationships, and although he'd never had trouble finding women to date, none had ever lasted beyond a few weeks. Now, perversely, he was thankful for that. What must it have been like for these poor fuckers around him who had family back home? A cursory glance around the canteen told him they were the ones whose voices were loudest, and whose faces were the most strained.

'What will you do, Bret?' asked Mirsaad.

He was about to throw out the standard reply of 'My job', when it occurred to him what a ridiculous answer that would be. Did he even have a job anymore? His month's salary and travel allowance were due to be paid overnight – would it go through? He had no idea. 'I don't know,' he answered honestly, raising his voice to be heard over the tumult. 'What about you?'

Mirsaad seemed almost ashamed. 'I have an assignment in Palestine,' he said. 'They are celebrating there. Dancing in the streets. A big party. But soon I think there will be fighting, no?'

'Fighting?' muttered Bret Melton, as he contemplated the loss of his whole world and the prospect of what remained falling to pieces beneath his feet. 'I reckon so.'

6

A harried-looking man wearing a white coat over a dark suit appeared at the door and pushed past Maggie. Poleaxed by the TV news, she barely noticed him. The physician seemed to do his level best to ignore all of them, including Caitlin, even as he questioned her. A name-tag on his white jacket read *Colbert*.

'*Vous avez mal? Une douleur, un malaise?*' he said, asking whether she was experiencing any pain or discomfort. He addressed the query to his watch, which he was examining as though it was the most fascinating trinket in the world.

'*Oui, docteur. Quand j'essaie de tourner la tête, j'ai mal au cou, et ça me fait –* ' She stopped short. To judge by the wide-eyed surprise on Monique's face, the young woman had not known she could speak French.

Shit.

'*Oui? Vous sentez quoi exactement?*' Colbert encouraged her to continue.

'My neck . . . is very stiff and sore,' she said slowly, in English. 'It hurts so much to turn it, I get sick. And I have a terrible ache in my head all the time.'

Monique's hand fell away from hers. The young woman stared at her as if she had grown a new limb. The others were still fixated on the BBC. More commercial satellite imagery, from all over the North American continent, was becoming available every minute. Forty-five minutes after the short burst of white noise that shut down all communication with the richest, most powerful nation in the world – and big chunks of the countries bordering her to the north and south – the truth was unavoidable. They were gone.

Caitlin had woken into some sort of Kafkaesque nightmare and for a moment she clutched at the hope that it might just be an actual nightmare, or even a psychotic breakdown, perhaps the result of an acquired brain injury.

'But you told us you could not speak French,' Monique said.

'Fookin' 'ell, look't that.'

'*Mademoiselle Mercure, malheureusement j'ai une mauvaise nouvelle à vous annoncer . . .*' Dr Colbert, still mechanically checking his watch, had just told her he had more bad news.

No shit, Sherlock, thought Caitlin.

Monique, like the doctor, was also phase-locked in her own little world. 'But you *told* us. You told us you could not speak French.'

Caitlin stared back at her, as the world broke up into jagged mirror shards of meaning and insanity. She improvised as best she could. 'I don't speak it very well. It's embarrassing to even try. You guys are like so hard-core about it, with all the eye rolling and the shrugging. I mean, you know, *lighten up.*'

The doctor saved her by cutting in at that point, 'Excuse me. But my patient is very ill. Now is not twenty questions time. Now is – '

'Fook me!'

Aunty Celia's extra loud cry finally brought everyone's attention back to the TV, where a top-down image of Manhattan was displayed. Caitlin momentarily thought it might have been archival footage of the 9/11 attacks. Great plumes of black smoke curled away from collapsed high-rise buildings that burned at their cores like active volcanoes. But quickly she saw there were too many of them, too widely spread over the island, at least eight or nine that she could count immediately.

'. . . *if repeated across the country, the death toll might run into millions,*' read the anchorwoman.

'Everyone's gone,' said Maggie in a flat voice. 'This is fucked. *Where* have they gone?'

'. . . *At any one time many thousands of aircraft are aloft over the US, many of them above densely populated cities.*'

The coverage switched to grainy video taken from a weather cam, somewhere high above Manhattan. As Caitlin watched, numb and disbelieving, a Singapore Airlines jumbo jet ploughed into the side of the Chrysler Building, one wing spinning off screen.

Something snagged in Caitlin's conscious mind. Something that she had almost missed. 'I'm ill?' she said, suddenly picking up on the qualification the doctor had made. 'I'm *sick* – not just injured?' Irrationally, she reached for the thought, hoping it might explain the psychotic bullshit on the television.

Dr Colbert nodded distractedly. Now that he was watching the TV he seemed unable to wrench his attention away from it.

The screen switched to a series of shots detailing the moments just before and after a giant tanker had slammed into a wharf in a city she didn't recognise. Two frames showed it heading straight into the dockside. The next two captured the impact, with the front quarter of the supertanker crumpling back in on itself while the water around the vessel churned white and dockside cranes began to topple. A single frame caught the moment of detonation amidships, a blossom of white light spilling from the ruptured hull. And then the entire length of the supertanker was consumed by the birth of a dwarf star.

Maggie started swearing at the TV again, a stream of disconnected curses. Aunty Celia softly repeated the same thing over and over again: 'Fookin' 'ell . . . Fookin' 'ell . . .' Every time she said it, she folded and unfolded her arms, like a malfunctioning animatronic figure. Monique, however, was refusing to even look at the screen anymore.

'You said you could not speak French at all,' she said, challenging Caitlin once more.

Dr Colbert shook his head like a dog emerging from water and waved the young woman away with his clipboard, addressing himself only half to Caitlin. His eyes remained fixed on the catastrophe as it unfolded a few feet above the end of the bed.

'We have done scans while you were unconscious,' he told his patient, in English. 'You have a lesion on your hippocampus, a part of the brain intimately involved in the organisation of memory. It may be a tumour. But we need to take a biopsy to ascertain its nature. It may be serious. Much more serious than the injuries that brought you here. They are uncomfortable, but they can be dealt with.'

Caitlin Monroe had been an Echelon field agent for nearly five years. She had been intensively trained for three years before that. For her entire adult life, she had lived in a crazy maze where every step she took, every corner she turned, she faced the possibility of betrayal and death. She had adapted to a contingent existence where nothing was taken for granted. She had faced her own potential annihilation so many times that a doctor telling her she might be dying was completely passé. At least, on a normal day.

But this was a thousand miles from being a normal day, and for once Caitlin found the idea of her life ending to be a completely novel and unsettling experience. It stuck in her mind, a barbed, immovable object that tugged painfully whenever she tried to pull at it. 'I'm dying?' she asked him finally.

'No,' said Colbert. 'But – '

The television went blank, the screen a dead, black void.

'What the . . . ?'

Two words of white, plain type appeared.

TRANSMISSION INTERRUPTED.

'Holy shit, it's happening here now!' Maggie exclaimed.

'No!' said Caitlin, cutting off an outbreak of panic. They could all hear cries of alarm and distress from other rooms on the hospital floor. 'Just wait.'

STAND BY FOR AN ANNOUNCEMENT BY HM GOVERNMENT.

'Check the French news channels,' she said. 'See if they're still on. And the English sports channels.'

Monique abandoned the task of glaring at her to flip through the channels with the remote. As Caitlin had expected, the continental stations were still broadcasting, as was Sky Racing and the English football channels. Even the end of the world wouldn't be allowed to interfere with interminable replays of last year's Champions League.

'It's nothing,' Caitlin assured them, rubbing at her throbbing temples with one hand, the one trailing slightly fewer leads and sensors. 'The government has taken control of the news broadcasters. It's standard procedure in a national emergency. Just watch . . . And doc . . . what's your name again?'

'Colbert.'

'Dr Colbert. I'm not dying?'

He gave the impression of a man greatly relieved to find himself back on familiar ground. 'Not yet. But you could, without proper treatment. You are not yet incapacitated but the lesion might well require intensive therapy, and very soon. But we can treat you as an outpatient for the moment . . . We need your bed.' He shrugged, smiling for the first time, almost apologetically.

A single, high-pitched tone filled the room for one second before the TV screen came back to life. Tony Blair was sitting at a desk in a book-lined room, with a British flag prominently draped from a pole behind him. His eyes were haunted and, even beneath a very professional make-up job, his skin looked blotchy and sallow.

'*G-good evening . . .*' he stammered.

Colbert wasn't kidding about needing the bed. An hour later, still swaddled in bandages, and trailing one rogue sensor lead that had become entangled with her unwashed hair, Caitlin Monroe was still in-character as Cathy Mercure, attempting to sign herself out of the Pitié-Salpêtrière while shaking off what she'd come to think of as her Secret Squirrel detail. The motley collection of professional anti-warmongers had closed around her like a fist as she'd dragged herself out of bed, dressed, and pushed her way through corridors now crowded with fearful idiots.

Caitlin was surprised at the hysterical undertow that was running so strongly in the Pitié-Salpêtrière. But then again, the place was full of people who were already stressed out and had nothing much to do beyond watching television while they waited for some sort of traumatic medical procedure. On the way down to check out she witnessed any number of pedal-to-the-metal, full-bore freak-outs. One woman even barrelled right into her; a large, bug-eyed Parisian Mack Truck, she knocked Maggie right off her feet, screaming about the end of days, before disappearing down the hallway with her enormous, deeply dimpled butt swinging free in the rear of a badly strung hospital gown.

'I'll be a lot better off out of here,' Caitlin assured her companions.

Apart from Monique, who remained suspicious after discovering Caitlin's hidden gift for her native tongue, the secret squirrels weren't doing much better than any of the ranting, unbalanced Frenchies around them. Maggie, after picking herself up off the floor, was blabbering on about needing to phone her sister in Connecticut. And Aunty Celia had settled on a never-ending string of curses and oaths as her favoured response. They'd all made perfunctory efforts to get her to stay in the hospital, to argue with Colbert that she was too ill to move, but Caitlin could tell that each was spinning off into her own little world of free-floating and violently unstable anxiety. The whole city was probably going to be like this. The whole fucking world.

For her part, she didn't know what to think about the news out of the States. It was bordering on psychotic. But she did know that even if this all turned out to be some post-millennial *War of the Worlds* shakedown, if she'd been cut off from Echelon, she was travelling blind and unarmed in a world of predators. She had to run to ground as soon as possible, re-establish contact with Wales, her controller, and get some updated instructions. Christ only knew what had gone down while she'd been out of it. Plus, of course, Monique was eyeing her off with increasing suspicion.

A single television, suspended from the ceiling in the main waiting room, had drawn a huge pool of onlookers, all muttering and gasping at every new revelation from the French-language news service. Caitlin ignored it. She was having trouble negotiating her release with the large, distracted black woman on the front desk. Like everyone else, the woman seemed incapable of dragging her attention away from the TV for more than a few seconds. Monique tugged at her elbow, saying '*Cathy, je veux te parler,*' while Maggie, having spied a bank of payphones, exclaimed, 'All righty then!'

The American took off past Caitlin and Monique – and her head suddenly burst open. Ropey strands of blood, bone chips and gobbets of brain tissue splattered everybody within two metres.

As Maggie's oversized, badly dressed and utterly lifeless frame began to drop to the floor, Caitlin was already in midair, having launched herself without thought towards the nearest cover. She sailed over the counter, crashing bodily into the nurse with whom she'd been making so little headway. A cheap pink radio exploded on top of a filing cabinet. The screams began as the hundred or more people crammed into the foyer finally realised that some-body was shooting into their midst, but Caitlin was already on the move, belly-crawling towards an open door that she hoped would give onto another exit point.

'Wait!'

She felt a hand on her ankle and lashed back with a heel strike, only checking the move as she recognised the voice. Monique. The blow still caught the French girl heavily on one cheek and she cried out in pain. Caitlin swore and reached back behind her, grabbing Monique by her collar and roughly dragging her up into a crouching run. She slipped once, losing her footing and pain-fully twisting one knee. 'Move!' Caitlin yelled. 'If you want to live, move your ass!'

Behind them a riot had seemingly erupted. She heard two muffled shots and the crash of breaking glass, barely masked by the uproar of the terrorised crowd. A frightened nurse stood in their way, her eyes wide and staring. Caitlin elbowed her aside and made for a doorway behind her.

'What is happening?' cried Monique before Caitlin cut her off.

'Shut up and run!'

Crashing out into the corridor, they ran headlong into a couple of security guards, one fat and wheezing, the other looking like he might have started his career as a public security professional back in the days of the Maginot Line. 'That way,' shouted Caitlin, throwing a glance back over her shoulder, where she caught the briefest glimpse of pandemonium in the hospital foyer.

Snaking around the guards, she sped up again, turning left

and right, slamming through a series of swinging rubber doors without regard for who or what she might find on the other side. She'd let go of Monique and didn't much care whether the Frenchwoman was keeping up or not, as she blew through yet another set of swinging doors, crashing into an orderly and the trolley he'd been pushing. It tipped over and fell to the tiles with a great metallic clattering of medical instruments and stainless-steel bowls. Never stopping, Caitlin swooped down on a foil package, slipping it into her sleeve as she hurried on.

'Wait, Cathy, wait . . .'

Monique was still with her.

They'd found the treatment area of the hospital's emergency ward, and even by the usually chaotic standards of an ER unit, their entrance drew attention. With no televisions in this ward and most everyone distracted by whatever injuries or raging illnesses had gained them access to the overstretched facility, the sudden noisy appearance of two women, covered in gore and moving at great speed with no apparent regard for their own safety or anybody else's, caused heads to turn and all conversation to cease.

Monique was obviously about to start demanding answers and looked like she might just put down roots on the spot where she'd slid to a halt. A formidable grey-haired woman in a matron's uniform started moving towards them with her head down and eyes glaring murderously. She put Caitlin in mind of a big blue bulldozer.

'What the hell are you doing, Cathy?' asked Monique. 'What is going on?'

Before Caitlin could answer, or even just spin around and keep running, the same heavy rubber doors swung inwards and two men, both armed, muscled through. They were dressed in suits, one of them badly blood-stained, and their eyes swept the room, quickly settling on their quarry. Caitlin knew there was no chance of running.

Two bullets took the formidable-looking matron in the chest, throwing her through the air and rendering her a whole lot less formidable as her body crashed into a bed and dropped to the floor, twitching and pulsing extravagant amounts of blood onto the yellowing tiles. Monique screamed and ducked, covering her ears with both hands. Her cries were lost in the bedlam of the emergency room as patients and medical staff flew into a panic. Having no cover and no safe exit, Caitlin took the only option left. She attacked.

One of her assailants had been caught out with a nearly empty magazine, leaving his partner as the primary threat. She grabbed the only ranged weapon to hand – a couple of stainless-steel bowls – and launched them with great force like bright metal frisbees directly at his head. He had no choice but to duck and weave, firing anyway, the bullets heading down-range unaimed, uncontrolled. One splattered an IV bag. Another struck a patient in the arm. Taking the foil pack from inside the sleeve at her wrist as she charged, Caitlin stripped the silver wrapping away from a disposable scalpel and, focusing her *kiai*, her war shout, into the very centre of her target, she closed the short distance between them as quickly as she could.

To those normal, mortal beings around her, she moved as a fluid blur of violent action, suddenly airborne, one long leg pistoning out and into the sternum of the armed attacker. The gun fired again, bringing down a shower of plaster dust from the ceiling as he slammed backwards into a wall. His head struck a metal oxygen tap with a wet crunch and he began a slow drop to the ground, trailing a greasy organic smear down the wall.

Without pause, Caitlin's whole body swept around in a small, self-contained tornado, one foot lashing out to strike squarely at the gun hand of her second foe, who had just jacked in a fresh mag as she struck. The pistol, a Glock 23, discharged a single round, shattering an overhead fluorescent light. Turning tightly with the direction of the kick, getting right inside the circle of her man, Caitlin shot out her free hand, grabbing his wrist, extending it up and slamming her other arm in under the elbow to snap the vulnerable joint with a terrible crack. In a flash, her weapon hand whipped backwards and she opened up his throat with the razor-sharp scalpel. A geyser of hot blood spilled out in a rush as she continued to spin, dragging the bulk of her victim around between her and the first man. Only then did she strip the Glock from the weak, rubbery grip of the man who was already slumping out of her grasp. She felt fingers breaking as she wrenched it away.

In the space of less than three seconds she stood over her would-be killers. The pistol was already cocked. Two loud, flat cracks rang out and she finished off the prone figure by the wall. A slight shift in stance as she swung around, and she double-tapped the man at her feet, even though his life was already bleeding out of him. Almost no thought went into the actions. She hadn't indulged herself in the luxury of conscious thought since the two of them had burst into the ER. She simply reacted, her mind and body running along tracks that had been laid down for her by thousands of hours of training.

'*Non!*' screamed a voice. Monique's. 'What are you? You fucking monster!'

I'm Echelon, thought Caitlin as she took the weapon from the lifeless hand of the first man she had killed. The ER was unnaturally still all around her. Nobody had yet recovered from the shock of such extreme and unexpected violence. Her gun hand seemed to float towards the weeping French girl. A slow, inhuman movement, machine-like in its lack of compassion. Monique was no longer an asset, a resource to be exploited for the mission. She was a loose end.

7

The Cuban officer's salute was crisp, and his posture ramrod straight, but his eyes betrayed only confusion and anxiety. Musso returned the salute before dropping into a more relaxed posture. The two men stood in a bare office, borrowed for the meeting. Until two days ago it had been the domain of a navy lieutenant, but he had transferred back home and nobody had yet arrived to fill his berth. And five'll get you fifty that nobody ever would, Musso thought bleakly.

'Major,' he said, to open the discussion, 'welcome to Guantanamo Naval Base.'

Major Eladio Nuñez bobbed his head up and down in an agitated fashion.

'Would you care to sit?' asked Musso.

'*Sí*. Thank you.'

Nuñez dropped into a chair with some relief. His aide, a captain, remained at attention by the door. Lieutenant Colonel Stavros stood at ease by the cheap government-issue desk on which Musso had leaned back. Outside, the base was locked down on its highest alert. Two Marines in full battle gear doubled-timed past. They were ready. The question was simple enough: ready for what?

'This . . . ah . . . this is very difficult, you understand,' said Nuñez. He leaned forward, his hands rubbing together nervously. 'We do not . . . I don't . . .'

'You've lost contact with Havana,' Musso offered.

'*Sí*. But more than that. Something strange. A few miles to the north of my position – a sort of heat curtain. We can see the land behind it, through a haze, and it looks normal. But nothing, or no people, move there. There is a town, not far beyond the line, on the road north. Nothing. Not a soul.'

Musso nodded. Nuñez was deeply agitated but Musso was not so stupid as to make any judgments about the man's character on that basis. The major had been chosen by the Cuban military to face off a mortal enemy, squatting on the very soil of his motherland. He would be neither a fool nor a coward.

'Have you sent anybody in?' he asked. 'To investigate.'

The captain standing by the door moved fractionally. A tic flickered under one eye.

Nuñez nodded. 'Yes. I send in some scouts. They appear to, uh, to disappear in the heat haze. It was very thick, very powerful, no, near the effect? It seemed much hotter. And so my men they walk in, slowly. They . . .' He groped for the right word. 'They *shimmer*, yes? In the haze. And they are gone.'

'Just gone?' asked Stavros.

Nuñez nodded vigorously. 'Yes. Sometimes the haze seems to shift, like a curtain, just for a second, and we can see further down the road, say two hundred metres. It is like looking into a fish tank, yes, in a restaurant? It is a very strange sight. Like a curtain of air? I do not see how that can be but it . . . ah . . .' He rolled his hands in a helpless gesture, again seeking the right words. 'You can see this curtain. But the scouts, they never emerge on the far side. Their uniforms, they fall in a heap. Charred and smoking.'

Musso frowned. He thought he understood what Nuñez was describing. The heat wall sounded a little like a blast wave – the front of super-compressed air that moves outwards from the point of an explosion. But in this case it wasn't moving, or compressed. It merely hung in the air 'like a curtain', as Nuñez had called it.

Musso cleared his throat. 'Major, my own observers reported some of your men heading north . . .'

'*Sí*,' he said bitterly. 'They abandoned their posts.'

'And they ran into the haze?'

Nuñez nodded, looking almost satisfied. 'Yes. There was no need to shoot them. They have gone too.'

'I see,' replied Musso. 'And so what would you like us to do?'

The Cuban shifted uncomfortably in his seat, looking around, surprised at last to find himself in the devil's lair. He sighed. 'We would like help. We are not a tin-pot dictator's ship,' he said, forcing Musso to suppress a grin for the first time that morning. 'We have been intercepting your satellite news services. We know this is beyond the normal. Something terrible and large is happening. We need to know what. To prepare.'

Musso folded his arms and let his chin rest on his chest.

'This "curtain" of air,' he said after a brief moment of quiet, 'is it stable? Is it moving, expanding, at all?'

Nuñez appeared deeply troubled by the question. 'Like I said. It is a giant curtain, and like a curtain, it moves as if blown by the wind, sweeping over the countryside like a curtain blows in a window.'

Musso felt a shiver that started at the base of his spine and ran up into his shoulders. The idea of this thing moving an inch was disturbing at a cellular level. 'Major, how much is it moving?' he asked. 'Have you been able to determine any limits?'

Nuñez bobbed his head up and down. 'It seems to . . . *billow* . . . is that your word? It seems to billow like a sail, up to fifteen or twenty metres. It seems random. Just like a curtain or the branches of a tree moving in the breeze. But if it sweeps over you – poof! You are gone.'

'Well, we need to know more about it, about the parameters under which it operates. But neither of us can send any more of our people in.'

'I know,' Nuñez agreed. 'We have watched your planes and ships, no? The pilots and sailors, they have been taken too.'

'What about a Predator?' suggested Stavros. 'I understand there's a unit on base. The effect doesn't seem to interfere with electronics. Perhaps we could send one up and into the affected area.'

Musso gave Nuñez an enquiring look. 'How'd you feel about that, Major? We could send an unmanned drone up, but we'd be violating your airspace. I would need written authorisation from your senior officer.' Part of him marvelled at how deeply ingrained was the ass-covering reflex, but what the hell was he supposed to do?

'I am the senior officer now, General,' said Nuñez as he began patting his pockets. 'My colonel was in Havana, and Lieutenant Colonel Lorenz drove into the haze before we realised what it was. His car went off the road and burned.'

Stavros handed him a pen and a notepad, and the Cuban began scribbling immediately. Nobody spoke while he wrote.

Musso walked over to the window. It was coming on for midday and the sun beat down fiercely on the base. A flagpole across the compound cast only a short dagger of shadow, the Stars and Stripes hanging limp in the humidity. Guantanamo was not a major fleet base. It had been established as a coaling station – not the most glamorous of postings, even before it became famous as a prison camp. Down in the bay, a couple of tugs and a single minesweeper lay at anchor close to shore. It was a scene entirely normal, even banal.

'Here, Colonel,' said Nuñez, handing the slip of paper to Stavros. 'You may countersign as a witness. I have authorised Brigadier General Musso to deploy surveillance assets into Cuban territory on a temporary basis, with myself to administratively supervise such deployments in each and every instance.'

'Fine,' agreed Musso.

In fact there were any number of red flags sticking out of such an arrangement, but under normal circumstances Nuñez would have guaranteed himself a trip to prison, or even a blindfold and a last cigarette, by writing out such an order. If he was willing to put his nuts in the grinder, Musso could hardly quibble.

'Goddamn.' Lieutenant Colonel Stavros was the first to speak, and he said it all.

'Goddamn is right,' agreed Musso.

'*Madre de Dios*,' muttered Nuñez.

His very presence in the situation room would have been unthinkable only hours earlier, and two heavily built MPs did shadow his every move, but Musso wasn't expecting any trouble. Nor was he expecting any repercussions from having allowed an enemy officer into one of the nerve centres of the US military to watch some of its newest technology in action. There had been some quiet and very forceful dissent from the army's senior representatives on base – a Military Police colonel and a Signal Corps major, no less. But they had been overruled with extreme prejudice.

'Empty,' said Nuñez. 'Completely empty.'

'Goddamn,' whispered Stavros again. A single bead of sweat trickled down his temple even though the blue-lit room, buried thirty metres below ground, was nearly as cold as a beer fridge. Fear and sweat, sour and musky, filled the space.

Holguín, a city of more than three hundred thousand souls, scrolled down the plasma screen in front of them. It lay nearly a hundred klicks away to the north, well within the Predator's range. But Musso intended to push the aircraft on, deeper into Cuban airspace. It was going to go down in hostile territory. Or what had been hostile territory this morning. Musso was already thinking of it as no-man's-land now. Quite literally.

The sysop controlling the surveillance bird had dropped its altitude to three hundred metres, a height at which the Predator's cameras could easily pick out very fine detail on the streets below. In fact, so low was it flying and so close had the operator pulled in the view that the real-time feed was a blur, and Musso, like the other observers, was instead examining slo-mo replays on the other monitors. In one the Calixto García Park, right in the middle of the city's downtown area, rolled into view. Another showed the giant Ceverercia Bucanero brewery, a joint venture with the Canadian brewer Labatt. It was aflame, but nobody was fighting the blaze. On other monitors, beautifully decaying Spanish colonial architecture sat cheek by jowl with aesthetically worthless cement office blocks and warehouses. Winding streets gave onto cobblestone plazas and the town's surprisingly rich cultural district, wherein half-a-dozen museums, galleries and libraries all stood. Not a solitary human figure moved anywhere.

Unlike the satellite images they'd been watching on the European and Asian news services, the Predator fed live video, and although the streets of Holguín were not nearly as crowded with vehicular traffic as an American city of comparable size, they were still choked with the wreckage of hundreds of cars, many of them burning, all apparently having lost their drivers at the same time. A thickening layer of smoke hung over the city, stirred only slightly by a gathering breeze.

'General Musso, sir?'

'Yes, son,' Musso answered without looking away from the eerie scenes.

'I have PACOM on line for you, sir.'

Musso accepted a pair of headphones with a mike attached, fitting them on and walking over to a far corner. 'This is Musso,' he said quietly.

'General,' came a brusque reply in a rather refined New England accent, 'Admiral James Ritchie here. Glad to hear you're still with us. You seem to be on the front line of this . . . phenomenon.'

'Close enough, sir. It's touched down about seventy klicks north of here. Looks like a weird storm front. Admiral, if you don't mind me asking, do you have information about the situation in CONUS? All we're getting is the news feeds out of Europe and Asia.'

'No,' complained Ritchie. 'We're not doing much better. Some of my people have managed to take control of the Keyhole over Havana – that's what I'm pushing through to you now – but we've got nothing from home yet. I take it there's no chance we'll get a real pair of eyeballs on this today?'

Musso shook his head, holding the earphones in place as he did so. The set was way too small for him and kept slipping off. 'No, sir. Whatever this thing is, it's specifically targeted for an anti-personnel effect. We lost a few people to it before we realised. The Cubans lost a lot more, for what it's worth. But there seems to be no interference with electronic signals or equipment. I guess it's something akin to a neutron bomb – takes out the people and leaves the infrastructure in place.'

Even as he said it, the rational part of his mind rebelled. He was talking about his wife and children. They were part of the 'anti-personnel effect'. They had to have 'shimmered away', just like all of Nuñez's men. Just like everyone north of here. *They'll be fine*, he repeated over and over. *They'll be fine and they'll be home soon.*

Ritchie's voice crackled in the headset and Musso wondered if he'd spoken too soon about signals interference, but the audio came good again.

'Okay, well, have a look at the video my people are sending you. There's about twelve minutes' worth. Then we'll talk again. I'm going to call a videoconference of the . . . the available theatre commands in twenty minutes.'

The admiral sounded like an old man. He'd have family at home, too. But this was even worse than losing a family. Much, much worse.

The videoconference, hosted out of Pearl Harbor, drew in high-level participants from all the theatre commands, including himself as the senior officer 'available' from NORTHCOM. That's how they were putting it: not 'surviving', just 'available'. For Musso, the fact that he was sitting in was a bad, bad sign.

He was enthroned behind the desk of the 'unavailable' commander of Guantanamo Naval Base, in a small, bare office just off from the base war room. Beads of moisture sweated from grey concrete walls and no personal touches softened the utilitarian space. Even the Sony plasma screens on the desk had been set up by a couple of Navy techs ten minutes earlier, to give him some privacy during the link-up. One panel was layered with multiple windows running civilian news feeds and restricted military data channels. In one of these windows he saw live top-down footage of Washington, with English-language subtitles laid in over the original Cyrillic script. There was no explanation for the Russian source material. It may have been hacked, purchased or simply offered for free. Another small riddle to add to the all-enveloping mystery of why the city in the satellite footage was entirely devoid of human life. At least half of Washington was visible in the pop-up window. Musso could see dozens of fires burning out of control, unattended by a single soul. It was amazing how the human mind could adapt to the most irrational, outrageous insults. He'd already accepted, down in his bones, that what had happened was real, and there would be no reversing it. But his balls still tried to crawl up into his belly as he considered the vision of a depopulated American capital. Perhaps it was the Russian captioning.

'Links secure.' The disembodied female voice could have originated anywhere, but Musso supposed it belonged to a comms specialist somewhere in Pearl.

The screen devoted to the conference divided in two, with the face of Admiral James Ritchie taking up half the real estate, while four smaller windows carried the heads or acting heads of the unified theatre commands. Apart from General Jones, the Marine Corps officer in charge of US forces in Europe, Musso didn't know any of them personally. But of course he knew *of* Tommy Franks, the CENTCOM boss. The long, weathered face was famous the world over as commander of the Coalition arrayed against Saddam Hussein. Musso could only imagine what sort of pressure he must have been under right now. Franks had a naturally melancholy appearance to begin with, and Musso thought it even more deeply lined and puffy-eyed than usual.

By way of contrast, a fresh-faced woman, Lieutenant Colonel Susan Pileggi, occupied the frame set aside for the senior 'available' officer of the Southern Command. With SOUTHCOM's main HQ in Miami lying well behind the event horizon, seniority fell to her as acting commander of Joint Task Force Bravo in Honduras. She was based at Soto Cano Air Base, about ten miles south of Comayagua. Like Musso himself, and Admiral Ritchie, whose superior, Admiral Fargo, had been in Washington this morning, Pileggi had found herself thrust into the rumble seat by the absence of her own boss back in the US. It reminded him of war games in which he'd had a very minor part back at the start of his career, role-playing a massive Soviet nuclear strike that all but destroyed the United States and her government.

Franks was the ranking officer among them, but he deferred to Ritchie, who wasn't burdened with managing a looming war in the Middle East, and who had the full resources of PACOM at his disposal. The admiral, like all of them, appeared tense and when he spoke it was with a clipped tone that Musso recognised. He heard the same serrated edge on his own words whenever he opened his mouth at the moment.

'I'll recap what we *do* know,' said Ritchie, 'before moving on to the much greater issue of what we don't.'

Musso watched four heads, including his own, nod in acknowledgement.

'As of three hours, fourteen minutes ago, an event of unknown origin appears to have wiped human habitation from an area estimated at just over four million square miles . . .'

Tusk Musso found his throat closing involuntarily. His wife and children were deep inside that four million square miles. His whole country was, close enough. His life.

'We have not yet mapped the exact perimeter of the effect,' Ritchie continued. 'But we have good estimates that it lies in a very rough ovoid shape that covers ninety per cent of the contiguous US mainland states, half of Canada, and all of Mexico above a line extending from a point a few miles south of Chilpancingo on the west coast to Chetumal on the east, and extending through the Gulf to transect Cuba seventy thousand metres north of Guantanamo. Of the larger cities on the contiguous mainland US, only Seattle appears to lie outside the area. We're still checking on Olympia, a bit further south. Things are confused there. The Governor's office has declared a state of emergency, imposed a curfew and called out the National Guard.'

Musso couldn't keep the surprise off his face. Nor could Susan Pileggi, he noted. He hadn't seen any mention of Seattle in the news bulletins. As if reading his thoughts, Ritchie explained.

'General Blackstone at Fort Lewis sent troops into the local media outlets to forestall a panic. The . . . uh . . . Governor and deputy are . . . unaccounted for. So too are some of the city council people for Seattle. Apparently they were at some conference in Spokane, behind the event horizon. An estimated three hundred and fifty million people were caught within the affected zone,' Ritchie continued. 'At this stage we have no information or even speculation about what may have happened to them, whether the effect is permanent, or stable, a natural phenomenon, or technologically based. We've been monitoring the reaction from any potentially hostile governments and none are behaving in any way that would give rise to a suspicion that they played any role in this.'

'What's happening in Beijing?' asked General Franks.

Ritchie appeared to direct his answer to a spot just over

Musso's shoulder as he addressed the image of Franks on a screen thousands of miles away. 'The army is pouring onto the streets in every major provincial capital, General. Martial law has been declared but none of the PLA's force-projection assets have been mobilised. Nonetheless, our own counter-strike forces are at Defcon 2, just in case.'

Ice water pooled in Musso's guts. Ritchie had ordered his nuclear submarines to stand ready should the need arise to reduce the communist giant to a vast crematorium. It raised an immediate question: who would authorise any such strike? Again, Ritchie seemed to be one step ahead of him.

'I'm afraid, before we proceed any further,' he said, 'we need to discuss where the executive authority now lies.'

'There's no designated survivor?' asked Tommy Franks.

Ritchie shook his head.

The further into this they got, the bleaker it grew, thought Musso. The 'designated survivor' was a Cabinet member nominated to remain apart from the other – was it sixteen or seventeen? – people in the presidential line of succession, a civilian analogue of the chain of command. The system only really operated when the executive was gathered in one place, such as during a State of the Union address, but now wasn't the time to play semantics. If they couldn't legitimately find somebody to step into the office of President, then any military actions they took would have no legal basis.

'Elaine Chao, the Secretary of Labor, is in Geneva,' said Ritchie, 'at a UN conference. But she is specifically barred from the line of succession because she's not a natural-born citizen. As best we can tell, there is nobody from the line . . . available.'

'You mean "alive",' said Musso, unable to accept the euphemism any longer. 'There is nobody else *alive*. In the line of succession. Back home. Anywhere within the affected area. You'll excuse me for speaking out of turn, but I think we need to start responding to this on the basis of a worst-case scenario. It's permanent. We cannot change it. They are not coming back and if we screw up, a lot more people are going to die.'

Silence greeted him, and Musso immediately regretted his lack of tact. There was a reason why he was never going to ascend to the rarefied heights of a theatre command, the same reason he'd been slated for forced retirement in the next twelve months. Finally, General Jones broke the moment, speaking from Brussels.

'Well said, Tusk. The world's been knocked flat on its ass wondering what hit it. But that's going to change within a day or two. And all hell is going to cut loose. You can bet on it.'

'Gentlemen, if I might?'

The testosterone had been ramping up very quickly. The intrusion of a softer, female voice seemed to calm things a little. Lieutenant Colonel Pileggi smiled out of the monitor at Musso, at all of them.

'We all took an oath to defend the Constitution of the United States. No matter what catastrophe has overtaken us, that oath and the Constitution still stand. Millions of American citizens are still with us. Some of them back home, in the unaffected Northwest. Most of them scattered around the world. I don't know the exact figures but there must be, what, four or five million Americans overseas on any given day? There are embassies, consulates, military bases and personnel – the sinews of government, if you will. But it is a government *of the people*. Not of us. If we are to act, it must be as servants of the American people, no matter how few or far flung they may be.'

Pileggi spoke with controlled passion. Nobody spoke at all until Tommy Franks's thick Oklahoma drawl poured out of the speakers.

'Granted, Colonel, we can't just pick a President out of a hat. But we need to act, and damn quick. I've got close on a quarter-million men and women out here in the desert waiting on orders to go. Saddam has even more waiting to receive us, and a locker-ful of dirty weapons ready to fire off. I got millions of potential enemy combatants all around me – Israel sitting on top of her nukes, and that asshole bin Laden spooking around in the back of it all. Pretty soon I'm gonna have to shit or get off the pot, and either way now it's gonna make a helluva goddamn mess. You are right. It ain't my decision to make. But somebody *has* to make it, and I don't see anybody we can turn to.'

Pileggi nodded. 'In the end, we have to turn to our citizens,' she said. 'But given the extreme nature of the immediate crisis,

I suggest we return to first principles. We are a representative democracy. I suggest we find the senior surviving *elected* representative. If we can't lay our hands on anyone from the federal level, then we go to state, to the Governor of Alaska, or Hawaii, or Washington State. We frogmarch them into office if necessary, for a strictly limited period, pending an election of a new Congress and executive.'

'Sounds like a plan,' agreed Franks.

'Consider it done,' said Ritchie.

Musso watched him drop his hand to make a few notes.

'If and when we do find someone to assume executive responsibility,' the admiral continued, 'we will need to be ready to do whatever is needed of us. General Musso, you're the closest out of us to the phenomenon. It might be time to tell us what you know.'

What I know? he thought. *What I know is that we've been fucked three ways from Sunday.* When he spoke, however, it was in the same brusque style as his peers.

'The edge of the effect, the event horizon, manifested itself as an observable atmospheric phenomenon, seventy kilometres north of my position at Guantanamo,' he began.

8

'He's . . . Barb. The Air . . . Guard picked him . . . ago . . . and later . . . for now . . .'

'Barney? You're breaking up. I can't hear more than two words in five. Did you say Kip was fine? Is he okay?'

The phone beeped in her ear, the connection lost.

Barbara Kipper slammed the handset down in its cradle. It had taken her nearly an hour, trawling around in hellacious traffic, to find a payphone that actually worked. Twice she'd been stopped by soldiers who informed her, politely enough, that a curfew was in place and she'd need to get home. But Barb knew that, given the traffic, home wasn't going to be that easy to reach, and she *needed* to talk to Kip. Only for a moment. Just to make sure he was safe.

She was convinced the phone companies let their booths fall into disrepair to force everyone to buy a cell. Not that cell phones were worth anything today. The network was obviously melting down. She only got through to Barney Tench on her eighth attempt, and even then the interference had been so bad it was hardly worth it.

But Kip was okay, wasn't he? Barney had said that. The National Guard had picked him up somehow and were flying him back, right? Or driving. Or whatever. But he *would* be back 'later'. She realised she was shaking and close to tears.

'Are you all right, lady? Are you done with the phone? I really need to call my mom, is all. She's in San Francisco this week, visiting her pop. And, you know, I *really* need to call her now.'

Barb came out of her trance with a start. The young man in front of her, a boy really, had almost pushed his way into the booth. He was dressed in some sort of uniform. A Wendy's employee, she realised, and his eyes were large and fearful, darting over her shoulder to lock on the phone as if it were a life jacket in high seas.

'Can I just get in, ma'am? And use the phone? You made your call and . . .'

'It's okay. I'm sorry,' said Barb. 'Let me get out of your way.'

He waited until she was half out of the cramped space before pushing in past her. On any other day it would've set off all of her New York alarms, made her think she was being mugged. But the kid only had eyes for the phone.

'Good luck,' she said. 'With your mom.'

He muttered 'Thanks' and began feeding coins into the slot.

She hurried back to the car, where Suzie was sitting up in the front seat, keeping an eye on her. Barb had parked outside a bar and grill near the corner of Northeast 106th and 4th Street, far enough away from the Bellevue Square mall to have avoided the traffic snarl that had frozen the streets for a few blocks around there. But, even so, the road network here was peaked out also. Nobody, it seemed, wanted to be at their desk and thousands of people had poured onto the streets in their cars, all hoping to get home or to their kids or partners. Maybe it was the dumbass curfew too, she thought acidly. No one wanted to get stuck away from home today. The sun flared off windscreens in hundreds of small supernovae, horns blared and thousands more people on foot picked their way through the slow-moving traffic, all of them looking to be somewhere else. It was like 9/11 except in the 'burbs.

Barbara climbed back into the Honda and strapped in, keying the ignition and searching the radio band for a reasonable voice. The national stations were offline, and many of the locals had thrown open their switchboards to a rising cacophony of nutjobs and crazies.

'Mommy, did you get my treat?' asked Suzie.

Barb squeezed her eyes shut. She'd promised Suzie a small

chocolate bar or a piece of candy if she'd sat quietly through her mother's increasingly anxious search for a working public phone. And of course, in the rush and the worry, she'd completely forgotten. The sharp, rising inflection in Suzie's voice, which was quavering towards meltdown, meant she couldn't put it off.

'I'm sorry, sweetie. Mommy forgot. But, I've . . . uh . . . I've got some gum here. Would you like some gum?' She fished a packet of Double Bubble out of the coins and scrunched-up gas receipts in the cup holder.

'But Mommy, I'm not allowed to have gum. You know that I – '

'Today, you can have gum,' Barb said, more brusquely than she'd wanted to. 'Here, knock yourself out.'

She tossed back the packet and immediately regretted it. Suzie was always a little more sensitive to Barb than to Kip – admittedly, because Barb tended to have a sharper tongue. The little girl's lower lip was trembling and the glassy sheen in her eyes warned of imminent tears. A tension headache began drilling in behind Barbara's temples.

'. . . *estimates of the dead or missing run into the hundreds of millions,'* declared a sombre voice on the radio. '*A joint statement from the Governor's office and the commander of Fort Lewis advises people in the metro area to stay off the roads, keeping them clear for emergency service vehicles and military transport. The curfew will be enforce–* '

Barb flicked off the radio with some irritation. It couldn't have been helping Suzie's mood.

'I want Daddy,' she sobbed, as the tears finally came. 'I want Daddy home. I don't want him eaten.'

'It's all right, darling. It's all right.'

But the collapse had begun and within seconds her daughter was a heaving, squalling ball of misery in the back of the car.

Where the fuck are you, Kip?

'Goddamn. That mother's gotta be twenty miles high.'

'Higher, sir,' the airman informed him. 'Seems to fold over somewhere up in the mesosphere.'

James Kipper nodded but said nothing. Better to keep your mouth shut and be thought a fool, than to open it and confirm the fact, as his granddad used to say. Pops Kipper was full of such quips for all occasions like that. He used to keep a dictionary of quotations on the kitchen table at his place, ready to deploy somebody else's wit at a moment's notice.

Christ knows what he'd have said about this, thought Kip, as they banked down and away to the west to begin their long approach to Seattle. The C-130 wasn't designed for scenic flights, but even through its small, grimy windows he was afforded a scarifying view of the energy wave that ran in both directions right out to the very edge of the world, and over it. He was the only passenger in the plane, a service laid on especially for him by the military at the city's request. The loadmaster – that's what they were called, he was sure – stayed glued to the window nearest his perch at the rear ramp, jamming his head up hard against the Plexiglas to keep an eye on the phenomenon as their course change took it out of direct view. It was far enough away from Seattle that you couldn't see it from the ground, they told him, which Kip thought of as a small mercy. The city would've been a nuthouse if you could – probably was anyway, he reflected. The flight crew, after exhausting the possibilities of speculation and conspiracy theory when the vast, shimmering wall had first hove into view, were restricting themselves to terse monosyllables as they prepped the craft for descent and approach.

'I reckon it came from space,' said the airman, a native of New Orleans, to judge by his accent. 'Something like a black hole that brushed up against us.' He was young, with a smattering of pimples on his fleshy pink jowls.

'Black holes don't really brush up against anything,' replied Kipper. 'They suck in whole planets and crush them to a singularity.' He'd seen that on the Discovery Channel once. It made him feel better to have something to say.

'A singu-what now, sir?' asked the airman.

'A singularity,' Kipper repeated. 'It's, uh, where energy and matter get crushed down into a single state that is so small it's almost not even there.'

'Shit,' said the young man. 'Well, I guess that ain't no singularity out there.'

'Nope,' agreed Kipper. 'Guess not.'

'Do you know what we're gonna do about it, sir, to turn it off?'

Kipper could see from the strain around the boy's eyes that he was really asking another question. *How are we gonna make this better?* Or perhaps: *How are we going to get our world back?*

'Son,' said Kipper, who felt old enough to call the airman that, 'you and I are going to do our jobs. And somebody, somewhere else, is gonna see to punching the lights out on this motherfucker.'

'So you think it can be turned off, sir?'

The need in the boy's voice was almost painful. Kipper tried for a nonchalant shrug.

'I'm an engineer. I was always taught that if something can be turned on, it can be turned off,' he said.

But he didn't believe that for a second. Not after seeing the thing with his own eyes.

By the time the C-130 he'd transferred to on some no-name airstrip out in the boonies touched down at Sea-Tac, Kipper had almost forgotten the crash back in the Cascades. As the young Guardsman who'd strapped him into the Blackhawk back in the mountains had explained, there were almost certainly no people on that flight anyway – they'd been 'disappeared'. The phrase gave him a twitchy feeling. It was redolent of the bad old days in Chile, where he'd done some contract work for Arthur Andersen on a power station project back in the '80s. People by their thousands got 'disappeared' there. As frightening as that had been, however, it was also comprehensible: a bunch of assholes, looking like they'd been tricked out as opera villains in military drag, had simply decided to murder anyone who looked sideways at them.

What he'd seen today, as soon as the chopper lifted clear of the deep valley in which he'd been trekking, was entirely *in*comprehensible. The brooding mass of the Cascades still blocked from view a good deal of what the guardsmen were calling 'the Wave', but the goddamn thing was reared up so high he could still see it anyway, soaring off towards space, somewhere beyond the skyline of the ranges. That was bad enough, but what they'd told him about the effect of this 'Wave' had drilled a cold, dead finger bone into his heart. Hundreds of millions of people, gone. Whole cities – close enough to the whole country – empty. Ships ploughing into ports and exploding. Cars just veering off the road, uncontrolled, crashing into each other because nobody was behind the wheel. Planes falling out of the sky, like he'd seen with his very own eyes earlier that day. It had been happening all over. Still was, in fact. The Oregon Air National Guard had jets up right now, waiting for half-a-dozen flights whose tracks were due to take them over Seattle. They'd been authorised to shoot the planes down well short of the city.

Kipper caught himself obsessively twisting and wrenching one of the straps on his backpack as he tried to imagine what had happened, what bizarre correlation of physical forces might have done such a thing. He couldn't think of a single explanation. He was a civil engineer, a good one, just quietly, but he maintained a professional interest in related fields, and indeed in most of the hard sciences. As a young boy he'd wanted to be an astronaut (who doesn't?), but he wasn't one for uniforms and taking orders and sucking up a lot of chickenshit nonsense. So he'd refused to go down the path his old man had been pushing him towards – a career in the air force. He loved building things, not blowing them up. He'd never quite got the bug out of his system though, and a lot of his down time consisted of reading the sort of scientific journals to which he might have contributed had he pulled on a space suit for real, instead of just in his dreams.

But nothing he'd ever read, learned or seen in his private or professional experience went one inch towards explaining what the hell had happened while he'd been off on his precious fucking nature walk.

Kipper shook himself out of his thoughts. The plane had touched down on a patch of concrete apron north of the control tower, affording him a good view of both runways and the terminal complex. He could see right away that things weren't normal. There was an unusually large number of planes on the ground, and none taking off. In one glance he could make out the liveries of half-a-dozen stranded carriers. Midwest. Jetblue. Frontier. China Airlines. They all had flights parked by terminals they wouldn't normally have used. A bunch of 737s and MD80s from Alaskan Airlines had huddled together, a bit like an old wagon train, down near the fire station, while a collection of jumbos and long-haulers from overseas had laagered up at the southern end of the airport. As his transport rumbled along the tarmac, a United Airlines Airbus aborted a landing with a scream of turbines and a building roar while it heaved itself back into the sky again. Kipper craned out of the cabin to see if he could spot whatever had gone wrong, but the Guardsmen were already popping harnesses and hurrying him out of the aircraft.

'This way, sir,' a woman in a Nomex flight suit yelled at him, pressing a firm hand on his shoulder. 'Follow me.'

Kipper did as he was told, crouching slightly for no good reason. It just seemed appropriate. The airport was a thunderbowl of screaming engines, jet exhaust and speeding vehicles, all of it controlled in some vague chaotic way by hundreds of scurrying, shouting men and women in coveralls and headphones. There were a lot more military uniforms than he was used to seeing, as well. The engineer allowed himself to be led across to a waiting Ford pick-up with city markings, where Barney Tench, a huge shambolic figure in khaki drill pants and a faded blue shirt, was waiting for him, looking worried.

Tench came forward, holding out his hand and shaking his head. 'Man, am I glad to see you, buddy,' he called out over the background roar. 'Thought we might have lost you up there, Kip. We lost a lot of people. I think Locke's gone, Owen too. Nobody can find the mayor either, but Nickells wasn't scheduled to be out of town, so maybe he'll turn up. It's chaos, man. Fucking chaos.'

His friend sounded unbalanced – which was one of the more disturbing developments of the morning. Barney Tench was usually as phlegmatic as a stone statue. Nothing upset him. It was why Kipper had insisted on hauling him in all the way from Pittsburgh when he'd taken the city engineer's job. There'd been some grumbling about Kip hiring an old college beer buddy, but that had fallen away once Barn settled in to the job. You couldn't ask for a better right-hand man. Except that, at this moment, his strong right hand was trembling and pale.

Kipper threw his gear into the back of the pick-up, yelled his thanks to the aircrew, and climbed up into the driver's-side seat, motioning for Barney to follow suit.

'Okay, Barn, gimme the keys. I'll drive, you chill the fuck out and we'll deal with this like we would any problem. Step by step. First, has anyone spoken to Barbara since you got my number off her? She'll be freaking out, wanting to know I'm okay.'

Tench had the good grace to look guilty. 'I'm sorry, Kip. We tried. It's just been a hell of a morning. And I . . . well . . .'

'Okay. Give me your cell. I'll call her now.'

'No point, man,' Barney said, shaking his head. 'The nets are jammed. Your sat phone might work, though.'

He took a small, calming breath. 'Okay. Two minutes.'

Kipper hopped out again and hurried around to retrieve his phone from the backpack. The signal strength was good, and he was relieved to get a clear dial tone. The call to Barb's phone stalled before it began, however. A recorded message told him that due to higher than normal demand, his call could not be connected. Kip grunted and tried their home phone number, an old-fashioned land line. It went though to voicemail on the fifth ring.

'Hi honey, It's me. They got me. I'm back safe. I have to go into the city. When you get home and get this message, stay there. Don't go out again, okay? Things are gonna be crazy for a while. Love you. Love to Suzie, too.'

He hung up, hoping that would avoid a scene later on. If Barb wasn't at home, it probably meant they were caught up in a traffic jam somewhere – hopefully not for too long. Some of the roads had looked like parking lots on the flight in. It was going to take him and Barney a while to drive into town.

'Okay, let's get going,' he said, climbing back into the cabin.

They pulled away, with Kipper driving south, towards the main terminal building. As they approached, he could tell it was crowded, with thousands of people lining the big glass windows that looked out over the tarmac.

'You got any idea what's going on, Barn, beyond the headlines?' he asked his friend.

'Wish I did, Kip. This is like a horror movie. First I heard this morning was Ross Reynolds on KUOW saying he thought we'd been nuked or something. Communications went down. Civil Defense alarms went off. Chaos and fucking madness.'

'But it wasn't an attack?' As he spoke, Kipper threaded past a knot of distressed-looking travellers, who were making their way towards a transit bus from a Horizon Air Dash 8. That done, he accelerated towards a vehicle exit up ahead.

'You've seen that thing, haven't you?' said Tench, answering Kip's question with one of his own. 'Not unless we got attacked by the Death Star or the Goa'uld or something. Right now the whole fucking world is just as weirded out as us.'

Kipper waved off a security guard who seemed intent on holding them up, and accelerated past, paying no respect at all to his frantically waved clipboard.

The council F-100 bounced up and down as they hit the outer road surface and Kip wrenched it around before gunning it towards the next exit. There appeared to be a couple of dozen soldiers on duty around this part of the airport, although what role they were playing he couldn't tell. Mostly they seemed to be doing traffic control, barring any civilians from leaving the facility. That's gonna end in tears, he thought. Seattle wasn't the sort of town where folks took well to being dicked around by crew-cuts and camouflage. It was a righteous certainty that if he stuck his head outside right now, he'd hear some would-be grunge god caterwauling about fascists and nazis.

'I'm sorry, Barney,' said Kipper, breaking the silence. 'I didn't think – you got family back east.'

Tench breathed deeply and nodded. 'Everyone has somebody. So do you.'

Kipper said nothing. His immediate family was here, thank Christ. But his dad was in Kansas City and he had a sister in New York. Their mother had died three years back. New York and KC, of course, were both behind the Wave.

He knew now why Barney had sounded so bad on the phone. There were some good folks on the city council, as well as a fair leavening of pinheads. But if Seattle was in the front line of a fight against something that had the power to zap a whole continent, they were all in deep, deep shit.

9

MV *DIAMANTINA*, PACIFIC OCEAN, WEST OF ACAPULCO

'Man, I vote we stay the hell away from that,' said Fifi.

It looked like Hollywood's idea of a mid-ocean tsunami, a mind-fucking wall of water that stretched across the horizon and reached miles into the sky – which was utter bullshit, of course. The *Diamantina* had struck two tsunamis in the time that Pete had been her skipper, both of them over a thousand nautical miles away from any coast and neither one even noticeable as it had passed under the hull. The thing to the north was nothing like a tsunami. And, some five hundred and seventy nautical miles offshore from Acapulco, they were sailing closer to it with every minute.

'No arguments from me, sweetheart,' he agreed. 'We'll keep a safe distance.'

'That's not what I said,' she insisted.

'And how close is that, Pete?' asked Jules with a much cooler demeanour. 'That bloody thing starts *below* the horizon. God knows how high it is. If it wanted to reach out and grab us it probably could.'

Pete Holder swung under the boom of the main mast to get a better view. He frowned. 'I don't think it's going to grab anyone, Jules. It's not alive. It's not even moving.'

'Whatever,' she said, with real exasperation. Whenever she was pissed off with him, her voice became even more clipped and correct than normal. 'If we have to do this, let's get it done, and then get the hell out of here, shall we?'

By 'this' she meant boarding the luxury cruiser they'd intercepted on their run towards the Mexican coast. The vessel, an enormous aluminium and composite super-yacht, was obviously unmanned. It wasn't drifting, but the engines were pushing it along on a southerly heading at just a nudge over six knots. It had emerged from behind the screen of the energy wave two hours earlier, easily visible on the *Diamantina*'s radar. Pete had thought nothing of it until Mr Lee had come to drag him away from the news feed on the computer. Lee's incomparable pirate's eye had spotted something very special on the horizon.

The empty yacht – the crew had to be dead or 'gone' – presented as a brilliant white blade on the deep blue of the Pacific. It almost hurt to look at the thing, so brightly did it gleam in the tropical sun. From the bridge it dropped down through four decks before kissing the waterline, where, he would have guessed, it was maybe two hundred and thirty or even two forty feet in length. A big twin-engine sport fisher, hanging from two cranes in a dedicated docking bay at the stern, easily outsized the *Diamantina* all on its own. Instead, the super-yacht looked like a toy, which in a way it was. A rich man's plaything. Pete could see other, slightly smaller vessels stowed away in the rear dock.

'It's like a fucking amphibious assault ship for the go-go party crowd,' he mused.

Not a soul moved anywhere on the open decks, while behind the yacht the impossible, iridescent wall of coherent energy raised itself high into the heavens.

'You're going to steal it, aren't you?' said Jules in a resigned voice.

'No. I'm going to salvage her.' Pete was grinning, his first real, sunny smile in hours. 'Keep her safe from the sort of villainous rogues one meets around these parts. I'm sure if the owners ever make it back from the Twilight Zone, there'll be a more than generous reward for her return.'

Jules rolled her eyes.

Fifi nodded uncertainly, her eyes never leaving the horizon. 'I dunno, Pete. We're coming up on that thing, and we're much closer than you thought was safe a coupla hours back. It's like it's curving towards us or something.'

'Mr Lee, would you bring us alongside her,' said Pete, ignoring Fifi's quite reasonable point. Selective deafness was a useful skill he'd picked up from his mother.

The old Chinese pirate grinned and began to swing their helm over on a converging course with the slow, aimless track of the yacht. As they drew closer Pete noted the name on the stern. The *Aussie Rules*.

He whistled, both at the unexpected connection with home, and the very strong feeling that he knew this boat from somewhere. It was maddening though, he couldn't remember where. There was little time to ponder the mystery, as he busied himself with preparations for the boarding. Truth was, he was no happier than Fifi about their proximity to the vast standing wave that filled the northern sky, but if his instincts played out, this baby might be the answer to their prayers. It could be that the super-yacht was too hot to hold on to even with the world collapsing around his ears, but she'd be packed to the gunnels with all sorts of goodies they could trade for jewels or gold. He had a feeling that the world's definition of wealth was going to get back to basics very quickly.

'Steady as she goes, Mr Lee,' he called out. 'Steady now.'

Over the next five minutes Lee brought the *Diamantina* alongside the immense bulk of the yacht. Even with the sun high overhead, they sailed in the shade of the much larger boat. Lee matched his speed to that of their quarry, and then slowly dialled down the engines, slipping back towards the docking bay at the vessel's stern. Pete could tell the yacht had been well cared for. Anyone who could afford to buy such a magnificent craft could obviously afford to lavish attention on her. Her hull was free of any build-up below the waterline. The portholes were all crystal clear, their glass freshly cleaned, possibly even this morning.

As they drew level with the docking bay, Lee edged their speed back up again, holding position perfectly, just a foot away. Pete gave him a nod and a wink before stepping off. The little Chinaman stood at the wheel, as though organically connected to the *Diamantina* through it. He didn't move much, but when he did, it was in perfect synch with the swell, the light chop and the grosser, sluggish movement of the other vessel.

'We cool?' asked Pete.

Fifi and Jules, both of them back in their combat rigs, agreed in turn.

'Okay,' he said, 'let's fuck this cat.'

Julianne Balwyn was not, at first blush, the sort of fabulous creature one might expect to find gracing one of England's older landed families. She had the bearing, the soft beauty, and the polished vowels of a woman whose family had enjoyed hundreds of years of privilege and favour. But in her case, as with her father, something had gone wrong. Lord Balwyn, a spectacular wastrel and confidence man, often used to tell her that Sir Francis Drake had added his seed to the Balwyn family line, accounting for the freebooters and blackguards who regularly popped up in their history, and whether it was true or not – Jules was smart enough to take everything her father said with a mountain of salt – it was undeniable that in the last Lord Balwyn's eldest daughter, the family's propensity for throwing up the occasional black sheep had reached a very particular zenith.

As she cross-decked from the *Diamantina* to the *Aussie Rules*, however, she found herself once again grateful to her father for instilling in her such a bleak, pragmatic, Nietzschean view of humanity. While Pete, their putative leader, was lost in an uncontrolled moment of fan-boy worship, Jules kept her head down and her poo in one sock. A favourite saying of Daddy's.

'Holy shit,' cried Pete. 'You know what? I do know this tub. I remember reading about it now. I think this is Greg Norman's yacht.'

'Who?' asked Fifi.

'You know,' said Pete, who was now *very* excited. 'The golfer – "the Great White Shark"? A terrible fuckin' choker, actually, but a great businessman. I think he designed a lot of golf courses when he wasn't losing PGA play-offs. Talk about money for nothing and your chicks for free. Although, you know, with your lady golfers, there's a reason those chicks are free . . . Anyway, I'm pretty sure this is his yacht. Or was.'

'You think so?' Jules deadpanned, as they stood by a large swimming pool inlaid with a stylised shark motif. She was holding a solid gold putter in one hand and a white straw hat in the other, both items sporting the same cartoon outline of a great white.

'Greg who?' asked Fifi.

Pete shook his head despairingly. 'If it ain't Nascar it just ain't real for you, is it, sweetheart?'

'What's up with Nascar?'

Before Pete could answer, Jules cut him off, clicking her fingers in an effort to bring the others back to reality. 'Excuse me, people – end of the world over here. Greg Norman's yacht getting all *Mary Celeste* on us? Let's maintain our focus, shall we?'

'Sorry,' said Pete. 'It's just, you know, it's *the Shark*, baby!'

'Stupid fucking game anyway,' muttered Fifi. 'Buncha fat-ass white guys in ugly pants, driving around in those faggy little carts . . .'

'Fifi.' Jules's voice took on a warning edge. She was fond of her white-trash friend, but managing the bimbo eruptions was a full-time job.

'Got it, got it. Maintaining focus.'

'Come on, let's have a little look-see,' said Jules.

She slipped her carbine over one shoulder and took out a handgun, a Beretta Px4, even though she wasn't expecting to find anyone on board. They'd been calling out since boarding, but it had the same feeling as knocking on the door of an empty house. She knew they were alone. The ever-suspicious Fifi, however, kept a sawn-off shotgun to hand with a shell racked in the tube. Her thumb stroked the safety, ready to flick it off at the slightest provocation.

The three of them walked around the pool, located on the second of four upper decks, the sun glinting fiercely off the water as it slowly sloshed around with the gentle motion of the boat. The tip of the *Diamantina*'s main mast rolled through a small arc a few metres away. By leaning over the polished rail, Jules could see the top of Mr Lee's bald head a long way below. The pool looked to be about ten metres long, with four round, black stools peeping above the waterline at the far end, where they abutted a full bar with its own beer taps and all the fixings for a high-end cocktail party. A large plate of fruit salad, wilted in the heat, lay untouched in the centre of the polished hardwood bar-top. White padded cushions lay along both sides of the pool, with pillows scattered here and there. She could read Pete like a cheap novel and knew that it was all he could do to resist diving in and asking the girls to set him up a margarita. To move things along, she strode forward, taking the port-side companionway.

'*Hello*,' she called out once more. 'Is anyone on board? Do you need help?'

'Oh fuck . . . Oh, gross me out!'

Jules spun around at the sound of Fifi's distress, reaching for her weapon again, but no obvious threat had emerged from anywhere. Rather, Fifi was dancing about as if she'd trodden in something nasty. Which she had.

'Oh goddamn!' Fifi cursed again. 'This is worse than rendered hog fat.'

'What is it?' asked Jules, as she hurried over, just one step behind Pete.

'Gawd, that is nasty,' he said, suddenly pulling up.

Before them on the deck was a pile of burnt clothes, out of which leaked a couple of gallons of the vilest-looking greenish black substance Jules had ever seen.

'What is it?' shrieked Fifi. She was losing it, badly.

'I think it might have been the Shark.' Pete rubbed at his face and gingerly toed another straw hat away from the mess. 'Ugh . . . Hey darlin', I really think you ought to throw those shoes of yours over the side.'

Fifi shook her head, disgust acid-etched into her features. 'Man, I don't wanna touch that gunk. What the fuck is it?'

Jules leaned over and peered at the toxic ooze. 'I think Pete's right,' she said. 'I think it used to be a person.'

'So w-what happened to them?'

Fifi lit up a calming Marlboro with shaking hands. The only answer to her question was the hiss of the Pacific sliding past the hull a long way below them.

'How many of those things are there, do you think?' she asked, tiptoeing over to the gunwale and using a pistol to ease off her deck shoes.

'Careful you don't shoot yourself in the foot,' warned Pete.

She shuddered. 'Couldn't be no worse than getting this crap on me. What if it's like the Blob? What if I turn into that . . . stuff?'

Jules could hear clearly the approaching edge of hysteria in her friend's voice. She strode over, put a steadying hand on the other girl's shoulder, reached down and pulled off the shoe Fifi had been trying to dislodge, before tossing it into the sea. Some of the oozing substance ended up on her hand, but she wiped that off on her shirt.

'It's gross, Fi, but it's not the Blob,' Jules assured her. 'We'll need to have a good clean-up if they're all like this. It'll be a devilish health hazard otherwise. What do you think, Pete? How many people would have been on board?'

The Australian shrugged. 'Dunno, sweetheart. At a guess, a boat this size, well over a dozen, maybe even twenty, but some of them would have been cooks, bartenders, cleaners, and so on. Perhaps even a caddy. There'll be a crew manifest somewhere.'

'Do you think he was on it, you know, when they got zapped?' she asked, indicating the straw hat with a nod.

Pete stared at the obscene mess on the polished deck. He looked very grim. 'The Shark? I dunno, could've been. Unless he lent it out to someone, or ran charters. I don't think he did, though. I read somewhere he kept this baby very much to himself.'

It did raise other, more pressing questions in Jules's mind. If it was the golfer's yacht and the mess in front of them *wasn't* him, then he was definitely going to want it back. But if it was Norman and they had to make a run Down Under, to put some serious distance between themselves and whatever had happened to the US, there'd be no hiding this yacht anywhere. It *would* be noticed.

'Well, let's just be careful where we tread from now on, I suppose,' she said. 'Fifi, maybe you could find a pair of shoes somewhere.'

Fifi nodded, looking sickly, as they moved further up towards the bow. Another pile of clothes, a uniform belonging to a crew member, lay at the bottom of the steps up to the next deck, oozing the same putrescent substance.

'Man, I am so not looking forward to swabbing that up,' muttered Pete.

'Maybe we should blow this off,' Fifi suggested. 'It's freaking me out, guys. You know, this is the bit in the movie where you're sitting there yelling at the screen, "Get off the boat, you fucking dumbasses!"'

Jules and Pete both ignored her and stepped through the doorway ahead. A cool curtain of chilled air washed over them. The yacht's climate control system was obviously unaffected by the loss of the crew. It kept the interior of the boat at a perfect twenty-one degrees Celsius. A small readout just inside the hatch confirmed the fact.

Jules stopped in her tracks and whistled in appreciation. It wasn't the shock of cold air that had pulled her up short, but the full-blown opulence of the interior fit-out. Unlike the *Diamantina*, where you could never forget that you were on a small boat, Norman's yacht seemed designed to provide the experience of stepping into a grand European hotel at sea. Polished wood panelling glowed with a soft red warmth. Brass gleamed. Thick woollen carpets covered the floor. As she got over the surprise and moved on, Jules briefly caught sight of huge staterooms, lavishly furnished with antique tables and cabinets and massive, overstuffed armchairs. Oil paintings hung from the walls wherever they turned. Here a bush scene – from Australia, she presumed – there, an enormous portrait of four white dogs. A grand staircase connected the decks above and below this one, again looking as though it would not have been out of place in a French palace or a grand Italian villa.

She counted another seven piles of clothes and organic matter as they explored.

The surroundings seemed to overwhelm Fifi, who momentarily forgot her fear and disgust. 'Man, this is like a hotel or something,' she cooed. 'A real fancy hotel too, not just a Motel 6. This is more like a Holiday Inn.'

'In here,' said Jules, leading them into a private cinema where two rows of plush, royal-blue lounges faced a giant wide-screen TV. She thanked God there were no nausea-inducing rag piles in here. 'Pete, do you think you could work some video magic?'

'Mate, there's gotta be more than five hundred channels on this thing,' he replied, waving a black plastic remote control at the screen. Immediately, the sound came booming up, making them all jump.

'News would be good, Pete.'

'Okay, don't rush me.'

After some fiddling about, he brought up a news service. BBC World, according to the electronic watermark in the corner of the screen.

'. . . *broke out between riot police and residents of the largely Muslim suburb after a man was arrested for allegedly stopping cars and demanding that the occupants join in the celebrations.*'

'What the hell's that about?' said Fifi.

Jules took the control from Pete and thumbed off the sound as she searched for a program guide. 'It happened last time too.'

'Last time?'

'Nine/eleven.'

'That's great,' said Pete as the big flat Sony filled with images of burning cars and shops. 'But we need to move our arses before someone else tries to grab this boat out from under us.'

Fifi, now fully recovered from her earlier fright, shrugged and hefted her sawn-off shotty. 'Let 'em try.'

'Someone with more guns,' he added.

Mr Lee looked over the main controls in the bridge one last time, shaking his head. 'Yes, we can do this,' he said, somewhat paradoxically. 'But not for long. We will need engineering johnnies, for begin.'

Pete nodded. They'd just come from inspecting the lower decks, specifically the engine room, which – save for three more puddles of dark green sludge on the floor and their accompanying uniforms – had gleamed whiter and cleaner than any human space he'd ever seen before. It was like the photos you sometimes saw of microchip plants in Taiwan. Not a speck of dust or grease anywhere. The boat was running perfectly for the moment, following a computer-controlled track to the south, but it was such a huge, complicated piece of machinery that there was no guarantee they'd be able to cope if anything went wrong.

He allowed himself a little Captain Kirk moment, swivelling in the main command chair as Fifi and Jules reclined on a padded bench at the rear of the cabin. Late afternoon light flooded in through the huge windows, bathing them all in a deepening golden glow. All in all, it felt more like they were kicking back at the Bellagio in Vegas than scoping out a hijack at sea.

'We could get crew,' suggested Pete. 'I know some guys in Acapulco, and down Panama way. German Willy still runs out of the Canal zone. And there's Stan Lusevic, and Shoeless Dan.'

'Jesus Christ, Pete!' protested Jules. 'Are we putting together a crew or a sheltered workshop for retired drunks and dick pullers?'

'Yes,' Lee agreed. 'German Willy, too much drinking, too much willy. Other two – morons. Without shoes. No good, Mr Pete. No good.'

'Okay,' he conceded. 'I take your point. But, Mr Lee, you're also right about us needing crew if we're going to be doing anything other than selling this boat off at the first safe port we can find.'

Jules smiled wryly at him from deep inside the luxurious royal-blue padding of the bench, which occupied the entire rear bulkhead. 'Pete, I thought we were just minding this old tub for the Shark.'

The Aussie gave a sad smile in return and shook his head. 'The Shark's gone, baby.' He spared a glance at the viscous stains on the non-slip floor where Mr Lee had cleaned up another two pools of human ooze; true to form, it hadn't seemed to bother his first mate. 'Almost everyone north of here is gone for good,' Pete continued. 'You've seen the news. If we're *lucky*, this'll be some kind of space-monkey invasion, because at least then we'll have someone to maintain order.'

'Like in *Planet of the Apes*,' said Fifi, in all seriousness.

'Sure, sweetheart, if you like. But me, I reckon the universe, or merciful Allah or the Great Pumpkin or whatever, sneezed and blew the good ol' US of A right out of its arse – which, as we've seen, a lot of people think of as A Good Deal. But me, I reckon it means we're about three days away from a Hobbesian fucking meltdown.'

Fifi's blank look spoke volumes for a formal education that had ended when she was only thirteen years old.

'Thomas Hobbes, darling,' explained Jules. 'A Brit. He invented the idea of the violent clusterfuck, with everyone fighting each other. Like a Jackie Chan movie. Or a cage-wrestling free-for-all on the telly. You know, *Smackdown* or *Spankdown*, or whatever it's called.'

'Right,' Pete agreed, before waving his hand in the general direction of the energy wave. 'That thing out there, most people won't realise it yet, but that thing has thrown us into a state of fucking nature, a war of all against all. And I've been wondering whether the safest option might be to ride it out in the south Pacific for a couple of years. Island-hop, trade a bit. Stay one step ahead of the chaos – because it's coming, believe me.'

'Already here,' said Lee.

'What's that?' asked Pete, spinning in his captain's chair.

Mr Lee was standing a few feet away, splitting his attention between a radar screen and an enormous pair of Zeiss binoculars, mounted on a pivot stand, through which he'd been watching the southern horizon. He'd peer through the glasses, check the screen, and peer through the glasses again, finally grunting once, emphatically.

'Twelve miles sou'-sou'-east, Mr Peter. Three go-fast boats I see. They making over sixty knots.'

'Heading?' quizzed Jules before Pete could open his mouth.

'Straight for us, I'll bet,' said Pete in a flat, fatalistic voice.

Mr Lee nodded. 'Straight for us.'

'They packin'?' asked Fifi, suddenly on her feet, shotgun in hand. 'You think I should go get the worm?'

'Too far away, cannot see.'

'They're packin',' sighed Pete. 'Come on,' he said, pushing himself up out of the chair, 'it's started. And yeah, Fifi – go break out the worm. And get your cannon too.'

'*Awesome.*'

10

'*Non!*'

The French girl's shriek was a raw, animal sound. Within it roiled pain, violation, horror and outrage. Her face, a mask of dark, primal emotions, raged at Caitlin over the unwavering muzzle of the Glock 23. The assassin had long ago stopped counting the number of men and women whose last seconds she'd seen through crosshairs or iron gun sights, and she knew from that face that Monique's cry was not a plea for life. It was a scream of protest at what had already been taken from her. Trust and intimacy and a whole world in which Caitlin (or Cathy, as Monique knew her) was a friend, not a liar and a murderer.

A hot flush washed over the Echelon agent, dizzying, unexpected. She let her gun hand fall to her side, tired of it all. And she might still use Monique to get to al Banna. If that still mattered.

'If you stay here you will die,' she said. 'Come with me right now, and you might live.'

The emergency room remained a still life by Goya. The first cries of staff and patients had been silenced by the shots she'd fired into the heads of her would-be killers – or captors. As Caitlin turned for the exit, a spasm of movement passed through the onlookers, as each flinched away from the line of her gaze. One man in a white coat, a doctor most likely, took a few hesitant steps in her direction, but a shake of her head and a casual wave of the pistol in his direction arrested any further advance. Caitlin did not check to see whether Monique was following her as she exited the ER. She knew the girl would.

Walking quickly but calmly towards a set of sliding doors, she stripped off her bloodied chambray shirt. The white vest underneath was stained pink but she hid the worst of it with a black leather motorcycle jacket, lifted from the corner of a litter on which a man with a heavily bandaged head lay unconscious. It was too big for her but would have to do for now. The guns, identical models, went into a couple of zippered pockets and she plucked the last of the sensor leads from her filthy hair. A roll of thick surgical tape from a nurse's trolley went into another pocket. In the last few steps she turned and walked backwards, scanning the room quickly for any more pursuers. Monique was glaring at her with unalloyed loathing, but she was following just a few feet behind, victim of a type of Stockholm syndrome that Caitlin had seen and exploited many times before.

The doors closed on the Pitié-Salpêtrière with a chime and the protesting grumble of old rubber wheels in dirty guide rails. Early evening had come with a hard frost and she shivered inside the jacket, thankful for its warmth. Transport was her first and most urgent need, then shelter. When they were safely hidden away she would contact Wales, her overwatch coordinator. Her cover was blown. Her image and the fight in the emergency room had certainly been captured on hospital security video.

'Where the fuck are we going, Cathy? What are you going to do? You killed those men. *Murdered* them.' Monique's tone was shrill, accusatory.

Caitlin shrugged her off, scanning the cars parked in front of the building as she hastened down the steps. A blue Renault Fuego had caught her eye – a good car, easily stolen, and as close to invisible in Paris as she could get on short notice. The front passenger-side window was open a crack.

'It's not the same,' she said.

'What do you mean?' Monique demanded to know, hurrying to catch up beside her.

Sirens were audible, but there seemed to be hundreds of them, the distinctive warble and wail coming from all points of the compass. The city was alive with their discordant jangling sound.

Traffic along the roads around the hospital grounds was heavy, but grinding forward in fits and starts. Caitlin could see the strobing lights of both police and ambulance vehicles in three separate places. It was impossible to tell whether they were headed in her direction.

'Killing and murdering are not the same thing. I killed them, sure. But I had good reason. That isn't murder. It's self-defence.'

'Self-defence!' Monique made a grab for her arm but Caitlin slipped out of her grip with practised ease. 'You expect me to believe that? You attacked them and killed them like . . . a . . . machine! A thing. You are no activist. You are no surfer!' Monique spat the last word at her.

'Well, I used to surf, but I'm also a soldier,' Caitlin replied. 'Now, get in the fucking car, if you want to get out of this alive. Those men back there, they were soldiers too, like me. And there'll be more of them looking for us.'

Caitlin retrieved one of the pistols from the leather jacket and swung the butt of the handle into the window, smashing it open and causing Monique to jump with surprise. There were over a dozen witnesses watching her, but nobody made any attempt to intervene as she popped the lock. More people came spilling out of the ER doors, some of them pointing her way, but none made any move towards her. It wouldn't be long, however, before hospital security, the gendarmes or something worse turned up.

'Clock's a-tickin', Monique. Hop in.'

The front seat of the Fuego was cluttered with papers, a bag of onions and a purse from which spilled a chequebook, iPod, mobile phone, make-up and more keys.

'Jesus Christ,' said Caitlin. 'Why not just get a big fucking bumper sticker that says "Steal my stuff"?'

She snatched a sturdy-looking steel pen from the jumble of items and used it to lever her way into the car's accessory circuits, cracking open the plastic cover beneath the wheel with a couple of violent jerks. She sensed Monique hovering outside and swept the detritus from the seat. 'Just get in. We're running out of time.'

The French girl climbed in carefully, as if unwilling to touch the belongings of the unknown owner. Caitlin swore softly as she sparked the engine to life, giving herself a small electrical shock in the process. A brief glance over her shoulder revealed a growing knot of people on the steps of the hospital, all of them gesturing in her direction, some of them shouting. She threw the car into reverse, stamped on the gas and peeled out backwards from the parking spot with a squeal and the harsh smell of burnt rubber, reefing on the handbrake to tighten her turning circle. Both she and Monique jerked forward in their seats and she slammed the disc brakes, changed gear and accelerated away, barely missing the tail-lights of an adjacent Fiat.

'You are not Cathy Mercure, are you?' asked Monique as they negotiated a twisting course through the car park towards the exit and out into the traffic stream.

Caitlin's first, unthinking reaction was to lie. Deceit and betrayal were so deeply ingrained by her training and the demands of her work that they had become elements of her true nature. But unless she was psychotic, her mission concerns were no longer relevant. Something bigger had happened, something infinitely worse than anything she had been prepared to fight. A painful throbbing on the injured side of her head grew more insistent as she allowed herself to contemplate anything beyond fight or flight for the first time since the shooting had begun back at the hospital.

'No,' she conceded to Monique. 'I'm not Cathy Mercure. My name's Caitlin. That's all you need to know. That, and also that you're in a lot of trouble.'

Blaring horns and some muffled Gallic abuse greeted their high-speed entry into the crowded Parisian road net. Caitlin opted to cut across the main flow of traffic, and forced her way through an intersection onto a lesser boulevard. She wasn't familiar with the road but it had everything she wanted right at that moment. It was navigable at a good speed and it was taking them away from the place where somebody had just tried to put the zap on her.

'*I'm* in trouble?' Monique shot back. 'I have not killed anybody or stolen a car. *I* am not some sort of criminal. I did not get my friends shot back at . . .'

Her voice hitched and cracked as the emotional blow-back of the battle at the Pitié-Salpêtrière finally struck her. She had seen at least one of her friends shot down in front of her eyes, before watching another morph into a homicidal destroyer. Monique's mouth gaped and her shoulders trembled as a squall of wild animus blew through her.

Caitlin rammed the little blue car through a series of gear changes as she threaded a course through a thicker pulse of traffic. Once they'd cleared the moving obstruction, she plucked a couple of paper tissues from a box jammed into the cup holder that lay between them.

'I didn't get your friends killed, Monique,' she said firmly, but quietly. 'I didn't pull that trigger. But I took down the assholes who did. They're avenged, for what it's worth.'

'Nothing! It's worth *nothing*,' shouted Monique, as the tears came at last.

'Fair enough,' shrugged Caitlin, checking the mirrors for any sign of pursuit as she dialled back on their speed to blend in to the surrounding traffic flow, and began to look for a landmark with which she could place them. She didn't fancy asking the French girl for anything just yet.

The street had narrowed to just one lane running in each direction. Stunted, leafless trees lined the footpath, which was thick with people hurrying home from work, or out to dinner in one of the many bistros and wine bars that huddled up close together on the ground floors of the old four- and five-storey buildings. Warm, golden light spilled out through their windows, affording brief glimpses of packed tables and bars at which drinkers stood beneath thick clouds of cigarette smoke. For all the cosmopolitan charms, it was all so conventional. Had she been able to drive along here twenty-four hours earlier, Caitlin was certain she would have passed by almost exactly the same scene. Surely the only topic of conversation at those crowded tables would be the day's news from the US; from the driver's seat of the stolen Renault, however, she could not tell.

Beside her, Monique was trying valiantly to control her crying, but she had already gone through at least a third of the tissues. The young woman searched inside a pocket for a small flip-top cell phone, sniffling as she tried to key in a number. Caitlin slapped it out of her hands.

'What the fuck are you doing? Don't you read your own con-spiracy theories? You can be tracked with that thing. In fact . . .'

She reached over and roughly jammed her hand between Monique's legs to retrieve the little Samsung.

'I'm just calling Billy!' she protested. 'He can come for me. I don't want to be alone with you or anywhere near you – whoever you are.'

Monique gasped in shock as Caitlin threw the phone out of the window.

'It won't be Billy who comes for you if you make that call, darlin'. It'll be more guys in ties, toting big fucking guns.'

'You bitch! That was my phone!' cried Monique, genuinely affronted.

'No. That was a chip tracking your every movement,' Caitlin corrected her. 'And forget about your boyfriend. His phone is being monitored too.'

Caitlin checked her watch. They had been driving for nearly fifteen minutes, more than enough time for their descriptions and the car's licence plate to have been pushed out over the police nets.

'We have to change cars, Monique,' she said. 'I'm going to pull off the street up ahead at that corner and ditch this ride. I'm gonna ask you to come with me, but I'm not going to make you.'

She allowed herself a brief, measuring glance at her passenger. Monique's eyes were puffy and tear tracks had washed runnels of make-up from her face. It must have been expertly applied. Caitlin hadn't even noticed before. Monique was upset, naturally, but she was angry too. Very angry.

'Why should I come with you? I should go right to the police and report you.'

'You could do that,' Caitlin said as she turned the wheel to take them off the narrow street and into an even narrower alleyway. 'But those men I killed – the men who shot Maggie in the head – they were from your state security service. Secret police, if you like. If you walk into the gendarmes and tell them what happened, your details will go onto their network and within half an hour more guys like that will turn up at the police station and take you away. The cops won't stop them. But they will stop you leaving if you try.'

'But why? That is ridiculous.'

Caitlin pulled over, running the Fuego's wheels up onto the very narrow footpath. It couldn't have been more than two feet wide. She was glad she hadn't had to reverse-park. Her head and neck were aching.

'They were after me, Monique, and I was with you, so now they're after you too. You have family? They're being watched. Your boyfriend? Him too. It's not you they want, it's me. Your security service is conducting a hard target search for *me*, and as of half an hour ago, you are the key. Every phone call you have made for the last five years, every address you've lived at, or just stayed at, that can be tracked, is being tracked. Every movement across every border, every purchase with your credit card, every transaction in your bank account, every mailing list your name appears on, every email you've ever sent, every chat room or web-site you've ever visited, every net search you've ever done, they are all being sifted through and analysed right now, by people *way* smarter than you, because you are alive, and free, and running from them. With me.'

Monique shook her head, refusing to believe what she was hearing. As she spoke, her words became clipped and fiercer. 'This is bullshit. *You* are bullshit. You come to us as a friend. You say you are against the war. But you are part of the war. You are a killer just like Bush and Blair. Those men, if they were from the police or the secret service, it was their duty to arrest you. And you killed them and got Maggie killed as well.'

Monique's anger overwhelmed her and she emphasised her last point by slapping at Caitlin's face. The American brushed off the ineffectual blows with one swift hand, not even flinching as Monique cried out with frustration and attempted to rake out her eyes. Caitlin grabbed one of the girl's hands and turned it sharply back in on the wrist, making her gasp with pain and shock.

'Knock it off, princess,' Caitlin warned. 'I didn't come here to hurt you or your dumbass friends. I came to protect you.'

'What?'

At that point, three young men, obviously drunk and in high spirits, came around the corner and past the car, banging on the windows and calling out to the two women to come out and play, to have a drink and celebrate with them. Caitlin glared back, but they just laughed. One held up two fingers in a 'V' and stuck his tongue between them, waggling it obscenely. This was obviously the funniest thing his friends had seen all night and they fell into the cobbled roadway, laughing hysterically.

'Assholes,' muttered Caitlin.

'What did you – '

'I said, "Assholes".'

'*Non*. What did you say about "protecting" us?'

The drunks helped each other off the cold, damp road surface and continued on their way to the next bar, one of them turning awkwardly to grab his crotch and give it a bit of a squeeze for the benefit of the two dykes. Caitlin had no trouble translating the slurred words that followed, but the body language said it all: *See what you are missing, ladies?*

'How could you have been protecting us?' Monique repeated, ignoring her oafish countrymen. 'From those skinheads at the Tunnel? You couldn't have known about that.'

Caitlin opened the door and stepped out, taking a handful of banknotes from the handbag. She left the door ajar. The Renault would not be here for long. Monique squeezed out on the other side, the car's proximity to a brick wall making for a tight fit. The wall was covered with an inch of peeling posters, most of them for awful French rock bands, but the uppermost layer called for a 'National Day of Action' to stop the 'Anglo War'. That was the gig her merry little band had been headed for when set upon by the National Front thugs, who got lucky and put her in hospital. *Where I got lucky and caught a fucking brain tumour . . .*

Caitlin had to stop for a moment and lean against the wall as her head reeled. Whether from the illness, her injuries or an adrenalin backwash, she couldn't tell. She stood still, closed her eyes and sucked in a long draught of air. It was unpleasantly cold now, but the alleyway still reeked of garbage and dog shit – the signature smell of Paris behind the coffee and *pain au chocolat*.

'Are you all right?' Monique asked grudgingly.

'I'll be fine. Just give me a second.'

And the dizzy spell did pass quickly. She felt a little lightheaded as they stepped off towards the street again, but nothing too crippling. Monique supported Caitlin at the elbow anyway, a gesture she was happy to accept.

'You didn't answer my question,' the Frenchwoman said, a little petulantly. 'What did you mean before, about protecting us?'

'You wouldn't believe me, not yet.'

'Try me.'

'No. If we're still alive in a few days, I'll tell you – and you will believe me, every word I say. But for now, no. Come with me, or make your own way home, where they'll be waiting for you. It's all the same to me.'

They stopped at the intersection, where bright lights and heavy foot traffic created an effect a little like stepping back into the real world from some underground realm. A bus rumbled by, coughing thick gouts of acrid smoke into the air. Shoes scuffed and clicked on wet, grey flagstones, and around them roared hundreds of voices, all discussing the same thing: '*la Disparition*'. The Disappearance.

Caitlin's heart sank. She had been hoping, irrationally, that the apparent normality of the street scene implied there was some sort of disorder within her, some malady of the brain caused by her illness, and that it had manifested itself as a perverse hallucination of cataclysm. But no, the Parisians were agog with the news. And further confirmation for her that it was real was the sound of so many voices raised in good cheer and even merriment. That is what the three jerks who'd abused them before were drinking to: a world without America.

Fucking assholes.

'*Excuse-moi?*' Monique had stopped in her tracks, affronted enough to revert to her native tongue.

'Sorry. Didn't think I was speaking aloud,' said Caitlin. 'It's nothing. We've got to get moving. Let's go.'

They set off again, heading uphill. Caitlin's eyes swept the road and the footpath ahead of them on both sides of the street for any sign of hostile action, but all she could see was heavy traffic and throngs of boulevardiers, many of them seemingly toasting the day. Not all, admittedly. Here and there, arguments raged in that Gallic way, all sound and fury without any real danger of violent contention.

'. . . It is a disaster, I tell you, a world-ending disaster.'

'No. A second chance is what it is, gifted by the gods.'

'So, you are a believer now, eh?'

'. . . This will mean horror, horror on an unimaginable scale . . .'

'. . . I shall be leaving for my farm this very night. Mark my words, leave the city now or you will have – '

'All I will have is another glass of Billecart . . .'

Caitlin set her mouth in a grim, thin line and pushed on with her head down. Monique fell silent beside her. After a few minutes it became obvious that for each individual who saw the Disappearance as a malign catastrophe, another two or three thought it a fine thing. From the snatches of conversation she picked up as they hurried along, it seemed that in this part of the world at least, a rough consensus had settled on a conspiracy theory about the Americans having destroyed themselves when testing some super-weapon for use in Iraq. Nobody seemed to imagine that any such fate might befall them here in Paris. But then, if they did, they'd hardly be out scarfing down dinner and aperitifs, would they? Perhaps the freeways out of the city were jammed with more people like the man she'd heard planning to leave for his farm later that night. (Although, why he thought he'd be safe there from something that gobbled whole continents was a mystery.)

'I am sorry.'

Caitlin almost didn't hear her. Monique's voice was small and timid and nearly lost in the roar of the busy street. 'What?'

'I am sorry, Cathy – Caitlin. I can hear what they are saying as well as you. It is disgraceful. Drinking to a tragedy. Saying your people deserved it.'

'Oh, fuck that,' replied Caitlin in pitch-perfect French. She really didn't want to get tagged as an American at the moment. 'This is one street, Monique. One little neighbourhood where people of like minds will gather all the time. It's just human nature. If some Algerian madman set off a nuke in Paris, I could take you straight to a food court in any city in the US and it'd take me all of three seconds to find some fat, doughnut-sucking slob who said you deserved it. People everywhere are fucked, that's all.'

'No. Not everyone . . . Caitlin. Some people are led by the better angels.'

At that moment they passed a café outside which stood a small, elderly gentleman in a black jacket and red beret. Both of his hands were holding the crook of a walking stick, which he was banging into the ground for emphasis while arguing with a couple of men who looked to be a fraction of his age. 'I was with the Americans at Carentan. I saw them shed their blood for France. You dishonour them and you dishonour France with this rubbish talk . . .'

Caitlin gifted the old man with a sad smile and a wink as she passed by. A siren brought her head up slowly, lest she draw attention to herself, but it was a fire engine a block over. She caught a glimpse of it muscling through traffic as they crossed an intersection.

'Down here,' she said, veering off towards a line of parked cars in a street of private houses and apartments. Only one shop, a liquor store, was open.

'Are you going to steal another car?' Monique asked warily.

No, thought Caitlin. *I'm going to buy a couple of magnums of champagne and pass them around the surrender monkeys back there, to help celebrate the cosmic cornholing of the great Satan.* Aloud she simply went: 'You got it.'

Three minutes later they were cutting back across town in a grey Volvo station wagon, a late-model V40. A suction cap held a black plastic cradle to the windscreen just below the rear-view mirror. Caitlin leaned across Monique as they came to a red light, popping the glove box open.

'Sweet,' she said as she pulled out a small Magellan Meridian GPS receiver. 'Is there a power cord in there? Look for a sort of flexi cord and an adaptor to plug into the cigarette lighter.'

Monique couldn't find one, but the little yellow and black unit had three-quarters of a charge on it anyway. Caitlin powered it up as the lights changed and waited for the chime that would tell them it had linked to enough satellites to fix their position.

A frustrating few minutes passed, during which time she had to force herself to concentrate on the road. As full darkness covered the city, she could see the tell-tale glow of fires burning on the outskirts of the old centre, explaining the large number of emergency vehicles. Apparently not everyone was content to celebrate with a smirk and a snifter of Courvoisier.

The Magellan chimed once eliciting a small 'Oh!' from Monique. 'Is this us?' she asked. 'Here, near Rue Ricaut?'

'Yeah, that's us. Does it have a route function? Can you work out how to get us to –'

The window shattered inwards with a huge, hollow boom and a tinkling of glass.

11

As a boy, Tusk Musso had loved visiting the city with his grandfather. For the Musso clan, that meant New York, the greatest city in the world. In the whole goddamn history of the world – except maybe for Rome, according to his grandpa, Vinnie Musso. There was a game they played, which Grandpa insisted little Tusk never tell his mother about, where they quickly lay on the footpath at the base of the highest building they could find, and then they just stared up at this monster looming over them, looking like it went all the way to heaven. They had to be quick, before the cops or security guards chased them off. The very first time they'd done it, when Tusk was only six, it had been a cool, overcast day, with a slight breeze dragging clouds across a lowering sky, and it looked for all the world like the Chrysler Building was gonna fall right down on top of them. Tusk had squealed with laughter, and not a little fear. He wasn't allowed to say anything to Momma about it, of course, because she would've had a blue fit if she'd known that Grandpa Vinnie (whom she considered a very poor influence at best) had been letting her precious bundle roll around on the filthy pavement with the dog turds and cigarette butts.

Thank God they're long gone, he thought, as he stood about two hundred yards back from the base of the event horizon and craned his head back to watch it climb away to heaven, feeling as small and insignificant as he had all those years ago at the feet of the tallest buildings in the world. Clouds drifted overhead, just as they had back in New York with Grandpa Vinnie. But these were wispier, less substantial, and held no threat of rain or sleet. They didn't even hold out the promise of much shade from the late afternoon Caribbean sun. Musso narrowed his eyes against the still-intense glare of the day and watched as a patch of white that reminded him of a Spanish galleon floated serenely into the silvery haze at the edge of the affected area. At that distance, it created an effect similar to a stationary waterfall – all glistening silver, hanging down like a curtain.

And like a curtain, it moved. Not much, just a lazy drift back and forth across the ground, no more than a couple of yards in either direction. Just enough to wake up the primitive creature dwelling in the darkest parts of Musso's mind, to fill him with an atavistic fear of whatever danger lay in the darkness just outside the mouth of the cave.

Musso the modern, rational man, dressed in a short-sleeve khaki shirt and olive drab pants, ground down on that ancient terror and watched, fascinated, as the cloud drifted into the energy wave. It seemed completely unaffected as it passed through. Its form became less distinct on the far side, but it was discernibly the same shape and size as before.

'Seen any birds fly into it or out of it?' he asked, still peering upwards.

Major Nuñez shook his head. 'None. Some of my men say they saw large flights of birds moving away from here earlier today, but I do not know where they came from. And there are none here now. Not one.'

The brigadier general dropped his gaze. They were standing by the crumbling edge of a two-lane road, the bitumen surface shimmering in the heat a few hundred yards behind them, a natural phenomenon. The much more powerful haze directly in front was decidedly unnatural. The small convoy of Hummers and Cuban vehicles had pulled up here ten minutes ago and Musso's heart was still beating hard from the sight. Any last, lingering doubts placed in the way of belief by his rational mind had been banished. Visible from well over the horizon, it not only reached up to the stratosphere, it curved away towards the horizon in both directions like a giant standing wave, raised by an unknowable deity.

It was alien.

It sat there, in front of him, utterly removed from any human context to give it meaning. He had no idea what it was, and having seen it up close for himself now, he doubted that anybody ever would.

'You still got nothing, Lieutenant Kwan?' he said.

Lieutenant Jenny Kwan shook her head. She seemed too young to Musso, almost baby-faced, but she was one of the smartest, scariest individuals he'd ever met. An MIT grad, Kwan was a Marine first lieutenant, the boss of an Incident Response Unit, which was a bland name for a bunch of very smart people trained to look for and respond to some of the worst things in the world: chemical, biological and nuclear weapons. Her crew and equipment took up three of the seven Humvees that had driven deep into Cuban territory, escorted by Major Nuñez and a platoon of his men in a couple of old Soviet-era BMP-2s.

Musso had to hand it to the Cubans. This monstrosity wasn't an abstract proposition for them, something to be intuited from indirect evidence provided by web links or satellite data. It was sitting literally a stone's throw away, bisecting their country. Given all that, he was impressed by their professionalism and no-bullshit attitude, although Nuñez had probably picked his Praetorian guard for this gig. They helped Lieutenant Kwan whenever she asked for it, and kept to themselves when she didn't. Not that Kwan was having any luck with her equipment – no matter what sensors or sniffers or magic wands she waved at the haze, it made not a damn bit of difference.

'According to my readings, General, that thing isn't even here,' she told him.

'Uh-uh,' he muttered. They'd had the same result plugging into FAA and weather satellites back at Gitmo. As far as their technology was concerned, the haze didn't exist.

He could feel the warmth leaking out of the late afternoon as the sun dropped towards a line of low, scrubby hills in the west. There was a faint but noticeable dry heat radiating from the haze, but that was all.

'Care to take a closer look, Major?' he said.

Nuñez shook his head. 'No. But what else is to be done?'

The Cuban officer took the first steps away from the convoy, towards the new edge of the known world. Musso fell in beside him as they cautiously approached the barrier. The country hereabouts was little different from the area around Guantanamo. Both were nestled at the edge of the Sierra Maestra ranges, the remnants of huge fractured slabs of continental plate, raised from the ocean floor over millions of years by tectonic impact, volcanic eruptions and the 100,000-gigatonne blast of the Chicxulub comet punching into the surface of the planet just a short distance away, some 65 million years ago. The Maestra was perfect guerrilla territory, a vast contrary maze of steep valleys, volcanic dykes, abrupt fault lines and almost impenetrable karst areas, all riven with limestone caves and covered in dense forest. The ranges gave out on the far side of the haze, smoothing out into the low, rolling plains that made up nearly two-thirds of Cuba's land surface. For all of the earth-shattering violence that had gone into creating this environment over the eons, it was nothing compared to the immediate spectacle of the static energy wave.

Musso was able to make out the lowland steppes on the far side without much trouble. Nothing moved there. He had earlier compared it to looking through a waterfall, but now to his mind it was more like a few layers of plastic wrap. He stooped down to pick up a rock as they walked, wondering what would happen if he threw it in. Nuñez slowed as they approached the face. It appeared to billow, like a sail, just as the Cuban had described. They stopped about fifty yards away.

'I would not think it safe to get much closer,' Nuñez warned.

'I wouldn't argue with that, Major,' agreed Musso. 'Let's just accept we're both possessed of stainless-steel *cojones* and take it nice and careful from here.'

He could see a burnt-out car wreck on the far side, near a bend in the road, and wondered if that's where Nuñez's superior officer had disappeared. This close to it, he avoided looking up. The scale of the thing was enough to give him a teetering sense of vertigo without making it any worse by craning his head back. He turned around to check on his people. They were all watching anxiously, their bodies rigid with anticipation.

Suddenly there was a whooshing noise and he saw them all jump, like an audience in a horror movie frightened by a cheap stunt. 'What the fuck?' he said, turning to Nuñez.

But the Cuban was gone. Only his smouldering uniform remained.

The cries of his comrades and of Nuñez's men reached him a moment later. 'Run, General! Get the hell outta there!'

PACOM HQ, PEARL HARBOR, HAWAII

Admiral Ritchie found his eyes straying from the television news broadcast to the silver-framed picture of his daughter on the desk in front of him. The photograph was old. Nancy was nineteen now, but on his desk, she remained forever three, holding a small bear, sucking her thumb, and staring off a thousand miles into the distance.

He had to tear his eyes away. It was almost too painful to bear. She should be all right – she was supposed to fly out from Chicago for Europe very early this morning. But they had heard nothing from her. Had she made the flight? Had it escaped the Wave? He didn't know. His wife Amanda was frantically trying to find out, but without much luck. With a grinding effort of will, Ritchie turned his attention back to work.

Thank God for cable news at least, he thought. He had wondered if he might have to press the Governor's office for a declaration of martial law, fearing that violence would be inevitable as the population of the islands digested what was happening. But far from sending mobs onto the street, the wall-to-wall media coverage, all of it sourced from Asia and Europe, seemed to be keeping Hawaii's civilian population glued to their TV and computer screens. Every available police officer had been called in, and a battalion apiece of Marines and the army were hurriedly kitting out with crowd-control gear, just in case, although all of the reports he'd received so far had the streets half deserted. Hopefully they wouldn't be needed. The surf breaks off the north shore were a little less crowded than usual, but not much. Apparently even the end of the world wasn't going to interfere with some people's search for the perfect wave.

'Governor's office called, sir.'

Ritchie looked up from the drifts of paperwork that covered every square inch of his desk. A couple of pages had even dropped to the floor. His PA, Captain McKinney, bent forward and retrieved them.

'Yes, Andrew? Good news, I hope?'

'Mixed, Admiral. Curfew starts at 1800 sharp tonight. They couldn't agree on the rationing though. But they have organised emergency flights from Tokyo and Sydney for any perishables or medical supplies that run low. The National Security Committees of both the Japanese and Australian cabinets are still meeting, but their local liaison staff have passed on messages from both prime ministers that they'll give us whatever help we need.'

They're the ones who'll be needing help soon enough, thought Ritchie. But aloud he only said, 'Well, that's something at least. For now.'

The armed forces had considerable stockpiles of rations and medical supplies on the islands, but they didn't store items like insulin for diabetics, or drugs for cancer treatment or a dozen other common maladies. Ritchie couldn't help wondering just how much of a supply of antidepressants there was in Hawaii, and how many people were likely to kill themselves or suffer heart attacks or stress-related strokes in the next few days. Given the number of tourists from the mainland here, probably lots.

Nearly two-and-a-half decades earlier, he'd written his masters dissertation at Annapolis on the navy's crisis management at Pearl Harbor. He'd been scathing of their efforts on 7 December, 1941. Now, faced with his very own calamity, he had to wonder if he would have done any better. There was just so much to do and so little to do it with. Events had accelerated to a point where he would possibly never catch up.

'Thank you, Captain,' he grunted, dismissing young McKinney, just as an officer in Army greens appeared at his door.

'Colonel Maccomb, Admiral. I have your updates if you have a moment.'

Ritchie didn't, but waved the man in anyway. Maccomb looked

like he had run all the way over from the 500th Military Intelligence Brigade – a decent hike in the midday heat of the equatorial sun. PACOM was just months away from taking possession of a new headquarters, the Nimitz-MacArthur Pacific Command Center, which would have centralised everybody in one modern facility. It looked like they'd be sticking with the old campus now, however, necessitating a lot of time wasting as his subordinates remained scattered about all over the island.

'Sit down, Colonel,' he said. 'Give it to me as quickly as you can without losing track of the story.'

The intelligence officer nodded brusquely, snapped a sheaf of paper in his hand and worked down a series of bullet points. 'Both of our alliance partners in the AOR have either activated their treaties, or will have within twenty-four hours. Land elements of Japan's Self Defence Force have been recalled to barracks, their naval forces are making preparations to put out to sea, and the air force is already flying CAP over the home islands. The Aussies have called up their Reserves and moved all of their remaining high-readiness forces onto alert – '

'Remaining?'

'Yes, sir. They have a special forces group, a squadron of Hornets and a naval task force in the Gulf with us, for Iraq.'

Ritchie nodded.

'All of the other regional powers have gone to varying states of high alert,' Maccomb continued. 'Taiwan has been placed under martial law and the armed forces there have put Plan Orange into effect. South Korea has declared that a curfew will come into effect as of 2200 hours tonight. Their forces and ours are ready, watching the DMZ, but Pyongyang is sitting very, very still. There's been nothing on their media at all.'

'And China?'

Maccomb gnawed at the inside of his mouth like a man with a lifelong chaw habit, before replying. 'They've put a lot of troops onto the streets, sir, and our satellite cover shows a lot of activity around the Taiwan Strait batteries, but the force projection capabilities they do have remain dormant for the moment. They're as spooked as anyone, and they know we still have the forces in theatre to check them if necessary.'

Ritchie nodded, feeling a headache building behind his eyeballs. 'That's a dreadfully dangerous amount of hardware and armed men moving around.'

'Yes, sir,' agreed Maccomb. 'It is.'

'It just reached out and took him,' said Kwan, a little breathlessly. 'Like, I dunno, like a sort of liquid metal blob or something. Faster than anything I've ever seen.'

Musso nodded. He didn't trust himself to speak just yet. His heart was still going like a rat in a trap, and he recognised the hollow, shaky feeling of having dodged a bullet, or something just as nasty. Musso had been a Marine for longer than he had been anything else in his life. He knew war from the inside, the way an addict knows their poison. He knew what it was like to make a ball of himself, tight and small, like a clenched fist, as death zipped like a swarm of bees through the air all around him. He knew too well the fragility of the human body, the way that war respects not age, not courage, gender, righteousness, intelligence or any of the limitless personal touchstones that everyone thinks will get them through, just before everyone starts dying. He had held in his arms grown men, reduced to bloodied rags and cooling meat by a few dumb grams of flying metal. He had carried a little Somalian girl in his hands, no more than two she would have been, her poor tiny body burnt and disintegrating as he ran for a medic. He knew the filth and horror of war as a contagion buried just beneath the surface of his own skin. He knew fear.

But he had never known it as he had in the few seconds after Eladio Nuñez was consumed. Fear like a rancid, suppurating pustule that suddenly burst all sweet and bilious in his guts, flooding his mouth and throat and stomach with a distillation of terror in its primal state. He was going to take a few moments to get over it.

The Cubans, he saw, had freaked the hell out, but were holding it together under the lash of Nuñez's deputy, Captain someone-or-other. Musso couldn't recall his name. His own people were no less upset, although they were hiding it a little better. Everyone had withdrawn back up the road towards Guantanamo, pulling over to the side about five hundred metres from their original position. The energy wave hadn't altered in the slightest.

Musso released a ragged breath. 'Okay. As of now, nobody gets within five hundred metres of that thing, okay? I can't tell the Cubans what to do, of course, but I'm guessing they won't argue.'

Kwan nodded and looked around for the nameless captain. 'I don't even know if he speaks English, sir.'

'Me neither, Lieutenant,' he said. 'Get someone to translate. Your sergeant, Gutteres, he's sharp. Put him on liaison if you can spare him.'

'Guilio's specialty is binary nerve agents. I don't think I'll be needing him,' she replied flatly.

Kwan saluted and turned away to find their new translator. Musso took a sip of chilled sports drink from an insulated bottle. They had withdrawn to a spot on a slight rise where a small clearing allowed all of the vehicles to pull off onto the shoulder. The Americans still tended to their equipment, attempting to take readings from something that their equipment told them wasn't there. The Cubans had gathered into a loose line under the watchful, if anxious, gaze of their latest commanding officer. They were sure getting through them at a fair clip.

Musso calmed his breathing. His heart rate had dropped back to something a little more reasonable and the unpleasant low-grade voltage that had been buzzing away just under his skin had finally died down. He couldn't help but wonder where Nuñez had gone. If anywhere. That thought led naturally to thoughts of his wife and kids and what had happened to them. His stomach turned over again. Another slug from the drink bottle and he put it away, pushing himself off the side of the Humvee and walking over to his radio man, determinedly trying to ignore his personal anxieties.

'Corporal, can you hook me up with Pearl, via Gitmo?'

'No problems, General. Just give me a moment.'

Musso left him to it, taking a minute to go off and talk to the Cubans' new CO. Jenny Kwan and Sergeant Gutteres were deep in a three-way conference with the scared-looking officer, who snapped rigidly to attention when he saw Musso approaching. The marine gave him a tired smile and a nod in reply.

'How're we doing, Lieutenant?' he asked Kwan.

'Pretty good, sir. Captain Álvarez here speaks pretty good English. A hell of a lot better than my Spanish, at any rate. Sergeant Gutteres is filling in the blanks.'

Musso addressed the Cuban directly. 'I'm sorry about Major Nuñez. He seemed a good man and an excellent officer.'

'He was,' Álvarez replied. 'We liked him. All the men like him very much.'

'Well, Captain, I'm about to seek guidance from my superiors, but for myself, I'd like us to keep talking, to help each other out if and when we can. I'd suggest you try and find someone further up your chain of command to report to, but son, you need to prepare yourself for the possibility that you *are* it.'

Sergeant Gutteres had begun translating quietly as soon as he'd seen Álvarez struggling to keep up with Musso. He finished a few seconds after the general.

Captain Álvarez grimaced a little at the thought that he might well be the sole surviving authority figure in his country, but, to his credit, he sucked it up and gave the *Americano* his sternest warrior's face. 'Cooperation, yes, General,' he answered. 'Perhaps, in this emergency, we might discuss a joint command, no – a combination command?'

At the look of incomprehension on Musso's face, he launched into a burst of Spanish. Gutteres waited, taking it all in, before passing on the gist of what he'd said.

'Long story short, General, Captain Álvarez is offering to *temporarily* place his men under your command. He emphasises the temporary nature of the arrangement, sir.'

Musso nodded. He understood the Cuban was covering himself against the unlikely eventuality that they might all click their heels three times and find everything had returned to normal. In which case he'd probably need to seek immediate asylum.

'You do me an honour, Captain,' said Musso, nodding to Gutteres to make sure he translated the phrase literally. 'Your men have comported themselves with great bravery and forbearance today. They are a credit to your country and it would be a privilege to serve with them, however *temporary* the arrangement might be.'

Álvarez, who seemed more than happy with that, asked if he might borrow the sergeant to speak to his men. Musso agreed, laying a light hand on Gutteres's shoulder before he left them. 'Take it easy, son. A light touch is called for. Let Álvarez do any yelling and butt-kicking that's required.'

'Got it, General.'

His radio operator indicated from the command Humvee that he'd established the link to Pearl and Musso exchanged a salute and, less formally, a handshake with his newest subordinate before hurrying back.

'Admiral Ritchie on the line, sir.'

'Thank you,' said Musso, as he took the handset. 'Admiral, it's General Musso, sir. I'm afraid I have some more bad news.'

Ritchie hung up when he was done with Musso. He didn't know what was more disturbing, the way the energy barrier had reached out and snatched Major Nuñez when he strayed too close, or the fact that the surviving Cubans had been so neutered by the events of the day that they'd effectively surrendered control of their territory, or what was left of it, to the United States – or what was left of *her*.

A terrible melancholy had settled upon his spirit in the last hour or so. He hadn't noticed it stealing up on him, but having received Musso's report he found himself in such a bleak frame of mind as he couldn't recall ever having known before. He could hear an increasing hubbub outside his office as more and more people poured into PACOM headquarters. Hundreds of phones appeared to be ringing, and so many voices competed with one another to get their message through, to have their tiny part of this unfolding nightmare recognised as important, that the normally hushed environs of the command centre reminded him of the stock exchange in New York. He'd visited there with his wife and daughter a few months before 9/11.

'Admiral?'

'I'm sorry,' he said, a little roughly, pretending he'd been lost in thought about something more than his own personal tragedy. His PA was at the door.

'It's General Franks, sir. On a secure line from Qatar. He says elements of the Iraqi Army are leaving their entrenched positions and appear to be heading towards the border with Kuwait.'

Just for a second Ritchie thought his heart might have stopped. Then he realised it had simply jumped. It felt as though it had gathered itself up and tried to leap right out of his chest. He felt momentarily dizzy and covered it by nodding as he leaned back in his chair. 'Patch him through, Andrew, if you would,' he said quickly. 'Any other good news?'

'The Israelis have moved extra units into the Gaza Strip,' Captain McKinney reported. 'A street party there got out of hand and turned into a riot. One of their guys got shot trying to close it down.'

'A street party?' Ritchie couldn't keep the dismay out of his voice.

'They're breaking out all over, sir. *All* over. Plenty in the Mid' East, of course. But plenty more in Europe, even Britain, in some of the northern areas, with big . . . er . . . migrant populations.'

'You mean, big Muslim populations.'

'Yes, sir.'

'Very well. Patch General Franks through to me here.'

Ritchie had a few seconds alone before Tommy Franks came on the line. *My God*, he thought, silently. *This is going to turn bad even quicker than I thought.*

12

'Shoeless fuckin' Dan,' spat Pete, with no joy in his voice at the arrival of such an old, esteemed colleague.

'And all of his little toes,' said Mr Lee, shooting a wide, gap-toothed grin at Pete. To add to the effect, he raised one eyebrow and winked. A most disconcerting sight. 'Flippant humour, Mr Pete? To ease tensions before confrontation.'

Pete forced a wan smile in spite of himself. Shoeless Dan was no laughing matter. The dude dealt in some high-octane villainy. Word was, he'd once filled the hold of a Liberian freighter with a couple of hundred orphans for the Chechen maf. Unspoilt children paid off at the same dollar-per-kilo rate as good heroin, if you could get them into the right wholesale chain. Dan denied it, of course, but not all that strenuously. It added to his mystique – which he needed, given the incurable fungal infection that had turned his feet into putrescent, oozing slabs of meat. The things were grotesque, as big as footballs when they really swelled up, and never smelling any sweeter than a rancid wheel of Spanish cheese. He knew his boats, though. And he knew the smuggling biz.

'Flippant humour, Mr Lee,' Pete echoed with a nod, while watching the trio of go-fast boats split up and peel off to come at the yacht from opposite sides. 'Does Chinese culture even do flippancy?'

'Mr John Woo, yes. Central Committee of Communist Party, not so much.'

'Who is the more Confucian, then?' asked Pete, following Dan's boat through a pair of binoculars.

'Not Confucian,' Lee replied, raising both eyebrows and positively beaming at his skipper with all of his remaining teeth on show, 'just confusing.'

His punchline delivered, the old Chinaman held up a hand in triumph. Pete allowed himself a genuine smile that crinkled the net of lines at the corner of his eyes as he smacked out a high five. It might well be the last smile of his life.

'Mr Lee, John Woo doesn't know shit about Chinese action heroes if he doesn't know you . . . Now, let's deal with this shoeless fuckwit, shall we? I won't have his stinky fucking plates of meat oozing and peeling all over my new boat. Take her up to thirteen knots, if you will. We'll leave a little bit of tiger in the tank for later, if needed.'

Lee fitted a set of headphones over his ears, plugged them into a digital radio clipped onto his sun-faded canvas pants, and then opened the throttles on the big boat's massive Caterpillar engines, unleashing a stampede from the 1492 horsepower contained in each one. Acceleration was smooth and instantaneous. Pete felt himself rocking back on his heels as they leapt forward and Mr Lee began a series of sharp tacking manoeuvres, to make any boarding operations as difficult as possible.

The radio in Pete's hand crackled into life. It was Jules. 'We're in position, Pete.'

'Good work, Julesy. Keep your finger on the trigger. Big boys' rules today.'

He signed off and moved over to the port side of the bridge, where he could see one cigarette boat slowing down and looping in and out, attempting to match its course and speed to the yacht. There were six men crammed into the small cockpit, all of them toting weapons. Shoeless Dan was standing by the wheel, one hand on the windscreen, the other waving madly at the bridge of the *Aussie Rules*. He'd have known Pete was on board. The *Diamantina* was roped to the stern, bumping along in their wake.

Dan stood about six foot two in his perennially bare feet, but he added another nine or ten inches to his height with the largest afro Pete had ever seen on a white man. The fact that Dan was

afflicted with red hair made him stand out even more dramatically from his brown-skinned crew. He was yelling, to no effect,
and grinning like a hyena on crystal meth.

Pete glanced at Mr Lee, an unspoken question passing
between them. Lee nodded brusquely to say that, yes, he had
the helm under control. The Chinaman suddenly spun the wheel
hard a-port in response to a radio call from one of the girls. Pete
plucked a handset from the console a few feet down from Lee and
powered up the yacht's loudspeakers. He was going to tell Dan
to back off or get blown away. Unfortunately he hit the wrong
switch, instead punching through an audio feed from the media
room, where BBC World was running a trailer for an upcoming
repeat of *Pride and Prejudice* on UKTV.

'. . . *it is happy for you that you possess the talent of flattering with
delicacy,*' boomed the giant luxury yacht. '*May I ask whether these
pleasing attentions proceed from the impulse of the moment, or are the
result of previous study?*'

The effect upon the Mexicans was salutary. They began
shooting.

'Oh, for fuck's sake,' cursed Jules.

She didn't know whether Pete had done that on purpose or
not – he had a pretty inappropriate sense of humour – but the
result was the same. Whatever small chance they had of talking
Dan down suddenly disappeared and they were now committed
to a shoot-out in which they were outnumbered plenty to one.
Hunkered down on the pool deck, where she'd been quietly watching the boat in which Shoeless Dan was travelling, she popped up
from cover, and squeezed off a couple of bursts from the M16 as
the go-fast made an abrupt turn and ran in towards the docking
bay. Both vessels were moving erratically at speed and most of
her clip missed, but at least one of the men flew back in his seat as
his head suddenly appeared to lose its structural integrity. A red
mist painted the other passengers in the boat as it came around
violently and laid on speed for the bow, to get out of Jules's line
of fire.

She performed a quick and dirty bit of maths, swung the 16
around and angled the barrel upwards at about sixty degrees. The

grenade launcher triggered with a hollow thump, sending a single 40 mm high-explosive round down-range. Jules was running forward, crouched low and swapping out her spent mag, well before it hit. She tensed up, waiting for the detonation, but it never came. The round had dropped into the sea without exploding.

'Oh, for fuck's sake.'

Yes, she tended to repeat herself under pressure.

'Lee!' she yelled into the radio. 'Target One is heading forward.'

'I see him, Miss Julianne,' Mr Lee replied, his voice calm in her headphones, like a parent soothing a distressed child.

The yacht veered across the path of the smaller boat without warning, nearly throwing Jules over the safety rail. She'd just regained her footing when Pete crashed into her. He had emerged without warning from a doorway, carrying a sawn-off shotgun he'd taken from Fifi. The cut-down stock slammed painfully into her unprotected arm, numbing it.

'Jesus, Pete. Watch out!'

'Sorry, darlin', didn't see you. Heads down!' He quickly raised the weapon and fired, the blast making her ears ring.

Pete worked the slide and fired again and again, until he'd emptied the entire load, then he dropped and rolled onto his back as Jules jumped up and loosed off a series of clattering bursts. The first burst went nowhere near the go-fast. She'd had to squint into a lowering sun and had simply hosed out some fire in the general direction of the boat. The second went a little closer as she adjusted her aim, but the shots flew over the heads of the men as Lee tacked again and she lost balance. The third blast, which emptied her clip, raked the foredeck of the boat, sending bright chips of metal and polished fibreglass flying and twinkling into the salt air and late afternoon sun. A muffled *whoomp* and a satisfying flash told her something vital had gone up, but before she could nail them with a round from the grenade launcher, Pete dragged her down – just as a line of automatic fire ripped along the bulkhead behind her with a heavy, industrial hammering sound. A hot steel chip grazed one cheek, burning her.

'Shit,' she gasped. 'Thanks, Pete. Owe you a blowie for that one.'

'Consider me blown,' shouted Pete over the uproar. 'Now, gimme the 16, and a couple of mags. You take my shotty and get back to Fifi at the loading dock – she's got at least one of the pricks on her case. The crazy fucker jumped onto the diving platform on a fly-by.'

'Okay. Got it,' she yelled back, fishing two full magazines out of her combat harness. From the rear of the yacht she heard the unmistakable pounding of Fifi's favourite gun, a Russian PKM.

They quickly exchanged weapons and he stuffed the reloads into the pockets of his cargo pants as she spun around.

Pete headed forward.

Jules found her shipmate crouched low at the bow of a SeaVee dive boat, which hung next to the big custom-built sport fisher on the lower deck at the rear of the yacht.

'Sorry, Julesy,' said Fifi. 'Asshole got on board when his buds had me pinned down. I put a lot of fire down there but don't know whether I even winged him. A frag woulda been nice to roll down on him.'

It was hard to hear her words over the tumult of gunfire and snarling engine noise, but the meaning was clear enough. Jules patted her on the back, where she'd slung 'the worm' – a rocket launcher Pete had acquired on their last trip to the Maldives. It was stamped with Australian Army markings and serial numbers, and had probably been stolen from the garrison on Timor. They had only one warshot for it, and Pete forever had to remind Fifi that she couldn't fire off a practice round. She'd been desperate to light that sucker up since he'd bought the thing.

'You leave this guy to me, babe,' said Jules. 'We really need you to nail one of those fuckers out there. Pete's working on Shoeless Dan's ride, that leaves the other one for you. Think you can take him with that thing?' She indicated the launcher on Fifi's back.

Fifi suddenly hauled up her PKM and punched out a short, angry burst, chewing big, expensive chunks out of the yacht's panelling down by the steps to the diving platform. A heavy Soviet-era design, the gun was powerful enough to be used as an anti-aircraft weapon. The uproar when she fired it was enormous. Jules's ears were already ringing from the shotgun blasts a few minutes earlier and now they began to hum a single deep tone to let her know they'd suffered some real damage.

'Sorry!' shouted Fifi. 'Saw him again. Asshole has only two ways up onto the deck – those two sets of stairs down there. You have to move across from one side to the other all the fucking time to check he hasn't snuck up. Can't keep an eye on both at once, you see, but then he can't be in both places at once either. He's packing some kinda light fully auto. Maybe an Uzi or an MP5. And yeah, I can put a hurtin' on that other fucker out on the water, no problemo.'

'Okay,' said Jules. 'You go.' Her own voice sounded dull and very distant to her, as though her head had been packed in cotton wool.

She flicked the safety off her shotgun as Fifi moved away. The *Rules* was still weaving an erratic course, changing tack without warning as Mr Lee strived to prevent their attackers from boarding any more men. Bent low, Jules couldn't see the go-fast boats, but the deep growling of their engines as they manoeuvred around the larger vessel was loud and constant. And although distance and the sheer mass of the super-yacht at times muted the pop and crackle of gunfire from Shoeless Dan's men, the impact of their rounds hitting home was often deafening, as they crashed into metal or glass just overhead.

Jules shifted position, scowling furiously. The boat deck was crowded with three big vessels and at least half-a-dozen jet skis, all of which provided excellent cover, but also denied her a clear line of sight to her target. The whole area was a terrible fucking mess, totally ripped up by hundreds of rounds of ammunition. Her guy was trapped a level down, where he'd come aboard on the diving platform. Conceivably, if she was able to find a position that covered both sets of stairs up onto the boat deck, she could keep him pinned down until the others were free to help her. But then, she wasn't familiar with the design of the yacht, and it was more than possible that he might be able to work his way up and behind her via an internal route directly from the docking bay. She didn't see any way of avoiding a direct confrontation with the little prick.

Despite the late hour, the sun was still putting out a fierce heat that made all her clothes sticky with sweat. Her tongue felt dry and swollen, and she had trouble swallowing. The yacht swung hard a-starboard, almost throwing her to the deck, but Jules used the momentum to push forward a few more feet to where a couple of black jet skis lay under the keel of the biggest of the auxiliary vessels, the 42-footer. That gave her a better view – she could now see at least part of the other staircase – but it also left her a good deal more exposed.

She caught a flash of long matted hair and blasted away at it, to be rewarded with a strangled cry. Jules didn't think the wound was mortal. A Remington made a horrible mess of a human head when it struck with full force, and she saw no evidence of that. Most likely a couple of pellets had hit home and raked out some skin and bone. But nothing fatal.

'Time to double down, Lady Balwyn,' she muttered to herself, summoning up her courage with a phrase her father had often used.

A *whoosh* followed by a sudden explosive roar told her that Fifi had launched her rocket. Without thinking, without waiting, Jules leapt up and ran forward, racking another shell into the breech and squeezing it off. The shotgun boomed in her hands. She racked the slide again.

Boom.

She'd made the head of the stairs and now fired down into the well . . .

Boom.

But the boarder was nowhere to be seen. *Damn!*

Blood tracks led away to the other side of the boat. There was one particularly large splatter, but it wasn't flecked with bone chips or brain flecks, and so most likely wasn't evidence of a killing stroke. Still moving as quickly as she could in the pitching, treacherous conditions, she attempted to rack another shell, but the Remington clicked empty. *Oh, for fuck's –*

And then she was on top of him – a small wiry man, deeply tanned, his bare torso covered in dense, brightly coloured swirls of tattoo ink. He was waving a gun around, but apparently blinded. His face was bathed in blood, and the flesh from his nose up had been badly torn by a few pellets of buckshot.

He fired wildly at the sound of her approach, unloading the better part of an MP5 mag at her, but Jules was already diving before he pulled the trigger. Head tucked in, heart pounding, she crashed into his thighs and knocked him backwards into a set of air tanks on the diving platform. Awkwardly, but with all of her strength, she slammed the butt of the shotgun into the soft, fleshy part of his upper arm, paralysing it, and tried to lock the injured limb under her knee as they wrestled.

The rank, sour stink of his sweat mingled badly with the coppery smell of blood and something richer, nastier. He writhed about beneath her weight, much stronger and quicker than her, but badly wounded and handicapped by his lack of clear vision.

For her part, Jules was restricted by having to keep so much weight on his gun arm. Knowing she couldn't win a battle of strength or endurance, she dragged the empty shotgun around and smashed the stock into his face. He screamed with rage and pain, and redoubled his efforts to get out from under her, but three more blows, the last one caving in his forehead, ended any resistance. The body twitched and shuddered and then went limp as his bowels voided themselves all over her legs.

She gagged, but just managed to hold it together. Snatching the MP5 from his twitching fingers, she crawled to her feet with the muzzle trained on him the whole time. Her leg muscles were rubbery and weak, however, and her knees folded up beneath her as she backed away.

Sitting there with her legs splayed out in front of her, covered in gore and worse, it took her a minute or so to realise she couldn't hear any more gunfire. And then, after a few moments when all she could manage to do was breathe and tremble uncontrollably, Jules realised that, for the first time all day, she'd forgotten about the energy wave that had swept away most of America.

'Clubfoot dickhead,' Pete murmured through clenched teeth as he dived back inside the yacht to avoid getting his head shot off on his journey towards the bow. 'We didn't have to do it like this.'

They were taking on a terrifying amount of fire now, in spite of the damage Jules had done to Dan's boat. It spoke volumes for the benefit of simply having more fingers on triggers than the other guy. Dan was handing them some serious fucking grief, and it pissed Pete off mightily. He hadn't been allowed to enjoy a single day as the master of Greg Norman's super-yacht before some skanky barefoot shit-eater in a Carrot Top fright wig came along and ruined everything by poking holes in his beautiful new boat with a ridiculous amount of automatic gunfire. He had no idea how Dan had come to be out here – probably he'd just loaded up and headed out looking for targets of opportunity as soon as his tiny peabrain had realised that the *federales* and the USN were *desaparecidos permanentemente*. Frankly, Pete couldn't have given a shit. He'd happily have had Dan along as a sidekick, had they been able to berth unmolested at Acapulco, and so long as Dan agreed to a rigid schedule of foot-powder treatments. But this – he emerged onto a forward deck and immediately ducked beneath a couple of rounds from something heavy and unpleasant, a .45 most likely – *this* was bullshit, a total liberty, and tantamount to taking the fucking piss.

He kept low and swapped out the mag that Jules had been using. The sun was in the last stage of a long dive in the west, which gave him a momentary advantage as the go-fast sped out of the yacht's long shadow. He saw half of Dan's crew suddenly throw their hands up to shade their eyes from the burnt-orange brilliance of the sun's rays. This was it. Slowly, and with infinitely more calm than he actually felt, Pete Holder stood up, knees bent slightly to allow him to adjust to the movement of the deck. He took careful aim and squeezed off an entire clip in four discrete bursts, forcing himself to drop the iron sight back on the cockpit after each salvo.

'Excuse me, Daniel,' he said to himself. 'But cheeky little fuckers sometimes need a good smack on the arse.'

The effect of taking the time to aim properly rather than just banging away was devastating. The first round stitched up Shoeless Dan, raking a line of fire up his fat belly, punching him backwards out of the boat. The last that Pete saw of him was a pair of blackened, swollen feet as they spun up and over the side. The next two bursts cut down all of the remaining men, bar one, who had the presence of mind to duck out of sight. The yacht climbed up a small wave while he was hiding, but Pete bent loose at the knees, keeping the gun sight on the cockpit of the cigarette boat the whole time. His stomach clenched tightly, and he could feel his anus puckering in fear, but he maintained the stance, even as a couple of rounds strayed up from the battle at the stern of the ship.

'Come on,' he whispered, 'just pop your ugly mug up and . . .'

He'd fired before making any conscious decision to do so. The last surviving Mexican in Shoeless Dan's boat suddenly leapt up and tried to snap off a couple of shots while grabbing the steering wheel and spooling up the engines. It was a hopeless, desperate thing to do, and it killed him. Pete sent at least half-a-dozen rounds down-range, and while only three intersected the target, they hit him in the back of the neck, tearing through bone and meat with enough force to sever the head. The body was jerked upright and tossed over the side. The head appeared to drop to the floor of the boat.

Nausea and revulsion boiled up inside him, but Pete sucked in a mouthful of air. It reeked of smoke and gunpowder, which didn't really help, but there was nothing for it. He had to push on. He turned to run for the stern, just in time to see a line of white smoke snake out from the deck above him.

'Eat the worm, motherfuckers!' It was Fifi, yelling from somewhere up on the pool deck.

His eyes instinctively followed the path of the rocket down through the air and into the side of the second go-fast boat, which blew apart as the warhead speared into her, just above the waterline behind the cabin area. Pete ducked as debris and shrapnel flew out from the point of impact with enough speed to kill anyone who happened to be in the way. Unfortunately, that described his situation precisely. His old knees weren't as quick or as flexible as they'd once been, and a fist-sized chunk of red-hot steel neatly took off the top third of his head.

Pete staggered back a few steps before his knees buckled underneath him and he fell to the deck, vaguely aware in his last moments of life that he had, after all, been fucked by the fickle finger of fate.

'Bugger . . .' he croaked with his last breath.

The disinfectant stung, but it was the least of Jules's myriad hurts. She seemed to exist within a tornado of pain, of dull aches, and sharp, shooting agonies of bruised muscle and tortured bone. Apart from Mr Lee, who was smiling as he dabbed at the deep cut on her cheek, they had all taken damage during the fight with Shoeless Dan's mob. Fifi had one arm in a sling and was limping from a flesh wound to her thigh.

The Chinaman finished up by gently pressing a thick bandage in place high on her wounded cheek and handing her a couple of blue capsules. The small pharmacy on the yacht had given up a treasure trove of sedatives and balms. 'For the pain, Miss Julianne,' he explained.

'Thanks, Lee,' she replied in a dry, cracked voice. Jules popped her pills and washed them down with a mouthful of gin and tonic, prepared for her by Fifi. 'Would it be churlish, at this point, to remind everyone that a couple of hours ago Pete had Shoeless Dan tagged as a reliable chap and potential crew-mate?'

Fifi sniffed and shook her head. 'He was always a fucking softie, was Pete. I loved him so much.' Her face crumpled and she let herself go, releasing a high-pitched keening sound that turned into a series of wails and sobs.

'It would be ungracious and beneath a lady of your breeding, Miss Julianne,' said Lee, whose own face was a mask, carved from ancient teak.

Darkness had fallen outside, or a sort of darkness. It glowed with a noticeable red hue thrown off by the energy wave, which was now eighty nautical miles to their north, but still visible. The three survivors had bathed and changed after cleaning up the worst of the damage and bloodshed. While they were at it, they'd got rid of the remains of the former crew members too. It hadn't been such a bad job, all things considered, compared to washing away the carnage of battle.

They'd wrapped Pete's body in a blanket and stored him in one of the galley's huge freezer units. He had once told Jules that if he ever bought it, he'd want his ashes scattered at an awesome surf break somewhere. Wouldn't matter which one. Mavericks, Pipe, Margaret River . . . they were all good. Just as long as it was pumping when he took his last ride.

They had gathered in the upper salon, one of the magnificent yacht's cosier, less formal spaces. A couple of olive-green two-seater lounges, hugely overstuffed and obscenely comfortable, sat around two sides of a giant brown ottoman. A pair of white single-seaters took up another side, where floor-to-ceiling bi-fold windows offered an expansive view of the sea far below. Jules had bathed and showered for two hours, to rid herself of the stink of the man she'd killed and the irrational guilt she felt at living when Pete hadn't. A couple of hundred dollars' worth of French toiletries had helped a little with the former, although she still felt as if some corruption had worked its way under her skin. And she knew she was going to be down about Pete for weeks. It was harsh, but she was more affected by his death than by the weird shit happening to the north.

She sipped at her drink, feeling lonely and abandoned, as she stretched out on the lounge and burrowed deeper into the waffle-weave bathrobe she'd found in one of the cabins. 'You know what,' she sighed, 'Dan was always a bit of a maddy, but even he wouldn't start a fight like that without good reason.'

'He had good reason,' said Fifi, who'd recovered some of her composure. 'Fuckin' Jane Austen on full volume. Drives me nuts when you play those vids, Julesy.'

Jules managed a sad smile. Fifi still held a grudge about having to sit through *Sense and Sensibility* with Julianne a while back. She'd thought they were seeing the sequel to *Dumb and Dumber*.

'It'd make me go for the gun locker too. Stupid m . . . mo . . . motherfucker,' she mumbled before lapsing back into tears.

Jules downed her drink in one long pull and stood up unsteadily, looking for the gin bottle. 'I'm sorry about Pete,' she said. 'I'll cry myself to sleep later, but we don't have time to wallow. This Twilight Zone rubbish is going to upset the apple cart in the worst way possible, and it's likely to happen very quickly. I suspect Dan was simply ahead of the curve. Well, him or someone who paid him. His operation didn't normally run to go-fast boats and hired *bandidos*.'

'Shoeless Dan always most unimpressive,' declared Mr Lee as he cleared away the first-aid kit. 'First I ever hear of him was of red-headed giant trying to sell stolen dog food to Vietnam criminals. Tried to say real dog in can. Vietnam tie bag of cans to Shoeless Dan and throw him in water. Only escapes because they cannot tie knot well.'

'No,' said Jules as she handed Fifi a Tasmanian beer, 'they probably tied those knots fine. But there were some things Dan did know well. Knots, sails, boats, tides, who'd take a bribe and who wouldn't, the range and speed of every Coast Guard cutter in the Keys – anything to do with smuggling by sea and he was good for it. But piracy was not his gig.'

'Yeah, well, he surely wasn't worth a pinch of shit as one,' sniffed Fifi.

'So, what was the story today?' asked Jules, as she picked a sandwich from a silver platter on the ottoman in front of her. She wasn't really hungry. It was just something to do. Fifi had found half a turkey and a leg of Iberian ham in one of the giant double-door refrigerators down in the main galley and she'd thrown together a small feast of cold cuts and salad. She wasn't eating either, and Jules suspected that preparing the meal was more about therapy than hunger. Long before Fifi had taken up smuggling, she had qualified as a commercial chef.

Fresh bread rolls, slathered with melting butter, lay in a pile next to a big bowl of baby spinach leaves, walnuts and slivers of pear and Parmesan. The drugs Jules had taken had begun a slow waltz with her gin and tonic, and she let the warm waves of sleepiness wash over her.

'Yeats, my friends. The story today was Yeats,' she said, answering her own question, if somewhat impenetrably. '"The centre cannot hold; mere anarchy is loosed upon the world." That's where we are right now. On the edge of anarchy.'

13

The early evening drive down to the Governor's residence in downtown Honolulu was enough to convince James Ritchie that the Hawaiian islands were going to go down a tube at high speed unless someone got their act together. The curfew seemed to have had no effect and the state government no interest in enforcing it. Thousands of people were milling about the streets, many of them agitated and besieging any place where they could buy emergency supplies of food and water. Large, increasingly unstable crowds had gathered outside travel agencies and airline shopfronts, which remained open well after normal business hours. Every gas station had a trail of vehicles snaking away from its bowsers, leading Ritchie to wonder where the hell these people thought they were going to escape to in their SUVs and family sedans.

His latest reports from Gitmo and Canada spoke of a strange glow, as if from a distant furnace, emanating from the energy wave, and as their route down to the Capitol District allowed Ritchie glimpses of the Pacific reaching away back east, he couldn't shake the impression of a sunset that seemed denser and richer than normal. Long, slow lines of surf banked up in sets of three off the beach at Waikiki, a strong offshore breeze blowing thick foam back off the lip as they crested. The weird, almost ethereal light lent the spray a bright, burnished cherry colour, and seemed to paint the mass of surfers and body boarders bright pink as they carved up the barrels.

The Capitol District was less crowded, probably because it offered little in the way of supplies that could be bought up and hoarded. Police and state troopers were out in force, however, and the pulsing lights of over a dozen Honolulu PD squad cars bathed the district in a rich, electric red that overwhelmed the otherworldly light Ritchie had noticed before. His BlackBerry buzzed as the staff car swung off Beretania Street and in through the gates of Washington Place. It was his wife.

NANCY IS OK! FLEW OUT OF O'HARE THS MNG.
IN LONDON. WILL CALL L8R.

A hollow opened up in the admiral's chest and filled with heat, but it subsided quickly, and he was left with a loose feeling in his bowels and a giddy, almost guilty, sense of relief. His only child had been scheduled to fly out of the US this week for a year's travel through Europe and Asia. But Nancy was a bit of a free spirit – an 'airhead', he might have said were she anyone other than his own – and organisation was not her strong point. She was just as likely to miss a flight as catch one, and her trip had already been rescheduled twice for that very reason. Ritchie had spent the entire day trying to cope with the end of the world while stomping down on a feeling of utter hopelessness for his baby girl. He had spoken to nobody about it. Everyone had people somewhere back home and his first responsibility was to the nation, not to himself or even his family. But he shivered uncontrollably as tears filled his eyes, hot and stinging, and he had to hold his breath to forestall a sob.

Damn, he cursed silently. *What a time to crack up.*

'You all right, sir?'

He kept his eyes shielded from the driver by pretending to stare out the window at plastic barricades that were going up around the Govenor's mansion. What the hell were they in aid of? They wouldn't stop the Wave if it came rushing at them from over the horizon, and the populace was more likely to storm a well-stocked 7-Eleven than the state legislature.

'I'm okay,' he grunted, when he had his voice back under control. 'It's just a message from my wife, that's all. Our daughter is fine. She flew out of Chicago this morning, before this business hit.' Ritchie wasn't sure why he felt the need to say anything. Perhaps to make it seem real to himself. It wasn't the sort of thing he'd normally discuss with anyone outside of his family, let alone a driver from the car pool.

'That's great news, sir,' said the young sailor behind the wheel, a new guy Ritchie had met only forty minutes ago. He sounded genuinely happy and Ritchie couldn't help but wonder where the lad hailed from and whether he had family back Stateside himself.

'Thank you, son,' he said, as they pulled up at the edge of a crowded parking lot. 'But a lot of people weren't as lucky as me today.'

The lot was packed solid. Men and women in expensive-looking business wear hurried about with no apparent reason to their movements. He supposed that the civilian arm of government had gone over to emergency procedures as quickly and completely as the military. Until now, he'd been concerned only with the latter, but the Governor's office had requested his presence at this meeting as a matter of the highest urgency and Ritchie had seen no alternative to attending. Apart from Olympia and Seattle, which were perilously close to the event horizon, and Alaska, which was sparsely populated and still largely undeveloped, Hawaii was pretty much all that was left of the United States. But while she could defend herself, given the concentration of military forces in the islands, Ritchie wasn't sure she could feed herself for much more than a few days. And with a quarter of a million men and women to pull out of a war in the Middle East, he really didn't need to be distracted by food riots in his own back yard.

'Shall I park here, sir?' his driver asked. 'You don't want to get jammed in, is all, Admiral.'

'No,' said Ritchie. 'Good point. Take the car back out of here. Get yourself something to eat, and then park somewhere in the District, but not here. This place is a mess. I've got your number, I'll call you when I need you.'

'Yes, sir. Thank you, sir.'

Ritchie was pleased to see that the sailor checked the charge on the car's cell phone before answering. Just because he was young didn't mean he was dumb.

'I'm sorry, sailor. What's your name? I didn't catch it in the rush before.'

'Seaman Horvath, sir.'

'Okay. Good work, Horvath. Take a break. I suspect I'll be a little while.'

Stale sweat, fading perfume, and air re-breathed so many times it tasted sick and wrong. The contrast with his own headquarters couldn't have been starker. Ritchie hit the corridors of the state capitol and ran headlong into mayhem. Spiralling turmoil seemed to be the general operating principle, the sort of witless hysteria you might expect on amateurs night at a Chechen bordello. Ritchie was buffeted by staffers and aides as they double-timed from office to office. A woman swerved to miss him, all elbows and high heels, and crashed into a copying machine that had apparently been pushed into the hallway. She spilled a couple of hundred loose-leaf pages over the carpet, cursing like a chief petty officer as she dropped to the floor to gather them up.

Hundreds of voices competed in the cramped space as people spoke over and past each other, all of them convinced their own particular order, request or fragmented rumour was the most important piece of that moment's puzzle. The media were everywhere, wolf packs of TV and print reporters threading through the upheaval, firing up shoulder-mounted cameras and thrusting microphones into the face of anybody who seemed remotely responsible for anything. Ritchie gripped his briefcase a little harder and pushed forwards lest –

'Admiral. Yo! Admiral, is the military taking over? Is there going to be martial law?'

And before he could dive into a side passage or broom closet, one of the packs had suddenly fallen on him. Bright white light seared the backs of his eyes, temporarily blinding him and forcing him to squint against the harsh glare.

'Admiral, are you here to take over? Are you going to run the emergency response?'

Ritchie couldn't see who was asking the damn fool questions, but he could sense a sudden press in the crowd around him as maybe a dozen or more reporters turned their attention towards the only symbol of authority in the immediate area: a man in a short-sleeve khaki Navy uniform sporting four stars on his collar. A jabbering crush of journalists surged towards him and, without thinking, he barked out an order.

'Stand back, please. Have some dignity, would you!'

Ah, damn it . . . He'd reacted instinctively, allowing his dismay and surprise at the chaotic scene to get the better of him. But to his relief, it actually seemed to work. There was a noticeable lessening of the disarray immediately around him and Ritchie made an impulse decision to go with it.

'First off, drop the lights, please. I'm not answering any questions standing here like a piece of roadkill in the spotlight. Secondly, hell no – I'm not here to take over. What's up with you people? You're not children, so stop acting like them. Governor Lingle asked me here this evening to discuss what aid the armed forces of the United States of America might render to the civil power. And that is it. I don't declare martial law. I don't give orders – I follow them. And if you don't mind, I'm going to do just that.'

Before he could step off and continue his journey, however, a small bird-like woman with enormous black hair pushed a microphone into his path. 'What can you tell us about what's happened on the mainland, Admiral?' she asked. 'Have the military been monitoring the phenomenon? What are you going to do about it?'

Ritchie was tempted to push past her, but he couldn't help but notice how the ambient roar that had filled the entire building just a few minutes earlier had died away completely. A flicker of colour behind the phalanx of reporters answered any questions he might have had about why. He could see himself on a television monitor in a room across the hall. This was probably going out live across the island. Possibly around the world. The urge to sit down, sigh and rub his eyes was nearly overwhelming, but these people needed leadership and certainty just as much as any bunch of kids taking fire from the enemy. In the absence of anyone to provide that leadership, the buck seemed to have fetched up at his feet for the moment. The admiral didn't see any point in fudging the issue. He slowly bent down and carefully placed his briefcase on a desk, the black, dead eyes of the TV cameras following every move. It gave him time to compose his thoughts. When he stood up again he spoke into near silence.

'Something terrible has happened back home,' he said. 'If you'll excuse me – my family is originally from New Hampshire . . . I can't tell you a lot of what you need to know right now. I can't say exactly what has happened, how or why. But you are right. We have been looking hard at this thing, throwing every asset we have at it. We've lost some more people in doing that, but I want to emphasise one very important point: much of our armed forces were outside of the continental US as of this morning. They remain intact and ready to make any sacrifice, to take any action necessary to protect you, the American people who are listening to this. Our friends and allies are helping us too, and with that help we *will* get through this. I promise you.'

A beat of half a second's silence followed his speech before the media pack erupted again, firing questions and demands for information at him. He was just about to wave them away when a booming Southern accent cut through the pandemonium.

'That'll be all for now, thank you, ladies and gentlemen. You heard the admiral – he does have a very important meeting to get to. Governor Lingle will address you all live right after it. And no, I can't say for sure when that will be, but you've definitely got a couple of hours to go get your horses fed and watered.'

The man's voice was so powerful, his delivery so sure, it quelled the incipient press riot almost immediately. Ritchie was grateful, but bemused. As a resident of the islands, he was familiar with some of the public faces of the state administration, even though Governor Linda Lingle had not long been in office. But this massive, roaring bear of a man was new to him, and Ritchie didn't see how he could have missed such a figure – or a voice.

He was impeccably, if heavily, dressed in a three-piece, blue pinstriped suit and he took Ritchie gently but firmly by the elbow and propelled him through the ruck of journalists. 'Keep smiling,' the man muttered. 'Don't let your fingers get anywhere near their mouths. And check to see if you still have your wallet and watch on the other side.'

His self-appointed guardian operated as a gentle but unstoppable battering ram, carving a path not just through the crush of reporters and cameramen, but on through the throngs of civil servants beyond them, many of whom stood and gawped at Ritchie when he passed by, almost as if he were some kind of celebrity.

'Guess I've had my fifteen seconds of fame,' the admiral said.

'Not if you got any more performances like that up your sleeve,' his companion replied somewhat grimly. 'Wish I could get a few others to turn it on like that. Jed Culver, by the way. Of the Louisiana Bar. Originally – I run a consultancy out of DC of late.'

Ritchie awkwardly swapped his briefcase from one hand to the other and they shook. 'Admiral James Ritchie, Mr Culver. You didn't sound like a local boy.'

Culver steered him around a corner and past a couple of security guards. The two uniforms were doing a good job of pissing off a dozen or more staffers who insisted they had good reason to be admitted to the inner sanctum. That's what this part of the building felt like. It was less crowded, much quieter, and events didn't seem to be spinning out of control quite so badly here.

'I was lucky enough to be on holiday with my family,' Culver explained. 'My immediate family at least, thank God. Anyways, I saw the news this morning and figured I would lend a hand if they wanted. Lingle's main press handler was Stateside.'

'You've done a lot of press management then?'

'Oh yes. Real press too. Hard men like Jimmy Breslin and Chip Brown, not like these pussies. That was a great speech before, you know. Really nailed a few heads to the wall. That's what we need right now – a big goddamn hammer and a whole bucket o' nails to get things secured 'fore they start flying off all over.'

They pulled up outside a closed office door. There was an indefatigable energy to Culver that one couldn't help liking. A lot of spare mass was expensively hidden away under that designer suit, but he looked like a man who could plough on for days at a time without a break. The island was probably lucky to have him. The heavy-set lawyer rapped on the door and waited half a beat before pushing on into an anteroom furnished with two desks, behind which sat a couple of very stressed-out young women. One had three phones clamped to her ears and was writing notes on multiple pads. The other woman was stabbing at her telephone's keypad, listening for a second, slamming down the receiver, and repeating the process all over again.

'Governor ready?' asked Culver. 'I got the admiral. Pulled him from the mouths of the lions by my own hand.'

The second receptionist, the one having so much trouble making her call, nodded at them. 'Go on through, Mr Culver,' she said tersely. 'They're waiting.'

As the big man led him through, a thought occurred to Ritchie. 'Why pack the suit, if you're on holidays, Mr Culver?'

The lawyer smiled back over his shoulder. 'Ah, you're a man who thinks like my good wife, sir,' he replied. 'Come on, meet the Governor.'

Culver seemed unnaturally assured of his place, given that he was little more than an interloper, but he'd obviously been of some help to the administration through the madness of the last twelve hours. There was any number of legitimate government officers trapped behind the velvet rope down the corridor who had more claim to be here than him. But here he was, and there they were, frozen out by a couple of state-sponsored bouncers. In a way, it gave Ritchie some hope. Perhaps things weren't as shambolic as they seemed.

Governor Linda Lingle was waiting for them just inside the office, flanked by a couple of suits. Her eyes were framed by the same haunted appearance he was beginning to recognise on everyone. If he looked in the mirror he'd doubtless see the same expression staring back.

'Admiral, thank you for coming down,' said Lingle, sounding very tired. 'I understand you must be very busy. Please, sit down. We'll get on with this as quickly as we can.'

'Thank you, ma'am,' said Ritchie, shaking her hand and then those of the other people in the room, whom the governor introduced as heads of various departments.

'How did the city look to you, Admiral, on your drive down here?' she asked.

Ritchie didn't see any point in using weasel words. 'Your curfew isn't holding, ma'am. It's being widely ignored. The state troopers and police are using a very light hand. I wouldn't say there was panic on the streets, but the shops will run empty very soon, and then you'll see some real fear and probably some violence. There's a lot of people trying to get out, tourists, I suppose – although, who knows. If you want my advice, do everything you can to get them on a plane with all dispatch.'

Lingle nodded and pursed her lips. Her staffers' reactions were mixed. One bristled, two others nodded vigorously. Jed Culver remained impassive.

'I don't want to see any more troops on my streets. In fact, I'd prefer not to see any out there at all, Admiral, and I'm sure you'd rather not have to employ your people here either, but it might not be a bad idea to prepare for the worst anyway. I'm sure you must have a plan in some bottom drawer somewhere for this sort of thing.'

'Not really,' he replied, shaking his head. 'But there'll be something somewhere about aid to the civil power in situations of extreme crisis – such as a mega-tsunami or super-volcano, or similar catastrophes. It shouldn't be beyond our abilities to adapt. But, Madam Governor, if I may, there is a related issue I'd like to raise very briefly, that of executive authority.'

Culver and Lingle did an odd, unrehearsed double act. The lawyer leaned forward keenly on his chair, while the governor rubbed her eyes and sat back in her own.

'Go on, Admiral,' she said.

Ritchie snapped open his briefcase and handed over a sheaf of documents. 'I had the JAG office here run up this brief for you, ma'am. It's about the line of succession. Realistically, the President isn't coming back. Nor any of the cabinet or other nominated successors. In terms of elected officials who can assume the office of Presidency, as best we can tell right now it's you, the deputy governor in Anchorage, or maybe the Speaker of the state house in Washington.'

'Oh,' said Lingle, as an uncomfortable stillness wrapped itself around the room. 'So, which one of us?'

Ritchie glanced over at Culver, who was now watching him like a rattler. 'Frankly, ma'am, it could be any of you. There is no statute or precedent covering a disaster of this magnitude. Between you and me, we may have to make it up as we go.'

Jed Culver eased himself back a little. His shoulders, which had been noticeably hunched up, relaxed.

'He's right, Madam Governor,' the lawyer offered, unbidden. 'Elaine Chao, the Secretary of Labor, is in Geneva – I checked – but she is not a native-born citizen and so is specifically barred from the office. There is no procedure for dealing with this. Even a nuclear war would not have decapitated the government as cleanly and completely. The admiral is correct. We need to make it up as we go. And we *do* need to act. I'm sure Admiral Ritchie is thinking of his comrades in the Gulf, and that's only reasonable, but there are still millions of US citizens who haven't been taken up, or whatever, by this thing, and they need to be protected.'

'But can we protect them from the Wave?' she asked. 'My understanding is that you have no idea what it is, Admiral.'

Before Ritchie could answer, Culver butted in again. 'That may be so, ma'am, but that's not what I mean. Maybe that thing will gobble us all up before breakfast. In which case, too bad. But the world is a cruel and unusual enough place, even without bad *Star Trek* episodes suddenly leaping off the screen at us.'

One of the younger aides couldn't help himself. 'There was a *Star Trek* episode . . . ?'

Culver shrugged. 'I'm extemporising.'

'Oh. Okay.'

'Gentlemen,' said Lingle, raising the sheaf of papers. 'I'll read these tonight, I promise. But you've seen what's happening out there. My immediate responsibility is to the people of Hawaii. That's who I was elected to serve and protect, and, for now, that is the extent of my office. Admiral, I can understand, given the situation in Iraq, why you need to resolve this, but for now can I suggest that you simply use whatever chain of command has survived the day. You know what you have to do and how to do it. I presume you won't be going ahead with any attack?'

Everyone in the room was suddenly staring at him, hard. Ritchie had spent decades in the military and every cell in his body rebelled at the idea of having to discuss operational issues in a forum such as this, but what choice did he have?

'Madam Governor,' he began, 'given the circumstances, no, at this stage we are not intending to commence hostilities. For one thing, as I've made clear, we have no executive authority to begin a war.'

'Bush signing a bit of paper wouldn't have given you – '

'Quiet, Jim,' Lingle snapped at the staffer who'd spoken out of turn. 'It's not the time or the place. Go on, Admiral.'

Ritchie ignored the distraction. 'But in any event, that decision may be taken out of our hands if the Iraqis themselves attack.'

'Is that likely? It would be suicide for them.'

'Yes, ma'am, it would,' agreed Ritchie. 'But rationality went down the toilet today.'

A few moments' silence followed, with everyone locked inside their own thoughts.

'Well,' Lingle said at last. 'As I said, you have an intact chain of command – use it as necessary. For now, we have our own problem right here. These islands cannot feed themselves. There isn't going to be any food coming from the mainland and people are going to starve if we don't get it from somewhere else, and soon.'

14

The night-time desert was a crumpled drift of blue-white silk below the chopper, which was all hot metal and grease and the suffocating body odour of soldiers. In the gloom it enfolded him like an unpleasant memory. Bret Melton had jumped out of helicopters and into another war not far from here, not long ago, and at times while riding out towards the line he had wondered if he'd be doing the same thing in another ten years. And ten more after that, forever and ever, amen. Now he knew that he wouldn't.

The thundering engine and rotors made normal conversation impossible but the four troopers in the cabin with him all needed to talk, to know what was happening back in the real world. In the faint glow leaking through from the cockpit, their faces were hollowed out and haunted. They all knew him, or knew of him. As a former Ranger, Melton was a popular embed. His shit was stowed according to regs and he could be trusted. He was as close to a believer as an outsider could be. Hitching the flight back to 3rd Infantry Division, the questions started as soon as they recognised him.

'What the fuck's happening, man?'

'What about our families?'

'Is it a fucking attack or what, dude?'

He'd done his best to explain what he knew, but really, what *did* he know? As Melton had laid it out for them, bellowing over the thump of the rotor blades, the looks on their faces had made him feel like a mental case. They gaped in horror and disbelief as he described what he'd seen and heard – and how could he blame them? He couldn't really believe it himself. He sounded authentically mad. After twenty minutes they'd all lapsed into silence and the rest of the flight passed in a sort of stunned, half-catatonic state. Melton knew that by the time these guys relayed the news to their friends, it'd be totally bent out of shape, but he didn't see much point in holding anything back. Everything they were defending was gone. Their homes and loved ones – everything. They had a right to know. In fact, that was the only reason he was still here. He had open tickets back to Paris and could check out any time he wanted, but he could no more fly out to Paris than he could to New York now. He had no immediate family. No steady girlfriend. His relationships had always been short term and contingent. One woman he'd been closer to than most called him 'commitment phobic', but she was wrong. Melton wasn't scared of commitment; he just wasn't committed to her. Ever since he'd left the army after Somalia he'd had one faith, one love from which he could not be diverted: the telling of soldiers' stories.

The pilot's voice came through, a clipped monotone announcing they were five minutes out. Melton craned around on his perch and briefly popped his head out into the slipstream. The 1st Brigade Combat Team's desert base wasn't totally blacked out, but it was much darker than the last time he'd come in, three days ago. Even so, under the moon it still glowed as a bed of pearls in the wide vessel of shadows that was the desert at night. On a satellite image, the tent city and masses of equipment would show up as a vast glowing metropolis of blood and iron, but what the hell. There was no sense in making it easy for Saddam, hence the blackout.

They flew in low, flaring and pivoting for the touchdown on a steel-mesh landing pad. A storm of gritty, stinging sand blasted into the cabin, scouring any exposed skin and working its way in through the layers of clothing Melton had drawn tightly around himself. One of the soldiers slapped him on the shoulder and grimly mouthed, 'Thanks anyway, buddy', before leaping out and hurrying off, bent double. The *Army Times* correspondent – or was he a *former* correspondent now? – followed the others out into the chill darkness, intending to head for the tent where some of the journalists maintained a rudimentary press club with a small stash of carefully hoarded bourbon and beer.

'Mr Melton? Sir?'

'Lieutenant Euler?'

Melton recognised him immediately. The platoon commander, who, at six-and-a-half foot, was forced into a very exaggerated stoop by the Blackhawk's spinning rotors, hurried forward and took Melton by the elbow, steering him away from his intended heading.

'Captain wants to see you, sir. We're getting set to roll on fifteen minutes' notice.'

'Roll where?'

'Don't know, sir. But Captain Lohberger needs you over at headquarters. The squadron commander will want to hear what you have to say as well.'

'About what's happened back home?'

'Yes, sir.'

Both men carefully stood up as they cleared the track of the rotor blades. Melton hoisted his backpack into a slightly more comfortable position and tried to take in as much as he could of his surroundings. Something was going to happen soon and the knowledge of it left a weird coppery taste in the back of his mouth. They hurried down from the rise of the makeshift helipad, diving into a small tent city laid out in a strict grid pattern, much of it obscured by the tan camouflage nets. Away from the overwhelming din of the chopper, he began to hear shouts and curses as non-coms wrangled their squads towards assembly points while junior officers like Euler gathered up platoons and began clicking them into larger units for deployment in the field. He could hear the whine of Abrams gas turbines and the snarl of Bradley fighting vehicles somewhere nearby, and overlaying it all was the ceaseless thumping of rotor blades as dozens of helicopters pirouetted through the inky black sky above them. The metallic, oily taste of diesel mixed with the grit and dust kicked up by the Blackhawk filled his sinuses. He pulled out a rag and blew his nose, knowing that the snot would be blood-flecked from the dirt.

'Do you mind if I ask you a question, sir?' said Euler, as they double-timed past a tent where a group of men in uniforms and berets he recognised as British SAS were hunkered around a table. One of the commandos levelled a hard stare at him and flicked the tent flap closed. 'Is it true, sir, what we've been hearing?'

Melton squinted against the sand, which was already coating the inside of his mouth and nostrils. 'I don't know what you've heard, exactly, Lieutenant. But it's gone. Home. Everyone there has gone.'

Euler's face twisted into a mask of despair. 'I'd heard it was a jihad attack. Bio weapons or nukes, or something. Took out a bunch of cities.'

They turned a corner, nearly running into a couple of MPs.

'Watch where you're going, asshole,' one of them barked, surprising Melton with a female voice. She was built thicker and closer to the ground than him. He muttered a hasty apology and moved on.

'No, this is nothing to do with the jihadis. Unless it was merciful fucking Allah, of course, like Saddam is telling everyone. But nobody knows. Some kinda weird energy bubble or something. Seems to have zapped away all the primates inside its boundary.'

Euler looked aghast. 'Primates?'

'Just before I took off, that was the latest on CNN. Some Japanese blogger checking webcams of the San Diego Zoo noticed all the monkeys were gone. Didn't take long to work it out from there.'

'Holy shit,' said the lieutenant in a small, choked voice that was completely at odds with his towering frame.

The reporter knew exactly what was going through his mind. He'd seen that same reaction many times today. Lieutenant Euler was counting his losses. Children and partner, if he had them. Mom and dad, ditto. Brothers. Sisters. Old friends and new. Neighbours. Faces on the streets where he once lived, even if he didn't know their names. Ex-girlfriends. Classmates from school. A widening gyre of personal history, all of it sucked away in some freakish moment when the laws of physics got turned inside out. Any moment now he'd look around, like a child who'd woken up in a strange room, trying to figure out where he was and how to put everything back in its place. *There*.

'I'm sorry,' said Melton, but Euler just shook his head.

'This sucks,' he breathed. 'Everyone?'

'Most everyone,' he confirmed. 'Seattle's still there. Alaska. Hawaii. Coupla places in Canada. That's it, though.'

'Man . . . Oh shit, here we are.'

They stepped into a large frame tent, one of the newer types that came with power outlets and lighting. It was nicer than the Korean War–era GP Mediums he used to spend time in. Melton recognised the tense, guarded body language of men who were used to facing the worst possible situations, but had never really expected anything this bad. He was almost rocked back on his heels by the concentrated force of their attention when they recognised him.

'Come in, gentlemen,' a voice called out. 'We're pressed for time here, Bret.'

Melton nodded a quick greeting at Captain Christian Lohberger, Bravo Troop CO, 5-7th Cav, and the only man in the tent who routinely used Melton's first name. Everyone else referred to him as 'sir', or 'Mr Melton'. Being called 'sir' beat 'hooah' or 'Rangers lead the way', the last of which Melton found increasingly annoying over the years, especially hearing the Ranger war cry from pukes who most definitely were not Rangers and were never going to be Rangers. And as a former grunt, the 'sir' thing had greatly amused him at first. Nothing much amused him at the moment, however.

'I'm guessing Iraq's not why you wanted to see me,' he said.

Lohberger shook his head and cut straight to the bone. 'No. We're getting nothing but smoke blown up our asses from Division on down. What the hell is going on?'

Melton dropped his bag by the trestle table, on which a map of the Kuwait–Iraq borderlands rested. It was covered in a swirl of red and blue lines and unit markings. The faces around the tent were grim and focused entirely on him.

'Well,' he began, 'what I knew when I caught the chopper back this afternoon . . .'

By the time Bret finished, Lohberger's first sergeant had fetched the squadron's commander and command sergeant major.

'Sweet mother of God,' grunted Sergeant Major Bo Jaanson, a gnarled stump of old wood who looked like he might well have seen off the Nazis at Bastogne. Melton had given them the super-concentrated version of the hours he'd spent plugged into the European and Asian news feeds, finishing up with the news of the primate discovery – fresh when he'd stepped off the tarmac in Qatar, but probably superseded by some new madness in the hours since.

The leadership cadre was otherwise speechless. Outside the slowly billowing walls of the tent in which they stood, the squadron continued to gather its strength. Yesterday it had seemed utterly formidable. Now, Melton felt like an ant sitting on a mound kicked over by laughing, moronic gods.

'Thanks anyway,' said Lohberger at last. 'It's been hard not knowing anything.'

Bret shrugged helplessly. 'I'm only telling you what I got off the satellite feed and the web. I wouldn't call it gospel, but . . . you know . . .'

The men were all younger than him, the platoon commanders by a considerable margin. Some of them would have young families of their own. Lohberger, at thirty, was something of a grand old man. He sucked in a deep breath and looked at the map as though he'd found some kind of nasty porn stash in his daughter's bedroom.

'Okay. There's nothing we can do about it from here, not right now anyway,' the captain declared. 'We know a lot more than we did ten minutes ago, but nothing that changes what we have to do in the next couple of hours.'

His voice and manner were hard. Melton observed a stiffening of postures and facial expressions among the other men in the room, a turning away from anxiety and doubts, as men jammed them down somewhere deep, at least for the next little while.

'Do you mind if I ask what's gonna go down here?' said Melton.

'Nope,' Lohberger replied. 'You're gonna be in on it soon enough.'

He jabbed a finger at the map table. Melton read the map plan, named Oplan Katie. It looked like someone's joke, a Cold

War–era forward defence at Fulda Gap write-up. He started to feel ill.

'Saddam's moving towards us. He's pulled a lot of his guys out of those useless fucking trenches they dug, and put them on the road heading this way.'

'Holy shit.'

'Yeah. Like we don't have enough to think about.'

Melton leaned forward to examine Oplan Katie on the transparent acetate. The basic plan had all Coalition forces moving forward out of Kuwait as originally planned. On the map was one phase line, a graphic control measure called Phase Line Katie, that ran through the Sulaybat Depression. All of the units in the Coalition were to hold that phase line and attrit any Iraqi force approaching it. The Brits with the 1st UK Division were still assigned the chore of dealing with Basra. Melton choked back any criticism of the plan. Getting into an urban fire fight, especially now, didn't seem to make any sense at all. It negated almost all of the Coalition forces' technological and military advantages. The 5-7 Cav's objective was Jalibah Airfield, marked as Objective Marne three hundred and seventy klicks south of Baghdad. The Mog all over again, he thought. It explained why everyone in the tent looked pale and sweaty.

What idiot came up with this plan? But he kept that question to himself and asked a different one. 'Any idea which units?'

Command Sergeant Major Jaanson volunteered the answer. 'The crap ones – militia, Fedayeen, reserve forces. A couple of Republican Guard units as well, but from the way they're moving, they look like their job is to keep a gun at the back of those other guys heading into the meat grinder.'

The *Army Times* reporter glanced at Lohberger for confirmation and received a brusque nod. 'We've seen a couple of fire fights break out within the Iraqi ranks. Guard units chewing over militia who tried to break off the advance.'

Melton couldn't help it. He pointed at Phase Line Katie. 'Surely you're not going to attack them, are you?'

Captain Lohberger shrugged as his squadron commander, a lieutenant colonel, left the tent for a meeting with the brigade commander. 'Well, the Kuwaitis don't want us fighting on their soil,' he explained. 'So that is why we're moving forward. They are taking positions on the Coalition's western flank, inside Iraqi territory, just on the other side of Wadi al Batin. These base camps are not the best defensive positions anyway, so we may as well follow the first tenet of warfare.'

'Engage the enemy as far forward as possible,' Melton said, nodding.

'Hooah, Rangers lead the way.'

Lohberger had a Ranger tab on his uniform and thus, in Melton's mind, the right to talk like one. Still, Bret winced anyway while Lohberger continued.

'The plan is that Coalition air power will conduct the air war as before, going for command and control. They'll take out the bridges as well, which should make our life a bit easier. Close air will stomp anyone who gets over those obstacles, then our arty engages them. Whatever is left is our meat, Bret.'

Melton didn't ask the obvious question – *why?*

Why the hell did any of them have to be here now? Saddam was no longer a threat to America, was he? And if the wingnuts were right, and it was all just about the oil and fattening up Halliburton's balance sheet so that Dick Cheney could retire in comfort . . . well, again, so what? Cheney was gone. And Bush. And the hundreds of millions of Americans they said they were defending. Melton had to shake his head to clear the buzz of conflicting thoughts crowding each other out. Why the hell didn't they just pack up and leave the whole sorry mess behind?

Of course, that begged the question of where they might go. Hawaii? Alaska? The Pacific Northwest? Frankly, he couldn't see anyone staying there if they could find a way out. Not with that hungry fucking bubble buzzing away just down the road.

Lohberger finished and let the air force liaison start his portion of the briefing. Bret found his thoughts drifting once the ALO, a major who liked to dip Oreos in his scotch, had taken over. His private thoughts, a tangle of confused memories and fresh trauma, were interrupted by Jaanson and Euler.

'You all right, sir?' Sergeant Major Jaanson asked.

The briefing was over. Melton blushed at having been caught out so badly. He'd seen plenty of others zoning out through the day. Men and women just standing, staring into the middle distance, eyes unfocused and faces slack. The worst ones looked like they'd come out of a session of electroconvulsive therapy. It was a mild form of shock, he supposed, as the rational mind shut down its higher functions to let the hindbrain deal with the violation it had experienced. In millions of years of evolution, humans had never been confronted by a threat like the energy wave. It was going to take some adapting, some getting used to – assuming the goddamn thing didn't end up swallowing the whole world, of course.

'Sorry,' he replied. 'It's been a helluva day. I'm a bit out of it.'

'That's fine,' said Lieutenant Euler, who looked to have recovered a good deal of his composure since their conversation on the way to the tent. 'You'll have time to shower, change and get some food into you, sir. Then you'll need to get your gear together and find my Bradley. We're on thirty minutes' readiness, but I want my guys ready to rock in ten.'

'Outstanding.' Melton's voice was flat with weariness and just a touch of sarcasm. The meeting was breaking up around them as Lohberger's men set to their duties with almost discernible relief that they had something to keep them busy.

'I'll send someone to get you from the reporters' billet, Mr Melton,' said Jaanson. 'Don't stray from there, okay?'

'Okay. I won't take long. I was already packed to move anyway.'

As they left the tent he could see that a change had come over the camp. The activity he'd noted on arriving had greatly intensified. Hundreds of men, all of them in full combat harness, hurried about in regimented groups, raising thick clouds of dust. The rattle of their equipment and the dull thudding of boots was loud enough to nearly drown out the shouts and curses of their NCOs. Nearly, but not quite. Humvees snarled and rumbled and a flight of jet fighters turned long, lazy circles high overhead.

Melton hurried back to his tent. He'd spent more than enough time in camp to move with confidence through the organised bedlam and located the six-man canvas shelter without trouble. Inside he found that his colleagues had already departed. There was a note from Patricia Mescalon on his cot, but otherwise nothing to show for the small civilian community they'd built up over the weeks. He slumped down on the bed and allowed himself a few moments of rest. He would need to eat, and a quick shower wouldn't be a bad idea. It might be weeks before he could wash again. Instead of moving, however, Melton found himself immobilised by a bone-deep lassitude.

What the fuck is the point of any of it now?

His throat tightened up and he felt tears beginning to well. Sitting up quickly, he rubbed the moisture from his eyes and sucked in a deep breath. Now was not the time to be falling to pieces. Chances were, things were gonna get a shitload worse in the next few weeks. Even if that bubble didn't move an inch, you couldn't punch a hole in the world like that and expect life to continue as normal. How long could the military hold together, for instance? They couldn't be resupplied for very long. And who was going to pay for them? Who was going to pay for *him*?

His paper was gone. He could ride out with the Cav and dutifully file his copy. For now the net was still working and his emails would zip through the myriad channels of fibre and copper wire all the way back to the *Army Times* server. But there they would sit, unread, forever. He had no idea whether his pay had gone into his account as scheduled. Possibly it had, if the process was automated. But how long would that last? And how long would anyone go on accepting US dollars anyway? For that matter, could the world economy even expect to survive the sudden disappearance of its beating heart? He didn't think so. Not when he gave it any real thought.

Sayad al Mirsaad had been right. This was the end of things.

15

Monique screamed as the windscreen crashed and bulged inwards, threatening to shatter. Rather than hitting the brakes, Caitlin sped up, awkwardly pawing inside her stolen leather jacket for one of the pistols she'd taken back at the hospital. The wheel jerked in her free hand and a dramatic shudder ran through the body of the Volvo as they struck something with a loud thud. She heard a cry and sensed, rather than saw, a dark shape fly through the air. The dense spider's web of cracks in the windshield made it impossible to know exactly what was going on outside. Caitlin hammered at the safety glass with the butt of the gun, using her peripheral vision and one-handed driving to keep to the road.

'Would you shut the fuck up and help me out here!' she yelled at the screaming Monique, eliciting a couple of ineffectual taps at the glass from the girl in the passenger seat.

The windscreen popped out just as they struck the tail end of a Mercedes with a massive metallic crash and a sudden jerk back into the middle of the road. Both women could now see dozens of people scattering from the roadway in front of their moving vehicle. They seemed to be fighting amongst each other, although a healthy number were focused solely on their car. Monique huddled down as more rocks came flying at them, one bouncing off the bonnet to slam into her shoulder. She cried out in pain and Caitlin reached across, grabbed a handful of her jacket and violently jerked the girl right down so that she was no longer exposed to the improvised missiles flying directly at them. The American enjoyed no such luxury and had to drive while dodging and weaving.

They had come around a sharp bend into a street fight, or riot. A normal person would have slowed down, fearful of injuring or perhaps killing a pedestrian, even as they were targeted with a fusillade of torn-up cobblestones, bottles and broken bricks. Caitlin set her mouth in a grim line and, hunching behind the wheel for the minimal protection it offered, she deliberately pointed the Volvo into the centre of a mass of youths blocking the road ahead of them. She didn't sound the horn or wave them away. She simply drove at them, implacably increasing her speed as they drew closer. A few of the braver (or dumber) among them hurled a couple more rocks, but they were poorly directed and none managed to hit the body of the car. The group lost its coherence rapidly as the men – they were all young, dark-skinned men – dived for the relative safety of the footpath. One, his head swathed in a black and white keffiyeh, was a fraction too late and the car's headlight caught his foot in midair, spinning him off the arc of his dive and into the side of a grocery van. His scream was snatched away by the speed of their passage.

'What is happening? Who are they?' cried Monique in distress.

'Arabs,' shouted Caitlin, over the roar of the wind pouring into the car. Youths from the city's outer suburbs, who were normally never found in the old quarters in such numbers.

In a few mad moments the car was through the confrontation and back into clear space, as Caitlin swung through a roundabout and took the exit furthest from the direction in which they'd just come. She tried to organise her impressions in a coherent fashion, arranging a random series of images into something she could understand and maybe even use. It wasn't just a riot, it was a brawl. The crowd, which she would have put at somewhere between seventy and a hundred strong, seemed almost evenly split between young white men and women, and perhaps a slightly larger number of African- and Arabic-looking youths. All of the latter had been males, as far as she could tell. The clash appeared undirected, and was probably a fight between the sort of moronic drunks she and Monique had encountered a little earlier,

intimation of the coming spring. She briefly consulted the GPS
again and took her bearings. The screen seemed overly bright
and she dimmed it a fraction, so as not to degrade her night
vision too badly. With time to think, she could finally place herself within a mental map of the city as she understood it: a matrix
of boltholes, safe houses, escape routes, dead drops, rat-runs,
friendly and hostile camps and, naturally, a matrix of history – a
personal and professional history of assignments, targets, milk
runs, black bag jobs, and wetwork. An ocean of wetwork these
past few years.

There was an apartment she could access on the Rue de la
Sablière, over in the next *arrondissement*, but it was a good hour's
walk away, possibly more, and Caitlin did not fancy being
exposed on foot for so long, especially not given her condition.
She had already taken to thinking of the tumour as 'my condition'. They would have to steal another vehicle, if possible. A car
door slammed behind her and she heard boot heels hammering
on the road surface as Monique chased after her.

'Please, wait for me. I am scared.'

'Everyone's scared,' said Caitlin as she drew up. 'Trick is to
push through anyway. Come on.'

They crossed an open area of the park, where the city put on
moonlight cinema in the summer, always showing French films,
and usually only those that had been filmed in the surrounding
district. And they call *us* insular, she thought, before experiencing a weird episode of doublethink. Of course, there was no 'us'
anymore.

This part of town was relatively quiet, but sirens still reached
them from across the metro area, and from the *banlieue*, she
imagined, the outer suburbs where generations of North African and Middle Eastern migrants had created their own pinched
and grim little fiefs in the tenements and public housing projects
. . . Caitlin was as familiar with them, with the slums and
. . . ed-up sharia towns like Clichy-sous-Bois, as
. . . e global Paris of Montmartre, the Louvre and
. . . gne.

. . . k everything will be all right?' Monique asked in
. . . voice.

Caitlin stopped dead in her tracks. They were halfway across the darkened park, two figures who stood out from the handful of wandering, self-obsessed lovers by the tension evident in their every exchange. Stiff limbs, jerky movements, voices pitched too high and sharp-edged like broken glass in the night.

'No, Monique. Everything is not going to be all right.' She faced her captive companion square on, hands on hips, jaw jutting out as her teeth ground together. Pain like a cold knife welled up from nowhere behind one eyeball. 'Start. Paying. Attention, sweetheart. Someone is trying to roll me up, and you with me. Hundreds of millions of people disappeared today. Important people, too. The guarantors of life as you know it. Even if they all get beamed back down tomorrow morning with nothing to show for it but a sore ass from the alien butt-probing they got, the world will still never be the same. Your city is falling apart. The whole fucking world is falling apart. What do you think will happen – that you'll all suck down a few celebratory bottles of Lafite now the left bank is the centre of the world again? That everyone will wake up tomorrow and go, "Hey, isn't this cool, we don't have to worry about big ol' fat-assed America ruining everything with her shitty fucking movies, and fast food and violence"? Is that what you think? Huh?'

Her delivery grew more intense and unbalanced with each question, until by the end of her little speech, Caitlin knew she was ranting but couldn't stop. Monique withered away under the lashing, shrinking into herself and dropping her eyes until she looked like a small child being shouted at by the scariest grown-up they'd ever met. Caitlin regretted her loss of control immediately. It was stupid and unprofessional – not at all the sort of thing she'd normally do, especially out in the field with hostiles on her case. She saw a couple of teenaged boys on pushbikes pointing at them, but there was no aggressive intent to the gesture. They merely seemed to be amused by the crazy woman speaking in English, and had probably picked up on her American accent.

'Look, I'm sorry,' she said, running a hand through lank, greasy hair. 'It's been a helluva day, and it ain't getting any better.'

'I am sorry too,' Monique replied in small, but surprisingly strong voice. 'You have lost everything, *non*? You had family?'

Caitlin nodded, a dark blue wave of sadness breaking over her at the thought of her family, now gone.

'What will you do . . . *Caitlin*?' She was still unsure of that name and pronounced it with extra care. 'You cannot go home and cannot stay here. You are a spy, yes? A killer? I suppose you know how to disappear?'

They resumed walking through the park, heading north-west, back towards the old centre of Paris, but still away from the hospital and the fighting they had happened across before.

Caitlin smiled sadly. 'I'm better at making people disappear than doing it myself. I have . . . well, let's not go there. You shouldn't even know any of this. It's only that things have changed so much, and . . . well . . . I'm sorta swinging out here on my own now.'

They passed a homeless man, making himself a bed on a wooden bench, balling up a copy of *Le Figaro* for a pillow. He smiled at them, a wide toothless grin, and doffed his filthy cloth cap as they passed. Monique stopped and handed him a couple of crumpled banknotes.

'*Merci, mademoiselle, merci.*'

'You know,' said Caitlin a minute later as they neared the edge of the Parc de Choisy, 'that guy back there doesn't know it, but he has a bunch of skill sets that are about to put him back at the top of the food chain.'

'Why?' asked Monique.

'He's a survivor.'

'I need to rest and eat,' Caitlin announced half an hour later, as they left behind the unattractive, modernist high-rise district of the Centre Commercial Italie on Rue Vandrezanne.

Seven roads met in a great starburst of an intersection a short distance away. Some of them were major arterials, like Rue Bobillot, which ran back into the huge roundabout at the Place d' Italie. Others were smaller tree-lined streets, on which cafés dealing in simple fare survived on local custom rather than the tourist trade. Monique steered her into one such venue, grabbing a table near the door, which Caitlin immediately rejected in favour of another where she could sit with her back to the wall and watch the entrance and the street.

'Does this place have a toilet out the back?' she asked. 'Do we have access through the kitchen?'

'I don't know,' said Monique with a shrug of her shoulders. 'I come here sometimes, but I've never had to ask. Why – do you need to go?'

'No. But we need another exit. Indulge me and ask them.'

Monique rolled her eyes, which Caitlin took as a good sign. She was throwing off her shock, reasserting herself. Still, she did as the American asked. While she chatted with the owner, Caitlin sat and leaned up against the red-brick wall. Faded posters of beach scenes in New Caledonia had been tacked up around the café and they looked mighty inviting. She felt her head swimming with exhaustion and forced her eyes open, gesturing to the one waiter and asking for a double shot of espresso.

'I'll teach this tumour to mess with me,' she muttered to herself.

After the violence at the hospital, and an hour or more on the run, she could have wept with relief at being able to just sit somewhere comfortable and warm, where people weren't hunting her. Nine other patrons were scattered about in ones and twos and such conversation as she could hear was all about *la Disparition*. She ignored it as best she could. The café smelled of baking bread, fried garlic and roast lamb. A man at the table next to her supped at a bowl of soup in which floated big white chunks of fish meat and black mussel shells. He tore small pieces of bread from a baguette and dipped them into the stock, washing it down with a glass of wine poured from a bottle with no label. Caitlin's stomach rumbled in protest and saliva leaked into her mouth. Her coffee arrived just as Monique returned.

'There is a convenience out the back. You have to go through the kitchen and they do not normally allow it, but I have told them you have just been diagnosed with cancer and they relented.'

Caitlin favoured her with a crooked half-smile. 'Nobody wants to disappoint the cancer girl. Good work, Monique. You're learning.'

'I am.' She nodded, even seeming a little pleased. 'The toilet is in a separate block, in a small yard that opens onto an alleyway.

The alleyway runs in both directions, linking up with Bobillot and Rue du Moulin des Prés.'

'Damn,' whistled the American. 'You could do this for a living, sweetheart.'

She spooned a single sugar into the coffee and threw the drink down in one go.

'I ordered some toasted sandwiches – *croque monsieur*,' said Monique. 'I thought you would want something simple.'

'And fast,' Caitlin added, dropping her voice. 'We have to get to the apartment as soon as we can, and see if I can contact anyone from my shop.'

Two straw baskets arrived, brimming with thick, toasted white bread wrapped around ham, gruyère cheese and French mustard. Two glasses and a bottle of house wine landed next to them, a nameless *vin blanc*. Monique poured herself a glass and drained it in two gulps before filling Caitlin's and refilling her own. Dark half-moons stood out under her eyes, which were puffy and red from crying. Her hand shook as she poured, but not so much that she spilled any.

Caitlin took a careful sip of her own but was more interested in the food. The bread had been dipped in egg and pan-fried in butter, with more melted cheese drizzled on the outside. Her eyes watered with the intensity of flavours as she bit into a moist, heavy slab. Right then it seemed like the finest meal she had ever tasted. She wanted to close her eyes and savour each moment, but her training demanded that she continually scan their surroundings and the entrance to the café for any threats. Apart from the heart attack she was holding in her greasy hands, however, there was nothing.

They ate in silence for five minutes, chewing through their meals and sipping at the wine. Unspoken, but lying between them like a dead curse, was the fate of Monique's friends. She had not mentioned them again, but Caitlin could tell they were on her mind. She didn't raise the issue herself, not wanting to unsettle the precarious emotional balance that Monique seemed to have achieved. There would be time for that later. Perhaps.

She ordered another coffee and paid for the entire bill when it came, but didn't finish her wine. Even a few mouthfuls had left her feeling light-headed and dizzy. It would have been luxurious to stay in the café for a few hours, drinking and smoking Gitanes as though all was right with the world, but Caitlin hauled herself to her feet as soon as she'd downed the second espresso. 'Come on,' she said. 'Let's go.'

The American headed out through the kitchen towards the rear of the café. The owner nodded and tutted and tried to look as sympathetic as he could for the pretty cancer girl. The kitchen was cramped and narrow, with crammed shelves running all the way up to a high ceiling. A woman in a stained apron gave them a querying look but the owner, her husband most likely, shushed her with one word: '*Cancer*.'

Caitlin shut her eyes for a few seconds before pushing open the flyscreen door and stepping out into the small darkened car park. A single pallid globe struggled to illuminate the courtyard, in which two scooters and a battered old van were parked. She had shifted the guns into easy reach, but there was nothing in the scene to alarm her.

'Well, my Spidey senses ain't tingling,' she told Monique, who gave her a weird look in return. 'We're fine,' she explained.

Two blocks later, she found a couple of bicycles chained to a cast-iron railing in front of a white, Moorish-looking tenement, and was pondering how to break the chains when Monique admonished her.

'Please, Cathy . . . sorry, *Caitlin*. Bicycles? Look at them. They are not expensive models, no? The people who ride these do so because they cannot afford a car. Do not steal them, please. They will not be insured. You will only be spreading more misery.'

Caitlin's irritation at the scolding was transitory. She was feeling quite ill now, and was coming to think she would need Monique to get through the next couple of days if she was unable to make contact with Echelon. It was better that the girl was feeling more confident, even if it meant she'd be less malleable and, frankly, more of a pain in the ass. 'Fine,' she conceded. 'No bikes. But we're gonna need some wheels soon. If we get caught out in the open on foot we're dead.'

They resumed their journey towards the 14th Arrondissement, walking against the flow of one-way traffic along the

Butte-aux-Cailles, which was alive with throngs of younger Parisians, all of them wealthy and well dressed, hopping from bars to clubs and restaurants as if this were a normal evening with a warm spring in the offing. The buildings here were smaller, with steeply pitched Alpine roofs, and tended to be given over to commercial concerns, chichi diners and exclusive clubs, so the two fugitives stood out in their cheap, unwashed clothes. A few bookstores remained open for late-night browsers, and apple trees lined the street, perfuming the air with sticky pink blossoms. The footpath in front of the cafés and bistros had been colonised by clusters of small round tables, all covered in immaculate white linen, and playing host to lovers, friends, gourmands and modern boulevardiers. Monique's cluster of angry political badges and sewn-on patches drew a score of withering glances and even open sneers. Caitlin tried to arrange her face in as neutral a fashion as possible, but something about her must have tripped warning beacons for most of those they passed by. In contrast with Monique, nobody looked her in the eye or dared make any snide, slanting comment about her bloodstained pants and leather jacket.

Two police cars and an ambulance went rushing by at one point, forcing Caitlin to softly squeeze Monique's arm and remind her to 'be cool'. She felt terribly exposed on the expensive strip, and wondered whether it might be wiser to dive into a side street, but the GPS indicated that the route they were walking would get them quickly to the apartment opposite Montparnasse Cemetery. The longer she was out on the street, the more imperative her need for shelter. She hadn't said anything yet, but her headache was getting worse, and now she was beginning to suffer from such severe nausea that it was possible she might lose her dinner all over the sidewalk. She had to get to that apartment. There, she'd find shelter, weapons, money, clothes and, just possibly, somebody from Echelon waiting to bring her in. Maybe even Wales. Although, what the fuck 'bringing her in' meant at the end of a day like this was a mystery. Perhaps a flight to London on one of the agency's black renditions – if the French were still allowing them. Nothing that had gone down in the last few hours gave her any confidence on that score. She was certain the muscle at the hospital had been French secret service. But she had no idea why they'd come in hot.

Even though she was an undeclared operative – an assassin, no less – working on their turf, there had been no call for that bullshit back at the Salpêtrière. This wasn't the movies. You didn't draw down on somebody and start banging away without serious fucking reason.

'Caitlin?' Monique's voice was quiet but thick with emotion.

They had passed out of the busy, well-lit entertainment district and were back on the quieter streets. Caitlin checked the navigator, estimating that they had about twenty minutes to go before reaching the apartment. She'd have to decide very soon about whether to steal another car or sneak up on the building through the cemetery, investing a couple of hours in surveillance before heading in. Beside her, Monique's eyes had welled up again and her shoulders were hitching beneath the thick jacket she wore.

'You thinking about your friends?' the American asked.

'They were your friends too, Caitlin. Or so I believed.'

They were my *mission*, she thought. But aloud she said, 'I liked them all right. Celia could be a self-righteous bore. And Maggie was kind of embarrassing, but . . .' She shrugged off the rest of whatever she had been planning to say, not wanting to upset Monique further, but not wanting to construct a series of defensive lies around her previous actions either.

Thunder, distant and muffled, rolled over the city, although there didn't appear to be a cloud anywhere in the sky. The city lights blotted out most of the stars, but only a few wispy strands of grey drifted across the face of the moon. Monique didn't appear to notice and Caitlin said nothing. The French girl was upset enough without being told that something big had just exploded a few miles away.

'I feel so guilty . . . about the hospital,' Monique confided. 'About Maggie and Celia and . . .'

'It's natural,' said Caitlin. 'It happens. You can't understand why they got zapped and you didn't. You keep telling yourself you should have done something, anything, to change it. You obsessively pick away at the memory like a wound, wondering if one small thing here or there might have changed it all, and kept them alive.'

'Yes,' she admitted in a small voice.

They stopped at the steps of a narrow-fronted apartment building. Flickering blue-green light behind a set of drawn curtains in the ground-floor flat indicated the presence of a television. Probably tuned into a news service. Sirens, police and fire service, swooped by a few streets away.

'Well, don't feel that way,' Caitlin continued. 'You're gonna have to let it go at some point, Monique. May as well be now. Your friends got taken out by a couple of guys you would've called "fascists" just yesterday. I took them down in return. For what it's worth, that's about as much balance as the world ever achieves.'

Monique's eyes looked hurt and almost resentful, but Caitlin continued anyway.

'This isn't over. I don't know why I've been targeted like this, or whether it has anything to do with what happened back home today. But it isn't over. They'll keep coming until they get what they want or we get away. You need to toughen up, Monique. And you need to understand that I will not let them take me or you without paying a heavy fucking price. Some people have been killed. Some more will go that way before I'm done. And that's just in our little world, which nobody knows about 'cept us and the guys who are hunting us. The rest of the world? It'll be a shit-load worse.'

They'd started walking again, slowly, passing under the branches of an ancient oak tree that covered a street corner in front of a small, darkened art gallery.

'What do you mean, "worse"?' asked Monique. 'How can that be so?'

Caitlin laughed, although it was more of a bitter little cough, really. 'Well, those guys at the hospital, and me, for that matter, we have our ways. You'd think them wrong, barbaric even. But if you understand the game and its rules, you can at least act with some sense of things playing themselves out right, one way or another.' Which was why that splatter-fest at the hospital was so fucking *out there*, she thought. It simply should not have gone down like that.

Caitlin stopped again, this time fixing Monique with a hard stare.

'But the Disappearance, you cannot underestimate how much that is going to fuck things up. I have to get out of Paris, out of France altogether. And so do you, if you want to survive. You ever read the English philosopher Hobbes? You're French, right – you read philosophy with your croissant in the morning, *non*? Man exists in a state of nature – a war of all against all? That's what modern society cured, at least so it didn't interfere with the lives of people like you. People like me, on the other hand, we were still out there, getting bloody with it. But Monique, listen to me – we're *all* outside now and a hard fuckin' rain is gonna fall. You need to find shelter.'

'How bad do you think it will be?' she asked.

'I'm a pessimist,' said Caitlin as they crossed a road where the traffic lights seemed to have failed. 'I think it'll be totally fucking medieval. Pogroms, food riots, blood in the streets. Maybe that's just me. Whatever. But, your friends, they're not gonna miss much in the next little while.'

'The living will envy the dead, you mean?'

'That's a bit too Metallica for me, but yeah, if you like. Economies are going to collapse all over the world. Not just slow down, or go a little wobbly. They will collapse like the Twin Towers into smoking fuckin' rubble, and anyone standing around underneath is gonna get smashed flat. Modern society is too complex to survive a shock like this. A simpler world, yeah, no worries – people would grow food in their back gardens, cart water from the well, live harder and closer to the bone for a few years. But you got, what, fifteen million people in the greater metro area of Paris? How are they going to move around, how are they going to feed themselves and their families in two weeks when the stores are empty because there's no more gas at the pumps?'

Monique tilted her head and gave Caitlin a quizzical look. 'But why would . . . ?'

'Why will the gas run out? Think of where it comes from, Monique. Think about what's going to happen there now that the evil global overlord is no longer around to oppress everyone into behaving themselves. Think about what's going to happen to the evil world financial system now that the planet's greatest debtor nation has winked out of existence and won't be meeting its mortgage payments to anyone. Think about what happens when you take the lid off Pandora's box and everything that we forgot about in history comes spilling out to bite you on the ass. Do you know how unusual it is in human history, for children to be able to grow up in a place like this?' She waved her hands around to take in the city. 'Never knowing the fear of someone riding over the horizon to steal their family's crops and burn their hut to the ground, and all as a prelude to being snatched up as slaves for the rest of their miserable fucking lives – *that's* normality, baby. *That's* life as it has been lived by most human beings through most of our history. *That's* what I've been fighting against my entire adult life, variations on *that* theme. *That's* what America protected you from. And now she's gone. And you are all alone in the world, Monique. Except for me.'

By now they had reached the edge of Montparnasse Cemetery, a vast pool of darkness in the city of light. Monique's lip was pushed out, giving her the appearance of a petulant child. She obviously didn't want to hear any more, but neither did she argue with Caitlin.

The assassin checked their position, relying on memory now rather than the GPS device. They were on the far side of the graveyard from the safe house. It was time to get to work.

'Listen,' she said. 'We're going in here, and I'll go ahead and check out the situation at the apartment. See if it's been tumbled. If they've got my number they might be rolling up the whole network. Are you going to be okay if I can stash you somewhere for a few hours?'

Monique looked alarmed. 'A few hours?'

'It's okay,' Caitlin assured her. 'I have a lay-up point near here, something I set up myself. You'll be safe there, but alone. I need to look over the place, otherwise we could be walking into something like the hospital all over again. Will you be okay with that? Are you strong enough?'

Monique shivered as she contemplated the fields of the dead stretching away from them into the dark. 'I will try,' she promised.

'Cool,' said Caitlin, slapping her on the shoulder. 'That's all anyone can ever ask. Let's go.'

Two vans had mounted the kerb outside the apartment, a no-parking zone, and lights burned inside the third-floor flat. Four or five men moved about inside without any pretence at stealth, turning the place over. Three hundred yards away, stretched out on a cracked, weed-covered gravesite overhung by an ancient elm, Caitlin was able to observe them unmolested. She had no scope or binoculars, but that hardly mattered. Their very presence was enough to alert her.

The apartment was an Echelon safe harbour, a first sanctum known only to her and her controller, Wales Larrison. He should have been waiting for her there. Indeed, he may well have been. He could be tied to a chair somewhere inside right now, taking the first of many beatings that lay in his immediate future. Caitlin had no way of telling unless she was willing to stake out the scene for much longer than was prudent. She closed her eyes and slowed her breathing as a new wave of dizziness and nausea rolled over her. She couldn't leave Monique on her own at the lay-up point further back in the cemetery for too much longer, and she couldn't interdict the search of the safe house in her current condition with no back-up, minimal equipment and no idea of what sort of opposing force she'd encounter.

'I'm sorry, Wales,' she mouthed silently, before slowly crawling backwards into the darkness of the cemetery.

She didn't know whether her illness was affecting her judgment as badly as she knew it had affected her physical abilities, but Caitlin was annoyed and not a little perturbed to find herself feeling scared and lost. The shooters at the hospital were state-sponsored muscle – of that she was sure. And the team at the apartment looked like pros too. From what little she could glimpse, they were taking the place apart in a precise, methodical fashion. If she had to bet on it, she'd lay down good money that they were French secret service, probably the Action Division of the DGSE, the designated point men for securing the Republic against the intrigues and depredations of Echelon.

What the hell they were up to, what greater scheme they

served, she had no idea. It was obviously related to the day's events – such frontal assaults on a 'sister' service were almost unprecedented – but she could not be sure how.

What she did know was that her control cell was compromised and she would need to get herself to safety. To a US or British military facility somewhere on the continent. Across the Channel, to friendly ground. Or, as a very last resort, to one of the diplomatic missions of Echelon's member nations, the old, English-speaking democracies.

As soon as the last idea occurred to her, she dismissed it. If the French were aggressively rolling up Echelon cells, they'd be staking out the embassies and consulates.

No. She was on her own.

ONE WEEK

21 MARCH, 2003

16

'I don't want you going out there again, Kip. You look *sick*.'

Barb looked worse than him, he thought, but it wouldn't be worth his life to point that out, of course. Her eyes stared at him from within dark hollows. She'd had little more than an hour or two of sleep a night for the last week. The old bathrobe clutched nervously just below her throat was dirty and her dark hair lank and greasy. Nobody had been allowed to run water for three days now, because of the contamination. They were living on what they had stored in pots and bottles and the old clawfoot tub upstairs in the half-renovated bathroom. Kipper needed to get into work to see if he could change that today.

'Barb, I'm not sick. I'm fine. They've been checking us every day. Army doctors, guys who specialise in chemical war and stuff – we're fine. We got those bio suits, but we don't even need them anymore.'

Unfortunately, she would not be dissuaded. 'Kip, you have a family to look after . . .'

'And I *am* looking after them,' he countered, with some irritation. 'I am the guy who can turn on your taps again. I am the guy who makes sure the power is there when you flick the switch. Me – nobody else. It's my *job*, Barb. I have to go.'

He wondered why she was so much worse this morning? The pollutant storms were clearing out. The toxic soup he'd had to brave on Tuesday to get into the city had been truly scary. The army had sent some sort of pressure-sealed armoured vehicle for him, something they were going to fight Saddam or the old Russians with, and all of the troops were suited up in NBC gear.

'This is insane, James.'

Uh-oh. He knew he was in trouble when she called him that.

'We should be thinking about getting out of here,' Barb continued. 'Not hanging around. Deb and Steve flew out for New Zealand yesterday. They're not coming back. They're too smart. But your martyr complex is going to see us die here. Isn't it?'

He controlled the anger that threatened to flare up between them, reminding himself that Barb had nothing to do but sit in the house, like the rest of the city, staring out of the windows at toxic rain. She must've been going batshit by now. And, he remembered at that very moment, she was also premenstrual.

'Okay,' he said, as calmly as he could without shading over into anything that might be mistaken for a patronising tone. 'Deb was born in New Zealand, so they could do that. They got out on a government charter. There aren't any other flights leaving, because no airlines will fly in here anymore. So leaving isn't an option. Yet.'

'But it's got to be, Kip. We can't feed ourselves. We'll starve soon.'

'We won't,' he said. 'I've got all those freeze-dried camping rations down in the basement. The ones you gave me all that grief over when I bought them cheap, remember? We've got at least two months' worth.'

She shook her head and her eyes hardened. 'That's not what I'm talking about and you know it. The city is starving. They're going to have to evacuate people before long. You know that, James. You must have been talking about it at council.'

He tried to speak but she rode in over him.

'And when it happens, *we're* going, mister. All of us. To New Zealand or Tasmania or fucking Bora Bora. Anywhere but here.'

'D-a-a-a-d-d-y!'

Suzie, who appeared at the kitchen door to complain that *Bear in the Big Blue House* wasn't on, saved him any further escalation. None of her shows were on. *Jo-Jo's Circus, Little Einsteins, The Wiggles,* they had all disappeared off the screen days ago. And every day she grew more upset with their absence. The only TV and radio now available carried Emergency Broadcast System updates, warnings about dangerous acid levels in the rain, information on food and gas rationing, handy hints for post-apocalypse home-owners about fortifying their neighbourhoods and establishing citizens' watch committees, and pleas for information on 'saboteurs and subversives' in the so-called Resistance. None of which impressed the hell out of a little girl who was bored and terrified in about equal measure.

'I want my shows back, Daddy,' she said. 'Can't you make the army men put them on?'

'Can't you watch a video, sweetheart? How about one of the movies I brought back?'

'I've watched them all a million times,' she complained, in a rising whine. 'It's not fair.'

He looked to Barb for help, but she wasn't giving him an inch. She simply folded her arms and raised one eyebrow. Very much aware that she'd be dealing with this all day, Kip didn't dare find fault with that response.

'Tell you what, princess,' he said as he dropped down to her level on one knee. 'I've got to get to work, but I promise I will bring home some new videos, ones you haven't seen yet. Okay?'

'Can you get *Piglet's Big Movie?*' she asked, suddenly brightening.

'Sure,' he replied, without thinking. '*Piglet's Big Movie*. No problemo.'

He felt, rather than saw, Barb tense up beside him.

'You run along and get dressed for Mommy, now. And no playing outside yet. Maybe tomorrow.'

'But D-a-a-a-d-d-y . . .'

'*Maybe* tomorrow. No promises.'

As she scampered away he rose to his feet again with a feeling of trepidation.

'Kip, you already made a promise you can't keep.'

'Sorry?'

'The Piglet movie. It's not on DVD. It was supposed to be on at the Cineplex this week. She's been looking forward to it all year. But you wouldn't know that, would you?' With that, his wife turned around and stalked off down the hall.

Damn!

Kipper stood in the kitchen, clenching and unclenching his fists, trying to breathe slowly. Blood was rushing through his head and he desperately wanted to say something stupid, but long, hard-won experience kept him quiet. He knew he should follow Barb and work things out, but he also knew that doing so would involve him in at least an hour's worth of apologies he didn't feel like making and maddening, circular discussions of his manifest failings on the home front. He was already late, and couldn't afford to miss the convoy out to the dam on Chester Morse Lake. Plus, he had to check on the food-aid distribution centres that were kicking off their operations this morning. One of them had been raided by some anarchist fools late last night. Kip hadn't gotten back to sleep after the cops had called him about it. There'd doubtless be interminable meetings about that today.

So he simply did not have time to get caught up in domestic trench warfare. It wasn't just a job anymore – people's lives rested on his decisions.

He knew he'd regret it before the day was done, but Kipper grabbed his car keys and travel pass and walked out through the kitchen door. The headache that had been building eased off a little as soon as he stepped outside and sucked in some fresh air. Well, not fresh, exactly. He could still taste the sharp, chemical tang in his mouth, in spite of the prevailing winds carrying away most of the pollutants from the south over the last twenty-four hours. A gigantic low over the Bering Strait had drawn up enormous volumes of ash and smoke from the conflagration in the Los Angeles Basin while a weird, contrary ridge of high pressure to the east had held the lowering toxic clouds over the Pacific Northwest for two days.

Seattle's chief engineer squinted into the morning sun for the first time in days, and tried not to think about what his family had been breathing into their lungs. He'd sealed the house as best he could – better than most would have managed – by rigging up an airlock and filter chamber in the spare room at the back. Barb had initially been none too impressed at the sacrifice of their best cotton sheets and the new Panasonic air-con unit they'd bought last summer, but the appearance of the towering, septic fogbank on the southern horizon quickly brought her around. When the power supply allowed, he maintained a rough overpressure by running the reverse-cycle heating and keeping the fireplace in the lounge room stoked at all times. Hopefully it would be enough.

Kipper stepped off the porch and started down the wet concrete pathway to his vehicle, the same F-100 pick-up he'd driven in from the airport a week ago today. He felt both guilt and relief at leaving Barb and Suzie behind. The house was large and comfortable, like most on Mercer Island, but it had felt like a cell while they'd been confined inside during the worst of the fallout period, as thousands of tonnes of toxic waste from the burning of LA had hung over the entire city and its surrounds. Barb's immaculately maintained garden had turned brown and died as though soaked in defoliant. Stopping at his front gate to survey the rest of the street, he could see they weren't alone. Mercer Island was a high-tone enclave, and Deerford Drive, perched on the edge of the lake and snuggled up against Groveland Park, was one of its better addresses. Truth be known, it was all a bit precious for Kipper, but Barb's family were Manhattan royalty – or had been, he reminded himself grimly – and she was used to moving among 'a better class of person'. 'People like us,' she would tease, smirking, knowing that the rude inhabitants of the cheap seats at a Larry the Cable Guy show were more Kip's sort of people than any of their opera-loving, sherry-sipping neighbours.

Thinking about her family made him feel even worse. She had cried all through that first night of the Disappearance, after wasting hours ringing every number she knew back on the East Coast. Her parents, her brothers and sisters, her uncles, aunts, old friends were all gone. Kip almost turned on his heels and went back inside, but momentum carried him forward. He *had* to get to work.

The street was sorry-looking and deserted. Nothing moved in a grey landscape of dying trees, brown lawn and wilted flowerbeds. Rain had washed away the worst of the fallout, but blackened, soggy clumps of mud and ash had collected at natural choke points in the gutter, behind the wheels of parked cars, and in small ponds of sludge where the ground dipped and run-off normally collected. Normally lush green and manicured to within an inch of its life, Deerford Drive was now sadly unkempt. Kipper shivered in the bleak chill of the morning. It had been unnaturally dark for most of the past week, with the sun completely blotted out, but prevailing weather patterns had finally pushed away the worst of the airborne waste, and although the day was by no means sunny, it was at least a good deal brighter. That wouldn't necessarily last, however.

Hundreds of cities and towns were ablaze across North America. The entire continent was pouring out vast noxious plumes as the infernos spread, with nobody and nothing to stop them, save for the occasional (and completely futile) automated firefighting system. He'd seen satellite photos of it on the web, and once on a local news show, before FEMA took over the airwaves. If he hadn't known better he'd have bet good money that an angry rash of super-sized volcanoes had suddenly erupted all over the US and up into Canada. Vast, slow-moving geysers of smoke, thousands of miles long, trailed away east from city after city. The Atlantic and most of Europe were now blanketed, with the wave front due to pass over the Urals in a day or two. It wouldn't be long before it had circled the northern hemisphere and reappeared back over Deerford Drive.

'Mr Kipper, Mr Kipper! Hello!'

Jolted by the unexpected cry, Kipper got his mask in place. He knew the voice only too well. Mrs Heinemann from number 43.

'Is it safe now? Is it safe to go out, Mr Kipper?'

'Well, you'd better hope so, Mrs Heinemann. Because you'll be in trouble otherwise, won't you?'

The woman was a wire-framed ninety-eight pounds of faded Jewish-American princess. Never married. Never got over it. At fifty-something, perhaps even sixty-odd, give or take some plastic surgery and a high degree of elasticity in her actual birth date, she'd poured all of her considerable energies into her self-appointed role as block kapo of the neighbourhood. Without a husband or children to harass and make miserable, she busied herself with other people's 'problems' – situations that, generally speaking, nobody had recognised as a problem until Mrs Heinemann became involved.

And yes, she was *Mrs* Heinemann. Unless you wanted an

earbashing out of your thoughtlessness and lack of consideration for the cruel vicissitudes that had left her single when so many other, undeserving women had chanced upon partners and off-spring. Dressed in a bright green and salmon-pink shell. suit, gathered at the ankles and wrists with elastic bands, and sporting a plastic shower cap and handkerchief face mask, she hurried up the slight incline in the street towards him, firing from the lip as she advanced.

'I'm so glad I caught you, Mr Kipper. I haven't seen anyone out and about all week. This terrible situation, you know. And the curfew. So is it safe now? Can we move about? It's just that I have very little food in the house. And so does everyone else. Mrs Deever at number 36, with her two little ones – she needs formula, Mr Kipper. And sweet Jane at 29, the retarded girl, she needs her medication. The Songnamichans – that very large Hindu family, he's a Microsoft manager – well, they must nearly be eating the wallpaper by now, with all of those children. What *is* to be done, Mr Kipper? *What is to be done?*'

She'd arrived right in front of him by now, yapping the whole time, a classic demonstration of fire and movement. He hadn't had a chance to speak or retreat. But her questions gave him the opportunity he needed.

'Mrs Heinemann,' he said forcefully. 'You need to get back inside right now. It is not safe out here, yet. We haven't had a chance to take any measurements of air or water quality. I'm only out here because it's my job. You need to get back inside where it's safe, this very minute. Go on. Right now. Don't delay. And don't drag any mud into the house with you. You'll need to strip off, bag up that outfit, and scrub yourself thoroughly. You still got water stored in the house? Good. Then, get going. Right now!'

He made sure his delivery was every bit as rapid and incontestable as her own. He waved her back towards her own house, shaking his head and brooking no backchat. In his peripheral vision he could see curtains twitching aside in a couple of houses and he made sure that everyone watching could see he didn't want anybody wandering around until it was safe.

'But Mr Kipper – '

'No! Move along now. Go on, Mrs Heinemann. You've no

business endangering yourself out here. Now git. Go and decontaminate yourself.' He took her upper arm in a deliberate grip and gave her a hurry-on towards home.

'Oh my. Oh dear,' she mumbled as she toddled off at high speed.

Shaking his head, he returned to the pick-up and climbed in, carefully knocking any mud from his boots before doing so, mostly for the benefit of his audience. The cabin was cold and still smelled of the McDonald's Family Meal he'd brought home late on day one. He'd also picked up a whole heap of canned fruit and eighty gallons of spring water in big ten-gallon plastic bottles, but that was the extent of any hoarding he felt necessary – because of all those freeze-dried, vacuum-sealed meals he'd bought in bulk near the end of last year, from some camping store that was closing down. Man, hadn't Barb changed her tune on that little purchase. He'd got himself a new one torn at the time.

The engine needed turning over a couple of times before the truck grumbled into life, sounding louder than usual in the unnatural stillness of the morning. He checked the fuel gauge as soon as he had power, making sure he hadn't been siphoned. The city council's Emergency Management Committee had banned the sale of gasoline for 'non-essential' purposes on the second day, but hadn't had the manpower – or the will, in his opinion – to enforce the measure when thousands of people ignored it and started queuing at gas stations. They bid up the price to almost fifty dollars a gallon at one point. That was when the army had rolled out of Fort Lewis to lock down the city and get everyone off the streets as the sky had blackened and the rain turned to acid.

Kipper's truck had three-quarters of a tank, and he could get more from a council depot without any trouble, yet. But that'd change. No commercial shipping or air traffic had come into Seattle for five days, and he didn't expect any in the foreseeable future. The only supplies they could draw on were aid shipments: food from Australia and New Zealand, one supertanker of petroleum so far from Taiwan, and more food and medical supplies from Japan. It was enough to keep things ticking over, if it kept coming, and if people didn't panic. Two big fucking 'if's.

The island was quiet, and people were sticking to the curfew.

Mostly. Kipper searched the radio dial for anything besides the recorded EBS messages, which told him nothing new, and said nothing about the raid on the food bank. He picked up a scratchy, inconsistent transmission from somewhere in Canada, but it was all electronic dance music, which in his book was worse than nothing. Sighing, he punched the button to cut off the radio and pulled away from the curb, wondering what the hell he was going to do about *Piglet's Big Movie*.

His route took him along West Mercer Way. Normally a quiet, tree-lined drive through some of the more exclusive real estate the island had to offer, it felt eerily deserted, with sodden rubbish and leaf litter strewn along its length. He took the Homer Hadley floating bridge across Lake Washington into the city, and again found it hard to get his head around the empty lanes. At this time on a Friday morning, traffic should have been crawling over the span, bumper to bumper.

There was some vehicular movement, however. Mobile army patrols stopped him three times. Then there were the roadblocks and checkpoints he hit on another four occasions. His pass, countersigned by three city councillors and the ubiquitous General Blackstone, carried him through each obstacle, but he understood why there were so few people about. After the food riot on day three down at Ivar's Salmon House, under the I-5 bridge, and a shoot-out at the 7-Eleven on Denny Way that left four people dead following an argument over who was going to get the last of the frozen pizza subs, the army had put away its smiley face. Three young men, who'd have been thought of as burglars a week earlier, got shot down as 'looters' while trying to make off with a carton of hot dogs from the Wendy's on Rainier Avenue that evening. A vagrant, emerging from a dumpster behind a KFC the following day, was cut in half by automatic weapons fire from an armoured fighting vehicle. Far from attempting to cover up the incidents, the same General Blackstone who'd scrawled the signature on Kipper's 'transit documents' appeared on television and the radio to detail exactly what had happened and to assure the citizens of Seattle it would happen again, to anyone who broke curfew and attempted to steal from their fellow citizens by 'subverting' the rationing system. Things went quiet around the city after that.

Talk-back radio and a couple of current affairs shows on the local TV networks had raged against the 'injustice', but that defiance was short-lived, lasting only as long as it took four Humvees full of troops to roll into their parking lots. Some lawyers who arrived at City Hall to serve papers on the administration for First Amendment violations were still in custody somewhere. There'd been no more open dissent and, incidentally, no more food riots or 'looting' either. But the self-proclaimed Resistance appeared shortly afterwards in the form of an email spammed throughout the city warning of a fascist takeover and promising to 'take back the streets'.

Kipper wasn't happy about any of it – how the hell could you be? But on the other hand he knew how desperate the situation was, and just how easily it could spin totally out of control. He really hoped this Blackstone asshole would see sense and ease off the thumbscrews a little. People were hurting and scared; you couldn't keep the whole city under house arrest indefinitely. And he could only pray that this dumbass Resistance thing turned out to be a bunch of dope-addled bullshit artists. God knows, Seattle was full of *them*. A few more stunts like last night's stupidity at the food bank and they could totally fuck things up.

Speaking of which . . . He hauled the wheel around, crossing over the median strip and pointing the truck towards 4th Avenue South, where the main food distribution centre for the CBD was located, at a Costco wholesale warehouse near the train yards. He wanted to see for himself how the food aid system was working.

The signal-strength meter on his cell phone read near full and he called Barney Tench on hands free as the pick-up swung around Rizal Park. It seemed a small wonder the call went through – until he remembered that 'unauthorised civilians' were barred from using the cell network for anything other than emergencies.

Kipper shook his head and scowled at a measure he thought of as totally unnecessary and counterproductive. It wasn't like the Wave had just appeared and people were going to be melting the phone-company servers with millions of calls. It was just more repression for no good reason. Exactly the sort of nonsense that fuelled the paranoid dementia of idiots and conspiracy loons.

His temper was building again as he chewed over the many poor decisions that had been made in the previous week, and it was only Barney's answering the call that short-circuited a bout of foul-mouthed, solitary cussing. His friend's voice filled the cabin, sounding flat and tinny as everyone did on speaker-phone.

'S'up, buddy?'

'Hey, Barn. I'm heading over to Costco right now to check things out. You on your way?'

'About four or five minutes away. I'm just coming over 1st Avenue Bridge. Heather should already be there. She overnighted in town to get there early.'

'Oh, okay. I didn't know that. Good for her.'

Kipper was taken aback for a second. Heather Cosgrove was a young civil engineering graduate on a six-month internship with his road maintenance guys, all of whom had been at a conference in Spokane when the Wave hit. If he was giving out a prize for Most Freaked Out, Heather was an unbackable favourite. She was from Minneapolis, and apart from her job, she had nothing left.

'It's spooky, isn't it,' said Tench, completely oblivious, 'without any traffic. Like a doomsday movie or something.'

'Yeah,' replied Kip, getting his head back in the game. 'Listen, did you hear about the raid last night?'

Barney snorted down the line. 'Dunno that I'd call it a raid, man. What I heard was two dreadlocked jerks got stoned and tried to steal a pallet of Cheetos from the food bank on South Graham.'

'Well, d'you hear they got shot?'

The speaker-phone hissed quietly for a second, as Kipper swung down the off ramp at South Forest Street.

'No. Sorry, I didn't hear that,' said Barney. 'Who told you?'

'Cops rang at about two this morning.'

'Why'd they call you? Why not one of the councillors?'

'Said they couldn't raise them.'

Tench laughed. 'That'd be right.'

17

'*Fedayeen!*'

The warning cry came from the man at point, a fraction of a second before the hammering of automatic weapons fire started up. The Cav troopers moved for cover as though every man had been jabbed with a stun gun. The dismounted cavalry scouts were fast and flowed like quicksilver, pouring themselves into doorways, around stone walls, and down behind piles of rubble that made vehicle movement all but impossible through the narrow streets of An Nasiriyah. The M3A2 Bradley Cavalry Fighting Vehicles followed them when and where they could. A couple of squads of infantry with their M2A2 Bradley Infantry Fighting Vehicles joined them when they moved into the town.

Bret Melton moved with them, the instincts and experience of his own time in the Rangers, and a decade of combat reportage since, rubbing up hard against fatigue and ageing muscles. He landed next to Specialist Vincent Alcibiades, burrowing in under the protection of a massive broken beam of concrete and rebar as small-arms fire chewed up the mud-brick walls of the street, zipping less than a foot overhead.

Melton had picked up an M4 for his own protection, moments before they entered Iraq. Nobody said one word to him. After the carbine, he picked up some MOLLE web gear and some ammo pouches. He already had a matching dark blue set of Level III body armour and a Kevlar helmet. The army issued him with a protective mask and MOPP gear in case someone dropped some germs or chemicals on them, but he'd always been one of the sceptics on the WMD front.

In any case, the fighting was simply too chaotic and disordered for Melton to be able to rely on anyone else to look after him. In the labyrinthine warren of souks, alleys, cut-throughs and ragged streets of the towns and villages in which they'd been fighting, you never knew when you were going to have some asshole suddenly appear right in front of you with murder in his eyes. He hadn't needed the carbine yet, for which he was grateful. Still, he flicked the selector from safe to semi and waited. Alcibiades let rip with two short bursts, holding his own M4 up over the cover and firing blind. The Bradleys added the hum and mechanical metal-punching beat to the chaotic audio mix, sending .25 mike-mike into buildings without a care for possible civilian casualties.

When the specialist came back down, he spat a green stream in the sand, his cheeks bulging from a wad of chew. 'Fuckin' ragheads.'

The volume of fire going down-range was impressive and deafening, nearly drowning out the shouts of Lieutenant Euler and his non-coms as they organised the counter-ambush with the infantry troops who had linked up with them.

Melton did his best to collect himself and commit to memory as many details as possible. He would write notes out later, when the immediate danger had passed, and his hands, hopefully, weren't shaking too much. As always, the head rush of contact was giddy and horrifying – a glassy funnel of light and colour down which you fell as soon as you realised somebody was trying to take your life. Melton found it harder to deal with as a reporter than he had when a soldier, perhaps because he was older and wiser, perhaps because now he had nothing to distract him from the experience. Indeed, having the experience and recording it for others were his sole reasons for being there. He couldn't shut down and get on with whatever task the sergeant or corporals assigned him. He played his part by opening up his senses to the madness of battle, letting it burn its terrors and banalities directly onto his cortex.

He savoured the taste of the dust in his mouth, the gritty, choking, dog-shit and tangy metallic diesel flavour of it. He noted the struggle of a green bejewelled bug caught in a wad of gum, stuck to the side of Alcibiades's boot; tried to freeze in his memory the smell of the man next to him, a cloying miasma of body odour, stale farts and wintergreen Skoal chewing tobacco. He studied the contours of the street, the way the ancient biscuit-coloured buildings snaked away, slightly uphill. The yellow-green, foul-smelling stream of raw sewage and trash that flowed down-slope towards him. The soldiers themselves – some cool and frosty, others sweating but focused, most of them scared out of their minds.

Lieutenant Euler took shelter behind a pockmarked stone pillar, which may well have stood on the same spot since the time of Mohammed. He was on the radio with a map in his hand, looking at something Melton couldn't see. The radio operator kept security, his carbine traversing along the rooftops, looking for snipers, RPG gunners or any other Iraqi in desperate need of a new weeping asshole in the middle of his forehead.

Bo Jaanson was doing the standard shoot, move and communicate drill, moving the soldiers, infantry and cavalry both, around the restricted battle space of the narrow street like a brutal chess master. Some soldiers would balk, while others would execute on command. With some, Jaanson calmed them with a pat on the shoulder and a few fatherly words, the way one would handle a terrified horse. With others, it was a boot imprint on the ass. Melton couldn't help but smile, having been there himself.

He saw a bird, swooping up and away to escape the sudden eruption of slaughter, suddenly fly apart in a spray of feather and blood as some stray round punched right through its frail body. The remains dropped into the dust, raising a small puff of dirt, and the body twitched for a few seconds as dumb electrical storms raged through its shattered nervous system.

Alcibiades saw it too. 'Fuck me, man. Not safe for man or beast in this motherfucker. I say call in Air and let them fucking hammer this place back to the Stone Age.'

'Hooah,' Melton said before he could stop himself. He tapped Al on the shoulder. 'Got any dip, Specialist?'

Alcibiades pulled a can from his hip pocket. 'Got a whole log before we left. I'm about half through it, so you'd better make me look good. Hooah?'

Melton took the can of Skoal and nodded. 'Hooah, Specialist. Fucking hooah.'

The dip in his mouth and the can returned to Alcibiades, he tried to lock himself down on reality. But no matter how hard he tried to anchor himself in the real world, time always seemed to warp and stretch before snapping back on these moments, almost as though it too had become an actor in the conflict, constantly turning and folding in on itself to better examine the deeds of the frail, ridiculous little creatures who raged through its currents. It may have been four minutes or many hours before the Apaches arrived overhead and announced themselves with a *whoosh* of rockets and the industrial *thumpety thump-thump-thump* of their chain guns. Half the street ahead of them disintegrated, quite literally, flying apart under the kinetic hammer of high-velocity explosive ordnance. Blocks of sandstone and dried mud shattered and crumbled, releasing their mass in the form of thick powdery clouds to drift away on the warm sirocco passing over the village.

'Apaches will do,' croaked Alcibiades. 'I feel like dancing every time they play my tune. Sing it, fuckers!'

Melton stayed down, rub-fucking the ground, as the fire from the soldiers of the Rock of the Marne tapered off. For a brief interlude, silence as heavy as an old coat lay over them. Then he heard the crunch of boots moving across broken masonry, through the ringing in his ears. The rattle of equipment as men darted forward. The metallic click and slide of a mag being swapped out.

Slowly, carefully, he raised his head over the cover. Their concrete beam had been badly chewed over by gunfire. Pockmarks and dark scores pitted and scarred the surface. One rusted spike of rebar glistened in the sun, a silver fang sliced out of its dull, reddish length by the impact of a single bullet. Melton let his peripheral vision take over for a second, scanning for any movement that would indicate the presence of a lingering threat. Perhaps a window pushed open to accommodate the barrel of a sniper's rifle. Or a door creaking backwards into a darkened hut, from whence some maniac in a dynamite vest might emerge shouting 'Saddam is great!' before detonating himself. But there was nothing. The Apaches had cleaned up the ambush, and probably a fair number of unlucky innocents as well.

Alcibiades arose beside him like an apparition, the muzzle of his rifle sweeping through a narrow arc in front of them, covering the men who were scoping out the rubble under which their attackers had died. Melton waited for the call of 'Medic!'

It never came. Whatever injuries the troopers had taken did not require immediate intervention. He kept his personal weapon to hand but consciously dialled back on the tension compressing his whole body into an impacted mass of nerve endings. They'd survived another one. The brigade and most of the 3rd Infantry Division had been remarkably lucky so far. Fewer than fifty KIA after days of fighting, and all of them lost in close-quarter battles like this one. Out on the desert plains, where they'd first engaged the Iraqis, it had been a pure slaughter of the foe. Nobody had any idea of the enemy's casualties, but in this sector alone it had run into the thousands. Perhaps more than ten thousand by now.

Lieutenant Leo Euler appeared beside him, handing back a receiver to his radio operator. 'D'you get all that, sir?' he asked the reporter. 'Gotta keep the folks at home informed.'

It was an attempt at light banter, but the young officer's eyes were too tired and far away to carry it off. 'Sleep when you are dead' became a soldier's unofficial motto.

Bret Melton nodded absently and spat onto the ground, the nicotine slowly infiltrating his wired nervous system. 'Any casualties, Lieutenant?' he said.

Euler shook his head. 'Nothing serious. No sucking chest wounds or lost limbs, so I'll count myself a happy man. Worthless Fedayeen fucktards. Sometimes I think they shoot high and wide, praying to get fucking captured.'

Saddam's volunteer militia had borne the brunt of the fighting in the crossroads towns and although they'd handed out some grief here and there, as a fighting force they seemed to be tasked with holding up the Coalition forces and making them 'waste' ammunition and lives. The Coalition didn't have the troops to provide POW facilities so without an order per se, the higher-ups let it be known that there would be no quarter. Some units in 3rd

ID had taken up the old practice of flying a black flag from an antenna. It didn't take long for the Iraqis to figure out what that meant.

As a tactic, Melton had to admit that sending your worthless troops forward as bullet-catchers made some sense. Everyone knew they weren't pushing on to Baghdad now, that'd be insane. The British and US forces executing Operation Katie in southern Iraq were planning to leave the whole leprous mess to fester on its own when they were gone. That was assuming they could kick the Kuwaitis and the Saudis off so they could actually get the hell out of Dodge. The tiny Polish and Australian special forces contingents were already gone, what missions they'd originally been assigned now irrelevant. And Saddam was openly mocking them from Baghdad, whipping up a perfect storm of pan-Arab hysteria at his 'defeat' of the infidel crusaders. Well, not openly – not since the Americans dropped that JDAM on Uday.

Saddam still made appearances in the open, but they were never televised live, and they never lasted very long. They did hit the mark, though. The allied air campaign went forward pretty much as originally planned, from what Bret had heard the Air Force liaison say, in an attempt to decapitate Iraq's command and control systems. The only difference was that Coalition air power had destroyed bridges they'd originally needed. But as long as the fat little fucker survived to taunt them, his stature only grew. He was openly comparing himself to Saladin now, declaring himself the reborn leader of the faithful.

The crackle of gunfire drifted in over the rooftops of the surviving buildings from somewhere to the west. It was another element of 3rd ID conducting sweep-and-clear ops to make sure that everyone – ladie dadie everyone – could withdraw through this shithole without getting nickel-and-dimed to death by snipers, suicide bombers and the half-assed incompetents tricked out like Arab ninjas who called themselves the Fedayeen Saddam.

Euler's men were moving towards one of the remaining intact bridges three blocks away, in tandem with another platoon taking a parallel route two streets over. Apaches from the squadron's air cav component buzzed about high overhead, waiting to pounce on any resistance. When Operation Katie went into effect, the rulebook was thrown out along with it. Melton remembered Captain Lohberger saying, 'Fuck the rules of engagement' before he buttoned up his Bradley so many days ago. Somebody seemed to have handed 3rd ID's commander, Major General Blount, an open checkbook.

No one took any chances. If a building needed to be swept, soldiers tossed frags through the door, then the M-249 SAW gunner sprayed the room before they went in. If the Iraqis decided a mosque prayer tower made a pretty good forward observation post, an MPAT round from one of 5-7's M-1 Abrams tanks chopped it down. If they used a school or a hospital for a fort, the division's artillery hammered it with 155 or MLRS rounds. No one took any chances anymore.

'Who you writin' for now, anyway, Bret?' Alcibiades was beside him, his eyes hidden behind the sliver of a pair of Ray-Bans. They gave him an insectile appearance as he scanned the blasted remains of the thoroughfare ahead, the muzzle of his rifle tracking the movements of his head with mechanical precision. '*Army Times* is gone, right? Like everything else.'

Unlike the officers, most of the grunts just called him by his first name. He didn't have to work hard to fit in with them.

'Headquarters is, but we've got field offices in Europe and Korea,' Melton replied, not that he'd had any luck getting in touch with any of them. 'And, worst comes to worst, there's always *Stars and Stripes*, I suppose. I had some contacts from my freelance days, foreign websites and magazines – you know, British mostly. I'm filing for them now and stringing for the BBC. The war's not nearly as big a story as it would have been. But it's up there.'

They formed up again with Alcibiades's scout team, picking their way through the rubble, stepping over tumble-down walls and mounds of pulverised mud brick. Melton stood on something soft and yielding, and before he could stop himself had glanced down and seen the tiny arm beneath his soiled boots. It ended in ragged flesh and a stump of white bone, just after the elbow joint.

He spat on the ground next to the remains and whispered, 'Yeah. Fuck the rules of engagement. Hooah.'

Lieutenant Euler's Bradley, *Fiddler's Green*, was burning a few hundred yards short of the bridge over the Euphrates. One of the crew had made it out, only to be shot down from a window in one of the low-rise ferroconcrete bunkers that passed for apartments in this part of Nasiriyah. His crew-mates had not escaped.

'They've got a fucking howitzer in one of those buildings, with the muzzle aimed into the street. Or maybe a T-72. I can't tell, damn it,' said Euler, who was blessed not to be in the Bradley at the time. The binoculars came down from his eyes as he turned away from the corner to address his squad leaders. 'Fuck me runnin'. Either it's Republican Guard or someone who has got their shit wired tight.'

Melton chanced a quick peek around the corner, darting his head out and back like a nervous chipmunk. He took a sight picture of the disabled Brad. The rear troop hatch was gone and the turret missing. Rounds cooked off in the main body, one at a time, with the sound of an M-80 firecracker under a steel bucket. It made a hollow *thump* with each cook-off. Thick, oily smoke poured from the commander's hatch and flames burned at the rear of the chassis.

Euler spoke quickly and privately with his platoon sergeant while Melton fell back to give the two some space. After a few words, Euler held a hand out to his radio operator for the handset of their SINCGARS.

'Air strike,' said Alcibiades as he spat into the ground. 'Betcha this week's pay the LT will call in some A-10s. Probably gonna flatten a coupla blocks.'

'We ain't getting paid this month,' said Bakic, one of his buddies.

'Still gonna be an – '

'What the fuck!'

Euler hadn't shouted, but the force of his exclamation had drawn all the attention back on him. He was talking on the radio, and everyone listened to his side of the exchange, which didn't tell them much.

'What d'you fucking mean . . . ?' Euler paused while the voice on the other end shouted loud enough for Melton to hear a time-honoured army phrase.

Remember your military bearing, soldier.

'Okay, if the ALO can't get me air, then what about . . . ?' Euler pulled off his k-pot and threw it at the wall across from him. 'You gotta be fucking kidding me,' Euler continued, obviously not impressed by the previous admonishment about military bearing. 'How about some goddamn fucking fire support then? . . . Oh, for fuck's sake . . .'

The handset shouted back, leaving Euler to shake his head some more. He signed off and threw the handset back at his radio operator. His non-coms pulled in closer, concern acid-etched into all of their faces. A few shook their heads as he relayed to them the details of whatever shit sandwich they'd just been handed.

'Goddamn,' muttered one of the sergeants, loud enough for Melton to hear. The enlisted men around him strained to pick up a few clues without being too obvious about it. They were spread out along a side street running between two shops, both of which had been cleared not fifteen minutes earlier. Euler had men inside both, and crawling around on the rooftops, denying the high ground to any hostiles. Anxiety crept stealthily down the line of soldiers, as men who'd been sitting in the dirt, catching a few minutes' respite, picked up on the changed vibe in the leadership group and slowly began to attend to them. Eyes that had been closed now cracked open, heads turned almost imperceptibly, bodies shifted just a little bit, leaning in towards the lieutenant, hoping to catch some scrap of information that might provide a clue as to what mess they'd stepped in now.

At last the NCOs dispersed down the line, carrying the news with them. Corporal Shetty – a short, dense, African-American version of The Thing from *The Fantastic Four* – rumbled over, his face a study in disgust.

'Choppers had to bug out,' he informed them. Suddenly Melton realised for the first time that the constant droning thud of the Apaches and Blackhawks that had shepherded them through the dusty maze of An Nasiriyah was missing. He saw men craning their heads upwards all along the shadowed alleyway as they heard the news.

Alcibiades asked the obvious question. 'Why?'

Shetty glared at him, like the absence was his fault. 'Fucking Iranians,' he said, as if those two words were enough. When they were found to be patently not enough, however, he continued. 'Iran declared war on America an hour ago. Their air force is up and trying to punch through, to get to us. It is a full-on fur ball out in the Gulf. Hundreds of speed boats and jet skis. All of 'em suicide runners. They been swarmin' the navy. Air force and some British units are mixing it up with the Iranian planes right now, trying to keep 'em off us here.'

'Holy shit,' cursed Alcibiades, his swarthy features paling noticeably.

'Yeah, anyway. Choppers are outta here for the moment. If we want air cover, we gotta call in A-10s, and they're only coming when they can get their own cover. It's fucked up.'

'Shit, what about arty then?' Some private, he was a replacement pulled out of the division's 123rd Signal Battalion and it showed every time he nearly shot himself in the foot with his M16. Melton stayed far away from him, because it was going to end in tears for that commo puke. He knew it in his bones.

'They're busy hammering a column of Republican Guard who are trying to get to us,' Shetty said. 'So no artillery, no air, nothing but Buffalo Soldiers and the grunts.'

Melton yawned so hard he nearly swallowed his stale wad of chew. He was exhausted but it was a nervous gesture too, one of his personal 'tells' that he was under pressure. He fingered the crap out of his mouth, took a sip from his camel-back and tapped Corporal Shetty on the shoulder.

'Corporal, is it just Iran?' he asked. 'Do we know if anyone else is moving? Syria, Israel maybe?'

The non-com's head swivelled like a gun turret. Back and forth, once. 'Dunno, Mr Melton. You'd be better placed to find out than any of us, if your satellite phone is working.'

'Battery's dead. Went down yesterday and I haven't been able to recharge,' Melton said. 'Sat coverage has gotten awfully spotty of late anyway.'

Shetty took that piece of news like a dustbowl farmer absorbing yet another month without rain. Such was life. 'Lieutenant's talking with Lohberger, getting instructions,' he went on. 'If we can't hammer down the bad guys with air support, it makes this whole deal a lot fucking harder.'

'But the brass still wants this bridge,' Melton said without any real enthusiasm.

'Yep. They still want it. Why they want it, I've no fucking clue, but they still want it.'

'Man, this is totally fucked,' said Bakic. 'What the fuck are we even doing here? It sure as shit ain't paying the rent anymore.'

'What we're *doing here*, bitch,' growled Shetty, 'is trying to get the fuck outta the 'hood without losing too many worthless motherfuckers like you along the way. That good enough reason for you? Or would you like to just lay down your fucking arms and walk out there and tell the towel heads, "Yo, dogs, it's my bad. I'm gonna ease on up outta here and head back to my new crib up in Alaska, yo"? Is that what you want to do, Private?'

The chastened soldier mumbled something like 'Sorry Corporal, no Corporal' and devoted himself to the intense study of the dirt at his feet. Up and down the line, similar scenes played themselves out as the men dealt with the shock of losing their air cover and gaining a new enemy.

Melton checked his watch. It was late afternoon, shading towards sunset in maybe an hour or so. He wondered if 3rd ID would wait until dark, when the Americans' night-vision equipment would return to them a significant advantage. On the other hand, the power of a unit like 5-7 Cav lay in its mobility. It was a 'terrible swift sword' in movement, cutting through anything that got in its way. Sitting here like this merely invited the Iraqis to gather their forces around them, especially when they couldn't be targeted for destruction from the air.

Euler was back on the radio within a few minutes, his head bent and shoulders hunched tightly forward as though he was attempting to contain some new piece of shit news from getting free. Figuring on being stationary for a while, Melton opened a chilli mac MRE and stuck the shit-brown spoon down into its contents. He chewed on the meaty mac combo joylessly and washed it down with a drink of warm water. The other men all used the break as best suited them. Some ate, some dozed, one pissed his name up against an ancient wall. Everyone sipped some water or mixed some flavoured drink from their MREs in a water bottle. Most of their store-bought pougie bait had run out days ago.

At least the shade of the alleyway was a blessed relief from the oppressive heat of day. Even with the sun dropping towards the edge of the world, fighting in this temperature was a crippling business. Keeping the troops' fluids up was proving as difficult as clearing a block of Fedayeen. Melton craned back his neck, stretching it far enough to work out a few kinks with a distinct cracking sound. The sky was lightly clouded and the glare had faded somewhat from its painful intensity in the middle of the day. He searched in vain for any sign of the so-called Disappearance Effect, the nuclear winter that had fallen on Western Europe with the arrival of billions of tons of particulate matter, released into the atmosphere by the burning cities of North America. Maybe it was all bullshit. He couldn't tell. He was as cut off from the wider world as everyone else in the unit.

It was in that position, leaning back against the wall of the gutted building, squinting slightly into the hot grey sky, that he saw the dark blur of the mortar round as it dropped towards them. The cry of 'Incoming!' arose in his head but never reached his mouth, as another round smacked into the rooftop corner at the far end of the alleyway, detonating with a bone-cracking roar and a deadly spray of shrapnel. Men screamed out warnings and dived for what little cover existed in the narrow passageway. A few made it through a single door halfway down. A couple of others scrambled through a hole in the wall blown out by a grenade some hours earlier.

Oh fuck, Melton thought. He got down and tried to become one with the ground while he looked for a better patch of cover than nothing at all. An open shopfront across the street looked promising.

He was on his feet then, unaware of how he'd made it up off his ass so quickly. More rounds were dropping on their position with enough accuracy to suggest they'd been pre-sighted by the Iraqis, who had been waiting for just such an opportunity Many of the rounds impacted the roofline but one speared right down into the constricted space, exploding with a terrible force that lifted Melton off the ground, turning him over and over.

He twisted slowly, impossibly, through the air. His mind, detached from the dead, stringless puppet of his body, pulled free with a discernible tug. He watched himself falling back to earth with bricks and clods of dirt, with the disembodied arms and legs of his friends, with clattering pieces of steel and burning splinters of wood.

Bret Melton, formerly of the US Army Rangers, twirled oh so slowly through clear air. Up so high he imagined he could see the entire town of An Nasiriyah below him. The savage close-quarter battles that still raged around choke points and contested streets. The ruined block where they had been ambushed in another life. Hundreds of Iraqi soldiers and militia fighters running towards his position. And beyond that. He could see the deserts stretching away towards the mountains in the far north. He could see the ships of the US fleet as they raked at skies full of Iranian fighters. And perhaps, at the dimmest edge of vision and consciousness, he could see an empty realm, the burning land that he had once known as home. The lost continent of North America.

Bret saw all of these things. Or thought he did, before he fell back to earth and into darkness.

18

She was sick. Increasingly nauseous, and occasionally close to vomiting. Caitlin had no idea whether it was a side effect of the headache, which had been constant for three days now, or an entirely new symptom of whatever was eating her brain from the inside out. Of course, it could also be a result of breathing in the soupy miasma of toxins and burnt chemicals that had rolled over the city on Tuesday and stayed for the last three days. The charred, atomised memory of America. Some *Guardian* writer with a very dark sense of humour and a taste for DeLillo had named it 'the airborne toxic event', and the tag had stuck.

French government warnings played on a loop across every radio station, advising listeners to stay indoors whenever possible. Caitlin couldn't believe anyone would need telling twice. Millions of dead seabirds had washed up on the coast of western France just before the tsunami of pollutants arrived, and thousands of pigeons – flying rats, as she thought of them – had been dropping from the sick, leaden skies over Paris ever since. She could see dozens of little grey carcasses from the apartment window. City council workers had already cleaned the streets below of twitching, broken birds, but that was on Wednesday, and they hadn't been back.

The few times Caitlin had ventured outside to stock up on fresh food, she'd returned with her eyes stinging and her airways burnt. It reminded her of the time she'd done a job in Linfen, a

city in China's Shanxi Province, where you could feel the acids and poisons leaching through your skin every extra minute you were exposed.

She splashed a handful of cold water on her waxy face. She looked bad. Bruised, puffy eyes; hollow cheeked. All the lines on her face etched too long and deep. Then again, almost everyone in Paris looked like that now. There weren't too many parties celebrating the new world order these days. People were either keeping to themselves, holed up with their families, or they were out in mobs, heedless of the poisoned atmosphere. The ring of fire that surrounded the old core of the city was down to them. What had begun as small-scale opportunistic looting had escalated into a rolling series of street battles between the police and ever-greater numbers of rioters from the *banlieue*. In the last twenty-four hours, the radio had carried reports of wider clashes, between 'migrant gangs' and 'white youths'.

Between Muslim whackjobs and fascist skinheads, Caitlin thought to herself. The first sparks.

She scrubbed her face with a damp cloth before towelling off.

The old bathroom at the rear of the apartment, a dark, depressing closet tiled in deep green and featuring a small faded yellow tub, wasn't the most flattering place in which to examine herself in a mirror. But there was nowhere else in the tiny flat. The fit-out was very basic, funded entirely from a black, discretionary account that she'd kept off the books at Echelon. One bed; a couch and a table; a bar fridge in the kitchenette, a two-ring gas burner, a microwave oven. And a small armoury under the floorboards in the bathroom where she had also stashed some money – increasingly useless – and three passports – ditto. Nobody knew about this place, not even Wales.

And for now at least, it remained off the grid, undiscovered by her hunters and relatively safe, unlike the first sanctum near the cemetery. It made sense, she supposed. If they'd known to try grabbing her up at the hospital, they had probably taken down her control cell, and possibly even the whole Echelon network.

Normally, she'd be gone by now. Disappeared off the map. But her illness seemed to grow worse by the day, and she had realised with horror some time ago that she actually needed

Monique's help just to get through the day. A lone run through hostile territory was out of the question.

And anyway, where could she go? Wales was uncontactable, probably because they'd grabbed him. The cell structure of Echelon's wetwork sections meant she was floating, alone. There were no convenient fronts or trapdoors through which she could slip. Beyond a few dead drops and compromised lay-up points, the network had no permanent presence on the continent. No outposts or operational centres. Just a transient pool of operators like her, who came and went with each mission. And she was being hunted.

But why now? What was the fucking point?

A small tic tugged at her cheek in the fly-spotted bathroom mirror. 'Relatively safe' didn't really mean much in Paris at the moment. Caitlin pulled down on a string, killing the power to the bare bulb that hung from the ceiling. She couldn't be sure it would come back on when next she needed it. The city's electricity supply was getting patchy. They'd been blacked out for three hours yesterday, and this morning the water had run brown and cold from all of the taps.

She padded down the short hallway so as not to disturb Monique, who was sleeping in the single bedroom. It was well after midnight and the only light in the apartment spilled in through the large windows overlooking an intersection. She moved up to the nearest one, careful not to silhouette herself. Dead birds still littered the cobblestones. She watched as a thin, scabrous dog carried off one of the bodies. The lights of the old city centre provided a pale illumination under the thick blanket of smog, while the fires burning out in the otherwise darkened suburbs threw a harder, eldritch glare over the world below.

Caitlin had never had to use the hide-out before. She only ever leased these places as a fail safe, a fall-back position, taking them for a maximum of six months before switching to a new address. After setting one up she would almost never return, unless her cover was blown, and that had happened only once, three years earlier in Berlin. That episode had convinced her of the need for a bolthole, no matter how much expense and hassle were involved in maintaining one without the direct logistical support of Echelon.

After staring out the window for a few minutes she realised that her nausea had eased, replaced by a hollow feeling in her stomach. Hunger. With one last glance at the deserted streets outside, Caitlin padded through to the kitchen to prepare a meal. It was late, but if she didn't feed herself now, she may not have the chance for another day. She'd been eating when she could, to fuel up for the long periods when her body simply rejected anything but water and breath mints. For some reason the mints seemed to help with the queasiness. She suppressed a sigh as she entered the tiny kitchen, not bothering with the light, which had blown earlier.

Besides the small box of prohibitively expensive fruit and vegetables Monique had bought on her last expedition, two weeks' worth of dried and tinned food remained – although, given Caitlin's reduced appetite, it would probably last longer, maybe even a month. She ran the tap for a minute, which helped to thin out the brown tea-stained tint of the water. Satisfied the quality wouldn't improve any more, she filled a pot and added a pinch of salt, setting it down on a gas burner. The pretty blue flame that flared up at the touch of a match was a pleasant surprise. The building's gas supply had been interrupted the previous day. As she worked, her hunger came roaring back and she decided to chance a slightly heavier meal.

She diced a brown onion and set it aside before opening a can of Italian tuna and breaking the chunks into a bowl. Another tin gave up four deep-red Roma tomatoes swimming in their own thick sauce. Saliva began to squirt into her mouth and she felt almost dizzy with new hunger and the prospect of a decent meal. She had no idea why her nausea had cleared, but she wasn't going to waste the opportunity. There was a hunk of nearly dried-out bacon in the small fridge and Caitlin diced that up, frying it with the onion in the oil from the tuna. One last shrivelled mushroom went into the pan, which was spitting and popping as the meat cooked.

Once the water had boiled, Caitlin added a thick sheaf of dried spaghetti, pushing the long yellow stalks under as they softened. The tuna went into the frying pan, followed by the tomatoes and their sauce. She turned the heat right down to a simmer while the pasta cooked. It was an old and much-loved dish, one of only three meals her dad had been able to cook. One-eyed Egyptians. Shit on a shingle. And this bad boy right here. She knew nowadays that the recipe was a variation on an old Italian standard, usually made with porcini mushrooms and their soak, but for Caitlin it had always been 'Dad's big pasta sauce'. As a teenager, she'd begged him to cook up buckets of the stuff to freeze and take away with her on surfing holidays. After seven or eight hours of carving up the big sets off northern California, she could inhale three big bowls' worth.

The small domestic scene in front of her blurred and disappeared behind diamonds and blue sapphires of light as tears filled her eyes. She rubbed away the moisture with the back of her hand. Her parents, of course, hadn't known the exact nature of her work, but her dad, an old air force man, had filled in some of the blanks for himself. He never asked Caitlin why a bureaucrat from the US Information Service had to travel so frequently or spend so much time out of contact. He never asked how a junior civil servant came to acquire such an impressive array of scars, broken bones and deep-tissue injuries over the years, and when other family members did, she explained them away as surf injuries. But he had taken her aside at a family wedding a while ago, just after she'd returned from four months 'out of contact' in the aftermath of 9/11, and he'd told her that he knew his little girl was doing 'good work', and that she needed to know her family loved her and were very, very proud of her. Dave Monroe, a veteran of Tricky Dick Nixon's undeclared war in Cambodia, had held his daughter's gaze for what felt like an eternity, and while no more words had passed between them, understanding did. He knew his daughter was a soldier.

'Caitlin?'

She had heard Monique shuffling up the hallway and rubbed the last of her tears away before the French girl caught her in a moment of weakness. Still, her eyes were red-rimmed and glassy as she turned around, holding the onion skin, by way of explanation. Monique seemed to think nothing of it. She herself was very sensitive to the smell. It had probably woken her.

'You are hungry then?' she asked. 'You don't feel sick anymore?'

There was a keen edge of hope to Monique's questions. For a muddle-headed idealist, she had proven herself to be a lot tougher and more reliable than the American had thought possible. Long accustomed to isolation and loneliness, Caitlin had allowed herself to relax just a little around her companion.

She drained the pasta and poured it into a large serving bowl, tipping the rich, steaming sauce over it straight away. 'Right now I'm fine,' she replied. 'So I'm going to eat, if you want to join me. A bit late for dinner, I know, but I have to take what I can get at the moment.'

'I'm hungry too,' Monique conceded. 'I have not eaten since this morning. It is so difficult to get good food, *non*?'

Caitlin ladled two large serves of the meal into a couple of old china bowls that had seen better days. 'It doesn't help that we can't move about freely because of me,' she said. 'I'm sorry about that, Monique. I'm sorry you got caught up in all this.'

'All this?' The French girl gestured expansively, taking in the disintegrating city, and a whole world of hurt beyond it. '*This* is not your doing. This would have happened whether we had ever met or not. Look out there. It is so sad. People behaving so badly towards each other. That is not your doing.'

She was gesturing towards the window where Caitlin had been standing earlier. With the apartment in darkness, the fires burning through the outer 'burbs stood out prominently against large swathes of blacked-out city. Here and there, blue and red strobes marked the passage of emergency vehicles, but they looked . . . inadequate. Paris was heading towards a tipping point. Caitlin doubted most of the city's residents realised that yet. Not down in their marrow, anyway. As soon as they truly understood what was coming, the unrest of the present moment would probably give way to savage anarchy. It would be a little while yet, however. The civilised mind was slow and deeply reluctant to throw off the habits of a lifetime, which meant that Caitlin and Monique still had a chance to escape.

They moved through to stand by the window as they forked up the pasta. It had become something of a ritual between them, a way to push back the walls. It wasn't so much a problem for Caitlin, but Monique felt very much the press of claustrophobia as their time in the hide-out dragged on, and the city itself seemed to contract around them, the sky lowering, the streets becoming mean and pinched and increasingly filthy. And of course, there were hunters, somewhere out there, still looking for them. The lack of a police response to the events at the Pitié-Salpêtrière, the appearance of more anonymous gunned-up suits and the vans outside Caitlin's other 'official' safe house did more to convince Monique that she'd been caught up in something weird and dangerous than anything Caitlin had said. She was not a believer. She hadn't gone across to the dark side, as the American wryly put it. But she was more trusting of Caitlin than she had been, more willing to go along with her call.

The two women ate in silence, enjoying the luxury of being warm, dry and well fed in a world that had turned inexplicably hostile, just a few inches away, on the other side of a windowpane.

The recipe wasn't perfect, but it was close enough to her dad's to be both comforting and upsetting to Caitlin. She had accepted the fact of her family's death. They were gone and the shock of it was doubly unsettling because she had never expected to outlive them. The familiar scent and taste of the dish brought home a flood of memories and threatened an even greater flood of tears. She would allow herself to grieve later. She knew that such feelings couldn't be bottled up without doing damage. But likewise, she was not ready to let her guard down in front of Monique, no matter how much closer they had become under the stresses of the last week. In the end, she told herself, the French girl was just a contact on a job that had gone wrong.

'We can't stay here, you know, Monique. We will have to get going, and soon.'

'But where? And how? Travel is so difficult for everyone right now. And for you it is worse. Where would you even go?'

Caitlin nodded. Three men ran through the intersection below, all of them young and white. Two had shaved heads while the third wore his lank, dark hair in a ponytail. They seemed to be laughing, but running as fast as they could. Whether towards or away from something, she could not tell. She waited for some further development but the cobbled street, wet with acidic rain and glowing a sick, jaundiced yellow under the street lamps, remained deserted.

'Things are better in England,' said Caitlin. 'The government seems to have a stronger grip.'

'Social fascists,' replied Monique with a shrug. 'And racist too. Putting the army on the streets like that. And only in the Muslim districts, of course.'

Caitlin didn't rise to the bait. There was no passion in the delivery. It was almost as though her companion was reciting a lesson by rote. A few days ago Caitlin would have argued with her, pointed out that the army had gone where the violence was worst. But she stayed silent and Monique abandoned her polemic, switching to a practical protest.

'How would you get there, to England?' she asked. 'The border is closed.'

'I'm not a tourist, baby.'

'No. I suppose not. But you are still hunted, *non*?'

'*We* are still being hunted,' Caitlin reminded her.

'Do you think? Really? Don't you think they have bigger problems? After all, you are no longer working on your mission, are you?'

For the first time in many days, an accusing tone crept back into Monique's voice, but unlike the first twenty-four hours after their escape from the hospital, it was unaccompanied by any whining or hectoring. If Caitlin wasn't mistaken, Monique was almost gently mocking her.

'No,' she admitted. 'The mission's been scrubbed. By me, by circumstance, or whatever. My priority now is getting the hell out, and I will take you with me, if you still want to come. But if you believe you're safe here, I'll go alone.'

Monique held her gaze for a long moment, lifting her chin in an almost defiant gesture. 'What was your mission, Caitlin? Why did you lie to us? And why did those men kill Maggie and the others?'

Caitlin shook her head as she put down the empty bowl. 'I don't know why they were killed, Monique. I've told you that. It was probably just a fuck-up. I don't think it had anything to do with my mission, although it obviously had something to do with me, since I'm the one they were trying to grab.'

'But we were your mission. Your *target*.' She said the word with more venom than Caitlin was expecting.

'No, you weren't,' the American replied, trying to sound soothing without being patronising. She paused then, on the verge of
a significant departure. To go on would be to acknowledge that
not just the mission, but her whole world, had been scrubbed. She
stared out of the window, looking at but not really seeing the bleak
scene below. She missed Wales, missed the security of knowing he
was out there somewhere, watching her back, keeping her safe.

She felt guilty at being unable to help him, but of course there
was no way of knowing whether he was even in the country when
the Disappearance went down. He may well have been out of
Paris or out of France altogether, especially with her laid up at the
hospital for so long. He may have been in Washington.

Her training reasserted itself. Putting aside pointless speculation, she had to go with what she knew, addressing the situation
right in front of her. 'You were going to lead me to my target,' she
explained. 'To a man, a blind recruiter, called al Banna.'

Monique looked confused. 'But I don't know any blind men.'

Caitlin shook her head. 'Sorry – jargon. Al Banna's not blind.
You are. He had targeted your group as mules, carriers. You were
going to take something back to the UK for him.'

'What bullshit.' And in an instant, the old Monique was back,
her face an angry mask of disbelief. 'I've never heard of this al
Banna. None of the others mentioned such a name. Do you take
us for fools?'

Caitlin kept her face professionally blank at that question, but
Monique seemed not to notice. A switch had flipped over somewhere and a torrent of impacted rage was released.

'We are not idiots, you know, Caitlin. We are not *blind* or even
one-eyed, like *some*. We saw oppression and violence on all sides,
not just from you and your masters. I have worked as a volunteer
in a women's shelter; I have seen what happens under the burqa,
non? The broken arms, the smashed ribs and bruises everywhere.
Do not imagine that just because we opposed your stupid oil war,
we did not understand the nature of your enemies. You were as
bad as each other. They may even have been worse, possibly, but
they lacked your *means*. So please, this stupid conspiracy of yours,
don't imagine that – '

'Monique,' Caitlin sighed, tired from a bone-deep weariness.

The inertia and fatigue in her voice seemed to trip the other girl up.

'What?'

She shook her head. 'Sweetheart, you'd already been recruited.'

'What do you mean?' Monique demanded to know. 'By who?'

Caitlin squared off and gave it to her cold. 'By your boyfriend.'

19

The Gurkhas were a real find, the first stroke of good luck they'd had in a week. The Nepalese warriors were long famed as members of one of the finest regiments in the British Army. Fearsomeness alone did not make them special, however – the world wasn't short of violent men. The Gurkhas were special because they combined a well-deserved reputation for savagery in battle with an equally well-founded renown for disciplined professionalism.

The British Army had recruited Gurkha infantry since the 1850s, and thousands still served in the regiment named for them. Such fame had they earned that former members were in high demand by private security concerns all over the world. Of course, this too made them little different from old boys of any of the world's A-list military outfits, but for Julianne Balwyn the five Gurkha warriors standing before her were of singular appeal because they had, until a week ago, been employed as shipboard security by Carnival Cruise Lines, headquartered in Florida.

Unfortunately, the Disappearance had robbed them of an employer and any way of getting home from Acapulco. Jules chewed at the stub of a pencil while she pondered exactly how much *legitimate* work she might have for them, but she pushed that thought to one side. For now, she needed some tough, reliable men who wouldn't fall apart if you pointed a gun at them, and who, just as importantly, she could trust not to sell her out.

'So, Mr Shah, how long did your serve in the regiment?'

'Twelve years, ma'am,' replied the short but powerful-looking man who acted as the group leader. His accent was quite polished, for a sergeant from Nepal. 'Four years as a private soldier. Eight as a non-commissioned officer.'

'A sergeant?'

'For the last six, yes, ma'am.'

Jules nodded as she scanned the employment history of the five men. The minimum any of them had served was six years. Shah had the longest stretch, at twelve. He was the only one who'd risen above corporal, making him the natural leader, even though they no longer took Her Majesty's coin. Jules was thankful for that last point – it made negotiating with them a simpler affair.

She leaned back in the old wooden chair behind a scarred table on which sat a small pile of papers, the men's résumés, and a loaded handgun within easy reach. A big shiny Mac 10, unsafed and set to full auto, for which she had traded away her former skipper's beloved yacht, the *Diamantina*. The beautiful wooden cruiser had been worth the gun, a thousand rounds of ammunition, two Mexican Army M16s, one crate of 5.56 mm reloads, and a half-pallet of rice, milk biscuits and flour, all packed tightly into bags stamped *A Gift from the People of America – USAID*. The guns and stores were secured in a cage behind the Gurkhas. She would've preferred to have transferred them to the super-yacht, but had decided with Fifi and Mr Lee that hiring reliable security was their first priority.

'Do you mind if I ask why you left the Cunard Line?' she asked. The men had all been employed by the premier British cruise liner, and some had even worked on the *QE2*. In her admittedly biased opinion, signing on with the Florida-based party-boat operators, Carnival, was not the first step on the happy staircase to success.

'Downsizing,' said Shah. Coming from him, the western technobabble sounded almost alien. 'The labour hire firm that subcontracted our services to Cunard was bought out by P&O, who were taken over by Carnival a year later. We were transferred to their Caribbean operations a fortnight ago. We were to pick up our next berth here at Acapulco.' The former sergeant shrugged as a way of finishing his explanation.

Jules sighed. 'Say no more.'

The dockside warehouse she'd hired was a long way from the resort town's tourist centre, but she could make out the beachfront apartments and hotels through a greasy, unwashed window to her right. One of the bigger towers was ablaze, with flames leaping high over the top floor. It was a moot point whether anybody was trying to put it out. Most likely not. The lower floors were probably being looted as she sat there.

'Well, Mr Shah. My father would have been impressed with your regimental connections. He was a Navy man, but he didn't hold with all that inter-service rubbish. And he thought very highly of Cunard. It's a pity you got shafted like that.'

She didn't mention that the old rogue had been banned by Cunard for cheating at cards on a cruise through the Med ten years earlier, and how only a swift return by his lordship of the swindled funds and an abject apology to his victims had kept the rozzers from becoming involved. Shah looked like the sort of chap who'd throw card cheats over the side.

Instead she continued: 'I'd be very keen to take on you and your men, Mr Shah, but there are two issues we need to settle. One I don't see causing much difficulty; the other, however, we'll have to see.'

Julianne spoke directly and forcefully, never taking her eyes off the man she was addressing. Behind him, his companions remained as immobile as stone dogs.

'Firstly, this won't be a pleasure cruise. My ship – which, you should know straight off, we boarded and took over after the original crew disappeared behind the event horizon last week – has already been attacked once. My captain was killed, and in turn we killed every one of the pirates attempting to seize the vessel. I do not expect that will be the last trouble we see. I cannot guarantee anyone's safety, quite the contrary, but we will endeavour to avoid whatever hazards we can.' She gestured back over his shoulder to the view of downtown Acapulco. 'I probably don't need to tell you that things are going to get worse, do I?'

'No,' agreed Shah. 'The risks are acceptable. And your second point?'

'Payment,' she said. 'And length of contract. Without a stable currency in which to negotiate, we are stuck with bartering for your services. As a minimum I promise free passage to the port of your choosing in Asia, at which point our business together will be deemed complete. Right now, I cannot give you a schedule. We might get there in a few weeks, it could be six months. Over and above passage, you'll require payment. I'm happy to hear any suggestions you might have about how we calculate a reasonable figure.'

Shah nodded slowly, his eyes peering into an unknowable future. She noted he didn't consult his men.

'Gold,' he said at last. 'We shall settle on an amount of gold, the value to be calculated at the end of the cruise, based on an equivalent pay scale to that which we would have earned with Carnival, plus hazard pay at current regimental rates, for each day spent in combat. The pay of any man killed or totally and permanently disabled to be delivered to his family by those surviving, along with a compensation payment to the value of his entire contracted fee. As to length of service, we would insist on an end to the contract within twelve months of its commencement.'

It was Jules's turn to nod sagely and give the impression of hard thought. She quickly toted up what she was getting into and figured it to be worth about half of their current liquid assets. A lot, in other words. On the other hand, there would doubtless be ample opportunity for 'salvage' in the near future. And, if she could just get to the Caymans before everything turned completely pear-shaped, she might be able to access her own accounts, and maybe even Pete's. Beyond that broad-brush plan to cash up and lay in stores, she wasn't sure what they would do. Lee was no more interested in returning to his home village than she was in heading for England, where there were still warrants out for her arrest on charges relating to the money her father had sent her. As for Fifi, whatever sorry excuse for home and hearth she'd once had was now lost behind the energy wave. It was possible they might well end up going with Pete's original plan and heading for Tasmania. It was far enough from everywhere to be safe, surely, and he'd insisted it was one of the few places in the world that would still be able to feed itself following a core meltdown of the old world order.

After a moment's consideration she glanced at the men behind Shah. 'Do you mind if I talk to your men?' she asked him.

'No. Ask them what you will.'

'Are you men okay with that offer? Do you need to discuss it?'

The briefest of nonverbal conferences took place, with each man quickly exchanging glances, shrugs and nods with each other.

'That will be acceptable,' replied the man standing nearest to Mr Shah. Jules was pretty certain it was the former corporal, Birendra. His first name was as long as a Himalayan mountain path, and just as difficult to negotiate.

'Good-o, then,' said Jules. 'Mr Shah, if you would like to work out the precise figures, we shall draw up a contract today. I'd like to get some of your men out to the yacht as soon as possible, but I will need two of you here with me over the next couple of days as we take on crew.'

Shah grunted in affirmation and, she was sure, nearly saluted her. 'Corporal Birendra will take Subba and Sharma out to the vessel. I will remain with Thapa and you.'

'Okay,' said Jules, still unsure who was who, other than Shah and possibly Birendra. She did note the use of the military rank, too. 'I imagine you fellows will have personal effects you want to pick up. And I suppose there's a bill for your accommodation to be worked out?'

'Yes and no,' replied Shah. 'We have personal items to gather. For the last week, however, we have provided security to our hotel in return for lodging. No bill.'

And soon after you're gone, no hotel, Jules thought to herself. 'Just one other thing, Mr Shah – or would you prefer "Sergeant"?'

'That is your choice, Miss.'

'Okay then. Your men here – I'm sorry to have to ask, and I mean no disrespect – but do they all speak good English? It's just that it could be an issue in a tight spot, couldn't it?'

Shah's face split open into a wide grin. 'The Queen's English, ma'am. With a touch of sarf London, from the instructor in their barracks.'

'All right,' Jules smiled. 'That will do fine. If you would like to detail a small party to pick up your gear from the hotel, I'll draft up some papers for you to check and sign if acceptable. Then I'll need your help transferring those stores behind you to my boat. We'll run out to the yacht, you can meet the others, secure the ship, and then you and I and Mr . . . Thapa, was it? – we'll get back on shore and round up some reliable crew.'

Shah indicated his agreement but he had one more question. 'Do we have a destination, Miss?'

'Please, "Jules" will be fine. And no, I have no idea where we are headed initially. Just the hell away from here and that bloody wave.'

It was late before they returned to port. Shah's men loaded the cruiser in less than an hour, but motoring to and from the *Aussie Rules* was a nine-hour round trip. For now the marina's own security staff, boosted by some freelance heavies, were more than up to the task of securing her boat and the small dockside lock-up against any looters, but that wouldn't always be the case. She was quietly relieved when Thapa took up watch on the 42-footer, while she and Mr Shah plotted out their next move.

It was coming up on ten at night, and the dock was well lit, courtesy of a diesel-fired generator she could hear droning away in the distance. Incredibly, she could also hear music, laughter and the tinkle of glasses drifting across from the more expensive berths, where a large number of luxury yachts were docked, one of them as big as her own. Apparently the owners and their guests had enough money and muscle to convince themselves they could remain unaffected by events outside the marina. Not all of the berths were occupied, however. Jules calculated that a third were empty, the boats that normally filled them having lit out already. But of those who had stayed, it seemed most were intent on pretending they could hold back reality with good cheer and hired guns.

Acapulco proper, though, was a patchwork of light and dark. From the flying deck of the cruiser, parts of the city looked entirely normal. Lights twinkled in houses and apartments, traffic streamed along the waterfront, and throngs of people were visible through the big pair of Zeiss binoculars she'd brought back from the *Rules*. Elsewhere, chaos reigned. Buildings burned and the pop and crackle of gunfire was constant. Sirens had wailed through the first few nights, but they were becoming less frequent. In fact, Jules couldn't recall the last time she'd noticed one. She poured three cups of coffee and silently thanked God that the thick blanket of toxic waste released by the burning of hundreds of empty American cities had drifted east, and not south. She was convinced this place would be falling apart a lot more quickly if a nuclear winter had descended as it had in Europe.

'Thapa, come get your brew,' barked Shah, as he handed a steaming mug down to the heavily armed rifleman on the deck below. Thapa took his drink with a grateful bow of the head and a smile for Jules, making her feel much better about having to hire and trust so many strangers with guns.

She couldn't help wondering how Pete would have played all this. Badly, she guessed, given that his first thought had been to team up with Shoeless Dan, just a couple of hours before Dan had attacked and killed him. She still missed the old fool, though. They'd been good friends, even if Pete had just a little too much of the surf bum about him to trust in a situation like this. He took his business seriously, and he was a smart bloke who'd played the odds as well as anyone she knew of. But in the end he was like so many Australians she'd met – ultimately prone to falling back on a naïve, almost childish belief that everything would work out for the best.

Nothing in Julianne Balwyn's life led her to believe that. To an outsider, to someone like Shah, for instance, she must surely have appeared as just one more rich oik, the lucky child of old landed gentry, wasting the advantages of the best schools, an ancient title, and a thousand years of hereditary privilege. For Jules, however, her old life was an anxious, contingent affair, where the pressure to maintain appearances was grossly aggravated by the manifest inadequacies of two parents whose laziness and selfishness were exceeded only by their sense of entitlement. She was well rid of all that bullshit.

'Okay,' she said. 'We're not going to need bartenders or butlers, but looking over the old crew manifest, we will easily need more than a dozen warm bods to run the engine room, the bridge, the IT systems, and do general deck duties. Probably be an idea to have a ship's doctor too, if we can find one. A proper helmsman who could handle the tub in a bad blow. A navigator for when the GPS goes down ... I mean, where does it end? How do I pay them all?'

Shah swallowed his coffee in one long draw. 'You don't,' he replied with a single, emphatic shake of the head. 'They pay you.'

'Beg your pardon?' Jules was perplexed, but intrigued.

In reply her new security chief held up the empty mug. 'This coffee, Miss Julianne, it came from your own stores. But if you had bought it here today, on shore it would have cost you twenty-five euros.'

That caused a raised eyebrow, but on reflection it shouldn't have. She already knew that raging inflation and currency collapse had reduced the worth of the greenbacks they'd stowed away in the *Diamantina* to a fraction of their face value. That's why she'd got rid of them so quickly. The small office and waterfront store she'd rented here for five days had cost fifty thousand US dollars upfront. Now it would probably be a six-figure sum, but she was a lot more sanguine about that than she had been a week earlier. As soon as they'd hit port she'd moved to unload most of the cash as quickly as possible, and had managed to get forty cents on the dollar, taken in the form of fuel, stores, gold, medicine and arms, most of it now safely aboard the *Aussie Rules*.

Shah moved to the railing of the boat's flying bridge and gestured at the party scenes around the marina. 'For now, these people are comfortable,' he said. 'They have food, shelter, safety, power.'

He turned away and pointed to the brighter, more chaotic night-time scene of Acapulco central, where uncontrolled fires duelled with neon and fluorescent light to hold back the darkness. 'Over there,' he continued, 'some people are still fine, but many are beginning to suffer and to fear for themselves. Soon, everyone will be afraid. A cup of coffee, a loaf of bread, it could be worth more than your life. People will pay you to get them away from that.'

'American refugees?' she pondered aloud. The richest, whitest refugees in the world. It was a bizarre thought, but entirely logical when you considered where events were headed, or indeed where they were right now. 'Where would we take them?

Alaska? Hawaii? The last I heard people were leaving Hawaii, not going there. I don't think they're even letting new people in. Same with Seattle, I think. Aid shipments in, flights out, and that's it.'

Shah moved his shoulder almost imperceptibly. His version of a shrug. 'If you have English-speaking passengers, take them to an English-speaking port. England, New Zealand, Australia. They are not closed and they will accept refugees, especially with money.'

'By the time we get there, though, any money they have will be worthless,' countered Jules.

'US dollars, certainly,' he agreed. 'But yen or pounds or euros – some surviving currency – they will be acceptable. At least to us, in the short term, for the purposes of provisioning. It would help you too, Miss Julianne,' he added, with a knowing smile.

'How so?'

'The yacht is not yours, no? The owner, a famous man, the original passengers and crew, they are gone. But even so, you will need to have some legitimate reason for having taken her over. Ferrying refugees away from danger, especially Americans, to friendly countries – to friendly *frightened* countries – it could make your passage into any harbour much less difficult. You could be a hero, a rescuer, not a villain and a smuggler.' His eyes glinted with real humour in the dark.

'You're not quite the ramrod-straight, do-it-by-the-book type you first appear, are you, Sergeant?'

'No good sergeant is, Miss Julianne.'

Jules let her eyes wander over the distant vista of the city as it disintegrated. Long strings of beaded light, the headlights of cars leaving town, wound up into the hills behind the bay. Camp-fires burned here and there, pushing back the blackness, while occasional flashes of light betrayed either cameras or gunfire. A huge blaze had engulfed a high-rise tower, the flames shoot-ing upwards like a giant roman candle, and yet not far away she could see candy-coloured neon and a pair of searchlights, picking out a nightclub where (local rumour had it) you could still dine and drink as though nothing had happened, as long as you could meet the very steep cover charge.

'Okay,' she said, making up her mind. 'Crew first. They work for their passage or they get left behind. We'll start here, at the marina, by putting out word we're offering a berth to qualified hands. But you and I might head out tonight, hit the right bars, gather the first of our flock. We can trawl the international hotels tomorrow, looking for passengers.'

'And where will we offer passage to, Miss Julianne?'

'Somewhere big and safe and far away. Somewhere the toxic cloud won't reach. Somewhere that can feed itself. Defend itself, if need be.'

Shah gave her a quizzical look, inviting her to go on. Jules nodded at a framed photograph fixed to the starboard bulkhead. It showed the boat's previous owner, Greg Norman, teeing off at Royal Sydney.

'In for a penny, in for a pound. Let's take his boat back home for him, shall we?'

20

The scientist droned on, baffling everyone with his impenetrable waffle and jargon-bluster, and in the end it all came to 'We don't know shit'.

'The phenomenon remains non-responsive to magnetic resonance scans,' said Professor Griffiths. He was a small, round, red-headed toad of a man who'd added yet one more element of misery to Tusk Musso's existence since his arrival at Gitmo with the National Laboratory team to study the Wave. 'The precise mechanism by which the phenomenon effects the transubstantiation of certain organic matter to energistic potential remains non-obvious . . .'

As he burbled on, the general surreptitiously checked his watch. Griffiths and his eggheads had flown in a few days earlier from Seattle, via Pearl, and Musso remained convinced that Mad Jack Blackstone had facilitated the move as some sort of malicious practical joke. Given the paucity of findings the Nat Lab guys had so far turned up, Griffiths chewed up an enormous amount of Musso's time and energy with resource requests he simply could not fulfil.

'Our investigations continue,' the scientist concluded.

Man, I hope that's a conclusion, thought Tusk. 'Any questions?' asked the Marine, getting to his feet and addressing the room.

Everyone remained unnaturally still. They had learned never to give Griffiths an opening. Ask him how high the Wave went, and you were liable to get a half-hour dissertation on electron orbits.

'Very good,' said Musso hurriedly. 'Bang up presentation there, doc, as always. You keep at it. Get back to us with anything new, of course. But don't feel the need to interrupt your research otherwise –'

'Well, about my research, General. This exclusion zone you've established along the line of the phenomenon – '

'Is not open for discussion . . . Sergeant!'

A Marine Corps gunny rolled up to the podium like an Abrams tank with the throttles thrown wide open. He double-timed Professor Griffiths out of the conference room, closing the door firmly behind them.

Tusk relaxed slightly. He wasn't being unfair. Everyone had been intrigued and even a little excited when Griffiths had arrived with two pallets full of scientific equipment, but exposure to the man, coupled with a rapid realisation that neither he nor anyone else had yet figured out jack shit about the Wave, tended to dampen that enthusiasm.

He was a five-star pain in the ass.

'Okay,' said Musso, with more relief than was seemly. 'I can see we lost two or three KIA from boredom there. Not a bad result. Ensign Oschin, you got my PowerPoint files ready?'

'Coming online now, sir.'

'Thank you, Oschin. Put it straight up.'

General Musso rubbed at a freshly scabbed-over bloodspot on his shaved head. He'd knocked a small divot out of himself fucking around under a desk earlier, fixing up a data cable that'd come loose. His fingers came away with a few tacky spots of blood and he had to pat down the wound with a piece of tissue paper while he waited for the vision from the Global Hawks.

Two of the giant, experimental UAVs were over the continental US at that moment, covering Miami and Kansas City. In contrast to the first moments after the Disappearance hit, when everyone had been wired and speeding on fear of the unknown, the feeling in the expanded op centre was now resigned and sombre. Everyone knew what to expect from the footage. Empty cities. Deserted streets. Massive pile-ups on the road networks. Some burning buildings, many more charred ruins. Stillness. Ditches and craters of burning ruin in the fields where aircraft had gone down over what many called 'Flyover Country', in the Midwest. Where there should have been cattle or horses, there were charred spots and grassfires, especially in west Texas.

Mega-fires still blazed across the length of America, spewing unknowable tonnages of pollution into the atmosphere. Thankfully, there had been only two meltdowns in a couple of older nuclear plants when the auto shutdowns failed – at Browns Ferry in Alabama and Hartsville, South Carolina. On the other hand, many coal-fired plants went up for want of human attention or computer intervention. But in these two metro centres at least, the worst of the conflagration was over. Indeed, it never really started. Cold, soaking rain had hosed down most of the initial outbreaks in Kansas City. An airliner had speared into a power station in Miami, killing the grid before an untended waffle iron or hair curler was able to burn down half the city. Satellite imagery confirmed similar strokes of luck had spared dozens of other cities, but hundreds more had been incinerated. The number of population centres lost came to thousands, however, once you counted all the minor towns and burgs that had gone up for one reason or another.

'Miami on the right-hand screen, KC to the left, General.'

Musso thanked Ensign Oschin again, even though the two cities didn't look much alike and there was no trouble telling one from the other. The footage of Kansas City was trisected by a meeting of the Kansas and Missouri rivers in the centre of the metropolis. No beaches, that was for certain. Musso had been to nearby Fort Leavenworth during the course of his career, for some joint-forces training with the US Army. It had been the coldest winter he had ever experienced and he certainly wasn't eager to go back there any time soon.

'Okay,' said Musso, as he turned to address the tightly packed group of officers seated on plastic chairs behind him. 'This is a highlights package, cut together an hour ago from twelve hours of coverage by our two Hawks.'

Fifteen men and women had squeezed into the small room for the briefing, including Lieutenant Colonel Pileggi, who'd flown up from Joint Task Force Bravo in Honduras the previous day. The senior SOUTHCOM representative sat in the front row with a notepad and pen at the ready. She and Musso were supposed to present a plan to Ritchie that evening to evacuate any and all US citizens who wanted to go, from South and Central America to an as-yet-undetermined location. It meant moving hundreds of thousands of people God only knew where. But certainly not to Gitmo. It already had a diabolical refugee problem.

Musso thumbed a control stick and brought up the first set of images. Still shots from the downtown areas of both cities. 'I'm afraid there's nothing new to report here,' he announced. 'Just better imaging than we've had so far. The power grid in both cities has failed, meaning there's less chance of a catastrophic urban firestorm starting up, although spot fires continue to break out here and there for whatever reason.'

Musso examined the Kansas City screen, which displayed the footage of a burnt-out Quiktrip on Armour Boulevard, across from a post office and a couple of larger buildings in Northtown. He never could keep all of Kansas City's various townships and municipalities straight when he was there. The Heart of America Bridge along with the Paseo and Hannibal bridges showed evidence of multi-vehicle pile-ups, some of which had combusted and later burnt out in the schizophrenic weather of the Midwest. A train had derailed on the ASB Bridge next to the Heart of America and dumped itself into the Muddy Mo. One of the towers, he couldn't tell which one, looked like it had been slashed with something – probably a Cessna or a Learjet from Downtown Airport.

On the other screen, a Walmart Supercenter on 88th Street in Miami had been reduced to a smouldering shell. Several watercraft in a variety of flavours and sizes had washed up on the beaches and canals. Musso couldn't help but be struck by the similarity between these images and those stolen from blasted landscapes throughout the Balkans and in Kuwait after the Iraqi invasion. There was one major difference, of course: no bodies.

'We chose these two cities for the Hawks, partly because they remain comparatively undamaged, and also because local weather patterns have temporarily cleared away some of the pollutants that are choking the air pretty much everywhere else. That won't last.'

He thumbed the control again, and the twin displays appeared to blink, as they switched to a different video stream.

'You're now looking at imaging taken from Montgomery, Memphis and St Louis as the first bird made its way up to KC.'

The screens reformatted into a series of windows, all showing bleak, grey landscapes that reminded Musso of photographs of old industrial towns, where soggy ash and acid rain permanently blanketed the landscape, leaching the colour from everything. A couple of low grunts and a curse or two were evidence that some capacity to be surprised remained in his audience.

'This nuclear-winter effect has been replicated across the continental US, although not uniformly. As you might expect, the concentrations of airborne pollutants are most dense at the source, and data from our weather satellites indicates that a significantly thick tail measuring about a hundred and fifty to two hundred miles extends east from each of the largest cities to have burned. In some areas of the country, in certain parts of the Rockies and on the West Coast well to the north and south of the LA Basin, the concentration of particulates is not yet at critical levels. Because of a low-pressure system sitting off the coast this last week, Seattle did suffer some contamination from the mega-fires that burnt out Portland and Spokane, but that system moved east and dragged a good deal of the plume with it.'

The scratch on his head was bleeding again, forcing Musso to reach for another tissue with which to dab it. He patted down his pockets, unable to find one, until Colonel Pileggi passed him a Kleenex from a handbag down by her feet.

'Thanks, Susan. Feels like I'm bleeding out here.'

'Don't worry, General. Chicks dig scars.'

A strained chuckle ran through the tightly packed group and eased just a little of the utter hopelessness that had begun to take hold. Musso turned back to the briefing with at least some sense of purpose.

'Okay. Average temperatures under the particulate cloud are up to twenty degrees cooler than average, although again, that varies from one locale to another. The variations are much more pronounced inland than by the sea, and proximity to a major source has an effect too.'

'That solves Gore's global-warming problem,' Major Clarence snorted.

'Quiet on deck!' Lieutenant Colonel Stavros shouted.

Musso ignored the distraction and brought up satellite coverage of the Eurasian landmass.

'The plume has moved across Europe and is within two days of reaching the eastern seaboard of China. It is largely contained within the northern hemisphere between thirty and sixty degrees latitude. The climatic effects are less severe than on the North American continent, but they remain significant, and I'm told they'll probably deteriorate for another two to three weeks, before stabilising for six to twelve months.'

'There's a lot of wriggle room in those figures, General,' said Pileggi, as she looked up from scribbling in her notebook.

'Enough of a margin to mean the difference between a lot of people living and dying,' he agreed. 'I've been on at PACOM to tighten them up, but that's as good as they'll commit to for now. You know what scientists are like,' he added, shaking his head. The spectre of Professor Griffiths still haunted the briefing room.

The display returned to top-down street scenes in Miami and KC. Not a living thing moved anywhere in either city.

'The weather data is important to us because it directly affects our mission: the evacuation of all US citizens who want it, to a secure location, *as yet to be determined*.' Musso turned to Pileggi while he dabbed at his cut again. 'Your airfield is going to be vital in that effort to move from the Pacific to the Atlantic, Colonel, especially if we evacuate to Australia, New Zealand or our allies in Asia.'

'I understand, sir. If I may – what about defence assets?' Pileggi asked. 'Castro is gone, but Chavez isn't. I do not have any air cover to speak of outside of our allies in the region, and their air power isn't quite up to dealing with Hugo if he gets froggy. Plus, we're going to need to secure the Canal.'

'I know,' agreed Musso. 'I've been on to PACOM about that too. Pearl's promising whatever they can spare, but at the moment, that's nothing.'

The colonel persisted anyway. 'If they're serious about the refugee problem they need to find that brigade to secure the Canal,' she said. 'My staff have planned our side of any evacuation based on being able to ship people through Panama. If the government collapses – which is a pretty good bet – that canal is going to stop working. These locks are a century old and require ground crew to run them. At some very narrow points, the ships are actually pulled by tugs. All of these locations are extremely vulnerable to attack.'

Musso threw up his hands. 'I know all about it, Colonel. But at the moment, it's a tenth-order issue for them. I'll see what I can do to change that. We need to plan for the worst, though.'

'There are some contingency plans, but they are almost uniformly awful,' Pileggi went on. 'Some ships could try to head to Nicaragua and cross there. Most of Nicaragua can be crossed by travelling upriver to a point where the trip overland to the Pacific side is maybe eight to ten miles. The navy could pick up folks on the other side, but it would require heavy combat power on the ground to secure any transit, especially if Nicaragua goes under. Alternately, a convoy could sail around the tip of South America. But that route is vulnerable to Chavez and his navy. I also imagine there will be a significant rise in piracy throughout those waters should there be a breakdown in state control. Another option is to disembark any civilians on the Atlantic side of the Canal Zone, where our own forces could establish a defensive position of sorts. Those civilians would then be escorted overland to the Pacific side or to a useable airfield. Another nightmare.'

'I'll talk to Ritchie,' said Musso.

There was no avoiding it. Over a hundred civilian craft lay at anchor down in the bay, most of them carrying US nationals who'd gravitated to the nearest and most obvious symbol of American power still in existence in this part of the world. Just feeding them and supplying enough fresh water each day was a Herculean challenge. They couldn't stay. But getting them there was a non-trivial problem too. From Musso's perspective, maintaining control of the Panama Canal was still a number-one priority for the United States. At least in the short term. He was responsible for the transport and protection of any American refugees who requested it, and that meant putting most of them through Panama. Where they went after that was a matter for diplomatic negotiations underway in Pearl.

PACOM HQ, PEARL HARBOR, HAWAII

'It's the low season for tourism, so we have plenty of spare beds, but nobody's figured out how it would work – who'd pay, what arrangements we might need over the longer course, and whether you'd be looking at permanent resettlement and residency or eventual citizenship. But Canberra has authorised me to assure you that we'll take as many as you can send.'

Admiral Ritchie thanked the Australian Ambassador – the new ambassador, of course. The previous one had disappeared in Washington. His colleague from New Zealand added that her government would likewise accommodate as many 'displaced US citizens' as possible. New Zealand's diplomat preferred not to use the term 'refugee' and had twisted herself into linguistic knots once or twice trying to avoid it.

Ritchie placed a tick in a small hand-drawn box next to the letters 'A/NZ'. He looked over to the Japanese Consul-General, seated near the window giving onto a pleasant view of the small garden outside his office. A riot of colour framed the small, dark-suited man, a pink and orange spray of flowering bougainvillea.

'Mr Ude?'

'My government is more than happy for you to initially house as many of your countrymen and women as you can within your military facilities on our soil. And with the suspension of the academic year, there are a number of temporary rooms available on some college campuses . . .'

Ritchie couldn't help but notice the heavy qualifications in that statement, and he could feel the 'but' coming somewhere in the next few seconds.

'However,' Mr Ude continued, 'you will appreciate that accommodation is severely limited on the home islands, and cultural factors mean that resettling many of your citizens within our borders is likely to be so difficult as to be . . . unfeasible.'

Ritchie stamped down on his annoyance and cut to the point. 'But you'll take them in, for now, if we bring them?'

Ude nodded, seemingly thankful for having something to offer. 'Yes. Within such limits as are to be confirmed by my government.'

Ritchie placed a tick in the box next to 'Japan' but then placed a small question mark after it and wrote *Limits*. A similar notation sat next to 'France', which maintained a number of colonial outposts in the Pacific, all of them well served by tourist infrastructure. In fact, a small forest of question marks surrounded the tick he'd placed next to France. His direct negotiations with the authorities in Noumea and the decolonised French territory of Vanuatu had initially gone well, but they had since referred all of his enquiries to Paris, and getting any kind of timely or useful response from Chirac or de Villepin was becoming nigh on impossible. Still, with firm commitments to help from Australia, New Zealand, Brazil and Chile, in addition to all of the larger independent island states such as Fiji, Ritchie could begin to stitch together a patchwork of temporary refuge for most of the five million souls in the American diaspora. He had about a quarter-of-a-million berths he could call on throughout the rest of the region, but Ude was right: countries like Japan and Korea weren't swimming in spare room, and many Westerners simply would not cope with the culture shock of being dropped in there even under the best of circumstances.

Ritchie twice tapped the ballpoint of his pen on the notepaper, as if sealing the deal, and leaned back from the conference table around which sat a dozen civilians, most of them foreigners. The only American not wearing a uniform was the lawyer, Jed Culver, sitting in for Governor Lingle's office. His blue pinstriped suit was every bit as crisp as the day they'd met at the state capitol, and Ritchie could only wonder where the man was getting it cleaned. He surely couldn't have brought more than one suit on vacation, could he?

Culver's presence, although much appreciated for the way he could smoothly negotiate a passage through the most impenetrable thicket of bullshit, only served to remind Ritchie that very little had been done to settle the issue of executive authority. Indeed, given the mess in Seattle, it was only getting worse. General Blackstone was cracking heads there, but Ritchie was beginning to wonder whether he was stomping down a little too hard. He'd virtually cut the state off from the outside world, save for aid shipments and chartered flights for foreign nationals. And under any other circumstances you'd have to describe some of his measures as a touch excessive. But Ritchie had no time to go meddling in Blackstone's command. Stopping that nuthatch city from imploding was probably beyond the abilities of any normal man. Mad Jack was welcome to the job.

Ritchie turned to the lawyer now, formally introducing him to the meeting. 'Mr Culver, who's here as a representative of the Governor, the highest civilian authority we have at the moment, has a number of issues he needs to work through with you, ladies and gentlemen, regarding humanitarian aid and any possible resettlement scheduling.'

'Thank you, Admiral,' said Culver, smiling at the group.

'But if you'll excuse me,' Ritchie added, 'I'm not needed for the next part of this meeting, and I do have an important video-conference. Please, stay seated . . .' He waved the Japanese Consul-General back down into his chair and withdrew as Culver thanked the diplomats for their countries' help so far.

An aide was waiting for him at the door and ushered Ritchie down the hallway to a temporary communications room he'd ordered set up a few days earlier. Running hither and yon across the scattered PACOM campus was a frustrating timewaster and he had moved quickly to consolidate his most important functions right here in the old white stone colonial building where he'd been quartered before the Disappearance.

'Generals Musso and Franks are on line, Admiral. But I'm afraid the secure link to Brussels is out, so we can't get General Jones in conference,' explained his aide, a navy commander called Oakshott. 'Also, I'm still having trouble getting Fort Lewis on line.'

'Well, keep on it. I know we've got links dropping out everywhere but this system was supposed to survive a first strike. So I don't see why it should be so goddamn flaky now.'

'No, sir. We're on it, but it's not just the links, Admiral.' Oakshott handed him a sealed envelope with a red stamp and marked, *Top Secret – Echelon. Your Eyes Only.*

'What the hell now?' grumbled Ritchie as they turned into the comms facility, which had quickly been christened 'the Radio Shack' by the lower ranks. 'Just excuse me for one moment, Commander. If you'll apologise to the generals for the delay.'

'Yes, sir.'

Ritchie took himself off into a small alcove attached to the main communications office, shutting a soundproof door behind him. The space was cramped, not much bigger than a closet, which indeed it had once been. He tore open the brown envelope and read the few lines of text, cursing under his breath as the import of the message became clear. 'That's all we fucking need.'

He crumpled the communiqué before regaining control of his temper, smoothing out the paper, and placing it back in the envelope. Then he hurried out of the alcove and over to the bank of monitors where he could see video images of Musso and Franks.

'Commander, safe-hand this back to my office, would you, and wait for me there. I'll reply when I'm done with the conference.'

'Aye, sir.'

Ritchie settled himself into a chair in front of the big flat screen, nodding at Musso and Franks. There were only four sysops in the small room, all of them cleared to the level of Top Secret Absolute. One of them handed him a headset, which he fitted himself before speaking.

'Please excuse the delay, gentlemen. Unavoidable, I'm afraid.'

On screen, both men nodded. They were all dealing with the unavoidable on a daily basis.

Ritchie continued. 'First point. This secure channel may not be secure. I'll explain by encrypted path later, but assume it's been compromised for now.'

He noted the immediate reaction of the two officers. They didn't go into a flap, but there was a noticeable stiffening of the sinews.

'Okay. We still have business to do. I've just come from a meeting with some of our regional allies and partners, and we now have firmed-up commitments from them to absorb any refugee flows. Some firmer than others, of course, but we can proceed with Operation Uplift.'

Musso's relief was palpable. He appeared to exhale a long, pent-up breath.

'General Musso, I'll send you a schedule of receiving ports in an hour. If you could get back to me soonest with a concept for getting any US nationals who want to go, out of the SOUTHCOM area, I'll start organising transport assets for you.'

Musso thanked him and appeared to scratch out a note to himself.

'General Franks, Uplift doesn't concern you as much in the immediate future, but it will when you've disengaged from the current operation. With a mind to my precaution about communications security, you want to update me with your latest?'

The commander of the Coalition forces in the Gulf looked as though he was chewing on nettleweed. He took a moment to gather his thoughts, obviously choosing what he could say over a possibly compromised channel. 'I have multiple situations evolving and deteriorating, Jim. Operation Katie is reaching the limits of its effectiveness. I have the Kuwaiti Government screaming at my liaison not to pull out of the theatre and citing line and verse of our treaty obligations. The Saudis and our other allies are doing the same.'

Marvellous, Ritchie thought. Just marvellous.

'The Kuwaiti armed forces are presently engaged along their front in the Wadi al Batin region, to the west of our lines. The British and the Marines are heavily engaged against an Iranian armoured sweep through al Basra towards their lines.' Franks ticked those items off a sheaf of paper. 'We are heavily attriting any force sent against us, regardless of their origin or nationality.'

Tommy Franks hadn't said anything that wasn't being reported by various surviving news networks. He was sticking to the public and the knowable. Ritchie wasn't surprised.

The general continued. 'The Iranians have contested our air supremacy over the theatre. At present, I've limited myself to asset defence.'

Ritchie pursed his lips and grunted an acknowledgement of Franks's vague allusions to the fact that the Iranian air force and navy were probably doing their best to try to sink every Coalition ship in the Persian Gulf.

Those Kilo subs of theirs will be a nightmare to find in the Gulf, Ritchie thought. He had half a mind to hammer America's so-called regional allies into sending their air and naval assets out to help hunt down the Iranians, citing the same treaties they were currently being hammered with.

'General, execute Oplan Damocles,' Ritchie said. No one

listening should know what that was. If they watched their news feeds, they'd know soon enough. But had he stepped over the line? he wondered. Hell, where was the line now?

Franks paused for a mere second before saying, 'Copy that, Admiral.'

See how the Iranians like that, Ritchie thought before he continued.

'We're in dangerous, unchartered waters here, gentlemen, if you'll forgive me the maritime analogy. This isn't just a military problem, it's political. But we have no political authority to lead us, and frankly I don't see that changing any time soon. The civilian leadership here is barely coping with local responsibilities. Just feeding the islands and maintaining order is keeping Governor Lingle busy twenty-five hours a day. She makes the point, quite reasonably, that she can do infinitely more in her current office. After all, her state government instrumentalities remain completely intact and functional, whereas almost everything at the federal level has disappeared. I get the same line from Alaska and Washington State. They might be bucketing out a sinking boat, but we're asking them to give up the bucket and the boat just to help us out. I don't think we should plan for a new executive to emerge any time soon. Certainly not soon enough to deal with your immediate concerns, General Franks.'

A brusque nod from Franks signalled his agreement. 'So, what do I do, Jim?' he asked.

The words seemed to come from outside Ritchie. 'If there is no political solution, we will have to find a military one. And fast.'

21

Sleep finally claimed her, but only after hours of pain, dulled in the end by a dangerously large dose of Advil. The argument with Monique had been titanic and galvanising, and she feared that it had cost her more than just a few hours' rest. Caitlin felt as though something vital had torn inside her head. She had lost her temper, and lashed out physically at one point, pushing Monique away from her, which only served to reinforce the French girl's certainty that she held the moral high ground. After Monique's initial shock at being pushed into the wall, Caitlin was sure she'd seen a smile and a small measure of triumph on her face.

'So, in the end it is always the same, Caitlin, yes?' she'd teased. 'If you cannot win by reason you will do so with violence.'

Caitlin had been unable to reply. She'd staggered backwards, suddenly losing her balance to a strong surge of nausea and a blinding stab of pain behind one eye. She'd collapsed and vomited up all of her dinner. Monique was beside her immediately.

She had to hand it to the chick, she didn't hold grudges. From a crazed harpy, screeching at Caitlin that she knew *nothing* about her boyfriend, she had switched without hesitation – propping her up, wiping the sick from Caitlin's face with the sleeve of her shirt and helping her over to the tatty, uncomfortable couch, where she lay, shivering, for the next hour, sipping a glass of cloudy, brackish tap-water. Monique had even apologised repeatedly for upsetting her when she was so sick.

She was genuinely remorseful. Caitlin didn't know whether to be aggravated or touched, and in the end it hadn't mattered. She was too sick to care. Sleep had only been possible after taking the painkillers, and she'd only managed that after three attempts. Her stomach was rebellious and disinclined to keep anything down. Eventually, however, she had drifted into a feverish, unsatisfying and fitful doze, waking frequently, or thinking she had, but never gaining full consciousness. The couch was just a few inches too short for her to stretch out comfortably, and the cushions were old and hard. She was so tired and drained, though, that it didn't matter. Her body needed to rest.

She found some peace by emptying her mind of all the troubles piling up around them, and imagining herself young again. Really young. Perhaps fifteen or sixteen, on a family beach holiday in Baja. Her dad was newly retired. Her older brother, Dom, was just about to leave home to take up a basketball scholarship all the way over in Vermont. Mom was still healthy. Caitlin lay shivering now in the darkness of the small, unheated apartment in a city tearing itself apart, and recalled an endless couple of weeks, surfing, swimming and hiking with her family. She managed a sad, lonesome smile at the memory of the surfing lessons she'd tried to give her parents. Her mother had wisely begged off after ten minutes, but Dad, he'd always been up for anything, and without the air force telling him what he could do with his life twenty-four/ seven, Dave Monroe vowed that he would spend whatever was left of it living as a surf bum. He was *probably* joking. He already had a civilian job lined up with an air-freight company run by some buds who'd handed in their uniforms a couple of years before he did. But it was nice, Caitlin thought, to have him there to herself, with no prospect that he would ever again be called away to some third-world suckhole to get shot at by whackjobs and savages. It was nice to think of him living a life of ease, if only for a little while. And it was a pure delight when she finally taught him to stand up and dial into a little baby wave that carried him all of ten or twelve feet, whooping and hollering before he went A-over-T into the drink. She fell asleep with that happy memory as her last thought.

It didn't last. Nightmares tormented her, some vivid, some half remembered. Her family was gone and she was left to wander a world denuded of love and kindness. She dreamed herself in a city she did not quite recognise, where decomposing bodies hung from lampposts. Swinging on rotted ropes, they twisted in the breeze and revealed themselves as her family – then Wales, even Monique. She ran and ran through the dream, deeper into a city where children laboured under the whip and scourge to build pyramids of severed heads, where monsters capered and ghouls in human form held dominion over all. Every barbarous malignancy of human nature was free to bloom and run free. She passed through this landscape of horrors as a shadow, unable to act, invisible to victim and tormentor alike. Every now and then she would come awake with her heart hammering and her mouth dry and she would attempt to find the happy place where she'd swum and played with her father in the surf off Baja, but to close her eyes meant falling back into dreams where the whole world had become a charnel house.

In the early hours of morning, sometime before the inky blankness of night gave way to the slightest hint of grey dawn she dreamed herself imprisoned in a cell, somewhere in the old fortress of Noisy-le-Sec. Her captors had beaten her, told her that as a 'floater', a deniable asset, she was already dead. She lay on an old cobblestone floor, in a pool of her own vomit and blood, her eyes closed almost shut by swelling. Two teeth were loose, probably knocked free of their roots. The pain from them alone was a hard, white supernova burning one side of her face. She could hear voices discussing her. Gutteral French, a smattering of German, and a few snatches of Arabic.

'She is already a ghost. Let us be finished with it now.'

'But the Americans, they know . . .'

'But they can do nothing! She is Echelon. She does not exist.'

'They dare to send her against us. They should learn such impudence is always punished.'

'There will be reprisals.'

'But of course!'

'Oh, it is fine for you, al Banna, you are not . . .'

She tried to wrench herself back towards consciousness. Al Banna. Her target. Monique's 'boyfriend'.

'It is all right for you. You are safe.'

'Nobody is safe.'

'She is not just a spy – she is a killer of the most dangerous kind.'

'Then ensure she does not kill again.'

'Bilal, it is not easy . . .'

Caitlin's head felt as though it was wrapped in heavy blankets. Exhaustion and illness weighed her down, pressing her back into sleep, but a small part of her, an echo of her waking consciousness, forced her up out of the troubled sleep. The dream came apart like mist before a hard wind. Her head reeled with dizziness, but she was immediately aware that the horrendous pain and nausea had gone. Not just eased, but gone, at least for the moment.

She became aware of everything. Her position, jackknifed on the short, uncomfortable couch. The threadbare blanket with which Monique had covered her. The smell of the meal she had cooked some hours before, and the rank stench of her having thrown it up. The pre-dawn darkness, tinted just the faintest orange by the glow of a far-off blaze. The ticking of a wind-up clock. Footsteps padding about in the apartment above her. And Monique's voice, talking to someone. Just her voice and occasional blank spots in the rhythm of a muttered conversation. She was on the phone.

A jolt ran though Caitlin's body, propelling her up off the couch and across the room. The sudden change left her balance reeling and she barked her shin painfully on a table leg, cursing but hurrying on. A phone call!

'Mother of Christ,' she hissed.

She heard Monique's voice falter, just before the *beep* of a terminated cell-phone call reached her.

'What the fuck are you doing? I said no calls! Who was that, Monique? Who was it?' Caitlin found her in the kitchen, pressed into a corner, looking scared.

'I am sorry. I'm so sorry, it's just I was frightened.'

The room was dark, the only light the residual glow of the tiny screen. It painted her features a garish yellow, before winking out and leaving them in darkness.

'Did you call your boyfriend, Monique?' Caitlin's voice was

flat and hard, a sheet of stamped iron slamming down between them. 'Did you call Bilal?'

Her reply was an almost inaudible squeak. 'I'm sorry, Caitlin. It is a new phone. Prepaid. I had to talk to him. I had . . .'

'Jesus Christ, Monique. How many times did I tell you, *no calls to anyone*? Let alone your boyfriend the terrorist.'

'He is *not* a terrorist . . .'

'Oh, I'm sorry. Did he pinky promise you that? Cross his heart and hope to die? Well then, I guess that's all right. I'll just go back to bed.'

Caitlin spun on her heels and stalked away, heading for the bathroom, where she tugged on the string to power up the one exposed bulb, before bending down to rip back a sheet of mouldy linoleum, exposing the wooden floorboards beneath. She reached one finger through a knothole, gave a tug, and the board came away. Another pull removed the piece of wood beside it. A thick, buff-coloured folder came out first. She sensed Monique coming up behind her but said nothing, busying herself with emptying the small arsenal she had stashed away beneath the floor.

No conversation passed between them. The only sound was Caitlin's breathing and the metallic rattle of weaponry and ammunition coming up out of the hiding place. She could feel Monique' wanting to say something, the air was almost alive with the tension growing between them. Caitlin didn't trust herself to respond rationally, however, so she decided to short-circuit any confrontation. 'There's a sports bag in the bedroom, would you please get it for me?' she asked, in as reasonable a tone as she could manage.

'Okay,' replied Monique in a small, frightened voice.

She returned a few moments later with an old Adidas bag, empty save for a few shopping items from their last trip out. Batteries, a flashlight, some energy bars. Caitlin began stuffing the guns and ammo into the holdall.

'I am sorry, Caitlin . . . It's just . . .'

'Forget it,' she snapped. 'It's my fault. *I* should have found the phone and taken it off you. You were always going to call someone. I should be apologising. I've lost my edge. This fucking tumour, the Disappearance, or whatever – it's fucked me up and we are going to get killed because of it. Not because you made a mistake. That's just . . . you. You're not trained. You have no experience. You don't think things through the way you need to now.'

She finished topping off the bag with the three passports and a stack of currency. After a pause, she tossed the greenbacks. They were just deadweight. The euros, about fifteen grand's worth, still had some residual value. Probably about half the purchasing power they'd had before Friday, 14 March. Caitlin hurried through to the small living area.

'I'm outta here. You can stay or come with me. If you stay, there's a good chance men will be here with guns very soon.'

'Because of my call.'

'Because of your call. To *Bilal*.' Caitlin turned and looked at her with real anger. 'If you come, there'll still be men with guns. At first it'll be like at the hospital – professionals, playing by the rules. Even if the rules have changed, and I don't know what the fuck they are anymore, there *will* be rules. But soon, very soon . . . no more rules. Just violence like you cannot imagine. You will have to change, Monique. You will have to grow up.'

'To be more like you?' Her tone was reproachful, almost sarcastic.

'To be like me. And Bilal.'

At that Monique rolled her eyes again and Caitlin pushed past her, not wanting to be delayed by another tantrum. She retrieved a small backpack from the bedroom and began cramming food into it. Trail food that she'd picked up from a camping store: freeze-dried meals, more energy bars and a couple of British-surplus MRE packages. It was getting lighter outside, the glow of the fires beyond the edge of the old city were throwing less of a dramatic light on the low, scudding toxic clouds that hung over Paris. Which hung over everything, she reminded herself.

'I am sorry . . .'

'Would you for chrissakes stop saying that and pack. We have to get out of here,' Caitlin insisted. 'Come on.' She led Monique through to the bedroom and pointed at another small backpack. 'Pack clothes and food. More of the latter,' she ordered.

'Okay, okay. But you are wrong about Bilal. I told him what you said . . .'

'A week ago that would have got you killed, but right now,

slow packing is what's threatening to end your life. Come on – move.'

Caitlin's ears pricked up at the sound of a distant siren. Her heart jumped forward a beat, but the sound tapered off. As Monique began to fill her pack with more supplies, the American retrieved a pistol from the holdall. A Glock 19 for herself and a .38 revolver for Monique, if needed.

'So what did he say exactly, your boyfriend, that is?'

Monique cinched shut the top flap, and flapped her arms theatrically. 'He said you were crazy. He was very understanding. He thought the Disappearance had driven you mad. There have been many instances amongst the Americans in Germany. Suicides, breakdowns and such.'

'So he's in Germany? At Neukölln, perhaps?'

Monique froze, a suspicious glare fixed on her face.

Caitlin smiled. 'That's right, I know where he lives. With his mom. Be cool – he is so off my to-do list now. Remember, I'm unemployed as of last week.'

The other woman eyed her doubtfully but finally swung the pack over her shoulder, ready to go. Caitlin rushed to put on a fresh pair of socks. She slipped into her old boots, donned the leather jacket she'd stolen from the hospital and loaded up. She wouldn't normally hit the streets weighed down with so much artillery, but any encounter they had with the cops was going to turn nasty. She had no doubt that both she and Monique were on watch lists with every agency of the state by now. The only question for her was whether the state would fall apart before it laid hands on them.

She checked her watch – 5.45 a.m. Fifteen minutes until the curfew was over. Fifteen minutes they probably didn't have.

At least the drizzle had stopped for now. She could see that the pavement and the road were still slick with acidic rain, but for now they could move about without the irritation of burning skin and stinging eyes. Caitlin checked the room for the last time, making sure they weren't leaving some vital piece of kit behind in the rush. The GPS batteries were dead but the satellite system itself, or at least the link to it, was increasingly sketchy, so the unit stayed on the table where she'd dropped it. Between them, they knew enough of the city to get away.

There was nothing to identify her. Unless the French security service had her DNA on file somewhere, and anyway, that sort of obsessiveness was no longer necessary. She'd already been blown. Echelon was gone. She was simply looking to save her own skin now, not to maintain operational security. It was liberating in a way – she could play a lot faster and looser because there were no rules. They might just make it.

If her illness didn't finish her off first.

As soon as they hit the street, both women were struck by the strength of the contamination still befouling the air. Caitlin had a flashback to her first time in India, when she'd stepped into a small curry house and had to step out again immediately, her eyes streaming and her throat burning from the dense mist of powdered chilli dust she'd inhaled. This wasn't quite that bad. It was at least bearable. But the deterioration in the atmosphere was still severe. At ground level the number of dead birds was spectacular. Perhaps the night had claimed more of them. They didn't quite carpet the ground, but it was impossible to walk in a straight line for more than a few metres without stepping on one.

'Man,' said Caitlin. 'This sucks. We should have masks. Let's get going. I want to find us a car with good filters.'

A week ago Monique would have protested and held them up. Now she nodded sombrely and hurried to keep up with her companion. Avoiding the birds, many of which still twitched and flapped feebly with the last sparks of life, slowed them down somewhat, and the noxious ether quickly burned their lungs and air passages. Caitlin had chosen an apartment in the 17th Arrondissement, north-west of the city centre, where the working-class tenements of Place de Clichy edged into the red-light district of Pigalle. There was still an abundance of smaller, cheaper rooms to be had in the area, one of the most densely populated in the capital. The brothels and strip clubs, the unlicensed bars and underground gaming halls all helped to create an outré environment where the police and other, more dangerous state actors were unwelcome.

'Why are you doing this, Caitlin?' Monique asked as they walked. 'Why are you helping? Surely you could move more quickly on your own. You must still have friends left in the city, or on the continent? You could disappear.'

'My friends have been *disappeared* already, Monique. My network's been rolled up. Remember those guys at the first apartment I tried to take us to? They were turning it over. My controller should have been there, to get me out. Maybe he was and they grabbed him, maybe he wasn't, but I haven't been able to contact him or anyone. The numbers I had, the internet addresses – they're all dead. And the net's useless anyway. It's falling apart. The people are gone, if they were back home, and missing, if they were here. But mostly they're gone. And I have to assume that all of my contacts have been compromised. I'm on my own, and in case you hadn't noticed, I'm a cot case. An invalid.'

They stopped outside a patisserie. It should have been open by now but the shopfront remained closed and the blinds were shut.

'I could sell you some line of bullshit, darlin'. That was a specialty of mine. You might not believe it, but I'm a bit of an empath. I have no trouble putting myself in somebody else's shoes. Just before I kill them, or arrange to have someone else kill them.'

Monique blanched and moved on, picking her way through more dead birds. Caitlin stepped up beside her, scanning the streets ahead for a vehicle. In this part of town, however, few people drove, and cars were few and far between. The streets were narrow and there was no garaging available for them. Everyone took the Métro or walked.

Caitlin went on. 'But there's no point shitting you, is there? You know the deal already. What I am, what I was doing.'

'*Oui*,' shrugged Monique.

'Bottom line is, I need you. I'm fucked up with this . . . tumour. The effects come and go. I'm fine right now but I still feel like shit. And I can never tell when I'm gonna lose it – fall on my ass, pass out, who knows what? So I could give you a line about how I'm responsible for you, how I got you into this mess and how honour demands I get us both out. But fact is, I'm fucked and I need your help. I have nobody else in what's left of the world.'

They came around a bend in the street and spied a minibus up ahead. A man was loading his family into it, with about a month's worth of supplies by the look of all the boxes and bags of food he was manhandling into the cabin. Monique caught Caitlin' scoping them out and was about to object but the assassin smiled crookedly.

'Don't worry. I'm not about to wax a bunch of kids and steal their ride. You have to have more faith in me. I know it's hard for you to believe, but people like that – normal, decent folks – in the end *they* were my mission. Protecting them.'

Monique examined her with wry detachment, almost tripping on a dead pigeon from not watching her footing. 'Not them so much, Caitlin,' she replied. 'They are French, and you are not. I know enough now about your world to understand what that means. You told me about Noisy-le-Sec, remember. And this Echelon is no secret. There have been books and news stories written, and a French government investigation. I read about it in *Le Monde*. Not so secret, no? It is a well-documented conspiracy of the English-speaking world.'

Caitlin smiled. 'There are knowns and there are unknowns, Monique. But you're right in one sense. Sometimes governments, agencies, whatever, they might set themselves against each other, but I'm talking about the wider picture. People like that . . .' – she nodded ahead at the family now loading the last of their number into the bus – 'people who want nothing more than to go about their own business, raising their kids, keeping them safe, giving them whatever chances they can to do better. The world they want to make is worth fighting for. They are worth defending.'

'Against my boyfriend?' asked Monique, giving full vent to her sarcasm.

Caitlin stopped and held her gaze. 'Yes.'

'*Merde alors* . . .'

They started moving again. Monique's shoulders had hunched forward and she was holding her arms stiffly by her sides. Caitlin recognised it as one of her tells: she was furious again.

She sighed. 'Bilal Hans Baumer,' she said, and immediately caught Monique's attention.

'You know his full name?' She looked both surprised and wary.

'Of course I know his name, darlin'. He was my target.' She dropped into her best Schwarzenegger. 'I haaf extensiff files.'

The French girl didn't get the reference. Caitlin pushed on regardless.

'Bilal Hans Baumer. Born 5 May, 1974 in Hamburg, Germany. Parents, separated. A German auto mechanic, Hans Baumer, and Turkish mother, Fabia Shah. His father named him Wilhelm, but Hans was a drinker and abandoned the family after losing his job in 1978. His mother was a reformist Muslim. Her brother Abu came to act as a surrogate father for the boy after Hans took off. Abu had always called him Bilal instead of Wilhelm. The name stuck – don't stop walking. Come on, we've got a lot of ground to cover.'

Monique had come to a halt just metres from the back of the minibus. The father, who'd been about to climb into the driver's seat, caught her eye. He looked guilty, as though she had found him out doing something shameful. Monique favoured him with a shaky smile, and he nodded, taking in their backpacks and the appearance of flight that hung about them.

'*Bonjour*,' said Caitlin as they passed. '*Bon chance.*'

'*Bon chance, mademoiselles*,' he nodded back, before climbing in and closing the door with a slam. Caitlin scanned the back of the van, thinking of asking for a lift, but it was crammed full with children, adults, boxes, suitcases and food.

'Why are you telling me this?' asked Monique as the minibus pulled away.

Caitlin kept walking. 'Through his uncle, Abu, Bilal came to meet other lost boys, most of them the products of failed unions between German men and migrant women. His mother stills lives in Neukölln in the council flat where he grew up. She works for the Berlin City Council records department. She is inordinately proud of his achievements. He is one of the few young men in the neighbourhood to finish school, let alone university. He has a real job, and would have represented Germany in volleyball at the Athens Olympics.'

A few people were beginning to show up on the streets now, some of them also dressed for hiking. Another family emerged from an apartment block just across the street. The children were crying, complaining about the way their eyes stung and how it hurt to breathe. A young man rode past on a bicycle, wearing goggles and a painter's disposable mask. He rang his bell as he passed them, fluttering his eyebrows. It drew a brief smile from Caitlin, made her feel a little better. But still she continued.

'Bilal is tall and rangy with light olive skin and thick, wiry hair, coloured darker, almost caramel blonde. He has wide shoulders, long well-muscled arms and legs. No fat. Deep brown eyes, so brown they almost appear black from more than a few feet away. A ready smile that seems to spark off a high level of nervous energy. He rarely sits still for more than a moment and is given to little jumps and skips when he's excited. He talks with his hands.'

Monique was staring at her now, almost walking into a pole at one point. Her eyes were wide, and anxious. As far as she knew Caitlin had never met Bilal, of course, but she had just described him perfectly.

'Uncle Abu encouraged him to remain in school and proceed to university while many of the young men around him had simply gone onto welfare. Abu funded the boy's education and supported his mother. As Bilal Baumer, he studied the German equivalent of sports science and became a qualified personal-fitness instructor, first working for a health insurance company, providing physiotherapy and rehab training for older clients, and later moving to a gym, where he proved very popular with the female clientele. I believe that is how you met, in fact, when he took you for a complimentary training session at a women-only gym in Berlin. When you were in the city eight months ago.'

Monique now looked physically ill, but Caitlin gave her no respite.

'Bilal took up beach volleyball after a trip to Sardinia in 1995 and became a German regional champion with his partner Jurgen Müller. Their run to the Olympics was cut short by Müller's acceptance into the Deutsche Marine.'

They had stopped walking again, and now stood on the edge of the gutter while Caitlin quickly checked up and down the street for any signs that they were being followed. It seemed clear. She spoke without emotion, simply recalling the facts from the dossier she had committed to memory as soon as her case controller had handed her the file on the al-Qaeda recruiter known as al Banna.

'He grew up in Neukölln, in south-east Berlin, where migrants form just under half of the total population. Three generations of Turks are mixed in with Eastern Europeans and some North Africans. Most of the Turks don't speak German or even go to school. Unemployment is at eighty per cent and the city spends three-quarters of its budget on welfare. Baumer has German citizenship because of his father. His mother retains hers because they are not lawfully divorced. Most of the migrants in Neukölln live in fear of immigration raids, which are hugely violent events.'

'Stop it, please. Just stop,' begged Monique. 'What is the point of all this?'

'The point, Monique, is that Bilal Baumer is not your boyfriend. Do you know why he has never agreed to move to be closer to you?'

'His work, he . . .'

Caitlin smiled gently. 'His work, or at least the job he uses as a cover, his personal training, could follow him anywhere. He's good at his job, his cover job, and has EU citizenship. The health funds who employ him would do so anywhere. You know all this. You've always known.'

Caitlin stepped closer, moving into Monique's personal space. Her voice, which she had kept flat and free of emotion while reciting from her memory of the target file, now grew softer, more understanding. 'Like a lot of women, you don't have perfect self-esteem. You could not believe that such a good-looking, intelligent, caring man, a good man, would be attracted to you. Part of you always believed you didn't really deserve somebody like *Billy*, and you assumed, possibly without ever thinking it aloud, that he was keeping his distance until someone better came along.'

Monique's eyes had filled with tears and she was shaking her head in jerky little spasms. 'No.'

'So you wore all his bullshit excuses about work and his mother and needing to stay in contact with his community. You were pathetically grateful when he travelled to see you, but *you* covered most of the miles in that relationship, didn't you, honey? And you had to wonder sometimes, when he was away with a client, or travelling for work, whether there might be some other girl he was stringing along – because he was a catch and a half, wasn't he?'

A nod this time, just the smallest movement, but a crucial acknowledgement that Caitlin wasn't entirely wrong. She could have said something about how Monique was also drawn to Bilal because he was simultaneously dangerous and safe. A young man from a Muslim background, politically aware if not active, but fiercely secular in his outlook. Not at all like the bearded wingnuts whose medieval views on women would've made it impossible for an enlightened feminist like Monique Duroc to have had anything to do with them. But of course, to lay it out as brutally as that would break the tenuous connection she had established.

'Monique, you were right,' the American continued. 'You were not his only one.'

A small groan escaped the throat of the distressed young woman.

Judging the time to be right, Caitlin reached into her jacket and produced the envelope she'd removed from the folder hidden under the floorboards back at the apartment. She shook out a handful of surveillance shots, good-quality hi-def colour photos of Baumer entwined with two separate women. The date stamps marked them as having been taken in the last six months.

'He also successfully targeted a Belgian student,' said Caitlin as Monique took the photographs with a shaking hand. 'Anya Delvaux, a part-time canvasser for Greenpeace in Brussels, and Sofía Calderón, an activist documentary-maker from Barcelona.'

Monique had started to sway on her feet and her face grew blotchy, with irregular patches of high colour fading quickly into bloodlessness. 'An auteur?' she asked.

'Well, a would-be auteur. Sofía's posted a few vids on the net, entered a competition or two, but she stills pays the bills as a waitress.'

The first photograph showed Baumer and the Spaniard, a tall, rather extravagant beauty, dry-humping each other in a park. Monique's tears were flowing freely now, but silently, as she attempted to control her free-falling emotions. 'You . . . you seem to know them well, these women.' She leafed through the other photographs with an unsteady hand, blinking large tears onto them and gasping at some of the more intimate encounters.

'Oh my god,' she said in a tiny voice. 'You must have similar photographs of . . .'

'Of you,' Caitlin finished for her. 'I'm sorry, but yes, I do. Or I did. When I selected you as my objective, my target, I filed them.'

The effort to dam up her feelings failed at last, and with a series of hitching sobs, Monique came apart, wailing and crying like a child who suddenly realises she is lost and alone. Caitlin placed a hand on her elbow and steered her through the carpet of twitching birds towards a side street, which was still deserted. The avenue on which they stood was beginning to come to life. It was nowhere near as busy as it would have been on a normal day, but here and there individuals were venturing out.

The photos spilled from Monique's fingers, falling into the contaminated mud and refuse of the street. Caitlin was forced to bend over and pick them up. It saved her life.

22

Everything came back slowly, from a great distance. Awareness, senses, memory – and pain. Oh yeah, there was plenty of that. Everything was so dim and far away that the actual transition to consciousness was not immediately real and for an age he hovered on the far side of a morphine dream unable and unwilling to pull himself back to reality. In the end, the pain made it impossible to hide. Whatever drugs he'd been given were beginning to wear off and Bret Melton had a dizzying, sick-making instant of realisation that he was in pain. Real pain, seated in more places throughout his broken body than he cared to catalogue.

'Goddamn,' he muttered.

'Hurts like a bitch, don't it, sir?'

The voice was loud and obnoxiously cheerful. Familiar too, in its smooth rap cadences. But he felt as though everything in his head, every thought and memory, had been violently jostled out of place by the explosion that must have put him here.

Where?

His eyelids were gummy and difficult to force open, but force them he did, blinking and raising a hand to rub away the crust that had formed while he slept. Or at least he tried to. His shoulder throbbed abysmally, as though he'd reinjured the old wound picked up so many moons ago at Ranger parachute school. 'Damn!'

'Yeah. You'll want to lie still, until the nurse comes to get you.

Don't go getting no ideas, though – it's a male nurse. Skinny, ugly little fucker too. He'll jam a bedpan sideways up your ass if you give him any stick.'

'Corporal Shetty?'

'Uh-uh. What's left of me.'

Their surroundings slowly came into focus. Melton was lying on a cot in a tent. On either side of him lay more men in uniform, some heavily bandaged, some apparently undamaged, at least on the outside. A fine layer of sand covered the plywood floors, and through a flap a short distance away he could see the fierce white light of the desert. He noticed the thrum of a heavy-duty air-con unit, keeping them cool. It looked as hot as a furnace outside. He slowly turned his head towards Shetty's voice, noticing immediately that the corporal was short one limb. His left arm had disappeared just above the elbow.

'Yeah, gonna have to work extra hard scratching my ass now,' he said. 'And that was my natural ass-scratching hand, too. Least I still got an ass, though. And my nuts.' He gave his groin a reassuring squeeze with his remaining hand.

'Where are we?' asked Melton. His voice was cracked and he reached for a squeeze bottle of water on the small stand next to his bed. It was warm and tasted slightly metallic, but still felt like sweet dew in his parched mouth.

'We scored an evac slot,' Shetty told him. 'Don't know where from exactly, they're not saying. But I'd bet Kuwait or Qatar if I had to . . . if I had any money. Germany is our next stop.'

Now fully awake, if still groggy at the edges, Melton found himself unpleasantly aware of just how much he hurt. His entire body seemed to ache, but here and there, more intense pain warned him of some very special hurts he'd picked up. Shetty seemed to read his mind.

'You're not doing too badly, Mr Melton,' he explained. 'Doc told me you lost a finger off your right hand. A big chunk of shoulder meat. You lost about half of your Ranger tattoo. And you got peppered with shrapnel and one big hunk of wooden window casement. Had a splinter as big as Florida stuck in your ass, apparently. Doc said that hunk of wood coulda been a thousand years old. Said they shoulda had an archeologist dig it outta your butt.'

Melton forced a weak smile, more in recognition of Shetty's attempt to cheer him up than from any genuine amusement. He carefully levered himself up on his elbows to have a look around. The tent was about as big as a tennis court and housed something like sixty or seventy cots. All of them were occupied. He was surrounded by a forest of IV lines and blood bags, but very little specialised equipment.

Shetty was on the other side of his cot, propped up on a couple of dirty-looking pillows, one stump of an arm heavily bandaged. He was smoking Kools with his free, intact hand.

'Glad to have you back, Mr Melton. You're the only familiar face in here. They got guys from all over, but nobody from my platoon.'

'How bad?' asked Melton.

Shetty's eyes clouded over slightly. 'They fucked us up three ways from Sunday, sir. The lieutenant's dead, Sarn't Jaanson, everyone in my squad. About fifteen guys all up, most of 'em in that alley. There just weren't nowhere to go. You and me, we got blown clear into a little shop. That's what saved us.'

'Holy shit,' he muttered. 'I'm sorry, Corporal. I really am.'

'I know, sir. You're a good guy. The boys, they liked having you along with them.'

A jet flew low overhead, the screaming whine cycling up quickly and shaking Melton's rib cage from the inside out. The dull thud of chopper blades emerged from the tail end of the cacophony. He tried to move around to face Shetty but only succeeded in hurting his left shoulder. Waves of grey washed out his vision and a thin layer of sweat broke out all over his body. He started shaking.

'Take it easy, sir,' said the wounded non-com. 'You're going to be a while getting better.'

Somewhere down the row of cots to his left a man began screaming. There was no warning, no cycling up. His shrieks suddenly filled the entire tent and brought two orderlies running. Melton turned his head as far as he dared but could only see what was happening in the very limit of his peripheral vision. The medics appeared to inject the soldier, and a few seconds later he slipped back into unconsciousness. The reporter gave up and eased himself onto his pillows.

'So, you know what's been happening here, Corporal? Or back home? Anywhere?'

Shetty drew on his cigarette and shrugged. Melton wondered idly how he'd managed to get one in and light up. There were no oxygen tents nearby or flammable chemicals that he could see, but he was sure there had to be a rule against smoking in a hospital tent. Yeah, there would definitely be A Rule.

'You were out of it a coupla days, sir. You missed a lot of stuff. We're fighting Iran and Iraq now. Expecting to have to fight pretty much everyone between here and wherever we're bugging out to – probably Europe, maybe the Pacific somewhere. But the Kuwaitis and the Saudis aren't too happy about that, so it's all up in the air. And it ain't just us. Israel has called up all of its reserves. Everything they got is ready to go, on a fucking hair trigger, is what I heard. Had my first walk outta here just this morning. Over to the mess tent. Guy there, a reporter like you, he told me the only reason the Arabs ain't invaded Israel so far, or tried to, is the bomb. That Ariel Sharon, he went on Al Jazeera and just straight up said, "Yep, we got it, in fact we got over two hundred of 'em", and then he read out a list of cities they'd nuke if anyone so much as looked at 'em wrong.'

'Holy shit,' muttered Melton.

'Yeah. Rules are changing. Even so, the Israeli army is fighting right now. They've gone into those Palestinian areas – what is it again? – that Left Bank Gaza joint, I can never keep that shit straight. Anyway, Israelis have put a world of hurt on 'em. They're fighting Hamas, the PLO, a whole bunch of fruit-and-nut-bar Islamic whackjobs. They pretty much hammered Arafat's guys flat. But Hamas is shooting loadsa rockets at 'em from Lebanon or something. Everyone thinks they're gonna get nuked.'

Melton felt dizzy and had to sip at his water bottle and lie back with his eyes closed. 'What about Iraq?' he asked. 'What's happening with them? You said we're fighting Iran too now. I sort of remember something about that before getting clobbered, but it's all hazy. My head feels like mush, you know.'

'Well, they ain't allies or anything. It's more like a street fight where everyone's piling in. Do you remember the Iranians had sent all them little speedboats into the Gulf waters, half of them suicide bombers? They got some good fucking licks in early, too, before we started sinking anything that didn't belong to the Coalition. They got a coupla our cruisers, sank a British destroyer, tagged some Australian boat full of clearance divers. It was fucking chaos for an hour or so, and then the skies were full of fucking MiGs: Iranian, Iraqi. Our guys were raking 'em out of the air, but these things are unloading hundreds of bombs and missiles, and some of 'em got through. Fucking scuds start landing on us – well, not us here, but right on some port where the Brits were fighting a bunch of Republican Guards and those Fedayeen motherfuckers. Those fucking scuds, man, they don't discriminate – they're dropping like rain, killing everybody. Iraqis, Brits, a buncha Marines who happened to be in the wrong place. It's fucking madness. A brawl, not a war.'

Melton was about to say, 'What about Washington?' when he remembered that Washington was gone, or empty at least. Instead he asked: 'So, what happened? Is it sorted now?'

Shetty smiled without humour. 'You know how I said the rules have changed? Well, of course, there ain't nobody in Washington to prod us in the ass with no 12,000-mile-long screwdriver. General Franks, he just gets on the blower to some admiral back in Pearl – he's like the new Chairman of the Joint Chiefs or something – and Franks says, "I'm gonna kill these motherfuckers if it's cool with you". And the admiral didn't have to run it past no senate committee or congressional circle jerk. He just goes, "Yeah, sure, kill 'em all."'

Shetty drew in the last of his smoke, and with one quick little move, almost like a magic trick, he twisted and squeezed out the butt between his fingers, before pocketing the remains to throw away later.

'So?' asked Melton. 'What happened?'

'It's happening right now,' said the nuggety corporal. 'Navy and air force turned around, dismantled the Iranians' air defence net. Then they demolished their fields. Last I heard, Baghdad and Tehran were getting taken apart by cruise missiles, and . . .' – he leaned over as if to impart some grave national secret – 'I heard there's a hundred or more B-52s flying in from the Pacific right now and they're gonna carpet-bomb what's left of both cities.

None of this pinprick surgical-strike bullshit. We're just gonna smash 'em flat. Give those raghead motherfuckers something to think about next time they feel like pissing us off. Lets the Chinese know the big dog's still in the yard, too. I heard they tossed a coupla missiles over Taiwan's way this morning.'

Melton tried to take it all in. He doubted there were a hundred B-52s available now, but he suspected that Shetty probably had the broad outlines of what was happening more or less right. Everything was beginning to unravel. The politics of it were pretty much irrelevant. All that mattered now was getting the hell out and hunkering down somewhere safe. But where?

He drifted off into a long fitful doze and when he awoke, Shetty was sleeping, the ward seemed quieter and the bright, hard edge had come off the day outside. Melton felt a little better, a little less muddle-headed and fragile. He still hurt all over, but being able to identify the injuries behind his pain allowed him to put each of his many hurts into a box and file it away. It didn't decrease the pain, but it sure helped dealing with it. Pain could be endured a lot more easily when you knew where it came from and when it was likely to recede.

'Mr Melton, you're awake. That's good.'

Bret turned his head carefully towards the male voice. A thin, exhausted-looking corpsman, with deep purple smudges under his eyes, appeared to have just noticed him and was advancing with a clipboard. He looked to be of Italian or maybe Greek extraction, and was obviously running too close to the ragged edge of a complete physical breakdown. It was a look you got used to around soldiers. When you saw it on rear-echelon personnel, however, it was never a good sign.

'What's your name, son?' Melton asked him. He had about fifteen years on the kid, and probably had more time in service than him too, so he felt comfortable taking the liberty.

'Deftereos, sir. Tony Deftereos.' Then he seemed to remember himself. 'Hospital corpsman, 15th MEU, sir . . . I've been told to watch out for you.'

'You're navy? What are you doing here?'

'Oh, you know. Chaos. Madness. The usual. My ship got hit by a jet ski.'

'A what?'

'A fucking jet ski, sir – pardon my language. Full of explosives. So here I am, looking after you, as per my orders.'

'From who?' asked Melton, somewhat nonplussed.

'Corporal Shetty, sir. He said he'd stomp me if he woke up and found out anything had happened to you.'

Melton looked across at the maimed black soldier lying in the bed next to his, and realised that Shetty was the closest thing he had to family or friend. At least in this part of the world. Possibly anywhere. He felt that familiar, irrational swelling of affection for someone he didn't really know, beyond having faced mortal danger with them.

'I'm sure he didn't mean it, Corpsman,' Melton said with a smile. 'Corporal Shetty is a gentle soul, a friend of lost animals and small children. He wouldn't hurt anyone.'

Deftereos looked most uncertain. 'Well, I promised him I'd keep an eye on you, sir. If you feel up to it, the doc would like you to answer some questions for him.'

'I'd shrug, but I've got a big hole in my shoulder and it really hurts. What d'you need to know?'

Deftereos took him through a standard post-trauma questionnaire, which wasn't all that different from the experience a civilian might have answering an ER survey at hospital, except for the questions about exposure to chemical or biological weapons and so on. By the time they were done, Melton felt a little hungry and asked if he might have something to eat.

The corpsman checked a note at the end of his bed and nodded. 'Nothing heavy, sir. A cup of soup maybe, to begin with.'

'Thanks. Listen . . . Tony, wasn't it? You hear anything from back home about what happened? Have there been any developments in the last few days while I've been out of it?'

A sad shake of the head was the initial reaction to that. 'No, sir,' Deftereos replied. 'Nobody's had any word out of home. And the news coverage we were getting – you know, satellite photos, webcams and stuff – it's drying up, because of the firestorms over there. Some whole cities have gone up. Not just a couple of blocks here and there – the whole thing, sir. They reckon the clouds are like a nuclear winter or something over Europe. Like when Saddam torched those oil wells in the last war, only much worse.'

Melton remembered that from before he checked out. He recalled resting in the alleyway, looking straight up at a hard blue sky and wishing some of those clouds would drift south and cool things down a bit. He tried to recall some more details but it was like pushing those same dirty, polluted clouds around the inside of his head. Nothing really cleared up.

'I'm not feeling too bad,' he told the corpsman. 'D'you think I could get up and walk over to the mess tent for my soup?'

Deftereos grimaced slightly. 'In fact, I was gonna ask if you could, sir. We're real shorthanded here. Doc's written that you should be mobile by now. You got no leg or spinal injuries, nothing internal. Just have to watch your sutures on the shoulder and some stitching on your rear end, where they took out some real big splinter. You'll have to move slowly, is all. I'm sorry, sir . . .'

'That's fine,' grunted Melton as he pulled himself up. 'If you could just give me a hand up, that'd be great.'

He bit down hard on the pain that welled up as he rose from the bed. No stranger to injuries and discomfort, he knew he'd have to get used to moving around with both. He was very much a non-essential part of this operation and considered himself lucky to have made it this far. It seemed a lot of the boys he'd been covering hadn't. A mild headspin unbalanced him and he leaned against Deftereos, but it passed with a few deep breaths.

'You gonna be okay, sir?' asked the corpsman.

Melton nodded. 'I'll be fine, Tony. You get back to looking after your patients. Just give me some directions.'

Deftereos pointed at the main tent flap as a puff of wind caught it. Melton could see a throng of uniformed personnel hurrying in both directions outside. 'You head out, turn left, and move through three intersections, then it's on your left again. About a hundred and fifty yards. You won't miss it.'

Melton thanked him and began the slow shuffle out of the tent. It remained quiet in there, with most of the wounded men sleeping in their cots. A few orderlies and corpsmen moved about checking on them. Some were in scrubs, others in their desert fatigues, a mix of various services, something that wouldn't normally happen in an army combat support hospital. But regardless of their branch, not one spared him as much as a glance. He was walking and mostly in one piece. He just wasn't a priority.

He felt adrift, disconnected from the world. He understood Shetty's feelings about not wanting to let go of the familiar. Melton had never been part of a unit that'd been shattered before, but it sounded like that's what had happened to Euler's platoon. He'd embedded with them, nearly died with them, been right there in amongst them as they fought their way through southern Iraq. It had been such a bullshit mission in one way, rushing forward to engage the Iraqis who'd attacked them, just to give themselves enough elbow room to get the hell out of Iraq when the war was all but called off by events – or just *the event* – back home.

The hospital tent opened up onto a thoroughfare, a wide street of sand in yet another huge military camp, laid out as always in a grid pattern. Soldiers and Marines moved about in groups of two or more, all in full battle rattle, many with a bad case of the thousand-yard stare. Melton blinked at the raw power of the sun after the relative gloom of the tent's interior. The field hospital enjoyed the benefit of a slight rise in an otherwise flat landscape, affording a view of the frame tents, generators and vehicles. The combat support hospital was attached to a number of other units in the area, near as he could tell. A five-ton truck rolled past him, filled with body bags, the bumper number clearly defined. *HHC 703rd MSB.*

'Jesus,' he muttered, watching the REMF vehicle roll down towards a container. 'I've died and gone to the rear.'

The truck stopped in front of the container, where a detail of soldiers waited. With great care, two soldiers at a time would remove a single body bag from the truck and carry it into the container. Melton could see a refrigeration unit attached to the side. A couple of soldiers from 3rd ID glanced at the body, then looked away. Melton overheard them talking as they passed.

'Those poor dumb bastards really got zapped,' one specialist said.

'Glad I wasn't there,' the other, a private first class, replied. 'Stupid fucking mission anyway.'

'Amen to that,' Melton said under his breath.

He gazed over a vista of thousands of tents and makeshift arrangements of prefab huts, motorised trailers, converted shipping containers, vehicle parks, supply depots and chopper pads. A cluster of antennas sprouted next to a tight knot of command vehicles and shelters. The camp had to cover a couple of klicks of real estate, thought Melton. He cautiously craned his head skywards, and was able to pick out the twinkling points and occasional contrails of at least a dozen jets flying Combat Air Patrol.

'Division main will want that on the double,' someone said to an underling. The underling nodded to the soldier, who was standing in the back of a communications shelter. Melton read the bumper number without thinking: *123 Sig BN*.

'Guess that commo puke didn't have to worry about shooting himself in the foot after all,' he thought aloud. 'I must be at 3rd ID's main camp.' Now where that was exactly, he had no idea.

The ground was rockier, harder, than he remembered from that last big post. It made walking a little more treacherous for someone with his injuries, but it also meant that there was marginally less grit and sand in the air. From the lowering position of the sun, he estimated the time as being quite late in the day, maybe 1600 hours or more. His watch was missing. There was only room enough for foot traffic in this part of the base, and it was heavily congested. Everyone was fully armed, as though expecting the enemy to appear around the corner at any moment, but people made way for him as he shuffled off in the direction of the mess tent.

It was slow going. His whole body was stiff and every movement seemed to threaten new rips and tears in those parts of him that had already been sundered apart and put back together. Melton desperately wanted to know what had happened while he'd been out of it. What had become of 'his' platoon? Who'd lived and who'd died? And what had gone down in the wider world? The little he'd picked up from Shetty and Deftereos wasn't reassuring. He had the impression of a world that had already tipped over the brink and was now falling towards destruction.

It took him a while and a good deal of discomfort to cover the short distance to the mess and he felt worn out when he'd done it, but satisfied too, as if he'd proved to himself that he wasn't a total cot case. Pushing in through the flyscreen doors, he found about half of the tables occupied by service men and women whose working routines obviously had them out of synch with the bulk of the camp. He recognised Marines and army personnel, and some foreign uniforms, possibly Australian special forces. There was even a table of USN sailors looking very much out of place. The hum of the room was subdued, with many of the diners watching a television that hung from a pole near one end of the space. Nobody appeared to be enjoying the show – some sort of news broadcast.

Melton was desperate for information, but also weak with hunger. His appetite had come roaring up as he'd shuffled towards the mess and its familiar smell of fried meat, grease and instant coffee. He was salivating heavily now, and his stomach actually seemed to twist itself into a knot in an effort to move him towards a fold-out table where a female on KP duty smiled at him.

'Can I help you, sir?' the specialist asked. Melton couldn't read her name-tag. It was covered by her body armour. 'We got some burgers and fries that are sorta fresh. And you look like you need feeding up.'

He shook his head but smiled. 'You got any soup?'

She turned towards the giant metal pots sitting on a big field oven behind her. 'Got some beef stew in one of them, sir. I could add a bit of water if you like. That'd almost be like soup, wouldn't it? Just chunkier.'

'Chunky is good,' said Melton.

The Army specialist even helped him over to a table where he could watch the TV, which surprised him. No one was ever cheerful to be put on KP duty.

A minute or two later he was sitting on a poncho liner she'd loaned him, trying to ignore the sharp pain from his butt sutures while dunking a bread roll into the thick dark stew of chuck steak and vegetables. His Ranger buddies would have given him a ration of shit for accepting the snivel gear, but his ass hurt, and as far as he was concerned, he wasn't a Ranger anymore.

'You ain't a Ranger with that haircut.'

Melton turned to see an air force sergeant, at the same time noticing that the remains of his Ranger tattoo were clearly visible on his left shoulder. For some, those would have been fighting words, but Melton just wasn't wired that way. The sergeant inhaled a chilli mac and green beans with a good-natured grin as Bret reached his hand over to shake.

'Reporter these days. Bret Melton, *Army Times* – or I was until last week,' Melton said. 'But no, I'm not in the army anymore.'

'Sergeant Anderson – Michael Anderson,' the man replied. 'But you can call me Micky if you want. You look pretty badly shot up there, Bret – mind if I call you Bret? You get caught up with the Marines?'

He shook his head. 'Nope, 5-7 Cav. At An Nasiriyah.'

The sergeant nodded sagely but said, 'Didn't hear about that. But then, there's been a helluva lotta fighting here and there. They're still patching my C-130 back together after all the fire we took from the Iranians on our way here. Co-pilot didn't make it. Hell of a ride, I'll tell you. Two burning and two turning, and I don't mean jets. Your guys, the ones you embedded with, they okay?'

'Afraid not. We got caught in a bad spot. They mortared the shit out of us . . . I don't even know how we got out.'

The realisation had just struck him. He really had no idea why he was alive. Shetty hadn't explained how the two of them escaped, only that they'd been blown into a building of some sort. A shop or something. One of the other platoons must have fought their way over to drag them out. Hadn't they lost air support just before the mortars started to fall . . . ?

He found himself slipping away into reverie and consciously pulled himself back into the present. 'Sorry, Sergeant . . . I mean, Micky. I've only just woken up. Been out of it since we got hit. But no, I don't think many guys made it.'

'I'm sorry,' Anderson said quietly. 'But at least you weren't with the Marines at Abadan. Man, what a fucking mess.' He didn't explain further. Another forkful of chilli mac effectively silenced him.

Melton gingerly dunked his bread into the rich broth of beef stew and tried to focus on the TV screen. He recognised BBC World's business news presenter, Dharshini David, on the screen. Her normally dark, full lips seemed pale and pressed tightly together, and her eyes were haunted and nervous. It was hard to hear what she was saying, but a tagline rolling across the bottom of the screen and a small picture window hovering beside her head gave him the impression that there had been a massive banking collapse in Europe. The little video window carried footage of black-clad riot police, whom Melton recognised as French CRS, baton-charging a huge crowd laying siege to an old colonnaded building. He assumed it was a financial institution that had run out of money. The scene switched to London, where even bigger crowds waited, a lot more patiently, outside a large Barclays bank in the City. A man in a dark blue suit made some sort of announcement to them and they reacted with catcalls and jeering, but there was no violence. The presenter then threw to an interview with a frightened-looking woman who was nursing two children.

'Any idea what that's about, Micky?'

Sergeant Anderson glanced quickly over his shoulder at the television and shrugged. 'Something about the banks falling over.' He grunted in disgust. 'Welcome to my world. I haven't been paid yet – not that it matters, since my ex gets half of it. Or . . . she used to, I suppose.' He stabbed at his food. 'But at least I'm not going hungry.'

Yet, thought Melton.

23

He could tell there was a problem from a couple of blocks away. Two women, one of them covered in blood, ran past his truck, hair streaming behind, eyes bugging out. Kipper nearly gift-wrapped a telephone pole trying to follow them in his mirror. When he looked up and saw the danger, he jerked the pick-up back onto a safe course with one wrenching pull on the steering wheel. He could see more people running towards him, many of them pounding up the middle of the road, which was free of any vehicles save his own. With his heart beating quickly, Kip pulled over and wound down his window, immediately becoming aware of a distant siren.

He hopped out of the vehicle and tried to flag down somebody to ask what had happened. It had to be a problem with the food bank, but nobody would stop. A couple of young men abused him when he tried to block their path.

'Get out of the way, you crazy old fuck! D'you wanna get killed too?'

And then he realised that the crackling, popping sound he could hear was gunfire. *Shit*.

Kipper jumped back into his truck, but before stomping on the gas, he redialled Barney, who answered on the second ring.

'What's happening, boss man?'

'Something's gone wrong, Barn. Very fucking wrong. I'm about two blocks from Costco and I can hear shots and there's all sorts of people running past me. Some of them bleeding.'

A string of oaths burst out of the earpiece.

'It sounds like the cops are coming, but get on the phone anyway. Make sure they get here before the army – those assholes should have been here already. If the army turn up now, they're just as likely to kill anyone they see moving . . . Oh, and send some ambulances, too. I think we're gonna need lots of ambulances.'

At that moment, a weeping woman ran past, holding up one hand from which a couple of fingers had clearly been removed by a gunshot. Kipper had no idea how she kept going, given the amount of blood she was losing.

Tench didn't answer. He'd already hung up.

Kipper's head was reeling and he felt distinctly ill. This was his fault. The food banks had been his idea, a way to ensure that the aid shipments coming in from across the Pacific were distributed in a rational, effective manner. It wasn't the sort of thing he should have been involved with; as the city engineer, he already had a full dance card handling the utilities. But the elected councillors had frozen like rabbits on the road and they'd let him run with the program. He'd personally negotiated the use of the Costco facilities with company management, who'd assigned dozens of their own stock-control specialists to the job and cleared their warehouse space of any non-essential items. He and Barney had been expecting all sorts of teething problems on the first day, but nothing like this.

Heather. An image of his nervy intern sprang up unbidden: a big pair of Bambi eyes staring out at him from under a short blonde bob, as her hands twisted in her lap like small white otters, constantly moving over and around each other.

'Oh fuck,' he muttered, stamping on the accelerator and punching the horn. The F-100 leapt forward, scattering the mob immediately in front of it.

Many of the people running towards him still paid no heed to his truck, however, in their desire to flee whatever had happened at Costco, forcing him to slow down some. By the time he made South Bradford Street, the crowds were thinning out, with most people having already escaped the scene. He rolled down his window and listened for gunfire, but heard only screams and cries and the growing wail of sirens.

Kipper threw the pick-up onto the footpath and into the parking lot at the northern end of the giant wholesale warehouse. Immediately he saw bodies, a lot of them lying still, and people who were so badly wounded they could not flee. But no shooting. Costco warehouse staff were everywhere, easily identifiable by their brightly coloured vests, many of them tending to the injured. Of the army, who were supposed to have provided a security detail, there was no sign. Nor of the cops and other emergency services, although he could hear them on approach.

Kip turned off the engine and stepped down warily. His senses seemed to be unnaturally alive, and even though this part of the city was a grey industrial area, he could never recall seeing colours so vibrant as the red and blue of the giant Costco sign high up on the building. His hearing too was amped up, with every cry and moan disturbingly clear. Small stones crunched on the tarmac beneath his feet; the engine block of the F-100 ticked loudly as it cooled down. And he gagged as the smell of violent death flooded his nostrils.

Barney Tench's car, an old mud-splattered Chevy C10, came flying up the road and screeched to a halt under the tree at the entrance to the lot. The squeal of his tyres caused some people to jump and shy away a few steps. Barney climbed out and raised one massive hand, pointing towards the warehouse. Kipper saw Heather standing there, a small, forlorn figure in blue jeans and a Minneapolis Twins sweater. Even from a distance, Kip could see she was shaking violently. The two men hurried over to her, picking their way through the carnage.

'Heather! Yo, Heather!' Tench called out.

She didn't seem to hear him at first, but her slack features became animated when she finally recognised her colleagues. She immediately burst into tears as Kipper folded the quivering young woman up in his arms.

'It's all right, kid. Everything's gonna be fine. It's all right.'

He didn't attempt to question her for at least two minutes. Barney stood by and occasionally patted her shoulder, but obviously felt the need to be doing more.

'Kip, I'm gonna see if I can scare up somebody from the company,' he suggested. 'See if they can tell me what happened.'

'Good idea,' agreed Kipper. 'I'll be here. You got the cops and the ambulance, right?'

'Done deal.'

In fact the first squad cars were already screaming to a halt at the edge of the lot, disgorging officers who emerged with guns at the ready, but unsure of where to aim them. Barney kept his hands held up in clear view and walked carefully over towards them.

'Can you tell me what happened, Heather? Can you do that yet, darlin'?' asked Kip.

A small, tentative nod was all he got in reply. Her whole body was still shaking uncontrollably. As she pushed away from him, she rubbed at her arms, folded them, and started rubbing again. 'There was m-maybe a thousand people here, when I got in at six,' she began, unsteadily. 'They all had transit passes and ration vouchers, just like we planned.'

Heather stared around the car park as if seeing it for the first time. Her face contorted and Kip was sure she was about to start crying again, but she got it under control. Her voice was small and seemed forever on the edge of breaking into a thousand little shards.

'Th . . . they were just fine, everyone waiting their turn, until these three pick-ups arrived.' She pointed with a shaky hand at a couple of abandoned trucks a hundred yards away. Kipper could only see two of them, but didn't interrupt her. 'A-about a dozen guys,' she stammered. 'All armed, and they like, just *pushed in*.'

Kipper shook his head. 'What about the army, the cops – where were they? There was supposed to be a platoon of soldiers here to help out.'

Heather volleyed back his headshake with one of her own, throwing in a nervous, exaggerated shrug for good measure. 'I don't know. But these guys, like I said, they just started pushing their way to the front, and some people are yelling at them, some are just getting out of the way. And this one guy, some big guy in a lumber-jacket, a big red lumber-jacket, he just steps in front of them and puts his hand up like a traffic cop or something.'

'Okay,' said Kipper. 'Go on,' he added in a quiet voice.

'Well, one of these jerks, from the pick-ups, he had like an axe handle or something, and he just butt-swipes this dude with it. Totally wipes him out. He goes down and then the shooting starts.'

'The pick-up truck guys, the looters, they started shooting people?' asked Kipper, his voice rising.

'Nope. They *got* shot. Or at least the one with the axe handle did. He dropped the lumberjack dude, looked like he was about to start pounding on him with that club, next thing you know, somebody blew him away. Two or three shots – I'm not sure. But there's blood everywhere, people screaming and *then* the real shooting started.'

Kipper felt as though he was going to vomit. There had to be more than a dozen lifeless bodies lying around in the parking lot. There'd probably be more in the streets beyond. *Where the fuck were the army guys?* They were supposed to have been here – they'd insisted on it, in fact.

'How about you, Heather?' he asked her. 'Are you okay? You got a little blood on you, darlin'. You're not hurt, are you?'

'I don't know where all the guns came from,' she said, ignoring his concern. 'But once they were out, it was like everyone was armed. Everyone was shooting. I've never seen anything like it. There was a little girl . . . standing just near me . . . She was screaming and crying for . . . for her mom . . . and . . .' The young woman broke down completely now, as the morning's blood and horror overwhelmed her.

Barney reappeared with a police officer, an older-looking man with sergeant's stripes. 'You in charge here, sir?' the policeman asked, almost accusingly.

'What? Yes, no . . . well, I . . .' Kipper pulled himself together. 'My name's Kipper,' he said. 'James Kipper, city engineer. We were starting our food aid program here this morning. The city's running the program, with help from Costco, here at least, but the army were meant to be doing the site management and security. So, no, I'm not in charge. Nobody was, by the look of things.'

The cop took in the scene with unalloyed disgust on his face. 'You know, the fucking city could have just used *us*. This wouldn't have happened on my watch, I tell you.'

More cops were arriving and the first of the paramedics were charging around, doing triage.

'I don't make these choices, Sergeant,' Kip replied. 'I'm like you – a civil servant. We do as we're told.' It sounded weak and worthless as it came out of his mouth, and he immediately regretted speaking.

The cop fixed him with a baleful glare. 'Well, don't you be wandering off, Mr Kipper. I'll be needing to speak to you again.' He turned his back on the three engineers with that, and trotted over to a couple of uniformed officers, barking orders as he went.

'Jesus, what a fucking mess,' said Barney.

'Uh-uh,' grunted Kip. 'We'd better find out what broke down, do what we can to help, then get back to council. We'll call the city councillors, tell them what's happened.'

Tench looked troubled. 'I tried, Kip. But none of them are available.'

'What d'you mean?' he snapped, instantly regretting it. 'Sorry. It's just I keep hearing this – it's bullshit. Where are they?'

His friend shrugged. 'I even tried a few home phones and their cells, but nothing. And if you call Municipal Tower you just get routed into phone-menu hell out at Fort Lewis.'

'Why? How come our calls are going out there?'

'Not *ours*, just the councillors'. When you call them direct, I mean.'

Kip started walking Heather over towards an ambulance. She had zoned out. She was looking shocked and pale and he wanted to get her cared for as quickly as possible. The paramedics, however, had their hands full with more serious casualties.

'Heather, I'm going to get someone to run you out to the hospital,' he told her. 'No, scratch that – they'll be completely overloaded. Do you have a doctor in town? Someone we can call?'

She shook her head. 'No, but I've been to a clinic near my apartment a couple of times. I got food poisoning my first week here.'

'Jeez, Seattle's been good to you, hasn't it . . . Okay. Barn, you think you could drive Heather over to this clinic and get her checked out? Don't take any shit from them – it's city business.'

'No problem,' replied Tench.

'Okay, you guys go now. Fuck the cops, they know where to find you. I'll deal with them. Off you go.' He shooed them away, keeping an eye on the sergeant, who had his back turned to them.

A long line of ambulances was speeding down 4th Avenue South towards them and he could hear a chopper, more than one, approaching from the city. Hopefully it would be a medical flight. The media couldn't take their helicopters anywhere without written authority from Fort Lewis. The entire state had been declared a no-fly zone, in order to 'secure' the city's airspace and approaches. It was bullshit, of course. There were no more unpiloted, empty aircraft headed for Seattle. They'd all crashed within hours of the Disappearance. But General Blackstone hadn't got around to removing the restrictions.

Well, for once, Kipper was glad of it. He could really do without having to deal with a lot of jackass reporters this morning.

Nearly six hours later, he finally made it through the last checkpoint on 5th Avenue, where a couple of Humvees with ring-mounted machine-guns blocked access to the Municipal Tower, the city's administrative centre. A kid with the name-tag *Meyer* read his papers, stamping his feet in the cold while his breath plumed in the frigid air. He didn't look at all pleased to be out in the open. The sun had disappeared again, and a light drizzle was drifting down from the leaden sky. It stung Kipper's eyes as he waited for his papers, taking him back to childhood memories of swimming in pools with way too much chlorine.

'Looks fine, sir,' said Private Meyer. Or was it Specialist Meyer? Kip never really knew where he was with these military types. 'Just park as normal and head on through. Major McCutcheon is waiting to see you.'

Kipper was about to walk away when he pulled himself up. 'Sorry, who's waiting to see me?'

Young Meyer consulted his clipboard again. 'Major McCutcheon, sir,' he repeated.

'I don't know any McCutcheon, son, Major or otherwise. What's it about? Unless he's come here to explain where your guys got to this morning when they should've been guarding my food bank, I'm not interested.'

Meyer looked severely discomforted. 'Sorry, sir. I don't know why he came to see you. He's General Blackstone's aide, if that helps.'

Kipper blinked away the burning rain that was running into his eyes. 'Well no, it doesn't . . . but . . . Damn it. McCutcheon, you said?'

'Yes, sir. Major Ty McCutcheon. He's waiting for you inside, sir, in the . . . er . . . deputy mayor's office.'

'Okay. Thanks.' He stalked off. If nothing else, this McCutcheon might make a convenient punching bag. God knows he needed one after this morning.

Forced to take a parking spot a good long walk from the tower, he didn't recognise many of the vehicles, and noted that a fair amount of military transport had fetched up here, too. The thin mist of rain started to thicken up, falling heavier and forcing him to hurry. He no more wanted to be out in it than poor Private Meyer. Two more guards, both of them toting rifles, greeted him at the door, eyeballed his papers, and reminded him that he had an appointment with Major McCutcheon. Kipper tried to shake off his anger with the rain and pushed past them into the heated and slightly humid interior of the building.

He could tell immediately that many more folks were in residence than was normal, a good number of them, perhaps most, out-of-towners. Every fourth man or woman was dressed in a military uniform. A couple of very expensive suits were wrapped around some very polished Eastern accents, too, he noticed. And Canadians seemed to pop up at each corner, announcing their presence with a rising inflection and an 'eh!' for every occasion. None of the newcomers recognised him, but here and there he caught a despairing look from a city employee. He had no idea how many people knew about the fuck-up at Costco – it certainly hadn't been on the radio as he'd driven in. Those stations still operating were given over to official announcements spliced in between wall-to-wall music, and none of the announcements made any mention of the trouble this morning.

By the time he reached the deputy mayor's office, he'd calmed down a little, and decided to ditch the meeting with this McCutcheon guy. He was going to be far too busy with all the blow-back from the food bank disaster and opted instead to attempt an end-zone run to his own office.

'Yo! Kipper, you made it, man, good to see. Come in, dude. We need to talk.'

The engineer nearly jumped out of his boots.

The army officer (or *was* he army? They had majors in the air force too, didn't they?) was a lean, forty-something man with a bristling grey crew-cut. He looked the part, but sounded like a surf bum. A Californian, maybe? There was no avoiding him though, so Kipper set his features and made the best of it.

'You're McCutcheon, right? Did you come in here to explain what the hell happened at Costco? You guys were supposed to be there guarding the handout. You *insisted* on it, as I recall.' As soon as Kipper started to speak, all of his bottled-up rage and frustration spilled out. He was nearly shouting by the time he'd finished. 'All that bullshit about major security operations being an army gig now – but I got *eighteen people dead*, and the entire fucking city locked down again! It's not good enough, Major!'

'No it's not,' countered a gruff voice from somewhere behind McCutcheon. 'Now get your ass in here, son, and help us sort it out.'

Kipper pushed in through the door, surprised to find another uniformed man in the chair behind the deputy mayor's desk. This one was older, bald, and much more thick-set than McCutcheon. 'Who the hell are you?' Kip asked, as the major pushed the door to slightly.

The man, who was dressed in fatigues like McCutcheon, gestured to a chair for the engineer to sit in. 'General Jackson Blackstone,' he said. 'Take a seat.'

Kipper blinked and froze. 'You. You're the fucking idiot who insisted that the army would handle security this morning. Great fucking work out there, guys. Top-shelf effort.'

'Sit. Down.' Blackstone's voice came out in a low growl.

McCutcheon pressed Kipper towards the chair, placing a hand gently on his elbow. 'Yeah, sorry, not our finest hour,' he said. 'We sent two platoons over to that marketplace that got hit last night. It's a snafu, Kipper – I'm sorry, it happens. Come on, we need to talk.'

'You're damn right we need to talk,' replied Kip. 'And what's with the invasion?' He gestured to take in the hordes of military personnel swarming the building. 'Is the army taking over or something?'

McCutcheon remained unaffected by his hostility. 'Naw. We just stand out because of our superior grooming and fashion sense. Really, if it weren't for that, you wouldn't even know we were here. Come on . . . I'm not army, by the way, I'm air force. Special liaison to the civil power, for now. General Blackstone is army, and co-chair of the Special Means Committee.'

The air force officer fetched a coffee pot from the sideboard. The office was crowded with paper files, maps and electronic equipment, all of it military issue. Blackstone sat as quietly and impassively as if he were a log on the forest floor.

'You want java?' asked McCutcheon. 'It's fresh. But the milk's not. I got some very nasty military-issue creamer, if you want.' He held up a drab olive container with a white plastic slide top on it, by way of explanation.

Kipper grunted, asking for a mug of black, no sugar.

'Damn, that's hard-core. You sure you've never been in the service?'

The chief engineer nodded grumpily. 'I'm certain. People shouting at me just pisses me off.'

'Well, fair enough then. You gotta love the shouting, or it's just not the life for you. How's your family, by the way? They pulling through okay, got enough supplies?'

Kipper shook his head in exasperation. 'Look, what the fuck is this? I have a major disaster on my hands. Eighteen people dead. And you call me in here to make fucking small talk.'

The major walked over to the door and carefully closed it, cutting off the growing hubbub from the corridor outside.

General Blackstone spoke up as he did so. 'The last time I checked,' he said, 'we had a lot more than eighteen dead. When last I checked, our casualty count was well over three hundred million, Mr Kipper. So I have some sour news for you, sir. This morning was a minor fuck-up, and there will be more of them.'

'A minor –'

'That's right. And there will be more of them. More death. More chaos. Get used to it, and get used to dealing with it. Because if we don't deal, it's game over here. In this city. Everywhere.'

Kipper waved away the cup of coffee McCutcheon held out.

'What are you talking about, General? If this morning was your idea of *dealing* with things, then yeah, we're fucked.'

'Look, this is kinda delicate,' said the air force man, taking a perch on the edge of the desk, where he could look down on Kipper. 'We've got a bit of a problem with the council, I'm afraid.'

Kipper shrugged. He'd wondered how on earth the military was going to continue working so closely with a group of people who were almost their antithesis. 'Well, apart from this morning, things seem to be getting done,' he offered. 'All my department's requests are going straight through the Special Means Committee and getting approved without any questions. What's the problem?'

Major McCutcheon sort of whistled inwards, which Kipper recognised as the universal sign of bad news coming. 'Well, the thing is, we don't really have a Special Means Committee,' he confessed.

'What?' asked Kipper, completely dumbfounded.

Blackstone leaned forward. 'I had them arrested three days ago.'

McCutcheon actually looked embarrassed for a second. 'Yeah. And we've been kinda winging it ever since.'

24

The roadblock was almost professional. Four old cars arranged in a herringbone pattern that forced any oncoming traffic to slow to a crawl as it negotiated a winding course through the obstruction. A dozen armed men, locals by the look of them, lounged on the bonnets and inside the vehicles, passing around bottles of no-name tequila and Dos Equis lager, and smoking an assortment of cigarettes and reefers.

'We could take that left,' suggested Fifi, pointing to a narrow side street that remained open to traffic, just before the roadblock.

'No,' replied Shah without hesitation. 'Too narrow. Nowhere to go. And they have enfilading fire from the roof-line and windows above. We must reverse immediately or go through.'

'Drive on,' said Jules. 'But slowly. Don't spook them. They're probably just shaking down the *turistas*. I'm sure we can talk them around to leaving us be.'

She lifted the dark grey Franchi SPAS 12 auto shotgun from the improvised gun rack that Shah had installed on the dashboard of the Jeep Cherokee, and jacked a round into the chamber. Behind the wheel, Sergeant Shah – they'd all taken to calling him that now – slowed the vehicle and made sure his own weapons cache, a pair of MP5s, was close to hand. In the back seat, Thapa and Fifi readied themselves.

They had almost managed to drive right up to the edge of

Acapulco Diamante, the most exclusive tourist enclave in the city, but the roadblock brought them to a halt a couple of hundred metres from the start of the private resorts and clubs. Jules had been expecting trouble even earlier, which is why the Jeep was kitted out with so much firepower. Until now, however, the sight of a few gun barrels lazily produced out of the Cherokee's windows had been enough to negotiate their passage through the town, where most of the violence they encountered was still small-scale and anarchic.

'Sergeant Shah, if you wouldn't mind, I think Fifi and I will handle the negotiations. A prominent display of your willingness to kill anybody who interferes with us would help, of course.'

'Of course, Miss Julianne.'

The former non-com brought them to a halt at least twenty-five metres from the blockade. A lot of the men up ahead were carrying rusty revolvers and .45s, which were unlikely to hit anything they aimed at over ten metres away. And most of them appeared to be drunk or stoned, which further called into doubt their chances of deliberately targeting anybody. There was a lot to be said for volume of fire, though, and they had plenty of that to go around.

Jules slipped a pair of sunglasses down over her eyes and stepped out of the cabin, fitting a radio headset. Fifi emerged behind her, already wearing her commo gear, the same sets they'd used back on the *Rules*. Immediately the wolf whistles and catcalls began. It was almost comical, really. It was a hot, bright day and both women were dressed in shorts and hiking boots. Jules wore a Level III A armoured vest over a white tee-shirt, but Fifi had only a sleeveless checked L.L. Bean to protect her. She'd knotted it, exposing a long expanse of tanned, finely muscled midriff, and most of the would-be desperadoes were torn between which of the *chiquitas* they wanted to objectify and harass the most.

One guy stood out from the rest, simply because he didn't ogle them or grab his crotch. He just stared cold and hard at the four gunned-up intruders.

'That'd be our guy,' Jules whispered into the mike. 'He's mine.'

'Gotcha,' said Fifi, who took her much-loved Russian PKM from Thapa at that moment. Jules was almost certain she felt the ambient temperature drop as blood began to run cold. 'What's happening back at the car?' she asked.

'Both Shah and Thapa are good to go, if they have to.'

'Are they being obvious about it?'

'Yup.'

'Excellent, *and* . . . Good morning, señor. This is your turf now, I suppose?' Jules favoured the gang leader with the full wattage of her smile, holding the shotgun so as to squeeze just a little more cleavage up towards his face.

'You presume I speak English, no?' he said in reply.

'You look like an intelligent, educated man, well travelled and worldly wise. It's a reasonable assumption.' She beamed at him. 'Especially when you use big words like presume.'

In fact, he looked like the worst sort of bad news. Sober and mean and not likely to be sweet-talked or bullshitted into anything he didn't fully intend to do.

'I am the block *capitán* here now,' he informed her. 'I coordinate security for the Mayan and Fairmont resorts.'

You mean you're shaking them down for protection, she thought. 'Well, that's excellent,' said Jules. 'Because that is where we are headed this morning. So if you'd like to provide an escort for me and my friend here . . .'

Fifi winked and grinned, while never taking her finger off the trigger of the PKM. 'Howdy, *Capitán.*'

'. . . we'll be on our way,' Jules continued. 'We have business up there, Mr . . . ?'

'What business?'

He was instantly on guard, alive to the possibility that somebody might trespass on his turf. She wondered about his background. He seemed too smart for a street thug, and yet he'd gathered a vintage crop of them around him. There seemed no obvious structure to his crew, no settled hierarchy of lieutenants or enforcers. He might be telling the truth about them providing a form of security to the resorts. After all, Shah and his men had hired themselves out to do just that to pay for their former lodgings, and of course they were now doing the same for her.

'There are some American citizens in the resorts,' she improvised. 'Their government has arranged evacuation and we're providing – '

'They have no government,' he cut in. 'It is gone, *desaparecido*.'

'Not all of it.' Jules smiled disarmingly. 'Not the part with all the guns and tanks and stuff. You know, *los militares*. There's a good many of them still hanging around, and if you can still get a news service you'll see they're organising safe passage for any US citizen who wants it. We're just part of that service. We're . . . contractors.'

She shifted the Franchi, a big heavy-hitting piece of artillery, just to remind him of his proximity to it. She dropped her voice, however, so that only she and the *capitán* could hear. 'Let me guess what's happening here, *puta* . . .'

Jules noted the instant flush of anger to his face. She could tell he wanted to bitch-slap her for that, but the presence of the shotgun stayed his hand.

She continued in the same low tone. 'You probably had a couple of your crew back there take a few pot shots at some of the guests. Maybe they roughed up a *gringo* or two. And then you magically appeared to offer your services, to preserve them from the attentions of such dreadful ruffians. Of course, a premium service like you're providing, it doesn't come cheap. There's all the men to pay, the equipment to maintain – and the smokes and beers and three-dollar whores don't come cheap, do they? Well, maybe the whores. And you plan on, what, holding them here until you've bled them dry? Is that right?'

A quiet smile was all the reply she received. Jules stepped in a little closer now. Spoke a little more softly.

'You're obviously the brains of this operation. You look about a hundred times smarter than anybody here. What were you last week – a cop, a soldier, or something?'

He didn't answer, but then he didn't smack her down either. He was listening.

'So think about this, *profesor*. Think about how much more it costs you to buy a cup of coffee, or a beer, or a taco, than it did two days ago. Think about how the money you've been taking off these fat white fools is worth less every day than the one before. You've noticed that, haven't you? Because you're the smart one here.'

He nodded, almost imperceptibly.

'Think about how *quickly* that's happening. Ask yourself how long it's going to be before the money they have in there . . .' – Jules motioned behind him, towards the protected enclave – 'isn't good for anything but wiping your arse. How long will that be? Another week, maybe two? Their money is going to be worthless a long time before you relieve them of it.'

Jules could see she'd struck a nerve point; now she had to act quickly before he made the logical connection and turned his guns around on the resorts. She moved right into his personal space now, but not in a threatening way. He had a good two or three inches of height on her, and she used it by turning her face up towards his and widening her eyes just a little more.

'This city is falling to pieces,' she went on. 'You're part of that, aren't you? You know how it's going to be here very soon, and you're setting yourself up as a new power. But you know what? It's not just you. We drove in here this morning. Some places are burning, some looted. We saw a couple of bodies on the streets here and there – saw plenty of guys like you, too. At the marina where my boat's tied up, they've hired some muscle who would take these faggots of yours down in less than a minute. That's not meant to be insulting. They're just better equipped, better trained – better paid too, I'd guess. Looks like a lot of ex-military types down at the marina. Like my Mr Shah and his friend back there.'

The gang leader flicked a glance back at the Jeep, where the two Gurkhas stood, squat and utterly still. Between them they were more heavily armed than his entire crew. They fairly bristled with automatic weaponry and Thapa even sported a kukri dagger at one hip.

Jules was almost whispering now, softly and gently, like an old lover. 'Not many ex-mil types here though – are there, *Capitán*? Just you, really. You're the only true pro here, which means you know what'll happen if my guys back there open up on you. I'll get shot, almost certainly, just because I'm standing so close to you. My friend Fifi, with that enormous Russian machine-gun, she'll probably make it to cover because she'll put out enough fire to make sure nobody draws a bead on her. And Shah and Thapa, well, look at them – they're cold motherfuckers. They'll do the job. But your guys . . . well . . . I think we both know what'll happen when thousands of rounds of ammunition start heading towards them, don't we? So let's not even go there. Let's see if we can work something out between us, you and me, so that everyone's a winner. Perhaps you could start by telling me your name.'

'Miguel Pieraro,' he said quietly. 'I am not police, no. I was *vaquero* – a cowboy . . . a boss of cowboys.' His shoulders straightened with real pride. 'But that was before. I worked in the north, by the border. I worked for an American cattleman, with large herds below the Rio Grande. I ran his business there. He supplied *McDonald's*.' Pieraro invoked the name of the Golden Arches with reverence and awe.

Jules eased back a little, giving him some room. He was a proud man and very obviously cut from finer cloth than his comrades. His grasp of English was excellent. The chorus of sexual taunts and whistles from the makeshift barricade had died away completely now. All of Pieraro's men watched him closely, straining to hear what had passed between *el jefe* and the white slut.

'I will take you in myself,' he declared. 'We will discuss your proposal. You have a proposal, yes?'

'I do,' she confirmed.

He nodded and called out to another man who was sitting on the bonnet of an old '79 Camaro, reclining back against the dirty windscreen. The car was a dinosaur, with faded red racing stripes to match a thick coating of rust and dust. 'Roberto, you are in charge here! I will take our new friends through to the Fairmont. Call me on the radio if you need to. The phones are useless.'

Jules noted that like Miguel, Roberto was notable for being clean-shaven and sober. Where his boss was a tightly wrapped bundle of steel cord and knotted muscle, however, Roberto slid from the bonnet of the car in one fluid movement. He reminded her of a snake, uncoiling in the sun. In Miguel's position, she wouldn't have trusted him to sit the right way around on a toilet seat. Oh well, not her problem.

A few hand gestures from the two men saw their followers hurrying to turn over engines and reverse the cars out of their herringbone arrangement. Pieraro indicated that Jules should follow him, so she signalled to Fifi to hurry back to the Jeep. 'It's cool,' she said over the radio. 'We're going in with this chap.'

With the tension evaporating, she allowed herself a few moments to check out the locale as she followed the former cowboy through the gauntlet of leering street toughs. They'd set up their barricade across an avenue that most of them would never have seen before. Twee little fashion shops, jewellery stores and cafés lined both sides of a street that recently had been a well-manicured boulevard. She noted Givenchy, Prada and Armani boutiques, all looted and burnt out. Rubbish choked the gutters and footpaths, and a couple of spent brass shell casings twinkled in the mid-morning sun.

Pieraro stopped at his car, forcing Jules to suppress a snigger. It was a micro, some sort of courtesy vehicle from the Fairmont resort, according to the livery; not much more than two doors and four dinky little wheels. Pieraro caught her sceptical expression.

'It is new,' he said. 'And environ . . . *environo-mentally* sustainable.'

'Does it run on tanning butter or something?' she smirked. She would have taken him for a muscle-car tragic. But then she'd taken him for a crooked cop too, hadn't she?

'It is just for running about . . . with work,' he emphasised.

She made sure the safety was engaged on the shotgun and then climbed in. A misfire would probably peel off the entire roof. 'My name is Julianne, by the way – Jules, if you like,' she told him as they fastened their seatbelts. 'Do you mind if I ask you something?'

'Will you mind if I don't answer, should the question be none of your business?' he said. 'I am an honest person . . . Not like you, *sí*?' he added pointedly.

'Really? Your little shakedown racket here – you're earning an honest peso with this, are you?'

He started the car but didn't drive off. 'I have a family. Three children. I am providing for them. Those men back there, *my* men now, they have their own to look out for too. Unlike these people . . .' he waved a hand to take in all of the Diamante district, 'my men have nothing to fall back with. *La Desaparición*, it will hurt the poorest the most.'

Pieraro pressed on the accelerator and they pulled away. 'Your question, *señorita*?' he asked eventually.

Jules shrugged. 'I was just wondering how you ended up on that roadblock, but I guess you answered it. Three children. You were, what, holidaying? Visiting relatives?'

Pieraro snorted at the first suggestion. 'My wages, they would not have allowed me to clean the streets of *el Diamante*. I could not holiday here. We were visiting my wife's cousins further south for a wedding when everyone disappeared. I came as far north as I dared to find work to support them. We have lost everything but our lives.'

Jules glanced in the side mirror to check that the others were still with her. The Jeep was only a few metres behind. She couldn't get a read on Pieraro at all. He looked like a hard case yet she could detect none of the primitive fear in his eyes that was such a part of the make-up of almost all street thugs – the knowledge that there was always someone harder and meaner than you just around the corner. She could sense anxiety leaking out of him, at the edges, where he couldn't keep his emotions completely nailed down, but it didn't seem personalised. If he was telling the truth about his family, that might well explain it. She would have to play him very carefully. In many ways, it would have been a lot easier if he were a simple gang boss.

'I suppose I should ask how you ended up *running* that operation. Not a lot of call for herringbone roadblocks, snipers and intersecting fields of fire in the cattle business, is there? Not even when working for Mickey D.'

'Mickey D? I do not understand . . . Oh, McDonald's. I see.' An arid smile cracked open the dark, sunburnt rock of the cowboy's face. 'The catering manager of the resort, an American, once worked for McDonald's in Houston,' he explained. 'I met him on business many years ago. We drank a lot of tequila and he embarrassed himself, eating the worm like a college boy. Well, he was a college boy, I suppose. But I looked after him. I knew he had taken the job here, so this week I came looking for work. Any work.'

'I see,' said Jules, nodding. 'But security work? That's not your business.'

'Men are my business. Running cattle and running men. You have never bossed twenty *vaquero*, no? I have bossed many more.

Hard men, not to be crossed. Much harder than those idiotas.'
Pieraro threw a contemptuous look back over his shoulder.

'Yeah, I get that. But that Roberto guy, he really is ex-military
or something, right? He handles the tactical side, yes – where to
place your good shooters and how to set up the roadblock?'

The cowboy remained quiet for a moment before finally muttering: 'He is Colombian. AUC – *Autodefensas Unidas de Colombia*.'

'What's that, some sort of fascist coke-smuggling outfit?'

'Paramilitaries,' said Pieraro before hurrying on. 'So, you have
a proposal, Julianne.' He pronounced the first portion of her name
as *Chooley*.

As the little car wound its way down towards Revolcadero
Beach, the signs of breakdown and chaos in the social order
became much less evident. The streets remained free of rubbish
and any indication of conflict. Huge villas and gated resorts sat
quietly underneath palms and soaring canopies of transplanted
tropicals. Few people moved about, apparently preferring to hunker down behind their high walls, but those who did, did not
seem especially fearful or concerned. Jules scanned the scene for
any obvious signs of things beginning to fray, but found none.
Perhaps Miguel and his gang were helping to hold it back for now.
She decided to take a punt on his honesty.

'You have three children, Miguel, right?'

'Yes,' he replied. 'Two girls and a little boy.'

'Would you like to get them away from here? From Mexico, I
mean.'

There was a slight delay before he answered. 'Very much so.
What you said before, it was not all true. But some was – about
how things will soon turn for the worse. I have seen the worst of
people. I know what to expect.'

They began to travel downhill through a neighbourhood of
large modern houses, some of them set back within vast grounds.
Jules caught the first sparkles of sunlight on water as glimpses of
the bay showed through the verdant surroundings.

'Okay, here's your deal. Passage out of Mexico for you and
your family if you can help me put together a passenger list. A
short one. People who can pay upfront, right away, in euros, British pounds or trade goods. Stones and jewellery, high-end stuff

only – gold, platinum, diamonds, and so on. I have a yacht that can accommodate two-dozen passengers and the same number of crew . . . well, I can accommodate a hell of a lot more, but I'm not interested in more. I'm not running a budget operation.'

It was Pieraro's turn to fix her with a measured, vaguely contemptuous look. 'You have misread me, today, Julianne,' he told her. 'Taken me for something I am not. You, however, I can read very well. I have met your type before. You are not an honest person. You are not good. Good, honest people do not carry themselves with weapons into danger, real danger, like you did before, with such . . . composure, *no*? You are familiar with men such as that.' Again, he jerked his head back in the direction from which they'd come. 'You have used weapons such as this.' A nod now towards the SPAS 12. 'You have killed people before. Yes?'

'When I had to,' she said tightly. 'When it was them or me.'

'This I understand,' he conceded. 'But you must understand me now. If I help you, if I entrust to you the lives of my wife and children, your own life, it is entrusted to me then. It is held within my hands. Do you understand? If you give me reason, I will close my hands and take that life from you.'

'I understand,' said Jules.

Pieraro slowed down and stared into her eyes. 'Good. Then we have a deal.'

25

Monique grunted and dropped to the still-wet ground like a puppet cut loose from its strings. A single round had felled her. Caitlin went down on the dirt under the angry buzz of bullets zipping overhead.

'Son of a bitch!'

She rolled over Monique and grabbed her by the backpack. Strap in hand, juggling her own hold-all, Caitlin hauled the young woman towards the door of the nearest apartment block. She didn't pause to think, to examine her surroundings, to question the choices she was already making. Her largest handgun, the Glock 19, had quickly appeared in her free hand and it roared, biting huge chunks of wood and masonry from the solid timber door.

Rather than screaming, Monique was gasping and grinding out an arrhythmic series of grunts, like somebody punched in the stomach trying and failing to draw air into their lungs.

Glass shattered as rounds zipped and cracked past Caitlin's head to chew up the brick façade of the old, run-down tenement. The gunfire echoed against the bricks and mortar of the surrounding apartment buildings. She logged the direction and volume of fire, and part of her mind calculated that they faced maybe three attackers.

Three? She looked out of the corner of her eye. *No, four shooters.* They'd emerged from a white van that had turned down onto this wide street just a minute ago. Four, she could be certain of – but were there more? A second vehicle perhaps? A lookout who'd been scoping the street for hours?

Her boot slammed into the door, which flew open and crashed into the wall, and they were suddenly through, into a darkened passage that smelled of boiled cabbage and dog hair. She dropped Monique on the threadbare carpet running down the long, poorly lit hall and spun back towards the street.

Caitlin holstered her Glock and hauled out both of her Steyr TMPs from the shoulder rigs under her jacket. With the safetys flicked off, she held the weapons out around the corner of the door and unloaded both of them into the free fire zone of Route d'Asnières in the direction of the van. The outgoing fire sounded like canvas sheets ripping in the high wind.

After three bursts, she took a quick peek to her left around the doorway to check her surroundings and see what she'd caught.

A civilian, on a bicycle, lying in the centre of the road, probably dead. Head shot. *Shit.*

A small Fiat, faded blue paint, up on the footpath down near the railway tracks, smoke or steam pouring out from under the bonnet. One flat tyre.

And birds – dead and dying birds everywhere.

A woman in a bright floral headscarf, cowering in the doorway of an empty boarded-up shop, shielding what looked like a child with her body.

Across the road from her, a dirty white van, parked at a slight angle in the gutter about fifty metres away, cabin door slid open. One leg hanging out of the interior, twitching. Windshield smashed, horn blaring.

Three identified shooters there. All white males, dressed casually, armed with FAMAS G2 assault rifles. One behind the van – possible leg wound. One crouched behind another vehicle, a grey, ageing Volvo. The last man, running, aiming for a deeply recessed doorway fifty yards away.

She snapped off two quick bursts at the figure heading for the doorway.

G2 rounds crashed around her once more, pulverising the ancient red brickwork and forcing her to fire blind again. Caitlin emptied the rest of the Steyr magazines with much greater accuracy this time, however, having sighted her targets, then she turned back into the building and shoulder-charged the first door on the right. It gave way with a crack of splintered wood and she tumbled into the small sitting room, taking cover below the window ledge, crunching broken glass under foot.

In one quicksilver motion, Caitlin slipped off her backpack and poured half a magazine of 9 mm hollow-point from the Glock through the smashed windowpane into the street outside, mostly aimed at the shooter behind the Volvo – the closest, easiest target. Chances of nailing him were low, but she could at least keep the fucker bottled up.

Monique moaned loudly just outside the room, and glancing back over her shoulder, Caitlin saw her legs begin to scythe and kick in reaction to the burning pain that would now be making itself felt. Gut shot by a military assault rifle. There was gore and leakage everywhere. Caitlin knew the exact location of a couple of morphine syrettes in one of the bags, but to attend to Monique now would have meant ceding the initiative to their would-be killers.

She opened her oversized hold-all and pulled out the artillery. The pistol-grip Benelli shotgun came first: customised 12-gauge, extended mag with a side-saddle shell carrier. Next was the deal closer, a specially cut-down Heckler & Koch UMP .45, with an extended box mag housing thirty rounds of .45-calibre Smith & Wesson goodness. She slung the HK over her shoulder. It was a large, excessive arsenal for just one young lady to haul around, but Caitlin Monroe very much adhered to her daddy's rule that when it came to guns it was always better to have 'em and not need 'em than the other way around.

She picked up the shotty, jacked a cartridge into the chamber, and poked the muzzle out through the shattered window. The Benelli was loaded with a buck 'n' ball combo that gave her a nice spread for quick and dirty area clearance, but still packed a nasty surprise in the form of one larger, molybdenum disulphide–coated brass slug at the centre of the load. Unlike softer malleable rounds, it was armour piercing and would slice through a car door or ballistic vest without bothering to slow down much.

She methodically pumped half-a-dozen rounds of buck 'n' ball down-range, angling to do some damage to the men behind the vehicles, but occasionally raking a shot along the front of the building to shut down their partner in the recessed doorway. She briefly heard a few distressed cries and more shouting upstairs, and the hammering of feet on bare wooden boards, but then the uproar of her sustained gunfire drowned out everything else.

I need to get a handle on this fucking mess, she thought. She was still firing blind, however, attempting to disrupt the flow of her opponents' advance and hoping for a lucky hit.

The briefest of lulls drew her attention upwards again, to the sounds of renewed panic. Caitlin let loose out of the window with another four shells from the shotgun and then ran, reloading, clearing the ruined sitting room and bouncing off the slimy, plastered wall of the apartment's main corridor. She leapt over Monique, who was writhing and crying pitiably – 'Hold on, baby,' the American muttered, 'these fuckers are gonna regret getting out of bed today,' before speeding towards the staircase, slipping the shotgun over her shoulder and bringing the Heckler & Koch into play.

Bounding up the stairs she swung around at the first level and raced for the front of the building. An open door led onto a small bedroom just ahead and she rushed in, grateful to find there was no baby in the cot that was pushed up against one wall. She thumbed the selector on the machine-gun to full auto. One of the reasons she liked the H&K was its relatively low rate of fire, a modest 600 rounds per minute, which, in the hands of an expert operator, made the burst mode all but superfluous.

Caitlin looked out the window with a black widow's smile. Two of the three shooters were crossing the road, giving her a clear line of fire. 'Thank you, gentlemen,' she said. 'Much obliged.'

The operatives both squeezed off covering fire at the ground-floor position she'd just left as they crossed the Route d'Asnières. The dense, rapid crack of their FAMAS rifles was painfully loud. They edged forward, right into her sights.

Her movements were quick and machine-like. One sharp pull on the trigger shattered the bedroom window, and as the two men instinctively looked up, she nailed the pair of them with short auto bursts, aiming for the centre mass and letting the muzzle drift upwards to punch a couple of rounds into each of their skulls.

The first man simply looked surprised, his eyebrows raised comically and mouth a perfect 'O' shape before five rounds stitched him up from the sternum to the forehead. His head all but disintegrated. The second attacker was fast, well trained – but doomed. He managed to lift his muzzle up a few inches, and even squeezed off one misdirected round, before Caitlin nailed him in the same way. A fan of blood and brain matter painted the side of the car next to which he died.

One more. There's one more, at least, she screamed silently at herself.

She didn't pause, instead leaning back from the exposed position and holding the gun forward, angled down, to let rip at the guy who had been sheltering in the doorway. There was no direct line of sight, but Caitlin fired from memory, confident she could at least keep him pinned down. A woman was screaming nearby, and downstairs she could hear Monique's guttural cries of pain becoming more ragged and intense, more animalistic in their abandonment.

'Shitfire!' spat Caitlin.

She took half a second to scan her immediate surroundings and plug them into a larger mental map of the world outside. A triangular block, typical of the streets of Paris, was her battlefield. *Time to slip backasswards.*

Setting off at a sprint, she exited the room and charged down the first-floor corridor – a dank, evil-smelling space. She headed away from Monique, away from the cries of the tenement's occupants, moving as fast as possible for the rear of the building. A closed wooden door loomed ahead of her, and she went straight through it, shoulder-charging the old frame, which disintegrated in a storm of splinters and dust. A faraway part of her mind thought, *Termites.*

She'd been expecting either a small storeroom or a water closet. It was the latter, as filthy and unkempt as the rest of the place, but she didn't care. A sash-window, grey and completely opaque with grime, opened onto a rear courtyard below. The pulley ropes were broken and hung uselessly, one of them trailing its frayed end through a petrified blob of toothpaste. Caitlin ignored it, safed and shouldered her weapons, and hauled herself awkwardly through the window.

It was a straight drop into the muddy courtyard, with no shed or ledge to step on. She levered herself out, and hung down as far as possible; then she pushed out and dropped. Her knees folded up under her, just as she had been trained to do by the good folks at the US Army Airborne School at Fort Benning.

There was nothing elegant about the move, which ended with her rolling in the wet earth. The submachine-gun squelched underneath her, digging painfully into her ribs, but she mostly kept the Benelli out of the muck, and with no time to check and clean the guns, she chose that as her primary. Pulling out more shells from the side saddle, she finished reloading on the run towards the small wooden fence that separated the courtyard from the property behind.

The muted rattling cough of the FAMAS reached her, adding urgency to her flight. But as she stood, a wave of disorientation swept over her and threatened to steal her balance. Caitlin took one precious second to stand perfectly still, draw in a fresh breath and attempt to centre herself, to gain some measure of control over her traitorous body. Then there was nothing for it but to forge on, leaning forward into the vertigo that had seized her and biting down a rising tide of bile that was trying to erupt upwards out of her stomach.

She leapt over the wooden fence, catching her jeans and almost crashing down in a heap on the other side as she lost her footing on a dead pigeon. Her momentum was enough to carry her forward, however, and she brought the shotgun around, flicked off the safety and jacked a round into the chamber.

In front of her now was the rear door of a building that faced onto the Rue du Bac d'Asnières, the other side of the elongated triangular block formed by its convergence with the similarly named route – from her point of view, the quiet, uncontested side. The van was at the apex of the triangle, flat tyres and all. An empty bakery stood before her, if she recalled correctly. *This just might work . . .*

The small frosted window embedded in the door was covered with a wire grill, but there were no other obvious security measures. No wires, no cams, no back-to-base relays that she could spot. Her head was still spinning and her balance was off, but the door was a stationary target. She drove a powerful side kick into it, just inches below the rusted key lock. It gave way with a report like a gunshot and she hurried inside as the sound of more automatic fire drifted over the roof line from the street behind her.

She entered a storeroom, mostly empty, with just two large paper bags of flour lying on the concrete floor. Rats had chewed both of them open. A doorway led through to the baking room, where big commercial ovens stood cold and unattended, presumably for want of supplies. Or perhaps the *boulanger*, more closely attuned to the city's increasingly serious hunger, had already taken his family and left.

Caitlin didn't give a shit. She found the door she was looking for – the shop's front door – punched through it, and emerged into the flat dismal light that leached through the thick blanket of toxic clouds now overhead. Rain started to spatter down again, burning her eyes and exposed skin. A black crow, seemingly unaffected by the pollution, picked at the carcass of a squirrel in the gutter just in front of her. She swore at her lack of goggles, a pair of which lay in the bag she'd left with Monique.

The assassin was caught unawares by the strength of her feelings for the girl. They were not comrades, more allies of convenience, thrown together only because of the extreme circumstances of the last week. And she had never allowed herself to grow attached to a target or an asset, but nor had she ever been diagnosed with a brain tumour or woken up to discover her whole world had vanished like a dream. As she ignored the increasingly difficult symptoms of her illness and pushed herself to the limits of endurance, Caitlin tried to convince herself she was simply worried, quite reasonably, at losing the vital support of a key asset.

A rising, ungovernable anger threatened to overwhelm her as she remembered her last sighting of Monique, jackknifed in pain, bleeding out onto the filthy floor of the old tenement. The girl was a ditz, but she had stuck by Caitlin when, really, she would have been better off lighting out on her own. If nothing else, the American owed her a settlement with whoever had shot her.

There were a dozen or more people milling about nervously on this street, flinching at the gunfire. Seeing her approaching, a young man called out a warning – '*Attention, elle a une arme!*' – and they scattered like birds startled from a tree. Caitlin ran five doors down the street, back towards the hairpin corner around which she'd walked with Monique a lifetime ago. When she judged herself far enough along, she diverted in through the open garage doors of an auto repair business, yelling that she was the police and warning everyone to get down. '*Tout le monde, planquez vouz!*' She heard more cries of alarm and noted two figures in coveralls cowering out of her way, but ignored them.

This building sat on the point formed by the meeting of the two roadways, so it had no back courtyard. The only open ground it boasted was a triangular concrete apron at the apex of the two streets, which appeared to be used as a parking bay for the business. It was possible to cut right across the workshop and emerge, hopefully, behind the white van and the last shooter. She quickly weaved her way through, dodging around a couple of pits over which sat a new Honda Accord and an ancient Trabant. A pair of double doors, identical to the ones she'd come through from the Rue du Bac, stood ajar, opening onto the wider thoroughfare of the Route d'Asnières. She could just make out the rear of the van, splattered with blood, and an outstretched hand, lifeless on the sidewalk.

The FAMAS roared again, a long guttural snarl of fully automatic fire, none of it directed at her. Nonetheless, her heart lurched forward. She saw smoke and a muzzle flash light up the darkened cave of the tenement entrance where the last shooter had holed up – the doorway of the building in which Monique lay, disintegrated as the bullets struck.

Clearing burst, she thought. *Right where she's lying.*

Caitlin took a second to check the shotgun and finish racking shells into the magazine. It was good to go, as near as she could tell. After she reloaded her Glock with a full mag, she stopped to think for a moment. What if there *were* more of them? There had to be more . . . Her eyes scanned the windows and rooftops, into stopped cars, taking in the few people still crazy enough to be on the street.

'Nothing for it,' she told herself. 'Surprise is everything.'

The shooters lying on the footpath and roadway in front of her were dead. She hurried past the van, covering the man whose legs protruded from the rear cabin, but he too was gone. Bled out. The last known gunman was inside the building, just out of her sight.

She sped up, crouching to drop below the line of the windowsill as she reached the front door. Shotgun up, trigger on a half-pull, she took in the sight of Monique lying as still as a fallen log in the dark pool of her own fluids. Her head was a shattered mess of blood, gristle and grey matter. She was identifiable only because of the stupid little protest badges she still wore on her old jacket. Fury boiled over inside Caitlin's head.

Oh, you filthy cocksucker. You and I will most certainly have a reckoning here directly.

Bloody footprints led away up the stairs and she heard the creak of a footfall overhead. *Oh yes*, Caitlin thought, pointing her shotgun at the ceiling. *We'll have that reckoning right now.*

She pulled the trigger two, three, four times without giving a second thought to any collateral damage. Not a thought about the families who lived in the building or the crib she had fired beside. Each blast gouged giant plumes of plaster dust and atomised floorboard, which erupted and dropped down, coating the two women like a snowfall. She was rewarded with a strangled cry and a brief, uncontrolled snarl of gunfire, before a dead weight dropped to the floor above.

She looked over her shoulder, out the door behind her, still wary that someone else might show up. But there was no one in sight.

Taking off at speed again, she rushed up the stairs for the second time that morning. A round in the chamber, the Benelli's muzzle described tight little arcs, as she aimed where she expected to find the body.

He was lying face down and still moving, but barely so. The last shooter, she hoped. Struck three times, once in the femoral artery, to judge by the rivers of rich, almost purple, lifeblood flowing out of him and onto the tacky brown carpet. He'd dropped the assault rifle in his dying spasm and Caitlin used her boot to kick it away, never once taking her aim off the back of his head.

She heard a door open somewhere and yelled out again: '*Police. Revenez, maintenant!*'

The door slammed shut. A child screamed endlessly elsewhere in the building.

Cautiously approaching the downed man, Caitlin kept her eyes on all of his hands and feet, aware that even now he might lash out at her. In his position, if at all possible, she would have. But a thick, glutinous, gargling sound told her he was on the way out. She shouldered the Benelli again, where it clanked against the barrel of the Heckler & Koch. Her pistol replaced the long guns and she dropped a knee right into the small of the man's back, jamming the Glock up against the base of his ear. A pellet had torn off a bite-sized chunk and she ground the gun sight into the bleeding wound for emphasis. He groaned pitiably, but there was very little fight left in him.

'You don't have long, Pepé Le Pew. We both know that,' she snarled, addressing the killer in French. 'But I could make the last few minutes of your miserable fucking life feel like an eternity.' To drive the point home, she shifted her balance to focus her weight onto a rib that was protruding from an ugly chest wound. A weak, liquid groan escaped from the man beneath her as she felt a nub of bone dig into her knee.

'Okay, questions. First one: did you shoot my friend downstairs?'

'I don't . . .'

The Glock gouged out a chunk of meat from his ruined ear and he found the strength for a full-bodied scream.

'Yes. Yes. I did,' he babbled in heavily accented English.

'Question two: who sent you?'

Lighter pressure was all that was required this time. The answer told her half of what she needed to know. 'Noisy-le-Sec.'

An iceberg in her stomach. Just as she'd thought – they were from the Action Division of the DGSE.

She didn't bother with her last unanswered question: why? This loser wouldn't have a clue, only a target. Her and Monique. But she had a new enquiry.

'Last question: how many in your team altogether? How many shooters? How many on overwatch?'

'Fuck you,' he groaned.

Caitlin drove a short, sharp punch into his injured rib cage and he screamed.

'How many?'

But his howling did not abate. If anything it grew worse.

Her skin crawled and every nerve ending under it seemed to tingle. *Time to go.*

She stood up carefully, making sure to give him no chance of entangling her legs or feet, and then she fired once into the back of his head, silencing the caterwauling cries, before turning and hurrying back downstairs to Monique.

Not that she needed to hurry. She already knew her friend – and yes, 'friend' *was* appropriate – she already knew that her friend was dead.

The body lay still and heavy in that telltale way, as though slowly melting into the floor under the pressure of its own dead weight. Black petals of light bloomed in Caitlin's vision and her head began to spin again, this time around the axis of a bright, sharp pain. She staggered against the wall, which seemed to fall away from her. She had to get out; she had to abandon her friend. More killers would be on their way.

As the floor rushed up to slam into her face, she thought she heard the dull metallic thudding of a helicopter. But it could have been her own heartbeat.

26

He was getting used to the chaotic, tumbling, whitewater rush of events, to waking up in different cots or beds, or a plastic picnic chair at some random transit point. Of course, Melton had experienced plenty of hurry up and wait during his time as a Ranger, and although he enjoyed a much greater degree of autonomy in his later career as a civilian correspondent, he was, in the end, still hanging around the army, which had raised 'hanging around' to an Olympic-standard event, interspersed with short bouts of furious ass haulage and seemingly pointless tail chasing. The thirty-six hours after he awoke in the field hospital featured plenty of each.

He'd been upset on returning from the mess tent to discover Corporal Shetty was gone, evacuated on a medical flight to Ramstein. He was alone again, without friends or colleagues or even a passing acquaintance, until Corpsman Deftereos returned, this time bringing with him a set of three-pattern desert BDUs and a standard-issue brown undershirt and underwear. The young orderly was accompanied by an exhausted-looking female doctor, who gave the reporter a perfunctory once-over, checked his stitches, wrote him a prescription for some antibiotics and signed off a travel order, ripped from a clipboard and pushed into Melton's pocket.

'Congratulations,' she said in a voice devoid of any spark. 'You win a no-expenses-paid trip out of my ward and on into the next exciting phase of your own personal mystery tour.'

He hadn't even drawn breath to ask what the fuck she was talking about before the doc was gone, administering more scripts and travel documents like some sort of malfunctioning vending machine. Deftereos at least had been a little more helpful, gesturing for him to stay exactly where he was for the next couple of minutes. Melton felt abandoned and more alone than he had in a long time as the two of them swept out of the ward, and he was on the verge of simply climbing back into his cot when the corpsman rushed back in, grabbing him by the arm and pulling him upright.

'No, really, you gotta get the hell outta here, right now, sir.'

'Why? What's up, Tony?'

'What, you think they tell me anything? I don't fucking know – excuse my language, sir.'

Deftereos was babbling, and noticeably distracted. 'Look, we just got word through that we're shifting at least a third of our cot cases,' he said. 'Corporal Shetty scored a golden ticket with the 86th Airlift while you were out. And you just lucked in with a civilian charter, to London. If I was you, I wouldn't even be here anymore. I'd be a dust ball, on my way to the fucking helipad. Now go!'

He pushed a small bottle of pills into Melton's hand. Vicodin. 'It'll help, with the shoulder and your finger,' he added. 'Don't worry about your kit. All your stuff has gone ahead. Now you gotta get going too.'

And with that Melton had changed out of his scrubs and been given the bum's rush out of the tent and into the dust and harsh sunlight, to join a small throng of the walking wounded, all recently displaced and as thoroughly nonplussed as himself. They had just enough time to work up some really wild theories about battles gone wrong, bio-weapon exchanges, hundreds of thousands of American dead and wounded, when a white bus with dark blue Hilton Hotel insignias pulled around the corner formed by a pod of air-conditioned shipping containers a hundred yards away, and a navy chief stuck his head out of the rear door, roaring at them to get their worthless carcasses into the vehicle or they'd get left behind for good.

Bret remembered a short ride out to a vast helipad where civilian choppers of all manner and description vied with US military helicopters for landing and take-off slots. He remembered shuffling onto a Vietnam-era Chinook with Australian aircrew, but missed a lot of that flight after downing two of the Vicodin with a swig of warm, bottled water. He vaguely recalled half an hour spent in some lavish civilian airport where he was at least able to fill the prescription for his antibiotics, at a mark-up of about a thousand per cent.

Melton slept through a C-130 flight to Qatar, and fetched up for a long spell in a giant hangar where hundreds of wounded Marines and soldiers were laid out on stretchers if they were lucky, or if they weren't, on a makeshift line of bright orange moulded plastic chairs. Groggy from the Vicodin and creeping exhaustion, Melton made his way towards a small mound of duffel bags that had been colonised by half-a-dozen Polish commandos. They all seemed in fine fettle, with their equipment stowed neatly in a pile to one side, guarded by one of their own – a huge blond stone monolith of a man.

'*Witam!*' Melton smiled in greeting, before holding up his hands to forestall a Polish-language landslide. 'Sorry, that's all the Polish I know. Besides *piwo* and *piękna dzie . . . dzi . . .*'

'*Dziewczyna?*' The small, wiry, heavily moustachioed man grinned back at him. The men's sergeant, judging by his chevrons. 'Not much beer or beautiful ladies around here, my friend. Just stinky American boxheads, yes? Apologies if you are boxhead too. I say it with love in my heart. And sorrow too, great sorrow. Please sit, you are wounded, yes?'

Two of the Poles crabbed around and Melton eased himself down on a couple of kitbags. They seemed wonderfully soft.

'Boxhead? No,' he grunted with relief at getting off his feet. 'Not for a long time, anyway. Wounded, yes. Not too bad, though, just missing a few bits and pieces.'

'Nothing to stop you enjoying *piwo* or *dziewczyna* then?'

'No, nothing that bad. My name is Melton, by the way. Bret Melton. I'm a reporter, or was . . .' He shrugged awkwardly and trailed off. It was simply too much effort to go into his CV, to explain his shift from *Army Times* staffer to itinerant freelancer for a slew of British media outlets. 'You guys been waiting long for transport?' he asked instead.

'Eight hours. Not long. Some here have been waiting many days. Some have died here – not joking now. I am Sergeant Fryderyk Milosz, I do not joke. Pleased to meet you Melton By-the-way . . . Okay, that was joke. Polish joke, yes? The best kind. By Pole.'

Milosz flashed him a blindingly white grin and raised his eyebrows with such comic élan that Melton couldn't help laughing out loud. It hurt his shoulder dreadfully but he gave into it anyway. It had been a long time since he'd enjoyed the abandon of real laughter. It seemed to loosen up Milosz's men as well, with some of them smiling and nodding, as their own tension and stresses eased off a little.

'We are going home soon,' the sergeant said. 'But you, my friend, where do you go now?' The man's eyes were dark pools of sympathy.

'London, I think,' said Melton. 'That's what my travel chit says, anyway. After that, well, I don't know that there is an "after that".'

'No,' agreed Milosz, nodding as though Melton had revealed some deeper truth. 'Maybe nothing after that, no.'

Leaning back and taking in his surroundings, the reporter couldn't help but dwell on how things were unravelling. There had to be nearly a thousand guys crammed into the baking heat of this hangar at the edge of a temporary base in the middle of nowhere. A lot of desert MARPAT, which meant Marines. Mixed in with the MARPAT were some army and air force personnel dressed in three-pattern desert BDUs like the fresh set Melton wore.

Marine, army or the few navy and air force he saw, all had the same look. The long stare, the slumped shoulders, postures crumpled in upon themselves. A few were crying openly, quietly, regardless of the severity of their wounds. Here and there, Melton would spot a soldier looking at a snapshot or a Marine watching a saved video file on his laptop. Some were by the door, chain-smoking for lack of anything better to do.

One soldier, from the 101st Airborne, had a collection of dog tags in his fist. He rocked himself back and forth until someone passed him, at which point he'd ask, 'Who should I give these to, do you know?' Even when he got an answer, he didn't seem to hear it. He'd go back to rocking, back and forth, until someone else walked past.

A female Marine over by a Coke machine covered in Arabic script was smiling, flirting with a half-comatose man on a cot. 'When I get home to see my baby girl, it'll be all right. She lives in North Dakota with my grandma. I heard they made it.'

Oh boy, Melton thought, taking in the glazed green eyes of the Marine, a lance corporal. She looked right past him, not seeing anything but her dead girl smiling back from the past.

To Melton, they looked beaten. Like men and women with nothing to live for. Milosz and his small band of brothers, however, they were still tight and looking forward to something. Home, family, a simple fucking ride out of the furnace. It was enough to keep their spirits up. Melton shook his head. Any place where soldiers gathered in great numbers always ended up reeking of sweat and stale breath, cigarettes, ration farts and something more elemental – an animal smell of violence waiting to turn loose upon the world. But that musky scent had turned rancid and cloying in here. Even Somalia wasn't this bad, Melton recalled. The Rangers on the whole weren't beaten, nor were those pogues from 10th Mountain, who'd done better than anyone ever thought they would.

Desertions, he thought. *These folks will desert or simply collapse if someone doesn't give them their spines back real soon.*

The giant metal fans droning away at the edge of the hangar merely pushed the vile atmosphere around, a gaseous slough of ill feeling and desolation. He was familiar with this. It was what happened when men faced the hopelessness of their circumstances and shrugged away any chance of redemption. It was what happened when men who were used to fighting for their lives gave up and said, 'What's the point?'

Milosz left him alone for a few moments. But perhaps uncomfortable with the brooding presence that had just insinuated itself into his little group, he toed Melton's boot to regain his attention. 'So, Melton By-the-way. You have a theory, yes?'

It was such a weird, unexpected question that Bret shook his head as if a bug had crawled into his ear. 'Sorry. What do you mean?'

'A theory, about the Disappearance, no?' the sergeant

elaborated. 'I am interested in theories. Real theories with science and learning, not bugaboo magic, for explanation. Like these Muslim pigs and their stupidity about Allah's will. So, your theory. Tell me.'

Melton opened his mouth to say something but simply shut it again, shaking his head. Fact was, he'd heard any number of bullshit explanations and crazy-talk gibberish about what might have been behind the catastrophe. He'd heard as many backwoods Christians lay it all at the foot of God as there were bug-eyed imams rejoicing in Allah's vengeance on the infidel. He'd heard whispers of secret government experiments gone wrong, black-hole laboratories, portals to hell, and alien space-bat biology missions that had scooped up hundreds of millions of lives with something akin to a giant butterfly net. He hadn't given any of them a second thought.

'I don't know, Sergeant,' he confessed. 'I don't even begin to know what happened, or why, or whether it can ever be reversed. I figure the best analogy is we're like ants whose nest got hit by a lightning strike, or by a kid with a magnifying glass on a sunny day. We're *ants* – what would we know about anything? Either of those things, they'd be the end of the world to us, but you stand outside the situation, you get the context in a way that we don't have, and it's probably something really simple . . . that we're a thousand years from understanding. Possibly we'll never understand it. My bet is that a thousand years from now we'll be living in caves again, banging rocks together for a living.'

The Polish non-com narrowed his eyes and dipped his head in acknowledgement. '*This* is a wise man,' he said to his troops. 'You see, he knows what he cannot know and does not pretend otherwise. This is wisdom, Jerzy.'

Milosz pointed to a younger, black-haired youth and spoke in a rapid garble of Polish. Melton had the impression he was repeating what he'd just said. The young commando shrugged, conceding a point.

'So what about you, Sergeant? No theories for you?'

Milosz smiled sadly. 'It is like you say. People groping through the dark, grasping at this and that, trying to explain what cannot be understood. My question, I ask it of people because it tells me how they are now. Whether they will get through or not.'

'You think people will "get through" based on whether they believe in conspiracy theories, or magic, or the will of God?'

'No. People will survive this because of luck. If you have no food to eat, no warmth in the deep of winter, it doesn't matter whether you think little green men or Mohammed broke your world. You will still die frozen and hungry. But if you have enough to eat, just enough, and if you have some shelter and safety – again, just enough – then maybe your living or dying might have something to do with whether you fall to madness and superstition, or whether you hold on to your rationality.'

A small, indulgent grin sketched itself onto Melton's weathered features. 'You're a materialist, then? Of the dialectic school? I thought Poland was done with all that.'

'Yes, I am a material thinker, like my father, a mathematician. And you are no boxhead, Melton.'

'It's foolish to assume that just because somebody puts on a uniform and takes orders, they turn off their brains. You didn't.'

'Excellent,' beamed Milosz. 'It is good to talk like this, Melton. So much of soldiering is crudity and ugliness, yes? But there is more to the profession of arms, and to life itself. We soldier so our children won't. For us, guns; for them, books and easier lives.'

Melton gestured helplessly. 'I never had any kids. Gotta say I'm real happy about that now.'

He didn't look back over at the Marine lance corporal as he spoke. She was still talking about her daughter in North Dakota. Someone came over, checked the man on the cot, took his pulse. The orderly then pulled a blanket over the man's head and made a note on the clipboard, but the lance corporal didn't notice.

'But if I had,' he continued, 'and they hadn't disappeared, I don't know that they'd be looking at an easier life than I had.'

'Not now, no,' conceded the Pole.

Three trucks pulled up at the vast hangar bay doors and soon able-bodied troopers began unloading more litters from their rear cabins. Corpsmen and a few nurses appeared and hurried over to help, but otherwise there was no appreciable reaction to their arrival. Men still sat and talked in low voices in their own small, closed groups. Country-and-western crooners still clashed with speed-metal shrieks and hardcore rap from dozens of portable stereos. Listless card games of hearts and spades continued without pause. The *bleep-blee-bloop* of Game Boy systems never faltered.

'And what now for you guys, Sergeant? Home to your families?'

Milosz nodded, but there was a severity to his expression that belied any sense of release or deliverance. A couple of the other Poles appeared just as sombre.

'Home, yes. We hope.' He waved his hands in the air, a concession of helplessness. 'If we have not been forgotten. Or abandoned. Or lost . . . But we may not see our families even if we do get home. There will be much work to be done. Our sort of work.'

'Fighting.'

'Of course. You have seen what happens when things go bad, Melton. In Polish history, there is much fighting – Russians, Germans. Who knows who will come now? Maybe Tartars and Ottomans again. Once, even the Swedes invaded. I doubt they would again. They are a soft people now. But not everyone is soft, no? The jihadi pigs I am fighting in Afghanistan, they are crazy men, but hard. The Iraqis – not so hard, but bad, and led badly. Weak men are often the cruellest. And Russia, a sick place, but still peopled with ruthless commissars and tyrants. This Putin, watch him. He is an iron fist hanging over all of us.

'So yes, Melton, fighting. Always fighting. Fighting big, between states, and small, between people for little things. Food, water – basic things. My brother, I spoke to him for three minutes on American phone yesterday. Nothing he has to eat for two days. Just some dried crackers and a little tinned food for his children. Nothing in market. It is like communism again. And now, with the poison clouds, no harvests, I think.'

His men were nodding, and Melton wondered about their grasp of English. If he recalled correctly, GROM operators had to have a working knowledge of at least two languages other than Polish. He supposed there was a fair chance all of these men did speak English with some fluency, given the anglophone nature of the Coalition. And doubtless this was a topic that had been chewed down to the gristle among them. He wished he had taken notes, or recorded the sergeant's lament. He was sure he could sell a story based solely on snatches of interviews taken with the men in this hangar, or with those men and women with whom he'd travelled to get here. An old, nearly burnt-out spark flickered somewhere inside him and he reached inside his jacket pocket, searching for the Sony digital recorder he kept there. It was gone, but he had a pen and a notebook that he had lifted off someone's desk over the course of his journey from Kuwait. His writing hand was uninjured, but holding the pad in his heavily bandaged left hand was awkward.

He looked at the lance corporal by the Arabic Coke machine. *Don't end up like her*, he swore to himself.

Melton raised an eyebrow at Milosz and asked, 'Would you mind? I don't have any of my gear. My newspaper is gone, but I'm still a reporter. I shouldn't be sitting here on my ass feeling sorry for myself – I should be telling stories. Your stories. Would you mind?'

'Of course not!' the sergeant cried out, holding his arms wide. 'I am always interested in hearing myself talk. And these, my poor little bastards, they have no choice – they have to listen. Why should they suffer alone? Yes, Melton, of course you can tell my stories. Where should I start? With our attack on the Mukarayin Dam? Yes, that was us. We flooded Baghdad. Everyone thinks it was Green Berets, pah, Hollywood pussies! It was GROM.'

Melton couldn't help glancing around to see if any Army Special Forces were around to hear that remark. If they were and heard, they didn't make themselves known.

Still struggling with his pen and paper, Melton came up short. The Polish special forces were not an old and venerable outfit. They had only been established in 1991. But they already had a rep as a very closed-up shop. You rarely heard about them, and they never did press. Yet here was one of the senior enlisted men, suddenly happy to give up details of a mission that he would have denied even happened a week or so back.

Milosz had no trouble translating the American's puzzled look. 'Do not be surprised, Melton,' he said. 'Everything has changed now. I will tell you about Mukarayin because it suits our purposes.'

'How so?'

'It is like I said – there will be much more evil in the world soon. There is already, yes? My country, she has suffered more than most through her history. But not this time. Or not without making others suffer for what they might do to us. I will tell you about Mukarayin because you will tell the world, and then she will know that we Poles, we will not be ploughed under again. You know what most people see when they imagine Polish Army? They see horsemen galloping off to charge Hitler's tanks. Brave, but stupid, and doomed. But now, if you tell them about Muka- rayin, in future when people think about Polish fighting man, they maybe think about that dam blowing high into sky and that mountain of water flooding out and drowning city of Baghdad. They will think twice about wishing evil upon us, yes?'

'Yes,' agreed Melton. 'I think they will.'

It was more than he had imagined writing about. He'd been more interested in Milosz's story of calling home and talking to his brother, of being trapped in the broken machinery of a vast war machine, suddenly cut off and alone in a hostile world. And he did do that interview, but he also filled half of his notebook with stories from every man in the sergeant's extended squad – GROM usually operated in teams of four – about blowing the dam that flooded Baghdad.

As he did so, the strangest thing happened. A small audience began to gather around them – just two passing Cav troopers at first, but increasingly building up into a circle of attentive listeners that drew in even more men and women by virtue of its novelty. After ten minutes Melton was sure that over two hundred people surrounded them, perhaps the majority of the walking wounded in the hangar space. The Polish operators spoke into a rapt silence, but occasionally someone would call out, confirming a detail of their story, or others would clap and cheer like believers at a revival meeting.

The specialist from the 101st Airborne stood over him, his fist full of dog tags, his eyes clear now. 'Sir?'

'Yes, Specialist?'

'Can I . . . Would it be okay if I told you . . . ?' The soldier held up the identity discs. There must have been twenty or more of the tags, some with blood and skin on them.

'Sure, Specialist,' Melton replied. 'Tell me what happened.'

A Marine stepped forward. 'Hey, need a recorder, Mr Melton?' he asked.

The reporter took it and smiled. 'Just call me Bret.'

When the dog tags were connected to formerly breathing, living, loving people, the army specialist moved away. The batteries were low, but an Australian commando contributed a set of triple A batteries. Bret then talked to the Marine who'd loaned him the tape recorder, until the tape ran out. He ejected the mini-cassette and passed the recorder back to its owner, who had a boy, a girl and a horse called Eagle back home, but the man shook his head.

'No, Bret, you keep it,' the Marine said. 'You need it more than I do.' He fished around in his pocket and pulled out some fresh tapes. 'I don't have anyone to record messages for anymore.' He then stood up, squared his shoulders, and moved out of the hangar. At the bay doors he collected a rifle and a helmet from another Marine, and they walked out into the searing Qatar daylight.

Melton had no idea where he would place the interviews, or what form they might take. But he kept scribbling and taping, encouraging people to talk about . . . well, about whatever they wanted. And they did.

'So the bastard was up in the ceiling,' one Private Adrian Bennet said. 'He popped four in my squad before we finally figured out where he was hiding . . .'

'Our convoy got cut off,' a Native American army private by the name of Piewesta told him, shaking her head. 'We took a hell of a lot of fire and my friend Jessie, she was in the back of the Hummer when we got hit. She didn't make it.'

'That was a helluva mess,' someone added. 'You with 507th Support Battalion, right?'

Piewesta nodded.

'The bullets came flying from everywhere,' an Apache pilot, half of his left foot missing, recalled. 'Hell of a thing, Bret. I thought I was home safe after knocking down those three Iranian helicopters, but then all of this ground fire comes up. Like being trapped in a mason jar full of lighting bugs. Just wasn't my day to be flying.'

Melton noticed that the pilot didn't mention his gunner. Probably didn't make it, he decided.

'She just wouldn't sink,' a sailor from the USS *Belleau Wood* said. 'That Iranian sub put three torpedoes into her, but she wouldn't go down. We were trying to get the fires under control when we got word to abandon ship. We could've saved her but they said resources were tight. Better to scuttle her.'

A Tarawa class LHA lost – scuttled. The US Navy hadn't lost a ship that large in combat since World War II.

The sailor smiled. 'We got that fucking Kilo sub, though. ASW guys from the *Nimitz* got us some payback on that bitch.'

'Hell, yeah,' someone else said. Others took up the chorus: 'Hell, yeah! Payback!'

He heard a seemingly endless stream of combat horror stories. Units cut off or abandoned. Enemies materialising out of nowhere. Supplies running out. Air cover disappearing. Waves of Iraqi troops flowing towards them, then suddenly disappearing inside great roiling walls of flame, or enormous volcanic eruptions of high-explosive dropped from miles overhead. He heard small, intimate stories about men killing each other with whatever weapon came to hand. About a female truck driver, trapped in a hostile village, crawling out via the thousand-year-old sewage system, and souveniring a couple of old Roman coins she discovered on the way.

Night had fallen, and half of the hangar's floating population had been spirited away before he finally stopped. Both hands ached, but his missing finger tormented him with a particular ferocity and the wounded shoulder throbbed with a deep, agonising bass line from his having sat hunched over the notepad for so long. But Melton thought he had enough material for a whole book, including a wrenching series of personal stories about what people had already lost. Families, home, friends, everything.

He made an effort to gather testimonials from the handful of Europeans present, such as Milosz and his men, and some British tankers whose Challenger had been crippled by a buried mine. Fact was, their stories would sell the piece in whatever form it took, the domestic market for American stories having literally disappeared. When the Poles finally got their ride out, he was reading back over the tale of a Scottish infantryman who'd been separated from his platoon in al Basra for two days, but whose main concern remained the fate of his family's trout farm after a week of acid rain had killed off the entire stock. They all shook hands and wished each other well.

'Make them understand that there is a new Poland,' said Milosz as they parted.

Melton looked around at those who remained. Not quite so many tears now. A few of them were snoring, sound asleep, jerking in the fit of a nightmare somewhere in their past. He heard a couple of guys laughing about a canoe trip they had been on – how drunk they'd been, and the silly idiot with the yellow swimming trunks who wouldn't fall into the raft full of college co-eds.

It was mid evening; a cool, almost chilly night, alive with the rumble of distant air operations. He was tired and very hungry, and getting shack-whacky, having been trapped inside for so long, even in such a large building. The last thing he'd eaten had been a protein bar, four hours earlier, and he just knew the table service in this place was going to suck big-time. Until his transport batch number was called, there was nothing for it but to wait. Having lost the pile of Polish duffel bags on which he'd been resting contentedly, he'd since moved to one of the uncomfortable plastic chairs dotted about the facility. He remembered the poncho liner, which he still had, gifted by the specialist on KP back in Kuwait.

Melton wrapped himself in the woodland-green camo snivel gear as the earlier desert heat turned to night-time frigid. It was there, half asleep, haunted by visions of the mortar attack that had put him in hospital, that Sayad al Mirsaad found him.

27

'You've gotta be fucking kidding me!' Kipper was incredulous, outraged even. In fact, half-a-dozen emotions blasted through him like a hot desert zephyr on finding out that the military had arrested the elected city councillors, but mostly his feelings arranged themselves around 'incredulous' and 'outraged'. 'You can't do that. It's . . . it's . . .'

'Wrong?' offered General Blackstone.

'Yeah, that's right. It's *wrong*. It's fucking wrong in so many ways I can't even begin to count them. What, you guys couldn't get your own way so you just threw the switch on a military coup? For Christ's sake, you're dealing with a bunch of frightened, fucked-up nimrods who take three hours to decide which sort of cookies they're gonna serve up at council meetings.'

'We knew you'd understand,' McCutcheon replied, without a hint of irony. 'That's exactly why we put 'em in the bag. They really do argue about the cookies, don't they? I watched them do it last week. Amazing, man. Truly fucking amazing. Anyway, while they're banging heads over the catering arrangements, *PEOPLE ARE DYING.*'

The last part of his routine he delivered in a parade-ground roar, emphasised by pounding a fist down on a stack of folders that burst out from under the blow in an explosion of paper. Kipper jumped and looked over to Blackstone, but the general remained impassive. It was a bad-cop bad-cop routine.

'Look,' the major said, instantly switching back to his usual calm and spookily cheery self. 'They haven't been arrested as such, just detained preventively.'

'What the hell do you mean, "preventively"?'

Blackstone answered for him. 'To prevent them being arrested when they fuck up so badly they really do get a lot of people killed.'

'Like this morning?'

'Oh grow up, Kipper,' snarled Blackstone. 'This is serious. We don't want to take over here. We don't want to take over anywhere. Hell, we're desperate for someone to tell us what to do, but nobody's putting a hand up. Everyone's arguing about fucking cookies.'

'Bullshit, General, that's an exaggeration.'

'No,' said McCutcheon, tag-teaming again. 'It's a metaphor. For "pointless, infuriating contention about complete fucking inanities". Like cookies – which I can assure you they did argue about. Somebody said they needed to start conserving food, so they spent three-quarters of an hour debating whether they were entitled to a packet of fucking Oreos at their meetings. This was just last Thursday, by phone hook-up, during the worst of the pollutant storm. By phone hook-up, Kipper – they were all *at home*. They could have eaten *their own fucking cookies*.'

Kipper rubbed his tired, burning eyes, but it only made them sting all the worse. 'So what are you gonna do, Major,' he asked, 'keep arresting people until you get someone you can work with? You gonna go all the way down to the dogcatcher?'

'If we have to. But really, I've met that guy. He's a freak – got that gimpy eye, and half of one ear chewed off. Wouldn't be a good look for the next President.'

'President?'

'Yeah, that's what I'm talking about. We need a President, and pronto. If we don't get a handle on this situation, we're all going to hell in a hand-basket.'

Kipper bumped up against a filing cabinet, jarring his elbow on the corner. 'Shit! Who the fuck talks like that? "Hell in a *hand-basket*"?'

The air force man's eyes twinkled. 'Granny Mae McCutcheon.

Eighty-six this year and still skinning her own beaver . . . Oh man, that didn't come out right. She's a trapper's wife – or she was. Granddaddy McCutcheon passed away back in '92. It was Clinton that eventually killed him. Seeing that gladhanding cocksucker take the oath, it was too much . . .'

'Back on message, Major,' said Blackstone. 'Mr Kipper, we have some command and control issues here, and elsewhere. Here it's bad enough, elsewhere it gets worse by an order of magnitude. That mess at your food bank this morning was a C-3 issue. That's what happens when command, control and communication break down. Blood. Gets. Spilled.'

Kipper's head was reeling. He wondered if the heating had been turned up too high or if any contamination had made it into the building through the filters.

'Do you know anything about the line of succession, Kipper?' asked Blackstone.

'The line of what?'

'Succession,' echoed McCutcheon. 'You know, the President gets whacked in a motorcade, the Veep steps up to the plate and *bam!* – any hopes the enemies of freedom had of exploiting our temporary constitutional befuddlement are right down the crapper.'

'Are you sure you're an air force guy?'

'Sure, born and bred. Anyway, the line of succession – focus, dude. Right? You with me? It's toast. We got nada. Nobody. Everyone we could've tapped for the top job is gone. Everyone we've approached since is like: "*Oh no, don't ask me, I'm too fucking busy. I got this fucking cookie crisis exploding in my face here.*"'

The engineer exhaled a deep breath he hadn't even realised he'd been holding in. That probably explained his dizziness. 'So, what do you want me to do about it?'

'About that? Nothing,' said Blackstone. 'That's our problem for now. But this city is yours. Kipper, you're now on the Executive Committee. You and your department heads. I need you to do a better job running this place than we've seen so far.'

'Whoa! Wait on a second. That's a *political* appointment. Only elected officials can sit on the committee.'

McCutcheon shrugged. 'Only elected officials on the civilian side, and they're all unavailable now. So General Blackstone is the senior member, and he's appointing you and the other department heads.'

'What are we – your Good Germans?'

'No, you're the only people we can rely on to keep this place from falling apart.'

'You don't get a choice, Kipper,' growled Blackstone. 'The days of easy choices are over. You've been drafted. You can either get with the program or you can fuck off and we'll find someone who will.'

'Jesus Christ, you people . . .'

'Yeah, wrestle with your conscience in bed, if you have to. But you need to decide whether you're going to help pull your city through, or walk away.'

It was too much. Kipper turned and stormed out of the door.

Was it his imagination or did the Municipal Tower seem to be even more overrun with military uniforms than he'd thought when he first came in? Kipper shook off the thought. No sense getting paranoid. A lot of the support staff were scurrying about on fast forward. A few saw him and looked relieved, others seemed even more frightened and just put their heads down, hurrying past.

The soldiers didn't seem to be intimidating anyone. Indeed, some of them looked pretty well spooked, too. But their very presence, in full combat gear, including their weapons, was enough to put the zap on anyone's head. And what the fuck were they carrying arms for anyway, what did –

Kipper pulled up in confusion. He'd been so angry, so unbalanced by the meeting with Blackstone and McCutcheon, that he'd stomped right around the corner into the Planning Department. Cursing quietly, he retraced his steps to the city engineer's office, his office, a small suite of rooms behind a plain dark wooden door inset with marbled glass. It felt like a holy sanctuary right now. He pushed through, praying that he'd find no military people inside, with their feet up on his desk and guns lying on top of the filing cabinets.

Instead he found Rhonda, his secretary, a large and formidable African-American presence in a room full of frightened white folk.

'Kipper! Thank the Lord at last!' she cried out when she saw him. 'We were beginning to worry they'd arrested you as well.'

'Not yet, Ronnie. Not just yet. So you've heard then?'

He smiled wearily at his team, or what was left of it. Barney Tench, his deputy and old college bud, who looked about as glum as Kipper had ever seen him; Marv Basco, the sanitation chief, a dead ringer for Larry from the Three Stooges; Dave Chugg, water, who looked a lot like Curly to Marv's Larry, at least when you stood them next to each other; and Heather Cosgrove. Sweet, fragile, freaked-out little Heather.

'Whoa. What are you doing here, darlin'?' Kip asked in surprise. 'You should be at home.'

'I wanted to come in,' she said, sounding preternaturally calm. He wondered if she'd been medicated.

Barney shrugged and shook his head. 'I dropped her at her apartment, Kip. But she talked some dumb grunt into giving her a lift back in.'

Kipper sighed. 'Okay. Heather, I'm not sending you home again. But you shouldn't be here. You're in shock. Go and sit yourself down on that couch over there and do not get up again. Ronnie?'

His PA nodded and bustled the girl as gently as she could over to the old brown couch in the corner. Heather didn't really protest or resist. When he thought about it, Kip understood. She had no friends or family in Seattle. Her work colleagues had been caught behind the Wave in Spokane. The only people she had left in the world were here, in this office. It would have been cruel to send her out again.

'So. You've heard about the council?' he said, addressing the room.

They all nodded and mumbled that yes, they knew about the arrests now.

'Did you know you've been drafted?' he asked Basco and Chugg. 'You're on the Executive Committee now.'

'No. Nobody's told us anything,' replied Chugg.

Kipper rubbed his neck, which felt stiff and very sore. He noticed he still had a smear of dried blood on the back of his hand. 'Well, I met the guy behind the coup d'état a few minutes ago. General Blackstone.'

'He's here?' asked Barney.

'Yeah. Hiding down in the deputy mayor's office.'

'Did he have any explanation for this morning?'

'Said it was a fuck-up, and we should get over it.'

'Good Lord!' exclaimed Ronnie, who considered 'heck' and 'gosh, darn it' to be pushing the boundaries of decent language. 'He said that?'

'Close enough,' said Kipper, as he leaned back on his desk. 'He pretty much threw everything back on us. Said if we didn't want the city to die, we'd have to step up to the plate.'

'And what about the councillors?' asked Barney.

'I have no idea. He's got them detained for protection or some crap, somewhere. I dunno what that means, short or long term.'

'Well, it sounds like this asshole feels perfectly free locking up people he doesn't get on with,' said Tench. 'What'd you tell him, Kip?'

'I didn't give him an answer either way,' he replied, chewing his lip. 'And I'm not happy. I'm a thousand fucking miles from happy. But he's right about one thing: no matter what we think of him, we have a responsibility to the city. We still need to get a handle on food distribution. As of right now, there is no market solution to the problem of empty shelves, because most of the market disappeared behind the energy wave on March 14. Priority number one is food. We have enough in aid shipments coming through, if it's distributed rationally. If not, this city will die. It'll tear itself apart before we can work out how to feed ourselves.'

He paused to look around. Heather had closed her eyes on the couch, but he had everyone else's undivided attention.

'I can't do anything about the politics. I'll talk to the army about letting the councillors go, but we have to proceed on the assumption that they won't. So, despite the fact that everything has changed, I don't see that anything has changed. We have a good plan to pull the city and the state through this. We just need to make it work. Which means we *are* going to need the military's help, no matter how difficult that might be to swallow for now.'

Barney Tench shook his head firmly. 'I don't know about that, Kip,' he said. 'What these guys look like to me is fascists.

My mom's family, way back when, they came from Croatia. You only got two types in Croatia: fascists and commies. That's why Grandpa moved here – to get away from that bullshit. And arresting elected officials, no matter how useless, just because it's convenient, that's fascism. And I can't have any part of it.'

'So what are you saying, Barn? You're going on strike? I need you, buddy. The city needs you.'

Barney shook his head. 'You think I don't know that, Kip? My family live here. Anything I won't do for you, I can't do for them either. But this dictatorial bullshit, I can't do. I'm sorry, man. Some things are just too important. I'll leave you a formal letter of resignation before I go. But I will go, and there's nothing you can do to stop me.'

Marv Basco dipped his head. 'Damn,' he said. 'Do you think Barney's right, Kip? Do you think we should all just walk off until the army agrees to get back in its box?'

Again, Kipper felt the weight of everybody's anxiety and expectations settle upon him. 'I don't know, Marv. I got no fuckin' idea. But I do know that if there had been a truckload of soldiers at South Street this morning like there was supposed to be, a lot of people would have lived, instead of getting shot down. I admire Barney's strength of conviction, but I can't afford it. I've got half-a-million people to look after, to feed and shelter. Half-a-million terrified people at that, all of them looking over their shoulder at that Wave wondering if it's gonna decide to gobble them up any time soon. The only reason most of them haven't bugged out overseas is that nobody's willing to come in here and get them. If we still had transport out of here, they'd be gone. Hell, *I'd* be gone. Nobody wants to be here, but here we are anyway, trapped. You ever seen what a trapped, hungry, frightened animal can do to itself, or to anyone who gets too close? It's not pretty. So, if I can't get them out of here right away, I can at least do something about keeping them fed and keeping them safe from the things I can guard against, like mass fucking psychosis.'

He paused then, to calm himself down a bit. He was beginning to lose it, raising his voice and barking his words out. He sighed, and shook his head in apology.

'I'm sorry. But, does anybody else feel like Barney? I need to know right now.'

Nobody answered.

The burning rain had closed in again, early in the evening. The army's weather guys told him it was down to an isolated pocket of toxins caused by a series of fires that had ripped through Portland two days earlier.

Kipper was glad of the weather in one way. It meant he couldn't see the glow from the Wave. It was visible at night, high up in the tower, as if the devil had thrown open a furnace door on the far side of the mountains to the south. It was a good thing most people couldn't see it – that Barb in particular couldn't see it. He was supposed to go out with some of Blackstone's people tomorrow to inspect the thing 'from a safe distance'. Whatever the hell that meant. He didn't think he'd be telling Barb about that little day trip. Her idea of a safe distance probably meant Guam.

'I'll be going now, Kip, if that's okay with you? I'll take Heather back to my place. She can sleep on our couch for a while. Poor child, she don't need to be alone.'

He turned fractionally and smiled at Ronnie. 'Thanks for staying and helping out, Ron. It was kind of a madhouse here today, wasn't it?'

'It surely was,' she agreed. 'And are you okay now, boss? Should I be pushing you out this door to your beautiful wife and child?'

'I'll be leaving soon, don't worry. I got no appetite for hanging around here at the moment. It's just that I have no choice.'

Ronnie frowned at him. 'Don't talk like that, Kip. There's always choices.'

'Yeah, but sometimes they all suck.'

'Ha!' she laughed. 'You sure you ain't a black man?'

Kipper pressed his face against the cool glass of the window pane, beaded with millions of starry droplets of poison. 'Barney won't be the last one, you know.'

'How's that?' asked Ronnie.

'A town like Seattle, people aren't going to stand for this takeover. And that's what it is, Ronnie. A military takeover, pure and simple. And I'm helping them do it. I should be stopping them.'

'Oh, horse hockey! All you're doing is keeping people warm and safe and fed and watered.'

'Keeping the trains running on time?'

'What trains?'

'Sorry. I was being obtuse. What I mean, Ronnie, is that I don't know if I can hold this place together. The council, let alone the city. I wonder if we shouldn't be planning to get the hell out of Dodge. I mean, look at that thing . . .'

She kept her eyes on him, rather than looking at the eldritch glow coming from just over the horizon.

'It took everyone, Ronnie. *Everyone*. Who's to say it's not going to jump out here and take the rest of us in two minutes?'

'Nothing,' she replied quietly. 'Nothing but my faith in the Lord. I know you're not a praying man, Kip. But I say some extra prayers on your behalf every Sunday to make up. And what the good Lord tells me is that nothing he does is without meaning. It all serves a purpose in the end. His purpose. And I do not believe his purpose would be served by laying another tribulation upon us. What is, *is*. This is for us to endure. For you to bear, Kipper. Whether you're a believer or not.'

'I wish I was, Ronnie,' he said. 'I wish I was.'

'So does Jesus, Kipper.'

From anyone else, he'd have taken offence. But Ronnie and he went way back and he knew she meant only the best.

'You coming in tomorrow?' he asked.

'As if you need to ask.'

'I'm sorry. I'm on the edge of a decision here. I think I'm going to front Blackstone. Demand he release the councillors and ease off the restrictions on people.'

'Set my people free?' Ronnie smiled.

'Something like that.'

'And what if he throws you in the clink, too?'

'Well, we all have our choices to make, don't we?'

'We do. And I'm sure you'll make the right ones.'

Kipper didn't reply at first, instead looking out the window at the largely empty city centre. 'You look after Heather,' he said at last. 'She's a good girl, but she's lost.'

'She wouldn't be the first stray we took under our care. Or the last, I'll wager. And you look after yourself, Kip. Don't sit here all night. Get yourself home. Your family need you too.'

'I will, Ronnie. Good night.'

He turned back to the window as she left, staring out into the rain. The city was dark, with only a few lights burning here and there in offices where he could see other people moving around working. As he watched, a few of the lights flickered out too. He tried to pick out the smouldering red light of the Wave but failed. The weather was really closing in.

Ronnie was right. Time to go home.

The walk back to his car was uncomfortable, the rain constant and stinging. They said a big chemical plant had gone up in the Portland blaze, and he thought he could feel it in the pores of his skin where the water soaked through.

It was an uneventful drive home to Mercer Island, thankfully. No riots. No ambushes. Only the usual military checkpoints, through which he sailed without delay, thanks to a new upgraded pass from Blackstone. He tortured himself the whole way, wondering if he should have followed Barney out the door. If they all should have.

He could see candles burning in the kitchen at home as he pulled up, and a curtain twitched aside. He turned off the motor and hurried up the driveway as the door opened.

'Come in, Kip. Hurry up. That rain's gone bad again, they say.'

'Hang on, Barb,' he said, shaking off as much moisture as he could on the porch, and removing his muddy boots.

'Come on. I've kept some dinner warm by the fire. And I poured you a whisky.'

'Thanks, darlin'. That's just what I need.'

'Barney called,' she said.

'Oh. He told you?'

'Everything . . . I'm so sorry, Kip. All those people killed. You must feel awful.'

He dried off with an old towel she handed him, and closed the door. It felt good to shut out the weather.

'Yeah. It wasn't a great day,' he replied wearily. 'And this thing with Barney and the council, I'm just – '

Barb shushed him and took him by the arm through to the lounge room, where a small fire crackled and glowed in the hearth. A plate, covered in foil, sat near the flames, and a tumbler of whisky waited for him on the coffee table.

'I'm sorry about this morning,' said Barb. 'I was a bitch. I shouldn't have put all that pressure on you. I'm sorry.'

'Damn.' He squeezed his eyes shut.

'What?'

He looked at his wife helplessly. 'I forgot the fucking *Piglet* DVD.'

She stared at him for a full second before they both burst out laughing.

28

Admiral Ritchie was wrong. Jedediah Armstrong Culver, of the Louisiana Bar, did not take three or four business suits along with him on vacation. He only ever took one, just in case. As soon as he'd learned of the Disappearance, however, he'd gone straight downtown and bought four new outfits, off-the-rack, but quickly tailored to fit his ample frame. As always, they were either blue pin-striped and single-breasted, or charcoal grey, ditto. Two Brooks Brothers, one Zegna and a rather subdued Armani. He put the charge on one of his European cards, a Visa issued by Barclays Bank in London, where he had worked for three years as an equity partner with Baker & McKenzie before moving home to set up his own firm. The Barclays Visa he normally saved for annual trips to Europe with Marilyn, but none of his US-issued plastic was working. Diners, Amex and Mastercard, none of them were any good. The local merchants had stopped taking them in payment or their billing systems simply locked up when presented with the account details.

For now, at least, there was no such problem with his English credit card. Even so, aware that some might think his use of credit an imposition on the goodwill and touching naïveté of Mr Rajiv Singh, the owner of the swish gentlemen's outfitter on Beretania Street where he bought all four suits, Culver had explained exactly how quickly Singh needed to lodge his accounts this month. Which was to say, immediately.

'And don't take no guff from those sons a bitches neither,' he'd advised. 'Get your money fast, and if you're in the market for some further and better advice – get the hell out of the suit business, too. Ain't gonna be much call for all these fancy duds soon.'

Mr Singh had not needed telling twice. Eighty per cent of his business came from mainland tourists dropping disgraceful amounts of money on exclusive leisurewear. Business attire was a sideline. The next time Jed Culver drove past the shop it was closed. He never saw Singh again.

'Best damn investment I ever made,' he said to himself while climbing into the jacket of his new favourite, the Armani.

'What's that, Jedi Master?' his wife called out, distracted, from the lounge room where she was glued to the television.

Culver tugged at his shirt cuffs as he walked through into the main living area of the Embassy Suites serviced apartment. Marilyn, his third wife, and definitely his favourite, sat curled up at the end of the lounge nearest the TV, ignoring the glorious vista of Waikiki Beach and Mamala Bay in the floor-to-ceiling picture windows. The pollution storm had not yet reached this far around the world, and the advice they had was that the worst of it probably wouldn't drift so far south anyway. Intensifying low-pressure systems were likely to draw the poisoned banks of cloud back up to the northern latitudes. Even so, Marilyn, a forty-year-old who looked thirty and sometimes acted twenty, remained at the end of the sofa, a black three-seater covered in a strikingly dense pineapple motif.

She was, he thought fondly, a bear of little brain, but such a beautiful bear, and so cuddly and loving that he couldn't help but love her all the more. She was just so much easier to live with than the harsh, angular carnivorous bitches he'd married by mistake the first two times. (And if there was one upside to the otherwise unmitigated horror of the last week, it was realising that those two life-sucking trolls had winked out of existence.)

In comparison to Vanda and Louise, Marilyn's needs were simple, if expensive, and she gave him so much in return that he could only worry at the change that had come over her since the Disappearance. What she lacked in book smarts, his wife more than made up for in a vast store of emotional, physical and spiritual resources. She was a woman who rushed at the edge of life, gleefully, like a child chasing soap bubbles on the breeze.

Jed had never known her to vague out in front of the tube for such a long stretch of time – unless it was in front of Fashion TV in the weeks before they decamped to London and Paris each year. This last week, however, she'd camped in front of the box, channel surfing between BBC World, CNN Hong Kong, Sky News and whatever crisis-of-the-moment bulletins the local network affiliates were putting to air. Right now, she was seemingly mesmerised by an interview with some retired British admiral who wanted to blow up the Channel Tunnel and deploy the Royal Navy 'to secure the approaches'. Distracted by his murmuring in the bedroom for only a moment, she had now sunk back into video torpor. Jed shook his head and let her be.

Of his children, there was no sign, for which he was happy. Melanie, aged sixteen and the only positive reminder of his first marriage, had taken the loss of her world like a physical blow. She hadn't wanted to come to Hawaii, and as soon as she realised that all of her friends back home were gone, she'd spiralled into a black whirlpool of survivor guilt, crying in her bedroom for two days. Roger, three years younger, from one marriage down the line, dealt with the shock by putting on a brittle and entirely counterfeit stoicism as his game face. Jed was worried about it cracking open at some point.

'Have you seen Rog around?' he asked Marilyn, interrupting the Chunnel bomber.

'He's with Debbie,' she said, only half paying attention.

'Debbie?'

'A pretty little thing. Down on one of the lower floors. You know – with the girls' choir from Iowa.' As Marilyn spoke she seemed to emerge from a daze, sitting up and actually dragging her eyes off the screen. 'You met her mom, the air force lady,' she reminded him. 'Remember? At breakfast the other day? When they ran out of muffins and toast.'

He remembered now. All of the choirgirls had at least one parent with them as a chaperone, and a few had come with all of their immediate family, dampening the shock a little. But Debbie's mother, an air force reservist, had been called back to active duty two days ago, and had been forced to leave her daughter in the care of the tour leaders.

'Oh yes, I remember her. And Debbie. She's a pretty thing, isn't she?'

He was glad that Roger and Debbie had met. Because, like kids everywhere, they were totally self-obsessed, and given the current circumstances, that was a form of strength.

Marilyn stood up, brightening. 'Yes, she's lovely. And Jedi, the girls are doing a concert tonight, down in the restaurant. Do you think you could get back for that? It would be lovely, don't you think, to do something nice? Everyone will be there, and the hotel manager will be hosting drinks afterwards. To keep up our morality. I could wear a new dress. If I went out to buy one.'

Another man might have wearied of such vacuous babble, but Culver smiled indulgently. The curfew had been lifted somewhat in the islands, allowing people to get out for strictly rationed supplies, but he had no idea whether Marilyn would be able to find a clothing boutique that was still open or accepting her credit cards. Doubtless, knowing her, she would have a wonderful adventure trying, however.

'You knock yourself out, honey. And I will move heaven and earth to be at that concert.'

He kissed Marilyn on the top of her head and loitered briefly by the window, squinting into the morning glare in the hope of picking his kids out of the small, scattered crowds down on the beach. A large but orderly swell pushed regular sets of clean barrelling waves up onto the sand and he knew that they would be somewhere down there: his children, Debbie, a handful of choirgirls and at least one or two parental chaperones, all playing in the surf, trying to keep their minds away from dark places. They were doing well at it too, all things considered, and he sent a quick, silent prayer of thanks up to the Lord for that small mercy. Especially for his daughter, who had found in her new friends a salve for the loss of so many old ones.

On the television the blustering admiral was gone, replaced by a handsome but harried-looking middle-aged man in a white shirt and bright yellow tie. He stood on what looked like the trading floor of some bank or brokerage house and his thick East London accent was difficult to follow, but certain words tolled like funeral bells. '*Meltdown . . . crisis . . . credit shocks . . . market collapse . . .*' A ticker line of breaking news items scrolled across the bottom of the screen. Massed rocket attacks on Israel from southern Lebanon. 'Pre-emptive' Israeli air strikes on dozens of targets in Syria, Iran and even Egypt. Another American cruiser, the USS *Hopper*, swarmed by Hamas suicide bombers on jet skis. Food riots in Berlin. Street fighting between thousands of youths in Paris. More refugees pouring into Guantanamo Bay. A declaration of martial law in six Chinese provinces. A toxic supercell storm forming in the Bay of Biscay.

There was no question in Jed's mind what everyone was doing down on the beach below him. They were trying to ignore the end of the world.

'Bye-bye, honey,' he said to Marilyn as he picked up his briefcase and kissed her again, on the forehead this time.

'Okay. I'll see you later, darlin',' she replied, surprising him with a fierce hug that almost pulled the 205-pound lawyer off his feet. When they separated, her eyes were puffy and haunted. 'Everything's gonna be cool, ain't it, Jedi Master?'

It was one of those questions he wasn't meant to answer truthfully.

'Sure, honey. Everything's gonna be cool.'

And he wasn't lying *exactly*. Things would probably be better for his family than for most survivors, because Jed Culver had come flying out of the starter's gate, throwing himself at an overwhelmed administration, impressing the hell out of them with his extensive background in disaster management and civil–military relations – two bits of fluff on his résumé that might best be described as completely fictitious. Didn't matter. Nobody was going to be checking his bona fides for a long time, if ever, and fact was, if you had to put a realistic description on Jed Culver's colourful employment history you could do no better than saying: Jedediah Armstrong Culver got things done and made sure they stayed done.

Indeed, he couldn't think of anyone better qualified to stick his hands into the fire and haul everybody's asses out with a minimum of singeing and whingeing. And if the price of that was his family getting looked after because he'd snuggled up tight to the surviving power structure, well, then that was just a win-win situation, wasn't it? As he squared his shoulders, still powerful from years of college wrestling, and headed out of the apartment, he was already thinking about that power structure, which was becoming one of his more difficult projects. In his briefcase he had letters from four ambassadors each putting himself forward as interim President, until a new Congress or election could be organised. It wasn't a bad idea, stiff-arming a senior diplomat into the job for a strictly limited amount of time. There were decisions that needed making at a national executive level that simply weren't getting made. But the four bozos in his briefcase were all political appointments – one of whom he'd actually played a very sly hand in getting up – and Culver didn't rate a single one of them much higher than a stale sack of shit. Frankly, anyone seeking power at the moment definitely couldn't be trusted with it.

No, they were going to need someone who actually didn't want the job. Someone who was available but who was nothing like him or any of his peers in the shark tank. They were going to need someone honest. As honest as George Washington, or at least a good enough actor that he, or she, could pull it off. But who?

He was going to have to start doing some digging, finding out what was happening beyond the Hawaiian Islands. The Alaskan state government was consumed with the job of making sure its people didn't starve and freeze to death. Seattle and those parts of Washington outside of the Wave's effect seemed to be muddling through after some unpleasantness with riots and looting, although it was hard to tell with news coming out of there in a drip feed. Perhaps that might be the place to start looking.

Culver stalked through the hotel corridors towards the lift at the end of the hall, brooding on a tangle of competing thoughts, among them how much emptier the Embassy Suites seemed compared to just a few days ago. Almost all of the foreign guests had checked out, but there seemed to be fewer Americans in residence, too. Operation Uplift hadn't started yet and he wondered where they might have gone, since most would have hailed from the mainland. That was less of an issue, however, than the lack of maids. Every morning when he'd emerged from his rooms, at least three housekeeping trolleys were parked somewhere on his family's floor, but this morning, nada. Of course, it might mean nothing, but he made a mental note to check with some of the staff whether there were problems with their pay, whether some people had just stopped turning up to work, or whether there might be any signs of order and organisation starting to fall apart. Of the three surviving US states, Hawaii was the least able to sustain itself. Without massive amounts of external assistance, the islands would probably be ungovernable, even with a huge armed-forces presence. Both the civilian and military authorities were alive to the very real possibility of starvation and a rapid fraying of the social fabric. Given the shit going down in Europe, nobody was sanguine about just muddling through anymore.

He walked into the elevator, which was empty, and punched in the button for the lobby. The lift stopped only once during the descent, to pick up a German couple and their luggage.

'Howdy.' He smiled as they wrestled their bags in. 'Heading home?'

'No,' the man responded in perfect, clipped English. 'We have relatives in Australia we are to visit. Winemakers in the Barossa Valley. Do you know it?'

'No,' he admitted. 'Not much of a wine drinker, though.'

The Germans both nodded as though he'd said something profound.

'So, you think you'll be going home any time soon?' Jed asked when the silence began to stretch out.

'No,' the man replied just as quickly, as they reached the ground floor. He bowed his head brusquely and said, 'My sympathies for your loss,' as they squeezed out with their suitcases.

The foyer would normally have been crowded at this time, with guests checking out and conference-goers arriving for seminars and meetings, but apart from the Germans and half-a-dozen cabin crew from some Asian airline, the lobby was mostly deserted. A couple of wet tourists wandered in from the beach with towels thrown over their shoulders, and the glassy, frozen grins of people desperately trying to avoid looking at the yawning abyss that had lately opened up in front of them. It was a look that Jed Culver was becoming used to. His eyes scanned the floor and he spied his driver standing just outside, sneaking in a last-minute cigarette.

He'd given the cancer sticks up himself twenty years ago, after successfully representing British and American Tobacco in a suit against one of their many former customers. Or victims, as even the executives called them in private.

Bobby Kua, his driver, was a native Hawaiian, a surfer. Jed shook his head ruefully as he watched the boy suck extra hard on the Marlboro, to drag in every last precious carcinogenic lungful, as soon as he saw the lawyer approaching.

'I'm telling you, Bobby, you'd be a much better surfer if you gave those things away.'

'No way, boss,' Kua said with a smile. 'I'm already a weapon. Couldn't get any better.'

He drew one last, long puff before stubbing out the butt and flicking it into a nearby bin. Jed wondered how long it would be before the young man was pinching off his half-smoked butts to finish them later. He made a mental note to buy up a few cartons. Within a week or two, some people would sell their souls for nicotine, he was sure.

'So where to, boss?'

'Pearl today,' replied Culver. 'We'll be there most of the day, then out to the Capitol at about three-thirty for a meeting. You could probably get away for an hour or so if you needed to. But I'm on a promise to get back here for drinks. Say, seven.'

'Got it,' said Bobby, leading him over to the nondescript white Chevy Aveo from the government fleet. Gas rationing meant that only the smallest, most fuel-efficient cars could be signed out of the pool for official business, while civilian motorists were restricted to just a few gallons a week, which could only be purchased on alternate days. Rationing had quickly become an unpleasant reality that everyone had to deal with. Armed troopers posted at supermarkets and gas stations made sure of that. Appeals to fairness and civic mindedness shortly after the start of the Disappearance had achieved nothing but the rapid emptying of grocery-store shelves and at least a dozen incidents of serious violence, including one macadamia-caramel-popcorn-related multiple homicide at a supermarket on Kalakaua Avenue.

Culver was grateful that he had no responsibility for the rationing system. It had quickly come to challenge the Disappearance as *the* open wound on talk radio. The first time an American was told by a heavily armed man in combat gear that they couldn't buy *all* of the Twinkies they wanted, it tended to come as a deep, existential shock every bit as unnerving as the still unexplained cataclysm back on the mainland. Jed himself had quickly emptied the small bar fridge of liquor back at the hotel and filled it up with emergency food supplies, as soon as he'd noticed the breakfast buffet in the restaurant was looking a bit spare. Frankly, he'd have been much happier if he could have relocated Marilyn and the kids to Pearl Harbor, just in case things got totally out of hand. But they all insisted on staying at the Embassy Suites, and he was reasonably confident of making himself important enough to grab up a safe berth in the event of any European-style uprising.

To that end, he strapped himself into the back seat of the car, with room to spread out his documents, and got to work while Bobby drove him through Honolulu. More shops were closed every day now. In fact, apart from bars and heavily guarded food outlets, there was very little open at all and very few people on the streets. Marilyn was probably going to be disappointed in her search for a new cocktail dress.

Soldiers and cops comprised most of the foot traffic in contrast to the first few days after 14 March, when huge unruly crowds had gathered and surged back and forth, almost like people running without real purpose on the deck of a sinking ship. Together the rationing and curfew systems tended to keep people at home most of the time.

They slowed down to negotiate a large but docile crowd that had gathered at the Fort DeRussy parklands for a food-distribution point run by the army. A dozen trucks were parked in a line before an avenue of olive-drab tents. Soldiers were unloading hundreds of boxes, stacking them in neat piles guarded by colleagues toting rifles. It was still a bizarre, unnatural sight – Americans lined up like victims of a Honduran earthquake to score a bowl of rice or a milk biscuit. Culver pushed the images out of his mind and returned to his papers, making some untidy margin notes on a briefing he had to deliver later that day at a telephone hook-up between the attorneys-general of the surviving states.

Admiral Ritchie was adamant that the armed forces could not

continue drifting through the constitutional limbo into which they had been cast. It was not simply a matter of requiring political direction for the course of the hot war they were now fighting in the Middle East. There were security nightmares springing up like poison weeds all over the world, as well as some very basic and uncomfortable questions of sustainability for those forces that remained in existence.

'How do we keep going?' Ritchie had asked Jed late last night.

Culver thought the admiral might as well have asked, 'Why should we keep going?' He couldn't imagine what was holding together a fighting force that had nothing to fight for anymore, and increasingly lacked the money to do so.

Immediate survival, he supposed. But if and when the immediate peril was no longer there, what then? A nation of ten million people – that was the rough estimate of living, breathing American citizens left in the world – a nation that small could not sustain a military even a fraction the size of the one it had at the moment. Especially not with most of the country sealed off behind an impenetrable and utterly mysterious barrier. Frankly, Culver doubted whether the area that remained unaffected on the continent was viable in the medium term anyway. He grunted almost imperceptibly as he briefly thought of all those people stuck in Seattle and just across the border in Vancouver. None of them could be certain some natural fluctuation in the event horizon wouldn't gobble them up in the blink of an eye, although, by that measure of course, nobody on the planet could really feel safe.

You had to wonder how much of the chaos wrapping itself like giant bat wings around the world was down to the effect of that uncertainty rather than the unsettling effect of simply removing at one stroke the massive political ballast represented by America . . . Oh, screw it. It was undergrad bullshitting, all of it. The only thing that mattered was fixing the problems he could fix, and for now that meant stabilising the remnant power of the United States and securing the immediate future of his family.

The lawyer flipped open his laptop and began to compose an email to Ritchie. He wanted to bounce a few ideas off the admiral before the conference call in the afternoon.

'*Hey Ritch,*' he began, very deliberately using the informal style of address he'd cultivated in his dealings with the navy man.

You asked for my thoughts on the line of succession before I wrote them up for the reference group. Well, I'm thinking the only way to punch through all this is to go back to first principles. We've got us a constitutional boondoggle. We need us a constitutional convention to stamp it flat. A short, sharp, butt-kicking convention.

Normally you'd require a vote of two-thirds of the state legislatures just to get everyone together. It's the only amendatory process available in the absence of a functioning Congress and Senate. The intent of the relevant section of the Constitution, Article 5, is that the 'two-thirds' would be 'two-thirds' of all of the states, but that is impossible under present circumstances.

The only available option would be for the three surviving states to declare themselves the only three states and to then call a convention or, more likely, to declare themselves trustees for the 'missing' forty-seven states, and vote those states' interests at a convention called to address the current emergency. The result is the same, and it is the only mechanism available in my estimation to reconstitute a federal government within the letter of the Constitution.

Jed stopped tapping the keys and stared out of the window at the passing scenery for a moment. They had turned onto the freeway, which was largely deserted, save for a few Hummers heading downtown from Pearl, and the National Memorial Cemetery was slipping by on the right. He had a great-uncle buried up there. Uncle Lou, on his mom's side. He'd meant to visit the grave sometime during his vacation but had never made it. He was sure his forebear would understand. Lou Stafford had been killed on Wake Island, the same day the Japanese bombed Pearl Harbor. He'd fought when all seemed hopeless, given his life so that Jed and his kids could live free. You had to wonder what the old guy would have made of all this, thought Culver – before reminding himself that Lou Stafford was only nineteen when he died. Not much of an old guy, really. The lawyer nodded a quick greeting, which would have to do for now.

He went back to his screen, wondering about the difficulties of assembling a convention along the lines he was proposing. The very nature of the three surviving states might pose problems. Hawaii and Washington, particularly the western half of the state, were very liberal, Democratic leaning, and in the case of the latter, not particularly pro-military. Seattle he found notoriously smug and self-righteous, although that may have changed now. The eastern, agricultural portion of Washington, right up to the event horizon, was heavily Republican, although many of those people had already relocated into temporary shelters in Seattle. Hawaii had no oil, no real agriculture and no industry, but it did have a strong military presence. The maritime power alone concentrated here was still greater than that of any other country in the world. Washington had agriculture, industry and refining capacity, but no oil. Alaska had no agriculture, plenty of oil and decent refining capacity, but very little else, particularly people; and what people it did have tended to be very conservative, libertarian Republicans. He just didn't know whether they could all get together.

With Massachusetts and Mississippi gone, you could award a blue ribbon to Alaska and Washington for taking out the Polar Opposites prize. Jed figured that Washington, with its much larger population and resource base, would resist Alaska having a virtual veto over any measures necessary to act within a constitutional framework. And Alaska, for its part, might well see itself as the last bastion of rugged individualism, and so would have limited interest in submitting to a drastically revised federal system highly tilted toward nanny-statism.

It was going to be worse than the First and Second Continental Congress, that was for certain. It was going to make the argument over issues like the Article of Confederation and how much of a person a slave represented look like a middle-school debate class. There wasn't any George Washington around to hold the delegates together or come up with the various compromises they'd need. Any constitutional convention with the three remaining players was going to be a first-class WWE smackdown cage match.

Culver sighed, already exhausted at the prospect of tying all this together into a neat package with a bright bow that everyone would want to own. He returned to his keyboard for one last sentence for Ritchie's benefit.

The trick to making this work will be to cram all the wild cats into the bag before they know what's happening.

The key, he thought to himself, is George Washington. If a modern George Dubya didn't exist, Jed Culver was going to have to invent him.

29

He was an operator, possibly a crook, and definitely not to be left alone with the small-change jar. But Admiral James Ritchie couldn't help but warm to Culver the more time he spent with him. There was no reason they should get on, a patrician New Englander from old money with a long family history of noblesse oblige, and a scheming carpetbagger from the bad end of the bayou. Certainly, naïveté didn't come into it. Thanks to Colonel Maccomb of the 500th Military Intelligence Brigade, Ritchie was well aware of what kind of a creature Jed Culver was. A fixer.

He was the operator your troubled multi-billion-dollar company called in to quickly and quietly clean up the mess left behind by your recently departed and grotesquely incompetent CEO. He was the man who procured the difficult export licence in the hopelessly corrupt, but fabulously oil-rich, third-world shithole. Or the development approval for your six-star resort on the ecologically fragile tropical island. Or the seemingly impossible negotiated truce between the warring Stone Age tribes that was interfering with the profit margins of your hardwood logging operations in the New Guinea highlands. If that didn't work, he hired the heavy hitters who protected your oil-drilling operations in Africa without cutting too deep into your budget.

Jed Culver was a rolled-gold son of a bitch.

That said, Ritchie had a gut feeling that when the big questions were asked, this gladhanding sack of shit would actually give you a straight answer, especially if that answer was something you didn't want to hear. Perhaps he was a bit like old Joe Kennedy in that way. Ritchie, an avid reader of historical biographies, thought he recognised something in Culver that FDR might have seen in the old bootlegger when appointing him to head up the SEC way back in the Depression – a thief you could trust.

The admiral kept all these thoughts to himself, of course, as Culver walked around his office speaking from notes, with his expensive jacket off, shirt sleeves rolled up and tie raffishly askew. Was the ruffled, big-doofus thing just part of his routine? Probably. With a guy like Culver you had to figure that *everything* was part of the routine. But still, he seemed blessed, if that was the right word, with a frightening appreciation for the worst aspects of human nature, and how they might still be turned to everyone's advantage.

'The only intact chain of command we have left,' the lawyer said, in his soft Southern brogue, 'is, of course, your own. But by constitutional tradition, your entire chain remains subordinate to civilian rule and, let me just check-back with you, ladies and gentlemen . . .' Culver looked up from his notes and smiled at the small group of military officers in the room. 'Y'all ain't planning a coup d' état, are you?'

From anyone else, it would have been a dangerous gamble, an insult to people who had pledged their lives to defending the Constitution. But Jed Culver had a way of smiling and somehow twinkling his eyes that added an unspoken *Naw, of course you ain't – you're good ol' boys and gals. The best.*

Ritchie even noticed a smile attempting to creep around the corners of the deeply fissured face of Lieutenant General Murphy, Commander, US Army Pacific, and the senior army officer on the islands. But, for professional reasons, Murphy had long ago banned any semblance of a sunny disposition from his person, and he managed now to crush the small grin stone dead. It had no discernible effect on Culver, who carried on.

'Fact is though, folks, given the scale of disaster we face, precise legality *will* have to give way almost immediately to practicality. As the esteemed Justice Jackson pointed out in *Terminiello v. Chicago*, the Constitution is not a goddamn suicide pact. If we are going to survive, we need good government, and quick. And given that nobody is much interested in fashioning a military dictatorship out of the ashes of the old Republic, I would suggest that for practical purposes it will initially resemble a patchwork of small- and big-town mayors, the surviving political and administrative leadership, law enforcement, and perhaps – no, *definitely* – some religious and community leaders with a large following. Whatever government comes into being out of this nightmare has to *arise* from the ground up, rather than be *imposed* from above.'

'Fine words, Mr Culver,' rumbled Murphy. 'Brings a tear to the eye. But we're in deep shit and we need to dig ourselves out of it, *muy pronto*. Adapt, overcome and drive on.'

There were nine military officers in the room. The commander of the army's 25th Infantry Division and the senior Marine nodded in agreement with Murphy's brusque comment. Again, however, Ritchie watched with sneaking admiration as the lawyer let the rebuke wash over him, even turning it around.

'Damn straight,' said Culver. 'We need this done yesterday. Hell, we needed it as soon as that energy thing crashed down on top of us. But we have to accept that as scared and fucked up as people are right now, especially those poor bastards who are close enough to the Wave to be able to see it, they *will* adapt. There *will* come a day when it's not the first thing they think of when they wake up in the morning. And they will go back to the old ways of doing things, of each against the other and damn anyone in between. It's just our nature. So whatever we set up now has to have the elegance of our first constitutional principles. It has to allow for the better angels of our nature to sing, because, Lord knows, the demons are going to be a massed fucking choir over the next little while.'

'What exactly are you suggesting, Mr Culver? Could you take us through your proposal, step by step?'

'Of course, Admiral,' the lawyer replied. 'Basically, some laws are going to get bruised, if not broken, but even Jefferson would have been cool with that. You know, his purchase of my home state, Louisiana, was, to put it bluntly, completely illegal – and he *knew* it. But he also knew that the strict observance of the written law, while one of the high duties of a good citizen, is not *the* highest.'

Culver stood up straight and appeared to stare off into space, obviously quoting from the third President of the United States. 'The laws of necessity, of self-preservation, of saving our country when in danger, are of higher obligation. To lose our country by a scrupulous adherence to the written law, would be to lose the law itself, with life, liberty, property and all those who are enjoying them with us; thus absurdly sacrificing the ends to the means.'

Having finished, he leaned forward and placed his hands on the edge of the conference table where they all sat. 'What that means, ladies and gentlemen, is that we're gonna crack some heads together. And fast. And by "we" I mean the American people, what's left of us.'

'I think it might be better if nobody showed up in uniform, flashing their medals and . . . what d'you call that stuff – fruit salad?' Culver gestured towards the campaign ribbons on Ritchie's uniform. He didn't wait for the admiral to reply. 'Fact is, we already got blood spilled in Seattle. People are skittish. Yeah, you guys are the only outfit with the chops to put boot to ass and get it all done, but I promise you that anything that looks even halfway like a military takeover will mean the end of *everything*.'

Ritchie clamped down on his surging frustration. Only he and Culver remained in the office, all of the other attendees having returned to their duties. He was hungry and tired and didn't see himself being able to do anything about either any time soon. The austerity measures he'd ordered for every military establishment in Hawaii were not merely window dressing. Food shortages would become dangerous if strict rationing was not enforced. The islands' airfields were running around the clock, shuttling aid in and people out, but a cascading series of economic crises ripping through global money markets was beginning to bite hard in the real world. In the last twenty-four hours, both the Chinese and Japanese governments had quietly ordered container ships loaded with food and medical aid bound for Hawaii to turn around and head home. Ritchie had savoured his cup of coffee at breakfast this morning with sad relish, because he wasn't sure when he might get another one.

'Yes, I understand, Mr Culver,' he said, still refusing to give in to the lawyer's insistence that he was just 'plain ol' Jed'. 'But I am fighting an illegal war. Men and women are going to their deaths on my say-so and not much else. Why are they doing that? No reason. No good reason, anyway. We're there because we're there and we can't get our sorry asses out in good order. Hell, we can't even turn to the United Nations for guidance.'

'I know you got pressures, Admiral. I know –'

'Do you? Really?' Admiral Ritchie stood up and walked over to the window. He stared out at the afternoon sunlight, took a deep breath and turned on Culver. 'I have bagmen from every tin-pot, oil-drenched Dark Ages dictatorship in the Middle East, including the ones we're fighting at this very minute, all banging on my door demanding to know what US government policy towards them and their vile little country is now. Doesn't matter how many times I tell them I'm not the President, not the government – they don't care. They won't listen. To them, I am the man with my finger on the trigger of what is still a very big gun. Big enough to blow them to hell and back. And the worst of it is, I can't just tell them to take a leap because some of them, at least, I need. I cannot get our people out of there without the help of the Saudis and Kuwaitis and Turks, and half-a-dozen others. But of course, none of them want us to go, because they know the whole place will melt down three minutes later. I need clarity, Jed . . .'

Damn it. You're losing it, he thought. *Get your bearing back.*

'I need orders from a properly constituted executive. I need to get my people out of that septic mess in the Gulf. I need to know what role we're going to play here, in CONUS, wherever we end up. I need to know what resources we'll have. I need to get on the phone to Tommy Franks and give him and his people some *hope.*'

Culver absorbed the mini tirade with equanimity, waiting him out. When Ritchie was finished, he nodded, slowly. 'Okay then. That's what you need. Now this is what I need to get it for you.'

Dealing with Culver's Machiavellian schemes was enough to bring his headache roaring back from the dull middle distance, where he'd banished it with a couple of Advils. Ritchie was not at all comfortable being so closely involved in political manoeuvres, but the lawyer was right. The United States had been gutted and

one of the very few working and half-intact institutions it had left
was the military. He was also right that it would be an intoler-
able violation of the country's founding principles if the Republic
became a militarised autarchy in the mad rush of a catastrophe.
And then, in mocking contrast to these high ideals, there was
brute reality.

'The Israeli envoy is here, Admiral.'

Ritchie popped another painkiller and washed it down with
a mouthful of tap-water from his beloved old VF-84 coffee mug.
'Send him in.'

The man who entered the room carrying a briefcase was
relatively short and his grey, wiry hair had retreated at least halfway back over his head. Tel Aviv had dispatched him as their
new ambassador, but Ritchie was adamant that he could not be
addressed as such because he had not yet formally presented himself to the President. (The navy man had flat refused to stand in
for the latter role himself.) Nonetheless, Asher Warat was the chosen representative of his government, and as such was deserving
of good manners and what few diplomatic niceties Ritchie could
extend to him.

'Admiral, thank you for seeing me.' The Israeli smiled, lighting up his wide brown eyes. 'I understand the demands on your
time must be horrendous.'

Ritchie gestured for him to take one of the two armchairs
directly in front of his desk. Warat did so, placing the briefcase
by his feet. Through the windows behind the envoy, the old sailor
enjoyed a sweeping view from Halawa Heights down to the harbour, which looked magnificent under a high sun. A few wisps
of cloud drifted across a hard blue sky and the waters of the base
sparkled bright silver on dark blue. Stare at it long enough and
you could almost believe nothing was wrong with the world. The
long, drawn features of his visitor, sitting smack in the middle of
that view, indicated otherwise.

'Everyone has their own troubles, Mr Warat. I'm sure yours
are as difficult as mine in their own way.'

Warat bobbed his head up and down, and his eyes seemed
even more watery and forlorn than normal, which was saying
something. 'Life is trouble, Admiral,' he replied. 'Especially these

days. And I am afraid I am about to make more for you. Much more – or less, maybe.'

Ritchie was instantly alert, the fatigue of the last ten days sluicing out of him. The small adrenalin surge didn't help with his headache, however. That just grew worse. 'How so, sir?' he asked guardedly.

Warat consulted his watch and seemed to hesitate. He rubbed his fingers together and shifted nervously in his place, before checking the time again. 'You will be aware, Admiral, that the strategic circumstances faced by my country have declined precipitously due to the cataclysm, the absolute cataclysm, that befell your own.'

'Yes,' said Ritchie slowly, as his heart seemed to slow down and grow to about twice its normal size, pressing painfully against the confines of his chest.

Warat hitched his shoulders and chewed at his lower lip. The man was a veritable Wal-Mart for nervous tics and tells.

'Your own forces in the region have come under attack from Saddam, from the mullahs, and from a whore's parlour full of opportunists and crazy men. Hamas, Islamic Jihad, al-Qaeda . . .'

Ritchie nodded but said nothing. Just that morning they had lost the USS *Hopper* and two hundred men to a swarm of jihadi suicide attackers on jet skis. You don't lose an Aegis cruiser every day, and he wasn't certain when he'd get a replacement. Probably never. It was the sort of thing that would have made headlines all over the world before the Wave. Now it was a minor irrelevancy to most news agencies, obsessed as they were with the accelerating collapse of their own societies.

The Israeli envoy glanced quickly at his watch again. 'Your plans to withdraw Coalition forces from Iraq and Kuwait, and US forces from the region in general, are understandable,' he continued, 'if short-sighted in the opinion of my government.'

'Well, sir,' said Ritchie, 'I am afraid the withdrawal is an operational necessity at the moment. It is not US Government policy, as you would be aware. I would characterise it as a tactical withdrawal, not a strategic retreat.'

'Or abandonment,' prompted Warat.

'No,' agreed Ritchie. 'I would not call it abandonment. But

right now, our presence there is making things infinitely worse, and I shouldn't have to explain to you, sir, that we cannot sustain our forces even in the short term. Our base is gone. Every missile we fire, every ship we lose, every soldier or sailor or airman who *dies* is a true loss. They *cannot* be replaced.'

The Israeli shrugged and sighed. 'We understand, Admiral. We have lost too. America was our arsenal and we find ourselves in the same position. Unlike you, however, we can stage no tactical withdrawal. We are trapped within our borders, with nowhere to go, and the barbarians at the gate. You will be aware of that. We are already fighting them. It will be a war of annihilation for one or the other.'

Ritchie ceded the point with a wave of the hand, an almost preternatural dread creeping up on him. It was a physical sensation, something he could feel crawling through his body like ice water rising from his nuts. The diplomat checked his watch one last time. He squared his shoulders and looked Ritchie in the eyes without flinching. His voice firmed up, losing the quaver and uncertainty that had haunted it until now.

'Twelve hours ago, we received a secure data package from our highest placed source within the Republican Guard. His information was so critical that it was cross-checked independently, even though doing so revealed the identity of other sources we have cultivated within the Hussein regime and the Iranian Revolutionary Guards. I am afraid those sources have now been exposed and eliminated. Before losing them, however, they confirmed that a convoy of civilian vehicles crossed the border with Iran and travelled without a military escort, but still heavily guarded, arriving at a warehouse on the outskirts of Mosul at 0300 hours local time yesterday. If you will excuse me, Admiral . . .' Warat leaned over and picked up his briefcase, popping the lid and pulling out a sheaf of papers which he handed across to Ritchie.

They were photographs mostly, with a few pages of printed material that appeared to be chemical analyses. The pictures were obviously close surveillance shots, the admiral noted, taken covertly by somebody at the warehouse.

'The large vehicles you can see in these pictures are standard commercial trucks,' Warat went on. 'Two Scania transporters, a

Volvo, a Mack Truck, and a Hino heavy diesel. The utility vehicles – SUVs, I believe you call them – provided the escort. The Hino truck carried a shipping container in which was stored an unknown quantity of uranium hexafluoride. I am afraid we have lost track of it. The other trucks, which we were able to continue tracking from Mosul and on to an Iraqi missile battery, contained weaponised anthrax and botulinum.'

Ritchie glanced briefly at the typewritten pages, but he was not a chemist and they meant nothing to him. He assumed they somehow attested to the contents of the trucks.

'We have no sources within the Iraqi battery, and the exposure of our other assets will have caused Saddam to alter his plans anyway. But we must presume that we now face the mortal danger of a missile strike on Israel with biological agents. Our policy in the face of such threats has always been stated clearly. We will not just retaliate, we will strike pre-emptively.'

Ritchie placed the documents very carefully on his desk. His hand was shaking and there was nothing he could do to stop it.

'So, my government hereby informs you, Admiral Ritchie, as the commander of friendly forces in the region, that as of one hour ago, the Israel Defense Forces have commenced Operation Megiddo. I am informed by my government that Israeli Air Force units are currently en route to twelve centres. I have here a list of the targets.'

The envoy passed across a single sheet of paper, which Ritchie took with a trembling hand. Warat, he noticed, seemed abnormally calm by comparison. The Israeli had apparently done all his sweating and shaking when he'd first come in.

The list was divided into two parts, labelled *Counter Force* and *Counter Value*. The former was a catalogue of military bases and suspected WMD sites such as the Iranian Revolutionary Guard training facility at Hamadan, long suspected to also be the Guards' principal WMD depository. 'Counter Value' comprised a short list of cities. The American officer found it hard to breathe. Baghdad, Tehran and Damascus in Syria were slated for destruction within hours.

'You can't do this,' croaked Ritchie. 'You'll kill millions, tens of millions, of innocent people.'

Warat's face was ashen and drawn, but firm. 'Yes, Admiral. We will. It is either that or millions of our people will die.'

'But . . .' Ritchie found it hard to speak. Blood rushed through his ears and dark spots bloomed in front of his eyes.

The other man sensed his difficulty and pressed on. 'We have drawn up the target list in such a way that it should not expose your forces to significant radiological effects, and it will not be necessary to fly through airspace controlled by the Coalition. This will not be like 1991, Admiral. We will not require IFF transponder codes; however, the range of some of the longer strikes means that without midair refuelling, our planes cannot return home. My government therefore requests the cooperation of the US Air Force in assigning such in-flight refuelling assets as we would require to successfully complete all of these missions without needlessly sacrificing our personnel. For many of them, it will be a one-way trip otherwise.'

'Are you mad?' Ritchie stared at the man, who had the good grace to look embarrassed.

'My government did not expect to receive a positive response to this request, but instructed me to make it anyway.'

'Mr Ambassador . . .' Ritchie faltered, forgetting that Warat had not been formally received and confirmed as ambassador. 'Mr Warat, I am afraid I cannot allow this plan to go ahead. Your government must call its planes back.'

'I am afraid they will not do that, Admiral. Under any circum-stances. My government is convinced that we face annihilation as a people if we do not act immediately.'

'You will be annihilated if you *do*,' protested Ritchie.

The Israeli nodded glumly. 'Anything is possible these days, Admiral.'

Ritchie's heart was still thundering in his chest, but his head was at last clearing of the shock and disorientation. He took a deep breath and leaned back in his chair.

'Sir, I am afraid I must inform you that I will direct US forces in theatre to interdict this strike and stop it by any means possi-ble. I will further contact our Coalition partners and request any and all cooperation they might provide. And, I will immediately inform the governments of the targeted nations that your strike is inbound and that I will assist them in whatever way possible to repel it.'

Warat received the rebuke with stoic reserve. Behind him, through the wide glass windows, life went on. Not normally. But it did go on. Some traffic moved through the streets. Children would be playing in suburban back yards as parents did their best to insulate them from the horror of a world collapsing in on itself. High above the idyllic panorama, Ritchie saw the sun glint on the wings of a commercial airliner, outbound. For where, he had no idea, but it was undoubtedly full. The Israeli envoy sighed and quickly recovered his composure.

'My government expected you might react in this fashion, Admiral,' he said. 'It would be the honourable thing for you. However, I must point out that your own forces have degraded the air defence nets of Iran and Iraq to the point where they cannot deny our air force. And the IAF has done the same to the Syrian Air Force over the last week of fighting. By warning them, you will do no more than condemn millions to spend their last hours in abject fear.'

Ritchie slammed an open hand down on the desk with a thunderous crash. 'Goddamn you, will you *listen*? You cannot do this and you *must* not. I am ordering my theatre commanders to interdict your sorties with deadly force. We *will* shoot you down!'

Warat's chin moved up and down like a bobble-headed doll on a dashboard. His shoulders twitched and when he spoke he did not look Ritchie in the eye. 'My government has prepared for such an eventuality, Admiral. The weapons packages will be delivered with an escort of IAF fighters. They will engage *any* hostile force that tries to prevent them from accomplishing their mission. Any. Hostile. Force.'

'My God,' breathed Ritchie. 'You'll kill us all. If you do this, how long do you imagine it will be before some maniac in New Delhi or Islamabad decides they need to get the drop on their nemesis? How long will it be before Russia and China decide things will be a lot simpler with us, here in Hawaii, out of the picture?'

'I cannot answer these questions, Admiral, as you well know. But I can tell you that if we do not act, the Jewish people and their state will be wiped out in a second Holocaust. And you *know* that I speak the truth.'

Ritchie dropped his head into his hands and rubbed at eyes that burned with a lack of sleep. 'Get out,' he said quietly.

30

The envoy had lied. Or rather, he had not told the whole truth because he did not know it. The target list that Asher Warat supplied Ritchie with was incomplete, as were other details of the attack, including the fact that many of the warheads would be delivered by Jericho II missiles, not piloted aircraft. In addition to the cities and military facilities on the list, the Israeli Cabinet had added a further thirty-eight sites. Suspected Iranian nuclear centres in Natanz, Ardekan, Saghand, Gashin, Bushehr, Aral and Lashkar A'bad were all slated for destruction, along with the cities of Tabriz, Qazvin, Shiraz, Yazd, Kerman, Qom, Ahwaz and Kermanshah. Five of the nuclear-tipped missiles were inbound on Libya as the ambassador had sat down with Admiral Ritchie, while another three were headed for military bases near heavily populated Egyptian cities. But one mission, the last to depart, had a very different target. The Aswan High Dam.

Colonel Rudi Molenz sat quietly in the cockpit of his F-15I Ra'am at the end of the main runway of Hatzerim Air Base in the Negev desert. Tel Aviv and his family lay fifty miles to the north, but the bejewelled cluster of lights would be dimmed tonight, as the city hid itself in the dark. He would not be able to glance back over his shoulder after take-off and smile at the thought of his two little children safely in bed, somewhere in that mass of glowing pearls, surrounded by soft toys and dreaming of Daddy's return. Because there was no guarantee that Daddy would ever be coming home. And worse than that, no certainty that home itself would survive the night or the next day. Behind him, his weapons system officer, Lieutenant Ephron, hummed tunelessly, irritating Molenz, who said nothing. Ephron was nervous and the flat, atonal droning was his release valve. It was the same before all of their missions. When they finally had a release from the control tower, the little putz would shut the fuck up and do his job flawlessly. He always had before.

A brief crackle sounded in the earphones of his bulbous DASH helmet. 'Attention Reach One Ninety, please stand by . . .'

Molenz felt his balls shrivel and became acutely aware of silence in the back of the cockpit.

The voice crackled in his Display and Sight Helmet again. 'You have clearance to execute Plan Magenta. Preliminary release codes: Echo Kilo Four Niner Three Niner Foxtrot.'

Molenz had burned the one-use code into his memory but checked the mission pad velcroed to his leg anyway. 'Release confirmed,' he replied. 'Reach One Ninety away.'

The enormous power of the aircraft's two F-100 Pratt & Whitney engines came roaring up like an angry leviathan as the pilot's heads-up display blinked into life. The caged fury of the jet fighter completely enfolded him and as always he felt the deep-body thrill of having so much potential power in his hands. Beneath the old familiar sensation, however, lay a dread that ran deeper than anything he had experienced in all the years he had been flying combat missions. It was not the fear of his own death, but of becoming Death itself, because attached to the underside of his Strike Eagle was a thirty-kiloton nuclear warhead in a specially hardened penetrator casing. It was designed to slam into the base of the Aswan High Dam, drilling down through ten metres of concrete, before birthing a small supernova to atomise much of the dam's solid mass, releasing the superheated waters behind to roar down the Nile Valley like a mega-tsunami towards Cairo.

Part of him could not believe he was doing this, that it was even happening. But the two aircraft ripping down the tarmac right after his were real. As were the dozen flights he'd watched leaving earlier for much farther flung locations. He'd known many of those pilots. Commanded some of them, trained others. Their goodbyes were restrained but heartfelt. Unlike Molenz, they were flying single-engine F-16s with modified drop tanks to get them all the way to Iran while flying low and fast through the wastes of northern Iraq. They would traverse the edge of the Kurdish regions, where years of British and American enforcement of the no-fly zone had denuded Iraq of air defence assets. Even with drop tanks, however, there would not be enough fuel for them to return. Extraction teams were standing by to evac anyone who made it to the preset rendezvous points. But Molenz knew from looking into the men's eyes as they shook hands, and in some cases hugged, that they were going to their deaths.

The Israeli Air Force flights left in groups of three. One F-15 carried the warhead while the two escorts carried air-to-air load-outs. Those headed for targets in Iran and Iraq did not expect to encounter any significant resistance en route. The top-secret electronic warfare suites installed for this mission were designed to maximise the escorts' effectiveness against any allied planes they might encounter. It was possible that Coalition aircraft might try to stop them, but Molenz and his peers figured they had enough on their plate as it was. They were no threat.

The colonel pulled back on the stick and the Strike Eagle clawed its way up into the stars. At twenty thousand feet he performed his usual contortionist feat anyway, straining to catch a glimpse of the capital off on the northern horizon. It was definitely dimmer, but not completely blacked out. What would be the point? Modern sensors meant that pilots no longer had to feel their way through darkened enemy airspace, seeking out targets to bomb. Iraqi Scuds had been landing in Israel for days, despite the best efforts of the Patriot batteries and the promises of General Franks that Coalition special forces would own the western deserts, from where the missile threat originated. The promises meant nothing. The threats issuing from the Iraqi dictator in hiding, however, they had to be taken seriously, and ever since the flooding of Baghdad those threats had become increasingly shrill and apocalyptic. It almost seemed as though Hussein and the Iranian president were racing each other towards a rhetorical abyss. *And now*, thought Molenz, *the abyss races towards them*.

Behind him, Ephron ran through another check of the Elisra

SPS-2110/A Modified Electronic Warfare System and the LAN-TIRN pods while Molenz checked the APG 70 terrain-mapping radar. Even in the foulest weather, in the darkest hours of night, the radar provided him with a picture-perfect return from the ground, making it possible to pick out even small targets like mobile batteries tucked away in a dry wadi. At just under 4000 metres in length, and 114 metres tall, containing 43 million cubic metres of concrete and fill, there wasn't much chance of him missing the dam.

Molenz edged their nose around to the south, to skirt Beersheba and trace the length of the border with Jordan, on a course for the headwaters of the Gulf of Aqaba. The three jets flew low and fast, operating up near the edge of full military power, shrieking over the ghostly blue-black desert at Mach 2.5. They maintained radio silence, each man alone with his thoughts, as the demands of the mission allowed.

A few minutes before they would overfly the resort city of Eilat, he pushed the stick over and sent them rocketing towards the Egyptian border. Beyond lay the Sinai Peninsula and the rocky wastes of the biblical Wilderness where David and the Israelites wandered for so many years. Mountains lay ahead, a jagged-edged void of darkness blotting out the stars, corresponding to the image scrolling down the APG 70 screen, bathing him in the softest of glows.

During a brief interlude, they traversed a particularly desolate and empty stretch of mountainous wasteland, and the pilot became aware of the beating of his heart. For one perverse second he couldn't help thinking of the millions of hearts he was about to still forever. Pushing the thought away like a fearful spectre, he concentrated on the return from the radar and the threat boards. Nothing untoward. The Egyptian Air Force was steadfastly refusing to offer even the slightest provocation to its neighbour, for fear of unleashing exactly the sort of hellfire that Molenz now carried with him. They didn't seem to know he was even in their airspace.

Whatever moral qualms Molenz had suffered before accepting this mission – and there had been many – he had nonetheless volunteered for it. They all had. He would destroy the dam and doom millions tonight, none of whom had raised a hand against him or his country. But there were millions more who would, who wanted to, and who even now were battling with the Egyptian Government's security forces on the streets of a dozen cities, attempting to overthrow the Mubarak regime because of its supine response to what they called Zionist aggression. And they were winning. That was the hell of it. They were winning and very soon they would sit in the Presidential Palace in the north-east of Cairo and turn their blood-dimmed eyes on his home and his family – and it was wrong and it was tragic, and he might well burn for the sin he was about to commit. But Rudi Molenz was convinced that if Israel did not reach out now, at this very moment, and hammer its mortal enemies into the dust, then the Jewish state and race would surely perish.

He shook his head, a quick, constrained movement inside the helmet. They were coming up on the Gulf of Suez, one of the trip points in the fight, where they would be exposed to the radar and weapons of the western naval forces operating in the area. They had no IFF codes for this flight; and as lead planner for the squadron, he knew that an envoy had been dispatched to Hawaii to inform the Americans at the last possible minute of what was about to happen under Operation Megiddo. But they would not know just yet.

He checked the mission clock. Fifteen minutes. In fifteen minutes they would find out, via the diplomatic envoy.

But in half that time he would be over the target.

The Gulf flashed beneath them and Ephron sat quietly waiting for the warning tones and pings that would tell them they had been painted by the sophisticated arrays of the naval vessels below. The warning was not long in coming. Three harsh, discordant tones sounded and Lieutenant Ephron went to work, firing up jamming sets and countermeasures. Molenz focused his attention down to a stiletto point, determined to see them through this passing hazard.

It was over as quickly as it had begun. The waters dropped away and suddenly the giant wind farm at Zafarana appeared in the crisp aquamarine glow of his terrain-rendering APG screen. Huge, alien-looking structures blurred beneath them, recalling for

Molenz an unbidden childhood memory of running alongside a picket fence through which a setting sun had cast its dying rays.

Behind him, Ephron requested permission to arm the warhead.

'Granted,' said Molenz. 'Primary release code: Alpha Two Four Delta Zero Two November Three Two Five One Echo. Confirm.'

'Confirmed.'

'You are released to arm.'

Ephron, whose voice was shaking, busied himself on a small keyboard, tapping out a long series of commands before announcing, 'The weapon is armed.'

Molenz dry-swallowed.

The port wing dipped thirty degrees and the plane began to track to the south as he levelled off, dropping the flight into the folds of a long valley that ran roughly parallel to the Nile. The faintest silver crescent of light bleeding over the ridgeline to the west would be Luxor, often acclaimed as the world's greatest open-air museum. The temple at Karnak, the Valley of the Kings, the ruins of Thebes, they were all just a few minutes' flying time away.

Molenz pressed on, allowing the Strike Eagle to begin its climb to a safe release height.

As all three birds emerged, screaming from the folds of the ancient valley, he finally saw what he was about to do. Towns and villages clung to the edge of the Nile, their weak, twinkling lights marking its sinuous path through the night like illuminated buoys. The IAF colonel pressed back into the flight seat as he poured on power for altitude.

Ephron announced from behind him that the automatic targeting system had a lock and requested that Molenz release control of the aircraft to him. The pilot agreed and felt that brief, awful moment of loss as microprocessors took over. The Eagle rolled and turned to bear down on its target, just like the bird of prey for which it was named.

There was an audible clunk and the plane jumped, suddenly free of the dreadful burden that had fallen away from beneath them. All three aircraft then pitched over and raced due east, away from the terrible thing they had just done.

The warhead slipped quietly down through the warm moist air. It did not whistle or shriek to announce its death dive. A passing sibilant hiss and the whirring of guidance fins at the tail were the only sounds it made. In the nose of the bomb, a small electronic device slavishly tracked the laser-designated aim point at the base of the dam, for as long as the warplanes were able to maintain the link. By the time they broke contact to escape the blast, the weapon had already settled into a stable descent. It struck the angled concrete wall of the Aswan High Dam at near supersonic speed with a thunderous boom that shook the entire structure.

Designed to spear deep into extremely hard, multilayered underground facilities, the penetrator – an elongated narrow-diameter spike of superhardened nickel-cobalt steel alloy – was enhanced with a void-sensing hard target Smart Fuze that measured the progress of the warhead into the body of the dam, delaying detonation until an optimal depth had been reached. Israel had long ago learned the art of reducing the size of its nuclear devices without sacrificing their destructive power. Some of the bombs falling on cities throughout the Middle East at that very moment topped out in the megaton range. The blast and heat and radiation effects they yielded were vastly greater than the primitive bombs that the US had dropped on Japan in 1945.

The device that lay, for all of a millisecond, sleeping beneath millions of tons of cement, was modest in comparison, although twice as powerful as the Nagasaki and Hiroshima bombs. It did not need to be a city-killer, however. It merely needed to bring down a wall, and did so by instantly turning a significant portion of it into white-hot plasma. The Smart Fuze, having determined that an optimum penetration had been reached, signalled the bomb to compress a sphere of subcritical explosive material around a plutonium core, setting off a fission reaction.

Surrounded as it was by the crushing mass of the Aswan High Dam, the initial burst of radiation could not escape and so began to rapidly heat the encasing medium to tens of millions of degrees, vaporising everything within the expanding sphere of gas. Growing towards its maximum size, the fireball cooled rapidly, until it no longer possessed the heat to transform solid mass into gaseous residue. Having disintegrated the wall, though, it did have more than enough thermal power to flash-boil the waters of the dam. With nowhere to easily dissipate, the blast front transferred much of its energy into a shockwave that sped outwards from ground zero, imitating the effect of an earth-shattering quake. It struck the smaller, original dam wall a little further downstream like a hammer of the gods. A few thousand people who lived in the small settlements around the dams died instantly in the explosion, leaving nobody on the ground to witness what happened as the Nile was set free.

High above, however, Molenz had a perfect view and whispered a prayer, asking forgiveness for what he had done. As the immediate effects of the explosion cleared, a mountainous wall of hot, irradiated water was unleashed on the valley below. A giant, boiling wave, over a hundred metres high, began its journey to the sea; it roared out of the huge lake, punched through the mushroom cloud that rose inexorably over the void where one of the great engineering marvels of the world had stood just a few seconds earlier. He could hear nothing in the cockpit, over the roar of the Eagle's twin engines, but the pilot imagined that hearing that monstrous wall of angry, super-hot white water rushing towards you would have to sound something like sticking your head inside the F-15's afterburner.

He watched the progress of the wave for as long as he could, saw it sweep over Luxor like a giant ocean dumper rolling over a child's toy at the beach, before something even more terrible caught his eye. The rising of a new sun, hours before dawn, far off to the north.

Where Cairo had once stood.

The tremor in Admiral James Ritchie's hand was obvious as he read from the briefing note. He managed to keep his voice steady, though – wouldn't do to be caught pissing his pants in a roomful of civilians.

'Casualties from the immediate effects of the first strike are estimated at eighty-five million,' he said. 'Further casualties from the breaching of the Aswan dams may double that.'

The dozen men and women arrayed around the grand oak table

in the Governor's dining room were ashen-faced. And some of them *were* visibly shaking. Governor Lingle had tears in her eyes. The room was crowded and hot, partly because of the amount of audiovisual equipment that had been brought in to effect the videoconference with Anchorage and Olympia, the Washington state capital.

The surviving civilian authorities of the United States of America were in shock. Perhaps even more traumatised than they had been by the Disappearance. Ritchie wasn't sure why. Perhaps it had something to do with the completely inexplicable nature of that event. Perhaps they were all still in a sort of denial. Everyone in this room, however, everyone involved in the conference, had grown up with the spectre of nuclear war lurking at the edge of their consciousness. It was not merely explicable, it was familiar.

'Indirect deaths, in the short term, from radiation poisoning and injuries, are estimated by our modelling to climb as high as another thirty million over the next month.' He heard somebody curse softly but continued on. 'Medium-term fatalities, from the collapse of governing and societal systems, may double or triple that again. There may be unquantifiable effects, further afield. Millions of bodies and radioactive debris have been flushed out of the Nile Delta and into the Mediterranean, for instance, where they will contaminate the environment and enter the marine food chain.'

A woman sitting by Governor Lingle covered her mouth and ran from the room.

Jed Culver, who had been standing near the door, waiting to speak, yanked it open to let her through. He was sweating profusely and appeared blotchy and unwell.

'General Franks reports that coordinated attacks on US forces in the area have ceased,' said Ritchie. 'Iraqi forces are requesting ceasefires or surrendering en masse. Iranian forces are withdrawing. Further, there seems to be no evidence of any national command authority in either country having survived the Israeli strike. In the areas of Iraq still under our nominal control as part of Operation Katie, local Iraqi government leaders have requested humanitarian aid. We have had similar requests from the surviving civilian leadership in both Syria and Egypt. Iran has also requested our assistance.'

He paused as a Republican state senator from Alaska swore loudly and colourfully.

'Uncoordinated attacks by non state actors continue off the coast of Lebanon and in Afghanistan. General Musharraf survived yet another assassination attempt this morning in the aftermath of the attacks. He informed me personally that Pakistan has now gone to full readiness to retaliate against anyone – Israel, India, anyone – who even remotely threatens his country,' he went on.

Ritchie let his hand drop and looked around the room, taking in the cameras beaming his image across the Pacific to Olympia and Anchorage as well.

'I have no national command authority to whom I can turn for orders,' he said. 'Our own nuclear deterrent is effectively useless without said authority. I can give orders to fire all day and night long, but the commanders of our ballistic-missile subs will not follow them without Presidential authority. That is why we originally scheduled this meeting. I believe that if we had such an authority, if we had a President and even the semblance of an emergency government, that this . . . *holocaust* could have been avoided.'

He had spoken the word without forethought, but having done so, did not regret it.

'This is not your fault,' he added, with a mounting and voluble anger that seemed to imply just the opposite. 'You have all had a hell of a time dealing with the impossible demands of our own emergency. But I promise you, if you cannot come to some sort of working arrangement, if you do not leave this room tonight with a plan to immediately rebuild some basic form of national government, then what happened today will happen again and again and again until the only evidence that civilisation ever arose on this planet will be its radioactive ruins.'

And with that, he turned and stormed out of the room.

31

Suzie was in the lounge room, watching *Toy Story* with her friend Emma, when Kip heard the news. Emma's mom had a transit pass and a voucher for the food bank in Bellevue and the chief engineer had spent the morning on the phone to Fort Lewis – another 'privilege' of his newly elevated status – making sure that this time all of the security that should have been in place was in place. He was just running through a checklist of the local aid centres with a Lieutenant Somebody-or-other when he heard Barbara cry out from across the kitchen.

'Just hang on . . . I'll call you back,' he said.

She had the radio on, listening to a news bulletin – which Kipper never put much stock in because of the army's control of the airwaves. Yesterday's shootings at Costco, for instance, had been reported as a 'serious disturbance', possibly 'Resistance related', that had halted food distribution for the day. Nothing more.

Whatever Barb had just heard, though, had to be something more than the anodyne pap and propaganda that Blackstone's people let out. She was pale-skinned by nature, but at that very moment she looked almost translucent, as though every drop of blood had rushed away from her face. Her hands shook visibly as she raised them to her mouth.

'What is it, Mommy?'

Suzie and Emma had appeared at the door, drawn by the cry of an adult. Both of them wore very grown-up frowns. Kip hustled them back into the lounge room with a promise of 'emergency chocolate' from the camping rations, before hurrying back to his wife.

'What's up?' he asked. Her eyes were wide with fear.

'A war,' she said. 'A nuclear war has started.'

Kipper's stomach flipped over. 'What d'you mean?'

'It's on the radio,' she said in a quavering voice.

He cast a quick look over his shoulder but the kids were back watching the movie. He stood next to Barb, who grabbed on and held him tightly. She seemed even more scared than she'd been after the Disappearance.

'. . . of sixty million dead in the Nile Delta. Israel remains on the highest state of alert, and the Israeli Cabinet is meeting in secret. Full-scale fighting continues in the Gaza Strip, on the West Bank and in southern Lebanon, but hostilities elsewhere in the region have ceased . . .'

The report was short, sourced from somewhere in England, to judge by the accent; and frustrating in the brief details it gave of American forces, which were reported to be unaffected, for the moment.

'What if they bomb here, Kip? What will happen?'

'Shh. That's not gonna happen. This is a local thing, over there. It's been coming for over a week now. It won't affect us.'

'But the Chinese or the Russians . . .'

'Barb, we didn't do it. They weren't our bombs. It's not our issue, and even if it was, all of the navy's missile boats are still at sea. I think. Most of them, anyway. Nobody is going to bomb us.'

She was shivering violently, and kept looking over his shoulder to the lounge room, where Kip could now hear Buzz Lightyear hamming it up. 'To infinity . . . and beyond!'

'You're seeing Blackstone today, right?' said Barbara, almost accusingly.

'Right,' he replied, with some care.

'Well, if you get one thing out of that useless cocksucker today, make sure it's a good idea about whether we're on a target list. Because I mean it, Kip, we're so gone. We are out of here if he even hints that Seattle might get hit.'

'Okay,' he said, still holding her. 'I can do that. It's the sort of thing I would ask anyway. But you need to stay calm, all right?

Don't go losing it in front of the kids. Do you still have everyone coming around for the home-school thing today?'

Barb shook her head, but didn't look up. 'I don't know now.'

Kip pushed her away gently. 'You should. Suzie needs it. That rain's cleared out and people will be looking for you. They'll be looking *to* you. You need to hang tough, Bub,' he said, invoking a pet name he used only in the rarest of circumstances. 'I'm not going to sit here for the sake of it. If we had to leave, we would. Straight away. But if people panic, this place will unravel so quickly that nobody will get out. Do you understand?'

His wife looked up and wiped away a few tears. Her eyes were swollen and red and she had to sniff to clear her nose. But she nodded. 'I'm sorry. It's just . . . on top of everything, you know?'

'I know. Be strong, okay? I do have to go. I have to get to Fort Lewis this morning and pick up a bunch of guys coming up from Olympia.'

'You're not driving down there, are you?' she asked, suddenly fearful again. 'Olympia's much closer to the Wave.'

'No,' he assured her. 'They stayed in town overnight. They're just coming out to coordinate the relief effort through the rest of the state. What there is of it, anyway.'

Kipper kept his misgivings to himself, but he really didn't know how much use they'd be. The state government had lost about a third of its people and was still reeling around in shock. He couldn't blame them. The city would be exactly the same in their position. He just didn't want to get sucked into their death spiral.

'I'll be late, but I will be back. Don't worry. And don't spend the day hovering over the radio while we have power. That stuff means nothing to us now. It's somebody else's problem.'

He saw Barbara gather her forces and quell her fears. She was so much smaller than him, but stronger in many ways. He wished he could have taken her to sort out General Blackstone. One of Barb's patented maulings and the old prick would run up the white flag for certain.

He kissed her on both eyelids and went through to say good-bye to Suzie and Emma, knowing it would probably be the last pleasant moment of the day.

FORT LEWIS, I CORPS HQ, WASHINGTON STATE

'Release them now!'

'Now is not the right time.'

'Now is completely the right fucking time, or I walk. My people walk. Every fucking city council employee walks and you can deal with the consequences,' said Kipper, stabbing at the tabletop for emphasis.

General Blackstone, half hidden in shadow under the shaded light, folded his arms and leaned back, disappearing further into the darkness. 'The consequences will be that you go down in history as the man who destroyed America,' he replied, just as implacably.

Kipper snorted. There were at least twice as many military personnel as there were civilians in the underground conference room at Fort Lewis. Blackstone had obviously insisted on scheduling the meeting here to keep them off balance, but Kip was determined it wasn't going to work. He wished he had Barney with him, though. Two axe handles across the shoulders, and dangerously impatient with bullshitters and idiots, he'd have made a great shotgun rider for this mission.

'America is more than just a name on a map or a bunch of business interests,' said Kipper. 'It's not the military. It's not the President. In fact, it's none of those things anymore. It hasn't been since they disappeared. I'm not destroying America, you are, General. America is an idea – of the people, by the people. You do the math on the rest of it. Because locking up the people's representatives, no matter how useless and fucked up they might be, *that* is destroying the idea of America. And I'm here to tell you that we won't stand for it. Release the councillors now.'

Blackstone, who had been sitting back, absorbing Kipper's attack, suddenly exploded forward into the light and slammed both open palms down on the table. 'How dare you! You march in here, under the pretence of amity, and lay down a subversive agenda . . .'

'Oh please – what are you, channelling McCarthy? The only subversives here, my friend, are toting guns and pretending the fucking Constitution doesn't exist. Well, it does, and if you won't defend it, we will.'

Blackstone gaped as though struck and Kip wondered if he might have gone too far. But no, damn it, he would be heard. Even if it meant he ended up in the cells too. He didn't dare take his eyes off Blackstone, lest it be interpreted as weakness, but he could sense the presence of Dave Chugg and Marv Basco on either side of him, and of the state government people beyond them. They weren't exactly supporting him yet, but they weren't backing Blackstone either.

'Haven't you seen the news, son?' asked the General. 'Are you a complete imbecile?'

Kipper smiled, but without warmth. 'The news? Is that what you call it? I've seen the censored bulletins your media people let out.'

'Uh-huh. And did you happen to notice anything about a nuclear war starting overnight? You think that might affect how you see things? Do you really want to turn the city over to a bunch of headless fucking chickens who couldn't even decide what cookies to eat the last time the world was ending? What'll it be this time, Kipper, as the fallout cloud closes in? Deadlock over flavoured milk or Kool-Aid?'

'I don't know, General. That'll be up to them. And they'll be judged on their performance or lack of it the next time they go to the polls . . .'

'Oh my god, man! There won't *be* a next time!'

'Why, you getting rid of the vote while you're at it?' countered the engineer.

'Don't be obtuse.'

Kipper closed the manila folder in front of him and scanned the ranks of military personnel arrayed around and behind the general. The only one he recognised was Ty McCutcheon, on Blackstone's right. What could they all be thinking? he wondered. They had to take off those uniforms sometime – surely they didn't want to live in a prison camp at the end of the day.

At least Blackstone hadn't ordered him thrown in irons yet. He let his eyes wander around the room, playing for time. It was an unremarkable breeze-block structure, somewhere deep underground. Maps of Seattle and the local area covered all the walls. Some others had been obscured by hastily hung drop cloths. He had no idea why. Perhaps it was time to roll a hard six.

'How about we ask Admiral Ritchie?' Kip suggested, turning back to let Blackstone get the full wattage of his stare.

The general wouldn't have made much of a poker player. His lips curved downwards, his shoulder rolled, a vein stood out on his neck. He did everything but run a finger around the inside of his collar and make an exaggerated cartoon gulp. A few of his uniformed offsiders shifted noticeably in their seats too. Major McCutcheon, Kip noted, was as still and quiet as a stone dog.

'Holy crap!' The engineer smiled, chancing his hand again. 'You haven't told Ritchie, have you?'

'I have full authority for line management of the tactical situation here and I . . .'

The blustering tone nailed it. 'Oh, General,' said Kipper. 'Oh, dear me . . . We are in trouble, aren't we? My apologies – I mean it. I came in here all ready to beat you down. But now I see what I need to do is give you an *exit plan*, right?'

A long, uncomfortable silence greeted that, broken in the end by McCutcheon.

'Keep talking.'

'An offer?' said Kip. 'Truth be known, I don't have one. This has sort of caught me by surprise, but if my colleagues agree to let me take this on the fly . . .' He glanced sideways at Dave and Marv, who nodded, and at the state government people, who were now more obviously behind him. 'Look, I guess, if you let the councillors go, and apologise for the inconvenience, I could do my very best to make sure that they don't make a meal of it. Unless you've tortured them or something – you haven't done that, have you?'

He was joking but Blackstone took genuine umbrage. 'They've been quartered more comfortably than any of my people, I'll tell you that.'

'They had Xbox and satellite TV,' offered McCutcheon.

'Well then, I'm sure they'll see the upside of their

imprisonment,' quipped the engineer. 'Look, being serious, I can understand why you felt the need to take them out of the decision loop, but you just can't do that. Let them go. Put them back on the Executive Committee . . .' He held a hand up to stave off any objections. 'But in the meantime we'll set up an *Operational* Committee, with my heads of department, some guys from the state capital, and whoever you feel the need to have on it, and the OC can do the actual grunt work of ensuring the power stays on and people get fed. Okay? Executive can discuss . . . I dunno . . . the meaning of life . . . but at Operations we'll actually get stuff done. Like assigning security to food distribution,' he finished, pointedly.

Blackstone let out a long breath and leaned across to consult in a lowered voice with Major McCutcheon. After a few moments of muttered discussion, he leaned forward and nodded. 'All right. You square it with the councillors, or it doesn't happen. Believe me, Admiral Ritchie is going to be a lot less interested in what's happening here than the Middle East for the next little while.'

'Well, let's hope for your sake we don't have to find out.'

'Is that all, Mr Kipper?' asked Blackstone. 'Can we get on with the meeting now?'

'No,' he said. 'All this *1984* bullshit has to stop, too. Travel permits, monitoring people's phone calls and shutting down the media. It's convenient in the short term – God knows I understand that – but it is a road to hell, General. And it has to stop here and now.'

'Are you crazy?' replied Blackstone. 'Even in normal times, during natural disasters, the government reserved the right to temporarily restrict travel, to federalise services, ration supplies and limit communications. You surely can't be serious about letting people run around as they please? Think how that scene at your food bank the other morning would've turned out if just anybody had been allowed to turn up. Some controls are necessary. Especially given that we have a fallout cloud from the Middle East making its way around the world.'

Kipper leaned back and tapped his pen on the table. Some of what Blackstone said made sense, but he couldn't help but feel they were paving a path to their own doom with good intentions.

'The fallout, we'll deal with,' he said. 'We have some experience of it now, thanks to the pollutant storms. They were a bit of a left-handed gift that way, I suppose. But I am serious, General – this police-state bullshit won't stand. It weakens us in the long run. I'm going to suggest that one of the first things the Executive Committee could do – when it's re-formed with its original, *elected* members, is look at exactly what restrictions are necessary.'

Blackstone looked like he was going to choke.

'Or we can take it up the line to Admiral Ritchie,' Kip suggested helpfully.

'Goddamn, this is why we need a proper chain of command,' grumbled Blackstone. 'These decisions should be no-brainers. Instead, I've got a bunch of no-brain pen-pushers telling me how to do my job.'

Kip sensed Marv Basco stirring beside him. His sanitation chief was slow to anger, but he did hold grudges and he wasn't one for ignoring a personal slight. There was no sense in letting this get out of hand, seeing as how things had gone so much better than they'd expected.

'Listen, if an elected official tried on this KGB stuff, fine. There's checks and balances to constrain them, and they can always get ass-whupped at the polls. But you're not elected, General. You have force. But you have no power. Nobody *consented* to being ruled by you, and that's what's been happening. Rule by decree. It has to end. We have to get back to first principles, now more than ever.'

Blackstone's hands were clasped, thick fingers knitted together, but they barely moved. He had stilled himself again. 'We will agree to disagree on the necessity of certain emergency measures, Mr Kipper,' he said slowly. 'For now, martial law will remain in place, as it remains in place throughout Alaska and Hawaii, without all of the amateur dramatics we've endured here. But I will release your councillors – on the proviso that they understand the extremity of our situation, and the absolute necessity of matching ends to means.'

'I will do my best, General,' replied Kipper, in as conciliatory a manner as he could. 'I guess we can get on with business. And I guess that business has to be the Middle East and any fallout that might reach us.' He felt Marv Basco nudge him with an elbow. 'Oh . . . and on a sort of related topic, we really need to talk about the nuclear plants back behind the Wave. Marv here thinks some of them are going to melt down.'

32

Everything had been going so well. Pieraro had spoken very quietly to a deputy manager at the Fairmont (the manager being a complete wanker) and between them they had quietly drawn up a short list of potential passengers for Julianne. The deputy manager did not seek transport, merely a cut of the shakedown. A sum was agreed upon, discreet contacts were made, and a meeting was duly arranged in one of the resort's more expensive bars. It had all taken about four hours but everything was going swimmingly. And then some fucker turned on the telly.

Even Jules, who had an unnatural ability to maintain her focus under the worst of circumstances, was blind-sided by the reports coming out of the Middle East. If there'd been any upside to recent events, it was the sudden collapse of the media's obsession with that benighted shithole. Even the Iraqi war news still ran a poor second to the Disappearance. But sixty, maybe seventy million dead in a nuclear strike . . . that did get your attention.

She had gathered a small group of potential customers around a table, sipping cocktails at hyper-inflated prices, and eating macadamias that weren't *quite* worth their weight in gold. The bar filled up as the day waned, mostly with displaced Americans and wealthy vacationers from Mexico City. Her grandfather, Lord Rupert, had been in Singapore just before the Japanese took it in '42 and Jules wondered idly if Raffles had felt like this. A genteel outpost surrounded by a gathering darkness. It was hard to tell which group was more desperate: the Americans, who filled up the room with booming voices and sheer physical presence; or the Mexican elite, whose anxiety was quieter and, if possible, much more extreme. For her purposes, however, only the *gringos* held any interest.

Jules had been following enough of the news to know that she could get the displaced Yanks into port legitimately at a number of places around the Pacific as part of some deal called Operation Uplift. She could even hit up the remains of the American Government for her fuel and supply costs if she felt really cheeky – and could be arsed filling out the appropriate forms for lodgement at the nearest consulate or embassy. The wealthy Mexicans, however, had nothing even resembling the wreckage of a government to lobby foreign capitals on their behalf, and Jules wasn't willing to take the risk of running them all the way to Sydney only to have some little immigration Nazi with a clipboard tell her they couldn't land. Miguel and his family, she'd get in somewhere by other means, but that marked the outer limits of her largesse.

So they'd been sitting at a table in the coolest, darkest corner of the bar, a small band of super-rich refugees, negotiating payment for passage, when the background buzz in the place suddenly spiked upwards and drowned out all conversation. Somebody screamed 'No!' and Jules tensed up, instinctively reaching for the pistol hidden in her small carry-all, but staying her hand once she realised nothing was going down. A small crowd had gathered under a television fixed high in another corner of the bar and something had set them off. Briefly she fought down a surge of panic, like a rat twisting in her mind, terrified that the Wave had expanded again.

A barman turned up the volume as people argued and shushed each other, and Jules recognised the voice of the BBC World presenter Mishal Husain. Poor old Pete'd had the hots for her. Jules smiled sadly at the memory of him drunk on Jamaican rum, stoned on hash and growling at the TV about exactly what he'd like to be doing to Ms Husain while she burbled on about some EU trade meeting. She missed him terribly.

'*In Tehran alone,*' read Husain, '*it is estimated that three million died in the initial blast and firestorm, which extended more than a dozen miles from ground zero. Many more died quickly from radiation exposure, and experts say that the final toll in that city alone may reach six million. Other Iranian cities destroyed in the attack include Qom, Isfahan . . .'*

Pieraro crossed himself as the news silenced the entire bar for a second. Her Gurkhas, Shah and Thapa, standing a few feet away, providing a formidable barrier to anybody wanting to approach them, did not visibly react. Their eyes continued to sweep the room like cameras.

'That's it. I'm not going to Hawaii,' said the construction magnate.

'What?' asked Jules, still straining to hear the television.

'Pearl Harbor. That's in Hawaii. If there's gonna be a nuclear war, it'll get hit for sure. I'm not paying you everything I have left just to get my family turned into fucking shadows on a wall by some Chinese A-bomb.'

Cesky was his name. Henry Cesky. A squat, powerful-looking man with coarse black hair and a nose that had obviously been broken more than once. He owned a hundred-plus building cranes towering over twelve North American cities. Within half an hour of hearing about the Disappearance, he'd transferred as much available cash as he could from his US accounts to a series of shelf companies registered in Vanuatu, using that money to buy gold and diamonds in Acapulco. Cesky was travelling with his second wife and four children, all girls, and as soon as he and Jules had met, the construction king had demanded passage to Hawaii for them and then Seattle for himself.

'I still got an office in Seattle,' he'd said in a deep, rasping voice that was just barely inflected with a trace of Eastern Europe under his harsh Brooklyn accent. 'My girls, they can't go to Seattle – too close to that fucking wave, it is. But I don't mind that. I don't think that fucking thing is going nowhere. So you take me there. Lotta fucking work to be done in the Northwest now. Lotta money too be made, to make up what I lost and what you fucking pirates are stealing from me. But my girls, they go somewhere I know they're safe. Hawaii.'

That had been half an hour ago. Now Cesky's tune was entirely different.

'No fucking way do they set foot on those islands! No fucking way do they get within a *hundred thousand miles*. You take them as far away from this bullshit as you can.' He was pointing at the TV screen. 'New Zealand – they filmed that *Lord of the Rings* there. Got some great fucking six-star lodges built for the movie stars. End of the fucking earth, it is. Went fishing there once. That'd be good. Or Tasmania – where they got that devil in the cartoon – that's even further away. But no fucking Pearl Harbor. Not now.'

Jules felt like her head was going to spin off. Cesky wasn't the worst of them, not by a long shot. That'd be the porn king, Larry Zood. He didn't look like a porn king, possibly because he was an internet porn king, and so looked more like a crooked real-estate broker. But he oozed a sort of pre-emptive creepiness that assured her he would one day weigh three hundred pounds, wear a bad hairpiece, and still insist on bouncing hotties on his knee.

Having arrived at the table an hour ago with a small imitation Fabergé egg, Zood had tossed it to Jules like a golf ball, demanding to know upfront how many of his 'bitches' he could take with him. 'I'll give you one egg per bitch,' he'd offered. 'They're fakes, from Thailand, but the jewels are real. I can leave a few bitches behind. They know that. Makes 'em extra keen to please, if you know what I mean. But I *will* need some with me. I don't like the water – I don't even like the hot tub they got by the pool over there – so a fucking sea voyage? Shit, if you don't mind I'm just gonna bomb myself with crystal meth and stay in my suite getting blown. That's why I need some bitches with me.'

The Brit was tempted to shoot him right there and then, and she wasn't the only one.

He'd been trying to get Fifi to climb on board since finding out that her mother had been one of the original *Hustler* babes. 'Larry Flynt was a great American hero,' Zood announced now in all earnestness, before grabbing one of Fifi's boobs and squeezing experimentally. When she peeled his hand away with a painful jujitsu technique he simply laughed. 'Ow! What a fucking rack. That was totally worth it.'

'Jules,' said Fifi, between thinly pressed lips, 'if this fucking nimrod gets on the boat, he pays twice the going rate.'

'Fine by me,' she agreed.

'Hey!' protested the porn king.

Jules leaned forward and fixed him with a glare like a pin pushed into a butterfly's back. 'Understand this, Mr Zood. We are not your bitches, we are people smugglers. Criminals. If you touch any of my crew, or any other passenger, like that again, I will have Mr Shah take out his pistol and shoot you in the head. And, yes, you will now pay double the asking rate if you wish to leave this city with us.'

Zood held her glare for a few seconds before breaking into an oily grin. 'Money schmoney,' he mugged. 'I still got plenty to blow. I didn't even have my dough stashed in the US – legally I don't exist there. For tax purposes, you know. Legally I got *disappeared* years ago.'

He was drinking heavily and very much amused by his own wit, but Jules could detect a slightly anxious edge to his demeanour.

'If you don't mind, Jules,' said Fifi, 'I've got crew to interview back at the marina. I'll see you back there. Better company if you ask me.'

'Sure, baby, you go. Thapa can escort you to town. Sergeant Shah and I will catch a ride with Miguel.'

Fifi left the table without a backward glance. An uncomfortable silence ensued for a moment as Julianne regarded Zood with cold contempt.

Not that her other candidates were much less odious. A property developer and his wife – no kids. Some guy whose family owned a health fund; he had his third wife and one small child with him. A merchant banker, with his very own bank, based in Basel, Switzerland; plus his mistress. An oil broker. And a couple of trust-fund delinquents, a brother and sister, who seemed not at all put out that their entire family back in Boston were gone. The siblings, like everyone else at the table, had distinguished themselves by striking like rattlers as soon as they knew the score. Cashing up and converting to exactly the sort of high-end trade goods Jules had known would hold or even increase their value, at least in the short term.

She had trouble keeping their names straight, and was seriously thinking of a cull. Maybe dumping the porn king and his posse of bitches, and possibly Cesky, who struck her as trouble. They were all very demanding people. The trust-fund duo, Phoebe and Jason, had an especially noxious sense of entitlement, one she recalled from the useless rich kids of her own childhood.

'Will there be staff?' Phoebe had asked, before nodding towards the two Gurkhas. 'Other than them.'

'We could bring our own, I suppose,' her brother had mused, not even bothering to run it by Jules. 'Hire them here, perhaps, from the resort?'

But Cesky, he was the real quandary. Although she knew nothing about the construction industry, she figured it had to be a tough game. Wasn't it rotten with mafia money and crooked unions? To make a fortune in it, you'd have to be as hard as tungsten, which wouldn't necessarily count him out as a prospective passenger. But she just had a feeling with this bastard that if he got off the leash, you'd suddenly have something like a 300-pound bull mastiff with amphetamine psychosis tearing at your throat.

Then again, she supposed, she could always have Shah just throw him over the side.

'*Israeli Prime Minister Ariel Sharon has warned other regional powers that they will have to disarm immediately, if they do not wish to be attacked in a second round of strikes. The Saudi government has already agreed to immediate talks with Tel Aviv and has stood down its military, which had been on high alert since the outbreak of hostilities with Iraq and Iran.*'

'Man's a fucking genius,' said Cesky. 'A fucking devil, but a genius.'

'You think he's a *genius*?' Zood arced up without warning. 'A fucking Hitler is more like it. He's a fucking war criminal, Cesky. A mass murderer. He should be fucking stoned to death for the rest of his life.'

Cesky laughed in the pornographer's face. 'With a name like Zood, you would think that, wouldn't you? Where'd your family come from again? No, lemme guess – they were ass-fucking goats in the Bekaa Valley for the last three thousand years, right?'

'You fucking Jewish pig!'

Jules caught Pieraro's eye for half a second, just long enough for an unspoken question. *Where the hell did you find these idiots?*

And then the two men were on each other, punching and clawing. Their chairs tipped over and drinks crashed to the floor. The

banker's mistress screamed, knocked down in the sudden eruption. The trust-fund brats simply pushed themselves back to a safe
distance and smiled, enjoying the entertainment. Shah moved like
a pouncing tiger but Miguel beat him into the fray. A flurry of
blows from the Mexican cowboy, a blur of short, vicious punches,
laid both of the tourists out flat.

Without consulting anyone, he stood over the prone figures
and announced, 'You will not be travelling on Ms Julianne's boat.
You will need to make your own arrangements. Do not attempt to
answer me back or get to your feet.'

Zood opened his mouth to speak and Pieraro suddenly pis-
toned out one booted foot and kicked him in the face. The man's
head flew back with a nasty click and he flipped over, landing on
his back. The *vaquero* turned a stone face on Cesky, who was glaring
at him murderously, reminding Jules of an enraged bull. Pieraro
absorbed the full force of the man's enmity, never breaking eye contact. Eventually Cesky folded, crabbing away from the table on all
fours until he felt he was at a safe enough distance to stand up.

A couple of security guards appeared, pushing their way
through the throng, which had momentarily turned away from
the television. The two Fairmont employees stopped in their
tracks, however, at a single glance from the Mexican.

'Man,' said Phoebe, a little breathlessly. 'That was so fucking
hot.'

'Do you wish to come on the boat, señorita, to escape?' Pieraro
asked her.

She flushed noticeably at his attention. Jules recognised it as a
purely sexual response. 'Yes,' she replied.

'Then you will shut the fuck up!' he barked. 'And do what you
are told when you are told. All of you! *Comprende*?'

The girl flinched, but nodded. The others all muttered and
mumbled their assent. Back at the bar, with the prospect of personal
violence abated, the crowd reluctantly turned back to the TV.

Jules saw Shah acknowledge the *vaquero*'s handling of the situation with the slightest dip of his head. She had to admit, it was
pretty fucking cool. None of these rich bastards would give them
another moment's trouble, she was sure of it.

But she was wrong.

ACAPULCO BAY

Fifi was never comfortable around mucky-mucks, as she referred to anyone wealthier than a gas-station attendant. Except for Jules, of course – her fall from societal grace and favour meant that she very much met with Fifi's approval. 'You're like Paris or Britney,' she often told the English exile. 'Rich but cool.'

The Oregonian was pleased to be away from that crowd up at Acapulco Diamante and back at the marina.

And she liked Mr Lee. He reminded her of old Lenny Wah, the man who rescued her after she'd fled her stepfather's dream of a family threesome and cable TV fame via the agency of Jerry Springer. Lenny ran a super-cheap Chinese take-out in San Francisco's East Bay, where she'd fetched up looking for a cheap meal after running out of money. The meal she got, a confronting fried rice/chow mein combo with a rock-hard spring roll, for $3.50. She also got a job offer, washing dishes in a huge clawfoot tub that stood out of view of the customers, in a weed-choked yard behind the café. The last dish-monkey had quit two days earlier and Lenny had let the pile of washing-up grow under a layer of cold, grey, fat-caked water.

'But Lenny was kinda nice,' she told Lee. 'He had real soft skin and he smelled of jasmine rice.'

'Lenny sounds like a bum, Miss Fifi. He try to make jiggy-jig for dishwashing?'

She snickered. 'Only every fucking day. But he was real nice about it. He didn't get upset when I said no.'

'You always said no?' he asked protectively.

'Not always.'

The old Chinese sea dog rolled his eyes as Thapa showed the next man through to see them. They sat behind a folding card table on the dock of the marina where Jules had berthed the sport fisher while the *Rules* lay well offshore, guarded by the remainder of Shah's men. The hasty patch-up work occasioned by the gunfight with Shoeless Dan stood out on the fibreglass hull, and more than a few of their potential recruits spent their interviews nervously eyeing the damage.

The next guy through – an older, pot-bellied American, with a dense map of broken blood vessels colouring his swollen nose, and a fat cigar perched in one corner of his mouth – snorted when he saw it. 'Hot damn! I guess I wouldn't want to see the other guy, eh?'

Fifi glanced over her shoulder briefly at the scorch marks and bullet holes. She tried to find the man's name on the list Thapa had provided, but the piece of paper seemed to have blown away, leaving her with nothing but a cup of flat ginger beer and a bowl of pretzels in front of her.

'The other guy is dead,' she replied. 'And who're you, Salty Sam?'

The man grinned, showing off uneven yellow teeth, but his smile seemed warm enough and contained none of the leering suggestion in Larry Zood's eyes. 'Rhino Ross, young lady. Chief petty officer, United States Coast Guard, once upon a time. These days, I've been running a fishing charter round these parts. And whom might I have the pleasure of addressing?'

'"Fifi" will do. And this is Mr Lee, who's *our* chief . . . petty . . . guy. So we already got one a them. What else can you do for us, *Rhino*?' She paused and regarded him through narrowed eyes. 'And did your parents really call you that, or something really gay that you just changed to Rhino?'

Ross smiled again and blew a perfect smoke ring. 'Rhino A. Ross. It's on my passport and birth certificate. Makes me kinda unique, don't you think?' He leaned forward. 'And lest you have any doubt whatsoever, it is *good* to be the Rhino. Now, let's get down to brass tacks. A little birdie told me you were looking to crew an ocean-going vessel. Bridge crew in particular, am I right?'

'A little birdie?'

'Yup. Ran his mouth right up to the point I ran a stick through his ass, and toasted him up medium rare over some hickory coals. A little scrawny, but good eatin' – beak was a little crunchy, though.' Another smoke ring punctuated the comment.

Lee said nothing, contenting himself with his kretek cigarette and a contemplative air. He gazed past Ross, away down the marina, where Fifi could see Thapa standing watch over a dozen men who'd also turned up to apply for berths on the yacht.

Something about the Rhino's demeanour changed. His eyes

hardened and his voice took on a commanding, almost military, tone. 'Now, given the size of that sport fisher you got all shot up over there, I figure you've got yourself a real ocean liner stowed away somewhere. And it's gonna have all manner of sensors, radar, communications gear and other assorted technological doodads, none of which you know a damn thing about – am I right? Looks more like the starship *Enterprise* than a sailboat to you, right? No, don't answer. The Rhino is always right. And of course, given all the holes some douche bag has already shot in your runabout, you know what sort of trouble is waiting for you up ahead. So here's the Rhino's iron-clad guaran-goddamn-tee: you take me out to your boat, I'll prove to you that I can run your systems, and then you can get me the hell out of here before it blows up. I need to get out of Acapulco, and you need a pro out there, Miss Fifi. Someone who knows these waters and the sort of lowlife scum that swims in 'em sometimes. Seems to me that the last thing you need to be worrying about is which button to press when a bunch of bad guys come charging over the horizon with knives between their teeth.' With that the Rhino sat back and puffed contentedly on his cigar, releasing a swirling cloud of thick white smoke with a self-satisfied whoosh.

Fifi leaned forward now, bunching her boobs up between her arms, to see if Ross would drop his gaze. He didn't. 'Would I be right in assuming you'd know one end of a gun from the other, Rhino?' she asked.

'Twenty years in service, ma'am. You can assume away, but you know what they say about people who "assume".'

She nodded. 'So, y'all said you ran charters. What happened to your boat? Why don't you just get the hell out under your own power?'

The Rhino folded his massive forearms and gestured towards her vessel. 'See all the holes in your hull? The ones in mine were a lot bigger. I ran a legitimate business, miss. I don't know what you did before all this, but the fact that you're sitting here tells me it probably wasn't legit, and you had the guns and the balls to fight off whoever came after you. I wasn't so lucky.'

Lee exhaled a thin stream of fragrant smoke. 'Mr Rhino,' he said. 'Your lost boat, do you know who attacked you?'

The former Coast Guard chief nodded. 'I do. A local pecker-head, working for a toothfish poacher down south. Said he was recruiting for his bossman. Wouldn't take no for an answer, so he shot up my boat when that was the only answer I had for him.'

'Why didn't he shoot you?' asked Fifi.

'Shooting my boat hurt more,' he said, quite honestly, she believed.

A lot of folks made the error of mistaking Fifi for some kind of life-sized Sluttymuch Barbie. But she'd been looking out for herself long enough to have developed a wild dog's instinct for sniffing out troublesome men. The job at Lenny Wah's take-out, which quickly morphed into cooking as well as cleaning, had scored her a spot on a catering-industry training course run by a Bay Area businessmen's charity – 'guilty fags', she called them – sponsoring college degrees for homeless kids. Her army-surplus cot in the storeroom at Lenny's counted as homeless. She graduated in the top five of her class, and landed a gig with an LA-based catering firm that specialised in providing 'nutritional services' for the military in shitholes-of-the-week like Bosnia and Mogadishu.

Fifi moved a lot more easily through that sort of crowd than the five-star ghetto of West Coast fine dining, and after shacking up with an Army Ranger for twelve months in the Balkans, she could field-strip an M4 carbine blindfolded. She'd also had a lot of experience with men like the Rhino; hard, uncompromising, and occasionally stupid men who were, nonetheless, decent at heart.

She leaned over to Mr Lee. 'What d'you think?' she whispered.

'He'll eat too much, but he's okay,' replied the Chinaman. 'Mr Pete would have liked him.'

'Okay, Rhino.' She turned back to face the old chief, who had heard everything. 'If you've brought any kit with you, stow it over there by the ramp. You can start out by helping to load some stores while we finish talking to these other guys.' Fifi waved towards the small crowd of hopefuls gathered by the marina gate and watched over by Thapa.

The Rhino nodded brusquely and said 'Thanks' before looking around. 'You said you wanted some stores loaded?'

'Inside,' she said, gesturing to the wooden shed in front of which they sat. 'Bags of rice, beans, lots of canned foods. Heavy work. But that won't bother you – you're the Rhino.'

'No,' he agreed, flashing a stagy grin and tucking his cigar firmly into the corner of his mouth. He pointed at one of his massive biceps and said, around the cigar, 'Yeah, it'll be no bother at all since I didn't get these from pettin' kitty cats.'

Ross paused before ducking his head into the shed. 'Oh, one other thing. You got a humidor on that boat?'

Fifi gave a quizzical look. 'Like a hot tub, you mean?'

'No, darlin', it's a little storage compartment for my Cuban friends here.' The Rhino blew a thin stream of blue smoke into the sky.

Fifi shrugged. 'I reckon so. It has everything else.'

The last thing she heard as the Rhino signified his approval and disappeared into the shed was, 'Oh yeah, it's good to be the Rhino.'

The lambent glow of Acapulco, a soft dome of light defining a horizon at the edge of the world in the absolute blackness of night at sea, had changed character to Jules's eye. It looked less artificial now, less fixed. Suffused by a burnt-orange tincture, it flickered and even flared at times.

'Another high-rise going up,' said Fifi.

'I imagine so.'

They worked by starlight and the pale illumination of a red moon. It had been that bloodstained colour since the Wave appeared. The *Aussie Rules* remained blacked out, a precaution against more attacks, as the new crew members that Fifi and Mr Lee had chosen helped to move supplies from the sport fisher to its mother ship.

Jules was generally pleased with the haul of men and cargo. She'd been a bit taken aback by the Rhino when she'd first met him, especially by the perpetual wreath of cigar smoke that preceded and followed him like London fog, but had quickly come to accept his bluster and bullshit as a well-polished routine. He'd probably been practising it on tourists for years and had forgotten how not to be in character. She couldn't fault his work ethic or his skill sets, however. He'd fired up whole suites of sensors and arrays in the bridge that had proven completely impenetrable to everyone else. And having done so, he'd gone right back to hauling sacks of rice and freshly killed meat – very expensive, freshly killed meat – onto the boat deck of the *Rules* and from there off to the freezers. Another odd thing: every so often he would stop one of the other workers, point to one of his enormous biceps and say, 'You don't get these from pettin' kitty cats', whatever that meant. Odd, very odd.

He stayed out of the ice room with Pete's body in, though. For now, that was sealed off.

'I'm glad Miguel kicked the shit out of those assholes,' said Fifi as she picked up an LNG canister and hoisted it over her shoulder.

Jules grunted after catching a sack of potatoes that had been tossed up by Thapa as though it was no heavier than a bag of fairy floss. 'Bloody hell,' she cursed, struggling not to fall over.

A German man, short but powerful-looking, caught her gently by the elbow. 'Not so good to be falling overboard, no?' He grinned, his teeth standing out in the wine-red light.

'No. Thank you . . .' replied Jules, reaching for his name. The yacht was beginning to fill up with strangers, and although she tried to commit all their names and potted histories to memory, there was just so much for her to do each day that she never really felt as if she was getting on top of any one job.

'This is Dietmar,' Fifi said, rescuing her. 'He's German, you know, like hot-dogs used to be. He's our navigator now. Used to work on a container ship.'

The German, who looked to be in his thirties, nodded enthusiastically as he wrestled the heavy bag of potatoes off Jules, before flinging them over his shoulder with as little apparent trouble as Thapa had experienced.

'Okay,' she said. 'You'll do.'

'Yo, Boss Jules!' called out a hoarse, rasping voice. The Rhino. 'Where do you want me to stow your boom sticks?'

Jules smiled and nodded at Dietmar, to thank him for his help. She peered down onto the boat deck, swarming with Gurkhas and new crew-mates, and found the Rhino shouldering a wooden box of Mexican Army rifles that Shah had secured from somewhere.

The number of things she didn't know about on this yacht was growing bigger and bigger every minute.

'Take them through to the gym, Rhino,' she called down. 'We're using that as an armoury for now. One of the Gurkhas will show you where it is, if you need.'

'Don't worry. I'll follow my horn, it always knows the way,' he replied. 'Oh, and where the hell is the humidor that Cap'n Fifi told me about? I've got four boxes of Davidoff Anniversario number 1s in my ruck and if they dry out, you'll find out up close and personal why rhinos are such surly beasts.'

'Library,' she called back at his retreating form as another newcomer, an Indian by the look of him, smiled and nodded shyly.

'Engine room, please?' he asked.

'Follow the Rhino, sailor, but take the second stairwell down two decks. You won't miss it.'

She turned around to ask Fifi if she could spare a few minutes to take her through the crew manifest again, but she was gone. Probably chatting up Dietmar on the way to the galley. Julianne took a few moments to just lean on the starboard rail and stare back towards the coastline. They were still a good twenty miles out from shore, giving them enough time to see anyone coming at them. The radar, which was now working much more effectively thanks to the Rhino, was showing dozens of vessels within a few nautical miles, but Mr Lee constantly adjusted their position to maintain a safe distance from any possible contacts. And, she had to admit, she felt much more secure with Shah's men and all the new arrivals on board.

Not that she'd be staying tonight. They had to take the smaller boat back to the marina later, stay the night there, and then pick up their passengers and the Pieraro clan in the morning.

Although, looking at the baleful light of the burning city, she had to wonder what sort of fresh hell she'd be sailing into, and whether Miguel would even make it back in time. He had a 400-mile round trip to retrieve his family, and the night-time roads, if not choked with refugees, would almost certainly be stalked by brigands and highwaymen. She wondered whether he'd make it, and how long she could afford to wait.

College students. More than a thousand of them.

They formed a moat around the entrance of the Fairmont when Jules returned with Shah to pick up her passengers and Pieraro. Security had deteriorated all over Acapulco during the night, as though news of the Israeli attack had somehow finally uncapped all the base animal fears stirred up by the Disappearance.

While Mr Lee and three of Shah's men supervised her newly hired crew in final preparations on board the *Aussie Rules*, now ten miles offshore, at the marina Fifi and Thapa prepped the launch for a quick dash across the bay. Jules had chosen a rendezvous point much closer to the Fairmont, to avoid a confrontation with the mob that had gathered at the gates of the marina demanding to be let in. Driving through the city, she could understand their motivation. Anarchy was loose.

Whatever remnant of order had prevailed until yesterday was gone and the madness she had been expecting was finally upon them. It was like moving through a city at war with itself. No, it was worse than that, because there were no sides, just a general eruption, a battle of all against all. Packs of young men fell on individuals caught out alone. Larger gangs fell on them in turn. There had been no uniformed police or city authorities visible for days, but even the sort of organised private muscle that had protected places like the marina and Acapulco Diamante were much less in evidence, either hunkered down behind high walls and barricades, or simply dissipated as men flaked away to protect their own immediate interests and families. Gunfire, thick oily smoke, occasional explosions and the mob sounds of fear and rage lay over the entire city.

Driving was a nightmare, with streets frequently choked and impassable. Only Shah's handling of the all-terrain SUV had allowed them any headway through the worst of the snarls. At times he simply mounted the kerb and rolled through private homes to dodge some of the blockages. When the roads opened up, the former soldier drove fast and aggressively, twice knocking down small groups of men armed with improvised weapons who attempted to bar their passage along the Escenica carriageway as it ran through scrubland in the hills to the west of Revolcadero

Beach. The thud of impact as the Toyota struck human flesh made her shudder and close her eyes. It was somehow much worse sitting passively in the seat beside Shah. The situation eased somewhat as they came down out of the hills and drove onto the long strip of dual laneway of the Costero de Las Palmas. Sprinklers still sprayed long arcs of recycled water over the empty, bright green golf courses to their left, and the beach-front resorts of Revolcadero on the right had not yet been touched by the violence that gripped the centre of Acapulco, but the evidence of accelerating collapse was everywhere. In the long lines of slow-moving cars piled high with personal goods. In the swarms of people sitting on the tarmac at the *aeropuerto internacional*, desperate for flights out, even though no aircraft remained there and none were flying in. And in the mob of seething, chanting American college students now laying siege to the gates of the Fairmont, where resort security led a grim effort to hold them at bay.

'What the fuck?' said Jules, as Shah slowed and pulled over to the side of the road, well away from the mob scene.

'Spring break,' Shah replied, by way of explanation. 'Many students on cruise ships from America. Cheap cruises. Very ugly.'

'That's great. But what are they doing *here*?'

She could see some of Pieraro's street toughs wielding canes and clubs to beat back the Americans, but many of the students seemed prepared to respond in kind. One group in particular had kitted themselves out with a mix of sporting equipment, protective gear and improvised weapons like baseball bats, and even one cricket bat that she could see. They appeared to work as a flying squad, charging from one spot to the next whenever the security men threatened more beatings and mayhem.

'Bit of a fucking cock-up then, Sergeant Shah.'

'A bit, Miss Julianne.'

He started the engine again and pulled back into the sluggish stream of traffic that rolled straight through the centre of the crowd.

'Don't stop,' she ordered him. 'I'll see if I can get Miguel's attention as we roll past.'

Shah crunched the stick into low gear. There was no moving any faster than a trot anyway, with the road and the dusty verge completely choked with foot traffic and hundreds of vehicles. Dozens of cars had stopped from want of gas and been pushed onto the verge, creating obstacles around which flowed the slow-moving mass of refugees. The exodus from the city poured through and past the huge knot of young Americans, who all seemed to be carrying expensive backpacks and luggage. More than a few were drunk. As Jules rolled down the window she was struck by the stench of so many people packed in closely together.

'It's bloody hopeless,' she said after a few minutes. 'I'll have to go in on foot. Turn off up ahead, Mr Shah, and take the car down to the sand. It can run on sand, can't it?'

The Gurkha nodded. 'I shall wait by the cabanas directly out the back. I will not move until you come for me.'

Jules thought about taking the shotgun, but settled instead on a concealed pistol, which she carried in a holster on her hip under a long shirt. She was dressed in desert boots, khaki shorts and a white sea-cotton top, and didn't look all that out of place in the young crowd. She waved off Shah and began to push her way forward. He was right. They were mostly young Americans, very obviously holidaying students. She supposed there had to be a few thousand of them in Acapulco at any time of year, but their numbers would probably swell during semester breaks. What the hell they were doing camped out in front of the Fairmont, she had no idea, but the deeper she moved into the crowd the uglier and more charged with menace the atmosphere grew, mostly thanks to the same street thugs they'd run into at the roadblock yesterday.

She recognised Pieraro's second in charge, Roberto, the Colombian guy, standing atop a stone wall, looking splendid in black combat pants and a matching wife-beater. His eyes were hidden behind silver sunglasses and he was sporting some fabulous new bling, but there was no mistaking the brute arrogance and cruelty of the man. He seemed to be enjoying himself, sooling small packs of his men onto the *gringos* whenever they threatened to push too far into the complex – although his goons seemed less enthusiastic about tangling with the mob of drunken, fired-up college jocks who had armed themselves with the sporting kit. They were pretty evenly matched.

It was a wonder that gunplay hadn't broken out, but then in

contrast with the day before, Roberto's men were all armed with clubs and axe handles. The pistols with which they'd manned the roadblock were nowhere in evidence. As Julianne elbowed and squeezed through the crush, she began to attend to the snatches of conversation she heard.

'They're picking us up here. Coast Guard or something . . .'

'It's the Marines, man – that's what I heard.'

'We're going to Seattle.'

'No way. It's Sydney.'

Oh no, thought Jules. *I have a very bad feeling about this.*

She decided to skirt around the heart of the mob, pushing out towards the edges and finally getting free of them about a hundred metres further down the road near the resort's tennis courts. Then, after cutting through a dense forest of artfully arranged palm trees, she looped around the rear of a large apartment complex and emerged near one of the half-dozen swimming pools. They were all deserted today, even the bars at the edge of the water, but over by the artificial lagoon, on the terrace of the Chula Vista restaurant, she found her passengers, their minder Pieraro, and his family. All fifteen of them.

The *vaquero* looked furious, but not nearly as angry as Jules. She stormed over, fists clenching and unclenching. Everyone but Pieraro flinched and shuffled aside.

'What the *fuck* is going on out there? And who the hell are these people, Miguel?' she demanded to know. 'You told me you had a wife and three kids. But now you've brought half the fucking village with you!'

The Mexican's extended family looked to him, with more than a little fear. Jules assumed the woman holding a toddler and clinging to his arm was the wife, and the girls crowded around her were their daughters, but the rest had to be a grab bag of aunts, uncles and grandparents – and possibly the village drunk, the village idiot and the village's drunken idiotic mayor all thrown in for good measure. None of them looked to have a fucking peso between them.

Pieraro disentangled himself from them and moved forward to intercept Julianne as she bulldozed her way through the tables and chairs overlooking the lagoon, knocking one over with a resounding crash. Normally the terrace would have been crowded with guests taking a late breakfast at this time, but the restaurant was closed and seemingly abandoned. She guessed that very few staff had bothered to show up.

'You've got a fucking nerve,' she hissed at him. 'I don't know what that balls-up out the front is about, but there are a thousand dumb-jock college students out there who seem to think they'll be hitching a ride out of here with us. But they won't, will they, because you've brought half the fucking village of *el Shithole del Diablo* with you!'

Pieraro didn't flare up or push back, instead replying in a steady voice, 'There is no need to be offensive, Miss Julianne. I am not responsible for the crowd out the front. That was Cesky's doing.'

'That putty-nosed toad. What the hell did – '

'It's true,' called out Phoebe, the trust-fund bimbo, looking appreciably less sure of herself than yesterday. 'He was so pissed off with you for cutting him out that he marched off yesterday and started telling everyone about the escape plan. It spread. I got three text messages about it.'

She held up a cell phone as if to explain. Jules was surprised it still worked. Hers had cut out days ago. She sighed inwardly. *The rich* – they always had a way. Her other five-star refugees all nodded glumly.

'Right,' said Jules, barely able to contain her exasperation. 'Well, we've still got to get you away from here. There's another lynch party back at the marina, waiting to do you all in for a ticket out of this madhouse, so listen up. You do exactly as I say or you *will* be left behind . . . Miguel? Transport. That was your job . . .'

'I have two buses,' he told her. 'They will take everyone.'

'Yeah, and how are they going to get out through that mob in front? I've got Sergeant Shah parked down on the beach waiting for us. There's no way your buses'll run on soft sand.'

'No. But I have not parked them here,' he said. 'When Miss St John' – he indicated Phoebe – 'warned me what had happened with Cesky, I hid them down the beach, at the Alberca Heritage. I know the security chief there. A good man.'

'How much did that cost?' asked Jules, rubbing her eyes.

'A hundred gallons of gasoline. He is leaving with his family this evening.'

'Fine,' she said through gritted teeth. 'And the mob out the front?'

'Roberto will hold them there. He has arranged with reception for a number of minibuses from the Fairmont. Everyone thinks they are the escape vehicles.'

'And he wants passage too?'

'No. He sees opportunities here,' Pieraro replied. 'Mostly he wants me gone. But some payment was involved.'

Jules closed her eyes. 'How much?'

The merchant banker, the one with the silicone-enhanced mistress, suddenly spoke up. 'It was nothing. Now can we get the hell out of here?'

Jules struggled for his name. Denby . . . Denby . . . Moorhouse. 'So you paid off Roberto, the coke-dealing paramilitary fascist?' she asked incredulously. 'Oh well, that'll turn out fine, I'm sure. He won't be back for another bite of the cherry, will he! I mean, do any of you actually need me? Everything seems to be running tickety fucking boo without my input. Perhaps I should just piss off and leave you to get on with it.'

'Listen,' said Moorhouse, stepping forward. He was a short man with all of the attendant psychological problems. Jules estimated that standing face to face with his girlfriend, he'd be smothered by her breast implants. His features were flushed and he was sweating profusely. 'We have had a very stressful morning here. Those people began arriving before dawn. The hotel has been locked down for hours by security men. We were stuck in our rooms, no air-conditioning, no cable, no idea what was happening. If it took a couple of trinkets and baubles to get that Colombian thug to run interference for us, that was well worth it. Now, I suggest you start earning your money and get us the hell out of Acapulco.'

Tempted to pistol-whip him, Jules merely nodded silently. She then turned her attention back to the *vaquero*. 'Miguel, can I talk to you? Privately. For two minutes. Do we have two minutes?'

The background roar was building, but not in a way that that made her think a boilover was imminent. Pieraro patted his wife on the shoulder and gently rubbed the head of his youngest child, a little boy, who was crying silently. He bent down to whisper a few words in his ear before kissing his forehead. With the child settled, for the moment, he and Jules walked off to the other side of the terrace.

'This conga line of relatives and . . . whatever,' she began, 'have you planned on provisions and stores for them? Because I haven't. We had an agreement – your wife and children. I don't recall agreeing to take all the supporting cast from *Three Amigos*.'

Pieraro looked physically pained. His next words came out like teeth extracted one after the other. 'If you cannot take them, you cannot. I will explain.'

The man's discomfort was so palpable, so deeply etched into the fissures of his sunburnt face, that Jules had to look away. She covered the moment of weakness by pretending to scan the hotel grounds for trouble. Unfortunately, standing right in her line of view were his family, the sorriest, most bedraggled-looking losers she'd seen in a long time. The crowd at the hotel gates were young, middle-class white people with a leavening of upper-echelon Mexicans; they were frightened, but still well fed and used to having their own way. Miguel's family looked like they'd turn around at one word from her and slouch off to their fate.

Jules risked a quick glance at her paying customers. They seemed entirely nonplussed, and she supposed they had no reason to question the arrival of the Pieraro clan. The *vaquero* had clearly established himself as a powerful figure in their eyes only yesterday. If that power meant he could drag along his extended family, they would probably accept that. After all, they were all too used to the privileges of power themselves.

The crowd noise intensified noticeably, spilling over and around the Fairmont's centrepiece architectural statement, the main hotel built in the form of a giant Aztec pyramid. She could see dozens of other guests on their balconies, hiding from the disturbance outside, and too many of them were pointing at her little group. Time to go.

'Listen,' she said. 'This isn't over, not by a fucking long shot. I cannot take all those people you've brought. I don't have stores for them and they won't be allowed off the boat at the other end – not to mention the trouble it's going to cause with everyone who actually paid for their passage. *But*, we don't have time to get into this

'Any trouble getting away from the marina?' asked Jules.

'Some,' admitted Fifi, who was dressed in a denim micro-skirt and distressed red tee-shirt emblazoned with the legend *Zombie Squad – We can handle it from here. We've talked about this on the internet.* A Marlboro dangled from her lips. Jules wondered what her friend would do when she finally ran out. 'But we got her done,' Fifi added, shifting up her PKM for effect.

Jules winced. 'You didn't kill anyone, did you?'

The other woman rolled her eyes. 'Just a few rounds downrange. Jeez, who died and made you Captain Sensible?'

Jules stared past her, into a place she wasn't even sure existed. Fifi caught the hint. 'Oh, yeah. Pete . . . Uh, sorry.'

'Right,' said Julianne, throwing up her hands. 'Let's just get them all on board before we draw another crowd, shall we?'

She could see cars had started to pull over to the side of the freeway on the hill up above them. Small groups of people were already picking their way down through the scrub, doubtless hoping to clamber onto the boat with them. To her west, across the confusion of the bay, the centre of Acapulco was a disaster movie. Fires blazed at so many locations that Jules couldn't count them, but it was eerily quiet, like watching TV with the sound down. After a second she realised why: no sirens, anywhere. The absence was chilling.

'Come on, move your arses!' she called out to the dawdling travellers. Phoebe had actually stopped to take pictures with a small digital camera. 'Excuse me, the fucking tour bus is leaving!' cried Jules in frustration. 'Move!'

Shah and Thapa started herding everyone towards the dock, occasionally glancing up towards the roadway behind them. A few more vehicles had pulled over. Pieraro spoke to an old man amongst his people, who nodded before firing off a scorching fusillade of native oaths and curses and clouting a teenaged boy, who'd stopped dead, transfixed by Fifi's tee-shirt. The Mexicans, all hauling heavy sacks of food by the looks of them, began to run awkwardly down the pier. The Americans, dropping some of their luggage as they went, followed suit as Thapa chivvied them along. 'If you would be so kind as to be hurrying your arses up now,' he said with some urgency.

'Mr Shah?' Jules called out. 'My gun, if you please.'

The Gurkha sergeant produced her shotgun from the cabin of the SUV, which they'd parked close to the start of the long pier. He racked a round into the chamber before handing it over to her.

'Thank you,' said Jules. She fired three shots into the air over the heads of the people swarming down the hillside towards them. It had a salutary effect on her own charges as well, speeding their passage down the jetty to a sprint.

'Hell yeah,' enthused Fifi. 'Time for a little redneck persuasion.' She let rip with a short, snarling burst from her heavy Russian machine-gun, firing into the windows of an abandoned building that overlooked the car park, shattering a dozen panes of glass. The sound was scarifying and the small horde descending the slopes stopped and dropped immediately.

'Go, go!' said Shah, waving the two women off towards the boat, where Thapa and Pieraro were hurriedly helping everyone aboard – in some cases by throwing them bodily over the side.

The girls didn't wait to be told twice. They set off at a sprint. Moments later, Jules heard the vehicle start up again, and looking back over her shoulder, she saw the former soldier driving it onto the jetty. He followed them, stopping halfway down, before turning the wheel to create a barrier across the pier.

'They'll just crawl over it,' said Fifi, levelling the PKM on the makeshift blockade.

'They won't,' promised Jules.

Shah climbed out, tossed something into the cabin and ran as quickly as she'd ever seen a short, refrigerator-shaped man run. A few seconds later, as the first of their desperate pursuers made it to the start of the pier, the grenade exploded, lifting the vehicle a few inches off the deck, but not moving it far enough to topple it into the water. Everyone ducked. When Jules straightened up, access from the shore was blocked by the burning wreckage.

'Nice work, buddy,' Fifi said as Shah trotted up to them. 'You like Nascar at all?'

Smiling like an imp, Shah lifted his shoulders. 'Nascar? Never heard of it. But I never liked Toyotas much.'

Fifi wondered if anyone even drove a Toyota in Nascar.

Out on the water, it was worse. The sport fisher was big and powerful enough to speed around or muscle through the occasional
logjams of smaller craft that blocked its way, and the sight of Pieraro, Thapa and Shah heavily tooled up and guarding against all
attempts to contest a boarding precluded any such misadventures.
But Jules still had a hell of a time clearing the bay, on which an
unknowable number of vessels jostled for primacy. Where the hell
most of them thought they were going, she couldn't say. The little runabouts, motorboats and inflatables that numbered in their
thousands would founder in even moderate seas, and word from
Mr Lee back on the *Rules* was that storms in the high latitudes had
whipped up a bitching four-metre swell on a nasty cross-chop of
at least another metre and a half. They were going to have a lot
of seasick passengers in less than half an hour. But at least they'd
survive the conditions.

Jules shook her head as she spun the wheel to dodge what
looked like a garbage barge barely able to stay afloat under the
weight of seven or eight hundred people, all tightly packed onto
the mounds of rubbish. They were throwing as much of the rot-
ting, malodorous ballast overboard as quickly as they could, but
the wake from her sudden turn set the flat-bottomed scow wallow-
ing dangerously, and at least a dozen men and women went over
the side. She nudged the throttles forward and tried to ignore their
flailing figures. They wouldn't be the last people to drown today.

A cacophony of horns, whistles, sirens and klaxons overlay the
constant screaming and calls for help. The further out into the bay
she took them, the worse it grew. Bodies began to appear in the
churning water, some floating near capsized boats, and some of
them obviously killed by gunfire. At one point she cut their speed
back to allow a small pod of surf-skiers to paddle by. They saluted
her with their oars before resuming their rhythmic progress.

'How did they get this far?' she said to nobody in particular.

Fifi appeared at her elbow with a couple of chilled Coronas.
She watched the surfers for a moment before shrugging. 'Surf
breaks get pretty crowded. They're probably used to it. Wanna
beer, Julesy?'

'You have to be fucking kidding . . . Oh . . . what the hell.
Could you open it for me?'

Fifi popped the tops and passed one of the bottles to Jules, who kept one hand on the wheel while draining half the *cerveza* in a few long pulls. The crisp, icy-cold bite was like an angel's kiss. Indeed, she couldn't recall ever having enjoyed a beer this much. It was almost obscene.

'You coulda waited, you know,' said Fifi. 'I cut up some limes.'

'Only poofs fruit the beer, sweetheart. What's happening below?'

Fifi finished her own drink and tossed the empty bottle overboard before answering. It crashed into the prow of a ferry, eliciting a raised fist and a long string of unintelligible curses from the skipper. She flipped him the finger. 'Miguel's got the mariachi band all stowed away down below,' she replied. 'They're cool. No problemo. That fucking prom queen, though, and her brother . . .'

'Phoebe and Jason?'

'Yeah, them. They're already arguing with the banker and his boob job about who gets the big cabin.'

Jules squeezed her eyes shut for just a second. It was dangerous to have them closed for any longer. 'As long as they keep it down there, I don't give a rat's arse.'

A deep, high-powered horn sounded off to starboard, where a large container ship had dropped dozens of lines over the side to pick up people struggling in the water. Another big ship, an oil tanker, was heading straight for it. Jules wondered why until she saw the telltale sparkle of gunfire around the tanker's bridge.

'Damn, Julesy,' said Fifi. 'Nobody's in charge of that son of a bitch. You'd better haul ass. This ain't gonna be pretty.'

Jules didn't need encouraging. As Shah came hammering up the steps to warn them of the impending disaster, she flicked on the boat's internal PA system. 'Hey, listen up everyone,' she began calmly. 'Get down low and grab something. I'm going to have to lay on some speed and do some rally driving.'

Another long, shrieking blast on the container ship's horn pounded at them, and all around it, those ships that could put on speed suddenly did so, leaping up at their bows and churning up white wakes.

'You have seen?' asked Shah.

Julianne pushed the throttles to three-quarter power and the sport fisher leapt ahead. 'I'm on it,' she cried out, over the rising clamour of horns and the screaming of thousands of people in the water and on nearby boats.

Stray rounds from the firefight on the tanker splattered against their vessel inches from Fifi's head. She unlimbered the PKM and spat a stream of tracers back at them. 'Fuckers!'

'Get down and stop arsing around!' Jules shouted.

Reefing the wheel to port, she narrowly avoided spearing into an old wooden yacht that looked a lot like the *Diamantina*. It was certainly of the same vintage and seemed to be crewed by three swimsuit models. Another sharp turn to starboard swept them around two more yachts, which had already collided with each other, and a bright yellow water taxi that was dangerously overloaded. The bow wave from her boat struck it amidships and the taxi went over.

Jules was sorry, but there was nothing she could do about it. Behind them the horns of both the tanker and the container ship roared in one long, deafening note.

Shah pointed her towards a stretch of slightly less crowded water and Jules opened the boat's engines all of the way. The massive bulk of the sixty-foot power craft lifted even higher in the water and she gripped the silver wheel hard, concentrating on not running into anyone. A few blasts on her own horn began to scatter and clear some room up ahead, but then the warning was lost in a huge, world-ending uproar as the two giant ships collided.

Risking a look back over the stern, she saw the container ship keel over violently. So great was the impact that the giant steel crates stacked high on its deck were thrown clear; those from the upper stacks describing long, slow arcs over the top of a few lucky boats, before crashing down and utterly destroying a host of smaller vessels further out. One rusted blue P&O container turned end over end and flew a good hundred metres before slamming amidships into the overcrowded garbage barge they'd left in their wake earlier. It struck like a giant fist, crushing hundreds of people instantly and cleaving the barge in two. Bow and stern folded up like a jackknife and the flat-bottomed craft sank in less than a minute. More and more of the massive steel boxes began to fall away as the container ship tilted over. They rained down over the side, falling directly on top of those vessels and people who'd been initially spared when the first containers had sailed well over their heads.

Jules flinched, expecting to hear the volcanic eruption of the oil tanker going up, but it never came. The thundering collision and the avalanche of containers gave way to torturous tearing and a grinding of steel plates as momentum crushed the two large ships together.

'Awesome,' said Fifi as Jules turned away from the spectacle to concentrate on threading their way through the pandemonium of fleeing craft.

Having hung back while she negotiated a safe passage, Shah appeared at her side now, just as the sport fisher finally swung out around the southern head of Acapulco Bay and got a little sea room around her. To port stood the high, wooded slopes through which they'd driven back from Revolcadero Beach less than an hour ago, and Jules made certain to maintain a safe distance from them. Twice they'd hit roadblocks while rolling through there and she didn't fancy getting sniped at by some resentful *bandido* sitting up on the bluffs.

Around them, the smaller craft began to suffer in the open seas. The cries of distress from hundreds of small boats suddenly swamped by the powerful and unruly ocean swell was distressing. Jules had seen a lot of children on some of those dinky little tubs, but she pushed it out of her mind. To stop and pick up anybody would mean getting swarmed by hundreds, possibly thousands, of people. She left the throttles open and brought them around to the south-west, heading for the rendezvous with Mr Lee.

'I have spoken to Thapa,' said Shah. 'As you asked, he did some work back on shore, investigating the attack on your vessel by this Shoeless Dan.'

'Whoa!' cried Fifi. 'He's cute *and* smart. Man, I'm gonna have to get me some of that later.'

From the way she was now eyeballing the small, well-muscled Gurkha standing at the stern, Jules knew it was no idle threat. 'Did he find out anything useful, Mr Shah?' she asked, as the towering Aztec pyramid of the Fairmont hove into view a few miles off the port bow. 'It's okay if he didn't. I wasn't expecting much, just wanted to cover our arses really.'

Shah, who seemed able to maintain his balance in the rough conditions by simply flexing at the knees, dismissed her last words with a shake of his head. 'It is his job, Miss Julianne, and mine. Private Thapa discovered nothing specific about the attack on your boat, but there are at least three syndicates, criminal enterprises, that moved very quickly to capitalise on the Disappearance. Most of their activities were restricted to land, but one of them already had a history of maritime criminality. Perhaps this was how they came to know your shoeless friend.'

'Makes sense,' Jules replied with a shrug. 'Maritime criminality was Shoeless Dan's special power.' She spun the wheel to take them on a long, looping course around a paddle-steamer that had somehow found itself blundering through the waves. It was nearly as badly overcrowded as the sunken garbage barge had been, and she wanted to give them a very wide berth. 'But there's not much of a piracy culture around here,' she added. 'Not like in parts of Asia. A lot of smuggling, yes, but not piracy. The Americans wouldn't have allowed it, even in Mexican waters. You think somebody's branching out? I mean, not that we'll be hanging around long enough for them to try their luck.'

The huge Gurkha bobbed and ducked quite comically to maintain his balance, without once needing to grab on to anything to steady himself. 'You will if you insist on hugging the coastline to drop Pieraro's people anywhere, Miss Julianne,' he said.

Jules frowned testily. 'Look, I'm really pissed off about that. But I didn't see any way around it. Miguel had that Colombian nutter holding the crowds off us and he could have very easily put us right in the poo if I'd cut up rough about his mariachi band.'

'His what?'

'Sorry. In-joke.'

Fifi produced another beer from an icebox on the flying deck and winked at Shah. 'They're cool with me,' she said. 'I think they're cute. Wanna brew, anyone?'

Both Jules and Shah answered at once: 'No.'

'They're not American citizens,' the Englishwoman continued. 'They're peasants. Nobody is going to take them in as genuine refugees. Even if we can get all the way across the Pacific with the rations we have on board – and, look, I suppose we can – Hawaii will not take them. They're shedding people at the moment. New Zealand might. Australia won't. And everybody else is just as likely to open fire on us as soon as we sail into view.'

Shah held both hands up as if to show her he had nothing left. 'I do not presume to tell you what you should do. But you have hired me to provide security, and I advise you now that heading back towards the coastline will be a very dangerous business.'

'Fifi, you've been out on the *Rules* with Lee a lot more than me. How's our provisioning?'

She drained half of the beer and burped. ''Scuse me. It's not bad, Julesy,' she replied. 'That golfer had some good shit in the fridge, and plenty of it. And we topped up the larder nicely. There's like two frozen pigs and couple of steer down there now. Plus, them Mexicans did bring plenty of food – not like those other fucking snobs. All they brought was expensive luggage and heaps of attitude. I don't see a problem. Really. Come on, it'll be fun. Be like Carnivale every night.'

Jules looked to Shah for support but he remained entirely impassive. 'I just ... it's just that ...' she faltered. 'Oh, I don't know ... my father taught me that helping people was wrong. It never ends well. We're not philanthropists here, we're smugglers – at best.'

'*Foxy* fucking smugglers.' Fifi saluted Julianne with her bottle. 'And anyway, your old man ate his pistol one night just before the cops grabbed him. Should you really be looking to him for advice?'

Jules looked completely lost. 'That was my mother's fault,' she said bitterly. 'If she hadn't tipped off Scotland Yard about Daddy diddling the tax man ...'

Shah regarded her with some confusion. 'Your mother informed on your father?' he asked.

'After a less than satisfying divorce settlement failed to provide for her in the style to which she'd *so* been looking forward,' Jules explained. She was surprised to find it hard to speak, with her throat suddenly locking. 'I was his favourite,' she said quietly.

34

The sutures in his butt made it all but impossible to run, and for a 'running high' junkie like Bret Melton, that was becoming every bit as uncomfortable as his assorted injuries. 'You'll have to excuse my irritability, Sadie. I've been folded, spindled *and* mutilated. Puts a man in a poor frame of mind.'

The Al Jazeera correspondent clicked his coffee cup against Melton's and smiled. The *Army Times* reporter was pathetically grateful to him for getting him out of that hangar in the boonies. 'It is nothing, really,' Mirsaad replied. 'Look at what is happening to the world. And you are worried about your manners.'

'Well, perhaps if people were possessed of a few more manners, they wouldn't go around killing each other with such abandon.'

Sayad al Mirsaad's eyes flickered nervously around the departure lounge. Kuwait International Airport was swarming with armed personnel from a dozen different countries, mostly American, however, and the atmosphere was twitchy and dangerous. Dense knots of travellers, civilian and military, crowded around every available television screen to follow the war news. There had already been one unpleasant incident where Mirsaad had been recognised from a report he'd just filed on the sinking of the USS *Hopper*. A couple of Marines didn't think he was suitably respectful in tone and Melton had been forced to intervene before the little Jordanian got stomped. It had put the American in a bad mood, arguing with his own people, even if they were a couple of Podunk assholes who would have left the world a better place had they stayed home and been zapped by the Wave. He'd been snappy and irritable ever since, and his inability to break out of the blue funk simply made it all the worse.

He needed to piss, his wounded hand throbbed like a bastard, and he'd had no sleep since the first Israeli warhead had gone off. He was grateful to Sayad for hauling his ass out of TRANSCOM limbo, especially so given the business-class ticket, paid for by BBC World, that his colleague had handed him.

'You're off to London, you lucky devil,' Mirsaad had said as he handed over the precious travel wallet. 'You don't deserve it, of course, what with your whoring and drinking and your disgraceful attitude to the Prophet and his faithful. I should really be going in your place. After all, I am much more virtuous.'

And behind his friend's twinkling eyes and ready smile, Melton had seen real fear at being left behind to burn in a nuclear furnace. It made it all the more affecting that he had agreed to track Melton down for the British broadcaster, which had lost contact with him when he was injured. Bret wondered whether he would have done the same thing in Mirsaad's place. The small coterie of full-time war correspondents tended to be close and unusually supportive of each other, but Mirsaad had spent days hunting him through the vast labyrinth of the US Transport Command and, having found him in that transit hangar out in the desert, had insisted on personally driving the injured reporter three hundred miles to Kuwait City.

'Don't you have a job?' asked Melton as they waited in the lounge for his BA flight to England.

'I am a roving reporter,' Mirsaad replied with a grin. 'I rove, therefore I am. And I will file many stories on the reaction to the Israeli bombs and to the American pull-out. Frankly, if it keeps me away from the bombsites themselves, I am grateful. I have heard from colleagues sent into Egypt and Syria about the conditions there. Many of them are now very sick. The network has suspended operations in the irradiated areas until they are safe. Well, *safer*. For now, Kuwait and Qatar are my beats, as you say. I shall fly out to Coalition headquarters when you have gone for a briefing on the ceasefire.'

Melton snorted. 'Not much of a ceasefire, Sadie. The Israelis wiped the field clean with a couple of airburst nukes. EMPs fried everything the Iranians had.'

Mirsaad's fragile smile fell away. 'You know, a lot of people are saying that if your government had not warned Tehran and the others, they would not have deployed all of their defences to be wiped out. Many people think it was a conspiracy, a plot between Washington and Tel Aviv to steal all of the oil, not just Saddam's.'

The American regarded his friend warily. 'Sadie,' he said in a gentle tone, 'Washington's gone. Bush, Cheney, all of them. All the petrol-company head offices, motor manufacturers, arms companies, all gone. If there was a conspiracy, it was a one-way street. Everything I've seen tells me the Israelis completely suckered Jim Ritchie. Iranian military doctrine is to throw everything at a threat. No reserves. They got an hour or so warning and put everything up. They tried to warn their own people, with the end result that the entire country lit up in panic. Computers, phones, radio, TV, every goddamn piece of electronic equipment in the place, and none of it hardened against a pulse.'

'So what you are really saying, Bret, is that they didn't need to bomb the cities. They had already destroyed their enemies as functioning modern societies.'

'Well, I wouldn't call them functioning or modern, but yes, I see your point,' Melton replied. 'Look, I don't condone it – who would? By the time the final butcher's bill is toted, they've probably killed, what, a hundred and fifty, two hundred million people. Christ only knows how many more if anybody else follows their lead. Possibly everyone, in the end. You know what that makes us – I mean, the US and the Disappearance? *Old news.*'

'You are right,' Mirsaad conceded. 'I apologise. I sound like some ill-bred street Arab falling on conspiracy talk like a scabrous dog on a bone. Tell me truthfully, Bret, what do you think your military will do?'

He shook his head. 'I have no idea, Sadie. Leave you all to it, I expect. We're out of the superpower business as of last week. Go ask the Chinese, or whoever's running India. If Pakistan hasn't nuked them yet.'

They fell into an uncomfortable silence as the PA called flights out to Paris, Rotterdam and Bangkok. Melton attempted to find a position in which he could recline without putting pressure on his injured butt cheek or shoulder. It was difficult. But at least for the first time in weeks he was clean, and dressed in luxuriously soft and well-fitting civilian clothes. The BBC had sent him payment in euros for the copy he'd filed before he was wounded, and had advanced him another, larger sum, on the basis of the interviews he had taken at the transit facility out in the desert. As he'd expected, they were most interested in any European angle.

Their money was still worth something in Kuwait, at least in the hermetically sealed environment of the international airport. He was able to buy clothes and replace some lost and damaged equipment. Even better than that, he'd managed to fill a few prescriptions at a pharmacy on the main concourse and, now that he had escaped the Kafkaesque frustrations of the military transport system, he could eat when he felt like it.

'What will you do when you get to London?' asked Mirsaad.

'I got a bunch of studio interviews to do,' he said. 'You know, glamorously wounded foreign correspondent stuff. I've promised to write up a couple of thousand words for their website, and I really want to push ahead with this book I've been thinking about. I wouldn't be surprised if they asked me to turn around and come right back, though. They lost a lot of people yesterday. Reporters in bureaux throughout the region. They're gonna be hiring, but it'll mean heading back here.'

'Do you want to?'

'Nope. Well . . . I don't know what I want. Something normal would be nice – do you miss normal, Sadie? I do. I can't go home, so all the conventional nostalgia bullshit is out. Truthfully? I'd just like to sit on my busted ass somewhere, write my book and, I dunno, look around and not see guys armed to the fucking teeth. How about you?'

'I am an Arab,' Mirsaad answered glumly. 'I grew up surrounded by men who were armed to the teeth.'

'Hey, I grew up in Kentucky. Me too.'

The PA system announced that his flight to London was boarding and Melton suddenly felt a soft pressure in his chest and throat. 'Well, Sadie, I gotta be going, bud. I might be back, but you know . . . I just want to say thanks for finding me. I think I might still be doing the zombie shuffle through TRANSCOM's twilight zone if you hadn't grabbed me up.'

Mirsaad stuck out his hand and they shook, awkwardly because of Bret's wounds.

'It was nothing, a trifling favour for a friend at the Beeb, and one I was happy to do as it helped another friend . . . I hope we still stay friends, Bret. If we live.'

'Yup. A big if, Sadie,' Melton agreed. 'Take care. I'll contact you through the network when I get settled.'

The Jordanian patted him gently on the arm and picked up his bags for the short walk to the departure gate. Most of the passengers lining up there were civilians, their numbers split evenly between Arabs and Europeans, although, Melton reminded himself, they might well all be British citizens. Nobody looked happy to be travelling. Either because of what they were heading towards – parts of England were under martial law, and it was being strictly and harshly enforced – or perhaps because of a well-founded fear they might never get there. Thousands of people had died when their aircraft were knocked out of the sky by the same electromagnetic pulses the Israelis had set off to cripple their enemies.

Neither reporter spoke again until Melton had swiped his boarding pass. The BA hostess was as smooth and pleasant as ever, which only served to heighten the sense of brittle weirdness and impending doom.

'Good luck. And thanks again,' said Melton.

'A safe journey to you, my friend, God willing,' replied Mirsaad.

He was pathetically grateful for a business-class seat. It was like settling into an overstuffed hotel bed compared to the steel benches, hard plastic seats and stinking kitbags on which he'd mostly fetched up while in transit. It was possible, while sipping at the complimentary orange juice, as they waited to taxi, to imagine that things were entirely normal. The business-class section was full, but remained decadently spacious and agreeable. His fellow bizoids, with one exception, were all male. The one woman looked like a banker or lawyer and had no sooner strapped in than she began opening files to work on. She plugged herself into an iPod and radiated a fierce repeller field, lest anyone should attempt to approach or interrupt her. An old hand, then.

The man sitting next to him, in the window seat, nodded brusquely before returning to his BlackBerry. He kept stabbing at the keyboard without any observable result. 'It was working this morning,' he kept muttering to himself. Melton ignored him all too easily.

A hostess, noticing his injuries as he'd levered himself into his seat, offered extra pillows and a blanket to lie on. A long time ago in a galaxy far, far away, he'd have derided such indulgences as 'snivel gear'; it took him a long time, after getting out, to throw off some of the dumber attitudes of his time in service. He took the pillows and thanked her, settling into them after washing down a couple of painkillers with the last of the orange juice. As the engines spooled up, the captain came on to announce that they would be taking a very circuitous route to avoid any hazards from hostilities to the north. Melton didn't bother to pay attention to the announcements. He didn't care how they got out of this mess, only that they did so.

He was going to miss Sayad, and felt yet again that he was simply allowing events to sweep him along and away from another friend, one whose own future looked very bleak. Melton didn't see anything good happening in this part of the world any time soon. There was no way the US could sustain a presence here, but it remained an area of vital importance to the surviving great powers. How long could it be before Chinese, Indian and Russian warships replaced the US Navy on permanent station in the Gulf? As his eyelids drooped and he tried to suppress the snoring he knew was going to piss off his fellow passengers, he sought to get his head around the strategic and economic wreckage of the Israeli strike, but he was too tired and the seat too comfortable, and before long he was asleep.

He woke briefly, thousands of miles later in Gibraltar, but popped another couple of pills, drank some water and went back to sleep. After that he didn't stir again until the plane began to descend. A flight attendant appeared at his elbow to gently rouse him and the BlackBerry addict, and to ask that they put their seats into the upright position for landing.

'We're in London?' he croaked.

The young woman, a rare beauty of Caribbean heritage by the look of her, seemed distracted and anxious. 'No,' she replied with a shake of her head. 'No. We're stopping in Paris. It's . . . unscheduled . . . but nothing to worry about. We'll refuel and be on our way.'

That brought him awake.

'We won't be going to London,' said his travelling companion, whom he'd avoided talking to so far.

'I've been out of it, sorry,' said Melton, still feeling groggy. 'I snore. Has something happened?'

The man, a young, nondescript-looking character with one of those weird Amish-style beards, shrugged and held up a pair of earphones. 'Sennheiser sound-cancelling technology,' he explained. 'Blocks out jet engines and loud snoring. Not a problem.'

Okay, so he wasn't Amish then.

'Britain's closed its borders,' he went on. 'They haven't told us yet.' He waved a hand towards the front of the plane to indicate he meant the flight crew. 'But I snuck a look at a news feed in the toilet. Everything's locked down. Air and sea ports, ferries, the Chunnel – all of it.'

Melton's head was clearing slowly because of the painkillers in his bloodstream. 'Why?' he asked.

BlackBerry guy folded his arms in obvious disgust. 'Blair's saying something about unrest spilling over the Channel. It's rubbish. I need to get home. Do you see any jihadi whackjobs on this plane? We're business people. This is just bullshit.'

'What unrest?' asked Bret. 'I didn't think those riots in Paris were so bad, considering.'

The man looked at him like he was dealing with a retarded child. 'You're kidding me, right? You've been out in the boonies, have you? Paris is on fire, man. All of France is. It's a civil war. And they're sending us into the middle of it.'

ONE MONTH

14 April, 2003

35

'So, you missing Uncle Sugar yet? Nostalgia sucks the big one, don't it?'

Caitlin's voiced cracked and she smiled through split, swollen lips, with teeth stained cherry red by her own blood. But the look on Reynard's face was totally worth it.

The Frenchman did his best to hold his feelings in check, but she'd struck a nerve point and his anguish spilled out in a slight downturn at the corners of his mouth, the merest pout of his lips and a hollowing of the cheeks, as he tilted his head back in an effort to disengage emotionally from his prisoner. He would not beat Caitlin for her insolence. The Algerian would be back later on to do that. Reynard – not his name, but to Caitlin he *looked* like a Reynard, like a hungry fox licking shit from a wire brush, as her old man would have said – he was too important to get her blood on his hands.

'The doctors tell me you are a very sick little girl,' he said, speaking to her in English as usual. 'We could help you. Your illness progresses, but it is not too late. Help us, so we can help you.'

She laughed, a wet, rattling sound that ended in a string of explosive, searingly painful coughs. They felt like phosphorous burns in her chest. Small gobbets of blood flew out and spotted his shirt and tie. 'Sorry Red just isn't your colour, is it, *Reynard?*' she said, before hawking up a mouthful of phlegm and blood to spit at him.

Caitlin had given him the name as soon as she realised he was not going to identify himself, not even with a false name. It was a cheap trick by the Frenchman to increase her feelings of powerlessness, and one easily countered by her simply calling him something and sticking to it. Hawking up blood clots to spit at him helped a little, too.

He held up a clipboard to protect himself, but she let fly anyway, hitting his fingers with a satisfyingly lurid chunk. He cursed her in French and stormed out of the cell, dragging the door closed behind him. A heavy iron cage, it slammed shut with a deafening clang.

Caitlin closed her eyes and smiled. A small victory. Not so long ago, Reynard would simply have absorbed the abuse and bored in on her, attempting to undermine her defences, all the time reminding her of how utterly alone she was in the world. Enraging him was a small victory. Possibly pyrrhic, but a victory nonetheless. She breathed in slowly. The air was stale and dank. She remembered her last stay in the cells beneath Noisy-le-Sec as being uncomfortable because of the cold. Her interrogators had maintained the temperature just above freezing, but on this occasion there had been no attempts to manipulate her environment. She put that down to power shortages. The lights flickered off and on irregularly, often going out for minutes at a time. The fort would have had its own generator but even so, the directorate would need to ration supply if the wider grid had gone offline.

Really though, she had no idea. She had been held incommunicado for three weeks now, and her captors told her nothing of the outside world save for those details that suited their ends, and of course, she could not necessarily believe them anyway. She could only trust what few miniscule scraps of reality came filtering through their control.

Time. They had tried to disconnect her from the flow of time. To impress upon her that she was adrift on the seas of eternity, and completely within their control. They were good, too. She had been trained to listen for any clues in their conversation, to try to catch a glimpse of any timepieces or watches that might stray into her field of view. But Reynard and his men were good. On their wrists she found only a tan line, and for a long time, lost in the haze of beatings and interrogation, she did lose track of the days and weeks. But of course there was one thing they could not take or hide from her: she was a woman and two weeks into her capture, her period arrived, weak but unmistakable.

It had since passed, marking three weeks since Monique had been killed and she had collapsed in the hallway of the apartment block back on the Route d'Asnières, betrayed by her own failing body. She kept the small morsel of knowledge, that she knew how long she'd been held, to herself. It was a small prize to covet in her ongoing battle with Reynard. And not the only one either. She knew things about him that he would not want her to know.

The Frenchman, for instance, was losing weight. She had taken note of where he notched his belt the first time he had interrogated her. It was two notches in from there now. At first, too, he had always been clean shaven, and his suits freshly dry-cleaned and pressed. Recently, however, he had once or twice sported a five o'clock shadow and she noted that his collars and cuffs were growing dark with grime. He, like her, was suffering. Dark bags had appeared under his eyes and he had chewed the skin around his left thumbnail quite ragged.

She could not know what was happening in the city outside the fortress walls, she didn't even know what was happening in the cells near her own, but Caitlin was willing to bet on a systemic collapse. And so she taunted him along those lines, finally eliciting the angered reaction of a few moments past. She would wait now for her punishment. She composed herself, a task made somewhat easier because today she was able to lie flat on the cold slab that served as her bed. She was naked, but she had long since grown used to that. Most importantly, they did not have her trussed into a stress position, sitting cross-legged, with her knees pulled right up and bound, and her hands cuffed behind her back. It had been excruciating after a while, and they'd forced her to maintain the posture by having two men stand over her with lengths of heavy rubber tubing, to hand out a beating whenever she attempted to alter position.

After a few days, however, pressure sores covered her buttocks and had become infected. That bought her respite for a day or two while a medic treated her. They then relented, in a fashion – resorting to a mix of stress positioning, water-boarding and sensory bombardment, rotated in such a way as to maintain her torment without the inconvenience of needing to halt for medical treatment. The combination had almost broken her, but they had stopped it after she sank her teeth into the wrist of a man who'd been attempting to place a hood over her head in preparation for another water-boarding session. Caitlin had bitten down as hard as she could, feeling the skin break and hot, salty blood start to flow, a split second before feeling the satisfying crack of a shattered bone. The asshole had screamed a lot louder than she ever did – something she'd been quick to point out to Reynard. Following that incident, they reverted to beatings for a couple of days.

Beatings she could handle, and she had even begun to goad her captors, holding on to the hope that somebody might lose control and kill her with an uncontrolled blow. Because Reynard was right about one thing: she was doomed. There was no point in hanging on for the sake of the mission. There was no mission, and there would be no deliverance.

Caitlin Monroe was refusing to break, simply because that's all she had left. The only choice that remained in her life was how she left it.

She released a lungful of infected breath, carefully, so as not to set off another round of racking coughs. Slowly breathing in, she kept her eyes closed and tried to imagine that the harsh, fluorescent light hanging from the bare stone ceiling of the cell was the sun. Her myriad agonies she repackaged as the well-earned scars of a hard day's surfing over some exposed reef in the Mentawis. She'd been there not twelve months ago, on a two-week vacation with her brother and some of his college friends. They had surfed for eight hours a day and she'd been pounded without mercy. Caitlin projected herself back there. She did not attempt to recall the entire trip, only one perfect ride, which she reconstructed from fragments of memory, recalling the kiss of warm tropical water flowing through her toes as she paddled out, the heat of the sun on her back, burning through a UV shirt, the salt spray in her mouth as she duck-dived through one broken wave after another, the tickle of bubbles she blew out through her nose while under the water, the –

'Dreaming of your mother's apple pie, Caitlin?'

She was too nerve-dead and exhausted to startle. But inside she fell through negative space, tumbling end over end. She knew who it was before opening her eyes. Her target. Bilal Baumer.

Al Banna.

'Are you an assassin, Willard?'

'What the fuck?'

'It's my Brando doing Colonel Kurtz,' laughed Baumer, a rich, stagy laugh that bounced off the damp, mouldy ceiling of her cell. He repeated the quote, amping up the grinding, nasal impersonation. 'Are *you* an assassin, Caitlin?'

Okay. Just go with it . . . She indulged him. 'I'm a soldier.'

'You're neither.' He smiled, dropping out of character, but staying with the quote. 'You're an errand girl sent by grocery clerks to collect a bill.'

She smiled back at him, all bloody teeth and cold eyes, a feral creature that had learned the trick of imitating a human being. 'Yeah,' she sneered, 'and you'll pay in full.'

'I don't think so.' It was Reynard. He had changed into a fresh shirt and now stood behind Baumer, regarding her with restrained enmity. 'These theatrics, they weary me, Miss Monroe. As they must weary you too, *non*? It is time, don't you think, that we shook off our roles. Me, the nameless interrogator – '

'"Reynard" will do fine . . .'

'*You*, the lone wolf, the hunter, who will never give in. It is all bullshit. You have nothing to fight for.'

'I didn't pick the fight,' she said, suddenly angry. The sight of Baumer had brought back memories of Monique, and a more painful moral sensibility, a recognition of her abject failure to protect the girl. 'You sent your people in after me. I don't know why. Or I didn't, until *he* showed up.'

'You still do not understand,' Reynard told her.

'What? That he belongs to you – he's a double? Big fucking deal.'

'No,' said Baumer. '*I* am not one of *his*.'

Caitlin levered herself up a little further, and fought down an urge to shield her naked body from Baumer. It would be an acknowledgement of weakness. She raised her cuffed hands to rub at her eyes. Her wrists were bound by plastic zip ties that had cut deeply into the skin. The wounds were raw in places, crusted over in others. Just another locus of pain to put in a box and hide far away at the back of her mind.

Her voice was faint and croaky, but she put as much strength into it as she had. 'Okay, so you're telling me ol' Reynard here really *is* a cheese-eating surrender monkey. He's sold out to Osama, right?'

'No.'

'You mean he doesn't like cheese?'

The Frenchman squeezed his eyes shut and sucked air in through his teeth. 'I have brought Bilal here to show you the futility of resistance,' he explained. 'The war you were fighting is over. Your country didn't lose – you lost your country. What is the point in clinging to ideas and loyalties that no longer exist? It is the definition of madness, Caitlin. Just tell us what you can of Echelon's operational structure in France and you can go. We understand you were no longer hunting Bilal. You are a stateless refugee. You need help. But we cannot do that until you help us.'

Caitlin sucked her bruised and broken lower lip. 'Yeah, look, about that, weren't you the guy torturing me the last few weeks? Why would I help you, exactly? And why would you let me go, if I did?'

Reynard sighed. 'Caitlin, you are not an imbecile. Stop pretending otherwise. We are all serious people, and the work we do, the measures we must all take, they are serious too – *non*? You killed three innocent people during your cowboy shoot-out. You did not know that, did you? No, of course not, you could not know. But the post-mortems put your bullets inside them, not ours.'

She shrugged. He could be lying, probably was.

'Caitlin, we need to know what you know about Echelon,' he went on. 'I understand you work in cells, and I am not expecting you to give me details you cannot provide. But even the most mundane of details might mean something to us while possibly meaning nothing to you. You have to understand, Caitlin, that your fellow agents are rogue operators now. They are more dangerous than ever. The situation outside is stable, but critical. There has been much unrest, much distrust between peoples, even bloodshed. Things have settled now, due to a great deal of effort and goodwill by all parties, but just one of your colleagues carrying forward a single mission, hitting just one target, they could bring everything down. You *must* understand this. They must be stopped, for everyone's sake.'

Bilal moved closer to the raised slab of concrete on which she lay. He seemed tired and stressed out, but he retained much of the easy, feline grace that she recalled from pre-op surveillance. He looked in much better shape than Reynard. An immature, irrational part of her wished that Monique could see him now, and could see that she had not been lying.

'Like you, Caitlin, I am merely a messenger,' he said, sitting himself down carefully on the edge of the concrete surface, keeping his eyes on her face and away from the bruises and wounds that covered her body. 'I obey a Lord who is compassionate, who will make you a partner in peace or war.'

Her mouth curved up in a vulpine sneer. 'Well, *Billy*, if you knew your Ibn Ishaq as well as your Coppola, you would know the full context of that reference. That before whispering sweet nothings about peace and mung beans, the Prophet's companion, Ubayy ibn Ka'b, first spoke of settling matters with the sword at Khaybar, where the faithful would bring death to those who struggled against them. Or something like that. Maybe I'm getting confused with Conan the Barbarian. That was a great flick.'

She had hoped to unsettle him, but Baumer nodded as though agreeing with her. He seemed almost pleased. 'So not just an errand girl, then,' he replied. 'A scholar of the book, no less. In which case you would also know that Ishaq was not just a historian, but almost a prophet of sorts. A small "p" prophet, if you like. What prescience he must have had, Caitlin, to write "Evil was the state of our enemy so they lost the day. We slew them and left them in the dust. Those who escaped were choked with terror. A multitude of them were slain. This is Allah's war in which those who do not accept Islam will have no helper."'

He reached out and brushed away a few matted strands of filthy hair that had fallen over her eyes. 'I understand you were a warrior, Caitlin Monroe. And you remain one. It is an honourable calling. But there is a time for war, and a time to put aside our swords and shields. The world has been wounded and it suffers gravely, Caitlin. We are all God's subjects and we must bind up those wounds together. But we cannot do so without trust. That is why I am here, why "Reynard" has invited me here – to make peace with my old enemies.'

Her feet and hands were still bound, but if she could lock her arms around his head, she might still have a chance, with one wrenching pull, of separating his head from his spinal column . . .

'I can trust you, Caitlin, because I know you,' Baumer continued. 'Just like you know me. I know you must be calculating the odds of lashing out at me now. You must be measuring your strength against the damage and pain you have endured in here for the last three weeks, perhaps weighing up what residual skills you retain from all your years of training, what strength of will you possess, even after Reynard has tried to break that will.'

He grinned and flicked one eyebrow up in a gesture of camaraderie.

Then his hand shot out in a blur and he gripped one of hers, turning it back on her cuffed, bleeding wrists so quickly that a spike of pure white fire ran up her arms. She almost screamed, biting deeply into the inside of her cheek in a desperate attempt to draw her mind off the agony of the wrist lock.

The holy warrior known as al Banna let her go. 'So, shall we stop fucking around?'

He drove a fist squarely into her face, a blow that detonated inside her head like shellfire. As the back of her skull hit the hard concrete slab, she felt his iron grip on her arms again, wrenching her bodily over onto her stomach.

'Or shall we *begin*?' he snarled.

She tried to lash out with a feeble kick but only scraped more skin off her legs. Another punch on the back of her neck stunned her and she came to understand just how weakened she was by weeks of torture and illness. His hands clawed at her hips, dragging her towards him, confirming the worst.

When Caitlin was a girl, maybe nine or ten years old, her family had travelled to California for a holiday, driving all the way from Charleston AFB in South Carolina, where her daddy had been stationed with an airlift squadron. They did all of the family things you do in California – visiting Disneyland, Hollywood, the beaches. But for her the standout memory had been climbing the bell tower on the Berkeley campus, just before the clock struck ten in the morning. The pealing of the bells was frighteningly loud, much louder than she had imagined it would be. She not only heard the thunderous clanging, she felt it, inside her chest and stomach, reverberating right down through her feet. The sensation, which was entirely unpleasant, remained with her ever after.

The rape lasted only a few minutes, but she was still shaking hours later.

Lying on her slab, under a harsh, flat white light in her cell at Noisy-le-Sec, she felt a powerful psychic echo of that same deep body shock.

Her limbs quivered and shook, sometimes so violently that she resembled a victim of late-stage Parkinson's disease, but it was inside that she felt herself being torn apart by a quaking, shuddering violence that was entirely psychological.

Nobody had entered the room since her violation. In her rational, calculating mind, the cold, mechanical killer's mind that had been honed to such a dangerous edge, she knew that was just part of 'the tactical questioning phase'. But she could not rid herself of the burning shame and humiliation she felt. As hard as she tried to control herself, the awful, nauseating tremors reminded her of that day in the bell tower, which naturally led to thoughts of her family, especially her father, and with them came more unutterable shame.

She tried to focus on something simple, some goal she might start working towards – like driving a stiffened sword handstrike into Baumer's throat at the first opportunity. But that only reminded her of how weak and unable to resist him she had been in the first place.

She was curled into a tight, shivering foetal ball when the lights went out.

It was so unexpected that Caitlin suffered a moment of total disorientation. She had been kept for so long in this cell flooded with bright, artificial light that the sudden fall of darkness was terrifying, as though her eyes had been put out. She squirmed far back into the corner of her cell, without being consciously aware she had done so. And then she heard something so familiar, but, like the sudden inky darkness, so unexpected it made her mind seize up for an instant.

Gunfire.

It was muted at first, far off in the distance somewhere in the underground maze of Noisy-le-Sec's interrogation cells. But it soon grew louder, and with it came other sounds. Boots running. Men cursing. More gunfire, the ripping snarl of automatic weapons and the crash of large-bore, single-shot rifles and pistols. A grenade exploded with a deafening roar in one of the enclosed tunnels outside her cell. She could see the flashes in the dark now and pick out individual voices; none of them familiar, all of them French.

Men ran past the heavy iron cage door that locked her in. One stopped, briefly, and fired in through the bars. A short wild burst that largely missed her, although a ricochet did rake a painful burning graze along one hip. She groaned and rolled off the slab, letting herself fall as a deadweight to the floor. In the pitch-blackness of the cell, nobody could see her, and whoever had stopped to finish her off rushed on. Muzzle flashes soon accompanied the crash and zip of bullets, which reached a crescendo as more men rushed past her cell, carrying their fight deeper into the prison complex.

In the darkness, Caitlin crawled into a blind corner, where she just might avoid getting shot, if she was lucky. She huddled there, naked, bleeding, and all alone, for what felt like a long time.

36

'My God, it looks like the seventh level of hell down there.'

'Down there' meant the Valley of the Nile, for thousands of years a seat of human civilisation, and now an eerie wasteland of oozing, radioactive mud dotted with the stubs of a few scattered ruins, both modern and ancient. To Jim Ritchie, it looked like nothing more than an endless sea of black garden mulch littered with tens of millions of corpses being picked over by every vulture in north-east Africa. The few American recon teams that had ventured in there described the buzzing of flies as being unbearably loud, something akin to a bandsaw. There were a handful of crazed survivors, one-in-ten-million lottery winners, of a sort. They were all, without exception, insane. The population of Egypt had been reduced to a few oasis dwellers deep in the Western Desert, and some wandering Bedouin, all moving south.

Ritchie stood grim-faced in front of the multi-panel displays, many of them recently arrived from Qatar, from the former headquarters of the Coalition. The Pacific Command's war room was fully engaged monitoring the dozen or more chaotic conflicts now scattered across Ritchie's theatre. This temporary facility had been constructed to maintain an overwatch of the former CENTCOM area, the nuclear wastelands of the Middle East. And as bad as the apocalyptic desolation of Egypt may have looked through the cameras of the two Global Hawks slowly circling above the Nile

Valley and Delta, it was by no means the most horrifying vista arrayed in front of him.

On other screens, smaller, more intimate and, in a way, more dreadful images played out. In Iraq, Syria, Lebanon and Iran, thousands of burnt and wounded victims of the atomic strikes had swarmed out of the charred husks of their cities and fallen upon the rural hinterlands. With no reliable supplies of fuel, power, or water in many areas, and with practically no functioning transport system to speak of, the farming lands of those countries, already poisoned by fallout, had since suffered an almost total collapse in their productivity. Whatever little edible stores the smaller settlements had, they now needed to be defended against the hordes falling upon them.

Ritchie had ordered that the worst of the footage not be allowed to run as a live feed. There was no tactical reason for having such grotesquery on display. But as the senior officer, he still had to view the edited intelligence take, which more often than not featured surveillance cover of village-level fratricide. It was heinous and terrible, disturbing at a cellular level, and it was repeated over and over again until he no longer possessed any moral capacity to react to the horror. It was all just pixels.

'Okay, I've seen enough,' General Franks told him.

The two men turned away as half of the video wall blinked out and switched over to standby feeds.

'I'm sorry,' said Ritchie as they left the room, dragging a short tail of aides behind them. 'Short of nuking the Israelis themselves, I didn't see what I could – '

'Forget about it,' growled Franks. 'They blindsided you. Me too. The warning I passed on to Tehran just made it worse for them, meant they lost everything to the EMP. I guess we can count ourselves lucky they didn't fry us as collateral damage.'

'There would have been consequences for that, Tommy.'

'Yeah,' Franks agreed. 'Wouldn't have made any difference to my guys, though, would it? And that bullshit target list – brilliant really. But now the Israelis have to live with what they've done, and they know they can't do it again. The Russians will nuke 'em, and we won't lift a finger in their defence.'

Ritchie said nothing to that. Three days after Armageddon, as the one-sided atomic war of March had been christened by the Western press, an emergency session of the reconstituted UN Security Council in Geneva had passed a unanimous resolution authorising member states to use 'all necessary means' to respond to any further nuclear strikes. In contrast to the usual ambiguity surrounding such things, the Russian and Chinese ambassadors had made it clear that this meant a massive nuclear attack on Israel. No other states had demurred.

'We still don't know where those other subs of theirs are hiding,' said Ritchie.

'Not our problem,' replied Franks. 'Not anymore. We're out of the world-policing business. Let the fucking French or the Brits find them. They have more to lose.'

The small pod of military brass turned into a large briefing room that had been prepared for their arrival. General Franks, the new Acting Chairman of the Joint Chiefs, waved everyone back to their seats as the assembled officers came to attention. He and Ritchie took their places at the head of the large conference table. There was no ceremony. Franks ordered the first briefer to the podium with another wave of his hand.

Colonel Maccomb nodded and smiled thinly at Ritchie as he moved around the table. The two men had seen a lot more of each other than their families in the last month. Ritchie had come to trust the intelligence man's judgement implicitly. He seemed able to read Jed Culver like an open book, for instance, and he'd warned of a possible Israeli strike days before it happened – which admittedly wasn't all that impressive, because the same predictions had been made many times in the press. But Maccomb had worked up a scenario that predicted the attack almost exactly as it transpired. Unfortunately, the report had not made it to Ritchie's desk before Asher Warat arrived in his office. The admiral made certain that the much-chastened commander of the 500th Military Intelligence Brigade understood he was never again to sit on any of Maccomb's reports if the colonel thought they should go up the line.

'Good morning, ladies and gentlemen,' Maccomb began. 'I have a number of points from each of the theatre commands to cover quickly before we discuss any particular issue in depth. Firstly, CENTCOM. Our latest best estimate puts half the population of the area dead, and it is likely that seventy-five per cent of the remainder are going to die within six months to a year.'

There was no evident reaction to the statement. Everyone had become inured to the horror story of the Middle East what felt like a long time ago.

'Major combat operations have ceased entirely, both between our forces, which have now left the region, and our former combatants, and between Israel and her former combatants. Israel remains under martial law, but we expect the state of emergency to be lifted within the next forty-eight hours as decontamination procedures are progressed far enough to allow some of the population to return to work.'

Maccomb thumbed a control stick and powered up a large flat-panel display on the wall behind him. A very familiar map of the Middle East appeared, with each of the atomic strikes clearly marked. Shaded areas of fallout stretched around the sites.

'A combined British, French, Russian and Chinese task force has arrived in Saudi Arabia to replace our own withdrawn forces,' the intelligence man continued. 'Smaller deployments have been made to various Gulf states to secure the surviving oil infrastructure. The Russian Federation's missile forces targeting Israel remain on the highest state of alert. British and French submarines also remain on station in the eastern Mediterranean, as a continued deterrent against further strikes by Tel Aviv. The future status of the French nuclear submarine *Le Triomphant* remains uncertain, however, dependent of the outcome of the struggle within France.'

Ritchie had some trouble containing a snort of surprise at Colonel Maccomb's talent for understatement. The 'struggle' he referred to had degenerated from incipient anarchy into civil war and from there into a confused and savage blood-swarm. Tracking the movements of the country's nuclear submarines was consuming almost as much attention from the surviving great powers as speculating on the disposition of those assets should the French Government finally succumb to the intifada.

'The situation within EUCOM is fluid,' said Maccomb, continuing with his penchant for understatement. 'The British Government is still enforcing its maritime exclusion zone and has secretly begun work to seal its end of the Channel Tunnel.'

That *was* a surprise to Ritchie. Since Franks had returned from Qatar and replaced him as Acting Chairman, he was no longer fully briefed on developments in Europe. Last he'd seen, Tony Blair was still denying that the Brits intended to do any such thing.

'The state of emergency remains in place throughout Britain, but we are informed that it will be lifted in Northern Ireland as of 0600 hours tomorrow. Our best information to hand is that the Blair Government will ignore the ultimatum from the European Union to release all of the so-called emergency detainees and is in fact planning to deport significant numbers of them.'

A murmur rippled around the table at this last revelation from Maccomb.

'With permission, General?' Ritchie asked Franks.

The chairman nodded. 'Make it quick, Jim.'

'Do you have anything more precise than just "significant numbers", Colonel?' asked Ritchie. 'Are they talking about flying out a couple of crazy mullahs or are we looking at mass deportations?' The admiral's daughter was in England, having escaped the Disappearance by a matter of hours. She was in no immediate danger, but the news coming out of the UK was growing darker every day.

'My information is that the forced relocations will probably take place on a greater rather than lesser scale, Admiral,' Maccomb replied. 'Much greater. They will probably involve a significant drain on the security forces. It will be a controversial policy.'

Sitting next to Ritchie, General Franks grunted and leaned forward. 'Ha. You know how to sugar-coat a shit sandwich, don't you, Colonel? It'll be a *bloodbath*. They're talking about deporting hundreds of thousands of second- and third-generation citizens. It's a pogrom, pure and simple. But,' he sighed, 'it's only our problem if it affects us operationally. What's your latest on the money Blair promised us?'

Colonel Maccomb coughed uncomfortably, and sipped from a glass of water by the podium before answering. 'General, the best information I have is that the special appropriations bill will pass with the help of the Conservatives. There are a hundred and thirty-four members of Blair's Labour Government who have publicly confirmed they will vote against it, but the

Conservative Party leader has pledged his support so it will go through.'

'And this little ethnic cleansing program of theirs, what's your reading of that?' Franks probed further. 'Is it likely to bring down the government? And if so, can we expect the same level of support from the British in future?'

Ritchie thought Maccomb looked even more uncomfortable at being asked to read the storm clouds of British politics, but it was a fair question. For the moment, at least, most of the day-to-day cost of running the US military was being met by alliance partners such as Britain and Japan. NATO was split on the issue, with countries like Poland stumping up support in cash and kind, while others, like France, were so busy falling apart they were worse than useless, as Ritchie knew all too well.

'The policy is supported by a clear majority of the British electorate,' said Maccomb. 'But the significant minority who oppose it can be expected to do so by all the means at their disposal. There will be bloodshed, yes. From our point of view, however, both the government and the opposition are committed to the supplementary appropriations process. So any change in government will not affect that. However, whether the UK can actually afford to maintain such outlays, even in the short term, is another matter entirely. And not one I am really qualified to discuss.'

Franks smiled grimly. 'Nice buck pass, Colonel. Damn, I never thought I'd see out my days as a gun for hire. Okay. We'll put that on the back burner. Continue.'

The intelligence officer returned to his notes and brought up a slide show of images culled from European news media.

'Fighting in France has intensified over the last two weeks. Elements of the state are in open conflict with each other, while large-scale street clashes that began as food and race riots have developed into open, disorganised tribal warfare – largely based on ethnic lines, but exacerbated by the involvement of some criminal syndicates in Marseilles and Lyons, and by the arrival of outside agitators from throughout the EU. Most official border crossing points have been closed, but that means nothing. France's borders aren't simply porous. They largely do not exist, and haven't for years. Additionally, we have very strong indications of

government-level assistance for some of this cross-border movement, especially of skinhead gangs from the eastern regions of
Germany into the main metropolitan areas of France. The numbers involved are not trivial, either. We tracked three train-loads
of neo-Nazis from Berlin and Dresden all the way to Paris. In total,
they numbered more than four thousand strong.'

'Good Lord,' muttered Ritchie. 'You mentioned these were
government-sanctioned movements. Which government?'

Maccomb pressed his lips together as though chewing over
something unpleasant. 'It is inaccurate to speak of a unitary
state authority in France right now,' he began, carefully. 'But one
bureau of their Direction centrale des renseignements généraux,
the General Information Service, has been in close and constant
contact with the BND, the German Government's foreign intelligence service, and the Russian FSB, which maintains extensive
networks in the former East German provinces. It's significant
because the GIS, as we call it, is the intelligence arm of the French
police, which answers directly to the Interior Minister, Mr Nicolas
Sarkozy. And, of course, his Emergency Committee has assumed,
or some would say *usurped*, responsibility for state security from
the Elysée Palace since President Chirac was wounded in the suicide bombing of March 25.'

Ritchie, who had privileged access to information about the
situation in France that nobody in the room other than Franks
enjoyed, still found Maccomb's explanation difficult to follow. 'I
don't see how this all hangs together, Colonel,' he objected. 'What
is your point?'

Maccomb shrugged before bringing up video footage copied
from a French news service. Up on the wall-mounted screen, a
hugely violent confrontation was playing out between thousands
of rioters in Clichy-sous-Bois, a poor commune in the east of Paris.
Hundreds of black-clad French riot police stood by as a wave of
shaven-headed thugs appeared from a maze of side streets in a
coordinated assault on a mass of dark-skinned rioters. Armed
with clubs and even-edged weapons, they cut a swathe through
their densely packed, inferior-armed opponents.

'The death toll from that one encounter was over two hundred,'
said Maccomb. 'It didn't rate as a news story for more than a day,

because there were bigger and more violent riots elsewhere in the city, and then the following day the first of the radioactive plumes from reactor meltdowns in CONUS crossed the French coast. The CRS – the French riot police – not only did not intervene, but they actually facilitated the attack and later the safe withdrawal of the neo-Nazi street fighters.'

The colonel then brought up footage of two police officers calmly chatting with a small number of fascist organisers, apparently giving them directions, while a murderous brawl took place a stone's throw away. The skinheads appeared to take a good deal of advice from the officers before running off to marshal their own forces.

'At no point in any of the clashes of the past weeks have the CRS decisively intervened to stop any major incidents of violence, *except* on those occasions where ultranationalist forces looked to be in trouble. I have a separate briefing note on this subject, and will cover it at length in due course, but for now I think it is reasonable to categorise the situation in France as a race war within the general population, and a civil war between some elements of the state security apparatus.'

Franks and Ritchie exchanged a quick, wordless glance. They had their own angle on the French troubles but it was not something they could discuss, even in this forum.

'Thank you, Colonel,' said Franks. 'It's fascinating, even a little satisfying, but we need to move on. You have a quick run-down on the Russian situation?'

Maccomb nodded. 'Russian military forces either remain at the highest level of alert or, in cases such as Georgia and Chechnya, have been deployed on active duty. None of the deployments raise any threat to American forces or interests, however, and the Russian Defence Ministry has been assiduous in keeping us informed of any developments that might impact upon our interests. They are treading very carefully around us, and trying hard not to generate too much friction along the Chinese border . . .' He glanced up at Ritchie before continuing. 'Which brings us to the Pacific Command.'

There was a noticeable shifting of postures around the table. PACOM was home. At least half of the officers in the conference belonged to Admiral Ritchie's theatre command.

'There are two serious flashpoints within PACOM,' Maccomb went on. 'I would have said three until recently, but the Korean peninsula is one of the few areas where tensions seems to have decreased in the last month, most likely due to the volume of aid shipments heading north from Seoul. For now, the bribes are working. For now, as well, there have been no calls from the north for the withdrawal of US forces. However, there will be an emergency session of the National Assembly in two days, to discuss an urgency motion requiring the withdrawal of all foreign forces from the Republic.'

Ritchie knew it was coming, but most people in the room did not. And, as much as a tightly controlled group of professional officers could descend instantly into uproar, they did – which is to say, an air force general swore under his breath and a Marine Corps colonel banged his water down a little too loudly.

'Get over it, people,' barked Franks. 'If they don't want us, we can't stay. They're already picking up our drinks tab and they can't afford it – their economy has imploded. Vote or no vote, we'd be leaving. Go on, Colonel. Give us some bad news for a change.'

Maccomb essayed a slight twitch of the mouth that may have been the ghost of a grin. 'India and Pakistan,' he said. 'The probability that one or the other will attempt a pre-emptive strike is approaching certainty. Their conventional forces have already clashed seriously on three occasions in the last month, and all cooperation with Islamabad over the Afghan situation has effectively ceased. Both sides have carried out proxy terror attacks approaching mass-casualty levels, and satellite cover indicates that each country has stepped up the readiness of its nuclear forces.'

'Jesus wept, did they learn nothing?' exclaimed the same Marine Corps officer.

'You can skip the details of any likely exchange, Colonel,' said Franks. 'We know what one of these wars looks like now, and how it affects the rest of the globe. Admiral Ritchie, what's our Uplift status for the subcontinental region?'

Ritchie didn't need to consult his notes or an aide. He'd been living Operation Uplift for nearly three weeks. 'Ninety per cent complete, General,' he answered. 'TRANSCOM has moved eighty-three thousand US citizens from India, Pakistan, Sri Lanka and

Bangladesh to reception facilities in Australia and New Zealand. We're still shifting up to a thousand a week, but the flow has really tapered off.'

'Anybody who's not out soon is going to get turned into an x-ray,' said Franks. 'We've done what we can. I don't want our people there in large numbers when one of those fools presses the button. I think we might put a deadline of this Friday local time for Uplift. After that, anyone dumb enough to hang around will be on their own. That timing sound right to you, Maccomb?'

'It's tight,' replied the briefer. 'The Indians have begun to prepare their launch sites. A lot of embassies are already shutting up and getting out. The Brits and Aussies have upgraded their travel advisories to the highest level, warning of immediate interstate conflict.'

'Okay. Wednesday – midnight. That's the end of it for us. Go on.'

'China.' Maccomb paused briefly as if that was all that was needed on the subject. 'While the People's Republic does not suffer from some of the ethnic division present in France, on our reading of the current situation its future is just as bleak. The economy hasn't imploded, it just ceased to be. There were already imbalances and rigidities building up before 14 March. Thousands of state-run enterprises were being propped up just to keep the rural poor fed and housed. Now, hundreds of millions of people have no income, and in the cities, no means of supporting even a subsistence level of existence. China was a net food importer when the Disappearance hit. It cannot feed itself. The PLA, which had begun to deploy some force projection assets around the Taiwan Strait, is now fully engaged within the country's borders. The government has imposed a media blackout and expelled all but a handful of foreign journalists, and their movements are tightly controlled. Most of our in-country assets were managed from CONUS and are of little use now. But we do have some access to British and Russian intel, and they are convinced that a schism has opened both between the army and the Communist Party, as well as within those institutions. At 0230 hours this morning, the FSB's Beijing station was reporting that major combat had broken out within the city between elements of the People's Armed Police and at least two divisions of Army

Group 6, including armoured and artillery units. Admiral Ritchie will have more on this, in a few minutes.'

Ritchie felt the weight of everyone's attention fall on him.

Franks met the admiral's gaze. 'Very quickly, Jim. You think they're going to turn this inwards, or out, on the rest of us?'

'Inwards,' he replied without hesitation. 'At least in the short term. Command and control of the Chinese state is failing – has failed. This is about re-establishing that control, but it won't be simple or easy, or something that happens very quickly. Like the colonel said, they have hundreds of millions of people who might well starve to death in the next few weeks. Jumping across the Taiwan Strait will not change that. It'll simply make dealing with it all the more difficult, and at any rate, the chain of command is broken. They can only fight among themselves, for now.'

'Okay,' said Franks. 'That'll do for the wrap-up. Let's start grinding our way through the to-do list, shall we?'

They met privately during a break in the all-day conference, Franks joining Ritchie in his office to share a cup of powdered coffee. There wasn't a drop of the real stuff to be had on the islands.

'This French business, we're gonna have to do something about it,' Franks told him. 'I wouldn't have believed it when you first told me, but this latest intelligence from the Brits nails it. We have to get that girl out, Jim.'

Ritchie drained the last of his lukewarm java and pondered the view out of his window. Another beautiful Hawaiian day. It seemed perverse, given the state of the world, but he knew that even out there, things were going badly. Most of the islands' non-residential population had already been moved on to resettlement facilities elsewhere in the Pacific. Almost none had volunteered to return to the mainland.

'Well, it explains a lot,' said Ritchie. 'Especially about what Blair has done, I suppose. How are we going to get her? She's dropped off the grid.'

Franks shook his head. 'We've found her again. Sarkozy's people grabbed her an hour ago.'

37

Jed Culver had scored himself three adjoining rooms at the Hotel Monaco, and standing in the centre suite, straining to listen to a CNN report on the nearby Constitutional Convention, he wondered if he should've grabbed a couple of spares. For the overflow. There had to be more than a hundred people in here. The roar of such a large crowd in so closely confined an area was loud enough to bury the sound of the television unless you knelt down in front of the set and jacked up the volume. He'd done that a couple of times, but within a few minutes the background noise had simply grown in response.

Dozens of people pressed in close around him, also trying to listen to the report, but their own cries of outrage drowned out the TV just as effectively as the background roar. On the screen, a doughy-faced man with an unfortunate comb-over banged his fist on a podium, shouting out his words. *'It would only be temporary . . . a three-year sunset clause, with . . . extension only if the emergency requires it. But we need . . . measures now. We face annihilation without . . .'*

A small band of type flashed up, identifying him as Reggie Guertson, whom Jed now knew of as a GOP mayor from some pissant burg out east that for the last month had been holding its breath right up against the edge of the Wave.

'The military got us through the worst of this,' yelled an increasingly red-faced Guertson, 'and they'll get us through the worst that is to come. But only if we give them what they need to get the job done.'

'He's a poet and don't know it,' cried out one of the hecklers standing behind Culver.

On screen, the camera panned around as the auditorium erupted with fierce catcalling and jeers, but Jed estimated that at least half of the howls of protest were directed against anyone who'd objected to Guertson's proposal to reserve a third of the new congressional seats for the armed forces. As an emergency measure.

The reaction behind him, in the hotel room, was uniformly negative. Deafeningly so. Nobody here was backing the idea. The Louisianan lawyer frowned and tried to get some more volume out of the television, but it seemed to have been programmed by the hotel to preclude inconsiderate or hard-of-hearing guests from annoying their neighbours. He could just make out a rising cacophony as Guertson attempted to shout down a sizeable chorus who were chanting over and over again, '*Sieg heil! Sieg heil!*' The image cut to a shot of the convention chairman, newly elected Anchorage mayor Mark Begich, banging his gavel and calling for order, entirely without effect.

Culver shook his head and pushed himself up to his feet. His knees hurt and he felt a little giddy, probably from all the smoke in the room. All three suites were choked with cigarette smoke, despite all of the non-smoking signs, and the whole space reeked of wet clothes, body odour, recirculated air and stale farts. The carpets had disappeared under an inch-thick mat of crushed potato chips and pizza rind, and every flat surface was full of empty bottles and paper cups. Clear plastic bottles of spring water stood next to crushed cans of Canadian beer. He wondered sometimes how many people were here simply because he had a proven supply of snack foods and free beverages.

Well, not free. There was nothing so gauche as a cover charge for entrance into Jed Culver's lair, but everyone in these rooms would pay a price for being here. Sometime, somewhere.

'Hey, Culver. Been looking for you.'

He turned, looking for the owner of the harsh Brooklyn accent. Or Brooklyn by way of Warsaw, to Jed's well-travelled hearing.

'Mr Cesky,' he called back, over the din. 'I've been looking for you too. Wanted to thank you for your help yesterday.'

Cesky, a short, thick-shouldered man, with the hardened hands and beaten-down features of somebody who'd worked in construction all of his life, waved him off with one hairy, bandaged paw. 'Nah. Fuggedaboutit,' he said. 'What's money for if you can't fuckin' spend it to gets what you want?'

Culver smiled but said nothing. For all of Cesky's two-fisted, roughneck routine, he'd found him to be quite a shrewd operator. A hard nut, his old man would have called him. Not likely to crack under the hammer. The businessman was covered in suture marks and bandages from whatever misadventures he'd endured getting himself and his family out of Central America. Cesky had said nothing to Jed, but the lawyer had done his background work before taking the man's favours, and he knew that after a couple of failed attempts, Henry Cesky had pulled off a remarkable escape from Acapulco, right in the middle of the city melting down. He had to have some kind of smarts, and he was obviously tough enough to have come through intact, if not unharmed.

Like all men, however, he was cursed with his own particular weaknesses. That crack about the money, for instance. That wasn't just for Jed's benefit, reminding him of how much credit he'd poured into the lawyer's 'discretionary account' – his black-bag fund, for want of a gentler euphemism. No, it also let everyone within hearing distance know that Henry Cesky was no fucking chump. Henry Cesky had somehow managed to salvage a good deal of his personal fortune and what was left of his business, and Henry-fucking-Cesky was still a fucking player. Especially by the much-reduced standards of the American body politic, as they were now being played out in the surviving seat of power, the Pacific Northwest.

The Brooklyn construction king slipped one of his heavy arms around Culver's shoulder. With Cesky's shirt sleeves rolled up, Jed could feel the thick mat of gorilla fur on the man's forearms tickling the back of his neck. He ignored it. Getting inside your personal space was a favoured ploy of Cesky's, and as the lawyer had about four inches and a good number of pounds on him, he let it slide.

'What I wanted to talk to you about was them fucking army

engineers,' said Cesky. 'They're doing a lot of work for the city at the moment and I can't help thinking that it could be done a lot fucking quicker and cheaper by the private sector, you know. By people who don't need to cross every fucking "i" and dot every fucking "t", if you know what I mean.'

Jed didn't correct him. He knew what the construction magnate meant. 'I hear you, Henry,' he bellowed back. 'I'm a hundred per cent behind you on that. But for now, at least, the army's a law unto themselves here. You've seen that. They're still running this place, really.'

And he had to wonder at that, given what he'd been hearing about relations between the city and Fort Lewis over the last month.

Cesky took his arm away. He'd had to reach up some, and it couldn't have been comfortable for him. 'Well, they need to get back in their fucking box,' he said. 'Or someone needs to put them there. I heard about what they did with the council guys. Coming the fucking heavy like that. No fucking wonder they got the contracts locked up for this joint, eh?'

Culver would have shaken his head in amazement. Another Henry Cesky weakness was a complete inability to see the world in terms other than his own. He honestly regarded the army as little more than a rival firm, undercutting him on his bids for city work. In their position, it's what Cesky himself would have done; so, obviously, that's what they'd been doing when they 'sequestered' the local councillors during the worst of the immediate crisis following the Disappearance. They were simply looking to do Cesky out of a buck. Un-fucking-believable.

Jed held up both palms. 'No argument from me, Henry. I can see why they moved the way they did at first. It was probably the only way to keep things together here. But we're past that now, aren't we?'

Cesky nodded sagely. Or in a manner that he obviously thought of as sagely, if he even knew what the word meant. 'Fucking lotta work to be done here, Culver,' he went on as they threaded their way through the heaving crush and heat of the crowd. 'Not just spade work neither. There's a lot of rebuilding up here, too,' he added, tapping the side of his head with two thick fingers.

Culver nodded, a little surprised at his insight. 'That's why this week is important,' he replied. 'It's why we need guys like you on side, Henry. Things are at tipping point, if you ask me. Could go either way. We could fuck this up, end up with Fort Lewis running everything and doing guys like you out of a job, or we could make a whole new start. And all this bullshit about giving the army seats in any government – that would be fucking things up, don't you think? That's third-world stuff.'

Cesky nodded vigorously. He grabbed a bottle of Molson Old Style Pilsener off a tray as it wobbled past at eye level. Whether he bought Jed's argument as a point of high principle, or whether he saw his main chance being cruelled by his major competitors getting their camouflaged butts into Congress, was a moot point. From Jed Culver's point of view, Henry Cesky was an ally because, like everyone else in this room, he was firmly in the 'No' camp when it came to the question of rewriting the Constitution.

'I dunno what these assholes are so frightened of,' declared Cesky. 'I don't see anywhere dealing with the fucking Wave as good as us, and we got hammered flat by the fucker. Look at them French assholes, killing each other in the street. Fucking China, falling apart like a cheap fucking toy. And England, it's a fucking prison camp. None of that happened here, and never will, unless we let it.'

Jed could have argued with him about some of the prison-camp aspects of post-Disappearance Seattle, but he let it go. 'Good man,' he said, as he slapped Cesky hard on the back. 'That's the spirit. Question is, though, what are we going to do about it? What are *you* going to do about it, Henry? The days when we could leave this stuff to the insiders and the beltway crowd are over. Those assholes are gone. Well, mostly gone. There's a few of them hanging around like farts in a phone booth at the convention, let me tell you. But that just means we've got to step up. *You* have to.'

'Hey, I'm doing my bit. I'm here, aren't I!'

'Yeah, but it's going to take more than standing around flapping our gums, Henry,' replied Culver, steering the smaller man into a makeshift alcove formed by a couple of couches. He leaned forward conspiratorially. 'Might come a time soon when we have to act . . . How would you feel about that?'

'What do you mean, "act"? You mean, break some fucking heads? If that's what it takes, Culver, that's what it takes.'

'Oh, I'm sure it won't come to that,' said Jed, moving them off again, towards a door connecting two of the hotel suites. 'There's no point butting heads with the army. You'll lose. But it's good to know, Henry, that if push comes to shove in some other way, we have you and your organisation behind us.'

Cesky stood a little taller and nodded emphatically. 'Six hundred guys I got on my payroll, Culver. Six hundred families I'm keeping fed and housed and warm at night. I'm fucking proud o' that, you know. It's not just about the money or my own family. It's what I can do for others. You need me to get out the vote – it's out. You need boots on the street – you got 'em. They're my people. They know who looks after them, and they know who's been trying to take food from their fucking tables, too.'

Cesky frowned and waved his beer at a TV in the next suite. Through a shifting mass of bodies, Culver could just make out somebody on the screen, wearing an army uniform.

'Mr Culver, Mr Culver.'

He gratefully embraced the distraction. Looking for an excuse to break free of Cesky, Jed craned his head around, searching for whoever was calling his name. Unfortunately, the builder saw the guy first.

'Over there. Faggy-looking mope.'

Culver saw him straight away then. Aaron Metz from Microsoft. He was attempting to cut a path through the tidal flow of the crowd, and not doing so well. Jed could see he was holding something aloft in one hand.

'Come on, make a fucking hole, would you,' shouted Cesky, bruting his way into the crush and virtually hauling the fragile-looking Metz out of it by force. 'Not you of course, buddy,' Cesky added, grinning at the Microsoft executive. 'Wouldn't want you making free with any holes around me, eh?'

The very obviously gay Aaron was both flustered and grateful, and chose to ignore the upfront homophobia of his rescuer's comment. 'Thank you,' he said. 'So many people here, Mr Culver. It's almost as mad as the convention floor. Not that I can get in of course, but – '

'How can I help, Aaron?' Jed asked, cutting him off before he started to babble. He'd learned the hard way not to let Aaron Metz get up a head of steam.

'Oh, Mr Ballmer wanted you to have this, sir, right away, Mr Culver. It's one of our new smart phones. Well, not *ours* – it's an iMate but it runs the Windows Mobile OS. It was still in development, you know, when . . .'

Culver nodded and waved off the rest of the explanation. 'Thanks, Aaron. You tell Steve it's greatly appreciated.'

'It has some special security features, Mr Culver . . .'

'I'm all over it, Aaron. Thanks again. Tell Steve and Bill, I *will* be in contact, later today.'

Metz looked even more flustered now than when Culver had first seen him. He gushed and flapped around, and even bowed at one point.

'What a bag of fruit,' grunted Cesky as soon as he was out of earshot.

'To each their own,' said the lawyer, pocketing the smart phone. 'I'm grateful for their help, Henry. I'm grateful for anyone's help, given the mess we're in.'

'So how come they're not here, then, those big software guys? You got a lot of corporate types here, Culver. Really heavy hitters, eh? You can't tell me there's anyone big enough in this town to put the fucking frighteners on Bill Gates. He's still richer than God.'

'You wouldn't think so, would you,' Jed replied, but not with enough volume for Cesky to hear him. 'You'll have to excuse me,' he said, a little louder. 'I have people I need to talk to. Now, as for you, Henry, I can count on you and your guys?'

'You bet, Culver. I'm not gonna get rolled over and ass-fucked without a fight.'

'Great. And your family, they're good? There's nothing I can do to help out there?' he asked, studiously avoiding the actual reason Cesky had fronted him – his complaint about getting shut out of city work by the Army Corps of Engineers.

Cesky shook his head and flexed one bandaged hand. 'We had some trouble getting out of Acapulco,' he said. 'Some people I gotta settle up with about that one day. But my girls are all in

Sydney now. They're safe. I don't have to worry about them if things get difficult around here.'

He cracked the knuckles on his undamaged hand and jutted his chin out. Culver gave him a comradely squeeze on the shoulder, excused himself and made for the nearest exit. As he muscled through, at least six or more people attempted to intercept him, but Jed shook them off with a smile and a wave of the smart phone that implied he had A Very Important Call to make, which he did.

Although it wasn't nearly as hectic and crowded out in the corridor, he was unsurprised to find a spillover crowd, working the space just as intently as the folks back in his trio of rooms. It was a weird vibe for an old hack like Culver. He saw figures he recognised from both the left and right of politics, some of them West Coast, others national figures who hadn't been caught by the Wave. Heads bent together, their devious minds were plotting against a new enemy – this cross-party faction in favour of a total rewrite of the Constitution and the Bill of Rights, paring them back, and ceding permanent powers of near autarchy to a smaller, militarised executive, all of it sold in terms of the dire need to protect the Republic from annihilation or anarchy or some such bullshit.

Culver had seen it all before. Frightened people driven to mortal foolishness by the extreme situation in which they found themselves. Well, not on my watch, buddy, he thought to himself.

He'd been blindsided by how bad things were politically, when he'd first arrived here in Seattle. But Jed Culver was nothing if not adaptable.

The future of the country was being fought out in this city, and he was a large part of the battle. As Governor Lingle's personal envoy to the surviving representatives of the civil authority in what was left of the mainland United States, he had driven the convention process harder and faster than anyone thought possible. And yes, he had to admit, to himself if nobody else, the whole push to institutionalise a role for the military in the new system of government had caught him unawares.

It certainly wasn't coming from any of the uniformed guys he'd dealt with back in Hawaii. That wasn't their style, and they had their hands full anyway. And it wasn't coming from the military power structure here in the Northwest, as best he could tell. Not publicly at least. That Blackstone asshole out at Fort Lewis – a real Captain Bligh character, thought Jed – even he was scrupulously careful not to be drawn into any political debate.

But then, as someone who'd perpetrated all manner of villainy in his professional life, Culver was well aware of how easy it was to use cut-outs and puppets to do your dirty work while you fronted the media, the investigators or some nitpicking Congressional committee with your halo shining and hands washed free of blood.

Somebody, somewhere was driving this madness, attempting to hijack *his* Constitutional Convention, and he'd be damned if they were going to get away with it.

He threaded through the hallway loiterers, smiling, waving and gladhanding everyone as he went. A part of Jed seemed to float outside of himself, marvelling that a fixer from the backwoods of Louisiana could find himself at the centre of a storm that had destroyed so much already. He spotted a few Alaskan delegates he would need to corral later in the day, and a couple of Canadian diplomats, who caught him by surprise. The lawyer made a mental note to investigate their presence, but hurried on around the corner and into the fire escape. Two floors up, he finally had some privacy.

The numbers were preloaded as arranged and he found the one he was looking for without trouble. He was a bit of a gadget freak, if truth be known, and the chance to play with a new toy was reward enough in itself. But the phone call he had to make was important. The connection went through on the third ring.

'Hey Bill, it's me, Jed Culver. I got your package. Thanks for that.'

The strangely youthful voice at the other end came through with great clarity, in spite of all the filters, washers and heavy encryption he knew had been packed into the phone. 'Oh hey, Jed. Good, that's great. I'm glad that got through to you.'

'So, I don't want to come on as a nattering nabob of negativism, but you're sure this is secure?' Culver asked.

The man on the other end laughed. 'My guys are sure, Jed. As sure as they can be, anyway. I'm confident, if that helps, and I am talking to you, after all. Some people in this town would consider that treason.'

'Okay. Good enough,' said Culver. 'So, you can get more of these units out where they're needed?'

'Already on their way. Six hundred of them, give or take a few. They'll be distributed by nightfall. The network will light up when you want it.'

'You sure, Bill? I understood the net was terribly patchy now. Not at all reliable. Do we want it sitting there as a weak link?'

'It's fine. At least here, it's fine. There are massive holes everywhere else, but the local nodes in the Northwest are good – we made sure of that. You can rely on them. Especially for this. We've taken precautions.'

'Okay,' replied Culver, almost convinced. 'If you say so, we'll proceed. I can't tell you how important this is, what a difference it could make.'

'I'm happy to help. It's important to do what you can. I've been here all along, remember – could have flown out, but I stayed. All my people stayed. We're not ready to give up yet.'

'That's the spirit,' said Jed.

'Okay. Well, anything you need, you have my number.'

'Thanks, I will be in touch.'

'I hope so,' said Bill Gates, before hanging up.

Culver studied the small piece of technology, wondering how long it would be before the appearance of such things, and the progress they spoke of, became commonplace again. Possibly never, if he didn't win the confrontation he knew was coming. He could feel it down in his meat.

He was confident of the alliance he was building up here in the city. In his quiet moments, he was even proud of what he'd achieved since arriving. But he knew it wasn't enough.

Jed Culver understood humans. He understood their baser, uglier nature, the way that fear could rob them of reason and send them rushing over the cliff like lemmings. Look around the world and you had proof enough of that. But he also knew that if led well, if led with some wisdom and just a modicum of courage, a frightened horde could rise above itself and act with outward

calm and considered grace that completely belied any inward turmoil. But they had to be led, and he was not a leader. He had come
here knowing he would need to find one, and fast.

He opened up the contacts file on the smart phone again and,
yes, the name and number he had asked for were there. He did
not dial, however. It was time to make contact, but he would have
to do so personally.

Everything he had heard about this man, everything he'd
learned since flying into Seattle, had only confirmed Jed's suspicion that he was the one. But because of that, he was not the sort
of man to be played like Henry Cesky.

This one would have to be given the opportunity to make a
choice. A real choice for good or ill. Culver was certain he'd choose
wisely.

The lawyer put the phone away and headed downstairs.

38

'I think we're probably okay to go,' said Jules.

Fifi agreed, and triggered a burst from the PKM. 'Yeah. I think you're probably right,'

Tracer rounds zipped away over the heads of the islanders, forcing them all to duck below the gunwales of the small fleet of lobster boats heading towards the *Rules*. Jules hit the press-to-talk button on her headset.

'Mr Lee, are those contacts still closing?'

The old pirate's voice came crackling back to her. 'They are still on a course to intercept us, Miss Julianne. In forty-two minutes, if we do not leave now.'

'Okay, Lee. Everyone's aboard. Let's get the hell out of here.'

Jules felt the deck thrum under her feet as the engines growled into life and she reached out for the handrail to steady herself against the inertia. The bow lifted appreciably as they thrust forward, adding their speed to the bluster of a freshening nor'-wester. Jules and Fifi crouched instinctively as a few puffs of white smoke from the decks of the lobster boats told of a couple of ancient shotguns being fired in their direction. Fifi responded with another snarling burst from the heavy Russian machine-gun. Again, she aimed well over the mast of the lead boat, and again their pursuers all ducked. It would've been a ridiculous pantomime were it not so serious. The islanders meant to delay them long enough for those radar contacts to close with them.

Jules was now certain they were being chased by one of the Peruvian syndicates.

She pressed the talk button on her headset again. 'Sergeant Shah. Have your men stand ready please. I don't think they'll be needed, but best we don't try our luck.'

'They are in position, Miss Julianne. The passengers have been secured below by Pieraro. He will join us on the boat deck.'

Jules thanked him. She didn't bother looking for the small squad of mercenaries. The super-yacht was too large and they were mostly arrayed on the lower decks towards the stern, giving them a clear field of fire over the heads of the lobster boats as the *Rules* came around.

Fifi safed her weapon when she could no longer draw a bead on the little wooden tubs. 'You want me to head on down there, Julesy?' she asked, referring to the Gurkhas' position below-deck. 'Be a shame to waste the ammo, though, if we're not trying to hit them. This 7.62 Eastern Bloc standard doesn't grow on trees, you know.'

Julianne shook her head, trailing a regretful look back over the retreating vista of the Juan Fernández Archipelago, the trio of islands located some four hundred miles west of the Chilean city of Valparaíso. 'No, save your fire, Fifi. We'll need it soon. And those guys are no real threat.'

Behind the tiny, bobbing armada of trawlers, the soaring peaks of the main landmass, Robinson Crusoe Island, knifed into a slate-grey sky above the village of San Juan Bautista. The lonely settlement, the only one anywhere in the archipelago, clung to the water's edge at the mouth of a steep valley that funnelled bitter winds down into Cumberland Bay. The uppermost reaches of the jagged volcanic mountains were lost inside a mass of scudding clouds. The gale roaring down on them had teeth and blew stinging salt spray into her face, but in spite of all that, it had been a great port in which to lay up and recover from the mad dash away from Acapulco and down the coast. Even more importantly, it had been about as far removed from the rest of the world as you could be, without pulling on your thermal knickers for a trip to the Antarctic. That had been the deal clincher after the Middle East went up. None of her passengers or crew had objected to the change in course. None of them wanted to be anywhere near a big city that might disappear inside a mushroom cloud.

Robinson Crusoe Island, a solitary fleck of volcanic rock in the vastness of the southern oceans, seemed a perfect bolthole. Too bad it hadn't worked out a little longer.

As the boat built up to its maximum speed, the muted pop of gunfire from astern was lost in the roar of the wind. Jules and Fifi remained on the flying bridge for the moment, wrapped in oilskin coats, taking in the view as they hastily exited Cumberland Bay.

'I can't believe they narked us out,' said Fifi sadly. 'After they gave us those lobsters and everything!'

Jules shrugged. 'Lobsters they have an abundance of, Fifi. But diesel, food, medicine – those they're running out of fast. Shah said the boat from Valparaíso hasn't been for two months. I don't think it'll be coming again.'

'So what, dropping a dime on us to the fucking syndicates is their idea of self-help?'

The Englishwoman lifted her hands in a gesture of resigned acceptance. 'What are they gonna do, Fi? We weren't part of the tribe. We're just a big shiny boat full of stuff they need and can't get anymore. These people are doomed and our time with them was up. Get over it, hon.'

Fifi looked like she wanted to argue, but eventually just deflated.

As much as San Juan Bautista had been an excellent place to sit out Armageddon, truth be told, it also creeped Jules out. It probably would've creeped her out even before the end of the world. It was a small, wind-ravaged speck of burnt rock out in the middle of a howling ocean. She found the villagers strange and remote, and San Juan itself was shrouded in a forgotten air that she was certain predated the recent catastrophe.

As Mr Lee took them out into the exposed waters again, the yacht began to pitch and roll on the much rougher swell. The bow climbed larger and larger waves, each time smashing down into the dark trough on the other side with an enormous boom. Jules took another look off to starboard at the wreath of funereal clouds gathering around the highest of the island's summits before motioning to Fifi to follow her inside.

Lee was at the helm in the gleaming bridge, joyfully directing the other crew members present – Dietmar, the German
navigator they'd picked up in Acapulco, along with Rhino Ross,
who was chewing the stub of a much-abused cigar. Apart from
a bag of clothes, his personal luggage consisted entirely of foul-
smelling stogies, which he insisted on smoking at all times, right
down to the nub. The smell reminded Jules of her father's library,
so she indulged the old Coast Guard chief, over the protests of
her passengers who objected to his 'second-hand carcinogens'.
And after all, there was plenty of room on board to escape the
smoke.

'How's it looking, Rhino?' asked Jules, as she shook off the
spray and slid the hatch closed behind her.

'Excellent. Just excellent, if you're in the market for an old-
fashioned ass-kicking today. Two boats. The lead vessel is making
about eleven knots, pulling away from the other one, which is topping out at about eight.'

'Any idea how big or how many of these hoodlums we might be
dealing with?' she said, without any hope of a positive answer.

The Rhino puffed on his cigar, firing up the embers right under
his nose. He shook his head. He was about fifty years old, and his
face was a bright-red relief map of broken blood vessels and sun-
spots. 'Sorry, Skip. They're not in visual range. I wouldn't have
seen them until they were on us if we'd been anchored any further
inside the bay. The mountains were blocking the return.'

She sucked the salt from her lip and thought it over. The *Rules*
had a comfortable cruising speed of fifteen knots, which they
could push out to seventeen and a bit for a while, especially now
she had some engineers she could trust. But if they had any trouble in the hugely complicated engineering plant, or if they hit foul
weather, their pursuers were highly likely to catch up. Plus, of
course, she'd burn through their fuel a lot quicker at top speed.
Jules rubbed her temples, which were beginning to throb. This
was not what she had planned when she'd agreed to soak a bunch
of rich tourists for as much as she could get. She wondered what
Pete would have done.

'Okay,' she said at last. 'I don't see this ending well. Fifi, let's
get everyone together, shall we. Anyone who can hold a weapon,

down in the main lounge. Mr Lee, you just keep as much distance between us and them as you can. I'll be back soon.'

She had one last look back towards the islands. A storm front was piling up to the south-east, smudging out the horizon. She was confident in the super-yacht's ability to handle a big blow and could only hope that whoever was chasing them didn't enjoy such a pimped-out ride. Perhaps they could lose them in bad weather.

It really was an incongruous sight. She'd never been taken with the fabulously over-egged opulence of the main lounge area on the *Aussie Rules* – it was a bit too clubby and try-hard for her tastes. But she had to admit she liked the sight of the half-dozen little village urchins who'd come on board with Miguel bouncing and leaping from one deep blue lounge chair to the next. Or rather, she liked the look of utter dismay on the faces of some of her wealthier passengers.

Fifi followed her in, toting the PKM. It brought a quick level of decorum to proceedings, with even the children stopping and pointing. They were experienced enough to know what it meant.

'All right. Listen up, everyone,' Jules cried out.

With all of the passengers and some crew gathered in there, she guesstimated that nearly thirty people were in the room. It held them comfortably. Pieraro's extended family, who'd proven themselves less trouble and much more help than her paying guests, were mostly clustered together quietly under the oil paintings of Greg Norman's dogs, with just a few of the youngest children still roaming around unleashed. Julianne subtracted them from her plans; they would need to be hidden away somewhere with a minder. Perhaps Grandma Ana, who was the oldest of the Mexicans and spent most of her days shelling beans and peeling vegetables in the weak sun up on the pool deck. Jules had no doubt that she'd cut the throat of anyone who tried to harm the little ones, but she was virtually immobile. The rest of the clan, though, she'd come to appreciate. They worked hard. Ate little. Some of the men were good shots. They were reliable in a fight and would do whatever Miguel ordered, without demur. Plus, they'd proven themselves diabolically effective traders whenever the *Rules* had put into shore for resupply. Jules was still adamant they would have to leave the boat at some point, but for the moment, she couldn't see her way clear to dropping them anywhere. The mainland, which they had now left behind anyway, was too dangerous, especially near any of the larger cities.

Her small crew, recruited in Acapulco and at a handful of trading stops at smaller, self-sufficient towns and villages on the way down to Crusoe, were all handy with weapons in one form or another, while Shah's men, it went without saying, were utterly formidable. As she totted up the number of potential shooters in the lounge, Shah himself appeared at the main entrance and nodded silently to her. His men had the situation in hand for the moment.

The problem, as always, was the passengers – the rich, skiving dilettantes she had taken on board to fund the trip and provide her with a fig leaf of respectability when she arrived in Hawaii or Sydney, or wherever they were headed. While some of them had proved themselves not completely odious, and one or two, such as Marc Unwin, the oil broker, had even brought some of their arcane skills to bear for the benefit of all, as a group they were a bunch of fucking oxygen thieves. The trust-fund brats, Phoebe and Jason, had alienated all of the crew by treating them like staff. Indeed, Jason still sported a black eye from one of the engineers. Moorhouse, the merchant banker, had become a virtual recluse as he'd come to realise that the old world, and his fortune within it, was never coming back. As for the others, they simply made pains of themselves at every opportunity, for want of anything better to do. Well, she had a job of work for them to do now.

'Okay,' she said simply. '*Pirates*. Looks like we have two shiploads of them bearing down on us from the north.'

A murmur surged through the adults, while some of the youngest began a chant of '*Piratas! Piratas!*', before Grandma Ana whacked one of them behind the ears and they all shut up quickly. Even the whackee held in his tears.

'We had our problems with these guys before we got to Crusoe, and it looks like we've got them again.'

'How?' asked the banker. 'How'd they find us out here?'

Fifi shrugged. 'Somebody on the island probably dropped a

dime on us. Five'll get you ten, one of the lobster boats chugged out of port and went looking for someone who'd be interested. They couldn't take us themselves . . .'

'But they sold us out to someone who could,' Jules finished for her.

More audible concern and a good deal of anxious muttering from the A-list passengers greeted that. Jules held up her hands to forestall any panic.

'They *could* take us, if they caught us sleeping on the job. But they won't. You have all seen these sorts of characters before. We chased them off then, we'll do it again now. I've only called everyone together because this time it looks like there's more of them, and they have a bigger, faster ship than before. It makes sense,' she explained. 'Things have turned to custard on the mainland. People are killing each other for a handful of beans in the big cities. In a situation like that, you will always get bandits who group together to prey on the weak . . . But we are not the weak.'

Fifi hoisted her large, ugly-looking Russian machine-gun to emphasise Julianne's point. Sergeant Shah folded his massive arms and allowed his solid granite head to dip once in a nod of agreement.

'We will try to outrun these guys,' Jules continued. 'One of their boats is already falling behind and the weather is closing in. That will help. They'll have to fight a storm instead of us. But they have a second vessel that could catch ours if we have any problems, and so we need to be ready. Everyone, and I mean *everyone*,' she repeated, eyeing off her American passengers, 'will be armed and ready to repel any boarders.'

She expected objections but the statement simply dropped into a fearful silence.

'I do not expect you to get into machete fights. You'll lose. But we have enough small arms and ammunition to distribute among you and you *will* defend the boat with them. That means you will have to shoot people. Dead. This is not something you can leave to Sergeant Shah and his men – there will be too many for them to handle on their own. No offence, Mr Shah . . .'

Shah smiled. None taken.

'Now, I need you to divide yourselves up into two groups:

those who are familiar with firearms and those who are not. Sergeant Shah and Corporal Birendra will give the latter a quick tutorial in how to pull a trigger. That's all we ask of you. The others will go with Fifi down to the gun lockers and arm your-selves appropriately. Do *not* panic. Whatever may happen, will not happen for many hours yet, possibly even a day or two. Familiarise yourself with your weapons and whatever firing station you are assigned. Learn its blind spots and weaknesses. Identify a fall-back route. And then get some rest. Watch a movie, hit the gym – whatever does it for you. If you have to fight, it's best you're not shagged out from running around like headless bloody chickens for half a day beforehand.'

At least some of them laughed. Nervously.

Jules took a few steps towards the group. 'It may not come to anything,' she said. 'We may outrun them. We have enough fuel for six thousand miles of cruising. Enough food stocks now for a month, with some rationing. We may lose them in the storm that's brewing up out there. But we may not.' She paused, very briefly, taking in the effect she was having.

The faces of the older Mexican men were unreadable, their eyes like black polished stones in a dark night. The women looked much more defiant, but also fearful for the children. Some of the younger men, boys really, looked excited. Her A-listers, on the other hand, were quietly freaking out.

'You need to understand this, most of all,' Julianne concluded. 'Anyone who steps onto this boat with hostile intentions will be cut down. They will be killed. And there will be no mercy shown them. Because we will receive none in return.'

39

GUANTANAMO BAY NAVAL BASE, CUBA

'We could let 'em loose about seventy-five miles north of here,' Stavros deadpanned.

Brigadier General Tusk Musso snorted softly. Yep, it would solve a few problems if he could just throw all of his prisoners into the Wave. But then what would the *New York Times* say? Nothing. Not now.

Goddamn, but he needed a rest.

Musso pushed the tips of his fingers under his sunglasses and rubbed at his sore, bloodshot eyes. He could feel bristle growing on his cheeks. The camp had run out of razor blades. He'd have to do something about that. They had to maintain standards.

They had run out of Kiwi boot polish as well, hard as that was to believe. Most combat boots looked as if they'd been polished with a Hershey bar, if at all. The general wore a pair of the new, now rare, suede tan Marine Corps boots. At least he didn't have to worry about spit and polish every night.

The afternoon sun was warm, but not uncomfortably so. Nonetheless, it glinted off the steel and wire of Camp 4 with a fierceness that made the sunglasses necessary. It was quiet today. The next call to prayer was still an hour away and the prisoners' initial excitement after the Disappearance had long since evaporated. The Israelis had made sure of that. Most of these humps were now as alone in the world as the Americans who still guarded them.

'I don't know what to do, George,' he admitted to his aide.

'Pearl wants this expedited. And that's the extent of their instructions. Except for Susan Pileggi's Uplift requirements, we really don't rate as a priority anymore, and the refugee flow has slowed up anyway. God knows, some of these losers really don't need to be here,' he said, waving a dismissive hand back towards the imprisoned jihadis. 'But, on the other hand, nobody's going to thank me for releasing a couple of hundred more lunatics onto the job market. So what do we do?'

'Don't know, General,' replied Stavros. 'That's why you make the *big* bucks.'

That really was a joke. Neither of them had been paid in weeks. Even if they had been, what use would they have for a dead, worthless currency?

'Okay, decision time. Let's set up a small review team. We'll do a quick and dirty study of each case. The really bad motherfuckers, like Khalid, we're going to try according to the laws of war. If convicted, they can be dealt with summarily.'

Lieutenant Colonel Stavros looked wary. 'But General, most of the personnel involved in the commission process were back home. Prosecutors, defence. And most of their files are gone too. What do we charge them with? How can we – '

Musso cut him off with a chopping hand gesture. 'I didn't say it'd be pretty, George. Just fast. Some of these guys need their necks stretched. Some of them don't belong here. Let's shake the box and see who falls out of which hole. I want it sorted in a month.'

'A month . . .' Stavros stammered. 'But General, we've got *hundreds* of cases . . . And where are we going to send them?'

'A lot of them can be repatriated to their homelands, assuming the Israelis didn't turn them into a slagheap. We got a lot of Pakistanis here – let Musharraf have them. We might even get lucky. India might nuke him as soon as they touch down. Most of the rest are Saudis, Jordanians, Afghanis – let's send 'em home. What happens then is up to their governments. Frankly, I don't think many of them will survive, but that's not my problem. A month, Colonel. This is one issue I don't need to think about anymore. There's plenty more that I do. Including this waste of space . . .'

Stavros turned to look over his shoulder where Musso had glowered at two approaching civilians. Professor Griffiths and his assistant Tibor, universally known as Igor. The pair were stomping up the road in front of Camp 4, sweating profusely.

Griffiths began carping as soon as he was in pistol-shot range. 'Found you at last, *General*. I must protest yet again about the lack of cooperation from your staff with my research. Do I have to remind you that my team and I were sent here by your superiors? I am supposed to be studying the phenomenon, instead I spend most of my time getting jerked around by you or your minions.'

'Good afternoon, Professor. Always lovely to see you,' said Musso. 'And no, you don't have to remind me. I've heard that particular song so many times now, it has its own neural pathway that lights up every time I see you. If this is about your field trip, my staff aren't thwarting you, Professor. They're simply following orders. They cannot go into the exclusion zone along the line of the Wave, because they have been ordered not to. The Wave is dangerous, sir. It eats people. It ate one of yours the first week you were here. Left a little pile of goo in a white coat, as I recall. It's not getting any more of mine.'

Musso's voice was rising and he could feel his anger slipping the leash. He pushed past the civilians and stomped over to where his driver and Humvee stood waiting on the small loop road in front of the camp. Brown, dried-out grass grew to knee length on the waste ground here and Musso made a note to himself to have that seen to. It was getting to be a fire hazard. He was aware of Stavros crunching up behind him, but his thoughts were elsewhere, sailing out across the blue waters he could just glimpse between the prison camp buildings as he attempted to calm down. Increasingly he found the fuse on his incendiary temper was burning way too quickly. He had once fancied himself the world's most patient man. Really, he was known for it. That's what made him a good lawyer. But he did have a temper, a foul one, and it had been running wild for weeks. Ever since the first shock had ebbed and he'd had time to really take in the enormity of the loss. Of his loss, personally.

He lay awake in his cot most nights, unable to sleep properly, tortured by the loss of his family. It was wrong, he knew, to feel their deaths so much more keenly than the hundreds of millions of lives snuffed out on that day and since. But that was just how people were. As each day went past, he found it more difficult to deal with their absence, not less. He often caught himself thinking irrationally of calling one of his boys or his wife. And then he'd remember . . . and his mood would implode.

'Well, let the Cubans escort me, General,' continued Griffiths, who was entirely oblivious to the needs of anyone but himself. 'They don't have to follow your orders, do they? I'm sure some of them would love a chance to travel back into their own country.'

Musso spun on him. 'Go ask them yourself, Professor, but first, tell me what the fuck have you actually learned while you've been here? Tell me what anyone has learned, here or anywhere else, about that thing.'

Griffiths staggered back one step and opened his mouth, but no words came out, because there was nothing to say. The Wave did not exist, at least not according to any instruments or sensor arrays currently available. The only evidence that it still sat there, squatting over the North American continent, was available by looking north. There it soared, miles into the sky. Mute, terrible and utterly impenetrable.

'Nobody is stopping you, Professor. Off you go, if you wish. But do not bother my people about it. I have lost half-a-dozen of them to that thing, not to mention the Cubans it's grabbed up. It's *random*. There is no safe distance within two thousand metres of it. People have been snatched from twenty feet away, and two klicks. You were told all of this, on arrival. Nothing has changed.'

Griffiths, a small man afflicted with receding red hair, appeared likely to blow a gasket. But unlike Musso he still had control of his temper. 'I am sorry for the loss of your men, General . . .'

'And women. Two of my Marines were women – Corporal Crist and Lieutenant Kwan.'

'Okay. I am sorry. But those casualties all predated my arrival. I do not need anyone to follow me into the exclusion zone. Entering is a risk I am willing to take. But I cannot get *out there* without an escort. There are simply too many bandits now. It is too dangerous.'

Musso made another conscious effort not to explode. He tried to climb down from the heights of his rage. Perhaps Griffiths was right. Nobody had ever been taken beyond two thousand metres. The survey stations in the Pacific Northwest and Canada confirmed that too. If the scientist had the nuts to take himself inside that safe, established perimeter on his own, who was he to argue? After all, if the Wave gobbled him up, it'd be one less headache for Musso to deal with.

'Okay,' the general replied, 'you can have an escort to within three thousand metres. After that, you're on your own. Even if you get nailed by bandits within clear sight of my people, if you are in the zone, you're on your own. See if you can remember that little rhyme. It'll help with your confusion when we don't come running to drag your ass out of trouble.'

Stavros stepped forward at that point. 'General, your meeting with the French consul, sir. You're going to be late.'

'Thanks, George,' he grunted. It wasn't even a set-up. He really did have a meeting, for which he was truly grateful. 'Dr Griffiths, if you don't mind, I have to sign off on the last of the refugee convoys today. Perhaps when they are gone, there will be time for dealing with your issues.'

That seemed to surprise and even mollify the scientist somewhat, and Musso climbed into the Humvee without delay. He didn't offer the civilians a ride anywhere.

'These won't be the last refugees we get, you know, General.'

'I know, Susie, but it will be the last big convoy the navy escorts anywhere. The word from Pearl is *finito*. It's been a month. From now on, people will have to make their own arrangements. We're losing more of our power-projection capability with each passing day.'

The midnight hour had long since passed and Musso was back in his office, enjoying the chill of the air-conditioning and the absence of pests. He nursed a precious cup of coffee. At least in this part of the world, it was still plentiful, if hard to get. Colonel Pileggi sat across from him, just outside the cone of light thrown down by his desk lamp, half hidden in the gloom, with an old-fashioned clipboard on her knee as she ticked off items on her checklist. Behind her, the waters of the bay twinkled under a bright moon and dozens of civilian craft of all sizes lay quietly at anchor, awaiting the departure of the final convoy for the Pacific.

A few small lighters still plied a path between them, distributing stores, collecting passenger lists, and handing out information on convoy protocols. In contrast with the first few crazed days of his time at Gitmo, a skeleton crew was on deck at the headquarters building. The base slumbered out in the darkness.

'So we can expect the escorts here tomorrow?' she asked doubtfully. There had been problems recently transiting the Canal. With the Panamanian Government's collapse, Pearl had finally put in a Brigade Combat Team to control the locks, but they were being pressed by an unknown number of criminal syndicates. Not a day went by without one or two casualties among the Americans. On the upside, though, the rules of engagement for the Canal Zone were robust. Anybody approaching the American-controlled locks was immediately engaged and destroyed without warning.

Musso nodded. 'It should be cool. Principal escort's French, coming up from Guyana. It's an F-70-class frigate, although it's big enough that we'd call it a destroyer. I spoke with their guy when he flew in late this afternoon from Cayenne. It won't have to transit the Canal until the convoy gets there and it has enough firepower to muscle through any parts we can't provide cover for. And a solid detachment of Marine infantry, for good measure. Our guys will pick them up on the other side. Then the French will split off with a smaller group for New Caledonia.'

Pileggi raised one eyebrow but remained silent.

Musso picked up on her reaction and shrugged to show his own. 'I know, I know. Surprised me too. I thought the French were too busy tearing each other apart to bother with helping anyone else, but Sarkozy's faction has been looking real hard at their Pacific territories. You want my opinion, there's going to be a lot of Frenchies opting out of food riots and ethnic cleansing for grass skirts and Gilligan's Island any day now.'

'Damn,' muttered Pileggi. 'Is that the good dope you're smoking? Straight from Pearl?'

'Yeah,' said Musso. 'There have been talks, apparently. Very quiet talks. This consular guy confirmed as much. We may be in business as a transit point in the future – assuming Sarkozy wins, of course.'

'That's quite an assumption from what I've read, General.' A new worry now etched itself into the deep lines of Pileggi's face, shadows pooled under her eyes. 'I've got a lot of my refugees bunking down in the French colonies. What's going to happen to them?'

'No idea. I guess there'll be more talks. Things are already pretty crowded in French Polynesia. For now, our problems are all here. We've got nigh on a hundred vessels to get out of the harbour and through the Panama Canal – are they going to be finished provisioning? You were having some trouble with supplies, as I recall.'

Pileggi tapped the clipboard with her pen. 'Those two big container ships that came in early this morning from Port-au-Spain declared a lot of stuff we could use. So I requisitioned their cargo. My guys are going to check them out in the morning and begin redistribution.'

'Uh-uh,' grunted Musso. 'How were the captains about that?'

She waved the question off with a hand gesture. 'Relaxed. They even sent over a complete cargo manifest to help out. They're Panamanian-flagged, with mostly Russian and Indian crews. The shipping line's gone out of business. They say they'll need some fuel and an escort to Australia, so I'd guess they're going to sell what they can in Sydney. The Indians will want to go home from there, the Russians will probably jump ship and try to disappear into the crowd.'

'Well, the crowd would be big enough, I imagine. Must be nearly two million displaced down there now.'

'Passed that last week,' the colonel replied, shaking her head. 'They're up to two point two, as of close of business yesterday. Two and a half if you count New Zealand. Mostly ours, but a fair number of Europeans too. Clean-shaven and fair-skinned, of course,' she added dryly. 'Don't bother knocking if your name is Mohammed.'

Musso felt instinctive disapproval stirring in his gut, just as he disapproved of the British Government's mass internment and deportation policies. It was ethnic cleansing by another name, or ethnic *filtering* perhaps Down Under. Racism cloaked as necessity, when you got right down to it. But it was hardly the worst thing

happening in the world today. And the Aussies had taken anyone
with an American passport, regardless of background. While their
motives were almost entirely selfish – just look at how much remnant US military power had been redeployed down there to protect
America's most precious asset, its remaining people – you couldn't
argue with the result. Refugee allocations to southern-hemisphere
locations were among the most precious things in the world at the
moment, the ecological catastrophe of the Disappearance being
mostly confined to the northern latitudes. Nobody in their right
mind wanted to go into the tribal slaughterhouse that was Africa.
And with so many South American countries succumbing to the
contagion of anarchy or military takeover, slots in the Australia and
New Zealand programs were the most avidly sought. Fortunes in
trade goods were being made smuggling people in there.

The Marine Corps lawyer was about to ask Pileggi for a run-
down on the civilian flights out of Soto Cano in Honduras, the
other leg of her role in Operation Uplift, when he suddenly blinked
in shock. A freighter, moored near the old fuelling station down
in the bay, exploded. There was no warning. It simply lifted a few
feet out of the water – a small dense blossom of white light cracking it amidships before flowering into a dark, oily orange ball of
flame that lit up the entire harbour. The sundered bow and stern
thumped back down, throwing up huge fantails of water, before
the vessel keeled over and started to sink.

'Motherfuck!' cried Musso.

Pileggi spun around in her chair, half raising herself as she
did so.

Musso didn't bother with the formalities of ending the meeting. They were both already heading for the door when a navy
lieutenant appeared, blocking their exit. She was holding a sheaf
of paper and appeared goggle-eyed with surprise.

'General Musso, there's a message for you, sir. From President
Chávez.'

'What?' He was tired, worn slick, and not firing on all
cylinders.

She handed the message across as more explosions ripped
through the night, muted by distance. A crackle of small-arms fire
resolved itself from the rolling thunder.

40

The soup was a simple broth, a thin brown liquid in which floated a few chunks of carrot, some onion and a little shredded meat, possibly beef, but to Caitlin it was heaven in a bowl. She sipped at the rim. Her hands shook too much to use the spoon they had given her, and she had already finished the small piece of bread that came with the meal.

'Thank you,' she said again. 'I'm afraid this place doesn't really deserve its Michelin star.'

Captain Rolland smiled kindly and effected a very Gallic lift of the shoulders. 'Standards are slipping everywhere, *mademoiselle*.'

Caitlin returned the smile. 'I dunno. My last stay here wasn't much better.'

She finished the bowl and placed it on the table in front of the old leather couch on which she sat, wrapped in a clean blanket and dressed for the first time in weeks. Rolland snapped his fingers and a young soldier appeared from outside the office to clear away the dish and plate. They did not speak while he was in the room.

Caitlin stood up and peered out of the window, over a rain-slicked parking lot below. A bus burned in one corner, and a couple of bodies lay nearby in pools of blood, which became lighter and pinker as the rain diluted them. She appeared to be about three storeys up, high enough to see over the red tiled roofs of the surrounding buildings to the eastern suburbs of Paris. A few fires burned in a desultory fashion here and there, dwarfed by a huge tower of smoke about five miles away. She couldn't see any movement in the streets, but she could hear gunfire. A lot of it.

'Sounds like Beirut. Or maybe the Mog,' she said.

Rolland, a handsome thirty-something man with a full head of black hair that was swept back and oiled in a very old-fashioned style, lit a cigarette and then stopped himself. 'Excuse me, do you mind?'

The pain in her head was wretched, but it was no worse than any of her other manifold agonies. 'Knock yourself out, *mon Capitaine*,' Caitlin replied as she returned to the couch, 'I doubt those things will kill me. They're at the back of a very long line.'

The Frenchman sat down across the coffee table from her and drew deeply on the unfiltered cigarette with evident pleasure. His army uniform was filthy and his boots caked with mud. He hadn't shaven in a few days.

'This is my first one all week,' he said, waving the cigarette around. 'And I had to take it from one of the jihadi pigs. It's Turkish. Not my blend. But what can one do?'

'Yeah, those jihadi pigs – you want to tell me what my target was doing in your dungeons? You know, besides raping me.'

Rolland shifted uncomfortably in his chair. 'I am sorry,' he said. 'It was a disgraceful thing. But, I am afraid, all too common these days. Monsieur Baumer, your target – and mine, as it transpires – he unfortunately escaped our net. We were hoping you might be able to help us find him. After all, you are the expert on "al Banna"?'

She laughed, a short, joyless sound. 'I'm the world expert on getting my ass kicked by him,' she replied. 'And I have to tell you, Rolland, the shape I'm in, I'd get it kicked all over again if we met. But you're not answering my question – what was he doing here? What were any of them doing here? And what the hell's been going on out there? Reynard told me you guys had things under control.' She nodded towards the city centre. 'But *that's* not under control. This place is dying.'

Momentary confusion passed over the soldier's face as he shook his head. 'Reynard? . . . Oh, you mean Lacan. No, it is not under control, *mademoiselle*. It has not been for weeks. Half of the city's population have fled into the countryside, but things are worse out there. All the cities have emptied out. You can imagine what that means. Some of them took tents and provisions for a few days' camping. Most just fled when the intifada and the *Résistance* began in earnest. Farms and villages have barricaded themselves off from the world, fought off everyone who seeks shelter or aid. It is a Dark Age again. There are bodies piling up in fields – possibly a million of them by now. With thousands more dying every day. Many, many are dead.'

Caitlin was already dizzy with exhaustion and moral collapse, but Rolland was making her head spin. She imagined a host of totally unprepared urbanites swarming over the French countryside expecting to live off stolen eggs and wild berries. They'd have stripped the fields bare in days. She began shaking again, the same deep body tremors that had seized her after being raped by al Banna. 'S-sorry,' she stuttered.

Rolland reached into his blood-smeared tunic and removed a silver flask. 'Here, drink some,' he said. 'It is brandy. Good brandy, not like the hospital disinfectant you are familiar with. And my battalion surgeon, he said these may help too.'

A small blister pack of tablets dropped onto the tabletop. Half of them had already been popped.

'They will calm your nerves,' he explained. 'But should not dull your senses.'

Caitlin briefly wondered whether she might react to them, given her medical condition. Then she thought, *What the hell*, and downed two with a swig from Rolland's flask. The liquor burned softly and warmed her upper body. As she handed back the brandy, a jet suddenly screamed through the air nearby, the noise arcing up from a distant whine to a deafening shriek in mere seconds. A very short time later she heard the unmistakable crump of air-dropped munitions detonating within a few miles.

'So, things haven't gone as well as I was led to believe?'

The captain took a long draw on the harsh-smelling cigarette. 'I am afraid not,' he admitted. 'The situation remains . . . confused.'

'Not as confused as me. Why don't you try explaining – you could start with Baumer. He was one of yours, right, so is that why I was targeted?'

'A double agent? No, I am afraid not.'

Caitlin's head felt as though it had been wrapped in old towels soaked in chloroform. She had trouble concentrating and holding her thoughts. 'But, what was he doing here at the fort?' she asked, trying again. 'Are you saying that Reynard ... sorry, what did you call him?'

'Lacan. Bernard Lacan, second-in-charge of the Action Division.'

'Okay. Lacan then – you're saying he'd sold out to the intifada?'

Rolland waved his hands in a frustrated manner, as if trying to shoo a fly. 'It is not so simple, no,' he replied. 'You have been out of contact for a long time, Caitlin. Do you mind if I call you Caitlin?'

'It's not the worst liberty that's been taken with me recently. Go on.'

'Lacan was working with Baumer's network, yes. But not just Lacan. And not just with one jihadi cell. It is difficult, Caitlin, this situation I must explain. Please bear with me. You will be aware of some of the history of the DGSE, your rival service, *non*?'

She leaned back against the arm of the leather sofa and pulled the blanket around to a more comfortable position. Outside, the rain began to pick up, strongly enough to wash much of the blood from the courtyard, she imagined. The pills hadn't kicked in yet, but the brandy was having a soothing effect. Rolland used the opportunity to light up another cigarette as he continued.

'Unlike your CIA, and despite its name, the Action Division does not maintain a standing section of paramilitary covert operatives. When such skills are required, it draws on what we call a "tank" of operators from the army, mostly the special forces and commandos.'

She nodded. The information wasn't new to her.

'Do you know the original battalion on which the Action Division relied, Caitlin?'

She searched her battered memory and came up with some fragment. 'Some paratroop regiment?'

'Very good,' said Rolland, with a nod of his own. 'Almost right. *Le 11-ième Bataillon Parachutiste de Choc* – "the Shock Parachutist

Battalion", as you would say. It was first raised in 1946, then disbanded in 1963 because its officers were collaborators, supporters of French Algeria.'

'Okay. That means they backed whitey, right? The *pieds-noirs*. Ancient history, but go on.'

'Ancient for you, young lady, not for France. The Algerian war nearly destroyed us. It collapsed the Fourth Republic, brought back the Gaullists, and forever changed our view of France as *une puissance musulmane*. Do you know the phrase?'

'A Muslim power,' she replied. 'Again, so what? A hundred years ago you wanted to lord it over the Arabs, because the Brits scarfed up all the good colonies for themselves.'

He favoured her with a lopsided smile. 'I had been told you are a difficult woman.'

'I prefer to think of myself as challenging,' she quipped back.

'Your American psychology betrays you, Caitlin. *Une puissance musulmane* does not just mean to wield power over the House of Peace. It means to hold that power in . . . how would you phrase it? . . . In agreement, in accordance – a sort of *entente cordiale* with the Islamic world itself. You and the British often described your filial bond as a special relationship. Indeed, that relationship extended across all of the English-speaking world. Your employer, Echelon, it was a perfect expression of that dysfunctional anglophone family, *non*? An alliance, a secret one, between the English-speaking powers, directed against *everyone* else. That is quite special, when you think about it. Well, our special relationship, our particular delusion, if you wish, was with the dar-al-Islam. Or so some thought.'

'Captain,' she said, as toxic rain began to patter against the windowpanes and the room became even gloomier, 'you're going to have to help me out here. I have a brain tumour and I'm having trouble putting two and two together.'

Rolland stood up and flicked on a light. He called out to one of his men stationed in the corridor and they spoke in murmurs for a moment before he returned.

'Excuse me, Caitlin. I am expecting someone . . . Yes, I am sorry – it is the continental way of narrative. Much more elliptical than your own. Let me "bottom-line" it for you, to borrow from your own vernacular. Since the accommodation in Algeria, there has been a school of thought, a quiet but powerful clique within the state, which has believed that accommodation with Islam is the only way forward. At first this group was centred on the Quai d'Orsay, here in Paris, and they applied their doctrine within their own sphere, often in conflict with other actors in the state realm.'

'Okay, so your Foreign Ministry was rub-fucking the Arabs. I have to say, this isn't breaking news.'

Rolland uncapped the brandy flask and took a swig for himself before offering it to Caitlin again. She joined him. The pills, whatever they were, had begun to smooth her rough edges and another drink seemed like a good idea. Sitting on this magnificent old sofa, drinking fine spirits and chatting with the handsome French officer, she finally began to get some distance on the horror of the previous weeks.

'I believe similar tensions existed between your own State Department and the military,' Rolland countered. 'It is the usual way between peacemakers and war fighters. But here in France, there was a complicating factor, which grew more complicated with every year.'

Caitlin nodded slowly. 'Your own Muslim population.'

'Quite so. Just as your country found that certain questionable policies and state activities initially carried out beyond your borders, say, in South-East Asia, tended to return home in one form or another . . .'

'We called it "blow-back".'

'How brutally elegant. Well, we too have discovered that a contagion, acquired in Algiers, transmitted itself to the body politic right here.'

'Rolland, this would be a fascinating discussion if we were Jean-Paul and Simone sucking down Gitanes and black coffee in a Montmartre café. But how about you ditch all the context and sell me your pitch.'

The captain leaned back and blew twin streams of blue smoke out through his nostrils. 'Betrayal, Caitlin,' he replied. 'I am talking about betrayal. The man who held you here, Lacan, did not do so on his own recognisance. Nor did he operate as part of a small, traitorous cell. I am afraid that Monsieur Lacan was part of a much larger, and very well organised network of state officials, the Algerian School, as we know them, who had determined that the only possible, rational option for dealing in the long term with the rise of Muslim power in the Middle East, and within France herself, was accommodation.'

'Appeasement, you mean.'

'*Non*, "appeasement" is not a strong enough word, Caitlin. To appease is simply to make morally compromised concessions in order to maintain one's own tenuous status. That is not what the School's philosophy now entertains. "Adaptation" is more apt. Although in your language it sounds rather bloodless, it is not. As practised by the Algerian School, it means to slowly adapt the French secular state to the brute realities of its future as an annexe to the dar-al-Islam, as a true Muslim power.'

'To convert.'

'Yes. To *convert*. And to that end they have allied themselves with the intifada, in which your target is a leading player.'

'Holy shit,' she said, impressed at last. 'And the Action Division, how many of them were . . . ?'

Rolland shook his head. 'Enough. Perhaps one-third. The others were quickly dealt with in the first days of fighting.'

'But you've got a civil war out there. Surely you can't have whole army divisions who've gone over . . .'

Another headshake from the Frenchman. 'No. There is fighting between many arms of the military and other organs of the state. But most of those involved see nothing beyond their gunsights. An army regiment is ordered to put down a mutiny by the Foreign Legion, for example, and the individual soldiers do not understand they are fighting an engagement to suit the ends of the conspiracy. To them, it is just a civil war, and now it is so far advanced that chaos reigns. Accusations, counter-claims, propaganda – all is confusion.'

He leaned forward and stubbed the butt of his cigarette.

'But this I do know, Caitlin. You can help stop it. Your target, Baumer, he is not the key, but he leads to the key – to the masters of the Algerian School. Take them down, and the intifada is leaderless, nothing more than a rabble. A huge rabble, yes – but not one that can match an army that is not divided against itself.'

'You want me to kill your own people?' she asked, still having some difficulty taking it all in.

A new voice spoke up from the doorway behind Rolland, startling her. An American voice. 'That was always going to be your next mission. That's why you were targeted.'

'*Wales*? Goddamn, Wales!'

As sick in body and soul as she was, Caitlin pushed herself up off the couch and ran over to hug Wales Larrison, almost knocking him off his feet as she threw her arms around his neck.

'Goddamn, Wales, it's been . . . it's just . . .' A small burning lump in her throat grew and grew, until it merged with the ache in her chest and for the first time since she had been captured, Caitlin Monroe let herself go and poured out a torrent of tears.

The rangy, silver-haired Nebraskan enfolded her within a generous bear hug and made no attempt to calm her down, as wretched, pitiful sobs and shudders racked her body.

'I'm s-s-sorry, Wales. I failed . . . and . . .'

He shushed her and stroked her head, patting down masses of thick dark hair still wet from the shower and smelling of cheap shampoo. 'It's all right, Cait, it's all right,' he said softly. 'You've been sick. I know. They told me. You shouldn't have been out in the field, let alone trussed up in this shithole . . . if you'll excuse my, er, French, Captain Rolland.'

'But of course, it *is* a shithole,' the Frenchman agreed.

Caitlin could feel Larrison's strong heartbeat through his suit jacket, and that strength flowed through his arms and into her. She slowly regained her composure and pushed herself away.

'How did you get here?' she asked shakily, wiping her nose on a shirt cuff. 'I thought they'd grabbed you, Wales. I thought they'd rolled up the whole network.'

Larrison put one finger on her lip and bade her to be quiet. He then led her back to the couch and eased her down, before sitting himself at the other end.

'I was in London when everything happened,' he said. 'I had to sit on my ass and watch it from there. I'm sorry, Caitlin. I tried to get an overwatch team to you, twice, but the DGSE had a legitimate counter-intel responsibility for shadowing us. We did spy on them, after all. They never penetrated a cell, but their Intelligence Division was aware of us. That's how they grabbed you the first time you were here. And they blocked both teams I sent in – wiped out the first, grabbed up the other one.'

Caitlin pulled the blanket closer around her shoulders. 'What's left of us, Wales? Of Echelon, I mean.'

He puffed out his cheeks. 'Every op we had running in France was taken down. Every one. With extreme prejudice. The Brits lost their people too. Would have caused a quiet, dirty little war if we hadn't known about the Algerian School. So now, in France, I'm afraid you're it. You're Echelon. Our last designated hitter.'

He indicated the fort around them with a wave of his hand. Somewhere many miles away, more bombs exploded.

'Lacan had people here, all over,' Wales went on. 'This Algerian School, it's like Captain Rolland told you, they were everywhere. When we sent you after Baumer, they stepped in. He was protected as part of the . . . accommodation. They were always going to try to keep you off him.'

Rolland put one muddy boot on the coffee table, leaned forward and retrieved his packet of pills. 'Normally you would have been detained, interrogated, the usual inconveniences,' he explained. 'But, the Disappearance, it changed everything. A massive, world-changing shock.'

'They had contingencies,' added Larrison. 'In the event of some foreseeable catastrophe that would cripple the US, or financial collapse, or a nuclear strike – whatever. The Disappearance wasn't foreseeable, but it was also a hell of a lot more than a simple catastrophe. It wiped us out.'

'And the contingency?' said Caitlin.

'To finish the work of Allah,' answered Rolland. 'As soon as it was confirmed what had happened in America, Lacan purged the Action Division and sent his trusted people out to roll up your network. It was not just you, of course. The British also maintained Echelon cadre in France, as Monsieur Larrison explained. They too were targeted. Even your junior partners, the Canadians, Australians and New Zealanders, all of them were smothered.'

'So, all the street fighting, the ethnic clashes – they were engineered by the School? That seems a bit far-fetched.'

Larrison, who looked so much older than the last time they had spoken, just two months ago, shook his head sadly. 'Not all of them, Cait. A lot of violence arose naturally. Once the capstone was off, the geyser blew. But yes, some incidents were engineered to bring on a wider confrontation. An uprising. Even then it may not have worked. Conspiracies often don't, as you would know. But Israel nuking half of the Arab world – that was a deal breaker. Race war, holy war, civil war, whatever you want to call it. It was inevitable after that. And people have been killing each other ever since.'

She moved her head carefully to look out of the windows again. The rain had turned the suburbs outside into a bleary, grey netherworld, but some elements did resolve themselves. There was no traffic, vehicular or pedestrian. The only aircraft aloft were military, and of course she had already noted that they were attacking targets within the city. There seemed to be fewer fires burning than she remembered, but the rain was heavy, and on looking more closely she could see that whole districts had already been burnt out.

Caitlin snuggled deeper into the sofa. It was strangely comforting. 'You said something about my next mission?'

Wales clicked his tongue. 'Yup. I did. We didn't tell you, because you didn't need to know, not at that point. But the file on Baumer was a joint operation with the DST, the intelligence arm of Sarkozy's Ministry of the Interior. Sarkozy had decided to move against the Algerian School and asked us to help. It was unprecedented. Echelon does not play outside of the family. But in this case, we did, because the strategic consequences could affect the family, generations down the line. The Brits were particularly gung-ho. Your mission was designed to shake out Baumer's contacts. To expose Bernard Lacan and his people. They were being monitored by the DST without their knowledge.'

'Or so we thought,' added Rolland.

'Or so we thought.'

'There was a leak?' asked Caitlin.

Larrison grunted. 'There was. We still don't know where from. But Lacan found out, and that's why he bet so much on grabbing you up. He needed you to start unravelling the op against him and the other School masters.'

'Son of a bitch,' muttered Caitlin.

'I'm sorry, Cait, but you know the rules.'

She waved away his apology. 'I'm not pissed at you, Wales. I know my job, and I know it's not always what it seems. I'm a pawn. I can be sacrificed. It's just . . . I dunno. I'm sick, Wales, really sick. And it's messing with my head, the way I think and see things.' A weak breath escaped from her lips, and she deflated. 'I made a friend. An asset. I shouldn't have, but I did. I'm not well . . . And I got her killed because I wasn't good enough to save her.'

The room broke up into a jewelled kaleidoscope as more tears came. Larrison leaned over and patted her on the knee. Her dad had done the same thing a thousand times, and it only served to deepen her sadness. Wales's voice was soft, like her father's had once been, but still hard with it.

'You're not a pawn, Caitlin,' he said. 'You're a knight. And you're still in play.'

41

The BBC offices in Paris were an armed compound, with every window covered in steel plating. It did nothing to dull the arrhythmic tom-tom beat of heavy machine-gun fire or the dense, percussive thud of high-explosive ordnance pounding the rubble in the 16th Arrondissement just a few minutes' drive away. A sandbagged gunpit and razor wire guarded the main entrance, secured by a rotating team of gunned-up heavies from Sandline, a British-based 'private military company'. Dave, one of the operators, was American, and Melton had initially attempted to forge some kind of relationship with him, but entirely without luck. All he ever received in return for his stream of 'howdy's, 'hi there's and 'how ya doin'?'s were grunts and the blank, dead stare of deep disinterest.

'He's not really a people person, is he?' said Monty Pearson, the chief of staff. 'Still, better than having every man and his mad dog wandering in, eh?'

Monty was a thirty-year veteran of war reporting, having cut his teeth on the Golan Heights all the way back in 1973, during the Yom Kippur War. Like most of the bureau staff, he was a new arrival, a volunteer, in his case from Kabul. Paris was considered a war posting, which was how Melton had moved from freelancer to staffer almost as soon as he'd put his foot in the door with his collection of Iraq War interviews. Very few people had the desire, experience and unique mix of skills that he brought to the table.

Even among the grizzled veterans of the Beeb's first-rank war correspondents, he stood out because of his own combat experience.

'Tea?' asked Monty, as they gathered in the second-floor conference room, a windowless box in the centre of the building. Along with the production studios down in the basement, it was one of the most secure areas in the building, but even so, every now and then a larger explosion nearby would shake flakes of plaster from the ceilings. Melton could feel the detonation through the soles of his shoes.

There was no coffee to be had, unfortunately, and Bret had noticed that the Brits really did seem to function a lot more effectively with just a cup or two of their weak, milky brew inside them. He had no idea where Barry, the office manager, sourced their supplies, but in a starving city riven by ethnic and civil warfare, he somehow kept the larder stocked and the teapots full. When Melton had complimented him on his scrounging chops, Barry had grinned back and said, 'If I can keep Jim Muir's fuckin' beer fridge full of fuckin' Boddingtons in Beirut, a cup of fuckin' char in Paris in't going to bovver me, is it, guvnor!'

'But a decent cup of java's impossible?' Melton asked.

'All but,' said Barry, in an apologetic tone. 'Frogs is killing each other over mouldy croissants and fuckin' Nescafé. So no, Mr Melton, no fuckin' coffee. Learn to drink somefin civilised, why doncha?'

The small team of correspondents and editors took their places around the conference table, most of them juggling papers and folders in one hand, and bone-china cups and saucers in the other. A packet of 'biscuits', as they insisted on calling all forms of cookie life, sat in the centre of the table, and Monty doled out one to each tea drinker, before carefully twisting the packet closed again and clamping it with a wooden clothes peg. The provenance of the peg was never explained. It was a peculiar ritual, one that Melton had rather come to look forward to each day. He was offered one of the McVitie's wholemeal 'bickies' to have with his glass of water, but again he turned it down.

'Couldn't get any Oreos, Barry?' he teased, only half in jest.

'Oh, I know where there's a whole warehouse of 'em, Mr Melton. Just couldn't be fucked dickerin' for 'em. Why, do you want some?'

'Oh no, don't put yourself out on my behalf,' Bret replied, smiling.

'Wasn't planning to, sir.'

Other exchanges rolled back and forth across and around the table as everyone settled in. The morning news conference was about something more than simply assigning new stories and monitoring those already in progress. It was the only time each day when the entire team was in one place, and it served as an opportunity for everyone to touch base, for the tribe to hunker down and count its blessings that once again their numbers had not been thinned out. The BBC had lost seventeen journalists killed or simply disappeared in the last month, not counting those who'd been vaporised in the Middle East. The Paris bureau, however, was charmed, having lost nobody since Jon Sopel was killed in the first week of fighting. The bureau had grown like topsy since then, and had taken the buildings on either side as they'd become abandoned, but only seasoned warcos and freelancers like Melton worked here now. He'd been hired on a twelve-month contract. It paid a fraction of his *Army Times* job, which hadn't been a great earner anyway, but because of the hazardous posting status, the former Ranger was guaranteed 'room and board' at the Paris compound. It seemed perverse, but he ate better and slept more securely than many people in England.

'Right then,' Monty called out in his down-to-business voice. 'What enchanting fripperies and puff pieces will we be filing from the City of Light today, then? Caroline, darlin', any chance of that interview with the blessed Sarko yet?'

Caroline Wyatt rolled her eyes up to the peeling paint of the high ceiling. 'His minders promised me I'd see him yesterday and I spent the whole bloody day in this wretched armoured car, roaring around from one bunker to the next, without ever actually managing to get anywhere near the little bugger. I'll stay on it, Monty, if you really wish, but I don't think Sarkozy's going to roll over for us until he has some genuinely good news to crow about.'

'Well, his armoured boys entered the old city last night. I'd have thought that was good enough.'

'Yes, it is a feel-good story, isn't it? Dozens of Leclerc main battle tanks crushing Arab street fighters under their treads in the Bois de Boulogne . . . I can't imagine why he wouldn't want to sit down and chat about that over a Pernod or two.'

'Well, keep at it, sweetheart. I have faith in your charms,' the chief of staff told her. 'Bret, are you all squared away with the Marines? London is super-keen to see you embed with them after they cleaned out Lyons.'

Melton tapped the point of his ballpoint pen on a Spirax writing pad. 'Soon as we're finished up here, I'm heading west to Suresnes,' he replied. 'The Marines – although, you know, they're really more like Army Rangers – they laid up last night at Mont-Valérien, the old fortress right next door. Parachuted in there when it was still full of jihadis. Pretty fucking hard-core. They'll have some good stories.'

Normally, in a room full of BBC reporters, he'd have kept his mouth shut and just grunted, 'Yeah, good to go.' But these guys weren't normal. Even Caroline Wyatt, who still spent an hour in make-up every day, nodded appreciatively. He didn't need to sex it up for them. They all knew what a godless blood-swarm the drop into Mont-Valérien would have been, and what the push eastwards into the city was going to be like from there. The clashes between rival elements of the French military were destructive in the extreme. Whole swathes of the suburbs had been gutted by collisions between main-force units siding with either Minister Sarkozy or the so-called Loyalist Committee. The blocks bordering the Bois de Boulogne parklands now looked like Stalingrad at the end of 1944. Those buildings still standing were mostly gutted and blackened, often with the upper floors sheared off by high explosives. The line of the ruined streetscape looked like broken teeth.

'It's bloody confusing, isn't it,' grumbled Monty. 'Rebels, renegades, mutineers, Loyalists – hard to keep them all straight some days. And if someone could do me a favour and explain why we're still calling them fucking "Loyalists" when it seems pretty obvious they've cut some sort of deal with the intifada crew, I'd be very grateful.'

Melton, who was idly sketching a rough map of the city centre, with various lines of advance and defence marked out, just as he'd been taught so long ago, looked up and shrugged. 'They self-identify as Loyalists, Monty, so it's only good manners. After all, Sarkozy did anoint himself boss hog when Chirac got whacked. Smart move or not, it was illegal. Shades of Napoleon grabbing the crown. Gotta figure most of the guys fighting for the Loyalist Committee think *they're* the ones protecting the Republic. The soldiers, at least. Sarko calling them all traitors and sell-outs to the intifada wouldn't have helped calm the matter down either. The jihadi, they're allies of convenience. It's all fucked up. Civil wars always are.'

'Do you believe him, though?' asked Caroline.

'Sarko? Who knows?'

'It seems a little incredible, don't you think, him accusing the Loyalists of treason? They seem rather less discriminating than that. Anyone in their way gets killed, no matter what their allegiance. Street gangs, neo-fascists, jihadis. They've cut them all down at one time or another.'

'Like I said, Caroline, it's confused. It's a mistake to think of this thing in terms of massed armies manoeuvring against each other. Alliances and loyalties are contingent. They can shift in minutes. An agreement negotiated at one level might have no effect at others, or further down a city block. I think this is going to be one of those times when the winners definitely write the history.'

'Well,' Monty interrupted the discussion, 'as another of your countrymen once pointed out, journalism is the first draft of history, and ours will be due in a few hours. So let's crack on, shall we?'

Leaving the office was no longer a matter of grabbing his equipment and stepping out to hail a cab. Melton didn't expect to see the compound again for a couple of days and he packed accordingly. At the bottom of a small black rucksack he stuffed a layer of spare socks and underwear, on top of which he placed some emergency rations, even though he'd be eating with his embedded unit, he hoped. On top of them went his equipment: a small handycam and twenty-four hours' worth of videotape, three notebooks and a couple of pens. He topped it off with two handfuls of carefully hoarded chocolate bars and cigarettes, which he planned to share with 'his' troops. He understood just how welcome an outsider with a small stash of luxuries could be.

It was raining outside again, quite heavily, enough to dull the sounds of close-quarter fighting. The steel plating that covered all the windows only served to magnify the sound of the downpour as the torrents hit the metal. He carefully pulled on his rain slicker over a BBC-issue ballistic vest and snagged a pair of goggles to protect his eyes. His injuries still troubled him. These days the toxic rain wasn't nearly as bad as it had been a few weeks back, but letting the water run into your eyes felt like swimming in a hideously over-chlorinated pool.

The last item, he took his time with. It was a controversial choice – a personal weapon. Some of the reporters, like Caroline and Adam Mynott, who'd arrived from Afghanistan with the last of NATO's returning contingent, refused to carry anything and tried very hard to talk Melton out of doing so. They argued that a journalist's best protection was their non-combatant status. In turn Melton insisted that nobody was playing by the Geneva Convention and cited at least three occasions in Iraq and two in Paris where he'd been forced to defend himself. It was an unresolved dispute, with some of the older hands writing him off as a fossil from the Cowboy Age, while a few of the younger ones quietly sought him out to ask his advice about how they might discreetly pack their own protection. It was telling, he thought, that Barry had scrounged him two spare magazines for the Fabrique Nationale 57 pistol.

He stripped, cleaned and rebuilt the handgun before slotting home a full mag. Safety on, it went into the holster on his right hip and disappeared under the slicker. Melton finished his packing with a fully charged cell phone, plugged into British Telecom's network and set to roam, but he noted that – as usual – there was no signal available. Service was spotty, at best. After a quick visit to Monty's cubicle for all the goodbyes and good-luck wishes, he signed out at the security desk, lodging a run-down of his expected movements over the next forty-eight hours, the name of the French unit he would be with, and the number of the all-but-useless cell phone in his breast pocket.

From there he hurried out to the internal courtyard where his ride was waiting, a custom-built six-wheeled Land Rover, with two armed guards and his driver, American Dave.

'Fantastic,' Bret muttered to himself. More loudly, on approaching the vehicle, he called out, 'Morning! You guys got my route map this morning? We're gonna be skirting around some contested ground.'

Dave, a chunky, dark-haired man with a short-cropped beard, continued chewing his gum and nodded. 'Yup.'

'Okay then. Drive on.'

Melton had mapped out a long, looping circuitous path through the district's quieter streets to avoid the fighting just north-east of the Bois de Boulogne, between Avenue Foch and the huge traffic roundabout at Place de la Porte Maillot. Within that area, fourteen irregularly shaped city blocks had been reduced to a wasteland of shattered buildings, burning ruins, and rubble through which no armour could pass and over which thousands of men and women now fought. The rain had dampened hostilities somewhat, but the rolling thunder of combat never completely abated. Soon after they set off, two jets screamed low overhead to unload their bombs on somebody. The air force was almost entirely behind Sarkozy, but even so, Melton flinched a little. Technically, they were still in Loyalist territory, and an armoured Land Rover would make an excellent target of opportunity.

It took them all of four minutes to deviate from the route and hit trouble. And the reason he didn't notice them veering off course was because American Dave surprised him by initiating a conversation as he popped a CD into the stereo. Melton checked out the cover. *Don Dudley's Truckin' Hits*.

'Gonna git bloody soon,' said Dave.

Okay, it wasn't much of a conversation, but it was a start.

'Yeah,' agreed Bret. 'Always gets kinda biblical whenever you get a lot of irregulars tangling with main force. These guys'll be desperate too. You got the Marines and tanks coming in from the park, and those two grunt divisions hit Romaine and Noisy-le-Sec yesterday. Loyalists are trapped.'

Dave snorted in disgust. 'Fucking Loyalists. Bullshit. Nobody loyal to nothing but Allah ever partnered up with those raghead motherfuckers.'

Melton let that one slide past. He had no idea what game plan the Loyalist Committee were running and wouldn't have been surprised to see them turn on the Arab street fighters and massacre them wholesale if the need arose.

The Land Rover rumbled down a deserted street in which all of the trees had died. The rain was still heavy, reducing visibility to about thirty yards, and he could tell from the neglected appearance of the buildings, with gaping broken windows and doors left ajar, that most of them were empty. Every now and then a figure would dart furtively from cover, but only for a few seconds at most. In the back, Dave's companions kept their weapons at the ready.

'You don't think?' said Dave.

'Sorry. I don't think what?'

'You don't think the ragheads and Loyalists are teamed up?'

Melton shrugged. 'They have a common enemy, but that doesn't make them friends or even allies. Loyalists are fighting Sarkozy because they think he's a dictator. A fascist. The street Arabs from the *banlieue* are fighting him because he sent his troops into their neighbourhoods and served up a big bowl of smackdown. As for the skinheads, they're fighting the Arabs because they're skinheads. The other white gangs are fighting the Arabs because fighting's all there is now. You fight, you eat. You eat, you live. Don't know that there's much more to it.'

Dave grunted and lapsed back into silence as Don Dudley started singing that he was king of the road.

And just out of the corner of his eye, Bret Melton saw the telltale, snaking smoke trail of an RPG round. A warning cry was in his throat but never got out.

Then the world turned upside down with a head-cracking roar and a geyser of hot fire.

42

It was raining, of course. Jed pulled his overcoat a little more tightly around his stout frame as he left the foyer of the Hotel Monaco. The caucus was still running in his three suites. It ran twenty-four/seven all week, forcing him to retain another private room on a different floor. He scowled at the weather and tugged his hat down a little more tightly, feeling like an extra from a B-grade film noir movie.

There was no avoiding it, though. The temperature had dropped away dramatically as spring succumbed to a 'Disappearance Fall' and a wide-brimmed hat was the only way to keep the acidic rain off one's face. For good measure, he popped open a large black umbrella as he stepped out onto the street. He had a four-block walk in front of him. Only the military and emergency services were getting any gas in Seattle, and they didn't rate Jed Culver's needs high enough to afford him a car and driver. He rather missed Hawaii.

The Monaco might have been one of the hippest little boutique joints in the world a month ago, but now it was full of rowdy conventioneers and tobacco-chewing soldiers who clomped so much mud through the place that the management had given up attempting to keep the public areas clean. Instead the hotel staff had laid down massive canvas tarpaulins everywhere. As Culver was leaving the establishment just now, he'd found a quartet of soldiers standing around one of the carpet-shampoo machines, trying to figure out how it worked. He overheard someone, probably a sergeant, saying he wanted to leave the place in a better condition than they'd found it. *If they left*, Culver thought, as he trudged through the quiet streets.

Huddled deep inside his coat, he shuffled quickly past an abandoned building site where oily water gathered in pools and dripped from torn plastic sheeting. Some locals had told him it would have been their new public library, but nobody expected it to be finished now. Jed walked on down 4th Avenue, with his free hand jammed into a coat pocket. He pressed a leather document wallet up against his body with that arm. Despite the thin leather gloves he wore to protect his hands from the burning rain, he preferred to keep them tucked away anyway.

The streets were quiet; save for a few council workers who all wore bright yellow ID laminates around their necks, and small groups of soldiers who tried to stay under cover at every street corner. Some managed a little respite under an awning or a bus shelter. Those who didn't looked as miserable as Jed Culver had ever seen grown men and women look. His own laminate, which guaranteed his passage through the downtown area, was an embarrassing hibiscus pink, identifying him as one of Governor Lingle's representatives to the convention.

A gust of wind, whipping through the canyons of the city, threw a spray of toxic water into his face, forcing Culver to stop and wipe it down with a handkerchief, one of a collection he carried for just that purpose. He had stopped outside Simon's Espresso Café, where he'd managed to score a quite decent prime-beef sandwich on his first day in Seattle, two weeks back. But between grousing about the 'fascist-pig-dog-maggots' who'd 'taken over' the city, and muttering darkly about the secret military experiment that had caused the Wave in the first place, his waiter – a life-support system for three hundred and ninety-two stainless steel ringlets, studs and spears – had advised him to enjoy the dead flesh. It was one of the last sandwiches Simon's would serve. And sure enough, the café was soon closed and dark, like most of the retail outlets in the city. As he wiped the stinging water from his face, Jed wondered idly what had happened to the freak with all the piercings. Probably joined 'the Resistance'.

He had to laugh at the studied pretension of those losers styling themselves on the French Underground. As bad as things were in Seattle, it wasn't Paris under the Nazis. And when you got down to it, these Resistance idiots were simply making things worse. Every time they hacked a server at Fort Lewis, every time they broke into a food bank to 'liberate' the supplies for 'the common people', every fucking time they chopped down a tree or spread small iron spikes on a road to 'deny' it to military traffic, they aggravated the situation. They weren't achieving anything – a major sin in Jed Culver's book – and they were handing Blackstone one rolled-gold opportunity after another to maintain martial law. What was worse, of course, was that they played right into the hands of the pinhead lobby who wanted to hijack the convention as the first step in reframing the Constitution, adapting it into something that Ferdinand Marcos or some Argentine general might have approved of in the 1970s.

Still, thought Jed, as he shuffled down the road, dabbing away the stinging water on his face, these Resistance characters were an element of the game, another piece on the board, and they could be played, too. That's why he had contact numbers and encrypted net addresses for some of the larger cells in his smart phone.

'Hey, buddy. Got a mouthful, did you?'

The lawyer looked up with a start. He had no idea where the man standing beside him had come from. Correction: the soldier standing beside him.

'Sorry, hope I didn't scare you. Ty McCutcheon's the name. Major Ty McCutcheon. But you can call me Mac, if that suits.'

'Uh-huh,' replied Culver, warily. He felt he'd been put off balance on purpose, but for what reason he wasn't sure.

'I've seen you at the convention,' said McCutcheon. 'I'm heading up there myself now if you'd like the company. It is kinda lonesome round here at the moment. I feel like the Omega Man some days.'

'The what?' asked Culver in a flat voice.

'You know, Charlton Heston? End of the world, last man alive – a great, great flick. Even with those dumbass hippie vampires. I'm telling you, Jed. They won't ever make 'em like that again.'

'No,' said Culver, who was about to point out that he had not introduced himself. He decided not to, though, wondering what game this character was into, and what role that little gambit with his name was supposed to play.

He scrunched up the damp handkerchief and jammed it deep into a pocket. He could feel the smart phone in there. Loaded with dozens of names and numbers, any one of which could see him hauled in by the military police for extended questioning. That's how things ran in this city.

'Well, I am headed that way, Captain . . . uh . . .' Culver knew what the gold oak leaf on the stranger's Gore-tex jacket represented.

'McCutcheon. Major McCutcheon,' the man replied, smiling. If he'd taken Jed's calculated affront to heart he gave no sign of it.

'So you're an army man, then, McCutcheon,' said Jed, even though he knew full well that wasn't the case. Precisely modulated buffoonery seemed to be the appropriate response to this gladhanding mountebank.

'Nope. Air force,' he replied as they continued towards the Municipal Tower, cutting across Marion into 5th Avenue.

'Well, that's all right too, I suppose. And what threat to national security are you dealing with down here, Major McCutcheon?'

'Oh, I'm just a humble liaison officer, Jed . . . You are Jed Culver, right – one of Governor Lingle's people? It is my job to know.'

Culver's smile was knowing, but he allowed just a small twinkle of admiration to light up his eyes too. This guy wasn't half bad. He certainly wasn't nearly as stupid as he pretended to be. It was telling that he'd referenced Culver's official designation as a Hawaiian delegate, and not his more infamous profile as the prime mover behind the 'No' lobby, the makeshift alliance opposed to any radical change in the nation's constitutional arrangements.

They turned the corner into Fifth, where a line of trees leading up to the Municipal Tower had shed all their leaves and died. The exposed branches called up an image of a witch's hands, clawing at the poisoned sky.

'I suppose the big pink calling card gives me away,' he conceded, fingering the ID laminate for emphasis. Jed had wondered who'd picked the colours for the laminate cards when he'd received his a fortnight ago. It certainly wouldn't have been his first choice, or Governor Lingle's for that matter.

Culver stopped and turned to face McCutcheon directly. 'But what gives *you* away, Major, is your non-regulation haircut, which is just a bit too close to the collar. Your whole hail-fellow-well-met routine, which is a little too practised at being a little too hip. And the small, almost unnoticeable hole in your left ear lobe, which tells me that at some point you had something stuck in there, possibly to fit in with an underground cell of Resistance nitwits or anarchist troublemakers. It was a nice save on the name, but I've been dealing with military people for weeks now, and none of them ever call me anything but "Mr Culver" or "sir". So why don't you stop trying to jam ten pounds of horseshit into a five-pound bag and tell me what it is you want.'

McCutcheon appeared to regard him with detached amusement. Staying in character then. Okay, thought Jed, one point for him.

'You're the guy that set this gig up, aren't you, *Jed*?' He smiled, with just a hint of steel in his voice.

'The Constitutional Convention, you mean?'

'Yeah. The clusterfuck down at the Municipal Tower of Babel.'

'No, I'm not the one who set it up, *Mac*,' Culver replied dryly. 'I think you'll find that the executive and legislative branches of the surviving states did that, in accordance with Article 5 of the Constitution. I'm just an observer for Governor Lingle's office.'

'Bullshit. Everyone knows what role you're playing. It's a dangerous game, Jed. Look at this place.' McCutcheon waved a gloved hand at the dead city lying in state around them. 'More'n half a million people bunkered down like rats, living on subsistence handouts. An active underground resistance, which is *this close* to flipping over into major violence, and the only goddamn thing keeping the lid on is martial law. And that's just here. You know what it's like back in Hawaii. You must have heard about the refugee camps down in Chile and Brazil. America isn't a functioning nation anymore. It's a fucking shambles, which is *this close* to going under. Do you honestly believe we can afford to indulge ourselves in partisan bullshit and self-seeking politics anymore – the whole fucking spin cycle, red state/blue state, inner/outer beltway psychosis? We are *this close* to going under.' He held up two fingers, pinching them together.

'No,' sighed Jed. 'You are *this close* to giving me a migraine. What are you, McCutcheon – Blackstone's Lord Chief Assassin? His Witch Finder General? What is it exactly that you want from me?'

'It's not what I want from you, Jed. It's what you can do for your – '

'Oh please, don't.'

Culver turned and resumed his steady stride down towards the convention. He half expected McCutcheon to grab him by the elbow and muscle him into a black van or down an alleyway. But the air force man – if that's what he really was – didn't even bother to follow. He simply called out after the lawyer, 'Room 1209.'

It took half a second for the significance to sink in, but when it did, Culver froze, almost comically, nearly pitching forward under his own momentum.

'That's where your family can be found, can't they? Room 1209 of the Embassy Suites.'

Jed had to summon all of his willpower not to spin around and fly back at McCutcheon. He was still a powerful man, in spite of years of fine living. His wrestler's physique had not run too badly to fat, and at that moment every nerve in his body was singing a high sweet song of madness. He wanted to tear one of McCutcheon's arms out of its socket and beat him down with it. Instead, he fixed a small vulpine smile on his face and walked back slowly.

'I don't know who you are, McCutcheon. Who you *really* are,' he said. 'I don't know what you really want. I'm going to do you the courtesy of presuming your intentions are honourable and that your means, like so much of what is happening in this city, are driven by the devils of necessity. But if you know about me, what I am and what I've done, you'll know I neither make nor accept threats idly. Our business here today is done. But you and I, my friend – we are not.'

And with that Jed Culver turned and walked away, wondering if he should continue with his planned meeting. Could he be under surveillance?

He wondered about McCutcheon's agenda. It seemed a hell of a risk, the major fronting him like that. What would happen if the lawyer walked up to a news crew at the convention now and started bleating about being monstered by a military officer, who had threatened his family?

And then he smiled. He knew what would happen. McCutcheon would produce a handful of impeccable witnesses, probably backed up with electronic evidence – say, date-stamped video coverage – 'proving' that he had been nowhere near the city at the time Culver alleged. Jed would be ridiculed as a fabulist and possibly as a fellow traveller with the subversives in the Resistance. His effectiveness as a backroom operator would be at an end.

He nodded in appreciation of the gambit, stopping and turning around. McCutcheon, of course, was gone.

'You sly son of a bitch,' muttered Jed. 'You're not half the fool you pretend to be, are you, boy?' He snorted with wry amusement and resumed his progress towards the Municipal Tower.

His back muscles, clenched against a bullet, only relaxed a block later.

His stash of freeze-dried rations at home was beginning to look mighty good as James Kipper surveyed the buffet in the main convention hall. The military had stocked trestle tables with light tan, plastic-wrapped MREs while a couple of ancient urns, dug out of the city council dungeons, hissed and steamed, providing hot water for powdered coffee. First cup free, then you had to supply your own makings. Kipper ripped open a sachet of army coffee, wondering if the navy's would've tasted any better. He'd heard that once. Too bad if it did, because the US Army had a lock on the coffee market in Seattle now.

The air in the hall was hot and cloying. That was his doing. Power restrictions meant that the air-conditioning had to be dialled right back and the lighting had been dimmed too. Kipper had taken a lot of grief for that decision, but every time some angry state congressman with three-day body odour harassed him about it, he just shrugged and pointed out that the citizens of Seattle were restricted to eight hours of power a day for the foreseeable future. The city engineer made up his one sachet of free powdered coffee and grabbed an army chocolate bar for his daughter to have later. The soldiers called them 'track pads', and after sampling one, he could understand why. They were as hard as bricks, but they seemed to mollify Suzie. Kip looked at the MREs and tried to figure out which one had either Skittles or M&M's in it. He'd learned that you could never tell.

He was getting ready to make a clean getaway when a Mack Truck in an expensive-looking three-piece suit suddenly blocked his way.

'Mr Kipper, the city engineer?'

Kip kept his face neutral, wondering if he was going to get in trouble for stealing the chocolate. As one of the city's senior administrators, he had unrestricted access to the conference floor – in case he had to speak urgently to any of the now-released city councillors – but he probably shouldn't have been grazing at the buffet. It had been laid out for delegates. He palmed the chocolate bar, or attempted to anyway.

'Oh, don't sweat it, son. I have a sweet tooth myself,' the suit said with a grin. 'Culver is the name. Jed Culver, with the Hawaiian delegation. And you're James Kipper, aren't you?'

'City engineer, yeah,' replied Kipper, who felt the need to explain himself. 'This, uh, this is for my daughter. She's six and . . .'

Culver held up his hand and shook his head. 'Say no more, I have two of my own. Although, they've moved on a bit in years now – terrible teens. Back in Honolulu, thank God. Listen, Mr Kipper, I wonder if I might bother you for a few moments of your time.'

Feeling as guilty as hell over the confectionery, Kip didn't feel he could say no. 'Is there something I can help you with, Mr Culver? I mean, I'm not a delegate. Not elected either – I'm just the city engineer. I'm trying to keep things running.'

Culver nodded. 'I know. That's why I wanted to talk, briefly. But not here. Do you have an office? Or, even better, somewhere we could talk that isn't likely to be bugged.'

Culver spoke in such a matter-of-fact way that the meaning of his question took a second to register with the engineer. Kip blinked and shook his head in surprise. 'I, uh . . . well.'

'I have good reason for caution, sir. Doesn't need to be anywhere special – indeed, the less special the better. Somewhere you wouldn't normally transact business. Somewhere your elected officials would be unlikely to frequent.'

'Somewhere not worth bugging?' said Kip.

'Yes,' replied Culver, nodding gently.

Kipper shrugged. 'Okay, I suppose so, if you want to follow me.'

'Tell you what, I understand it may be an inconvenience for a busy man, but could you meet me in half an hour? Wherever you think best.'

Kipper wasn't sure whether to be pissed off, intrigued or worried. A little of each perhaps. He gave Culver directions to an empty office on the twenty-ninth floor. An auditor had been working in there all last year, causing untold angst for the various department heads. But he was gone now, and the office had not been reallocated. It was a bare space full of paper files awaiting the shredder.

The chief engineer had enough time to squeeze in a quick meeting with his own section heads, detailing their priorities for the day – sanitation and sewerage were the new headaches – before excusing himself for ten minutes to call Barb. To his surprise, he found Culver waiting for him there, in his office. He wasn't entirely happy with that.

'Do you mind if I ask how you made it up here, Mr Culver? I mean, you're not really supposed to be on this floor.'

'Nope,' the big man admitted. 'But in my experience just looking like you should be somewhere is ninety per cent of the battle won. And you don't have any armed soldiers up on these floors, do you?'

Kipper released a deep breath out of his nostrils. 'No, we don't. Not since they released the councillors. Military's handling security downstairs, but the city looks after its own up here now.'

Culver seemed to chew this over. 'I hear tell you were the one who dragged this town through the worst of the aftermath. Heard you were the de facto mayor and governor.'

'City employs a lot of people, Mr Culver,' Kip replied, shrugging off the attempt at flattery. 'They all worked long days after the Disappearance hit. I wasn't unique. There are thousands of city and state-government workers, thousands more in private firms, tens of thousands of individual citizens, all of whom pitched in to help. Most of my people wouldn't have seen their families awake in a month.'

'And the military,' said Culver. 'Do you mind if I ask how they . . . fitted in?'

Kipper snorted. 'Fitted in? More like *stormed* in. Was a time there I was seriously thinking about following one of my guys out the door. He quit after Blackstone arrested the councillors. Said it was fascism, no less.'

'But you *didn't* quit.'

'How could I? The army are good at some things but not others. You want something destroyed, they're your guys. You want something saved, preserved, built, whatever – not so much. Believe me, Mr Culver, I had my doubts. But this place would've fallen apart if enough of us had just thrown up our hands on a point of politics. And it did get sorted out in the end.'

Jed Culver waited to see if Kipper claimed any credit for that. His sources told him the engineer was responsible for sorting out the 'misunderstanding' between the city and Fort Lewis, and for ensuring that everybody moved on from it as quickly as possible. A remarkable piece of hog trading, in Jed's considered opinion.

But the engineer said nothing. He didn't even raise it. Culver decided to nudge him.

'I have to say, Mr Kipper,' he began, 'I am surprised it got sorted, as you put it. People must have been a tad upset with General Blackstone, no? I would've thought a lot of folks might have wanted him arrested and court-martialled. Or at least relieved of duty.'

Kipper shrugged. 'Look, it's a tough call. Blackstone is an asshole. He shouldn't have done what he did, but he gets as much credit for pulling this place through the last month as anyone. More than most, really. I guess unusual times call for unusual methods.' The engineer checked his watch before going on. 'Look, I don't want to be rude, Mr Culver, but is there some reason we had to arrange such a cloak-and-dagger meeting for a conversation you could have a hundred times over down on the conference floor?'

Culver smiled. 'I'm sorry, Mr Kipper, I know you're very busy. There was one thing. Have you ever dealt with a Major Ty McCutcheon?'

43

GUANTANAMO BAY NAVAL BASE, CUBA

The screaming howl of turbines prompted Tusk Musso to dive for the floor, badly jarring his elbow and bruising a few ribs. Thunder struck the headquarters building. Windows shattered and the floor seemed to jump beneath him as a computer screen crashed down off the desk. Smoke poured into the office from down the hallway and dozens of phones rang as the base-alert siren trumpeted the end of the world. The shouts of Marines, sailors and soldiers in and out of the building reached Musso dully through the ringing in his ears.

'*Corpsman! Man down!*'

'*What the fuck, what the fuck . . .*'

'*The armoury – now, Gutteres . . .*'

Colonel Pileggi picked herself up, checked for any injuries while dusting off, and reached for one of the two ringing telephones. She began shouting into the mouthpiece just as Musso grabbed the other phone.

'Commanding officer,' Musso yelled, finger to his ears. He heard an unfamiliar voice, gruff and powerful, as someone attempted to make himself heard over the crash of rockets and gunfire.

'Gunnery Sergeant Miles Price, base security, sir. Orders?'

'What's our status, Gunny?' coughed Musso as he caught a lungful of dust and smoke.

The room glowed bright orange from the flames in the bay,

bright enough to blot out the stars and illuminate the panic of the civilians on the vessels crammed together down there. Their cries and screams registered faintly in the small spaces between the crash and roar of battle.

'Got a battalion-sized landing force in the bay, sir,' the gunner shouted back. 'They've split into two groups. One headed for the airfield, the other for your position. My Marines are scattered all over the base. It'll take at least fifteen minutes to get everyone up.'

Musso carried the phone with him over to the window, taking care not to present an easy target. He could see a column of six-wheeled armoured vehicles and amtracs rolling out of the bow of the beached container ship. Muzzle flashes twinkled from their gun mounts as long ropey arcs of tracer fire reached out for targets unseen in the night.

'Try to set up an anti-tank team and hit that column headed for headquarters,' he called down the phone. 'Colonel Pileggi's organising a security force to handle the airfield. Give every swinging dick a weapon – I don't care what branch they are or what their MOS is, I want everyone armed. Grab any willing civilians, too. Anyone who can and will pull a trigger. We're in the shit deep, Gunny. You read me?'

'Yes, sir, we are indeed in the shit,' Price replied. 'I'll get on that anti-tank team.'

'Okay. I'll keep someone on this line,' Musso promised. He turned to the navy lieutenant by the door. 'Lieutenant McCurry, man this phone.'

'Aye, sir,' barked McCurry, taking the handset from him.

Tusk watched as Pileggi continued to yell into her phone. 'No, hold those fuckers off the airfield, Sergeant!' she insisted. 'And if you've got civilians volunteering to fight, then let them. I don't have time for any bullshit about whether or not it's kosher – just do it!'

'Can you hold it?' Musso asked her as she slammed the receiver down.

'I have no idea, sir. I'm not over there, I'm here,' Pileggi said.

'Grab a couple of Marines as close protection, and a personal weapon, and go, Susie. You're my man out there.'

She stood to attention and ripped out a salute. Then she was gone, barking out orders at men in the hallway he couldn't see.

Turning back to the shattered window on the second floor of his headquarters building, Musso watched tracer fire flickering across the airfield, some of it going astray into the bay, skipping across the water. A C-5 Galaxy was trying to climb off the runway and claw its way into the air. Ice water flooded Musso's veins as tracer reached out from the perimeter of the airfield to pepper the fuselage of the massive cargo transport.

Climb, Musso prayed silently. *Climb.*

'Sir!' McCurry shouted over the chaos. 'I'm getting reports of two additional columns outside the base perimeter. Estimated time to contact is five minutes.'

The tracer fire lost interest in the Galaxy and focused again on earthbound targets. Musso allowed himself a sigh of relief.

Just then a missile zipped into the flank of the cargo plane at the wing root and exploded. The lost wing folded up and back over the top of the C-5, shearing off the tail section as the fuel ignited, engulfing the dying aircraft.

'Mother. Fucker . . .' said Musso.

He watched the wreckage plummet towards a Carnival cruise ship, which was already burning from a number of bomb strikes. Musso knew he would never be free of the image of children falling out of the belly of that burning Galaxy as it careened towards the ship.

'No,' Musso whispered. 'No, God . . .'

The plane hit the bow of the Carnival vessel, shearing it off completely. Burning fuel and white-hot shrapnel shredded the upper decks. Adding to the carnage, another aircraft, a Venezuelan jet, swooped in low, and began strafing the growing funeral pyre in the bay, catching some burning passengers in midair as they flung themselves from the cruise ship and tried to find safety in the waters of Guantanamo Bay. A second container ship pushed past the wreckage for the beach, only to be met by a couple of Navy Shore Patrol boats, gnats buzzing around a behemoth. Small-arms fire passed back and forth between the mayfly's quick adversaries and their lumbering prey, chopping up the water around the smaller boats where civilians were mixed in the fray.

'Got a fire fight between base police and some infiltrators at the McDonald's, sir,' McCurry reported. 'Another engagement is taking place up at base housing. Gunny Price says he's only got a third of his force under arms and maybe two-dozen civilians. That's it.'

'Where's that army commo puke?' Musso asked, as he stalked over to the doorway. 'Captain Birch!' he roared.

A scuffle of boots through the smoke-filled corridors produced a large, somewhat overweight man in army BDUs. 'Sir?'

'Do we still have comms with Pearl or the brigade in Panama?'

Birch seemed pale, a bit stunned.

'Comms with Pearl, Birch. Or the Canal. Get with the fucking program,' Musso said, resisting the urge to slap the man silly. 'I need air cover over our AO.'

'I'll check, sir . . . right away.' The captain turned to leave. 'Specialist Gibbs!' he called down the hallway. 'See if Pearl is –'

Birch's head exploded.

'Sniper!'

Pileggi, shepherded by two Marines and a stray Coast Guard chief, made the airstrip on the bay's western headland by virtue of a white-knuckle high-speed run in a little Trabant. The Cuban vehicle had been parked outside the headquarters block, and one of the Marines, Sergeant Gutteres, had hotwired it with practised ease. At times, tracer fire zipped and crackled all around them, while at others, on short stretches of road, everything seemed eerily still.

As they screeched around the last curve before the hangar buildings at the edge of the field, Gutteres pointed skywards and Pileggi's heart sank as she saw dozens of parachute canopies popped open, high in the air. A few lines of orange and green fire flicked up to cross-hatch the descending paratroopers, but not enough. It was a feeble, poorly guided effort compared to the volume of fire on the ground.

Chief Lundquist, who had the wheel, swerved a few times to avoid burnt-out vehicles and hastily erected firing positions, before slamming on the brakes next to a long concrete pipe behind which a small group of Marines seemed to be directing the defence of the airfield. Colonel Pileggi, still dressed in her office uniform, scrambled out and hurried over with her bodyguards right behind her. She was protected from the worst of the enemy's ground fire by the giant pipe, which stood at least six feet high, but she crouched almost double anyway, running to avoid getting picked off from above. A few of the Venezuelans were shooting from small hand-held weapons as they came down. The fire was inaccurate, but getting heavier.

'You Sergeant Carlyon?' she asked the senior non-com, throwing herself up against the pipe.

'Yes, ma'am,' he answered, reading her name-tag and adding, 'We spoke before, Colonel.'

'Okay, what's your situation, Sergeant? I'm not going to run your fight for you. I'll just see what I can do to help.'

Carlyon looked relieved. 'I have eight Marines with me, Colonel,' he replied. 'Only six have any ammo left. Around the base, I have less than fifty men. Some of them sailors, some airmen. They're not trained for this. Some MPs, who are.'

As he spoke, two of his men depleted their stocks even further by sniping at the Venezuelans dropping to earth beneath the billowing chutes.

'There's at least a platoon of hostiles on the ground already,' the sergeant continued, raising his voice over the steady gunfire and the more distant roar of the battle out in the bay. 'But they haven't consolidated. I think they came ashore in a couple of inflatable hulls, probably got split up, and haven't regrouped yet. We've got 'em pinned down behind two shipping containers on the far side of the strip. But tactical's changing, ma'am.' Carlyon looked upwards. Stepping away from the cover of the pipe and calmly raising his rifle, he put two shots into a paratrooper a hundred yards up and slightly north of them.

'Well, you got my guys here,' said Pileggi. 'Here, take my rifle – give it to one of your men. I'll make do.' She unholstered her pistol, as Carlyon passed her M 1 across to a grateful looking Marine.

'Thank you, Colonel. Much obliged.'

Just behind her, Lundquist raised a Remington shotgun and fired twice. She turned briefly to see a human leg falling from beneath a writhing, screaming paratrooper, not fifty yards away.

'You're going to need more men and guns,' she said. 'You got a radio?'

Carlyon shook his head and handed her a cell phone. 'It's still working, ma'am. On and off.'

'Okay. I'll see if I can round up some warm bodies. What happened to those civilians you had before?'

'They're dead.'

PACOM HQ, HAWAII

Admiral Ritchie watched the four 52-inch HDTV screens in the ad-hoc war room of the re-formed Joint Chiefs of Staff at Fort Shafter. Centre left displayed a real-time Keyhole satellite feed of the running battle at Guantanamo Bay; centre right, a live feed from some Venezuelan reporter on the scene, an embed from the government-run TVes network. The reporter was covering his country's Marines as they tried to fight their way towards base headquarters, and at that moment was speaking to camera, framed by the burning light of an amtrac. The satellite feed was choppy and slow, breaking into bursts of static, but Ritchie could see that the man looked terrified. He was also providing a constant stream of very useful information, which a small team of Marines here in Pearl were feeding right back to their colleagues at Gitmo.

On the screen to the far left, President Hugo Chávez pumped his fist in the air as he shouted cadenced beats of Spanish at the microphone. A running subtitle of translation tried to keep up, but Ritchie had long since given up reading it. Most of his attention was focused on the fourth screen, the videoconference taking place with the surviving senior officer of the *Nimitz* battle group, Captain Ted Branch. Lights flickered behind the master and commander of the wounded USS *Nimitz* as he gave his report to General Tommy Franks.

'I've got two cats up, and two-thirds of my air wing operational. However, we're still at half power and running on one screw. Additionally, the USS *Princeton* is trailing behind. We may have to scuttle her if we can't get flooding stabilised,' Captain Branch said.

Admiral Ritchie leaned forward. 'Captain, you'll transition into the Atlantic later this afternoon your time, correct?'

'Yes, sir. Barring any trouble at Gibraltar,' Branch replied. 'The Royal Navy tell me they still have things under control, but Morocco is a little too close for comfort. I estimate we can be in Cuban waters, earliest, in ten days.'

General Franks shook his head. 'This will be over long before then, Ted.'

Captain Branch nodded. The thin man didn't appear to have an ounce of body fat on him. Ritchie always thought the carrier commander looked more like an Army Ranger than a naval officer. Most in the navy were, well, a little heavier than they ought to be. Himself included.

'Ted, do you think you can spare any elements of your battle group?' Ritchie asked. 'Who can sprint away and arrive sooner?'

Branch rubbed the bridge of his nose, probably trying to clear his head or suppress a burning migraine, perhaps both. 'Sir, if you think it will do some good, I'm sure the battle group is willing to make the sacrifice. However, I do not think we can suffer the loss of our remaining combat power without endangering either the *Nimitz* or the *Princeton*. Furthermore, I do have a convoy of my own refugee vessels trailing my battle group. Some of them have been vetted by our Marine and navy boarding teams, some have not. There's no way of knowing whether or not one of them is a jack-in-the-box waiting to pop on us.'

Franks glanced over at Ritchie. 'Do you think it's worth it, Jim?'

Ritchie looked up at the paper map of the Atlantic area of operations. Here in the war room, they were already falling back to paper, acetate and coloured markers to indicate their force dispositions. It wasn't for a lack of computing power. It was the lack of secure communications and data sources that forced the fallback to more primitive methods.

'No, sir,' Ritchie concluded. '*Nimitz* should continue as planned. We'll have to try something else.'

Franks turned to the commander of the 25th Infantry Division, who had remained silent during the exchange. 'Francis, what's your take on Guantanamo?'

General Murphy snorted. 'They're well and truly fucked, sir. Civilians mixed into it, and us with our cocks in our hands . . . Musso is a smart man. He'll see it pretty clear as well.'

'You mean surrender,' Franks said. 'Right?'

Murphy couldn't bring himself to say it. He folded his arms and nodded.

'Sir?' An army specialist approached the officers. 'Gitmo on the line.'

Susan Pileggi exhaled, and with the hot, stale breath went some of the tension cramping her arms and shoulders. Not that she relaxed – that would have been impossible. But as she saw the end coming, with no chance of escape or redemption, she accepted it for the first time, and part of the fear and the strain of the last few weeks ebbed away.

She waited in the gun pit. The muzzle of her M-1, retrieved from the body of the Marine she'd lent it to a few hours ago, tracked the small group of Venezuelan paratroopers as they cautiously rounded the huge mound of burning rubble a hundred yards away. It had been a chemical storehouse; for what, she had no idea. But the stench was vile enough to blot out the smells of the base as it died around her. Burnt meat, corpses crawling with carpets of black flies, the unwashed bodies of the men around her, napalm smoke and festering wounds – the evil stink of the warehouse blotted them all out.

'Sergeant Carlyon. A head count, please.'

'Twenty-three friendly, ma'am. As of five minutes ago.'

Pileggi nodded. They were spread out over a hundred-yard front, some fucking the earth in a drainage ditch, others taking cover behind broken machinery or piles of concrete barriers. They held on. The enemy numbered in the hundreds now, but they still hadn't forced the issue, and in this failure had probably died in greater numbers than was necessary. They could've ploughed us under an hour back, she thought.

Carlyon popped up and squeezed off a three-round burst, and the reassuring boom of Lundquist's shotgun followed almost immediately. The volume of return fire was heavy, but poorly directed.

She followed the advance of the small party attempting to flank them to the north. Carlyon was aware of them too.

Gitmo was dying. The base had done so well to hold off against the sneak attack, but Lieutenant Colonel Pileggi knew it would be overrun, probably in the next few hours, and her small band of brothers were sure to die with her. She was aware, without turning to look at them, of the men in the firing pit next to her. Chief Lundquist was hunkered down, reloading his shotgun next to Jimbo Jamieson, a civilian who had joined them in the middle of some of the worst fighting; he'd pulled up in a Humvee full of sailors, carrying two boxes of ammo and, most precious of all, spare barrels for an M249 squad automatic weapon. Jamieson was watching the enemy creeping through the dark too. Never taking his eyes off them as they crept closer.

Even while concentrating so fiercely on the flankers, Pileggi remained unnaturally aware of other details. A patch of red hair peeking out beneath the curve of a helmet . . . The unnaturally straight line of a bayonet . . . A muted cough in the next foxhole, barely audible under the freight-train scream of battle all around.

Their lives had only one meaning now: to delay a catastrophe that was otherwise inevitable. Attackers were pouring onto the headland from three sides and they were going to take the strip. When they did, more would doubtless fly in, falling upon Guantanamo's remaining defenders and the unarmed refugees with equal ferocity.

God only knew what sort of shit rain and hellfire that would unleash, and Pileggi wasn't sorry she'd be missing it. She had already seen civilian boats targeted out on the bay, for no apparent reason other than that they made easier, more pleasing prey than armed Marines and soldiers. The atrocities, witnessed by everyone she'd managed to gather for the airfield defence, had doubtless hardened the Americans' resolve. Dozens of dead paratroopers lay on the tarmac as testimony to that.

She laid the cold iron sight of her weapon on the centre of the group of men, who were now coming at her with much greater confidence and speed. They hadn't seen Carlyon's ambush yet.

Good. Half a second telescoped out towards infinity. Susie Pileggi had plenty of time to examine the poor standard of their uniforms and the torn rubber shoes of the man in the lead. It spoke of a badly planned, hastily thrown-together plan of attack. A three-legged dog suddenly bounded in front of the advancing Venezuelans, spinning in circles, howling as though possessed by a demon. It was probably mad.

'Fire,' yelled Carlyon.

The dog exploded into a ball of hair and gore as the SAW opened up a short distance away. She heard cursing and saw Lundquist adjust his aim up a little. The attackers dispersed like startled rabbits, those who could anyway. An invisible wave swept over at least half them, cutting some down, throwing others into the air, completely disassembling one from the groin up.

'Pour it on, boys!' Carlyon yelled over the uproar.

The dense crump of exploding hand grenades momentarily smothered the rattle and snarl of gunfire. The battle for Gitmo, a vast conflagration, fell away from the minds of the men around her; the whole world was now contained on the small stage of this burning, rubble-strewn airstrip. They started to take return fire from the enemy, dug in all around them, and someone screamed as a round took him in the face.

Pileggi squeezed off discrete shots from the rifle – picking her targets, waiting until she had a clear line, and sending two or three rounds down-range. The bullets hit hard, punching out chunks of meat and bone when they struck. Pileggi dropped three men in just a few seconds before having to duck behind the shattered masonry she'd built up in front of her firing position.

Lundquist cried out and flew backwards. Gouts of dark red blood looped gracefully into the overcast sky. The ground shook and heaved violently as mortar bombs began dropping on their position. None of them had any overhead protection.

'They're coming!' screamed Carlyon. 'Get ready!' He emptied a whole magazine to give himself and his men some cover.

The Venezuelans had gathered themselves at last and were charging at them en masse, running into their own mortar barrage with bayonets drawn. Pileggi was almost certain she heard a bugle faintly beneath the din.

Pileggi changed magazines, rapidly, mechanically. Firing again as quickly as possible. Four of the attackers fell in front of their pit. Two more leapt forward and sailed over the edge, throwing themselves onto Jimbo Jamieson, who swung wildly at the closest intruder with a lump of wood. It connected with a hollow clunk that Pileggi heard quite clearly, despite all the noise. She swung her M-1 like a club too, driving the heavy wooden stock into the face of the second attacker. The man's nose collapsed with sickening ease as blood erupted from his torn flesh.

Carlyon fell on her, driving her down. She felt his dead weight, the terrible slackness of his limbs, and knew he was gone. Pileggi tried to lift him clear, to get back to her firing position, but he was so heavy. It was worse, much worse, than having a drunken lover fall asleep on top of you. It was crushing, painful.

And then he was gone. The weight suddenly flying away, and she was looking up into the muzzle of a gun, wondering what it was, and realising just before it flashed white.

'Pearl is up, sir,' a Marine private said, holding up a phone. 'A lot of static.'

Musso thanked the private and took the phone. 'General Musso.'

'Franks. This line secure?'

'I sorely doubt it,' Tusk replied. 'It's probably trailing across one of the sat news channels as we speak, sir.'

He looked around the underground command bunker. Some of the screens were running live feeds from Venezuelan TV. The static on the phone connection grew in intensity. Musso shook the phone, even though he knew it didn't do any good. It made him feel better.

'Say again, sir?'

'As a matter of fact, TVes is running us live, Musso,' Franks told him. 'Bastards. What is your status?'

The brigadier general rubbed his forehead and thought for a moment. If they were live on TVes, this conversation was going out to the world, a situation he might be able to use to his advantage. He couched his next words very carefully, trying to remember the lessons he was taught at charm school when he received his first star.

'Enemy forces are aggressively targeting civilian refugees at my position, sir,' Musso began. 'I've got multiple civilian vessels burning in the bay or sinking. We lost a C-5 Galaxy as it tried to take off. My air liaison officer tells me that over four hundred US civilians were on board. We're probably looking at upwards of a thousand civilian casualties minimum, perhaps more. My own casualties are climbing as well.'

'Any attempt to offer a ceasefire?' General Franks asked. 'To mitigate civilian casualties.'

Musso blinked. Every fibre in his soul screamed at him to fight it out, resist to the last, make the enemy pay, but the civilians were his priority. They were his boss, his reason for being in the first place.

'By us or by them, sir?'

'Either.'

'Negative, sir. I've not even had a chance to think about it,' Tusk admitted.

'The civilians need to be your top priority, General Musso,' said Franks. 'I'm ordering you to attempt to contact the enemy commander to seek terms for a ceasefire. We will try to do the same at our end. In the meantime, until you receive such a cease-fire, *resist with maximum effort*. Do you understand?'

'Yes, sir,' Musso replied. What other choice did he have if the Venezuelans weren't willing to accept terms? Even though he'd moved underground, he could still hear a savage battle chewing up the base above him.

'Also know this . . .' Franks paused for a moment. 'If you go under, we will exact retribution from the Venezuelans at a time and place of our own choosing. We will make this night very expensive for them. Do you understand, General Musso?'

Okay, I'm not the only one playing to the media then . . . 'I do, sir,' he replied.

'Carry on, Tusk. Franks out.'

Musso hung up the phone and found Lieutenant McCurry in front of him.

'We've lost the airfield, General,' she said.

That meant Susie Pileggi was probably dead, Musso realised. He nodded and hurried over to a display that carried security-cam vision of the airstrip area. He could see that the tracer fire across the bay had flickered out now. The burning hulks of civilian and military aircraft littered the runway. On a separate display, the Venezuelans' armoured column was stalled out, harassed by ambushes set up by Gunnery Sergeant Price's security teams.

Tusk Musso felt like he was falling into a deep well, an abyss of despair that seemed to know no end. From the depths of this descent, he heard himself speak the words. They sounded faint and weak to his ears.

'We need to find a white sheet.'

44

Mr Lee heaved on the wheel and took the *Aussie Rules* up the face of the giant wave at about forty degrees. Jules held on, wedging herself into a corner of the bridge, unaware she was clenching her teeth, willing the 228-feet super-yacht over the moving ridge of black, storm-tossed sea water. A force-eleven storm raged outside, reducing visibility to near zero as it hurled sheets of rain and ocean spume at the thick glass windows of the wheelhouse. Lightning strobed, followed almost immediately by the crash of thunder as Lee took them over the crest and down the other side, dropping so precipitously that Julianne had to hold on to the grab bars even more tightly to avoid having her head smashed into the ceiling.

'Nice work, Mr Lee,' she called out over the uproar.

The old Chinese helmsman did not reply, remaining steadfastly focused on trying to feel the heaving ocean beneath their keel.

'Radar, how we doing? Have we lost those cheeky fuckers yet?' Jules asked.

The Rhino, who had strapped himself into his chair, gave her a ready thumbs-up and raised his voice over the shrieking of the storm, speaking around the newly lit cigar that was fugging up the air in the bridge. 'Hard to tell, skipper, but I'd bet two inches of horn that they're losing contact. Slow but sure. Last time I had a good fix, it looked like they were having real fucking problems with the storm. We had about eighteen nautical miles on them.'

'But they weren't breaking off pursuit?'

'Afraid not, no, ma'am. Oh, and Boss Jules, is this a good time to ask about the location of the humidor? It's just I couldn't find it in the library, like you said, and – '

Julianne silenced him with a warning look.

'Alrighty then,' he said, conceding the point. 'We'll sort that out later.'

The ship suddenly tilted precipitously, as a rogue wave took them abeam and tried to roll the vessel over. Lee cursed in Mandarin and spun the wheel again, calling for more power.

Jules would never have admitted it, but her heart felt as though it might burst out of her rib cage. She took a deep, difficult breath and announced as calmly as she could, 'I'm going to go check on everybody down below. Shout out if there's any change at all, for better or worse. Good work, everyone. We'll outrun these blaggers yet.'

Lee didn't reply or even turn his head, so fiercely was he concentrating. He stood on the balls of his bare feet, knees flexing to meet the rise and fall of the deck, eyes seemingly unfocused, simply lost somewhere out in the dark and violence of the storm. The Rhino, by way of contrast, looked quietly pleased with himself. The bridge crew, Dietmar the navigator and Lars the Norwegian backpacker turned first mate of the *Aussie Rules*, both grinned like stupid dogs given a pat on the head. They were among the younger members of her pick-up crew, and even though they'd been shot at half-a-dozen times so far, the two Northern Europeans still seemed to think it was all just insane fun, a great story they couldn't wait to tell all the Helgas and Anyas at their next travellers' hostel. Nobody but Mr Lee and herself seemed to be too bothered by any of it. Jules wondered how they'd be feeling if things turned bloody and personal in a few days, should the Peruvians get close enough to board. The *Rules* enjoyed a speed advantage of a few knots and had put some good distance between them, but they were hanging on doggedly.

She clawed her way out of the corner she'd been jammed into and tried to roll out of the bridge and through to the companionway in synch with the movements of the yacht. With seas running at ten metres and whipped up into a frenzy by sixty-knot winds, her progress was slow and extremely hazardous. She found the conventional stairwells and wide corridors of the *Aussie Rules* to be more difficult in extreme weather than the cramped conditions she'd grown used to on Pete's little yacht. It was so much bigger here that the chances of being thrown clear across an open area by a particularly bad wave were significantly higher. As she proceeded towards the media centre, she climbed up a steep, pitching rise, levitated into the air, and crashed back onto a plunging deck as Lee took them through another boiling ravine on the surface of the southern oceans.

Having finally reached her destination after a trek that took three minutes instead of the usual one, Jules launched herself through the door and into the plush confines of the media room with a real sense of deliverance. She found Shah, Fifi and Pieraro there, all of them wedged deeply into the soft blue armchairs, talking amongst themselves, if somewhat volubly over the sound of the storm. The big screen was lit up with a feed from the Rhino's radar, showing a highly degraded image on which a lone vessel occasionally popped out – the giant trawler *Viarsa 1*, according to the Rhino, a toothfish poacher turned pirate raider.

'How's it goin', Julesy?' asked Fifi.

'Spiffing. They're holding on. I was really hoping we'd lose them in the storm, but Rhino says not. They're used to these conditions and worse. We're not.'

'No,' Fifi agreed.

They really weren't. On the *Diamantina*, they'd always run from big storms, harboured up or anchored on the leeside of an island wherever they could, and ridden them out. Only once or twice during their time together had Pete been caught out in open seas when a big blow started up, and that had been nothing like this.

'Miguel, how're your people hanging on?' she asked. 'They wouldn't see a lot of ocean storms back in the village, I'd imagine.'

The *vaquero*, whose face was a study in granite stoicism, shook his head almost imperceptibly. 'Very sick, Miss Julianne. The children are frightened. They are all frightened, but only the children admit so.'

Jules saw the *Viarsa 1* appear as an indistinct, faraway blip on the big screen. It must have climbed a crest at the same time as the *Rules* and been painted by the radar. She wondered if there was somebody on the other vessel hunched over a screen, hanging on for a fleeting glimpse of them through the fury of the storm. There had to be. Otherwise Lee would've lost them already.

She turned back to address the Mexican again. 'As soon as the weather calms down enough to get them out of their bunks, Miguel, I want you and Sergeant Shah to start training everyone again, especially the Yanks. Just the basics, as we discussed. Aiming, firing, reloading, clearing jams. Over and over and over, with every minute we have. These bastards may never get within a bee's willy of us, but if they do, I want to kick them so hard that their goolies pop out of their eye sockets.'

'The passengers will be fine, Miss Julianne,' Shah assured her. 'They did very well in their lessons before the storm. They understand what is required, and what will happen to them if the pirates get control. They will fight. All of them. Even the children, if you let them.'

She looked across at Miguel. Deep hollows under his eyes gave him a ghoulish appearance in the dim light of the room. The ship plunged and rolled again, forcing him to grab the arms of his deep padded chair with white knuckles that stood out starkly against the blue fabric.

'I have discussed this with Mariela, my wife, and the old ones,' he said. 'We have agreed that only the very youngest will go with Ana and one of the crew in the big launch if the worst happens. The other children will carry ammunition, and if they can hold a weapon, they may fire it too.'

It was hard to be certain in the half-light, but Jules thought he may have been on the verge of tears.

'My daughters, they will fight,' Pieraro went on. 'They must. Better for them to die quickly than to live out their years as a slave to some stinking Peruvian *cabrón*.'

'Miguel, I promised you safe passage for you and your family,' said Jules, as softly as she could and still be heard. 'The girls do not have to fight. If the *Viarsa 1* gets close enough, we can put them in the sport fisher with Lars or Dietmar and Grandma Ana. They would outrun any pursuit.'

Pieraro smiled sadly. 'And then what, Miss Julianne? How far are we from safe land? They would not survive a storm like this, and they would be heading into the bad weather. I told you I would hold you responsible for their safety, but I do not hold you responsible for this. You are not pursuing us. You did not bring the storm out of the skies.'

Shah clapped his hands together, a thunderous sound. 'Enough of this talk!' he declared. 'This will defeat us as surely as any man. How many of these monkeys have we seen off in these last weeks? They are desperate, foolish fishermen playing at pirates. Let me tell you what will happen if they should come alongside us: *we* will cut *them* down and take their stores for our own.'

'Hooah!' cried Fifi, grinning hugely. 'That's the spirit, mountain man!'

Julianne braced her back against one arm of her chair and her feet against the other as the *Rules* began another tumbling ride down a foaming summit. She glanced at the screen to see if they'd lost radar contact with the *Viarsa 1*, but it wasn't on screen to begin with. It must have been hidden in some shifting valley of water at that moment. The seas were large enough to tower over both vessels at times, hiding them from each other.

'Okay,' sighed Jules. 'Shah's right, Miguel. Now, if you'll all excuse me, I'd best get on with my King Henry routine.'

'I am sorry, Miss Julianne?' quizzed the Mexican, confused.

'A little Shakespeare, darling. Benefits of what classical education I received before Daddy pissed away his ill-gotten gains and all the family silver. "For forth he goes and visits all his host; Upon his royal face there is no note, how dread an army hath enrounded him."'

Pieraro was an intelligent man, but she could see she'd lost him.

'Don't bother none about her, Miguel,' said Fifi with good humour. 'She gets all thinky and stuff sometimes. Your girls, they'll be fine. I will personally take apart any motherfucker who tries to interfere with them.'

'You are kind, for one so fierce, Miss Fifi. But in the last extremes, I shall attend to my own family.'

'Enough!' barked Shah, clapping his hands together again with a thunderous report.

'Yes,' said Jules, 'enough.' She pushed herself up out of the chair with the momentum of the ship. 'Try to get some sleep.'

Her rounds of the ship took nearly an hour – a slow, difficult progression through all decks, moving hand over hand along companionways that violently plunged and rolled and shifted as the storm tossed the super-yacht about. Most of the passengers were in their beds, many of them strapped in against the violence of the night. Down in the engine room her grease monkeys – a Sri Lankan and two Dutch merchant mariners she'd picked up in Costa Rica – were tending to the *Rules*'s gleaming white plant with the universally pissed-off look of all engineering crew. The Sri Lankan, Pankesh, had one hand bandaged, the legacy of a fall against a steam conduit in the difficult conditions. She checked his burn, which seemed quite ghastly, but he insisted on remaining at his station.

The main lounge looked very bare now, with most of the fittings stowed away. There she found one half of the trust-fund brats, Phoebe, sitting with one of the village children. They'd wedged themselves into one of the heavily padded loungers. Before Jules could ask them what the fuck they were doing out of their cabins, Phoebe spoke up.

'Maya was scared,' she said. 'She got lost looking for the little girls' room – didn't you, sweetheart? – and wandered into my cabin. I said I'd sit with her a while.'

Julianne wondered if Maya was the only one who'd been scared, but she let it go. The last thing she needed now was hysterics over a lost child. 'Thank you, Phoebe. Good show,' she replied. 'But make sure you get her back to her bunk soon. I need everyone rested.'

She had turned around and was about to claw her way back to her own sleeping quarters when Phoebe called after her: 'Hey, Julianne?'

'Yes?'

'Do you mind if I ask you something?'

There was a neediness in the girl's eyes that answered Jules's earlier, unspoken question. 'What's up, Phoebe?'

The little village girl, Maya, no more than five or six years old, snuggled in tight, burying her face in the young woman's chest.

'You used to be rich once, didn't you?'

Jules couldn't help but smirk. 'So did you.'

'No,' said Phoebe, 'that's not what I mean. Before all of this, before the Disappearance, before you *found* this yacht. Before whatever it was you were doing with Fifi and that Chinese man. You used to be rich. Like me. I can tell from your voice and from the way you run your crew – like you were always meant to.'

The ship dipped and plunged again, unbalancing Jules and propelling her forward. She let herself fall into another lounger close to Phoebe, lest she get hurled out through the glass doors.

'Yes,' she sighed. 'My family had money. Old money. And my father stole a lot more. But it was never enough to fund his extravagant tastes, or to pay the upkeep on our estates.'

'I knew it,' said Phoebe with a note of triumph. 'So you, like, grew up in a castle?'

'Something like that. It's not nearly as much fun as it sounds. We had to throw the place open to the public every other weekend just to pay for heating.'

'And how did you end up doing, you know, whatever?'

Jules's smile was genuine now. '*Smuggling*, Phoebe. I was a smuggler – I still am, I suppose. It's one of the few jobs still paying these days.' Jules gave a quick shrug and settled deep into the safety and comfort of the chair. 'I loved my father, in spite of his faults. *Because* of them, in some ways. He was very different from the sort of people we mixed with. Or rather, he was just like them, but more honest about it.'

'But you said he stole money.'

Jules smiled again, fondly. 'He did. He was a terrible crook, but he only ever stole from the rich – and believe me, Phoebe, if your family has been rich for nine hundred years, somewhere some of that loot was stolen. Most of it, even.'

Lightning and thunder flared and crashed so closely together that Jules was unaware of any lag between them. The flat, white light illuminated a ghastly vision outside of the whole ocean in turmoil, of living, waterborne mountain ranges boiling up around the ship.

'You didn't tell me how you became a smuggler,' Phoebe continued, pressing for more.

'No, I didn't,' said Jules, who pushed herself up out of the chair and headed for the nearest grab bar. 'Don't worry, Phoebe,' she called back over her shoulder, 'you'll be fine. The only reason you're on this boat is because you were quick enough and smart enough to react to the Disappearance. You got some of your old money out and turned it into new money, very quickly. Most people aren't like that – they'll sit and wait for the situation to bury them. You, you're a survivor. Plus, a family like yours, it would've had investments all over the world, wouldn't it? Not all of them would have tanked.'

The American said nothing to that and Jules smiled again. 'Don't worry, sweetheart. You've paid for passage, I'm not going to ask for any more. But tomorrow, or the day after, when this storm clears and those Peruvians have a clear run at us, if we can't outpace them, you'll have to *earn* your passage. So get some rest.'

She pulled herself up the rising deck and out into the companionway. The journey to her own cabin, the former owner's quarters, was a hand-over-hand trek that took another six or more minutes and came close to exhausting her.

'Maya? Maya?'

A woman's voice, Mexican, made her look up. Mariela Pieraro was clawing her way along the corridor towards Jules, a frantic look haunting her eyes.

'It's all right,' Jules called out. 'Maya's in the big lounge. With Pheobe.'

The two women hauled themselves along, hand over hand, holding on to the safety rails that ran the length of the companionway. The look of animal fear disappeared from Mariela's face, but a deep, abiding worry remained. The storm, Jules supposed. Your first big storm at sea was always terrifying. How much more so would it be for a woman who had spent her life on the edge of a desert?

'Miss Julianne. I am . . . sorry . . . I . . . not to find her . . . I . . .'

The boat slipped sideways and Jules nearly lost her footing as she waved away the mother's concerns. Mariela didn't speak English with much confidence, although Jules didn't know why. Her grasp of the language seemed fine, but after the scene at the

Fairmont she and the other villagers had very much kept to themselves, doing everything asked of them but trying to remain as unobtrusive as possible.

'Just down there a little way,' Jules said, pointing back to the way she'd just come. 'Through the big doors. She went to the loo . . . to the toilet, sorry. And got lost. She is fine, Mariela.'

Pieraro's wife nodded gratefully. 'I worry. I cannot see her and I worry.'

'She's fine,' Jules repeated.

The woman grabbed at her arm as they passed each other, a strong, almost vice-like grip. 'You are a good person, yes?' she said. 'A good person to save my family. All of us. Thank you, thank you . . .'

Embarrassed, as any Englishwoman would be by flagrant neediness and raw emotion, especially from a stranger, Jules blushed slightly and tried to shrug it off.

'No,' insisted Mariela. 'You did not have to take us all, but you did. You helped when no one else would. You are good person, Miss Julianne. Good person.'

'It's fine,' replied Jules, not knowing what else to say. 'She's in the lounge. Best go get her.'

'Sí. Sí.'

Mariela continued on her way, muttering 'Thank you' repeatedly as she receded. It was the longest conversation Julianne had had with her or any of Miguel's people, save for Pieraro himself, of course. Truth be known, she had avoided them, not wanting to grow attached to people she had promised herself she would cut loose at the first opportunity.

Putting that uncomfortable thought out of her head, she resumed the journey to her cabin, taking another few minutes to get there. She was sticky with salt and sweat, and filthy from the day's exertions, but the sea was too rough to have a bath or shower. Instead, Julianne stripped down to her underwear, crawled under the covers and turned out the light.

There was nothing she could do about the storm or the men chasing them. The storm would pass. The men would not.

She fell asleep haunted by visions of the little girl called Maya being tortured by faceless ghouls.

45

Jed Culver stood at the back of the auditorium, stirring a sachet of Sweet 'N Low into his instant coffee, regarding the deteriorating fiasco of the convention with mute detachment.

Reggie Guertson had the call again. He'd firmed up as the point man for what Culver was calling 'the Beer Hall Putsch' – the broad-based faction of neo-con Democrats, national security fetishists, wingnut Republicans and a grab bag of survivalist whackjobs, chancers, urgers and shameless self-aggrandisers who had all come together behind the banner of the so-called Reform Movement. They were his enemies. That's how he thought of them. His enemies, and the enemies of the old Republic.

And they were winning, at least on the floor of the Constitutional Convention. Their crazy, fear-driven idea of a new Constitution, enshrining military representation at the heart of civilian government, was actually gaining traction. If he didn't have such a low opinion of human nature he'd have had a hard time believing it. Didn't these fools understand that the US military couldn't even sustain itself now, let alone run what remained of the country?

The hard truth didn't seem to matter to them, though. It was as if they'd all joined hands and stepped through the looking glass.

Up on stage, Mayor Guertson was haranguing a section of the audience that was attempting to shout him down. Spittle was flying from his lips and the public address system distorted every time he banged the podium with his fist. For their part, the hecklers were giving back as good as they got. Screeching and even throwing things at him.

'This is what we're fighting against!' railed Guertson. 'This sort of anarchy and subversion is what will destroy us all – it has to be stopped!'

'*Sieg heil. Sieg heil,*' chanted his detractors.

'This is going well then.'

Culver wasn't surprised to find James Kipper at his elbow. He'd been expecting him here. He knew Kipper often cruised the buffet tables looking for treats to take home to his daughter. In fact, before Jed could speak, the engineer fessed up.

'Just came up here looking for more army chocolate,' he admitted sheepishly.

'Here. For your kid,' said Culver, producing a carefully hoarded packet of Milk Duds. 'I traded my cigarette ration for them.'

The city engineer blushed and began to shake his head, but Culver waved off his objection.

'I don't smoke, and I'm diabetic. I just thought your little girl might like them.'

'Well, she would,' Kip admitted. 'But it doesn't feel right. Things are so tight at the moment.'

'What are you, a Catholic, with all that guilt? Take the fucking Milk Duds, Kip. They'll kill me if I eat them. Do you have any idea how hard it is to get insulin at the moment?'

The engineer thanked him and pocketed the small treat. 'Suzie'll love them.' He had to raise his voice to be heard over the din.

'This is a first-class shambles, isn't it?' said Culver.

Kipper nodded. He surveyed the scene as if discovering a bedroom left in chaos by a naughty child. The convention chairman was on his feet now, pointing his little wooden hammer at Guertson, demanding he give up the podium. The *Sieg heil* crew were being pushed around at the edges by a group of men who looked like they'd just come in from a logging mill, and at least two fist fights had broken out on the far side of the hall. Kipper muttered something, excused himself and hurried away. A minute or so later, all power to the room was cut, plunging it into darkness.

The effect was almost instant: a sudden change in tone from angry contention to confusion and surprise. After a short interval, the lights came up again, and when they did, Kipper was standing at the podium, smiling at Mayor Guertson, asking politely for the microphone. He got it and then spoke forcefully to the entire room.

'Sorry, folks. James Kipper, city engineer. We've had some trouble with relays from the power station and this place is a major drain on the grid. The whole building is set to flip off when we get a spike. Perhaps a ten-minute break while my guys sort this out would be a good idea. It won't take long, I promise.'

He flicked off the PA and waved a hand over at a man in overalls, standing by a junction box at the rear of the hall. His technician dimmed the lights and cut power to the sound system with an audible pop. Kipper hopped down from the stage, holding both hands up, with his fingers splayed. *Ten minutes.*

The crowd seemed to deflate as the malign energy that had been building up sluiced out of the room. Not entirely, but enough for everyone to retreat from their entrenched positions.

Culver stood to one side as a hundred or more people made straight for the coffee and sandwich tables where he was standing. He pushed through them, like a salmon swimming upstream, intent on catching Kipper before he disappeared again. He found the engineer, loitering by a side exit, watching over the room with a censorious air.

'So, mass psychology and creative bullshitting,' the lawyer said, impressed. 'I didn't realise the city engineer had to be so versatile.'

Kipper raised an eyebrow. 'Multitasking, Jed. It's all multitasking in today's go-go world of local government.'

'Uh-huh, so you're going to switch off the lights and send them to the naughty corner every time they get out of hand?'

The other man looked at a loss for words. 'I don't fucking know. I mean, what the hell is this about?' He waved a hand around to take in the entire auditorium. 'I don't know that we're gonna get through this, you know. You'd have thought that people would be pulling together, not trying to rip each other down.'

Culver smiled gently. 'Do you know much history, Mr Kipper? Do you know the Battle of Salamis?'

'Some Civil War thing?' Kip replied, looking slightly perplexed.

Culver shook his head. 'Most important battle in history. Gallant little ancient Greece versus the enormous, evil Persian Empire. If the Greeks had lost that battle, we wouldn't be standing here today. There would be no such thing as Western civilisation. Anyway, the point is, before the battle the Greeks looked a lot like the people in this room – beating on each other, calling each other dumb fucks and ignorant assholes. The only thing they could agree on was the need to kick Persian ass, but nobody could agree how. In the end, though, they did. And it was partly due to all that aggravating back and forth, as they sorted through their ideas. That and the fact that the Greeks all fought as free men, whereas the Persians were slaves to a God King.'

Kipper sort of squinted and sucked air in through his teeth. 'I don't really get it,' he said. 'We're not about to fight a battle. We're just trying to rebuild a working country.'

Culver leaned in closely now. 'We are fighting a battle, Kip. And this . . .' – he waved his hand at the room – 'this is just a skirmish.'

Suzie's squeal of delight was painfully, beautifully loud in the gloomy candle-lit kitchen.

'Oh thank you, Daddy! Thank you!' She hugged the bright yellow packet of Milk Duds to her chest. 'I'm going to have a tea party and share them with Barbie, and Big Teddy, and Daisy the horse, and . . .'

Barbara Kipper stroked her daughter's bobbing head and tried to calm her down. 'That's lovely, sweetheart, but remember, Daddy may not be able to get any more, so don't *share* them all at once. Maybe just one tonight?'

'Oh I know that, Mommy,' she insisted. 'I know that Milk Duds might not come back ever again. Or Oreos or Barney the Dinosaur. So I'll share mine for real with Sophie and Anna. Because they're sad.'

'That's very generous of you,' said Kip. 'That's very good, darling . . . You go have a play now, and let Mommy and Daddy talk, okay?'

The little girl flicked on her Scooby Doo flashlight, turned on a dime, and shot away up the darkened hall to set up a tea party with her stuffed toys.

'Any chance she won't scoff them all down tonight?' asked Barb sceptically.

'Oh, she's pretty good. She did share that army chocolate with her friends.'

'And she got in trouble for it, Kip. Remember? That asshole ration Nazi at the school had her wait outside his office for an hour. A fucking *hour* . . . !'

'Okay, honey, calm down,' he said. 'It's a good thing, you know. She gets so little now. And she's so good about it. It's nice that we can still get her these little things.'

'Nice for her, Kip, but you're not here every day dealing with the neighbours and the school moms.' Her voice hitched. 'The th-things they say . . .' Tears welled up in Barb's eyes and her face creased as she leaned forward into his chest, sobbing. She was like this so often now. Brittle and prone to emotional collapse.

They stood like that, in the soft, guttering light of a half-melted candle, for nearly a minute. The house did have power, for the next two hours, but like most people they kept their energy usage to a minimum. Barb had the rice cooker plugged in on the bench, with some vegetables in the steamer basket, but that was it for appliances. They would turn on the battery-operated radio at nine for the Emergency Broadcast update, and then switch it right off again.

His wife was just calming down when three hard knocks rattled the door leading out to the porch and made them both jump. Kip left Barbara to compose herself and peeked through the curtains to see who'd come by. Visitors were a rarity these days, because of the shortages. Everyone stayed close to home. There was no mistaking the mountain-sized moonlit silhouette on the porch, however. It was his friend and former deputy, Barney Tench.

'Holy crap, Barn, what are you doing all the way over on this side of town? How'd you get the gas?'

'Can I come in?' asked Barney, with a hint of urgency.

'Sure, buddy, come in. Hey Barb, look – it's Barn. Reckon we could break out the emergency bourbon?'

Tench hustled in, keen to be off the street. 'S'okay, I don't need a drink, Kip,' he said. 'Although a glass of water would be nice.'

Barb wiped the last of her tears away and fetched him a glass from the cupboard. She drew the water from a five-gallon plastic bottle on the bench by the sink. It didn't matter how many times Kip assured her that the water supply was all right, she refused to drink straight from the tap anymore. She handed the glass to Barney, who was abashed to see that she'd been crying.

'Oh man, I hope I'm not interrupting anything?'

Barb kissed him on the cheek. 'Don't worry, Barn. I'm just being silly. Ignore me, I'll go look after Suzie. She gets lonesome in the dark after a while.'

As his wife disappeared, Kip pulled out a couple of chairs from the kitchen table. 'You sure I can't offer you a drink, buddy?' he asked again. 'Wouldn't mind one myself, the day I've had. Well, the week, really.'

Barney sat down and said no. 'I have to keep a clear head, Kip.' He paused and looked his former boss in the eyes. 'I'm sort of on the run.'

'What?'

'It's Blackstone, Kip. There's a warrant for my arrest . . . Oh man, I hope you don't mind me coming here. I don't want to get you in trouble.'

'Don't be fucking ridiculous,' Kipper shot back. 'You're always welcome in my house. But what's going on? Is this another one of his stupid fucking games? I'd have thought he'd learned his lesson after the last time.'

Tench shook his head. 'The warrant is for sedition and sabotage – for aiding the Resistance. Specifically, for cutting off the power to Fort Lewis last week.'

Kip smacked his open palm down on the scarred oak table that Barb had dragged all the way over from New York. 'Son of a bitch,' he swore. 'Those assholes at Lewis – '

'Kipper, it's *true*,' said Barney, talking over the top of him. 'I was part of that. In fact, they couldn't have done it without my help.'

'Oh.'

An awkward moment followed, a hot uncomfortable silence broken in the end by Kipper.

'Well, they're still assholes . . . So why'd you do it, buddy? You would've known you couldn't really hurt them – crews had that supply back on within hours. It's like poking a wild bear with a stick. You're gonna get your ass bit.'

Barney rubbed his face and leaned forward, elbows on the table, a picture of desolation. 'I did it because it was the right thing to do, Kip,' he replied firmly. 'Even if it seemed pointless and made things even worse for me. And my family. They cut Lorraine and the kids off support – did you know that? After I left the department, Lorraine couldn't even get the food stamps that everyone else got. We had to live off the neighbours and her family. Church helped too, for a while. Then their stamps got cut off too.'

'Damn, Barney. I'm sorry . . . I didn't know.'

'You wouldn't, Kip. You've been too busy holding this city together. And I didn't want to put you in the shit by contacting you. They've been watching me pretty closely. I meant what I said when I left: I can't collaborate with a dictatorship. But I want you to know that I think what you've done for the city, for the people, that's been great.'

'Oh come on, Barney,' Kipper said, with a hint of irritation. 'Don't piss in my pocket. That was my job. It was yours too. I respect your reasons for going, but I couldn't agree with them – for myself, you know.'

'I know. I . . . Look, I don't want to sound like a nut, but do you think we could go somewhere I can't be seen from the door?'

Kipper was nonplussed, but Barney was so agitated and so genuinely concerned that he picked up the candle and led his guest through to the sitting room. He could hear Barb and Suzie playing tea parties upstairs, and thought about calling out that it was almost time for bed. But he kept his mouth shut. Barbara would probably put Suzie down in the next half-hour or so and crawl into bed with her. She'd been doing that most nights since the Disappearance.

The sitting room was dark, and the curtains drawn. A small fire in the hearth threw a flickering glow over the room. Kip blew out the candle he was carrying and placed it on an old plate that was already scummy with melted wax. 'Welcome to the new frontier,' he said dryly.

They took seats facing each other across a glass-topped coffee table, covered with Barb's old magazines. Past editions of *New Yorker* and *Vanity Fair*, and the February and March issues of *Vogue*. None of them would ever be published again.

'Okay,' said Kip. 'What have you got yourself caught up in, Barn?'

Before answering, Tench rubbed his palms on the knees of a pair of jeans that looked like they hadn't been washed in a long time. 'Like the arrest warrant says, Kip – the Resistance. That's what they call themselves. Frankly, I think it's a dumb name, a bit too Secret Squirrel for me, but there's a hell of a lot of them out there. Normal people, you know? Some, like me, worked for the city, some used to work for the feds, lots of business people too – but *normal*, Kip. Really normal people who just don't like the way this thing, this fucking Disappearance, has been used as an excuse to mess around with stuff, to start cutting off people's freedoms.'

'But Barney, we're not free to live as we did. You can surely see that?'

Tench leaned forward. 'We're not free to run our plasma TVs twenty-four hours a day, no. We're not free to gorge ourselves to death on junk food and Vanilla Coke, *no*. We're not free to travel anywhere we want. We're not free to fill up with gas and drive out to Disneyland. We're not free from hunger or fear or the threat of being eaten alive by that fucking thing out there, whatever it is. You're right. None of those freedoms are ours to enjoy anymore. But the basic freedom, Kip – the freedom to say what you think, and to act on it, the freedom to control your own life – that is being taken from us, too.'

Kipper was going to protest, but he had been at the convention when that blow-hard mayor had moved for an amendment to reserve thirty per cent of the congressional seats for the military as an emergency measure. To ensure stability. He'd sniggered when he heard – and then been gobsmacked as one speaker after another rose to support it. And the fact was, the city was still locked down. People were living on handouts and doing as they were told. Food stamps were the new currency. The movement of people and goods was closely vetted by the military. 'Production Committees' had been set up to allocate labour and resources where they were most needed. And the local media, although able to work again, was heavily constrained by 'D Notices', issued by the Acting Governor but countersigned by General Jackson Blackstone.

'Barney,' he said, feeling very uncomfortable, 'I work with these people every day. Some of them, sure, they're sons a' bitches. I wouldn't trust them with three dollars in change. But I can guarantee you, man, they are not doing these things because they're all little Hitlers in their hearts – they're doing it because they're *scared*. They're scared we're not gonna make it.'

'We're not. Not like this. We might *survive*,' but as what? And what about you, Kip? Be honest – do you think it's a good idea to just rope off a third of Congress for the military?'

'Well, of course not, Barn,' the chief engineer admitted. 'It sucks the big one. But if you'd been there today and seen the chaos on the convention floor . . . Man, I really don't know whether that's the way to go. I just –'

A thunderous hammering interrupted him. Tench blanched, visibly so, even in the poor light, and muttered, 'Oh God.'

'Open up,' called out a harsh voice. 'It's the police.'

The two men locked eyes and a whole conversation passed between them without a word being spoken.

Kipper placed a finger to his lips and gestured for Tench to follow him, leading his friend into the hallway and pointing to a door under the stairs that led down to the cellar. Barney needed no telling. He hurried over to the door as the pounding began again.

'Open up, please. Police.'

'I'm coming,' Kipper yelled back. 'But I'm not breaking a leg for you, so you can just fucking wait.'

Barb appeared at the top of the stairs and Kip waved her back, shaking his head emphatically. There was no time to explain to her any of what Barney had just said. He could only hope she wouldn't give anything away. Kipper moved into the kitchen and deliberately banged his leg on the table, sending a glass crashing to the floor. 'Son of a bitch!' he yelled, loud enough to be heard outside.

Then, reefing open the back door, he let his natural foul temper off the leash a little, surprising the two police officers who stood there, blocking his view of a small squad of soldiers. 'This better be fucking good, and quick,' he snarled. 'I have to get up at about three in the morning tomorrow and drive out to Fort Lewis.'

One of the cops actually blinked and said, 'Oh.' The other, older one didn't take a backward step.

'Mr Kipper, eh? My name is Sergeant Banks and this is Officer Curlewis. Sorry to bother you, sir, but we're looking for agitators who've been reported in this area. We need to have a look around your place.'

'What's going on, dear?'

Barb had appeared at his elbow. 'I dunno, some crap,' he told her. 'They think we've got someone here. Want to search the place.'

'Oh, that's ridiculous.'

'I'm sorry, Mrs Kipper, ma'am,' said Banks. 'I have my orders. Do you mind?'

'Well, I do, but that's hardly going to make a damn bit of difference, is it?'

The policeman didn't bother replying to that, but he at least waited until Kip had opened the door properly, rather than forcing his way in. His partner followed and the soldiers moved up the path, until Barb held up a hand.

'I'm sorry. I don't mind the police looking around, but you boys have the filthiest shoes I've ever seen. Would you mind awfully just waiting for the officers to do whatever it is they have to do? You're welcome to stand on the porch to keep out of that drizzle, and I could make you some cocoa if you'd like. It's powdered milk, though, I'm afraid.'

A corporal raised one eyebrow at the cops, who shrugged it all off. 'Yeah, whatever,' agreed Banks. 'If you don't mind us poking around, Mrs Kipper?'

Barb smiled sweetly, firing up her long-dormant Homecoming Queen charm. 'Well, if you could try not to wake my daughter. I've just put her down, and her sleep's been very disturbed since . . . you know.'

When James Kipper's wife felt like it, she could be all eyes, tits and teeth. Even the older cop was taken in by the display. 'We'll try not to disturb her, ma'am,' promised Sergeant Banks.

They padded through the kitchen, and Kip watched with a lurching heart as the two of them headed towards the cellar door. Curlewis, the younger one, flicked on the lights as he went, forcing Kip and Barbara to flinch and squint at the fierce glow. They hadn't had the place lit up in a month.

'So, would you boys like that cocoa?' she asked brightly.

Kip's heart was racing and he felt like his guilt must be writ large on his face, but the army corporal only smiled and nodded enthusiastically at the offer of a hot drink. 'That'd be awesome, ma'am.'

'Will you be out all night?' Barb asked as she set about fixing up their cocoa. 'It's going to be terribly cold, I think. It's been so chilly and awful, hasn't it, since the Wave came?'

Her husband tried not to look concerned as the police disappeared down into his cellar. He tried to imagine where Barney might have hidden himself away down there at such short notice. The place was a mess, with dozens of packing crates from their original move to Seattle still stored down there. But really, there weren't many places a grown man could hide himself.

'Who'd like a marshmallow?' trilled Barb.

His nuts felt like they were retracting inside his body as he heard the cops shifting boxes and talking to each other down there.

'Mr Kipper? Sir? Could you come here?' It was the older policeman, the sergeant.

Giddy and shaking ever so slightly, Kip excused himself and walked down the hallway. He stopped at the head of the staircase. They hadn't been able to find the light switch and the cellar was lit by two torch beams. 'Something I can help you with?' he asked, forcing the fear from his voice.

'Yes, there is. Could you come down here, sir?'

He trod carefully, descending the steps. 'Something up?'

'Yeah,' said Banks. 'You know there's an emergency ordinance against hoarding, don't you, sir?'

Kipper almost stammered in reply. 'What?'

'You've got a lot of rations stowed down here, sir. I hope you didn't stock up recently.'

'I . . . uh . . . I . . . no. No, I didn't, Sergeant. I'm a hiker. I got those supplies about six months ago, in Spokane, when a camping warehouse closed down.'

'Got receipts, Mr Kipper?' Curlewis called out in the semi-darkness.

Completely flummoxed now, Kip could only shake his head at first. 'Uh. No . . . No, wait – I paid for them with my Visa. It'll be on the statement, if you need to see it.'

He felt like he was trapped in some absurdist Eastern European play, one of those fuck-awful theatre-of-pain things he'd seen with Barb when they first started dating. Man, the things you do to get laid.

'Okay,' said Banks. 'That'll be fine. If you could fax it through to me on this number.' He handed Kipper a card. 'I'm afraid I do have to report it, sir. But if you've got that statement you'll be okay.'

'Great,' replied Kip.

The cops gave the cellar another once-over but seemed satisfied and picked their way through the clutter back towards the stairs. Kipper moved back and aside to let them up. He could smell the heady aroma of cocoa wafting in from the kitchen and hear the muffled voices of the troops as they thanked his wife. Banks and Curlewis then checked every room on the ground floor before moving towards the staircase up to the bedrooms.

'My daughter's room is the first on the right,' said Kip softly. 'If you could just, you know, be quiet up there . . .'

The three of them stepped lightly up the stairs and carefully pushed Suzie's door ajar. She was wrapped up in her Barbie quilt, with just a tuft of hair poking out. He could see that her room, normally quite neat, was an utter shambles, with toys all over the floor and clothes strewn everywhere. Banks gestured to his younger, more agile partner to get down and check under the bed, which Curlewis did by shining a light under there.

He shook his head. 'No bogeymen. No terrorists.'

The room had no cupboards – always a source of frustration to Barb – but every drawer in Suzie's dresser was open, with items of clothing hanging out. The lid was off her jumbo toybox, which had been crammed full of furry friends, dress-up costumes and an inflatable Barney the Dinosaur.

'Sorry about the mess,' Kip whispered. 'Kids, you know.'

Banks rolled his eyes. 'I got three.'

The officers searched the other bedrooms and the bathroom,

but without success. At last, with Kip's heart fit to burst out of his rib cage, the sergeant flicked off his torch.

'Think your wife has any cocoa left?' he asked.

'There's always some to spare,' said Kipper.

They didn't stay much longer. Just another five minutes, enough time for them to throw down a hot drink before heading out into the hard chill of the night. Barb smiled and waved them all the way down the drive, keeping her mask in place until she'd come back inside and closed the door. Then her act fell apart, and she rushed to the sink and vomited up a stomachful of warm cocoa.

Kipper quickly flicked off the lights so that they couldn't be seen from outside. 'Holy shit,' he breathed. 'Where the fuck is Barney?'

'Toy box, in Suzie's bedroom. I stashed him in there. Covered in Barbies and fairy wings. God, he's so fucking big, I didn't think he was going to fit in . . . Oh man, I have never been so fucking glad we got the monster-size toy box,' she grunted before hurling again.

Barb took a few seconds to gather herself. Kipper rubbed the back of her neck. 'I told Suzie it was a game,' she said, 'that she had to pretend to be asleep . . . Oh my God, Kip, what the *hell* was that about?'

'I'd better go get the Scarlet Pimpernel and let him tell you himself,' he said.

'Better wait a while first, honey,' she replied, wiping flecks of brown drool from her chin. 'In case they come back.'

But they didn't. Kipper peeked out once and saw them knocking on the door at Mrs Heinemann's place. They seemed to be working the whole street, which gave him some confidence that he hadn't been specifically targeted.

He gave it fifteen excruciating minutes before hurrying upstairs to rescue his friend. Suzie had fallen asleep for real while Barney stayed hidden in her toy stash. His legs had cramped painfully and he'd had a lot of trouble breathing in there. He emerged with a flushed purple complexion and a plastic tiara on his head.

'You see, Kip? You see what we've been reduced to?' he said, after he'd finished gasping for air.

Kip put one finger to his lips to quiet him down. 'Don't wake Suzie. Come on, we have to get you out of here.'

'I'm sorry, Kip, I'm real sorry,' Tench whispered. 'I shouldn't have come. I'm gonna get you in trouble.'

'Just shut up, Barn, and come out of Suzie's room.'

Barb was waiting outside in the hallway, looking terrified but angry with it. 'What the hell was all that about?' she said, repeating her earlier question.

'They were looking for me,' Barney admitted, shamefacedly.

'No shit, Sherlock? What the fuck's going on, Kip? Barney?'

'Just what I said would happen,' their visitor replied. He grabbed Kipper by the elbow. 'I can't thank you enough for helping me back there, Kip. But more people need help – they need *your* help, buddy. What d'you think now?'

Kip didn't answer. He was looking at his wife's eyes.

Her frightened, haunted eyes.

46

His mother tucking him into bed, patting down the blanket and making sure that Thumper, his stuffed corduroy kangaroo, was snuggled in tight. A fire crackling in the pot-belly stove. Bret's head hanging over the edge of the bed as he stared into the flames. Heat. Smoke.

Rough hands. Cursing.

He came to in the wreck of the Land Rover, American Dave's caved-in head on his lap, as heavy as a medicine ball, spilling its glutinous contents over his legs. A dark man, without a face, rummaging in his jacket, looting his body.

No. He was alive. He stirred, and the figure jumped and swore in Arabic.

Hands closed around his throat and tightened. He gagged and tried to gulp down air, but could not. A struggle ensued, one he couldn't hope to win, as Melton shot a hand out, reaching for the man's throat notch. He missed and struck a bristled cheekbone.

Flames licked at the back of his neck and smoke poured out of the rear of the wreckage. His hand scrabbled like a giant fleshy spider and quickly felt its way up his would-be killer's face, finding an eye socket into which he dug his thumb, gritting his teeth against the inescapable revulsion as he felt it push in between the eyelid and socket.

The man screamed, rearing back and hitting his head on something. Bret could see his hands, pawing at the injury. He lifted a leg and lashed out with one boot as best he could. Not a great kick, but enough to drive the man back another foot. The former soldier twisted and attempted to pull out his pistol, but pain, white fire, in his shoulder prevented him. Dark spots bloomed before his eyes, but he turned the other way and reached around with his good hand, reaching across his body and finding the weapon at his hip. Dave's ruined head turned up to stare at him. One side of his skull had been jellied by the impact of the rocket blast. Trying not to let the gnawing, twisting rat of panic get control of his mind, Melton drew the pistol as quickly as he could, thumbed off the safety and fired two shots into the centre mass of his looter. The man flew backwards and down, hitting the pavement with a heavy thud.

Melton scrabbled at the seatbelt, only to find it was already disengaged. He had no idea how – perhaps by the man he'd just killed. He couldn't get out of the driver's-side door since American Dave was blocking the way. With his one good hand, he attempted to open his own door, but it was buckled and jammed. Ammunition began to cook off in the rear of the vehicle . . . or was that shooting from outside?

The heat was unbearable and his eyes stung with acrid smoke. He levered himself around, drew up both legs and piston-kicked the door. He was unbalanced by the ease with which it flew open, and suffered a painful blow on his shins as the door bounced back and struck him heavily just below the knee. Swearing loudly, he butt-shuffled across the seat and fell onto the cobblestone road.

The air cleared instantly, at least compared to the smoke-choked interior of the Land Rover. Left arm dangling uselessly, Melton quickly checked for the other passengers. One was obviously dead, shredded by the RPG, the other was missing. He hurried away, making for the nearest doorway.

Unsure of where they were, disoriented by the blast and probably suffering concussion, he took in his surroundings as a dizzy, discontinuous swirl of images. Burnt-out vehicles. Gutted buildings. At least four bodies in the street. A wall of four- and five-storey terrace buildings in front of him. Old but well-maintained until recently. They were now pockmarked with bullet holes and disfigured by scorch marks. He was still in the old city. Somewhere near the BBC offices, he thought – but deep inside that jigsaw puzzle of irregularly shaped city blocks to which neither the Loyalists nor Sarkozy could lay claim.

Bullets spattered and caromed off the wreckage of the Land Rover, just as the fuel tank went up with a dense, hot *whump!* Melton hobbled as fast as he could for cover. A doorway, hanging from its hinges just in front of him.

'This is the last of them,' said Caitlin. 'If he's not here, or hasn't been here, I'm tapped out, *Capitaine*.'

The French infantry officer patted her gently on the shoulder. 'You have done well,' he told her. 'Better than we could have asked. Perhaps you should let us handle this now?'

Caitlin peered out through the window of the ruined apartment, across the street from the tenement where Baumer had met with English members of Hizb ut-Tahrir on three occasions. 'No, I don't think so,' she replied eventually. 'If that fucker turns up, there'll be a reckoning between him and me.'

'You are still very weak, Caitlin. If we are to get him, it will mean a struggle.'

'I'm strong enough to pull a trigger.'

Rolland pulled her around to face him. 'We need him alive. Both him and Lacan. We need to know the extent of the School Masters' influence.'

Caitlin folded her arms and leaned against the wet, peeling wallpaper. A bomb had damaged the upper floors of this building, letting in the elements. She was wrapped in a padded army jacket but she still shivered at the unseasonable chill. Three French commandos kept watch on the street while staying well hidden from view. It had been a hellish business, just getting them into the neighbourhood, let alone into this house opposite the last of Baumer's known addresses. For two whole days they had been on his trail, using her knowledge of al Banna's networks and contact nodes. Two days of scurrying like dump rats from one ruin to the next, avoiding all contact with the enemy, both uniformed and otherwise.

She felt much stronger in mind and body than she had for a long time, although her illness still weakened her, and it would take her months to fully recover from Noisy-le-Sec. In truth, she should not have been out here, but there was no choice. She was the expert on al Banna, and that meant being in on the hunt, no matter how damaged she may have been.

A wet, dank-smelling armchair, covered in plaster and mouse droppings, sat in the nearest corner. After one more glance at the street outside, she dropped into it. She could hear sporadic firing somewhere out there and the occasional shout, but the street was relatively quiet for now. A more distant thunder spoke of the pitched battle at the edge of the park, as Sarkozy's forces attempted to break into the heart of the old city.

'He may not come,' she said, forcing the weariness she felt out of her voice.

'No,' Rolland admitted. 'Maybe not. He may have fled the city already. But we must do what we will. Would you like a coffee, Caitlin? I saw some in the kitchen before. I could have one of my men heat up some water. We may be waiting a while.'

They did. It was not until night had fallen that any significant activity returned to the street. There had been a small explosion, during the afternoon, and a cloud of dirty black smoke rose over the roofline of the buildings opposite, but nothing came of it. Just another skirmish in a city of a thousand myriad clashes. She dozed through the afternoon, fitfully, for a few hours, waking in the early evening as Rolland's men ate a cold meal of MREs. She'd been hoping the French might have had better field rations than the US version, but there was no discernible difference in quality. It was all NATO standard slop, she supposed.

'Caitlin? Come here, please.'

She came fully awake with a start, and slid from the chair like a cat. Rolland stood by the window, narrowing his eyes, peering through the lace curtain.

'Those men, do you recognise any of them?'

She peered out. At least four men, all civilians, all Arabic or African in appearance, were gathered outside the target address across and down the street a little way. It was dark outside, but some of them smoked, and as they passed around a lighter she was pretty sure she recognised a couple of faces.

One in particular stood out. Short, round-shouldered, with a potbelly. Grey stringy beard but no moustache. His skin was dark brown, as though stained by tobacco juice. He smoked hand-rolled cigarettes and in her imagination she could smell the fragrant blend. Some acne pits blemished the left side of his face, but melted skin from a homemade bomb gone wrong marred his other profile. The permanent squint to his right eye was a result of the same disfiguration. She couldn't see from here, but she knew he would have yellowed, crooked teeth, with two of the lower incisors missing, thanks to a beating from the Malaysian Special Branch five years ago. Completing the picture were his powerful forearms and thighs from years of silat and karate training.

'The chunky-looking groover in the nasty grey acid-wash jeans and cheap vinyl jacket, his name's Noordim ul Haq. He's an Indonesian. Javanese. We called him "Doctor Noo". He's a Jemaah Islamiyah commander, a bomb maker too, but not a great one, as you can see from his pretty face.'

'He is part of Baumer's network?' Rolland asked. 'I have not heard of him.'

Caitlin frowned. 'Nope. But he and Baumer have met, twice that we know of. Once in Singapore in August 1998, and in Surabaya later that year. We're not sure to what end or if they ever met again under the radar. But the Doc there is a heavy hitter in Mantiki 3, the Jemaah Islamiyah franchise with responsibility for the Philippines and central Indonesia.'

Rolland looked lost.

'Sorry,' said Caitlin. 'I can be a bit of a fucking train spotter, can't I? Noordim's CV doesn't matter, the fact he's here does. He should be about ten thousand miles away, blowing up noodle shops in Jakarta for the glory of God.'

'Well, we don't have many noodle shops in Paris anymore.'

'You never did, Marcel. Not worth a pinch of shit anyway.'

'So, this Noordim,' said Rolland softly, peeking out into the dark again, 'if he is here, there must be something important going on.'

'Dude, if he's here, it's the end of the fucking world,' Caitlin replied before realising what she'd just said. 'Oh, wait . . . We already did that, didn't we? Okay, look, it's not just delicious noodles and opportunities for mass murder that kept Noordim

in Mantiki 3. This guy, he doesn't like whitey. His father was a
mid-level official in Golkar, the guys who put the "party" into
Indonesia's one-party state under Suharto. His mother was a
singer, but more importantly a second cousin to Tuk Tuk Suharto,
the big guy's daughter. The family controlled the distribution of
kretek cigarettes in East Timor and lost it all in the Australian takeover of '99. Doctor Noo was already into the whole jihad thing by
then and his family may well have been funding him, but Timor
pushed him right over. Ruined the family and put the zap on his
head. So he really hates whitey.'

She paused and Rolland took the hint. 'But?' he said.

'But,' she continued, 'he *really* fucking hates Arabs and resents
their control of international jihad. To his way of thinking, the
Arabs never recovered from the crusader attacks after 9/11. All
of the best jihadis since then have been Asian or African, but in
the mythology of the jihad, it is the Arabs who matter. And they
make sure their little rice-eating cousins know about it, too. Our
understanding was that Noordim got ass-fucked three ways from
Sunday while he was in Afghanistan. The camel humpers really
broke his balls. His raison d'être ever after has been to see himself
acknowledged as a player of equal importance to the likes of bin
Laden and Zawahiri.'

'So he blew up noodle shops?'

'Yeah. Lots and lots of noodle shops. Apparently Allah really
fuckin' hates noodles.'

Captain Rolland smiled, an exhausted, washed-out smile.

Caitlin watched the men in the street as they moved into the
building. 'Tell your guys they need to be on the stick now,' she
said. 'They need to . . .' She trailed off as a car appeared.

Gasoline was so scarce that any moving vehicle was invested
with significance. This one, a blue Volkswagen Passat with a
cracked windscreen, appeared to be full of passengers. She
motioned Rolland over to the gap in the curtains.

As they watched, saying nothing, the car came to a halt and
all four doors opened like insect wings. Heavily armed, unshaven
young men stepped out and scanned the street. Neither Caitlin
nor Rolland moved. Nobody pointed them out or paid anything
but scant attention to the ruined building in which they stood. As

a jet screamed overhead somewhere nearby, the last of the passengers exited the rear of the Passat.

Baumer and Lacan.

Melton was lying in a child's bed, his head pillowed by a mildew-riddled stuffed elephant. The room was dark and the multi-level house empty, abandoned. Or at least it had been.

As he came awake, he heard voices on the lower floors. Men talking in a ghetto mixture of Arabic and French. He was jolted awake as all of his body's remaining adrenalin reserves sluiced into his nervous system. A cool ball of ice seemed to form in his stomach, making his balls contract and loosening his bowels.

He wondered if some friends of the man he'd killed earlier had come looking for him, but the few snatches of conversation he heard clearly seemed to be all about the civil war.

A quick scan of the room where he'd hidden out, far above the street, told him there were no obvious hiding places. He slowly, carefully, eased himself up, fearful of a creaking bed spring that might give his presence away. For the same reason, he dared not put his feet on the floor as the boards would surely creak. Instead, he lay in darkness, straining to hear whatever he could pick up. He stroked his pistol for reassurance and checked that he still had the spare mags in his vest pocket. Not that a dinky little handgun would be much help if he'd woken up in a houseful of jihadi street fighters. And really, who the hell else was left in this part of Paris?

As the minutes ticked by with infuriating slowness, his heart rate began to calm a little and he even managed to relax. Nobody had come up to check on this room. He hadn't been discovered. Indeed, there didn't appear to be anybody on this attic level of the house. But he found that hard to accept. It commanded a good view of the street below and some of the approaching roads. If this were his show, he would have put a lookout up here, even if he was just running a small gang of looters. Then again, his instructors at Ranger school had probably drilled the basics into him with more alacrity than the towel-headed loser who'd trained these guys downstairs. If trained they had ever been. Judo rolls and paintball in the forest didn't really count.

Slowly, and as quietly as he possibly could, Melton eased himself off the bed and slid across to the door. He placed his ear against the cool wood for two minutes, straining to hear anything that might indicate he wasn't alone up here. After that, he gripped the old-fashioned brass knob and turned it gently but firmly until the door clunked open. It sounded as loud as a grenade to him, but there was no discernible change in the flow of conversation from downstairs. He was able to make out a lot more of what was being said, however – not that it did him much good. The men's French was heavily accented and their Arabic so guttural and fast spoken that his very basic understanding of the language was all but useless.

Then someone spoke whom he could understand. A Frenchman, with a polished, well-educated voice. Again, Melton's French wasn't great, but he was certain this guy was giving them a pep talk. Something about how well the fight had gone in the suburbs and how they had to delay the fascist Sarkozy forces long enough to get their leaders out of this area. Or at least, that was what Melton thought he said. He simply couldn't be sure, and it made no sense. He had no context in which to frame the conversation.

It was infuriating, but there was nothing he could do about it.

'They will be here in fifteen minutes,' said Captain Rolland, referring to the back-up he'd called in. 'They are coming through the stormwater drains. There is a . . . how do you call it . . . a *man's hole* in the rear courtyard of the building two doors down.'

Caitlin snickered despite the seriousness of the situation. 'Okay. You got any floor plans?'

Rolland removed a set of drawings from a plastic tube. 'There has been some remodelling of the property in the last five years,' he explained. 'These were lodged with the city archives. I had a devil's job getting them.'

'Yeah, but God bless continental bureaucracy,' said Caitlin. 'Now, what've we got here?'

They scoped out the plans of the house across the street by torchlight on a foldout card table, in a windowless room on the second floor of their own building. It looked like it may have been used as a storeroom until recently. A few cardboard packing boxes, folded flat, remained.

The target property was not so different from the one in which they stood. Same number of floors, and a similar layout of rooms, save for the ground floor, which had been opened up into one vast living space. It was not bomb-damaged either, as far as they could tell.

'This will be very hard,' said Rolland, 'getting them alive.'

Caitlin nodded. 'Like a hostage situation, where the hostage doesn't want to come with. And he's armed.'

'We would normally train in a mock-up facility first. But there is no time.'

'You could let me go in on my own,' she offered. 'I'm renowned as a sneaky bitch, you know.'

'You are renowned as an assassin, Caitlin. I have no doubt you could make it inside. But perhaps only you would come out, *non*?'

'Perhaps,' she conceded. 'But I could make it easier for you.'

'How so?'

Caitlin explained what she would need, and although the plan was crazy, to his credit, Rolland heard her out.

When she was finished she folded her arms and shrugged. 'Captain, it is the only way I can think of to kick down the doors, kill everyone who needs killing, and maybe, *just* maybe, keep Baumer and Lacan in one piece.'

Rolland pinched his lip between thumb and forefinger, a gesture she had already recognised as his giveaway. He was thinking of betting the pot.

47

'Oh, for fuck's sake . . .'

'I am sorry, Captain, but the storm, it put much stress on the engines, yes, much stress on everything, and this can be repaired but it will take time.'

Julianne examined the length of black steel-mesh tubing that was going to kill them all. It was less than an inch thick and just a foot long and it carried coolant to one of the *Aussie Rules*'s twin 1492-horsepower Caterpillar engines. Or rather, it would have were it not disconnected and dangling uselessly, having blown as a result of running at maximum pressure for way too long. Her Sri Lankan chief engineer shook his head sadly, as though betrayed by his wife.

'How much time do you need to fix this, Pankesh?' asked Jules. 'The truth. Don't underestimate the difficulty.'

'It is a very specialised fitting, ma'am,' he said as his two Dutch offsiders crowded in behind him, both of them looking equally despondent. 'Three hours, minimum. Possibly up to five. You can run the other engine at half power, but that is all.'

She closed her eyes and breathed deeply. Her temples were throbbing. They had a break of twenty nautical miles on the *Viarsa 1*, but their pursuers would eat that distance up in two hours. They were going to have to fight.

'Okay,' she said, standing up and turning away from the mess of spilled coolant. The engine room gleamed as white as ever, but it was eerily still with the power plant shut down. 'All three of you will work on this as fast as you have ever worked on anything in your fucking lives. Got me? Maybe you'll perform miracles. First, though, each of you get to the armoury and draw yourself a weapon. If they board us, we'll need every hand we have – except for you, Pankesh. You keep working here. You don't stop until one of them comes through that door, understood?'

The Sri Lankan's frightened eyes were comically wide as he bobbed his head up and down.

'Rohan, Urvan,' she went on, 'when I give the call to repel boarders, you'll have to down tools here and come help out on deck? You understand that?'

The Dutchmen were both in their thirties, veterans of North Sea oil-rig tenders, who'd been stranded in Ecuador by the collapse of the airline carrying them home from a sex tour of Bangkok. They nodded and tried to look resolute, but she could tell neither of them wanted to leave the relative security of the engine room.

'All right, everyone. Get your weapons, then get back to work. If you can pull a miracle out of your arses we won't have to fight.'

She moved from one handhold to the next, negotiating an exit with the engineers on her tail. They'd left the storm behind twelve hours ago, but the sea was still a vista of churning, mountainous waves. At least it would make any boarding difficult. When the Dutchmen headed aft to the gym-turned-armoury, she hurried as best she could up to the main lounge, where she found Shah and Birendra engaged in the interminable process of teaching her passengers how to kill. She held on to the doorway to steady herself and beckoned Shah over when she caught his eye. He moved with fluid grace across the pitching deck, barely needing to check himself against the movement of the ship.

'Yes, Miss Julianne? The engines, they are down?'

'Yeah, and I don't think we're getting them back any time soon. How're your pupils going, Mr Shah?'

'They do well, miss,' the Gurkha replied. 'Some of the Americans have guns at home. Moorhouse the banker hunts with a shotgun – I think we should arm him with one. The others should take the M16s. They are A2 models, quite reliable. We have seventeen of them and three thousand rounds of ammunition. I would suggest creating three fire teams. Pieraro can watch over one, two of my men will take the others. Volume of fire, Miss Julianne, that will be crucial.'

Jules had to agree. Even the Yanks, who may have had pistol club or hunting experience, would never have shot at another human being – and crucially, would never have been shot at. The decks were still heaving all over the place, and she knew from personal experience that firing from one unstable platform at another usually meant missing your target. Sergeant Shah was right: best to just throw up a wall of lead.

'Okay,' she agreed. 'Your guys and Miguel will need to run those teams, otherwise we'll fire off all of our ammo and hit nothing but waves and sky. What about the crew and your chaps? What's happening with them?'

Shah looked behind him to where Corporal Birendra was instructing the Mexican children in how to reload an M16 magazine. He was making a game of it, laughing and clapping along as they pushed the rounds in. Jules shook her head sadly. What a sight.

'We have spent much time on this, Miss Julianne,' the sergeant assured her. 'I will lead the reaction force. We will have the heavy weapons, including the rocket launchers. Three RPG7s and eight warheads, deployed from the upper decks. Depending on how the enemy attempts to effect their boarding, we shall use them to interrupt the assault or interdict any heavy-weapon crews on the *Viarsa 1*.'

'Fifi's gonna be pissed off,' replied Jules with a smile. 'She loves rocket launchers.'

'Miss Fifi will lead the fire team composed of crew members. She will also suppress any heavy-weapons fire from the *Viarsa* with her machine-gun. The crew I have divided up according to their levels of competence. She will take the best of them as a reserve, holding the pool deck and providing cover over the aft sections. If needed, they have been trained to split into two sections, one to hold the pool level and the other to be deployed as needed.'

'Okay. Sounds like a plan,' agreed Jules, slightly encouraged.

'What about those kids, though? I'm really not comfortable having children in the thick of it.'

Shah shook his head, frowning gravely. 'It is a bad business, Miss Julianne. But unavoidable. They cannot run away, not in this sea state, and they are very useful. Birendra has trained them well to load and to clear blockages. They know to keep their heads down. And Miss, remember too, they are not spoilt little brats – they are village children, from the edge of the desert. They have all worked from their earliest days, and their lives have been hard, sometimes violent. They will be scared, but I think they will endure the battle more calmly than some of the others.'

She rolled her eyes. 'I know what you're talking about, Sergeant. I'm really worried about some of my bigger dilettantes just going to pieces.'

The deck dipped sharply as they slid over another crest. One of the kids that Birendra was teaching rolled himself into a ball and tumbled across the thick woollen carpet in the empty lounge, squealing with laughter.

'Now roll back, roll back, little yeti!' called out Birendra.

Jules had to admire his patience. She found the children a challenge and was more than happy to have as little to do with them as possible.

'How long until we are intercepted?' asked Shah.

'Two to three hours, depending on how hard we can push the second engine. I don't want to blow it too, though. If we get stuck without any propulsion at all, we're royally buggered.'

'Then I shall take all of the civilians outside for a live fire exercise,' the Gurkha said. 'It would be best if they hear the guns before the real shooting starts.'

'Yes, it would be,' agreed Jules. 'Who knows, it might even put off our chasers.'

It didn't, but the live fire did give her some hope and, she supposed, her charges too. Sergeant Shah gathered everyone on the boat deck at the stern and had them fire off three rounds. One individually; one in their fire teams; and one en masse. It was the latter that gave everyone some heart. Shah had assembled quite an armoury for the yacht and the roar of so many guns firing all at once was more than impressive – it was actually frightening. The youngest children, who would be having nothing to do with the fight, as agreed, were all herded inside during the exercise, but it was still loud enough to upset them. Quite a few of the adults, too, Julianne thought.

But when the single crack of thunder had dissipated on the strong ocean breeze, what remained were forty-one people, most of whom were grinning like fools.

'Bring it on!' yelled Fifi, leaping onto a diving locker and waving her ass at the small dot of the pursuing vessel. 'You want some of this? Come and get it, baby!'

The younger members of the crew laughed and grinned, and some of the Mexican village boys began smacking their own behinds and crying out 'Brinning on, *sí*! Brinning on!'

'Maybe we should be the pirates,' said the Rhino, who stood beside Jules on the pool deck, above the display. He was wearing a side arm for the first time and his eyes were hidden behind a pair of dark aviator glasses. His face was flushed, but Jules couldn't smell any rum on his breath. He was smoking, of course.

'How long, Rhino?'

'Less than an hour.'

Julianne shaded her eyes against the sun and stared at the dark shape closing with them from astern. It was about twice the size it had been when last she checked.

First blood went to Fifi. As the *Viarsa 1*, a red-hulled 2000-tonne former toothfish poacher, muscled through a seven-metre swell to put itself within a few hundred metres of the *Rules*, Fifi lay under a tarpaulin on the pool deck, tented to allow her spent cartridges to eject, with only the barrel of her Russian tripod-mounted machine gun poking out. Shah had deployed everyone to their fighting positions and then ordered them to remain under cover. The *Aussie Rules* appeared deserted as it wallowed about under reduced power.

Fifi took her time, adjusting to the relative rise and fall of the two vessels. With the *Viarsa 1* coming up astern, she had a clear view of the vessel's foredeck and bridge. She had intended to unload a magazine into the wheelhouse, hopefully cutting down some of the more important crew members, but as the distance between hunter and prey collapsed, an infinitely more tempting target presented itself. At least a dozen men, all armed, began to gather near the bow of the *Viarsa*, pointing at the super-yacht and occasionally firing the odd random shot.

Fifi waited in her little tent, patiently tracking the closely grouped cluster of men with her sights. Three times she imagined squeezing off a burst – but she held her fire, waiting to see what the arrhythmic dance of the two ships did to her aim. Once, as the *Rules* fell hard a-port into a boiling black trench, she would've missed completely. The second and third times, however, were fine.

On the fourth occasion that the two ships lined up, she was ready. The battered, rusting trawler had pulled to within two hundred metres. The boarding party had stopped firing, possibly at the behest of a large bearded man who had just rushed down onto the deck. He was yelling and gesticulating, obviously warning them to move away. The eerie quiet of the *Rules*, the complete lack of any movement on deck, had apparently unnerved him. The poacher heaved itself over a line of black swell, shot through with streaks of dirty foam, just as the *Rules* began to climb a wall of water large enough to steady the yacht's ceaseless tossing from side to side. For three precious seconds, while the trawler slid down the face of the wave behind, Fifi enjoyed a relatively stable platform and an exposed, slow-moving target as the shooters headed back inside with great difficulty.

She breathed out and squeezed the trigger.

The PKM began its harsh industrial jackhammering and lines of tracer arced out across the ocean to kiss the bow of the *Viarsa 1*. She had a 200-round box mag loaded with Russian-standard 7.62 rifled cartridge and tracer. The long, whipping line of light ribboned across the gap between the ships almost instantly and tore the men apart. She fired in three separate bursts, as hot spent casings bounced off the tented tarpaulin and stung her whenever they touched exposed flesh. Only two of her prey survived. The bearded man who had rushed onto the deck to warn his comrades of the danger they faced, and another who dived for cover as soon as her first target disintegrated in a shower of blood and body pieces.

She noticed a twinkling light on the roof of the wheelhouse and rolled off her perch a split second before the tarpaulin was chewed to pieces by the line of return fire.

... *whump whump* ...

Two lines of grey smoke reached out for the *Viarsa*'s twinkling star, which disappeared inside twin explosions as the rocket-propelled grenades detonated, taking out the machine-gun. Fifi heard another snarling burst of automatic fire and wondered whether Shah or one of his men had also targeted the bridge, as she had intended to. Belly-crawling to her next firing station, where Dietmar waited with a fresh box of ammunition, she didn't dare put her head up to look.

The *Rules* was now taking fire from the length of the trawler.

Sergeant Narayan Shah, formerly of Her Majesty's Royal Gurkha Rifles, had disposed of his resources very well. Five independent fire teams, providing coverage for the length of the super-yacht, with the least experienced or reliable provided with the best cover.

Peering at the *Viarsa 1*, he had to wonder who was running things over there. As soon as Fifi had opened up on the fo'c'sle, more men had emerged from the rear of the wheelhouse and begun to spread out on the aft decks, taking cover here and there, and firing in an uncoordinated, indiscriminate fashion. *Stupid fishermen*, he thought again. His teams, all run by his own men or Pieraro, worked in concert and directed their fire onto specific targets.

'Blue barrels, aft,' he called out, and his shooters sent a torrent of gunfire into the rear of the ship, where two men had just popped up and started firing at the bridge of the *Aussie Rules*. One of the targets flipped over backwards as a dark fan of blood painted the white crane nearby. The other dropped straight down and didn't reappear.

Puffs of smoke appeared and the occasional tracer zapped across, punching into the aluminium skin of the yacht with a terrible clang.

'Smoke stack, aft,' Shah called out again, sending a lethal stream of automatic-weapons fire across the gulf between the ships. A distance, he noted, that was narrowing rapidly.

Armed with her trusted shotgun, Jules crouched in the entrance to the bridge, watching Mr Lee as he hunkered down and attempted to steer them away from the *Viarsa 1* with only limited power. He was also handicapped by having to keep his head below the line of the windows lest he get shot. Dozens of rounds had already smashed through the glass and wounded the Rhino, who was bleeding heavily from one arm, cursing up a storm and puffing rapidly on a new Davidoff.

'Apologies, Miss Julianne,' Lee cried out, as the whole ship rang like an iron bell.

The other vessel had just struck them broadside.

In her headset, Fifi's voice came through. 'Here they come, Julesy. Lots of them.'

'On my way.'

'Shoot them down!' said Pieraro, without any urgency or, he hoped, trace of fear in his voice as he spoke the words in Spanish. It was difficult to contain his marauding emotions, however. He was not leading some band of old seadogs or hardened mercenaries. His little fire team was composed entirely of men and boys from the village, and now they were fighting for their lives.

'As they climb across, shoot them down,' he repeated. 'Do not linger. Stand up, shoot and drop down again.'

His small group of fighters, six in all, did as they were told and had been taught, popping up and firing short bursts at the Peruvians, before scuttling like bugs to another hiding place. Miguel himself snapped up his M16 and squeezed off short bursts whenever a slow-moving Peruvian exposed himself. Well, he assumed they were *peruanos* . . . It was possible they might have been from anywhere.

All that mattered now, however, was that a small army of them appeared to be boiling up from the innards of their ship and attempting to board the ship where his family sheltered. Some threw grappling hooks and thick lines across. Others darted from cover as the two vessels banged together and they attempted to leap from one to the other. He flinched as one man missed his jump and fell between the converging vessels. The crunch of steel plate on aluminium was slightly muffled as his body was pulped by the collision. Pieraro could not help but see the flattened remains peel away from the flanks of the trawler and fall into the sea.

'They are getting on board!' cried Adolfo, one of the older men.

'Stay where you are. Keep firing. The others will take care of them,' yelled Miguel.

'The boat deck!'

Jules hurried up behind the racing forms of two Gurkhas as they headed aft to repel the first of the intruders. Doubled over to remain below the line of the gunwale, she moved as quickly as she could but had trouble keeping up with them. The uproar of the battle was enormous, much worse than anything she'd experienced before. Bullets whined and pinged around her, chewing huge pieces out of the yacht's superstructure. She kept her head down. And all the time, the vessel lurched up and down, dancing drunkenly on the huge waves.

A grappling hook clanged down in front of her and bit deeply into the fibreglass walls of the gunnel. She didn't stop to look, instead whipping out her machete and slamming the weapon down on the line as she passed. An ululating scream fell away into the churning maelstrom and Jules moved on to where she could hear the bark of automatic weapons starting up.

She found the two Gurkhas, Sharma and Thapa, taking cover behind a couple of jet skis and engaging at least three boarders who'd leapt across and hidden themselves behind one of the smaller runabouts. 'Coming up behind,' she cried out over the savage din.

'Please cover us from behind,' Thapa yelled, and Jules dropped low, aiming her shotgun back up the exposed passageway along which she had just run.

Less than two seconds later a man swung over the rail and dropped to the deck. She registered him as young, dark and rake-thin; he was wearing cut-off (or possibly rotted) denim shorts and his naked torso was covered in swirling, amateurish tattoos. Jules cut him down with one blast from the shotgun, tearing a football-sized chunk of meat from his stomach and rib cage.

Behind her, she heard the Gurkhas scream something, but could not turn – as another man dropped to the deck beside his fallen mate. The *Rules* pitched over, and before she could shoot him, he tumbled back into the sea with a terrified scream.

A quick look over her shoulder, and she saw a chromatic, disordered flicker of scenes. Thapa and Sharma leaping at the intruders with kukri daggers drawn. A flash of silver blade. Gouts of blood. A shot, and Thapa flying backwards and slamming into the side of the sport fisher.

Then movement in front of her again – two of them this time. The yacht plunged and her shot went high and wild. Their guns cracked and spat at her.

She racked another round into the shotty and squeezed the trigger again. The first man flew backwards as she fired twice without success. The dead man's body shielded his mate. She was going to run out of ammunition before she finished him.

A thunderclap and a spray of wet, organic matter.

Both pirates dropped to the deck.

Jules blinked and saw Denby Moorhouse, the banker, stick his head out of a hatchway and look her way. His grin was feral and he pumped his fist twice. 'Yessss!'

She flinched as bullets stitched up the hatchway and Moorhouse disappeared.

Fifi had lost two of her crew already. Dietmar was gone, shot in the throat. One of the engineers, Rohan or Urvan – she could never remember which was which – had died as soon as he'd stepped outside. She had two men left: a wounded Rhino, who had joined her from the bridge, and the surviving half of Rohan and Urvan. She was also out of ammunition.

No more boarders were pouring out of the *Viarsa 1*, but from the sounds of the struggle on the lower decks, there had to be more than enough of them on the *Rules* already.

'Rhino, your arm's fucked – gimme that 16, would you?' she yelled over the noise.

The old Coast Guard man readily handed over the weapon. His left arm dangled uselessly at his side, dripping blood through a makeshift tourniquet, and his normally ruddy complexion was grey. Fifi led them aft again, hunkered over, shuffling forward until they could pour fire down on the boat deck.

Popping up quickly, she spied Jules and one of Shah's men guarding a fallen Gurkha with about half-a-dozen boarders closing in on them. The conditions were so rough there was no point attempting to pick them off with single shots. She pointed to a couple of the boarders and indicated to Rohan, or Urvan, that he should draw a bead on them. Only then did she cry out: 'Julesy. Heads down, babe!'

She bobbed up and fired.

Dropped.

Moved, popped up and fired again.

She'd cleaned four of them up when a single bullet from the wheelhouse of the *Viarsa 1* blew out her brains.

Jules was out of ammo, curled up in a ball, under one of the boats with Sharma. The Gurkha was edging forward with his kukri dagger. A small lake of blood, thinned only slightly by salt water, sloshed about the deck. She gripped her machete and followed him as he advanced on a pair of bare, filthy feet a couple of metres away.

They were within an arm's length, close enough to see all of the open sores on the man's deep brown, stringy calves, when the shooting seemed to reach a crescendo. The feet lifted off the deck and a body, riddled with bullets, crashed down on top of a coil of rope. A few isolated, individual shots followed, and then silence.

She had no idea who had carried the day until she heard Pieraro's voice.

'Miss Julianne?'

48

Dawn rose over Guantanamo Bay, a blood-red shroud for the silent battlefield. Ships still burned in the water and wrecked aircraft smouldered on the airfield over which the flag of Venezuela now flew. Few civilians remained on the craft in the bay. Over four thousand had been rounded up and herded out onto the salt flats beyond the base perimeter, where they sat in the sun, surrounded by soldiers and marines of the Venezuelan armed forces.

In the base commandant's office, never truly his to begin with, Brigadier General Tusk Musso stared at his opposite number, who was seated behind a desk that wobbled precariously. It had been damaged in the fighting, and every time General Alano Salas leaned on it, the entire surface tilted. It made for a slightly ridiculous pantomime, but Salas seemed to think it important that he should be able to sit behind Musso's desk.

Lieutenant Colonel Stavros sat to Tusk's left, sporting a bandage over one eye, while two aides to the Venezuelan commander stood behind the desk, flanking Salas at each shoulder. They were armed. The Americans were not. Next to the shattered window, a Venezuelan soldier was recording the meeting with a large shoulder-mounted camera.

Musso tried to remember who, exactly, had been the last American general to surrender on a battlefield. General Lee was the most notable example, but hardly the last. If memory served correctly, he was reasonably certain that General Jonathan

Wainwright was the last man to surrender. He had an untenable situation as well, at Corregidor, after old Dugout Doug slipped away for Australia.

General Salas scribbled something onto a pad, signed it and looked up. 'My terms for the cessation of hostilities are explicit, General Musso. Unconditional surrender of all forces in Guantanamo Bay.'

Salas presented the piece of paper with a flourish. Musso wondered why he'd bothered to write down such a simple thing. For the National Museum in Caracas, perhaps. Hugo Chávez had cracked down hard on his country, but it was one of the few nations in South America still functioning, which made the Venezuelan president a major power in the hemisphere now. Perhaps *the* major power, for the foreseeable future. He would want this piece of paper for the archives. The marine officer ignored it.

'And what about safe passage for my civilian population?'

'Unconditional surrender, sir,' Salas insisted. 'I shall accept nothing less.'

Musso shook his head. 'That is unacceptable.' He then leaned forward, and the two men on either side of Salas shifted their stance perceptibly. 'Allow me to explain what will happen if you do not agree to negotiate,' Musso continued. 'While my tactical situation is untenable and deteriorating, my ability to resist is not. I extended an offer of a ceasefire entirely out of concern for my refugee population, whom you have deliberately targeted in violation of the laws of war . . .'

Salas glanced over his shoulder and appeared to consider saying something to the cameraman, but turned back to the American instead. 'That is a despicable lie,' he countered.

Musso sat back and shrugged. 'You're not the only one with a camera, General Salas. Returning to the matter at hand, however, I have dispersed my remaining forces throughout the base and surrounding area. The better part of a Marine brigade – three thousand armed men, including a component of special operations – capable personnel. You have not had much luck locating the majority of them as of yet.'

'We will.'

'I seriously doubt that. You will provide a guarantee of safe passage for the civilian population out of Guantanamo Bay. Furthermore, you will provide – '

Salas slammed his hand down on the desk, causing it to tip over again and spill a couple of pens onto the floor in front of the American officers. 'Surrender is to be unconditional, General Musso!' he shouted.

Musso raised his voice and continued. 'You *will* provide safe passage for our military personnel. In return, we will surrender our remaining holdings in Cuba.'

'We already hold your remaining holdings in Cuba.'

Musso jerked his thumb at the shattered window behind him. 'Three thousand of my Marines say you don't. And if they do not hear from me within the next twelve hours, this marvellous silence we have enjoyed will come to an end. More to the point, the United States will not rest until the civilian population of this facility is evacuated to safe harbour. Those three thousand will be joined by other forces within days.'

Salas laughed. Partly it was forced, but not entirely. 'The United States does not exist, you stupid man,' he replied. 'Where have you been this last month? You do not make threats anymore. The Muslims were chasing you out of their lands before your Jewish friends murdered them all. Just as we shall chase you out of our territory now. Your threats are empty and worthless.'

Musso reacted with another shake of his head. 'Really? General Salas, I'll be the first to admit we're down. However, we still have the bulk of our navy. We have our submarines and the majority of our armed forces were deployed overseas when the Disappearance took place. We are still strong, stronger than you will ever be. And *we will not leave anyone behind, sir.*'

'It is an empty threat.'

Musso decided to push his luck. 'You have raised the issue of what the Israelis did recently,' he began. 'They had less than two hundred nuclear weapons. We, my friend, have far more than that, and more to the point, we really do not need your oil anymore.'

Leaning forward again, Musso invested his voice with all of the growling threat he could muster. 'How many ballistic-missile submarines does the Venezuelan navy have, General Salas?'

Stavros looked as if he was holding his breath. Musso rolled on.

'You tell that little cocksucker *el presidente* of yours that if we do not get acceptable terms, we will atomise every major population centre in Venezuela by the end of the day.'

Salas turned pale. 'I . . . I-I'll need to consult my superiors,' he stammered.

'You do that.'

PACOM HQ, PEARL HARBOR, HAWAII

With Tommy Franks back in the top job, Admiral Ritchie found that many of the political calls he'd recently had to make could be passed up the line to his superior – a situation for which he was entirely grateful. He had even managed to get home for more than four hours and have a meal with Amanda this week, after which they'd spoken on the phone with Nancy, their daughter, for a few short but precious minutes. She was staying with a couple of college friends in Edinburgh, sharing an apartment rather than braving one of the American refugee camps in the south of England. It was a blessed relief to hear her voice again. It meant that he could set aside personal worries and concentrate on his much greater professional ones.

Ritchie had his hands full coordinating refugee flows throughout the Pacific, while standing watch over the strategic situation in Asia – a fancy way of saying he was holding his breath and watching the collapse of China and the north-east Asian economies, hoping it wouldn't spill over into the wider world. His ability to do anything about it was disappearing fast. He simply couldn't sustain the Pacific Fleet for much longer, even with the help of allies such as Japan, who were themselves teetering on the brink of collapse.

But Tusk Musso's gambit had dragged him right back into the centre of a purely political question. Would he be party to authorising a strategic interdiction? Damn the euphemisms, call it what it was: a nuclear attack.

deny it. That's one of the things that's changed: I don't have to give a damn anymore. Just tell him.'

Ritchie stood quietly in the underground command centre, listening to Franks as he talked on the phone to the American Ambassador in Venezuela. *Now, there's a job I'm glad I didn't get stuck with*, he thought.

Many of the screens in the room were blank, the workstations unmanned. Just behind Franks, a navy commander silently updated the positions of three Ohio-class ballistic-missile submarines in the south Atlantic, moving their pins on an old-fashioned paper map. All three were well within striking distance of Caracas. One of them, the *Tennessee*, had only just responded to flash traffic, having been silent since 14 March. There were two other boomers lurking somewhere in the Atlantic right then as well, but they had flatly refused Franks's request to put some bite into Musso's bluff, citing the launch protocol, line and verse. *Only the President of the United States, using the correct and verified launch codes . . .*

It didn't matter. They really only needed the ordnance of one Ohio-class submarine.

Franks appeared to be listening to some long and winding passage of dialogue from Ambassador Shapiro but then cut him off. 'Look. I can see this is getting us nowhere, Mr Ambassador. Can I suggest you take cover, sir? Franks out.' He hung up and turned to Ritchie. 'Do it.'

The admiral picked up a phone. He had expected his voice to sound shaky but it was remarkably steady. 'This is Ritchie,' he said. 'Patch me through to the *Tennessee*.'

General Alano Salas nodded and hung up his phone. 'It is not acceptable,' he told Musso. 'You impugn our honour with the very suggestion. To promise that we will not attack you as you flee, to imply that we would even consider such a thing, is to traduce our national reputation. Our very manhood.'

Musso would have snorted in derision but he was haunted by the awful sight of that C-5 spilling its precious human cargo into the night. So many children, hundreds of them. Their deaths had been confirmed by the light of dawn. It was a sight so gruesome he would never be free of it. What terror must have attended their last moments on earth? If he had been wearing a side-arm, the general's brains would probably be dripping down the wall behind him right now.

'Do not talk to me of your honour,' he said, slowly and carefully enunciating each word. 'I have seen your honour and it is a poor ragged fucking thing, which barely hides the crude ugliness of your intentions and deeds. The lowest of my Marines could not wipe his ass clean with your honour, General Salas. It would not be worth the effort of the rubbing. Now, I suggest you stop fucking everyone around and agree to what is a very reasonable request.' Musso looked at his watch. 'Time is running out.'

Salas regarded him with lidded eyes, a snake sizing up a scorpion for its dinner, weighing up the risks. 'And how long do you imagine that the civilians we are holding, some four thousand of them, I believe, how long do you think they will survive in any . . . cross-fire?'

Musso sneered openly. 'Those people are in your care, General,' he replied, 'and I would warn you to have a care for their safety. You, and every man under your command, will be held personally responsible for their fate. You keep telling me that things have changed, and you are right. There will be no diplomatic solution to this question, no Security Council meetings, no backroom deals – if you hurt them you will be hunted down. Your men will be hunted down. And your country will be laid to waste.'

'I think you overestimate yourself, General Musso. You are not the power you once were.'

'No. We're not,' said Musso. 'We're something infinitely worse now.'

'Active track, package inbound,' a staff officer announced. 'One minute to impact.'

Ritchie watched the centre-left screen, which showed a view of Caracas from the roof of the American Embassy. The Venezuelan capital sat high up in a valley of the Cordillera de la Costa Central, separated from the shores of the Caribbean by a ten- to twelve-mile stretch of national park. On a linked display, the ocean could be seen in a wide-angle shot sourced from the international airport, which lay on the water's edge in the smaller city of Maiquetía, a short distance away. The image looked benign, a pleasant scene of blue water and a few plodding boats. Ritchie wondered if there were people down by the water, taking in the fresh air. He didn't recall Caracas being famous for any beaches. The embassy had reported that the streets of the capital were not overly crowded, although there was a heavy and obvious military presence. But there was none of the violence and chaos that was rampant throughout so much of South America, or Europe for that matter.

Nobody in the command centre spoke. Ritchie could hear the blood rushing through his own head. It seemed perverse that he had just unleashed a nuclear warhead. It could not be real.

At 0706 hours a second sunrise blossomed out over the horizon from Maiquetía, as three bright flashes, one at a time, flared up, twenty miles offshore on the satellite feed.

'All weapons delivered, Admiral.'

The Venezuelan general looked ill as he put down the phone.

'S-s-afe passage out of the region is . . . assured, General Musso,' he said. 'But this isn't over. My government assures me that this isn't over.'

'It'd better be over,' Musso replied, rising from his seat. 'The next time it won't be warning shots. Good day.'

49

Caitlin wormed her way through the crawl-space, feeling nauseous and claustrophobic. The attic was a constricted geometric tangle of wooden beams, hundreds of years old, rendered into opalescent green by her borrowed night-vision goggles. She'd had three days to recover since her liberation from the cell, but at least two of those days she had spent on the move with Rolland and his small team, creeping through hostile territory, backtracking through a year's worth of surveillance of Bilal Baumer. Tight spaces had never bothered her before, but her heart felt as though it was being squeezed by a giant rubber band. Yet another symptom of her physical decay.

And so it came to this, as always. Caitlin Monroe, on her own, inching carefully towards her prey in the dark.

She'd reached the little access panel after an hour of snaking through the roof spaces along the line of tenements, ending up here at the four-storey house where Baumer and his companions were holed up. Her watch read 2.13 am, and although she could hear the rumble of a great battle in the distance, and even sense it vibrating up through the structure of the four-storey house, down below her, all seemed quiet. She had no idea what Baumer and his men were doing down there. Chances were, it was just a lay-up point, a place to regroup before escaping the city.

Caitlin adjusted her headset and hit the push-to-talk button on the secure digital radio. 'In position,' she reported quietly.

Rolland's voice came back in a brief crackle. 'No discernible movement inside. One guard at the front door. Sniper has him marked.'

'I'm going in.'

She cut the connection and carefully lifted the wooden panel, just a crack, giving her access to a hallway on the top floor. By threading through a thin black fibre-optic wire plugged into a hand-held display, she was able to recon the hallway. It was clear.

Caitlin removed the hatch and took a length of rope from the heavy utility belt she wore over her black coveralls. Then, tying it to a beam, she rappelled down silently and took a moment to orient herself, imagining Rolland's floor plans overlaid onto the glowing green setting in front of her. A narrow corridor leading to a stairwell. Two doors on the left, both closed.

A silenced handgun and a fighting knife appeared in her hands.

She glided over to the first door and inserted the fibre-optic wire through the old keyhole. The room appeared to be deserted. She turned the knob. Hinges creaked horribly and she sidestepped, bringing up the pistol. For two minutes she stood, ready to cut down anyone who appeared, but there was nobody inside.

She moved on and repeated the routine. This time her pulse accelerated, as the optic display unit showed her a low-light amplified image of a man, crouched in the corner of the room, pointing a pistol at the door.

A large caucasian male, with head and arm wounds field-dressed using torn bed sheets, if she was not mistaken. He seemed to be straining to hear any sound that might give away the position of someone in the corridor. Caitlin checked her exposure. Crouched low as she was, off to the side of the door, she was safely out of his line of fire. He was aiming for the centre mass of anyone who walked through the door.

Fuck.

With no idea who he was, or what he was doing there, the man was a complication she did not need. There was no going in and taking him down, though. This guy was primed for trouble.

She took a moment to examine him in the display screen again. He had a good firing position and held the gun as though it were an extension of his body. He didn't look nervous, self-conscious, or likely to hesitate if he needed to shoot.

He was clean-shaven, and wearing the sort of vest she'd often seen on press photographers. The image was not sharp, unfortunately, but in his pockets, she thought she could make out a notepad, some pens and possibly a small dictaphone, the sort of thing that took little micro-cassettes. If only she could've seen the back of his vest, there might have been an identifying logo or something. A lot of reporters used reflective tape to spell out 'PRESS' or the acronym of their media affiliates on their backs. Caitlin always thought that just made them easier targets, but journalists were weird. They had some fucked-up ideas.

She had to come to a decision quickly.

The man was almost certainly not part of the group downstairs. He was trapped in the room, doubtless due to their unexpected arrival. There was probably no way of getting in there without him firing off half a mag at the door.

She decided to leave him in place.

He disappeared from the screen as she withdrew the fibre-optic wire. For thirty seconds she crouched, waiting, but no sound or movement came from within. That was actually kind of impressive. This guy was no amateur – but he was not necessarily an ally either.

She began to edge away, eventually making the stairs, where she stood, adjusting herself to the sounds, to the feel of the house. It felt like an inhabited dwelling, but that wasn't down to any bullshit sixth sense. She already knew the lower floors were occupied. What she didn't know was where her targets were holed up.

She listened, willing her nausea to recede to the edge of her consciousness, breathing as she had been taught, to settle her nervous system.

She could hear the angry rumble of battle. A jet aircraft shrieking low to the west.

The creaking and settling of the building as the ground underneath moved fractionally in response to the pounding of high explosives and the grinding of heavy armour through streets no more than a mile away.

A radio, playing Arabic music.

Snoring. Some muttering, but not conversational – probably someone talking in their sleep.

The clink of china cups or glasses.

Quiet laughter.

And then a ringing in her ears, which had been constant for two weeks. Her pulse and heartbeat. The silent advance of the tumour that was eating her from the inside out.

Caitlin floated down the stairs, using a technique she had studied under the Ninjutsu master Harunaka Hoshino, who had trained her to cross a nightingale floor with a minimum of noise. There was no way to eliminate the singing of the boards, but Hoshino taught her to quieten its chirping. The stairs of the old French residence were no challenge after that.

She paused on the second last step. The house was dark, the power grid having failed long ago, but with her NVGs she could make out a weak, fluttering light emanating from under two of the four doors on this floor. She stilled herself, becoming as stone-like as a human being could, and opening all of her senses wide to let the world rush in.

She smelt old food. Meat gone cold. And coffee.

A body shifted and rolled over on the floor nearby, lifting up slightly, and settling back down with a light thump.

A sheet or blanket rustled.

A wind-up clock ticked.

In one of the lighted rooms a page turned.

Every hair on Caitlin's body bristled, in an ancient autonomic response to danger – a hangover from her animal ancestors.

She glided down the hallway to the door behind which she knew at least one man was awake and reading. Again, she settled into stillness and allowed the life of the building – just a soft heartbeat and a murmured breath here, at this dead hour – to flow into her.

Another page turned and she heard mumbling in Arabic from the same room: *'O ye who believe! When ye meet the Unbelievers in hostile array, never turn your backs on them. If any do turn his back to them on such a day – unless it be in a stratagem of war, or to retreat to his own troops – he draws on himself the wrath of Allah and his abode is Hell, an evil refuge indeed.'*

Caitlin visualised the small room on the other side of the door. A single bedroom, probably given to a child in happier days. A window overlooking the street behind. No connecting doors to either room beside it.

She examined the handle. An old-fashioned brass knob without a keyhole. There could be a latch on the other side, but of that she could not be certain.

There was only one thing for it. Caitlin sheathed her fighting knife. Powered down and raised her night-vision goggles. And waited.

The mumbling and page turning continued.

She stood, motionless, for six minutes until her opportunity arrived – another jet, roaring close overhead within a mile. As the whining howl reached its maximum intensity, she calmly reached out, opened the door, got a sight picture of one man – young and shirtless, sitting up in a small bed, leaning against a pillow, reading, and then looking up at her, all innocence and dawning bewilderment as the assassin raised a hand-tooled, frequency-shifting silenced pistol and squeezed the trigger twice.

Two muted clacks, almost like a stapler, and the subsonic .300 Whisper rounds left the muzzle of the weapon at about 980 feet per second, slowing only fractionally as they entered his brainpan and scattered the contents all over the room.

She swept the space automatically, but already knew it to be empty. A quick puff to blow out his candle, after which she pulled the door closed and turned down towards the next lighted room.

This one was silent. No muttering. No page turning. Again she waited.

Closer to the stairwell this time she could hear at least three voices down on the ground floor. Two spoke in rapid-fire Arabic; one was slower, polished, but heavily accented. *Lacan.*

Okay, that was a bitch. She'd been hoping to find him in bed, but filtering out his voice, she did determine that Baumer's German accent was not part of that conversation, which was the only talking in the house at the moment.

Caitlin returned to her vigil at the door. The flutter of a light leaking out told her there was a candle inside. She concentrated, leaning her ear to the wooden panelling, and waiting. After three minutes she was rewarded with a brief snore.

No jet fighters conveniently appeared to cover the sounds of murder this time. But when the voices downstairs rose and broke into laughter, she was able to repeat her actions of a few minutes earlier. Coolly opening the door, lining up a head shot, and double-tapping her victim – a slightly overweight, balding man who had fallen asleep with a pair of headphones plugged into an iPod. His body shuddered violently as the 250-grain bullets shredded his neocortex. Dousing this second candle, she plunged the floor back into darkness before refitting the NVGs.

Two other rooms remained on this level. According to the building plans, they were larger, possibly capable of taking more than one small bed. Caitlin moved to the door through which she could hear the loudest snoring.

She sniffed and caught the faintest trace of an earthy, familiar smell . . . *Kif.* A highly concentrated cannabis resin, popular among North African fighters. That was enough for her to take a calculated risk, unshipping the fibre-optic set and sliding the wire under the door for a quick scan of the room.

Inside she found three men, all asleep on the floor. There being no beds or other furniture, they had balled up clothes or used their bags to serve as pillows. Caitlin observed them until she was certain they were deeply asleep. She withdrew the surveillance device, and then quietly swapped out her mag, which unfortunately only ran to six rounds. It was one of the drawbacks of using the bespoke no-name handgun.

This time, however, she kept the goggles powered up as she eased through the door and closed it behind her, covering the three prone forms all the time. A damp towel lay on the floor and she carefully toed it along the gap between the bottom of the door and the floorboards.

Then she quickly and methodically executed every man in the room.

Only the last one came awake, and then only enough to prop himself up one elbow and squint into the darkness. His sudden movement put her aim off and the first bullet struck him in the throat. Caitlin took two silent steps towards him and cut off his gargling death rattle with her last shot.

A hard, steel spike of pain was drilling into her head from a point about an inch behind her left eye, intensifying her nausea and giddiness. She took a precious minute to centre herself, to breathe deeply and detach from the barbed emotional tendrils of her bloody work.

The last of her six-shot magazines went into the pistol and she replaced the suppressor with a new one taken from a slot on her belt. The silencers, unique to Echelon wetwork cells, relied on a customised combination of austenitic nickel-based superalloy baffles, foam wipes and carbon nanotube mesh to reduce the sound of weapon fire by diverting and cooling the hot, rapidly expanding gases created by the detonation of the gunpowder. After she had burnt out this one, she would have to rely on her knife for silent killing.

She drifted to a halt in front of the next door. Another darkened room, outside which she waited for a minute before threading through the optical fibre again. When the display lit up this time, her heartbeat jumped.

She could see Baumer, asleep on a mattress on the floor. Lying next to him was a woman she did not recognise. The woman had one leg draped over his thigh and a thin arm lay across his chest.

Billy, Billy, Billy, she thought. *Monique was too good for you, buddy.*

Caitlin removed a one-use syringe from a leather pouch at her hip, uncapped the needle-point and pressed the plunger until a small stream of fluid squirted out.

Lacan was talking downstairs. In French now, cursing Sarkozy as a fascist and a half-Greek Jew, a comment that gave rise to an animated rant by one of his companions about the Jewish state and the revenge that was coming its way.

Seizing the opportunity, she entered the room, and came face to face with the woman, who had awoken and sat up. Her wide eyes searched the darkness, bulging when she saw Caitlin's outline: a silhouetted figure in black overalls, wearing night-vision gear and carrying a weapon. She was dead before she could scream, two bullets taking the top of her skull off and painting the wall behind them.

Baumer came awake instantly and rolled out from under the falling corpse, crying out as he did so. He launched himself at Caitlin's knees and knocked her back off her feet with a crash. She drove the syringe into his neck and squeezed, smashing the butt of her pistol up against his head for good measure. It didn't knock him out, but it stunned him enough to allow her to piston a boot into his chest and push him away from her.

'Crusaders,' he shouted. 'Hurry, they're here!'

He tried to launch himself at her again, but the fast-acting drug had already robbed him of any coordination and he fell like a drunk into a heap at her feet.

'Not so tough now, are you, you rapist motherfucker?' she said before hitting the PTT button on her headset and speaking loudly. 'I'm blown, Rolland. I got Baumer. Third floor, first room on the left coming up. Possible civilian above us, armed. Hostiles below. Lacan is awake and unsecured.'

'You . . .' muttered Baumer mushily as he collapsed into a drugged stupor.

Caitlin heard the French commandos open fire on the ground floor. The guard out the front would be dropping to the ground, dead before he hit. Below her, the sounds of riot and tumult erupted as men awoke and reached for their guns, unsure of what was happening, but certain they were in mortal peril.

She holstered the silenced pistol and pulled her personal weapon around on its strap, an HK MP5. Feet thundered up the staircase below her and she darted from the room, all concern at stealth now departed. The house had no power, but torches and electric lamps dazzled in her NVGs. She loosened off two bursts from the submachine-gun down the stairs at the bobbing, moving sources of light. Two of the torches tumbled back down, while the third stopped and dropped as the man carrying it let go.

Fire came back up at her, automatic and single shot, describing beautiful emerald traces in her enhanced night vision. She stripped a hand grenade from her belt, while firing one-handed down the staircase, pulled the pin with her teeth – painfully cracking a filling as she did – and tossed the small bomb into the maelstrom below. She closed her eyes, backing away and firing blindly.

The grenade exploded with a roar, causing the spike of pain already drilling into her head to grow cruel thorns that raked at the back of her eyes and drove jagged spears deep into her brain stem.

Caitlin pitched over and vomited. 'Son of a bitch,' she grunted, struggling to regain her feet.

The volume of fire downstairs was deafening, drowned out only by the deep bass percussion of exploding grenades on the ground floor. The boards beneath her shook and shuddered so much she feared they might collapse. And still she couldn't get up. Her head spun as though she'd stepped off a fairground ride, and she could not control her weapon anymore. Two figures appeared at the top of the stairs, one of them the squat, powerful outline of the man she called Dr Noo.

He raised his weapon at her, a FAMAS assault rifle, and cried, 'Allahu Akbar!' – just before his face exploded and he toppled backwards onto the man behind him.

'Quick, come with me!'

A voice, coming from above her ... It was unfamiliar, but unmistakably American.

'Who the fuck ... ?' She gagged and choked again on a mouthful of bile, toppling sideways as she tried to stand. 'Can't go,' she protested. 'My target.'

'Leave him!'

The stranger, the man upstairs, leapt down beside her, stripped the MP5 from her grip and wrested a fresh magazine from the utility belt. He swapped out the mag in the dark without any trouble and moved over to the stairs to fire down on any approaching attackers. Three more grenades exploded in close succession and the uproar of automatic fire became unbearable.

Caitlin felt herself falling away into darkness.

50

No civilised man should ever be awake at this hour, thought Jed, as he waited in the darkened office for his last meeting of the night. Not unless he had a bottle of good champagne in one hand and a couple of exotic dancers in the other.

He stayed away from the window by habit now, but there wasn't that much to see. The downtown city centre was in darkness, save for a few buildings running on generators, one of them his own hotel, a few blocks away to the south. The never-ending caucus would still be in session there, his delegates – he did think of them as *his* now – working the phones and counting heads as they attempted to stave off defeat in the morning's vote.

But they would be defeated. Jed Culver had stolen enough votes in his time to know when the situation was hopeless. The Putsch were going to get their amendments up. They were going to turn the United States Government into something like a third-world junta. He shook his head at his own incompetence in not foreseeing this and aborting it at conception. But, looking back, he could understand. He'd been so focused on his own, much humbler agenda that he simply hadn't been prepared for the depth of feeling, the visceral fear that had infected everything here in a way it hadn't back in Hawaii. That was understandable. You couldn't see the Wave in Hawaii; you didn't live every minute with the prospect of it moving and just eating you alive. He should have factored that in.

'There is a tide in the affairs of men,' he muttered to himself, 'which, taken at the flood, leads on to fortune – but omitted, and all the voyage of their life is bound in shallows and in miseries.'

'What's that, Jed?'

Culver turned around to the doorway and was surprised to find a thin man standing there, silhouetted by the light of a small hand-held phone. Two larger companions, instantly recognisable as bodyguards, loomed a discreet distance behind him.

'Just mangling the bard, Bill,' the lawyer replied. 'It always helps me when creeping murmur and the pouring dark fill the wide vessel of the universe.'

Bill shrugged. 'Me, I like to read or play bridge. Golf's pretty good too. But not at this time of night.'

'No,' agreed Culver, who hadn't been expecting anyone like this. The others he'd met tonight had all been anonymous people. Quiet men and women. 'So . . . er . . .'

The figure chuckled in the gloom. 'I really threw you for a doozey, didn't I? Coming here, I mean.'

'Yes, you did,' Culver admitted. 'I was expecting some-one . . . lower down the food chain.'

'Someone expendable?'

'If you like.'

The man walked into the room while his bodyguards remained in the corridor. 'This is important, Jed,' he said. 'I have a lot invested in this venture. We all do. If it fails, we're sunk. If it plays out, who knows, maybe people will remember us hundreds of years from now. Assuming there's anybody left, of course.'

The lawyer shrugged. 'People would remember you anyway, Bill.'

'Not for something as cool as this, though, Jed. This is the sort of thing that ends up in oil paintings. Like Paul Revere's ride. It's *that* important.'

Culver couldn't argue with that.

'You did bring your phone, right?' asked Bill.

Jed pulled it out of his suit pocket and handed it over. The man's face was underlit by the glow of the screen as he keyed in a series of codes.

'Okay,' he said, as the smart phone beeped. 'The network is active.'

'And secure?'

'And secure.'

Culver thanked him as he took the phone back. He opened the message window and pressed a few buttons.

And with that, a single hard-encrypted message beamed out across the city to hundreds of identical devices.

'It's done,' he said. 'It's happening.'

Most of the delegates at the convention had succumbed to the lack of air-conditioning and removed their jackets; ties were loosened and, in some cases, dispensed with altogether. The atmosphere in the auditorium was sour, hot and rank, although partly that had to do with the split on the floor that was threatening to tear the whole process apart. James Kipper pressed his lips together in an effort to maintain his calm as some asshole from Spokane attempted to tell him how to do his job.

'This isn't how we would run things, let me tell you, Kipper. We'd have had this show wrapped up days ago, and there wouldn't have been any of this school-camp bullshit with lights out and no air, either. How the hell do you expect people to make decisions under these conditions? It is impossible.'

Kipper's jaw moved like he was chewing gum, which he wasn't. It was simply an old habit. He folded his arms and resisted the urge to tell this . . . Malcolm Vusevic, according to his name-tag – that he was full of shit because Spokane, lying behind the Wave, wouldn't be organising anything ever again.

He kept his mouth shut, because, in his experience, people who'd hailed from the dead zone tended to be a little sensitive about it, which was only reasonable. What wasn't reasonable was the delegates demanding that they get special treatment over and above what the rest of the city could expect.

'Not gonna happen, sir,' said Kip, resolutely shaking his head. 'Redmond, Finn Hill and North Creek are all on their allotted power-ups at the moment. If you want to turn up the air-con here, it means diverting grid power from those folks. I'm not going to do it. Not on your say-so.'

'Well, on whose then?' Vusevic demanded to know. 'Would an order from General Blackstone do it for you?'

'Nope.' Kipper shook his head equably. 'I work for the city, not the military. At least not yet.'

He instantly regretted the indiscretion as Vusevic's eyes lit up in triumph. 'Oh, I see . . . one of those anarchists, eh? You're just doing this to delay the inevitable. Whatsa matter, buddy – don't like losing a vote? Can't handle democracy?'

Kipper's shoulders and arms ached with the tension building up in them as he restrained a violent urge to beat this idiot into a pulp. 'It's none of my business, sir,' he replied flatly. 'City utilities are my business. And you're not getting any extra power.'

With that he turned and walked away from the delegate from Spokane, wondering how the fuck anyone from Spokane got a ticket here in the first place. All Vusevic represented was a burnt-out ruin of urban wasteland.

'*Whoa* there, Nelly! You're gonna throw a shoe, stomping off like that.'

Kipper pulled up at the sight of Jed Culver, who'd just emerged from the crush around the refreshments table. He seemed to live there, and it was taking its toll. The guy looked like he hadn't slept. His face was puffy and dark bags hung under his eyes.

'Sorry, Jed. Not today, man. I've got a world of fucking hurt on my shoulders.'

'Who doesn't, Kip, who doesn't? Just a word in your shell-like. Won't take a minute.'

Kipper frowned at the odd phrasing, until he remembered that Culver had worked in London for a couple of years. Or he said he had. Sometimes with Jed you were never quite sure when he was feeding you a line. The engineer sighed, exhausted. He really was buried by work, and being called down to the conference floor to get reamed out over the air-conditioning hadn't improved his mood. He hadn't slept last night, after the Gestapo, as Barb called them, had left. Partly because Barney Tench had stayed until just before dawn, attempting to win him over to the cause. His friend had left in a police cruiser of all things. 'Not everyone in uniform wants to be the Führer,' Barney had explained, winking.

Kip shook off Culver's guiding hand and continued on his way to the exit. The lawyer fell in beside him, not saying anything. Just grinning and waving at the other delegates as he passed them, even those who Kip knew for a fact he hated. How the hell he did that was a mystery for the ages. When James Kipper didn't like someone they didn't die wondering.

'You going back up to your office?' Jed asked, as they left the auditorium behind.

'Yes, I am, but . . .'

'Great. I'll come with you. Come on.'

'Don't you want to be here for the vote?' the engineer enquired. 'It's on soon, isn't it?'

'Already lost that one, Kip. So no, I have other plans, my friend. Come on.'

He reluctantly allowed Culver to tag along with him, mostly because he knew the man was congenitally incapable of taking no for an answer. Kip could have blown him off, but he knew that by the time he reached his office many floors above, this expensively suited fixer would most likely have been waiting in his chair with a big dumb grin on his face.

'That doesn't sound like you, Jed, giving up because you can't win.'

'Who says I'm giving up?' Culver asked in reply.

Kipper spared him a glance and was disturbed by the wolfish smile he found there. 'What's happening, Jed? This really isn't the morning for it.'

'No, that's where you're wrong, Kip. This is very much the morning for it. This is the morning the American people – what's left of 'em, God help us – take back their government.'

They entered the elevator, which Kipper had tried to shut down without success – the city councillors had baulked at that power-saving measure. Jed punched in the number for the Engineering Department's floor, before smiling graciously and using his arm to bar the way of a young woman who'd rushed up behind them to share the ride. 'Sorry, darlin'. Do you mind?'

She did, but there was nothing she could do about it as the doors slid shut.

Kipper bristled at the impoliteness. 'That wasn't very nice, Jed, and it was wasteful,' he chastised the lawyer. 'And what are you crapping on about anyway? You already said you were going down in that vote this morning. Blackstone is gonna get his congressmen, whether the rest of the army wants it or not.'

Jed put a finger to his lips before gesturing around the elevator. Kip sighed with exasperation, but after last night he wasn't so quick to dismiss paranoid speculation about surveillance.

The lawyer nodded. 'Well, you're right about one thing, Kip. Not all of the military wants this situation. Ritchie and Franks are dead against it.' Culver looked around as if addressing an unseen audience. 'And nobody in uniform is arguing in favour of it, of course. But in the end they'll accede to the wishes of the people.'

'But people don't want this,' Kipper said. 'Some people maybe, but not everyone. This is just fear and craziness.'

'Well, fear whispers loudly downstairs, my friend. Come on.'

A bell dinged as the elevator came to a stop. Kip made to step out and head for his office but Culver grabbed his arm and directed him towards another room.

'I had this one swept fifteen minutes ago,' he said quietly, pulling the door closed behind them.

'You what?'

'Found this . . .' Jed pulled a small electronic device from his breast pocket. 'Don't worry, it's been disabled.'

Kip stared at the tiny piece of technology as hackles rose on his back. 'Sons of bitches.'

'Nah, *amateurs*, Kip,' Culver corrected him. 'Rank fucking amateurs playing at big boys' games. Now, come to the window. I want you to see the sort of view you miss when you work indoors all the time.'

The chief engineer followed Culver to the window and looked down on his city. It was a relatively clear morning, the first in a while. A few grey clouds scudded out near the mountains to the east, but otherwise the sky was clear, save for two army helicopters holding position over the bridges across Lake Washington. And then he saw them – a sea of colour, a teeming, seething mass of humanity, streaming onto the bridges and heading for the city centre.

'What the hell?'

The crowd had already swept past a small army roadblock at

the eastern end of the bridge and were beginning to string out in a long procession that took up every available lane.

'The wishes of the people, Kip. I didn't think they were being heard downstairs either. So I invited them all here to have their say.'

The engineer was speechless.

'You're a local – how long do you think it will take them to walk that distance, Kip? To get them here, I mean, beating on the doors of the Municipal Tower?'

Kipper shook his head. 'Not long, I guess. If they're allowed.'

Jed Culver snorted. 'If they're allowed! What, did I wake up in Soviet Russia this morning? They're *American citizens* down there, Kip. Your neighbours and friends. Nobody tells them what they can or can't do. And sure as shit, nobody tells them how they're gonna govern themselves.'

Kipper pressed his head to the glass, which felt cool against his sweating brow. 'How did you do this, Jed, without anyone knowing?' he asked quietly.

'Without Blackstone knowing, you mean? I had some friends – some of them friends of yours, actually.'

'Hey buddy, sorry to keep dropping in like this.'

'Hello, sweetie!'

Kipper spun around to find Barney standing at the office door. And next to him was Barb, holding Suzie on one hip.

'Holy crap, Barn, they'll fucking lock you up, man! And Barb . . .'

'Daddy said the rude word!' squealed his daughter.

He pulled up, realising he'd just dropped an F-bomb in front of his six-year-old child. *Damn.*

'I'm sorry,' he said. 'Daddy shouldn't have done that, darlin'. It's just that he was a little . . . surprised. And kind of upset.' The bomb diffused, Kip turned to the two adult visitors. 'So, what's going on here?'

Barney was peering out of the doorway and back along the corridor, where his former co-workers had begun to gather and point at the slow-moving crowd snaking across the bridges. One or two saw him and waved. He smiled back before returning his attention to his old friend.

'I told you last night, Kip, that there were a lot of people involved in the Resistance. Some whackjobs, for sure – you know, commies and anarchists, just like you hear all the time – but a shit-load more decent folk. Guys who used to work for the media, the telecom companies, the government. Moms and dads.'

Barbara nodded as she carefully lowered Suzie to the ground. 'You run along, princess,' she said. 'Find some paper to draw on. See if you can find Ronnie, she'll help you.'

'I like Ronnie!' Suzie cried before dashing out of the office.

Kip stared at his wife. It was as though he didn't recognise her. 'You too, Barb? You were part of this?'

'I'm sorry, Kip, yes. Well, I'm not sorry for being part of it, but I am sorry I had to keep it from you.'

'But why?' he asked plaintively. 'Couldn't you trust me?'

She smiled sadly. 'It wasn't safe, honey. If you knew I was helping Barney and the others, how could you have come in here every day and faced off Blackstone? You're a lot of things, Kip, but you're not a liar. You couldn't have done it.'

Kipper turned on the lawyer. His head was an angry swirling mess of emotions. 'You knew about this, Jed? About my family being involved?'

Culver nodded. For once he wasn't smiling. 'I've had contact with a number of opposition cells,' he admitted. 'Your wife's was one.'

'You had a *cell*?' he asked Barbara. His voice rose with incredulity.

Barbara sniffed. 'You make it sound like a spy movie, Kip. It was just me and some of the moms from school, and some of our friends. People I could trust.'

'Jesus Christ . . .'

'They're down there, Kip,' she added, pointing out of the window. 'They're coming. Because they have to.'

Barney walked over from the door and looked down on the massing crowd. 'We've been waiting for this, Kip,' he said. 'Waiting for the right moment when those assholes downstairs would go just a bit too far. I thought they'd done it when they locked up the councillors, but people were still frightened out of their minds back then, willing to give up anything just to feel safe. That just isn't so, now. They've had enough and they want their country back. The little bit they have left, anyway.'

Kipper was stunned. Never would he have imagined the day turning out like this. He had kept his opinions private, but he'd been expecting a bleak and wretched day.

'We need your help, Kip,' Barney went on.

'Mine? What do you need me for?' He waved a hand at the window. 'Looks like you've got it all locked down.'

Culver answered his question. 'We need you to shut off power to the city, and to Fort Lewis. And we need it done now. We have to knock the legs out from under these idiots before they have a chance to get to their feet.'

'But they'll have their own back-up plans,' he protested.

'Everyone has back-up plans,' Culver smiled silkily.

'What about it, Kip?' Barney Tench implored. 'You saved this city once. You can save your country if you act right now.'

'Come on, honey,' added Barbara. 'You know what's right.'

Kipper turned back and gazed out of the window. The crowd looked to be hundreds of thousands strong. He could see them bunched up at the bottleneck of Faben Point, a great mass of people emerging from the suburbs. He could see a similar crowd heading over the Evergreen Point Bridge to the north.

Telephones began to ring all over the floor, as voices rose in confusion, surprise and even awe. His secretary, Rhonda, came bustling down the hallway and into the room with Suzie trailing behind her. She looked surprised and delighted.

'Barney!' she cried out. 'And Barb!'

'Hey Ronnie.'

'Hiya Ron.'

She turned her attention back to Kipper and said, 'I'm sorry, boss, but it's General Blackstone's office on the phone. They desperately need to talk to you and the other department heads. What should I tell them?'

Kipper smiled.

EPILOGUE

ONE DAY

The killer awoke, to find a stranger by her bed.

No, not a stranger, the guy who had saved her. The civilian in the room on the top floor. She could see him clearly now, as she blinked the sleep out of her eyes.

'Where am I?' asked Caitlin, her voice cracking in her dry throat.

'London,' replied the man. 'A special hospital. They had to operate on you.'

'My friend the tumour,' she said. 'Don't tell me he's gone.'

The man shrugged. 'I'm not a doctor so I don't know. Or a relative, so they won't tell me.'

'Who are you?'

'Name's Melton,' he said. 'Bret Melton.'

Caitlin tried to lever herself up but found she had no strength in her arms at all.

'Well, Bret Melton, thank you for saving my sorry ass. And to think I might have popped a cap in yours.'

He seemed to take that without offence.

'You probably saved mine, Miss Mercure. I holed up in that joint after my vehicle got hit by an RPG. I was pretty much out of it, just trying to get as far away from the street as possible. If those guys had been even half competent they'd have checked and found me unconscious up top. Probably would have cut my head off.'

'Probably,' she agreed. 'And my name's not Cathy Mercure, by the way. That's a cover. I'm sorry they felt the need to tell you that. My name is Caitlin.'

Melton took that without obvious concern, too.

'In my experience,' he said with a half-smile, 'ladies who sneak into snake pits and twist the heads off vipers can pretty well call themselves whatever they feel like. You should know, by the way, that I'm a reporter. I'm not going to write about you. Not even going to ask what went down in that house. They made me sign a piece of paper that says I lose my nuts if I do. But I just wanted to get that out there for you.'

Caitlin felt a wave of lassitude steal through her body. She was aware of great damage that had been done. 'Thank you, Bret,' she said weakly. 'But it's all right. I'm retired now, a lady of leisure, as of two minutes ago.'

'Okay then.' He nodded and they lapsed into silence.

Her eyelids fluttered heavily, and she felt herself drifting back towards sleep. 'Bret,' she said, 'did they get him? Did they get my guy?'

His voice seemed to come from far away. 'I don't know, Caitlin. They got a lot of guys.'

She forced her eyes open. For the first time she noticed the window off to the side of her bed. It opened onto a garden scene, although the trees were leafless and the grass had all died off.

'What are you going to do, Bret?' she asked. 'Will you go home?'

He shrugged again. 'What's home?'

'I don't know.'

She started to fade out again. 'I don't know.'

ONE WEEK

They buried their dead according to whatever beliefs the departed had lived by. Gathered on the heavily damaged boat deck at the stern of the *Aussie Rules*, the surviving passengers and crew said their prayers or quiet goodbyes for friends and loved ones who hadn't made it.

Julianne had never known Fifi or Pete to be in the slightest way religious, but while tidying Fifi's quarters in the days after the last battle, she found an old Gideon's bible, stolen from a motel somewhere, annotated by her lost friend's large, childlike script. The story of Noah and his ark had come in for a lot of attention. *That's just like us, except for all the animals*, she had written. Elsewhere, *Please Lord, smite that asshole Larry Zood* was followed in a different-coloured ink by: *Damn! This prayer shit really works!*

It was evidence of a secret, inner life that Jules would never have imagined of Fifi Lamont, and she asked Miguel to add a few Hail Marys to the endless rosaries his extended family were sending skyward for old Adolfo, the only casualty their party suffered. Dead of a heart attack a full day after the gunfight.

'Hail Mary, full of grace, the Lord is with thee, blessed art thou among women, and blessed is the fruit of thy womb Jesus . . .'

Grandma Ana smiled and nodded sadly at Jules and then at the two bundles that had been her friends, and she realised that Miguel's family, who had been praying in Spanish, had changed to English without her noticing. The Mexican matriarch waved a thin brown hand at Pete and Fifi's bodies, indicating that the change was for their sake. Out of reflex, an earlier, more cynical Julianne Balwyn would have smirked and rolled her eyes at the idea of an omniscient God needing a translation, but now, on this bright and cold morning, Jules let the tears come freely as the age-old prayer to the mother of Jesus was whipped away on a freshening southerly breeze.

The sea state had dropped down to a long, rolling swell and only a few wisps of cirrus cloud spoiled an otherwise perfect sky. Time at last for a burial. Eight bodies lay wrapped in sheets and blankets on the large, bullet-pocked diving platform at the stern. Fifi and Pete, the last two bundles on the starboard side, she had placed there herself with a lot of help from Shah and Mr Lee. The gravity and sorrow of the moment was undercut somewhat by the frozen stiffness of Pete's remains. He'd been lying in the largest of the galley freezers for over a month, and Jules wasn't sure she'd have been able to contemplate moving him had Shah and Lee not helped.

'Mr Pete, he would have loved this,' said the old Chinaman, as they struggled with his body. 'Would have laughed his *gweilo* anus right off, yes.'

And he would have, thought Jules, with a private smile and an involuntary hitching sob.

Fifi, though, she would've been really pissed off. Of all of them, Jules thought, her Oregonian friend had most easily dealt with everything that had happened. Perhaps because she'd been alone and fighting for herself most of her life. Mute and numb, staring at the inert swaddle of sheets in which the redneck princess was wrapped, Julianne could not help indulging in a small, bitter moment of self-loathing. If she had been smarter, if she had in any way been worthy of the trust everyone had placed in her, Fifi would still have been with them. Still grinning and shining and lighting up the face of everybody who encountered her.

'. . . Holy Mary, mother of God, pray for us sinners, now and at the hour of our death. Amen . . . Hail Mary, full of grace . . .'

She was shaking – a slight tremor at first, something she didn't really notice until it had spread through most of her body. She shivered inside her thick, dark oilskins, and her throat felt so tight she could not swallow. Beside her, the three surviving Gurkhas quietly sang a funeral song for their fallen comrades, Thapa and Birendra, which seemed to magnify the power of the Mexicans' rosary chant. Her American passengers mumbled along, all of them having made it through except for Denby Moorhouse, who lay next to Birendra on the diving platform, shot down after saving her life during the battle. His mistress – 'the boob job', as Fifi had once called her – had found a black cocktail dress somewhere for her mourning outfit, creating an incongruous effect under a yellow rain slicker. The young woman dabbed at dramatically running mascara, but, regarding her from within the depths of her own misery, Jules thought she was going through the motions of grief, rather than its reality. The presence of Jason St John's hand massaging her arse did detract somewhat from the air of decorous remembrance she was trying so hard to create. Moorhouse's former squeeze had already moved cabins to take up with the trust-fund delinquent, much to the chagrin of his sister Phoebe, who was now refusing to talk to him.

Jules sighed at the petty, meaningless nature of it all.

One would've thought that people could have put aside all the silly wretchedness and just pulled together, but no. They couldn't. Her father would have said it simply wasn't in their nature. He was an old villain, there was no denying that, but in his own strange way he had a good heart, and he never stole from anyone who couldn't afford it. There was even a spark of noblesse oblige in him, and he made sure that all of his children were raised to think of themselves as no better than anyone else. Because, as he so often told her, 'In the end, Julianne, we're all just as bad as each other.'

'Miss Jules?'

Lee's voice in her ear dragged her out of these reveries.

'It is a warship, Miss Jules. On the radio. From New Zealand.'

She excused herself with a brief hand on Shah's arm, and turned and left the funeral scene, secretly glad not to have to witness the dumping of the bodies into the deep.

'He wishes to speak with our captain,' said Lee, who had contented himself with just a few private words over the bodies of his comrades before everyone came together for the ceremony.

Our captain, thought Jules. How risible. 'What does he want?' she asked.

'Oh, it is nothing bad. I have told him we have Uplifted Americans on board. He asks if we need assistance, and whether we will be berthing in Auckland or proceeding to Sydney.'

'Okay, thanks, Mr Lee.' She stopped before climbing the stairs up to the next deck. 'What do you want to do, Lee, when we get there? They probably won't let us keep this boat, you know. It's not ours.'

Her one surviving friend shook his head sadly. 'No. They will not, Miss Jules,' he agreed.

'And you can't go home. Indonesia is a god-awful mess now.'

'Yes, miss.'

'So what will you do?'

He looked completely lost for the first time ever. 'What will *you* do, Miss Jules?' he asked in reply. 'Maybe I come too.'

'I don't know either, Lee. These last few weeks, they've really taken it out of me. I don't want to go home, I know that much. England looks nightmarish right now. A giant bloody jail, if you ask me, and not at all the sort of place for the likes of us.'

'No, miss. Foreign Johnnies not welcome anymore.'

She started the long climb up towards the bridge, stopping just once to look back towards the stern and say her last goodbye. From here, against the vastness of the southern ocean, her little group of seafarers and survivors looked so vulnerable and sad. Like the last people on earth. But at least they were still alive.

Daddy would have been proud, she thought. He'd have been so proud of her, for bringing the ship and all of these people safely home, wherever that might turn out to be.

'Don't worry, Mr Lee,' she said. 'We'll muddle through.'

ONE YEAR

The President of the United States was hunkered down over a small mountain of paperwork in the Oval Office of the newly christened Western White House. Of course, the office wasn't oval-shaped at all, but he felt it important to retain a link with the past. Something to give people hope that they might be able to reclaim some of the advantages and even a fraction of the glory that the past had once gifted them as a nation.

He read the summation of the reports from the high-energy physics lab into the latest investigations of the Wave, but they all boiled down to the same thing: nobody knew shit.

He leaned back and rubbed at his eyes. His chief scientist and the National Security Advisor waited quietly on him, as they sat in the bright yellow armchairs arranged in front of his desk. He had no idea where the Governor of Washington had retrieved them from, just before he 'gave up' his accommodation for the needs of the federal government, but they were suitably hideous. A parting fuck-you of exquisite eloquence.

'So, no change,' said the President.

'No.'

'Not in the slightest, sir.'

'Okay, thanks, guys. Send in the Secretary of State on your way out, would you? Thanks for your efforts anyway.'

The two men excused themselves and departed.

The President gazed out over the gardens of the former

Governor's mansion. They had recovered well as the environment had returned to normal. Better than normal, actually. The total collapse of the world economy had given the planet a breather, but at a terrible cost. He'd actually heard that some of the deep green nutjobs in the all-powerful state legislature next door had been saying that, on balance, the Disappearance was a good thing.

Of course, they never said so on the record. They'd be lynched. But he didn't doubt for a minute that some of them thought as much.

He tidied away the scientific reports and pulled over a tottering sheaf of folders dealing with the expatriate population. Most Americans still lived overseas, and tending to their needs and the demands of their host governments was about half of what he did nowadays. The Brits were looking for territorial concessions, pressuring him to give up US claims over the Antarctic oil fields. The Australian Prime Minister wanted him to visit to 'discuss' the future co-funding arrangements of the Pacific Fleet.

A dull pain was growing behind his left eye when his personal secretary burst into the office.

'Mr President! Mr President! You have to come, sir. Right away!'

'What's up?' he asked, suddenly worried.

Just then two secret service agents bustled past her into the room and urgently requested he come with them immediately.

'No, goddamn it, I won't. What the hell is going on?'

'We need to get you away from here, Mr President,' one of the men repeated. 'We'll explain on the way, sir.'

'Oh no you don't.' President James Kipper jumped up from his desk. 'I'm not going anywhere with anyone until you tell me exactly what's happening, right now.'

'It's the Wave, sir,' cried Ronnie. 'It's gone.'